EDGAR ALLAN POE

Edgar Allan Poe

SELECTED PROSE, POETRY, AND EUREKA

Edited with an Introduction by W. H. Auden

Holt, Rinehart and Winston, Inc.

NEW YORK • CHICAGO • SAN FRANCISCO • ATLANTA • DALLAS
MONTREAL • TORONTO • LONDON • SYDNEY

Typography Design by Stefan Salter
ISBN: 0-03-084241-7

Printed in the United States of America

2345 065 9876543

Introduction

What every author hopes to receive from posterity—a hope usually disappointed—is justice. Next to oblivion, the two fates which he most fears are becoming the name attached to two or three famous pieces while the rest of his work is unread and becoming the idol of a small circle which reads every word he wrote with the same uncritical reverence. The first fate is unjust because, even if the pieces known are indeed his best work, the reader has not earned the right to say so; the second fate is embarrassing and ridiculous, for no author believes he is that good.

Poe's shade must be more disappointed than most. Certain pieces—how he must hate these old war horses—are probably more familiar to non-Americans than are any pieces by any other American author. I myself cannot remember hearing any poetry before hearing "The Raven" and "The Bells"; and *The Pit and the Pendulum* was one of the first short stories I ever read. At the same time, the known works of no other author of comparable rank and productivity are so few and so invariably the same. In preparing to make this selection, for example, I asked a number of persons whom I knew to be widely read, but not specialists in American letters, if they had read *Gordon Pym* and *Eureka,* which seem to me to rank among Poe's most important works; not one of them had. On the other hand, I was informed by everyone that to omit *The Cask of Amontillado,* which for my taste is an inferior story, would be commercial suicide. Poor Poe! At first so forgotten that his grave went without a tombstone twenty-six years—when one was finally erected the only American author to attend the ceremony was Whitman; and today in danger of becoming the life study of a few professors. The professors are, of course, very necessary, for it is through their devoted labors that Poe may finally reach the kind of reader every author hopes for, who will read him all, good-humoredly willing to wade through much which is dull or inferior for the delight of discovering something new and admirable.

The Tales Varied in subject, treatment, style as Poe's stories are, they have one negative characteristic in common. There is no place in any of them for the human individual as he actually exists in space and time, that is, as simultaneously a natural creature subject in his feelings to the influences and limitations of the natural order, and an historical person, creating novelty and relations by his free choice and modified in unforeseen ways by the choices of others.

Poe's major stories fall roughly into two groups. The first group is concerned with states of willful being, the destructive passion of the lonely ego to merge with the ego of another (*Ligeia*), the passion of the conscious ego to be objective, to discover by pure reason the true relationships which sensory appearances and emotions would conceal (*The Purloined Letter*), self-destructive states in which the ego and the self are passionately hostile (*The Imp of the Perverse*), even the state of chimerical passion, that is, the passionate unrest of a self that lacks all passion (*The Man of the Crowd*). The horror tales and the tales of ratiocination belong together, for the heroes of both exist as unitary states—Roderick Usher reasons as little as Auguste Dupin feels. Personages who are the embodiment of such states cannot, of course, change or vary in intensity either through changes in themselves or their environment. The problem in writing stories of this kind is to prevent the reader from ever being reminded of historical existence, for, if he once thinks of real people whose passions are interrupted by a need for lunch or whose beauty can be temporarily and mildly impaired by the common cold, the intensity and timelessness become immediately comic. Poe is sometimes attacked for the operatic quality of the prose and *décor* in his tales, but they are essential to preserving the illusion. His heroes cannot exist except operatically. Take, for example, the following sentence from *William Wilson:*

> Let it suffice, that among spendthrifts I out-heroded Herod, and that, giving name to a multitude of novel follies, I added no brief appendix to the long catalogue of vices then usual in the most dissolute university of Europe.

In isolation, as a prose sentence, it is terrible, vague, verbose, the sense at the mercy of a conventional rhetorical rhythm. But dramatically, how right; how well it reveals the William Wilson who narrates the story in his real colors, as the fantastic self who hates and refuses contact with reality. Some of Poe's successors in stories about states of being, D. H. Lawrence for example, have tried to be realistic with fatal results.

In the second group, which includes such tales as *A Descent into the Maelstrom* and *Gordon Pym,* the relation of will to environment is reversed. While in the first group everything that happens is the consequence of a volition upon the freedom of which there are no natural limits, in these stories of pure adventure the hero is as purely passive as the I in dreams; nothing that happens is the result of his personal choice, everything happens *to* him. What the subject feels—interest, excitement, terror—are caused by events over which he has no control whatsoever. The first kind of hero has no history because he refuses to change with time; this kind has none because he cannot change, he can only experience.

The problem for the writer of adventure stories is to invent a succession of events which are both interesting and varied and to make the order of succession plausible. To secure variety without sacrificing coherence or vice versa is more difficult than it looks, and *Gordon Pym,* one of the finest adventure stories ever written, is an object lesson in the art. Every kind of adventure occurs—adventures of natural origin like shipwreck; adventures like mutiny, caused by familiar human beings, or, like the adventures on the island, by strange natives; and, finally, supernatural nightmare events—yet each leads credibly into the next. While in the stories of passionate states a certain vagueness of description is essential to the illusion, in the adventure story credibility is secured by the minutest details, figures, diagrams, and various other devices, as in Poe's description of the mysterious ravines.

> The total length of this chasm, commencing at the opening *a* and proceeding round the corner *b* to the extremity *d,* is five hundred and fifty yards.

Both these types of Poe story have had an extraordinary influence. His portraits of abnormal or self-destructive states contributed much to Dostoevski, his ratiocinating hero is the ancestor of Sherlock Holmes and his many successors, his tales of the future lead to H. G. Wells, his adventure stories to Jules Verne and Stevenson. It is not without interest that the development of such fiction in which the historical individual is missing should have coincided with the development of history as a science, with its own laws, and the appearance of the great nineteenth-century historians; further, that both these developments should accompany the industrialization and urbanization of social life in which the individual seems more and more the creation of historical forces while he himself feels less and less capable of directing his life by any historical choice of his own.

Poe's minor fiction also falls into two groups. The first is composed, not of narratives, but physical descriptions of Eden, of the Great Good Place *The Domain of Arnheim.* Such descriptions, whoever they may be written by, are bound to be more interesting as revelations of their authors than in themselves, for no one can imagine the ideal place, the ideal home, except in terms of his private fantasies and the good taste of his day. In Poe's case, in particular, his notions of the stylish and luxurious, if they are not to seem slightly vulgar and comic, must be read in the light of his history and the America of the first half of the nineteenth century. And, lastly there is the group of humorous-satiric pieces unrepresented in this selection. Though Poe is not so funny in them as in some of his criticism, at least one story, *A Predicament,* is of interest. A parody of the kind of popular horror story appearing in

Blackwood's, it is, in a sense, a parody of Poe's serious work in this vein; and it actually uses the same notion of the swinging descending knife which he was later to employ in *The Pit and the Pendulum.*

The Poems Poe's best poems are not his most typical or original. "To Helen," which could have been written by Landor, and "The City in the Sea," which could have been written by Hood, are more successfully realized than a poem like "Ulalume," which could have been written by none but Poe.

His difficulty as a poet was that he was interested in too many poetic problems and experiments at once for the time he had to give to them. To make the result conform to the intention—and the more experimental the intention, the more this is true—a writer has to keep his hand in by continual practice. The prose writer who must earn his living has this advantage, that even the purest hack work is practice in his craft; for the penniless poet there is no corresponding exercise. Without the leisure to write and rewrite he cannot develop to his full stature. When we find fault with Poe's poems we must never forget his own sad preface to them.

> In defence of my own taste, it is incumbent upon me to say that I think nothing in this volume of much value to the public, or very creditable to myself. Events not to be controlled have prevented me from making, at any time, any serious effort in what, under happier circumstances, would have been the field of my choice.

For faulty they must be admitted to be. The trouble with "The Raven," for example, is that the thematic interest and the prosodic interest, both of which are considerable, do not combine and are even often at odds.

In *The Philosophy of Composition* Poe discusses his difficulties in preventing the poem from becoming absurd and artificial. The artificiality of the lover asking the proper series of questions to which the refrain would be appropriate could be solved by making him a self-torturer. The difficulty of the speaker of the refrain, however, remained insoluble until the poet hit on the notion of something nonhuman. But the effect could still be ruined unless the narration of the story, as distinct from the questions and answers, flowed naturally; and the meter Poe chose, with its frequent feminine rhymes, so rare in English, works against this and at times defeats him.

> Not the least obeisance made he; not a minute stopped or stayed he;
> But with mien of lord or lady, perched above my chamber door.

Here it is the meter alone and nothing in the speaker or the situation which is responsible for the redundant alternatives of "stopped or stayed he" and "lord or lady."

Similarly, "Ulalume" is an interesting experiment in diction but only an experiment, for the poem is about something which never quite gets said because the sense is sacrificed to the vowel sounds. It is an accident if the sound of a place name corresponds to the emotion the place invokes, and the accidental is a comic quality. Edward Lear, the only poet, apparently, to be directly influenced by Poe, succeeds with such names as "The Hills of the Chankly Bore" because he is frankly writing "nonsense" poetry, but "Ulalume" has a serious subject and the comic is out of place. "The Bells," though much less interesting a conception than "Ulalume," is more successful because the subject is nothing but an excuse for onomatopoeic effects.

There remains, however, *Eureka*. The man who had flatly asserted that no poem should much exceed a hundred lines in length —"that music (in its modifications of rhythm and rhyme) is of so vast a moment to Poesy as never to be neglected by him who is truly poetical," that neither Truth, the satisfaction of the Intellect, nor Passion, the excitement of the Heart, are the province of Poetry but only Beauty, and that the most poetical topic in the world is the death of a beautiful woman—this man produces at the end of his life a work which he insists is a poem and commends to posterity as his crowning achievement, though it violates every article in his critical creed. It is many pages in length, it is written in prose, it handles scientific ideas in the truth of which the poet is passionately convinced, and the general subject is the origin and destiny of the universe.

Outside France the poem has been neglected, but I do not think Poe was wrong in the importance he attached to it. In the first place, it was a very daring and original notion to take the oldest of the poetic themes—older even than the story of the epic hero—namely, cosmology, the story of how things came to exist as they do, and treat it in a completely contemporary way, to do in English in the nineteenth century what Hesiod and Lucretius had done in Greek and Latin centuries before. Secondly, it is full of remarkable intuitive guesses that subsequent scientific discoveries have confirmed. As Paul Valéry says:

> It would not be exaggerating its importance to recognise, in his theory of consistency, a fairly definite attempt to describe the universe by its *intrinsic properties.* The following proposition can be found toward the end of *Eureka:* "Each law of nature depends at all points on all the other laws." This might easily be considered, if not as a formula, at least as the expression of a tendency toward generalized relativity.
>
> That its tendency approaches recent conceptions becomes evident when one discovers, in the poem under discussion, an affirmation of the *symmetrical* and reciprocal relationship of matter, time, space, gravity, and light.

Lastly, it combines in one work nearly all of Poe's characteristic obsessions: the passion for merging in union with the one which is at the root of tales like *Ligeia,* the passion for logic which dominates the detective and cryptographic studies, the passion for a final explanation and reconciliation which informs the melancholy of much of his verse—all are brought together in this poem of which the prose is as lucid, as untheatrical, as the best of his critical prose.

The Critical Writings Poe's critical work, like that of any significant critic, must be considered in the literary content which provoked it. No critic, however pontifical his tone, is really attempting to lay down eternal truths about art; he is always polemical, fighting a battle against the characteristic misconceptions, stupidities, and weaknesses of his contemporaries. He is always having, on the one hand, to defend tradition against the amateur who is ignorant of it and the crank who thinks it should be scrapped so that real art may begin anew with him and, on the other, to assert the real novelty of the present and to demonstrate, against the academic who imagines that carrying on the tradition means imitation, what modern tasks and achievements are truly analogues to those of the past.

Poe's condemnation of the long poem and of the didactic or true poem is essentially a demand that the poets of his time be themselves and admit that epic themes and intellectual or moral ideas did not in fact excite their poetic faculties and that what really interested them were emotions of melancholy, nostalgia, puzzled yearning, and the like that could find their proper expression in neither epic nor epigram but in lyrics of moderate length. Poe was forced to attack all long poems on principle, to be unfair, for example, to *Paradise Lost* or *An Essay on Criticism,* in order to shake the preconceived notions of poets and public that to be important a poet must write long poems and give bardic advice.

His rejection of passion is really a variation of Wordsworth's observation that, to be capable of embodiment in a poem, emotion must be recollected in tranquility; immediate passion is too obsessive, too attached to the self. Poe's attack is further directed against the popular and amateur notion of poetic inspiration which gives the poet himself no work to do, a reminder that the most inspired poem is also a contraption, a made thing.

> We do not hesitate to say that a man highly endowed with the powers of Causality—that is to say a man of metaphysical acumen—will, even with a very deficient share of Ideality, compose a finer poem than one without such metaphysical acumen, shall be gifted, in the most extraordinary degree, with the faculty of Ideality. For a poem is not the Poetic faculty, but the *means* of exciting it in mankind.

Through its influence on the French, Poe's general aesthetic is well known. The bulk of his critical writing, and perhaps that which was of the greatest service, is concerned with poetic technique and practical criticism of details. No one in his time put so much energy and insight into trying to make his contemporary poets take their craft seriously, know what they were doing prosodically, and avoid the faults of slovenly diction and inappropriate imagery that can be avoided by vigilance and hard work.

If Poe never developed to his potential full stature as a critic, this was entirely his misfortune, not his fault. Much of his best criticism will never be read widely because it lies buried in reviews of totally uninteresting authors. If he sometimes overpraised the second-rate like Mrs. Osgood or wasted time and energy in demolishing nonentities like Mr. English, such were inevitable consequences when a critical mind, equipped by nature for digesting the toughest of foods, is condemned by circumstances to feed on literary gruel. The first-rate critic needs critical issues of the first importance, and these were denied him. Think of the subjects that Baudelaire was granted—Delacroix, Constantin Guys, Wagner—and then of the kind of books Poe was assigned to review:

Mephistopheles in England, or the Confessions of a Prime Minister
The Christian Florist
Noble Deeds of Women
Ups and Downs in the Life of a Distressed Gentleman
The History of Texas
Sacred Philosophy of the Seasons
Sketches of Conspicuous Living Characters in France
Dashes at Life with a Free Pencil
Alice Day; A Romance in Rhyme
Wakondah; The Master of Life
Poetical Remains of the Late Lucretia Maria Davidson

One is astounded that he managed to remain a rational critic at all, let alone such a good one.

The Man If the Muses could lobby for their interest, all biographical research into the lives of artists would probably be prohibited by law, and historians of the individual would have to confine themselves to those who act but do not make—generals, criminals, eccentrics, courtesans, and the like, about whom information is not only more interesting but less misleading. Good artists—the artist *manqué* is another matter—never make satisfactory heroes for novelists, because their life stories, even when interesting in themselves, are peripheral and less significant than their productions.

As a person, for example, Poe is a much less interesting figure than is Griswold. Since Professor Quinn published side by side the original versions of Poe's letters and Griswold's doctored versions, one is left panting with curiosity to know more about the latter. That one man should dislike another and speak maliciously of him after his death would be natural enough, but to take so much trouble, to blacken a reputation so subtly, presupposes a sustained hatred which is always fascinating because the capacity for sustained emotion of any kind is rare, and, in this instance, particularly so since no reasonable cause for it has yet been found.

In his personal reputation, as in so much else, Poe has been singularly unfortunate. Before the true facts were known, he was dismissed by respectable men of letters as a dissolute rake and hailed by the antirespectable as a romantically doomed figure, the Flying Dutchman of Whitman's dream.

> In a dream I once had, I saw a vessel on the sea, at midnight in a storm . . . flying uncontrolled with torn sails and broken spars through the wild sleet and winds and waves of the night. On the deck was a slender, slight, beautiful figure, a dim man, apparently enjoying all the terror, the murk, and the dislocation of which he was the centre and the victim.

Today this portrait has been shown to be false, but the moral climate has changed, and Poe would be more respected if it had been true. Had he been a really bad lot like Villon or Marlowe or

Verlaine, someone who drank like a fish and was guilty of spectacular crimes and vices, we should rather admire him; but it turns out that he was only the kind of fellow whom one hesitates to invite to a party because after two drinks he is apt to become tiresome, an unmanly sort of man whose love-life seems to have been largely confined to crying in laps and playing house, that his weaknesses were of that unromantic kind for which our age has least tolerance, perhaps because they are typical of ourselves.

If our present conception of Poe as a person is correct, however, it makes Poe the artist a much odder figure. Nobody has a good word to say for his foster father, John Allan, who certainly does not seem to have been a very attractive gentleman; but if we imagine ourselves in his place in the year 1831, what sort of view would we have taken of Poe's future?

Remembering his behavior at the university, his pointless enlistment in the army, his behavior at West Point, his behavior to ourselves, would he not have seemed to us an obvious case of a certain kind of neurotic with which we are quite familiar—the talented youngster who never comes to anything because he will not or cannot work, whose masterpieces never get beyond the third page, who loses job after job because he cannot get to work on time or meet a date line? We might find psychological excuses for him in his heredity and early childhood—the incompetent, irresponsible father, the death of his mother when he was two—but our prognosis for his future not only as a man but also as a writer would hardly have been sanguine. At the very best we might have hoped that in the course of a lifetime he would produce one or two exquisitely polished lyrics.

But what in fact did happen? While remaining in his personal life just as difficult and self-destructive as we foresaw, he quickly became a very hard-working and conscientious professional writer. None of his colleagues on magazines seems to have had any professional difficulty with him. Indeed, when one compares the quality of most of the books he had to review with the quality of his reviews, one is inclined to wish that, for the sake of his own work, he had been less conscientious. The defects we find in his work are so often just the defects we should have least expected—the errors of a professional who is overtaxed and working against the clock.

As to his private life and personality, had it been more romantically wicked, his work would not have the importance it has as being, in some senses, the first modern work. He was one of the first to suffer *consciously* the impact of the destruction of the traditional community and its values, and he paid the heaviest price for this consciousness. As D. H. Lawrence says in an essay conspicuous for its insights:

> Poe had a pretty bitter doom. Doomed to seethe down his soul in a great continuous convulsion of disintegration, and doomed to register the process. And then doomed to be abused for it, when he had performed some of the bitterest tasks of human experience, that can be asked of a man. Necessary tasks too. For the human soul must suffer its own disintegration, consciously, if ever it is to survive.

To which one might add: "Abused?" No, a worse doom than that. Doomed to be used in school textbooks as a bait to interest the young in good literature, to be a respectable rival to the pulps.

Still, he has had some rewards. Not many authors have been invoked as intercessors with God in an hour of need, as Poe was named by Baudelaire when he felt himself going mad; not many have been celebrated in poems as beautiful as Mallarmé's Sonnet, of which this is Roger Fry's translation.

THE TOMB OF EDGAR POE

Such as to himself eternity's changed him,
The Poet arouses with his naked sword
His age fright-stricken for not having known
That Death was triumphing in that strange voice!

They, with a Hydra's vile spasm at hearing the angel
Giving a sense more pure to the words of their tribe

Proclaimed aloud the sortilege drunk
In the dishonored flow of some black brew.

Oh, Grief! From soil and from the hostile cloud,
If thence our idea cannot carve a relief
Wherewith to adorn Poe's shining tomb

Calm block fallen down here from some dark disaster
May this granite at least show forever their bourn
To the black flights of Blasphemy sparse in the future.

Capri W. H. Auden
June, 1950

CHRONOLOGY

1808 David Poe marries Elizabeth Arnold Hopkins. He is Irish, she English. Both in the theatrical profession.

1809 January 19. Edgar Poe born in Boston, Massachusetts. Father soon deserts his family.

1811 Poe's mother dies in Richmond. Poe taken into the home of Mr. and Mrs. John Allan.

1815–1820 Departure with the Allans to England. Poe attends school at The Manor House, Stoke, Newington.

1820 Return to Richmond.

1826 Student at the University of Virginia. Withdrawn by John Allan.

1827 Quarrel with his foster father.
Tamerlane and Other Poems

1827–1829 Enlistment in the U.S. Army. Honorable discharge.
Al Aaraaf

1830–1831 U.S. Military Academy at West Point. Expelled.
Poems

1833 *Ms. Found in a Bottle*

1835–1836 Assistant editor of the *Southern Literary Messenger*, Richmond.

1836 Marriage to Virginia Clemm (born 1822).

1837–1838 Residence in New York.
Gordon Pym

1838 Moves to Philadelphia.

1839–1842 Assistant editor of *Burton's Gentleman's Magazine,* then editor of *Graham's Magazine,* Philadelphia.

1840 *Tales of the Grotesque and Arabesque.*
Feud with Longfellow.

1842 Virginia Poe breaks a blood vessel while singing.

1844 Moves to New York.

1845 An editor, later proprietor, of the *Broadway Journal,* New York.
The Raven and Other Poems
Tales

1846 The *Broadway Journal* fails. Moves to cottage in Fordham.

1847 Death of Virginia Poe.

1848 *Eureka*
Friendship with Mrs. Richmond (Annie) and Mrs. Whitman.
Engagement to Mrs. Whitman broken off.

1849 August. Lectures in Richmond on the Poetic Principle.
October. Is found unconscious in the street in Baltimore and dies October 7.

TEXTUAL AND BIBLIOGRAPHICAL NOTE

Despite the significance of Poe's position in the history of modern writing, no truly complete edition of his works exists. The most comprehensive collection is that edited by James A. Harrison, *The Complete Works of Edgar Allan Poe* (N.Y., 1902), 17 vols. For the poetry, Killis Campbell's *The Poems of Edgar Allan Poe* (Boston, 1917) is by far the best, and these two editions are the ones on which this text is based. The prose is taken from the former, and the poetry from the latter. The text of each has been meticulously followed, though certain textual inconsistencies in each are open to question and indicate the desirability of truly definitive editing. His letters have been recently collected and edited by John Ward Ostrom, *The Letters of Edgar Allan Poe* (Cambridge, Mass., 1948), 2 vols. Of the biographical studies, the romantic treatment of Poe by Hervey Allen, *Israfel* (N.Y., 1926), 2 vols., has always been popular, while Arthur H. Quinn's *Edgar Allan Poe: A Critical Biography* (N.Y., 1941) is the most thorough from a scholarly point of view. George E. Woodberry's *The Life of Edgar Allan Poe, Personal and Literary, with His Chief Correspondence with Men of Letters* (Boston, 1885; rev. ed. Boston, 1909, 2 vols.) is still valuable.

Critical commentary on Poe's work has been extensive, particularly on his poetry. Few essays have been more perceptive than Charles Baudelaire's early estimates: "Edgar Allan Poe: Sa Vie et Ses Oeuvres," *Revue de Paris* (March-April, 1852); "Edgar Allan Poe: Sa Vie et Ses Oeuvres," *Histoires Extraordinaires par Edgar Poe* (Paris, 1856); and "Notes Nouvelles sur Edgar Poe" in the 1857 edition of the same book. The latter two have been reprinted in D. Parmée, ed., *Selected Critical Studies of Baudelaire*

(Cambridge, England, 1949), 25-69. Poe's impact on French writing is most fully treated in Célestin Pierre Cambiaire's *The Influence of Edgar Allan Poe in France* (N.Y., 1927). Paul Valéry's "Situation de Baudelaire," in *Variété II* (Paris, 1930), 141-74, shows the continuance of the interest. Paul Elmore More's "The Origins of Hawthorne and Poe," in *Shelburne Essays,* 1st series (N.Y., 1904), 51-70, and W. C. Brownell's "Poe" in *American Prose Masters* (N.Y., 1909), 207-67, are excellent examples of the most sensitive treatment of Poe at the beginning of the century. More recent, and variously stimulating, essays are those of D. H. Lawrence in *Studies in Classic American Literature* (N.Y., 1923), 93-120; Yvor Winters' "Edgar Allan Poe: a Crisis in the History of American Obscurantism," *In Defense of Reason* (N.Y., 1947), 234-61; Horace Gregory, "Within the Private View," *Partisan Review* (May-June, 1943), 263-74; Edmund Wilson, "Poe as a Literary Critic," *Nation* (Oct. 31, 1942), 452-53; and F. O. Matthiessen, "Edgar Allan Poe," in Spiller et al., *Literary History of the United States* (N.Y., 1948), I, 321-42. T. S. Eliot's essay *From Poe to Valéry* (N.Y., 1948) has recently appeared, and Allen Tate's forthcoming critical and biographical study of Poe should be a significant contribution.

The scholarship on Poe is extensive, and the particular contributions to knowledge and the suggestions of possible sources or interpretations can be found among the articles listed in Lewis Leary's *Articles on American Literature Appearing in Current Periodicals, 1920-1945* (Durham, N.C., 1947), 91-106; or in Spiller et al., *Literary History of the United States* (N.Y., 1948), III, 689-96. Of general interest and value are: Walter Blair's "Poe's Conception of Incident and Tone in the Tale," *Modern Philology* (May, 1944), 228-40; Norman Foerster, *American Criticism* (Boston, 1928), 1-51; Killis Campbell, *The Mind of Poe* (Cambridge, Mass., 1933); Margaret Alterton, *Origins of Poe's Critical Theory* (Iowa City, Iowa, 1925); and John E. Cooke, *Poe as a Literary Critic* (Baltimore, Md., 1946). Bradford

A. Booth and Claude E. Jones, *A Concordance of the Poetical Works of Edgar Allan Poe* (Baltimore, Md., 1941) is useful.

The chief bibliographies of Poe are those by Charles F. Heartman and James R. Canny, *A Bibliography of the First Printings of the Writings of Edgar Allan Poe* (Hattiesburg, Miss., 1943) and John W. Robertson, *Bibliography of the Writings of Edgar A. Poe* (San Francisco, 1934), 2 vols.

A critical and biographical study showing the influence of the theater on Poe's life and work is N. Bryllion Fagin's *The Histrionic Mr. Poe* (Baltimore, Md., 1949).

Contents

POETRY

EUREKA

SELECTED PROSE AND POETRY

Stories

THE FALL OF THE HOUSE OF USHER*

Son cœur est un luth suspendu;
Sitôt qu'on le touche il résonne.
De Béranger

DURING the whole of a dull, dark, and soundless day in the autumn of the year, when the clouds hung oppressively low in the heavens, I had been passing alone, on horseback, through a singularly dreary tract of country, and at length found myself, as the shades of the evening drew on, within view of the melancholy House of Usher. I know not how it was—but, with the first glimpse of the building, a sense of insufferable gloom pervaded my spirit. I say insufferable; for the feeling was unrelieved by any of that half-pleasurable, because poetic, sentiment with which the mind usually receives even the sternest natural images of the desolate or terrible. I looked upon the scene before me—upon the mere house, and the simple landscape features of the domain—upon the bleak walls—upon the vacant eye-like windows—upon a few rank sedges—and upon a few white trunks of decayed trees—with an utter depression of soul which I can compare to no earthly sensation more properly than to the after-dream of the reveller upon opium—the bitter lapse into every-day life—the hideous dropping off of the veil. There was an iciness, a sinking, a sickening of the heart—an unredeemed dreariness of thought which no goading of the imagination could torture into aught of the sublime.

* *Burton's Gentleman's Magazine,* September, 1839; 1840; 1845.

What was it—I paused to think—what was it that so unnerved me in the contemplation of the House of Usher? It was a mystery all insoluble; nor could I grapple with the shadowy fancies that crowded upon me as I pondered. I was forced to fall back upon the unsatisfactory conclusion, that while, beyond doubt, there *are* combinations of very simple natural objects which have the power of thus affecting us, still the analysis of this power lies among considerations beyond our depth. It was possible, I reflected, that a mere different arrangement of the particulars of the scene, of the details of the picture, would be sufficient to modify, or perhaps to annihilate its capacity for sorrowful impression; and, acting upon this idea, I reined my horse to the precipitous brink of a black and lurid tarn that lay in unruffled lustre by the dwelling, and gazed down—but with a shudder even more thrilling than before—upon the remodelled and inverted images of the gray sedge, and the ghastly tree-stems, and the vacant and eye-like windows.

Nevertheless, in this mansion of gloom I now proposed to myself a sojourn of some weeks. Its proprietor, Roderick Usher, had been one of my boon companions in boyhood; but many years had elapsed since our last meeting. A letter, however, had lately reached me in a distant part of the country—a letter from him—which, in its wildly importunate nature, had admitted of no other than a personal reply. The MS. gave evidence of nervous agitation. The writer spoke of acute bodily illness—of a mental disorder which oppressed him—and of an earnest desire to see me, as his best and indeed his only personal friend, with a view of attempting, by the cheerfulness of my society, some alleviation of his malady. It was the manner in which all this, and much more, was said—it was the apparent *heart* that went with his request—which allowed me no room for hesitation; and I accordingly obeyed forthwith what I still considered a very singular summons.

Although, as boys, we had been even intimate associates, yet I really knew little of my friend. His reserve had been always excessive and habitual. I was aware, however, that his very ancient family had been noted, time out of mind, for a peculiar sensibility of temperament, displaying itself, through long ages, in many works of exalted art, and manifested, of late, in repeated deeds of munificent yet unobtrusive charity, as well as in a passionate devotion to the intricacies, perhaps even more than to the orthodox and easily recognizable beauties, of musical science. I had learned, too, the very remarkable fact, that the stem of the Usher race, all time-honoured as it was, had put forth, at no period, any enduring branch; in other words, that the entire family lay in the direct line of descent, and had always, with very trifling and very temporary variation, so lain. It was this deficiency, I considered, while running over in thought the perfect keeping of the character of the premises with the accredited character of the people, and while speculating upon the possible influence which the one, in the long lapse of centuries, might have exercised upon the other—it was this deficiency, perhaps, of collateral issue, and the consequent undeviating transmission, from sire to son, of the patrimony with the name, which had, at length, so identified the two as to merge the original title of the estate in the quaint and equivocal appellation of the "House of Usher"—an appellation which seemed to include, in the minds of the peasantry who used it, both the family and the family mansion.

I have said that the sole effect of my somewhat childish experiment—that of looking down within the tarn—had been to deepen the first singular impression. There can be no doubt that the consciousness of the rapid increase of my superstition—for why should I not so term it?—served mainly to accelerate the increase itself. Such, I have long known, is the paradoxical law of all sentiments having terror as a basis. And it might have been for this reason only, that, when I again uplifted my eyes to the house itself, from its image in the pool, there grew in my mind a strange fancy—a fancy so ridiculous, indeed, that I but mention it to show the vivid force of the sensations which oppressed me. I had so worked upon my imagination as really to believe that about the whole mansion and domain there hung an atmosphere peculiar to themselves and their immediate vicinity—an atmosphere which had no affinity with the air of heaven, but which had reeked up from the decayed trees, and the gray wall, and the silent tarn—a pestilent and mystic vapour, dull, sluggish, faintly discernible, and leaden-hued.

Shaking off from my spirit what *must* have been a dream, I scanned more narrowly the real aspect of the building. Its principal feature seemed to be that of an excessive antiquity. The discoloration of ages had been great. Minute fungi overspread the whole exterior, hanging in a fine tangled web-work from the eaves. Yet all this was apart from any extraordinary dilapidation. No portion of the masonry had fallen; and there appeared to be a wild inconsistency between its still perfect adaptation of parts, and the crumbling condition of the individual stones. In this there was much that reminded me of the specious totality of old woodwork which has rotted for long years in some neglected vault, with no disturbance from the breath of the external air. Beyond this indication of extensive decay, however, the fabric gave little token of instability. Perhaps the eye of a scrutinizing observer might have discovered a barely perceptible fissure, which, extending from the roof of the building in front, made its way down the wall in a zigzag direction, until it became lost in the sullen waters of the tarn.

Noticing these things, I rode over a short causeway to the house. A servant in waiting took my horse, and I entered the Gothic archway of the hall. A valet, of stealthy step, thence conducted me, in silence, through many dark and intricate passages in my progress to the *studio* of his master. Much that I encountered on the way contributed, I know not how, to heighten the vague sentiments of which I have already spoken. While the objects around me—while the carvings of the ceilings, the sombre tapestries of the walls, the ebon blackness of the floors, and the phantasmagoric armorial trophies which rattled as I strode, were but matters to which, or to such as which, I had been accustomed from my infancy—while I hesitated not to acknowledge how familiar was all this—I still wondered to find how unfamiliar were the fancies which ordinary images were stirring up. On one of the staircases, I met the physician of the family. His countenance, I thought, wore a mingled expression of low cunning and perplexity. He accosted me with trepidation and passed on. The valet now threw open a door and ushered me into the presence of his master.

The room in which I found myself was very large and lofty. The windows were long, narrow, and pointed, and at so vast a distance from the black oaken floor as to be altogether inaccessible from within. Feeble gleams of encrimsoned light made their way through the trellissed panes, and served to render sufficiently distinct the more prominent objects around; the eye, however, struggled in vain to reach the remoter angles of the chamber, or the recesses of the vaulted and fretted ceiling. Dark draperies hung upon the walls. The general furniture was profuse, comfortless, antique, and tattered. Many books and musical instruments lay scattered about, but failed to give any vitality to the scene. I felt that I breathed an atmosphere of sorrow. An air of stern, deep, and irredeemable gloom hung over and pervaded all.

Upon my entrance, Usher arose from a sofa on which he had been lying at full length, and greeted me with a vivacious warmth which had much in it, I at first thought, of an overdone cordiality —of the constrained effort of the *ennuyé* man of the world. A glance, however, at his countenance convinced me of his perfect sincerity. We sat down; and for some moments, while he spoke not, I gazed upon him with a feeling half of pity, half of awe. Surely, man had never before so terribly altered, in so brief a period, as had Roderick Usher! It was with difficulty that I could bring myself to admit the identity of the wan being before me with the companion of my early boyhood. Yet the character of his face had been at all times remarkable. A cadaverousness of complexion; an eye large, liquid, and luminous beyond comparison; lips somewhat thin and very pallid, but of a surpassingly beautiful curve; a nose of a delicate Hebrew model, but with a breadth of nostril unusual in similar formations; a finely moulded chin, speaking, in its want of prominence, of a want of moral energy;

hair of a more than web-like softness and tenuity; these features, with an inordinate expansion above the regions of the temple, made up altogether a countenance not easily to be forgotten. And now in the mere exaggeration of the prevailing character of these features, and of the expression they were wont to convey, lay so much of change that I doubted to whom I spoke. The now ghastly pallor of the skin, and the now miraculous lustre of the eye, above all things startled and even awed me. The silken hair, too, had been suffered to grow all unheeded, and as, in its wild gossamer texture, it floated rather than fell about the face. I could not, even with effort, connect its Arabesque expression with any idea of simple humanity.

In the manner of my friend I was at once struck with an incoherence—an inconsistency; and I soon found this to arise from a series of feeble and futile struggles to overcome an habitual trepidancy—an excessive nervous agitation. For something of this nature I had indeed been prepared, no less by his letter, than by reminiscences of certain boyish traits, and by conclusions deduced from his peculiar physical conformation and temperament. His action was alternately vivacious and sullen. His voice varied rapidly from a tremulous indecision (when the animal spirits seemed utterly in abeyance) to that species of energetic concision —that abrupt, weighty, unhurried, and hollow-sounding enunciation—that leaden, self-balanced, and perfectly modulated guttural utterance, which may be observed in the lost drunkard, or the irreclaimable eater of opium, during the periods of his most intense excitement.

It was thus that he spoke of the object of my visit, of his earnest desire to see me, and of the solace he expected me to afford him. He entered, at some length, into what he conceived to be the nature of his malady. It was, he said, a constitutional and a family evil, and one for which he despaired to find a remedy—a mere nervous affection, he immediately added, which would undoubtedly soon pass off. It displayed itself in a host of unnatural sensations. Some of these, as he detailed them, interested and bewildered me; although, perhaps, the terms and the general manner of their narration had their weight. He suffered much from a morbid acuteness of the senses; the most insipid food was alone endurable; he could wear only garments of certain texture; the odours of all flowers were oppressive; his eyes were tortured by even a faint light; and there were but peculiar sounds, and these from stringed instruments, which did not inspire him with horror.

To an anomalous species of terror I found him a bounden slave. "I shall perish," said he, "I *must* perish in this deplorable folly. Thus, thus, and not otherwise, shall I be lost. I dread the events of the future, not in themselves, but in their results. I shudder at the thought of any, even the most trivial, incident, which may operate upon this intolerable agitation of soul. I have, indeed, no abhorrence of danger, except in its absolute effect—in terror. In this unnerved—in this pitiable condition—I feel that the period will sooner or later arrive when I must abandon life and reason together, in some struggle with the grim phantasm, FEAR."

I learned, moreover, at intervals, and through broken and equivocal hints, another singular feature of his mental condition. He was enchained by certain superstitious impressions in regard to the dwelling which he tenanted, and whence, for many years, he had never ventured forth—in regard to an influence whose supposititious force was conveyed in terms too shadowy here to be re-stated—an influence which some peculiarities in the mere form and substance of his family mansion had, by dint of long sufferance, he said, obtained over his spirit—an effect which the *physique* of the gray walls and turrets, and of the dim tarn into which they all looked down, had, at length, brought about upon the *morale* of his existence.

He admitted, however, although with hesitation, that much of the peculiar gloom which thus afflicted him could be traced to a more natural and far more palpable origin—to the severe and long-continued illness—indeed to the evidently approaching dissolution—of a tenderly beloved sister, his sole companion for long years, his last and only relative on earth. "Her decease," he said, with a bitterness which I can never forget, "would leave him (him, the hopeless and the frail) the last of the ancient race of the Ushers." While he spoke, the lady Madeline (for so was she called) passed slowly through a remote portion of the apartment, and, without having noticed my presence, disappeared. I regarded her with an utter astonishment not unmingled with dread; and yet I found it impossible to account for such feelings. A sensation of stupor oppressed me, as my eyes followed her retreating steps. When a door, at length, closed upon her, my glance sought instinctively and eagerly the countenance of the brother—but he had buried his face in his hands, and I could only perceive that a far more than ordinary wanness had overspread the emaciated fingers through which trickled many passionate tears.

The disease of the lady Madeline had long baffled the skill of her physicians. A settled apathy, a gradual wasting away of the person, and frequent although transient affections of a partially cataleptical character were the unusual diagnosis. Hitherto she had steadily borne up against the pressure of her malady, and had not betaken herself finally to bed; but on the closing in of the evening of my arrival at the house, she succumbed (as her brother told me at night with inexpressible agitation) to the prostrating power of the destroyer; and I learned that the glimpse I had obtained of her person would thus probably be the last I should obtain—that the lady, at least while living, would be seen by me no more.

For several days ensuing, her name was unmentioned by either Usher or myself: and during this period I was busied in earnest endeavours to alleviate the melancholy of my friend. We painted and read together, or I listened, as if in a dream, to the wild improvisations of his speaking guitar. And thus, as a closer and still closer intimacy admitted me more unreservedly into the recesses of his spirit, the more bitterly did I perceive the futility of all attempt at cheering a mind from which darkness, as if an inherent positive quality, poured forth upon all objects of the moral and physical universe in one unceasing radiation of gloom.

I shall ever bear about me a memory of the many solemn hours I thus spent alone with the master of the House of Usher. Yet I should fail in any attempt to convey an idea of the exact character of the studies, or of the occupations, in which he involved me, or led me the way. An excited and highly distempered ideality threw a sulphureous lustre over all. His long improvised dirges will ring forever in my ears. Among other things, I hold painfully in mind a certain singular perversion and amplification of the wild air of the last waltz of Von Weber. From the paintings over which his elaborate fancy brooded, and which grew, touch by touch, into vaguenesses at which I shuddered the more thrillingly, because I shuddered knowing not why;—from these paintings (vivid as their images now are before me) I would in vain endeavour to educe more than a small portion which should lie within the compass of merely written words. By the utter simplicity, by the nakedness of his designs, he arrested and overawed attention. If ever mortal painted an idea, that mortal was Roderick Usher. For me at least, in the circumstances then surrounding me, there arose out of the pure abstractions which the hypochondriac contrived to throw upon his canvas, an intensity of intolerable awe, no shadow of which felt I ever yet in the contemplation of the certainly glowing yet too concrete reveries of Fuseli.

One of the phantasmagoric conceptions of my friend, partaking not so rigidly of the spirit of abstraction, may be shadowed forth, although feebly, in words. A small picture presented the interior of an immensely long and rectangular vault or tunnel, with low walls, smooth, white, and without interruption or device. Certain accessory points of the design served well to convey the idea that this excavation lay at an exceeding depth below the surface of the earth. No outlet was observed in any portion of its vast extent, and no torch or other artificial source of light was discernible; yet a flood of intense rays rolled throughout, and bathed the whole in a ghastly and inappropriate splendour.

I have just spoken of that morbid condition of the auditory nerve which rendered all music intolerable to the sufferer, with the exception of certain effects of stringed instruments. It was, perhaps, the narrow limits to which he thus confined himself upon the guitar which gave birth, in great measure, to the fantastic character of his performances. But the fervid *facility* of his *impromptus* could not be so accounted for. They must have been, and were, in the notes, as well as in the words of his wild fantasias (for he not unfrequently accompanied himself with rhymed verbal improvisations), the result of that intense mental collectedness and concentration to which I have previously alluded as observable only in particular moments of the highest artificial excitement. The words of one of these rhapsodies I have easily remembered. I was, perhaps, the more forcibly impressed with it as he gave it, because, in the under or mystic current of its meaning, I fancied that I perceived, and for the first time, a full consciousness on the part of Usher of the tottering of his lofty reason upon her throne. The verses, which were entitled "The Haunted Palace," ran very nearly, if not accurately, thus:

I

In the greenest of our valleys, 6½
  By good angels tenanted,
Once a fair and stately palace—
  Radiant palace—reared its head.
In the monarch Thought's dominion—
  It stood there!
Never seraph spread a pinion
  Over fabric half so fair.

II

Banners yellow, glorious, golden,
  On its roof did float and flow
(This—all this—was in the olden
  Time long ago)
And every gentle air that dallied,

In that sweet day,
Along the ramparts plumed and pallid,
A winged odour went away.

III

Wanderers in that happy valley
Through two luminous windows saw
Spirits moving musically
To a lute's well-tunèd law,
Round about a throne, where sitting
(Porphyrogene!)
In state his glory well befitting,
The ruler of the realm was seen.

IV

And all with pearl and ruby glowing
Was the fair palace door,
Through which came flowing, flowing, flowing
And sparkling evermore,
A troop of Echoes whose sweet duty
Was but to sing,
In voices of surpassing beauty,
The wit and wisdom of their king.

V

But evil things, in robes of sorrow,
Assailed the monarch's high estate;
(Ah, let us mourn, for never morrow
Shall dawn upon him, desolate!)
And, round about his home, the glory
That blushed and bloomed
Is but a dim-remembered story
Of the old time entombed.

VI

And travellers now within that valley,
  Through the red-litten windows see
Vast forms that move fantastically
  To a discordant melody;
While, like a rapid ghastly river,
  Through the pale door,
A hideous throng rush out forever,
  And laugh—but smile no more.

I well remember that suggestions arising from this ballad, led us into a train of thought, wherein there became manifest an opinion of Usher's which I mention not so much on account of its novelty, (for other men have thought thus,) as on account of the pertinacity with which he maintained it. This opinion, in its general form, was that of the sentience of all vegetable things. But, in his disordered fancy, the idea had assumed a more daring character, and trespassed, under certain conditions, upon the kingdom of inorganization. I lack words to express the full extent, or the earnest *abandon* of his persuasion. The belief, however, was connected (as I have previously hinted) with the gray stones of the home of his forefathers. The conditions of the sentence had been here, he imagined, fulfilled in the method of collocation of these stones—in the order of their arrangement, as well as in that of the many *fungi* which overspread them, and of the decayed trees which stood around—above all, in the long undisturbed endurance of this arrangement, and in its reduplication in the still waters of the tarn. Its evidence—the evidence of the sentience—was to be seen, he said (and I here started as he spoke), in the gradual yet certain condensation of an atmosphere of their own about the waters and the walls. The result was discoverable, he added, in that silent yet importunate and terrible influence which for centuries had moulded the destinies of his family, and which made *him* what I now saw him—what he was. Such opinions need no comment, and I will make none.

Our books—the books which, for years, had formed no small portion of the mental existence of the invalid—were, as might be supposed, in strict keeping with this character of phantasm. We pored together over such works as the Ververt et Chartreuse of Gresset; the Belphegor of Machiavelli; the Heaven and Hell of Swedenborg; the Subterranean Voyage of Nicholas Klimm of Holberg; the Chiromancy of Robert Flud, of Jean D'Indaginé, and of De la Chambre; the Journey into the Blue Distance of Tieck; and the City of the Sun of Campanella. One favourite volume was a small octavo edition of the *Directorium Inquisitorum,* by the Dominican Eymeric de Gironne; and there were passages in Pomponius Mela, about the old African Satyrs and Œgipans, over which Usher would sit dreaming for hours. His chief delight, however, was found in the perusal of an exceedingly rare and curious book in quarto Gothic—the manual of a forgotten church—the *Vigiliæ Mortuorum secundum Chorum Ecclesiæ Maguntinæ.*

I could not help thinking of the wild ritual of this work, and of its probable influence upon the hypochondriac, when, one evening, having informed me abruptly that the lady Madeline was no more, he stated his intention of preserving her corpse for a fortnight, (previously to its final interment,) in one of the numerous vaults within the main walls of the building. The worldly reason, however, assigned for this singular proceeding, was one which I did not feel at liberty to dispute. The brother had been led to his resolution (so he told me) by consideration of the unusual character of the malady of the deceased, of certain obtrusive and eager inquiries on the part of her medical men, and of the remote and exposed situation of the burial-ground of the family. I will not deny that when I called to mind the sinister countenance of the person whom I met upon the staircase, on the day of my arrival at the house, I had no desire to oppose what I regarded as at best but a harmless, and by no means an unnatural, precaution.

At the request of Usher, I personally aided him in the arrangements for the temporary entombment. The body having been encoffined, we two alone bore it to its rest. The vault in which we placed it (and which had been so long unopened that our torches, half smothered in its oppressive atmosphere, gave us little opportunity for investigation) was small, damp, and entirely without means of admission for light; lying, at great depth, immediately beneath that portion of the building in which was my own sleeping apartment. It had been used, apparently, in remote feudal times, for the worst purposes of a donjon-keep, and, in later days, as a place of deposit for powder, or some other highly combustible substance, as a portion of its floor, and the whole interior of a long archway through which we reached it, were carefully sheathed with copper. The door, of massive iron, had been, also, similarly protected. Its immense weight caused an unusually sharp grating sound, as it moved upon its hinges.

Having deposited our mournful burden upon tressels within this region of horror, we partially turned aside the yet unscrewed lid of the coffin, and looked upon the face of the tenant. A striking similitude between the brother and sister now first arrested my attention; and Usher, divining, perhaps, my thoughts, murmured out some few words from which I learned that the deceased and himself had been twins, and that sympathies of a scarcely intelligible nature had always existed between them. Our glances, however, rested not long upon the dead—for we could not regard her unawed. The disease which had thus entombed the lady in the maturity of youth, had left, as usual in all maladies of a strictly cataleptical character, the mockery of a faint blush upon the bosom and the face, and that suspiciously lingering smile upon the lip which is so terrible in death. We replaced and screwed down the lid, and, having secured the door of iron, made our way, with toil, into the scarcely less gloomy apartments of the upper portion of the house.

And now, some days of bitter grief having elapsed, an observable change came over the features of the mental disorder of my friend. His ordinary manner had vanished. His ordinary occupations were neglected or forgotten. He roamed from chamber to chamber with hurried, unequal, and objectless step. The pallor of his countenance had assumed, if possible, a more ghastly hue—but the luminousness of his eye had utterly gone out. The once occasional huskiness of his tone was heard no more; and a tremulous quaver, as if of extreme terror, habitually characterized his utterance. There were times, indeed, when I thought his unceasingly agitated mind was labouring with some oppressive secret, to divulge which he struggled for the necessary courage. At times, again, I was obliged to resolve all into the mere inexplicable vagaries of madness, for I beheld him gazing upon vacancy for long hours, in an attitude of the profoundest attention, as if listening to some imaginary sound. It was no wonder that his condition terrified—that it infected me. I felt creeping upon me, by slow yet certain degrees, the wild influences of his own fantastic yet impressive superstitions.

It was, especially, upon retiring to bed late in the night of the seventh or eighth day after the placing of the lady Madeline within the donjon, that I experienced the full power of such feelings. Sleep came not near my couch—while the hours waned and waned away. I struggled to reason off the nervousness which had dominion over me. I endeavoured to believe that much, if not all of what I felt, was due to the bewildering influence of the gloomy furniture of the room—of the dark and tattered draperies, which, tortured into motion by the breath of a rising tempest, swayed fitfully to and fro upon the walls, and rustled uneasily about the decorations of the bed. But my efforts were fruitless. An irrepressible tremour gradually pervaded my frame; and, at length, there sat upon my very heart an incubus of utterly causeless alarm. Shaking this off with a gasp and a struggle, I uplifted myself upon the pillows, and, peering earnestly within the intense darkness of the chamber, hearkened—I know not why, except that an instinctive spirit prompted me—to certain low and indefinite sounds which came, through the pauses of the storm, at long intervals, I knew not whence. Overpowered by an intense sentiment of horror, unaccountable yet unendurable, I threw on my clothes with haste, (for I felt that I should sleep no more during the night,) and endeavoured to arouse myself from the pitiable condition into which I had fallen, by pacing rapidly to and fro through the apartment.

I had taken but few turns in this manner, when a light step on an adjoining staircase arrested my attention. I presently recognised it as that of Usher. In an instant afterward he rapped, with a gentle touch, at my door, and entered, bearing a lamp. His countenance was, as usual, cadaverously wan—but, moreover, there was a species of mad hilarity in his eyes—an evidently restrained *hysteria* in his whole demeanour. His air appalled me—but anything was preferable to the solitude which I had so long endured, and I even welcomed his presence as a relief.

"And you have not seen it?" he said abruptly, after having stared about him for some moments in silence—"you have not then seen it?—but, stay! you shall." Thus speaking, and having carefully shaded his lamp, he hurried to one of the casements, and threw it freely open to the storm.

The impetuous fury of the entering gust nearly lifted us from our feet. It was, indeed, a tempestuous yet sternly beautiful night, and one wildly singular in its terror and its beauty. A whirlwind had apparently collected its force in our vicinity; for there were frequent and violent alterations in the direction of the wind; and the exceeding density of the clouds (which hung so low as to press upon the turrets of the house) did not prevent our perceiving the life-like velocity with which they flew careering from all points against each other, without passing away into the distance. I say that even their exceeding density did not prevent our perceiving this—yet we had no glimpse of the moon or stars—nor was there any flashing forth of the lightning. But the under surfaces of the huge masses of agitated vapour, as well as all terrestrial objects immediately around us, were glowing in the unnatural light of a faintly luminous and distinctly visible gaseous exhalation which hung about and enshrouded the mansion.

"You must not—you shall not behold this!" said I, shuddering, to Usher, as I led him, with a gentle violence, from the window to a seat. "These appearances, which bewilder you, are merely electrical phenomena not uncommon—or it may be that they have their ghastly origin in the rank miasma of the tarn. Let us close this casement;—the air is chilling and dangerous to your frame. Here is one of your favourite romances. I will read, and you shall listen;—and so we will pass away this terrible night together."

The antique volume which I had taken up was the "Mad Trist" of Sir Launcelot Canning; but I had called it a favourite of Usher's more in sad jest than in earnest; for, in truth, there is little in its uncouth and unimaginative prolixity which could have had interest for the lofty and spiritual ideality of my friend. It was, however, the only book immediately at hand; and I indulged a vague hope that the excitement which now agitated the hypochondriac, might find relief (for the history of mental disorder is full of similar anomalies) even in the extremeness of the folly which I should read. Could I have judged, indeed, by the wild overstrained air of vivacity with which he hearkened, or apparently hearkened, to the words of the tale, I might well have congratulated myself upon the success of my design.

I had arrived at that well-known portion of the story where Ethelred, the hero of the Trist, having sought in vain for peaceable admission into the dwelling of the hermit, proceeds to make good an entrance by force. Here, it will be remembered, the words of the narrative run thus:

"And Ethelred, who was by nature of a doughty heart, and who was now mighty withal, on account of the powerfulness of the wine which he had drunken, waited no longer to hold parley with the hermit, who, in sooth, was of an obstinate and maliceful turn, but, feeling the rain upon his shoulders, and fearing the rising of the tempest, uplifted his mace outright, and, with blows, made quickly room in the plankings of the door for his gauntleted hand; and now pulling therewith sturdily, he so cracked, and ripped, and tore all asunder, that the noise of the dry and hollow-sounding wood alarumed and reverberated throughout the forest."

At the termination of this sentence I started and, for a moment, paused; for it appeared to me (although I at once concluded that my excited fancy had deceived me)—it appeared to me that, from some very remote portion of the mansion, there came, indistinctly, to my ears, what might have been, in its exact similarity of character, the echo (but a stifled and dull one certainly) of the very cracking and ripping sound which Sir Launcelot had so particularly described. It was, beyond doubt, the coincidence alone which had arrested my attention; for, amid the rattling of the sashes of the casements, and the ordinary commingled noises of the still increasing storm, the sound, in itself, had nothing, surely, which should have interested or disturbed me. I continued the story:

"But the good champion Ethelred, now entering within the door, was sore enraged and amazed to perceive no signal of the maliceful hermit; but, in the stead thereof, a dragon of a scaly and prodigious demeanour, and of a fiery tongue, which sate in guard before a palace of gold, with a floor of silver; and upon the wall there hung a shield of shining brass with this legend enwritten—

> Who entereth herein, a conqueror hath bin;
> Who slayeth the dragon, the shield he shall win.

And Ethelred uplifted his mace, and struck upon the head of the dragon, which fell before him, and gave up his pesty breath, with a shriek so horrid and harsh, and withal so piercing, that Ethelred had fain to close his ears with his hands against the dreadful noise of it, the like whereof was never before heard."

Here again I paused abruptly, and now with a feeling of wild amazement—for there could be no doubt whatever that, in this instance, I did actually hear (although from what direction it proceeded I found it impossible to say) a low and apparently distant, but harsh, protracted, and most unusual screaming or grating sound—the exact counterpart of what my fancy had already conjured up for the dragon's unnatural shriek as described by the romancer.

Oppressed, as I certainly was, upon the occurrence of this second and most extraordinary coincidence, by a thousand conflicting sensations, in which wonder and extreme terror were predominant, I still retained sufficient presence of mind to avoid exciting, by any observation, the sensitive nervousness of my companion. I was by no means certain that he had noticed the sounds in question; although, assuredly, a strange alteration had, during the last few minutes, taken place in his demeanour. From a position fronting my own, he had gradually brought round his chair, so as to sit with his face to the door of the chamber; and thus I could but partially perceive his features, although I saw that his lips trembled as if he were murmuring inaudibly. His head had dropped upon his breast—yet I knew that he was not asleep, from the wide and rigid opening of the eye as I caught a glance of it in profile. The motion of his body, too, was at variance with this idea—for he rocked from side to side with a gentle yet constant and uniform sway. Having rapidly taken notice of all this, I resumed the narrative of Sir Launcelot, which thus proceeded:

"And now, the champion, having escaped from the terrible fury of the dragon, bethinking himself of the brazen shield, and of the breaking up of the enchantment which was upon it, removed the carcass from out of the way before him, and approached valorously over the silver pavement of the castle to where the shield was upon the wall; which in sooth tarried not for his full coming, but fell down at his feet upon the silver floor, with a mighty great and terrible ringing sound."

No sooner had these syllables passed my lips, than—as if a shield of brass had indeed, at the moment, fallen heavily upon a floor of silver—I became aware of a distinct, hollow, metallic, and clangorous, yet apparently muffled, reverberation. Completely unnerved, I leaped to my feet; but the measured rocking movement of Usher was undisturbed. I rushed to the chair in which he sat. His eyes were bent fixedly before him, and throughout his whole countenance there reigned a stony rigidity. But, as I placed my hand upon his shoulder, there came a strong shudder over his whole person; a sickly smile quivered about his lips; and I saw that he spoke in a low, hurried, and gibbering murmur, as if unconscious of my presence. Bending closely over him, I at length drank in the hideous import of his words.

"Not hear it?—yes, I hear it, and *have* heard it. Long—long—long—many minutes, many hours, many days, have I heard it—yet I dared not—oh, pity me, miserable wretch that I am! —I dared not—I *dared* not speak! *We have put her living in the tomb!* Said I not that my senses were acute? I *now* tell you that I heard her first feeble movements in the hollow coffin. I heard them—many, many days ago—yet I dared not—I *dared not speak!* And now—to-night—Ethelred—ha! ha!—the breaking of the hermit's door, and the death-cry of the dragon, and the clangour of the shield!—say, rather, the rending of her coffin, and the grating of the iron hinges of her prison, and her struggles within the coppered archway of the vault! Oh whither shall I fly? Will she not be here anon? Is she not hurrying to upbraid me for my haste? Have I not heard her footstep on the stair? Do I not distinguish that heavy and horrible beating of her heart? MADMAN!" —here he sprang furiously to his feet, and shrieked out his syllables, as if in the effort he were giving up his soul—"MADMAN! I TELL YOU THAT SHE NOW STANDS WITHOUT THE DOOR!"

As if in the superhuman energy of his utterance there had been found the potency of a spell, the huge antique panels to which the speaker pointed threw slowly back, upon the instant, their ponderous and ebony jaws. It was the work of the rushing gust—but then without those doors there DID stand the lofty and enshrouded figure of the lady Madeline of Usher. There was blood upon her white robes, and the evidence of some bitter struggle upon every portion of her emaciated frame. For a moment she remained trembling and reeling to and fro upon the threshold, then, with a low moaning cry, fell heavily inward upon the person of her brother, and in her violent and now final death-agonies, bore him to the floor a corpse, and a victim to the terrors he had anticipated.

From that chamber, and from that mansion, I fled aghast. The storm was still abroad in all its wrath as I found myself crossing the old causeway. Suddenly there shot along the path a wild light, and I turned to see whence a gleam so unusual could have issued; for the vast house and its shadows were alone behind me. The radiance was that of the full, setting, and blood-red moon, which now shone vividly through that once barely discernible fissure, of which I have before spoken as extending from the roof of the building, in a zigzag direction, to the base. While I gazed, this fissure rapidly widened—there came a fierce breath of the whirlwind—the entire orb of the satellite burst at once upon my sight—my brain reeled as I saw the mighty walls rushing asunder—there was a long tumultuous shouting sound like the voice of a thousand waters—and the deep and dank tarn at my feet closed sullenly and silently over the fragments of the "House of Usher"

LIGEIA*

And the will therein lieth, which dieth not. Who knoweth the mysteries of the will, with its vigor? For God is but a great will pervading all things by nature of its intentness. Man doth not yield himself to the angels, nor unto death utterly, save only through the weakness of his feeble will. *Joseph Glanvill*

I CANNOT, for my soul, remember how, when, or even precisely where, I first became acquainted with the lady Ligeia. Long years have since elapsed, and my memory is feeble through much suffering. Or, perhaps, I cannot *now* bring these points to mind, because, in truth, the character of my beloved, her rare learning, her singular yet placid cast of beauty, and the thrilling and enthralling eloquence of her low musical language, made their way into my heart by paces so steadily and stealthily progressive that they have been unnoticed and unknown. Yet I believe that I met her first and most frequently in some large, old, decaying city nea. the Rhine. Of her family—I have surely heard her speak. That it is of a remotely ancient date cannot be doubted. Ligeia! Ligeia! Buried in studies of a nature more than all else adapted to deaden impressions of the outward world, it is by that swcet word alone—by Ligeia—that I bring before mine eyes in fancy the image of her who is no more. And now, while I write, a recollection flashes upon me that I have *never known* the paternal name of her who was my friend and my betrothed, and who became the partner of my studies, and finally the wife of my bosom. Was it a playful charge on the part of my Ligeia? or was it a test of my strength of affection, that I should institute no inquiries

* *The American Museum,* September, 1838; 1840; *Broadway Journal,* II. 12.—*Corrected by the Poe-Whitman-Ingram copy of B. Journal.*

upon this point? or was it rather a caprice of my own—a wildly romantic offering on the shrine of the most passionate devotion? I but indistinctly recall the fact itself—what wonder that I have utterly forgotten the circumstances which originated or attended it? And, indeed, if ever that spirit which is entitled *Romance*—if ever she, the wan and the misty-winged *Ashtophet* of idolatrous Egypt, presided, as they tell, over marriages ill-omened, then most surely she presided over mine.

There is one dear topic, however, on which my memory fails me not. It is the *person* of Ligeia. In stature she was tall, somewhat slender, and, in her latter days, even emaciated. I would in vain attempt to portray the majesty, the quiet ease of her demeanor, or the incomprehensible lightness and elasticity of her footfall. She came and departed as a shadow. I was never made aware of her entrance into my closed study save by the dear music of her low sweet voice, as she placed her marble hand upon my shoulder. In beauty of face no maiden ever equalled her. It was the radiance of an opium-dream—an airy and spirit-lifting vision more wildly divine than the phantasies which hovered about the slumbering souls of the daughters of Delos. Yet her features were not of that regular mould which we have been falsely taught to worship in the classical labors of the heathen. "There is no exquisite beauty," says Bacon, Lord Verulam, speaking truly of all the forms and *genera* of beauty, "without some *strangeness* in the proportion." Yet, although I saw that the features of Ligeia were not of a classic regularity—although I perceived that her loveliness was indeed "exquisite," and felt that there was much of "strangeness" pervading it, yet I have tried in vain to detect the irregularity and to trace home my own perception of "the strange." I examined the contour of the lofty and pale forehead—it was faultless—how cold indeed that word when applied to a majesty so divine!—the skin rivalling the purest ivory, the commanding extent and repose, the gentle prominence of the regions above the temples; and then the raven-black, the glossy, the luxuriant and naturally-curling tresses, setting forth the full force of the Homeric epithet, "hyacinthine!" I looked at the delicate outlines of the nose—and nowhere but in the graceful medallions of the Hebrews had I beheld a similar perfection. There were the same luxurious smoothness of surface, the same scarcely perceptible tendency to the aquiline, the same harmoniously curved nostrils speaking the free spirit. I regarded the sweet mouth. Here was indeed the triumph of all things heavenly—the magnificent turn of the short upper lip—the soft, voluptuous slumber of the under—the dimples which sported, and the color which spoke—the teeth glancing back, with a brilliancy almost startling, every ray of the holy light which fell upon them in her serene and placid yet most exultingly radiant of all smiles. I scrutinized the formation of the chin—and, here too, I found the gentleness of breadth, the softness and the majesty, the fulness and the spirituality, of the Greek—the contour which the god Apollo revealed but in a dream, to Cleomenes, the son of the Athenian. And then I peered into the large eyes of Ligeia.

For eyes we have no models in the remotely antique. It might have been, too, that in these eyes of my beloved lay the secret to which Lord Verulam alludes. They were, I must believe, far larger than the ordinary eyes of our own race. They were even fuller than the fullest of the gazelle eyes of the tribe of the valley of Nourjahad. Yet it was only at intervals—in moments of intense excitement—that this peculiarity became more than slightly noticeable in Ligeia. And at such moments was her beauty—in my heated fancy thus it appeared perhaps—the beauty of beings either above or apart from the earth—the beauty of the fabulous Houri of the Turk. The hue of the orbs was the most brilliant of black, and, far over them, hung jetty lashes of great length. The brows, slightly irregular in outline, had the same tint. The "strangeness," however, which I found in the eyes, was of a nature distinct from the formation, or the color, or the brilliancy of the features, and must, after all, be referred to the *expression*. Ah, word of no meaning! behind whose vast latitude of mere sound we intrench our ignorance of so much of the spiritual. The expression of the eyes of Ligeia! How for long hours have I pondered upon it! How have I, through the whole of a midsummer night, struggled to fathom it! What was it—that something more profound than the well of Democritus—which lay far within the pupils of my beloved? What *was* it? I was possessed with a passion to discover. Those eyes! those large, those shining, those divine orbs! they became to me twin stars of Leda, and I to them devoutest of astrologers.

There is no point, among the many imcomprehensible anomalies of the science of mind, more thrillingly exciting than the fact —never, I believe, noticed in the schools—that in our endeavors to recall to memory something long forgotten, we often find ourselves *upon the very verge* of remembrance, without being able, in the end, to remember. And thus how frequently, in my intense scrutiny of Ligeia's eyes, have I felt approaching the full knowledge of their expression—felt it approaching—yet not quite be mine—and so at length entirely depart! And (strange, oh strangest mystery of all!) I found, in the commonest objects of the universe, a circle of analogies to that expression. I mean to say that, subsequently to the period when Ligeia's beauty passed into my spirit, there dwelling as in a shrine, I derived, from many existences in the material world, a sentiment such as I felt always aroused, within me, by her large and luminous orbs. Yet not the more could I define that sentiment, or analyze, or even steadily view it. I recognized it, let me repeat, sometimes in the survey of a rapidly growing vine—in the contemplation of a moth, a butterfly, a chrysalis, a stream of running water. I have felt it in the ocean; in the falling of a meteor. I have felt it in the glances of unusually aged people. And there are one or two stars in heaven—(one especially, a star of the sixth magnitude, double and changeable, to be found near the large star in Lyra) in a telescopic scrutiny of which I have been made aware of the feeling. I have been filled with it by certain sounds from stringed instruments, and not unfrequently by passages from books. Among innumerable other instances, I well remember something in a volume of Joseph Glanvill, which (perhaps merely from its quaintness—who shall say?) never failed to inspire me with the sentiment;—"And the will therein lieth which dieth not. Who knoweth the mysteries of the will, with its vigor? For God is but a great will pervading all things by nature of its intentness. Man doth not yield him to the angels, nor unto death utterly, save only through the weakness of his feeble will."

Length of years and subsequent reflection, have enabled me to trace, indeed, some remote connection between this passage in the English moralist and a portion of the character of Ligeia. An *intensity* in thought, action, or speech, was possibly, in her, a result, or at least an index, of that gigantic volition which, during our long intercourse, failed to give other and more immediate evidence of its existence. Of all the women whom I have ever known, she, the outwardly calm, the ever-placid Ligeia, was the most violently a prey to the tumultuous vultures of stern passion. And of such passion I could form no estimate, save by the miraculous expansion of those eyes which at once so delighted and appalled me—by the almost magical melody, modulation, distinctness, and placidity of her very low voice—and by the fierce energy (rendered doubly effective by contrast with her manner of utterance) of the wild words which she habitually uttered.

I have spoken of the learning of Ligeia: it was immense—such as I have never known in woman. In the classical tongues was she deeply proficient, and as far as my own acquaintance extended in regard to the modern dialects of Europe, I have never known her at fault. Indeed upon any theme of the most admired, because simply the most abstruse of the boasted erudition of the academy, have I *ever* found Ligeia at fault? How singularly—how thrillingly, this one point in the nature of my wife has forced itself, at this late period only, upon my attention! I said her knowledge was such as I have never known in woman—but where breathes the man who has traversed, and successfully, *all* the wide areas of moral, physical, and mathematical science? I saw not then what I now clearly perceive, that the acquisitions of Ligeia were gigantic, were astounding; yet I was sufficiently aware of her infinite supremacy to resign myself, with a child-like confidence, to her guidance through the chaotic world of metaphysical investigation at which I was most busily occupied during the earlier years of our marriage. With how vast a triumph—with how vivid a delight—with how much of all that is ethereal in hope—did I *feel,* as she bent over me in studies but little sought—but less known—that delicious vista by slow degrees expanding before me, down whose long, gorgeous, and all untrodden path, I might at length pass onward to the goal of a wisdom too divinely precious not to be forbidden!

How poignant, then, must have been the grief with which, after some years, I beheld my well-grounded expectations take wings to themselves and fly away! Without Ligeia I was but as a child groping benighted. Her presence, her readings alone, rendered vividly luminous the many mysteries of the transcendentalism in which we were immersed. Wanting the radiant lustre of her eyes, letters, lambent and golden, grew duller than Saturnian lead. And now those eyes shone less and less frequently upon the pages over which I pored. Ligeia grew ill. The wild eyes blazed with a too—too glorious effulgence; the pale fingers became of the transparent waxen hue of the grave; and the blue veins upon the lofty forehead swelled and sank impetuously with the tides of the most gentle emotion. I saw that she must die—and I struggled desperately in spirit with the grim Azrael. And the struggles of the passionate wife were, to my astonishment, even more energetic than my own. There had been much in her stern nature to impress me with the belief that, to her, death would have come without its terrors; but not so. Words are impotent to convey any just idea of the fierceness of resistance with which she wrestled with the Shadow. I groaned in anguish at the pitiable spectacle. I would have soothed—I would have reasoned; but, in the intensity of her wild desire for life,—for life—*but* for life— solace and reason were alike the uttermost of folly. Yet not until the last instance, amid the most convulsive writhings of her fierce spirit, was shaken the external placidity of her demeanor. Her voice grew more gentle—grew more low—yet I would not wish to dwell upon the wild meaning of the quietly uttered words. My brain reeled as I hearkened entranced, to a melody more than mortal—to assumptions and aspirations which mortality had never before known.

That she loved me I should not have doubted; and I might have been easily aware that, in a bosom such as hers, love would have reigned no ordinary passion. But in death only was I fully impressed with the strength of her affection. For long hours, detaining my hand, would she pour out before me the overflowing of a heart whose more than passionate devotion amounted to idolatry. How had I deserved to be so blessed by such confessions?—how had I deserved to be so cursed with the removal of my beloved in the hour of my making them? But upon this subject I cannot bear to dilate. Let me say only, that in Ligeia's more than womanly abandonment to a love, alas! all unmerited, all unworthily bestowed, I at length recognized the principle of her longing with so wildly earnest a desire, for the life which was now fleeing so rapidly away. It is this wild longing—it is this eager vehemence of desire for life—*but* for life—that I have no power to portray—no utterance capable of expressing.

At high noon of the night in which she departed, beckoning me peremptorily, to her side, she bade me repeat certain verses composed by herself not many days before. I obeyed her.—They were these:—

Lo! 'tis a gala night 7
  Within the lonesome latter years!
An angel throng, bewinged, bedight
  In veils, and drowned in tears,
Sit in a theatre, to see
  A play of hopes and fears,
While the orchestra breathes fitfully
  The music of the spheres.

Mimes, in the form of God on high,
  Mutter and mumble low,
And hither and thither fly;
  Mere puppets they, who come and go
At bidding of vast formless things
  That shift the scenery to and fro,
Flapping from out their Condor wings
  Invisible Wo!

That motley drama!—oh, be sure
  It shall not be forgot!
With its Phantom chased for evermore,
  By a crowd that seize it not,
Through a circle that ever returneth in
  To the self-same spot,
And much of Madness and more of Sin
  And Horror the soul of the plot.

But see, amid the mimic rout,
  A crawling shape intrude!
A blood-red thing that writhes from out
  The scenic solitude!
It writhes!—it writhes!—with mortal pangs
  The mimes become its food,
And the seraphs sob at vermin fangs
  In human gore imbued.

Out—out are the lights—out all!
  And over each quivering form,
The curtain, a funeral pall,
  Comes down with the rush of a storm,
And the angels, all pallid and wan,
  Uprising, unveiling, affirm
That the play is the tragedy, "Man,"
  And its hero the Conqueror Worm.

"O God!" half shrieked Ligeia, leaping to her feet and extending her arms aloft with a spasmodic movement, as I made an end of these lines—"O God! O Divine Father!—shall these things be undeviatingly so?—shall this Conqueror be not once conquered? Are we not part and parcel in Thee? Who—who knoweth the mysteries of the will with its vigor? Man doth not yield him to the angels, *nor unto death utterly,* save only through the weakness of his feeble will."

And now, as if exhausted with emotion, she suffered her white arms to fall, and returned solemnly to her bed of death. And as she breathed her last sighs, there came mingled with them a low murmur from her lips. I bent to them my ear, and distinguished, again, the concluding words of the passage in Glanvill—"*Man doth not yield him to the angels, nor unto death utterly, save only through the weakness of his feeble will.*"

She died;—and I, crushed into the very dust with sorrow, could no longer endure the lonely desolation of my dwelling in the dim and decaying city by the Rhine. I had no lack of what the world calls wealth. Ligeia had brought me far more, very far more than ordinarily falls to the lot of mortals. After a few months, therefore, of weary and aimless wandering, I purchased, and put in some repair, an abbey, which I shall not name, in one of the wildest and least frequented portions of fair England. The gloomy and dreary grandeur of the building, the almost savage aspect of the domain, the many melancholy and time-honored memories connected with both, had much in unison with the feelings of utter abandonment which had driven me into that remote and unsocial region of the country. Yet although the external abbey, with its verdant decay hanging about it, suffered but little alteration, I gave way, with a child-like perversity, and perchance with a faint hope of alleviating my sorrows, to a display of more than regal magnificence within.—For such follies, even in childhood, I had imbibed a taste, and now they came back to me as if in the dotage of grief. Alas, I feel how much even of incipient madness might have been discovered in the gorgeous and fantastic draperies, in the solemn carvings of Egypt, in the wild cornices and furniture, in the Bedlam patterns of the carpets of tufted gold! I had become a bounden slave in the trammels of opium, and my labors and orders had taken a coloring from my dreams. But these absurdities I must not pause to detail. Let me speak only of that one chamber, ever accursed, whither, in a moment of mental alienation, I led from the altar as my bride—as the successor of the unforgotten Ligeia—the fair-haired and blue-eyed Lady Rowena Trevanion, of Tremaine.

There is no individual portion of the architecture and decoration of that bridal chamber which is not now visibly before me. Where were the souls of the haughty family of the bride, when, through thirst of gold, they permitted to pass the threshold of an apartment *so* bedecked, a maiden and a daughter so beloved? I have said that I minutely remember the details of the chamber—yet I am sadly forgetful on topics of deep moment—and here there was no system, no keeping, in the fantastic display, to take hold upon the memory. The room lay in a high turret of the castellated abbey, was pentagonal in shape, and of capacious size. Occupying the whole southern face of the pentagon was the sole window—an immense sheet of unbroken glass from Venice—a single pane, and tinted of a leaden hue, so that the rays of either the sun or moon passing through it, fell with a ghastly lustre on the objects within. Over the upper portion of this huge window, extended the trellis-work of an aged vine, which clambered up the massy walls of the turret. The ceiling, of gloomy-looking oak, was excessively lofty, vaulted, and elaborately fretted with the wildest and most grotesque specimens of a semi-Gothic, semi-Druidical device. From out the most central recess of this melancholy vaulting, depended, by a single chain of gold with long links, a huge censer of the same metal, Saracenic in pattern, and with many perforations so contrived that there writhed in and out of them, as if endued with a serpent vitality, a continual succession of parti-colored fires.

Some few ottomans and golden candelabra, of Eastern figure, were in various stations about—and there was the couch, too—the bridal couch—of an Indian model, and low, and sculptured of solid ebony, with a pall-like canopy above. In each of the angles of the chamber stood on end a gigantic sarcophagus of black granite, from the tombs of the kings over against Luxor, with their aged lids full of immemorial sculpture. But in the draping of the apartment lay, alas! the chief phantasy of all. The lofty walls, gigantic in height—even unproportionably so—were hung from summit to foot, in vast folds, with a heavy and massive-looking tapestry—tapestry of a material which was found alike as a carpet on the floor, as a covering for the ottomans and the ebony bed, as a canopy for the bed and as the gorgeous volutes of the curtains which partially shaded the window. The material was the richest cloth of gold. It was spotted all over, at irregular intervals, with arabesque figures, about a foot in diameter, and wrought upon the cloth in patterns of the most jetty black. But these figures partook of the true character of the arabesque only when regarded from a single point of view. By a contrivance now common, and indeed traceable to a very remote period of antiquity, they were made changeable in aspect. To one entering the room, they bore the appearance of simple monstrosities; but upon a farther advance, this appearance gradually departed; and step by step, as the visiter moved his station in the chamber, he saw himself surrounded by an endless succession of the ghastly forms which belong to the superstition of the Norman, or arise in the guilty slumbers of the monk. The phantasmagoric effect was vastly heightened by the artificial introduction of a strong continual current of wind behind the draperies—giving a hideous and uneasy animation to the whole.

In halls such as these—in a bridal chamber such as this—I passed, with the Lady of Tremaine, the unhallowed hours of the first month of our marriage—passed them with but little disquietude. That my wife dreaded the fierce moodiness of my temper—that she shunned me and loved me but little—I could not help perceiving; but it gave me rather pleasure than otherwise. I loathed her with a hatred belonging more to demon than to man.

My memory flew back, (oh, what intensity of regret!) to Ligeia, the beloved, the august, the beautiful, the entombed. I revelled in recollections of her purity, of her wisdom, of her lofty, her ethereal nature, of her passionate, her idolatrous love. Now, then, did my spirit fully and freely burn with more than all the fires of her own. In the excitement of my opium dreams (for I was habitually fettered in the shackles of the drug) I would call aloud upon her name, during the silence of the night, or among the sheltered recesses of the glens by day, as if, through the wild eagerness, the solemn passion, the consuming ardor of my longing for the departed, I could restore her to the pathways she had abandoned—ah, *could* it be forever?—upon the earth.

About the commencement of the second month of the marriage, the Lady Rowena was attacked with sudden illness, from which her recovery was slow. The fever which consumed her rendered her nights uneasy; and in her perturbed state of half-slumber, she spoke of sounds, and of motions, in and about the chamber of the turret, which I concluded had no origin save in the distemper of her fancy, or perhaps in the phantasmagoric influences of the chamber itself. She became at length convalescent—finally well. Yet but a brief period elapsed, ere a second more violent disorder again threw her upon a bed of suffering; and from this attack her frame, at all times feeble, never altogether recovered. Her illnesses were, after this epoch, of alarming character, and of more alarming recurrence, defying alike the knowledge and the great exertions of her physicians. With the increase of the chronic disease which had thus, apparently, taken too sure hold upon her constitution to be eradicated by human means, I could not fail to observe a similar increase in the nervous irritation of her temperament, and in her excitability by trivial causes of fear. She spoke again, and now more frequently and pertinaciously, of the sounds —of the slight sounds—and of the unusual motions among the tapestries, to which she had formerly alluded.

One night, near the closing in of September, she pressed this distressing subject with more than usual emphasis upon my attention. She had just awakened from an unquiet slumber, and I had been watching, with feelings half of anxiety, half of vague terror, the workings of her emaciated countenance. I sat by the side of her ebony bed, upon one of the ottomans of India. She partly arose, and spoke, in an earnest low whisper, of sounds which she *then* heard, but which I could not hear—of motions which she *then* saw, but which I could not perceive. The wind was rushing hurriedly behind the tapestries, and I wished to show her (what, let me confess it, I could not *all* believe) that those almost inarticulate breathings, and those very gentle variations of the figures upon the wall, were but the natural effects of that customary rushing of the wind. But a deadly pallor, overspreading her face, had proved to me that my exertions to reassure her would be fruitless. She appeared to be fainting, and no attendants were within call. I remembered where was deposited a decanter of light wine which had been ordered by her physicians, and hastened across the chamber to procure it. But, as I stepped beneath the light of the censer, two circumstances of a startling nature attracted my attention. I had felt that some palpable although invisible object had passed lightly by my person; and I saw that there lay upon the golden carpet, in the very middle of the rich lustre thrown from the censer, a shadow—a faint, indefinite shadow of angelic aspect—such as might be fancied for the shadow of a shade. But I was wild with the excitement of an immoderate dose of opium, and heeded these things but little, nor spoke of them to Rowena. Having found the wine, I recrossed the chamber, and poured out a gobletful, which I held to the lips of the fainting lady. She had now partially recovered, however, and took the vessel herself, while I sank upon an ottoman near me, with my eyes fastened upon her person. It was then that I became distinctly aware of a gentle foot-fall upon the carpet, and near the couch; and in a second thereafter, as Rowena was in the act of raising the wine to her lips, I saw, or may have dreamed that I saw, fall within the goblet, as if from some invisible spring in the atmosphere of the room, three or four large drops of a brilliant and ruby colored fluid. If this I saw—not so Rowena. She swallowed the wine unhesitatingly, and I forbore to speak to her of a circumstance which must, after all, I considered, have been but the suggestion of a vivid imagination, rendered morbidly active by the terror of the lady, by the opium, and by the hour.

Yet I cannot conceal it from my own perception that, immediately subsequent to the fall of the ruby-drops, a rapid change for the worse took place in the disorder of my wife; so that, on the third subsequent night, the hands of her menials prepared her for the tomb, and on the fourth, I sat alone, with her shrouded body, in that fantastic chamber which had received her as my bride.—Wild visions, opium-engendered, flitted, shadowlike, before me. I gazed with unquiet eye upon the sarcophagi in the angles of the room, upon the varying figures of the drapery, and upon the writhing of the parti-colored fires in the censer overhead. My eyes then fell, as I called to mind the circumstances of a former night, to the spot beneath the glare of the censer where I had seen the faint traces of the shadow. It was there, however, no longer; and breathing with greater freedom, I turned my glances to the pallid and rigid figure upon the bed. Then rushed upon me a thousand memories of Ligeia—and then came back upon my heart, with the turbulent violence of a flood, the whole of that unutterable wo with which I had regarded *her* thus enshrouded. The night waned; and still, with a bosom full of bitter thoughts of the one only and supremely beloved, I remained gazing upon the body of Rowena.

It might have been midnight, or perhaps earlier, or later, for I had taken no note of time, when a sob, low, gentle, but very distinct, startled me from my revery.—I *felt* that it came from the bed of ebony—the bed of death. I listened in an agony of superstitious terror—but there was no repetition of the sound. I strained my vision to detect any motion in the corpse—but there was not the slightest perceptible. Yet I could not have been deceived. I *had* heard the noise, however faint, and my soul was awakened within me. I resolutely and perseveringly kept my attention riveted upon the body. Many minutes elapsed before any circumstance occurred tending to throw light upon the mystery. At length it became evident that a slight, a very feeble, and barely noticeable tinge of color had flushed up within the cheeks, and along the sunken small veins of the eyelids. Through a species of unutterable horror and awe, for which the language of mortality has no sufficiently energetic expression, I felt my heart cease to beat, my limbs grow rigid where I sat. Yet a sense of duty finally operated to restore my self-possession. I could no longer doubt that we had been precipitate in our preparations—that Rowena still lived. It was necessary that some immediate exertion be made; yet the turret was altogether apart from the portion of the abbey tenanted by the servants—there were none within call—I had no means of summoning them to my aid without leaving the room for many minutes—and this I could not venture to do. I therefore struggled alone in my endeavors to call back the spirit still hovering. In a short period it was certain, however, that a relapse had taken place; the color disappeared from both eyelid and cheek, leaving a wanness even more than that of marble; the lips became doubly shrivelled and pinched up in the ghastly expression of death; a repulsive clamminess and coldness overspread rapidly the surface of the body; and all the usual rigorous stiffness immediately supervened. I fell back with a shudder upon the couch from which I had been so startlingly aroused, and again gave myself up to passionate waking visions of Ligeia.

An hour thus elapsed when (could it be possible?) I was a second time aware of some vague sound issuing from the region of the bed. I listened—in extremity of horror. The sound came again—it was a sigh. Rushing to the corpse, I saw—distinctly saw—a tremor upon the lips. In a minute afterward they relaxed, disclosing a bright line of the pearly teeth. Amazement now struggled in my bosom with the profound awe which had hitherto reigned there alone. I felt that my vision grew dim, that my reason wandered; and it was only by a violent effort that I at length succeeded in nerving myself to the task which duty thus once more had pointed out. There was now a partial glow upon the forehead and upon the cheek and throat; a perceptible warmth pervaded the whole frame; there was even a slight pulsation at the heart. The lady *lived;* and with redoubled ardor I betook myself to the task of restoration. I chafed and bathed the temples and the hands, and used every exertion which experience, and no little medical reading, could suggest. But in vain. Suddenly, the color fled, the pulsation ceased, the lips resumed the expression of the dead, and, in an instant afterward, the whole body took upon itself the icy chilliness, the livid hue, the intense rigidity, the sunken outline, and all the loathsome peculiarities of that which has been, for many days, a tenant of the tomb.

And again I sunk into visions of Ligeia—and again, (what marvel that I shudder while I write?) *again* there reached my ears a low sob from the region of the ebony bed. But why shall I minutely detail the unspeakable horrors of that night? Why shall I pause to relate how, time after time, until near the period of the gray dawn, this hideous drama of revivification was repeated; how each terrific relapse was only into a sterner and apparently more irredeemable death; how each agony wore the aspect of a struggle with some invisible foe; and how each struggle was succeeded by I know not what of wild change in the personal appearance of the corpse? Let me hurry to a conclusion.

The greater part of the fearful night had worn away, and she who had been dead once again stirred—and now more vigorously than hitherto, although arousing from a dissolution more appalling in its utter hopelessness than any. I had long ceased to struggle or to move, and remained sitting rigidly upon the ottoman, a helpless prey to a whirl of violent emotions, of which extreme awe was perhaps the least terrible, the least consuming. The corspe, I repeat, stirred, and now more vigorously than before. The hues of life flushed up with unwonted energy into the countenance—the limbs relaxed—and, save that the eyelids were yet pressed heavily together, and that the bandages and draperies of the grave still imparted their charnel character to the figure, I might have dreamed that Rowena had indeed shaken off, utterly, the fetters of Death. But if this idea was not, even then, altogether adopted, I could at least doubt no longer, when, arising from the bed, tottering, with feeble steps, with closed eyes, and with the manner of one bewildered in a dream, the thing that was enshrouded advanced boldly and palpably into the middle of the apartment.

I trembled not—I stirred not—for a crowd of unutterable fancies connected with the air, the stature, the demeanor of the figure, rushing hurriedly through my brain, had paralyzed—had chilled me into stone. I stirred not—but gazed upon the apparition. There was a mad disorder in my thoughts—a tumult unappeasable. Could it, indeed, be the *living* Rowena who confronted me? Could it, indeed, be Rowena *at all*—the fair-haired, the blue-eyed Lady Rowena Trevanion of Tremaine? Why, *why* should I doubt it? The bandage lay heavily about the mouth—but then might it not be the mouth of the breathing Lady of Tremaine? And the cheeks—there were the roses as in her noon of life—yes, these might indeed be the fair cheeks of the living Lady of Tremaine. And the chin, with its dimples, as in health, might it not be hers?—but *had she then grown taller since her malady?* What inexpressible madness seized me with that thought? One bound, and I had reached her feet! Shrinking from my touch, she let fall from her head, unloosened, the ghastly cerements which had confined it, and there streamed forth into the rushing atmosphere of the chamber huge masses of long and dishevelled hair; *it was blacker than the raven wings of midnight!* And now slowly opened *the eyes* of the figure which stood before me. "Here then, at least," I shrieked aloud, "can I never—can I never be mistaken—these are the full, and the black, and the wild eyes—of my lost love—of the Lady—of the LADY LIGEIA."

WILLIAM WILSON*

What say of it? what say [of] CONSCIENCE grim,
That spectre in my path?

CHAMBERLAYNE'S *"Pharronida"*

LET me call myself, for the present, William Wilson. The fair page now lying before me need not be sullied with my real appellation. This has been already too much an object for the scorn—for the horror—for the detestation of my race. To the uttermost regions of the globe have not the indignant winds bruited its unparalleled infamy? Oh, outcast of all outcasts most abandoned!—to the earth art thou not for ever dead? to its honors, to its flowers, to its golden aspirations?—and a cloud, dense, dismal, and limitless, does it not hang eternally between thy hopes and heaven?

I would not, if I could, here or to-day, embody a record of my later years of unspeakable misery, and unpardonable crime. This epoch—these later years—took unto themselves a sudden elevation in turpitude, whose origin alone it is my present purpose to assign. Men usually grow base by degrees. From me, in an instant, all virtue dropped bodily as a mantle. From comparatively trivial wickedness I passed, with the stride of a giant, into more than the enormities of an Elah-Gabalus. What chance—what one event brought this evil thing to pass, bear with me while I relate. Death approaches; and the shadow which foreruns him has thrown a softening influence over my spirit. I long, in passing

* *Burton's Gentleman's Magazine,* October, 1839; *The Gift,* 1840; 1840, *Broadway Journal,* II. 8.

through the dim valley, for the sympathy—I had nearly said for the pity—of my fellow men. I would fain have them believe that I have been, in some measure, the slave of circumstances beyond human control. I would wish them to seek out for me, in the details I am about to give, some little oasis of *fatality* amid a wilderness of error. I would have them allow—what they cannot refrain from allowing—that, although temptation may have erewhile existed as great, man was never *thus,* at least, tempted before—certainly, never *thus* fell. And is it therefore that he has never thus suffered? Have I not indeed been living in a dream? And am I not now dying a victim to the horror and the mystery of the wildest of all sublunary visions?

I am the descendant of a race whose imaginative and easily excitable temperament has at all times rendered them remarkable; and, in my earliest infancy, I gave evidence of having fully inherited the family character. As I advanced in years it was more strongly developed; becoming, for many reasons, a cause of serious disquietude to my friends, and of positive injury to myself. I grew self-willed, addicted to the wildest caprices, and a prey to the most ungovernable passions. Weak-minded, and beset with constitutional infirmities akin to my own, my parents could do but little to check the evil propensities which distinguished me. Some feeble and ill-directed efforts resulted in complete failure on their part, and, of course, in total triumph on mine. Thenceforward my voice was a household law; and at an age when few children have abandoned their leading-strings, I was left to the guidance of my own will, and became, in all but name, the master of my own actions.

My earliest recollections of a school-life, are connected with a large, rambling, Elizabethan house, in a misty-looking village of England, where were a vast number of gigantic and gnarled trees, and where all the houses were excessively ancient. In truth, it was a dream-like and spirit-soothing place, that venerable old town. At this moment, in fancy, I feel the refreshing chilliness of its deeply-shadowed avenues, inhale the fragrance of its thousand shrubberies, and thrill anew with undefinable delight, at the deep hollow note of the church-bell, breaking, each hour, with sullen and sudden roar, upon the stillness of the dusky atmosphere in which the fretted Gothic steeple lay imbedded and asleep.

It gives me, perhaps, as much of pleasure as I can now in any manner experience, to dwell upon minute recollections of the school and its concerns. Steeped in misery as I am—misery, alas! only too real—I shall be pardoned for seeking relief, however slight and temporary, in the weakness of a few rambling details. These, moreover, utterly trivial, and even ridiculous in themselves, assume, to my fancy, adventitious importance, as connected with a period and a locality when and where I recognize the first ambiguous monitions of the destiny which afterward so fully overshadowed me. Let me then remember.

The house, I have said, was old and irregular. The grounds were extensive, and a high and solid brick wall, topped with a bed of mortar and broken glass, encompassed the whole. This prison-like rampart formed the limit of our domain; beyond it we saw but thrice a week—once every Saturday afternoon, when, attended by two ushers, we were permitted to take brief walks in a body through some of the neighbouring fields—and twice during Sunday, when we were paraded in the same formal manner to the morning and evening service in the one church of the village. Of this church the principal of our school was pastor. With how deep a spirit of wonder and perplexity was I wont to regard him from our remote pew in the gallery, as, with step solemn and slow, he ascended the pulpit! This reverend man, with countenance so demurely benign, with robes so glossy and so clerically flowing, with wig so minutely powdered, so rigid and so vast,—could this be he who, of late, with sour visage, and in snuffy habiliments, administered, ferule in hand, the Draconian Laws of the academy? Oh, gigantic paradox, too utterly monstrous for solution!

At an angle of the ponderous wall frowned a more ponderous gate. It was riveted and studded with iron bolts, and surmounted with jagged iron spikes. What impressions of deep awe did it inspire! It was never opened save for the three periodical egressions and ingressions already mentioned; then, in every creak of its mighty hinges, we found a plenitude of mystery—a world of matter for solemn remark, or for more solemn meditation.

The extensive enclosure was irregular in form, having many capacious recesses. Of these, three or four of the largest constituted the play-ground. It was level, and covered with fine hard gravel. I well remember it had no trees, nor benches, nor any thing similar within it. Of course it was in the rear of the house. In front lay a small parterre, planted with box and other shrubs, but through this sacred division we passed only upon rare occasions indeed—such as a first advent to school or final departure thence, or perhaps, when a parent or friend having called for us, we joyfully took our way home for the Christmas or Midsummer holidays.

But the house!—how quaint an old building was this!—to me how veritably a palace of enchantment! There was really no end to its windings—to its incomprehensible subdivisions. It was difficult, at any given time, to say with certainty upon which of its two stories one happened to be. From each room to every other there were sure to be found three or four steps either in ascent or descent. Then the lateral branches were innumerable—inconceivable—and so returning in upon themselves, that our most exact ideas in regard to the whole mansion were not very far different from those with which we pondered upon infinity. During the five years of my residence here, I was never able to ascertain with precision, in what remote locality lay the little sleeping apartment assigned to myself and some eighteen or twenty other scholars.

The school-room was the largest in the house—I could not help thinking, in the world. It was very long, narrow, and dismally low, with pointed Gothic windows and a ceiling of oak. In a remote and terror-inspiring angle was a square enclosure of eight or ten feet, comprising the *sanctum*, "during hours," of our principal, the Reverend Dr. Bransby. It was a solid structure, with massy door, sooner than open which in the absence of the "Dominie," we would all have willingly perished by the *peine forte et dure.* In other angles were two other similar boxes, far less reverenced, indeed, but still greatly matters of awe. One of these was the pulpit of the "classical" usher, one of the "English and mathematical." Interspersed about the room, crossing and recrossing in endless irregularity, were innumerable benches and desks, black, ancient, and time-worn, piled desperately with much-bethumbed books, and so beseamed with initial letters, names at full length, grotesque figures, and other multiplied efforts of the knife, as to have entirely lost what little of original form might have been their portion in days long departed. A huge bucket with water stood at one extremity of the room, and a clock of stupendous dimensions at the other.

Encompassed by the massy walls of this venerable academy, I passed, yet not in tedium or disgust, the years of the third lustrum of my life. The teeming brain of childhood requires no external world of incident to occupy or amuse it; and the apparently dismal monotony of a school was replete with more intense excitement than my riper youth has derived from luxury, or my full manhood from crime. Yet I must believe that my first mental development had in it much of the uncommon—even much of the *outré.* Upon mankind at large the events of very early existence rarely leave in mature age any definite impression. All is gray shadow—a weak and irregular remembrance—an indistinct regathering of feeble pleasures and phantasmagoric pains. With me this is not so. In childhood I must have felt with the energy of a man what I now find stamped upon memory in lines as vivid, as deep, and as durable as the *exergues* of the Carthaginian medals.

Yet in fact—in the fact of the world's view—how little was there to remember! The morning's awakening, the nightly summons to bed; the connings, the recitations; the periodical half-holidays, and perambulations; the play-ground, with its broils, its pastimes, its intrigues;—these, by a mental sorcery long forgotten, were made to involve a wilderness of sensation, a world of rich incident, an universe of varied emotion, of excitement the most passionate and spirit-stirring. *"Oh, le bon temps, que ce siècle de fer!"*

In truth, the ardor, the enthusiasm, and the imperiousness of my disposition, soon rendered me a marked character among my schoolmates, and by slow, but natural gradations, gave me an ascendency over all not greatly older than myself;—over all with a single exception. This exception was found in the person of a scholar, who, although no relation, bore the same Christian and surname as myself;—a circumstance, in fact, little remarkable; for, notwithstanding a noble descent, mine was one of those every-day appellations which seem, by prescriptive right, to have been, time out of mind, the common property of the mob. In this narrative I have therefore designated myself as William Wilson,—a fictitious title not very dissimilar to the real. My namesake alone, of those who in school phraseology constituted "our set," presumed to compete with me in the studies of the class—in the sports and broils of the play-ground—to refuse implicit belief in my assertions, and submission to my will—indeed, to interfere with my arbitrary dictation in any respect whatsoever. If there is on earth a supreme and unqualified despotism, it is the despotism of a mastermind in boyhood over the less energetic spirits of its companions.

Wilson's rebellion was to me a source of the greatest embarrassment;—the more so as, in spite of the bravado with which in public I made a point of treating him and his pretensions, I secretly felt that I feared him, and could not help thinking the equality which he maintained so easily with myself, a proof of his true superiority; since not to be overcome, cost me a perpetual struggle. Yet this superiority—even this equality—was in truth acknowledged by no one but myself; our associates, by some unaccountable blindness, seemed not even to suspect it. Indeed, his competition, his resistance, and especially his impertinent and dogged interference with my purposes, were not more pointed than private. He appeared to be destitute alike of the ambition which urged, and of the passionate energy of mind which enabled me to excel. In his rivalry he might have been supposed actuated solely by a whimsical desire to thwart, astonish, or mortify myself; although there were times when I could not help observing, with a feeling made up of wonder, abasement, and pique, that he mingled with his injuries, his insults, or his contradictions, a certain most inappropriate, and assuredly most unwelcome *affectionateness* of manner. I could only conceive this singular behavior to arise from a consummate self-conceit assuming the vulgar airs of patronage and protection.

Perhaps it was this latter trait in Wilson's conduct, conjoined with our identity of name, and the mere accident of our having entered the school upon the same day, which set afloat the notion that we were brothers, among the senior classes in the academy. These do not usually inquire with much strictness into the affairs of their juniors. I have before said, or should have said, that Wilson was not, in a most remote degree, connected with my family. But assuredly if we *had* been brothers we must have been twins; for, after leaving Dr. Bransby's, I casually learned that my namesake was born on the nineteenth of January, 1813—and this is a somewhat remarkable coincidence; for the day is precisely that of my own nativity.

It may seem strange that in spite of the continual anxiety occasioned me by the rivalry of Wilson, and his intolerable spirit of contradiction, I could not bring myself to hate him altogether. We had, to be sure, nearly every day a quarrel in which, yielding me publicly the palm of victory, he, in some manner, contrived to make me feel that it was he who had deserved it; yet a sense of pride on my part, and a veritable dignity on his own, kept us always upon what are called "speaking terms," while there were many points of strong congeniality in our tempers, operating to awake in me a sentiment which our position alone, perhaps, prevented from ripening into friendship. It is difficult, indeed, to define, or even to describe, my real feelings toward him. They formed a motley and heterogeneous admixture;—some petulant animosity, which was not yet hatred, some esteem, more respect, much fear, with a world of uneasy curiosity. To the moralist it will be unnecessary to say, in addition, that Wilson and myself were the most inseparable of companions.

It was no doubt the anomalous state of affairs existing between us, which turned all my attacks upon him, (and there were many, either open or covert) into the channel of banter or practical joke (giving pain while assuming the aspect of mere fun) rather than into a more serious and determined hostility. But my endeavours on this head were by no means uniformly successful, even when my plans were the most wittily concocted; for my namesake had much about him, in character, of that unassuming and quiet austerity which, while enjoying the poignancy of its own jokes, has no heel of Achilles in itself, and absolutely refuses to be laughed at. I could find, indeed, but one vulnerable point, and that, lying in a personal peculiarity, arising, perhaps, from constitutional disease, would have been spared by any antagonist less at his wit's end than myself;—my rival had a weakness in the faucial or guttural organs, which precluded him from raising his voice at any time *above a very low whisper*. Of this defect I did not fail to take what poor advantage lay in my power.

Wilson's retaliations in kind were many; and there was one form of his practical wit that disturbed me beyond measure. How his sagacity first discovered at all that so petty a thing would vex me, is a question I never could solve; but having discovered, he habitually practised the annoyance. I had always felt aversion to my uncourtly patronymic, and its very common, if not plebeian prænomen. The words were venom in my ears; and when, upon the day of my arrival, a second William Wilson came also to the academy, I felt angry with him for bearing the name, and doubly disgusted with the name because a stranger bore it, who would be the cause of its twofold repetition, who would be constantly in my presence, and whose concerns, in the ordinary routine of the school business, must inevitably, on account of the detestable coincidence, be often confounded with my own.

The feeling of vexation thus engendered grew stronger with every circumstance tending to show resemblance, moral or physical, between my rival and myself. I had not then discovered the remarkable fact that we were of the same age; but I saw that we were of the same height, and I perceived that we were even singularly alike in general contour of person and outline of feature. I was galled, too, by the rumor touching a relationship, which had grown current in the upper forms. In a word, nothing could more seriously disturb me, (although I scrupulously concealed such disturbance,) than any allusions to a similarity of mind, person, or condition existing between us. But, in truth, I had no reason to believe that (with the exception of the matter of relationship, and in the case of Wilson himself) this similarity had ever been made a subject of comment, or even observed at all by our schoolfellows. That *he* observed it in all its bearings, and as fixedly as I, was apparent; but that he could discover in such circumstances so fruitful a field of annoyance, can only be attributed, as I said before, to his more than ordinary penetration.

His cue, which was to perfect an imitation of myself, lay both in words and in actions; and most admirably did he play his part. My dress it was an easy matter to copy; my gait and general manner were, without difficulty, appropriated; in spite of his constitutional defect, even my voice did not escape him. My louder tones were, of course, unattempted, but then the key, it was identical; *and his singular whisper, it grew the very echo of my own.*

How greatly this most exquisite portraiture harassed me, (for it could not justly be termed a caricature,) I will not now venture to describe. I had but one consolation—in the fact that the imitation, apparently, was noticed by myself alone, and that I had to endure only the knowing and strangely sarcastic smiles of my namesake himself. Satisfied with having produced in my bosom the intended effect, he seemed to chuckle in secret over the sting he had inflicted, and was characteristically disregardful of the public applause which the success of his witty endeavours might have so easily elicited. That the school, indeed, did not feel his design, perceive its accomplishment, and participate in his sneer, was, for many anxious months, a riddle I could not resolve. Perhaps the *gradation* of his copy rendered it not so readily perceptible; or, more possibly, I owed my security to the masterly air of the copyist, who, disdaining the letter, (which in a painting is all the obtuse can see,) gave but the full spirit of his original for my individual contemplation and chagrin.

I have already more than once spoken of the disgusting air of patronage which he assumed toward me, and of his frequent officious interference with my will. This interference often took the ungracious character of advice; advice not openly given, but hinted or insinuated. I received it with a repugnance which gained strength as I grew in years. Yet, at this distant day, let me do him the simple justice to acknowledge that I can recall no occasion when the suggestions of my rival were on the side of those errors or follies so usual to his immature age and seeming inexperience; that his moral sense, at least, if not his general talents and worldly wisdom, was far keener than my own; and that I might, to-day, have been a better and thus a happier man, had I less frequently rejected the counsels embodied in those meaning whispers which I then but too cordially hated and too bitterly despised.

As it was, I at length grew restive in the extreme under his distasteful supervision, and daily resented more and more openly what I considered his intolerable arrogance. I have said that, in the first years of our connection as schoolmates, my feelings in regard to him might have been easily ripened into friendship: but, in the latter months of my residence at the academy, although the intrusion of his ordinary manner had, beyond doubt, in some measure, abated, my sentiments, in nearly similar proportion, partook very much of positive hatred. Upon one occasion he saw this, I think, and afterward avoided, or made a show of avoiding me.

It was about the same period, if I remember aright, that, in an altercation of violence with him, in which he was more than usually thrown off his guard, and spoke and acted with an openness of demeanor rather foreign to his nature, I discovered, or fancied I discovered, in his accent, in his air, and general appearance, a something which first startled, and then deeply interested me, by bringing to mind dim visions of my earliest infancy—wild, confused and thronging memories of a time when memory herself was yet unborn. I cannot better describe the sensation which oppressed me than by saying that I could with difficulty shake off the belief of my having been acquainted with the being who stood before me, at some epoch very long ago—some point of the past even infinitely remote. The delusion, however, faded rapidly as it came; and I mention it at all but to define the day of the last conversation I there held with my singular namesake.

The huge old house, with its countless subdivisions, had several large chambers communicating with each other, where slept the greater number of the students. There were, however, (as must necessarily happen in a building so awkwardly planned,) many little nooks or recesses, the odds and ends of the structure; and these the economic ingenuity of Dr. Bransby had also fitted up as dormitories; although, being the merest closets, they were capable of accommodating but a single individual. One of these small apartments was occupied by Wilson.

One night, about the close of my fifth year at the school, and immediately after the altercation just mentioned, finding every one wrapped in sleep, I arose from bed, and, lamp in hand, stole through a wilderness of narrow passages, from my own bedroom to that of my rival. I had long been plotting one of those ill-natured pieces of practical wit at his expense in which I had hitherto been so uniformly unsuccessful. It was my intention, now, to put my scheme in operation, and I resolved to make him feel the whole extent of the malice with which I was imbued. Having reached his closet, I noiselessly entered, leaving the lamp, with a shade over it, on the outside. I advanced a step and listened to the sound of his tranquil breathing. Assured of his being asleep, I returned, took the light, and with it again approached the bed. Close curtains were around it, which, in the prosecution of my plan, I slowly and quietly withdrew, when the bright rays fell vividly upon the sleeper, and my eyes, at the same moment, upon his countenance. I looked;—and a numbness, an iciness of feeling instantly pervaded my frame. My breast heaved, my knees tottered, my whole spirit became possessed with an objectless yet intolerable horror. Gasping for breath, I lowered the lamp in still nearer proximity to the face. Were these—*these* the lineaments of William Wilson? I saw, indeed, that they were his, but I shook as if with a fit of the ague in fancying they were not. What *was* there about them to confound me in this manner? I gazed;—while my brain reeled with a multitude of incoherent thoughts. Not thus he appeared—assuredly not *thus*—in the vivacity of his waking hours. The same name! the same contour of person! the same day of arrival at the academy! And then his dogged and meaningless imitation of my gait, my voice, my habits, and my manner! Was it, in truth, within the bounds of human possibility, that *what I now saw* was the result, merely, of the habitual practice of this sarcastic imitation? Awe-stricken, and with a creeping shudder, I extinguished the lamp, passed silently from the chamber, and left, at once, the halls of that old academy, never to enter them again.

After a lapse of some months, spent at home in mere idleness, I found myself a student at Eton. The brief interval had been sufficient to enfeeble my remembrance of the events at Dr. Bransby's, or at least to effect a material change in the nature of the feelings with which I remembered them. The truth—the tragedy—of the drama was no more. I could now find room to doubt the evidence of my senses; and seldom called up the subject at all but with wonder at the extent of human credulity, and a smile at the vivid force of the imagination which I hereditarily possessed. Neither was this species of skepticism likely to be diminished by the character of the life I led at Eton. The vortex of thoughtless folly into which I there so immediately and so recklessly plunged, washed away all but the froth of my past hours, engulfed at once every solid or serious impression, and left to memory only the veriest levities of a former existence.

I do not wish, however, to trace the course of my miserable profligacy here—a profligacy which set at defiance the laws, while it eluded the vigilance of the institution. Three years of folly, passed without profit, had but given me rooted habits of vice, and added, in a somewhat unusual degree, to my bodily stature, when, after a week of soulless dissipation, I invited a small party of the most dissolute students to a secret carousal in my chambers. We met at a late hour of the night; for our debaucheries were to be faithfully protracted until morning. The wine flowed freely, and there were not wanting other and perhaps more dangerous seductions; so that the grey dawn had already faintly appeared in the east while our delirious extravagance was at its height. Madly flushed with cards and intoxication, I was in the act of insisting upon a toast of more than wonted profanity, when my attention was suddenly diverted by the violent, although partial, unclosing of the door of the apartment, and by the eager voice of a servant from without. He said that some person, apparently in great haste, demanded to speak with me in the hall.

Wildly excited with wine, the unexpected interruption rather delighted than surprised me. I staggered forward at once, and a few steps brought me to the vestibule of the building. In this low and small room there hung no lamp; and now no light at all was admitted, save that of the exceedingly feeble dawn which made its way through the semi-circular window. As I put my foot over the threshold, I became aware of the figure of a youth about my own height, and habited in a white kerseymere morning frock, cut in the novel fashion of the one I myself wore at the moment. This the faint light enabled me to perceive; but the features of his face I could not distinguish. Upon my entering he strode hurriedly up to me, and, seizing me by the arm with a gesture of petulant impatience, whispered the words "William Wilson!" in my ear.

I grew perfectly sober in an instant.

There was that in the manner of the stranger, and in the tremulous shake of his uplifted finger, as he held it between my eyes and the light, which filled me with unqualified amazement;

but it was not this which had so violently moved me. It was the pregnancy of solemn admonition in the singular, low, hissing utterance; and, above all, it was the character, the tone, *the key,* of those few, simple, and familiar, yet *whispered* syllables, which came with a thousand thronging memories of by-gone days, and struck upon my soul with the shock of a galvanic battery. Ere I could recover the use of my senses he was gone.

Although this event failed not of a vivid effect upon my disordered imagination, yet was it evanescent as vivid. For some weeks, indeed, I busied myself in earnest enquiry, or was wrapped in a cloud of morbid speculation. I did not pretend to disguise from my perception the identity of the singular individual who thus perseveringly interfered with my affairs, and harassed me with his insinuated counsel. But who and what was this Wilson? —and whence came he?—and what were his purposes? Upon neither of these points could I be satisfied; merely ascertaining, in regard to him, that a sudden accident in his family had caused his removal from Dr. Bransby's academy on the afternoon of the day in which I myself had eloped. But in a brief period I ceased to think upon the subject; my attention being all absorbed in a contemplated departure for Oxford. Thither I soon went, the uncalculating vanity of my parents furnishing me with an outfit and annual establishment, which would enable me to indulge at will in the luxury already so dear to my heart,—to vie in profuseness of expenditure with the haughtiest heirs of the wealthiest earldoms in Great Britain.

Excited by such appliances to vice, my constitutional temperament broke forth with redoubled ardor, and I spurned even the common restraints of decency in the mad infatuation of my revels. But it were absurd to pause in the detail of my extravagance. Let it suffice, that among spendthrifts I out-Heroded Herod, and that, giving name to a multitude of novel follies, I added no brief appendix to the long catalogue of vices then usual in the most dissolute university of Europe.

It could hardly be credited, however, that I had, even here, so utterly fallen from the gentlemanly estate, as to seek acquaintance with the vilest arts of the gambler by profession, and, having become an adept in his despicable science, to practice it habitually as a means of increasing my already enormous income at the expense of the weak-minded among my fellow-collegians. Such, nevertheless, was the fact. And the very enormity of this offence against all manly and honourable sentiment proved, beyond doubt, the main if not the sole reason of the impunity with which it was committed. Who, indeed, among my most abandoned associates, would not rather have disputed the clearest evidence of his senses, than have suspected of such courses, the gay, the frank, the generous William Wilson—the noblest and most liberal commoner at Oxford—him whose follies (said his parasites) were but the follies of youth and unbridled fancy—whose errors but inimitable whim—whose darkest vice but a careless and dashing extravagance?

I had been now two years successfully busied in this way, when there came to the university a young *parvenu nobleman,* Glendinning—rich, said report, as Herodes Atticus—his riches, too, as easily acquired. I soon found him of weak intellect, and, of course, marked him as a fitting subject for my skill. I frequently engaged him in play, and contrived, with the gambler's usual art, to let him win considerable sums, the more effectually to entangle him in my snares. At length, my schemes being ripe, I met him (with the full intention that this meeting should be final and decisive) at the chambers of a fellow-commoner, (Mr. Preston,) equally intimate with both, but who, to do him justice, entertained not even a remote suspicion of my design. To give to this a better colouring, I had contrived to have assembled a party of some eight or ten, and was solicitously careful that the introduction of cards should appear accidental, and originate in the proposal of my contemplated dupe himself. To be brief upon a vile topic, none of the low finesse was omitted, so customary upon similar occasions, that it is a just matter for wonder how any are still found so besotted as to fall its victim.

We had protracted our sitting far into the night, and I had at length effected the manœuvre of getting Glendinning as my sole antagonist. The game, too, was my favourite *écarté*. The rest of the company, interested in the extent of our play, had abandoned their own cards, and were standing around us as spectators. The *parvenu,* who had been induced by my artifices in the early part of the evening, to drink deeply, now shuffled, dealt, or played, with a wild nervousness of manner for which his intoxication, I thought, might partially, but could not altogether account. In a very short period he had become my debtor to a large amount, when, having taken a long draught of port, he did precisely what I had been coolly anticipating—he proposed to double our already extravagant stakes. With a well-feigned show of reluctance, and not until after my repeated refusal had seduced him into some angry words which gave a color of *pique* to my compliance, did I finally comply. The result, of course, did but prove how entirely the prey was in my toils; in less than an hour he had quadrupled his debt. For some time his countenance had been losing the florid tinge lent it by the wine; but now, to my astonishment, I perceived that it had grown to a pallor truly fearful. I say, to my astonishment. Glendinning had been represented to my eager inquiries as immeasurably wealthy; and the sums which he had as yet lost, although in themselves vast, could not, I supposed, very seriously annoy, much less so violently affect him. That he was overcome by the wine just swallowed, was the idea which most readily presented itself; and, rather with a view to the preservation of my own character in the eyes of my associates, than from any less interested motive, I was about to insist, peremptorily, upon a discontinuance of the play, when some expressions at my elbow from among the company, and an ejaculation evincing utter despair on the part of Glendinning, gave me to understand that I had effected his total ruin under circumstances which, rendering him an object for the pity of all, should have protected him from the ill offices even of a fiend.

What now might have been my conduct it is difficult to say. The pitiable condition of my dupe had thrown an air of embarrassed gloom over all; and, for some moments, a profound silence was maintained, during which I could not help feeling my cheeks tingle with the many burning glances of scorn or reproach cast upon me by the less abandoned of the party. I will even own that an intolerable weight of anxiety was for a brief instant lifted from my bosom by the sudden and extraordinary interruption which ensued. The wide, heavy folding doors of the apartment were all at once thrown open, to their full extent, with a vigorous and rushing impetuosity that extinguished, as if by magic, every candle in the room. Their light, in dying, enabled us just to perceive that a stranger had entered, about my own height, and closely muffled in a cloak. The darkness, however, was not total; and we could only *feel* that he was standing in our midst. Before any one of us could recover from the extreme astonishment into which this rudeness had thrown all, we heard the voice of the intruder.

"Gentlemen," he said, in a low, distinct, and never-to-be-forgotten *whisper* which thrilled to the very marrow of my bones, "Gentlemen, I make no apology for this behaviour, because in thus behaving, I am fulfilling a duty. You are, beyond doubt, uninformed of the true character of the person who has to-night won at *écarté* a large sum of money from Lord Glendinning. I will therefore put you upon an expeditious and decisive plan of obtaining this very necessary information. Please to examine, at your leisure, the inner linings of the cuff of his left sleeve, and the several little packages which may be found in the somewhat capacious pockets of his embroidered morning wrapper."

While he spoke, so profound was the stillness that one might have heard a pin drop upon the floor. In ceasing, he departed at once, and as abruptly as he had entered. Can I—shall I describe my sensations?—must I say that I felt all the horrors of the damned? Most assuredly I had little time given for reflection. Many hands roughly seized me upon the spot, and lights were immediately reprocured. A search ensued. In the lining of my sleeve were found all the court cards essential in *écarté,* and, in the pockets of my wrapper, a number of packs, fac-similes of those used at our sittings, with the single exception that mine were of the species called, technically, *arrondées;* the honours being slightly convex at the ends, the lower cards slightly convex at the sides. In this disposition, the dupe who cuts, as customary, at the length of the pack, will invariably find that he cuts his antagonist an honor; while the gambler, cutting at the breadth, will, as certainly, cut nothing for his victim which may count in the records of the game.

Any burst of indignation upon this discovery would have affected me less than the silent contempt, or the sarcastic composure, with which it was received.

"Mr. Wilson," said our host, stooping to remove from beneath his feet an exceedingly luxurious cloak of rare furs, "Mr. Wilson, this is your property." (The weather was cold; and, upon quitting my own room, I had thrown a cloak over my dressing wrapper, putting it off upon reaching the scene of play.) "I presume it is supererogatory to seek here (eyeing the folds of the garment with a bitter smile) for any farther evidence of your skill. Indeed, we have had enough. You will see the necessity, I hope, of quitting Oxford—at all events, of quitting instantly my chambers."

Abased, humbled to the dust as I then was, it is probable that I should have resented this galling language by immediate personal violence, had not my whole attention been at the moment arrested by a fact of the most startling character. The cloak which I had worn was of a rare description of fur; how rare, how extravagantly costly, I shall not venture to say. Its fashion, too, was of my own fantastic invention; for I was fastidious to an absurd degree of coxcombry, in matters of this frivolous nature. When, therefore, Mr. Preston reached me that which he had picked up upon the floor, and near the folding doors of the apartment, it was with an astonishment nearly bordering upon terror, that I perceived my own already hanging on my arm, (where I had no doubt unwittingly placed it,) and that the one presented me was but its exact counterpart in every, in even the minutest possible particular. The singular being who had so disastrously exposed me, had been muffled, I remembered, in a cloak; and none had been worn at all by any of the members of our party with the exception of myself. Retaining some presence of mind, I took the one offered me by Preston; placed it, unnoticed, over my own; left the apartment with a resolute scowl of defiance; and, next morning ere dawn of day, commenced a hurried journey from Oxford to the continent, in a perfect agony of horror and of shame.

I fled in vain. My evil destiny pursued me as if in exultation, and proved, indeed, that the exercise of its mysterious dominion had as yet only begun. Scarcely had I set foot in Paris, ere I had fresh evidence of the detestable interest taken by this Wilson in my concerns. Years flew, while I experienced no relief. Villain!—at Rome, with how untimely, yet with how spectral an officiousness, stepped he in between me and my ambition! at Vienna, too—at Berlin—and at Moscow! Where, in truth, had I *not* bitter cause to curse him within my heart? From his inscrutable tyranny did I at length flee, panic-stricken, as from a pestilence; and to the very ends of the earth *I fled in vain.*

And again, and again, in secret communion with my own spirit, would I demand the questions "Who is he?—whence came he?—and what are his objects?" But no answer was there found. And then I scrutinized, with a minute scrutiny, the forms, and the methods, and the leading traits of his impertinent supervision. But even here there was very little upon which to base a conjecture. It was noticeable, indeed, that, in no one of the multiplied instances in which he had of late crossed my path, had he so crossed it except to frustrate those schemes, or to disturb those actions, which, if fully carried out, might have resulted in bitter mischief. Poor justification this, in truth, for an authority so imperiously assumed! Poor indemnity for natural rights of self-agency so pertinaciously, so insultingly denied!

I had also been forced to notice that my tormentor, for a very long period of time, (while scrupulously and with miraculous dexterity maintaining his whim of an identity of apparel with myself,) had so contrived it, in the execution of his varied interference with my will, that I saw not, at any moment, the features of his face. Be Wilson what he might, *this,* at least, was but the veriest of affectation, or of folly. Could he, for an instant, have supposed that, in my admonisher at Eton—in the destroyer of my honor at Oxford,—in him who thwarted my ambition at Rome, my revenge at Paris, my passionate love at Naples, or what he falsely termed my avarice in Egypt,—that in this, my arch-enemy and evil genius, I could fail to recognize the William Wilson of my schoolboy days,—the namesake, the companion, the rival, —the hated and dreaded rival at Dr. Bransby's? Impossible!—But let me hasten to the last eventful scene of the drama.

Thus far I had succumbed supinely to this imperious domination. The sentiment of deep awe with which I habitually regarded the elevated character, the majestic wisdom, the apparent omnipresence and omnipotence of Wilson, added to a feeling of even terror, with which certain other traits in his nature and assumptions inspired me, had operated, hitherto, to impress me with an idea of my own utter weakness and helplessness, and to suggest an implicit, although bitterly reluctant submission to his arbitrary will. But, of late days, I had given myself up entirely to wine; and its maddening influence upon my hereditary temper rendered me more and more impatient of control. I began to murmur,—to hesitate,—to resist. And was it only fancy which induced me to believe that, with the increase of my own firmness, that of my tormentor underwent a proportional diminution? Be this as it may, I now began to feel the inspiration of a burning hope, and at length nurtured in my secret thoughts a stern and desperate resolution that I would submit no longer to be enslaved.

It was at Rome, during the Carnival of 18—, that I attended a masquerade in the palazzo of the Neapolitan Duke Di Broglio. I had indulged more freely than usual in the excesses of the wine-table; and now the suffocating atmosphere of the crowded rooms irritated me beyond endurance. The difficulty, too, of forcing my way through the mazes of the company contributed not a little to the ruffling of my temper; for I was anxiously seeking (let me not say with what unworthy motive) the young, the gay, the beautiful wife of the aged and doting Di Broglio. With a too unscrupulous confidence she had previously communicated to me the secret of the costume in which she would be habited and now, having caught a glimpse of her person, I was hurrying to make my way into her presence.—At this moment I felt a light hand placed upon my shoulder, and that ever-remembered, low, damnable *whisper* within my ear.

In an absolute frenzy of wrath, I turned at once upon him who had thus interrupted me, and seized him violently by the collar. He was attired, as I had expected, in a costume altogether similar to my own; wearing a Spanish cloak of blue velvet, begirt about the waist with a crimson belt sustaining a rapier. A mask of black silk entirely covered his face.

"Scoundrel!" I said, in a voice husky with rage, while every syllable I uttered seemed as new fuel to my fury, "scoundrel! impostor! accursed villain! you shall not—you *shall not* dog me unto death! Follow me, or I stab you where you stand!"—and I broke my way from the ballroom into a small antechamber adjoining, dragging him unresistingly with me as I went.

Upon entering, I thrust him furiously from me. He staggered against the wall, while I closed the door with an oath, and commanded him to draw. He hesitated but for an instant; then, with a slight sigh, drew in silence, and put himself upon his defence.

The contest was brief indeed. I was frantic with every species of wild excitement, and felt within my single arm the energy and power of a multitude. In a few seconds I forced him by sheer strength against the wainscotting, and thus, getting him at mercy, plunged my sword, with brute ferocity, repeatedly through and through his bosom.

At that instant some person tried the latch of the door. I hastened to prevent an intrusion, and then immediately returned to my dying antagonist. But what human language can adequately portray *that* astonishment, *that* horror which possessed me at the spectacle then presented to view? The brief moment in which I averted my eyes had been sufficient to produce, apparently, a material change in the arrangements at the upper or farther end of the room. A large mirror,—so at first it seemed to me in my confusion—now stood where none had been perceptible before; and as I stepped up to it in extremity of terror, mine own image, but with features all pale and dabbled in blood, advanced to meet me with a feeble and tottering gait.

Thus it appeared, I say, but was not. It was my antagonist—it was Wilson, who then stood before me in the agonies of his dissolution. His mask and cloak lay, where he had thrown them, upon the floor. Not a thread in all his raiment—not a line in all the marked and singular lineaments of his face which was not, even in the most absolute identity, *mine own!*

It was Wilson; but he spoke no longer in a whisper, and I could have fancied that I myself was speaking while he said:

"You have conquered, and I yield. Yet, hence forward art thou also dead—dead to the World, to Heaven, and to Hope! In me didst thou exist—and, in my death, see by this image, which is thine own, how utterly thou hast murdered thyself."

THE PIT AND THE PENDULUM*

Impie tortorum longos hic turba furores
Sanguinis innocui, non satiata, aluit.
Sospite nunc patriâ, fracto nunc funeris antro,
Mors ubi dira fuit vita salusque patent.

[*Quatrain composed for the gates of a market to be erected upon the site of the Jacobin Club House at Paris.*]

I WAS sick—sick unto death with that long agony; and when they at length unbound me, and I was permitted to sit, I felt that my senses were leaving me. The sentence—the dread sentence of death—was the last of distinct accentuation which reached my ears. After that, the sound of the inquisitorial voices seemed merged in one dreamy indeterminate hum. It conveyed to my soul the idea of *revolution*—perhaps from its association in fancy with the burr of a mill-wheel. This only for a brief period; for presently I heard no more. Yet, for a while, I saw; but with how terrible an exaggeration! I saw the lips of the black-robed judges. They appeared to me white—whiter than the sheet upon which I trace these words—and thin even to grotesqueness; thin with the intensity of their expression of firmness—of immovable resolution—of stern contempt of human torture. I saw that the decrees of what to me was Fate were still issuing from those lips. I saw them writhe with a deadly locution. I saw them fashion the syllables of my name; and I shuddered because no sound succeeded. I saw, too, for a few moments of delirious horror, the soft and nearly

* *The Gift,* 1843; *Broadway Journal,* I. 20.

imperceptible waving of the sable draperies which enwrapped the walls of the apartment. And then my vision fell upon the seven tall candles upon the table. At first they wore the aspect of charity, and seemed white slender angels who would save me; but then, all at once, there came a most deadly nausea over my spirit, and I felt every fibre in my frame thrill as if I had touched the wire of a galvanic battery, while the angel forms became meaningless spectres, with heads of flame, and I saw that from them there would be no help. And then there stole into my fancy, like a rich musical note, the thought of what sweet rest there must be in the grave. The thought came gently and stealthily, and it seemed long before it attained full appreciation; but just as my spirit came at length properly to feel and entertain it, the figures of the judges vanished, as if magically, from before me; the tall candles sank into nothingness; their flames went out utterly; the blackness of darkness supervened; all sensations appeared swallowed up in a mad rushing descent as of the soul into Hades. Then silence, and stillness, and night were the universe.

I had swooned; but still will not say that all of consciousness was lost. What of it there remained I will not attempt to define, or even to describe; yet all was not lost. In the deepest slumber—no! In delirium—no! In a swoon—no! In death—no! even in the grave all *is not* lost. Else there is no immortality for man. Arousing from the most profound of slumbers, we break the gossamer web of *some* dream. Yet in a second afterward, (so frail may that web have been) we remember not that we have dreamed. In the return to life from the swoon there are two stages; first, that of the sense of mental or spiritual; secondly, that of the sense of physical, existence. It seems probable that if, upon reaching the second stage, we could recall the impressions of the first, we should find these impressions eloquent in memories of the gulf beyond. And that gulf is—what? How at least shall we distinguish its shadows from those of the tomb? But if the impressions of what I have termed the first stage, are not, at will, recalled, yet, after long interval, do they not come unbidden, while we marvel whence they come? He who has never swooned, is not he who finds strange palaces and wildly familiar faces in coals that glow; is not he who beholds floating in mid-air the sad visions that the many may not view; is not he who ponders over the perfume of some novel flower; is not he whose brain grows bewildered with the meaning of some musical cadence which has never before arrested his attention.

Amid frequent and thoughtful endeavors to remember, amid earnest struggles to regather some token of the state of seeming nothingness into which my soul had lapsed, there have been moments when I have dreamed of success; there have been brief, very brief periods when I have conjured up remembrances which the lucid reason of a later epoch assures me could have had reference only to that condition of seeming unconsciousness. These shadows of memory tell, indistinctly, of tall figures that lifted and bore me in silence down—down—still down—till a hideous dizziness oppressed me at the mere idea of the interminableness of the descent. They tell also of a vague horror at my heart, on account of that heart's unnatural stillness. Then comes a sense of sudden motionlessness throughout all things; as if those who bore me (a ghastly train!) had outrun, in their descent, the limits of the limitless, and paused from the wearisomeness of their toil. After this I call to mind flatness and dampness; and then all is *madness*—the madness of a memory which busies itself among forbidden things.

Very suddenly there came back to my soul motion and sound—the tumultuous motion of the heart, and, in my ears, the sound of its beating. Then a pause in which all is blank. Then again sound, and motion, and touch—a tingling sensation pervading my frame. Then the mere consciousness of existence, without thought—a condition which lasted long. Then, very suddenly, *thought,* and shuddering terror, and earnest endeavor to comprehend my true state. Then a strong desire to lapse into insensibility. Then a rushing revival of soul and a successful effort to move. And now a full memory of the trial, of the judges, of the sable draperies, of the sentence, of the sickness, of the swoon. Then entire forgetfulness of all that followed; of all that a later day and much earnestness of endeavor have enabled me vaguely to recall.

So far, I had not opened my eyes. I felt that I lay upon my back, unbound. I reached out my hand, and it fell heavily upon something damp and hard. There I suffered it to remain for many minutes, while I strove to imagine where and *what* I could be. I longed, yet dared not, to employ my vision. I dreaded the first glance at objects around me. It was not that I feared to look upon things horrible, but that I grew aghast lest there should be *nothing* to see. At length, with a wild desperation at heart, I quickly unclosed my eyes. My worst thoughts, then, were confirmed. The blackness of eternal night encompassed me. I struggled for breath. The intensity of the darkness seemed to oppress and stifle me. The atmosphere was intolerably close. I still lay quietly, and made effort to exercise my reason. I brought to mind the inquisitorial proceedings, and attempted from that point to deduce my real condition. The sentence had passed; and it appeared to me that a very long interval of time had since elapsed. Yet not for a moment did I suppose myself actually dead. Such a supposition, notwithstanding what we read in fiction, is altogether inconsistent with real existence;—but where and in what state was I? The condemned to death, I knew, perished usually at the *autos-da-fé,* and one of these had been held on the very night of the day of my trial. Had I been remanded to my dungeon, to await the next sacrifice, which would not take place for many months? This I at once saw could not be. Victims had been in immediate demand. Moreover, my dungeon, as well as all the condemned cells at Toledo, had stone floors, and light was not altogether excluded.

A fearful idea now suddenly drove the blood in torrents upon my heart, and for a brief period I once more relapsed into insensibility. Upon recovering, I at once started to my feet, trembling convulsively in every fibre. I thrust my arms wildly above and around me in all directions. I felt nothing; yet dreaded to move a step, lest I should be impeded by the walls of a *tomb*. Perspiration burst from every pore, and stood in cold big beads upon my forehead. The agony of suspense grew at length intolerable, and I cautiously moved forward, with my arms extended, and my eyes straining from their sockets in the hope of catching some faint ray of light. I proceeded for many paces; but still all was blackness and vacancy. I breathed more freely. It seemed evident that mine was not, at least, the most hideous of fates.

And now, as I still continued to step cautiously onward, there came thronging upon my recollection a thousand vague rumors of the horrors of Toledo. Of the dungeons there had been strange things narrated—fables I had always deemed them,—but yet strange, and too ghastly to repeat, save in a whisper. Was I left to perish of starvation in this subterranean world of darkness; or what fate, perhaps even more fearful, awaited me? That the result would be death, and a death of more than customary bitterness, I knew too well the character of my judges to doubt. The mode and the hour were all that occupied or distracted me.

My outstretched hands at length encountered some solid obstruction. It was a wall, seemingly of stone masonry—very smooth, slimy, and cold. I followed it up; stepping with all the careful distrust with which certain antique narratives had inspired me. This process, however, afforded me no means of ascertaining the dimensions of my dungeon, as I might make its circuit and return to the point whence I set out without being aware of the fact, so perfectly uniform seemed the wall. I therefore sought the knife which had been in my pocket, when led into the inquisitorial chamber; but it was gone; my clothes had been exchanged for a wrapper of coarse serge. I had thought of forcing the blade in some minute crevice of the masonry, so as to identify my point of departure. The difficulty, nevertheless, was but trivial; although, in the disorder of my fancy, it seemed at first insuperable. I tore a part of the hem from the robe and placed the fragment at full length, and at right angles to the wall. In groping my way around the prison, I could not fail to encounter this rag upon completing the circuit. So, at least, I thought; but

I had not counted upon the extent of the dungeon, or upon my own weakness. The ground was moist and slippery. I staggered onward for some time, when I stumbled and fell. My excessive fatigue induced me to remain prostrate; and sleep soon overtook me as I lay.

Upon awaking, and stretching forth an arm, I found beside me a loaf and a pitcher with water. I was too much exhausted to reflect upon this circumstance, but ate and drank with avidity. Shortly afterward, I resumed my tour around the prison, and with much toil, came at last upon the fragment of the serge. Up to the period when I fell, I had counted fifty-two paces, and, upon resuming my walk, I had counted forty-eight more—when I arrived at the rag. There were in all, then, a hundred paces; and, admitting two paces to the yard, I presumed the dungeon to be fifty yards in circuit. I had met, however, with many angles in the wall, and thus I could form no guess at the shape of the vault, for vault I could not help supposing it to be.

I had little object—certainly no hope—in these researches; but a vague curiosity prompted me to continue them. Quitting the wall, I resolved to cross the area of the enclosure. At first, I proceeded with extreme caution, for the floor, although seemingly of solid material, was treacherous with slime. At length, however, I took courage, and did not hesitate to step firmly; endeavoring to cross in as direct a line as possible. I had advanced some ten or twelve paces in this manner, when the remnant of the torn hem of my robe became entangled between my legs. I stepped on it, and fell violently on my face.

In the confusion attending my fall, I did not immediately apprehend a somewhat startling circumstance, which yet, in a few seconds afterward, and while I still lay prostrate, arrested my attention. It was this—my chin rested upon the floor of the prison, but my lips, and the upper portion of my head, although seemingly at a less elevation than the chin, touched nothing. At the same time, my forehead seemed bathed in a clammy vapor, and the peculiar smell of decayed fungus arose to my nostrils. I put forward my arm, and shuddered to find that I had fallen at the very brink of a circular pit, whose extent, of course, I had no means of ascertaining at the moment. Groping about the masonry just below the margin, I succeeded in dislodging a small fragment, and let it fall into the abyss. For many seconds I hearkened to its reverberations as it dashed against the sides of the chasm in its descent; at length there was a sullen plunge into water, succeeded by loud echoes. At the same moment, there came a sound resembling the quick opening and as rapid closing of a door overhead, while a faint gleam of light flashed suddenly through the gloom, and as suddenly faded away.

I saw clearly the doom which had been prepared for me, and congratulated myself upon the timely accident by which I had escaped. Another step before my fall, and the world had seen me no more. And the death just avoided was of that very character which I had regarded as fabulous and frivolous in the tales respecting the Inquisition. To the victims of its tyranny, there was the choice of death with its direst physical agonies, or death with its most hideous moral horrors. I had been reserved for the latter. By long suffering my nerves had been unstrung, until I trembled at the sound of my own voice, and had become in every respect a fitting subject for the species of torture which awaited me.

Shaking in every limb, I groped my way back to the wall—resolving there to perish rather than risk the terrors of the wells, of which my imagination now pictured many in various positions about the dungeon. In other conditions of mind, I might have had courage to end my misery at once, by a plunge into one of these abysses; but now I was the veriest of cowards. Neither could I forget what I had read of these pits—that the *sudden* extinction of life formed no part of their most horrible plan.

Agitation of spirit kept me awake for many long hours, but at length I again slumbered. Upon arousing, I found by my side, as before, a loaf and a pitcher of water. A burning thirst consumed me, and I emptied the vessel at a draught. It must have been drugged—for scarcely had I drunk, before I became irresistibly drowsy. A deep sleep fell upon me—a sleep like that of death. How long it lasted of course, I know not; but when, once again, I unclosed my eyes, the objects around me were visible. By a wild, sulphurous lustre, the origin of which I could not at first determine, I was enabled to see the extent and aspect of the prison.

In its size I had been greatly mistaken. The whole circuit of its walls did not exceed twenty-five yards. For some minutes this fact occasioned me a world of vain trouble; vain indeed—for what could be of less importance, under the terrible circumstances which environed me, than the mere dimensions of my dungeon? But my soul took a wild interest in trifles, and I busied myself in endeavors to account for the error I had committed in my measurement. The truth at length flashed upon me. In my first attempt at exploration I had counted fifty-two paces, up to the period when I fell: I must then have been within a pace or two of the fragment of serge; in fact, I had nearly performed the circuit of the vault. I then slept—and, upon awaking, I must have returned upon my steps—thus supposing the circuit nearly double what it actually was. My confusion of mind prevented me from observing that I began my tour with the wall to the left, and ended it with the wall to the right.

I had been deceived, too, in respect to the shape of the enclosure. In feeling my way I had found many angles, and thus deduced an idea of great irregularity; so potent is the effect of total darkness upon one arousing from lethargy or sleep! The angles were simply those of a few slight depressions, or niches, at odd intervals. The general shape of the prison was square. What I had taken for masonry seemed now to be iron, or some other metal, in huge plates, whose sutures or joints occasioned the depression. The entire surface of this metallic enclosure was rudely daubed in all the hideous and repulsive devices to which the charnel superstition of the monks has given rise. The figures of fiends in aspects of menace, with skeleton forms, and other more really fearful images, overspread and disfigured the walls. I observed that the outlines of these monstrosities were sufficiently distinct, but that the colors seemed faded and blurred, as if from the effects of a damp atmosphere. I now noticed the floor, too, which was of stone. In the centre yawned the circular pit from whose jaws I had escaped; but it was the only one in the dungeon.

All this I saw indistinctly and by much effort: for my personal condition had been greatly changed during slumber. I now lay upon my back, and at full length, on a species of low framework of wood. To this I was securely bound by a long strap resembling a surcingle. It passed in many convolutions about my limbs and body, leaving at liberty only my head, and my left arm to such extent that I could, by dint of much exertion, supply myself with food from an earthen dish which lay by my side on the floor. I saw, to my horror, that the pitcher had been removed. I say to my horror—for I was consumed with intolerable thirst. This thirst it appeared to be the design of my persecutors to stimulate: for the food in the dish was meat pungently seasoned.

Looking upward, I surveyed the ceiling of my prison. It was some thirty or forty feet overhead, and constructed much as the side walls. In one of its panels a very singular figure riveted my whole attention. It was the painted figure of Time as he is commonly represented, save that, in lieu of a scythe, he held what, at a casual glance, I supposed to be the pictured image of a huge pendulum, such as we see on antique clocks. There was something, however, in the appearance of this machine which caused me to regard it more attentively. While I gazed directly upward at it (for its position was immediately over my own) I fancied that I saw it in motion. In an instant afterward the fancy was confirmed. Its sweep was brief, and of course slow. I watched it for some minutes, somewhat in fear, but more in wonder. Wearied at length with observing its dull movement, I turned my eyes upon the other objects in the cell.

A slight noise attracted my notice, and, looking to the floor, I saw several enormous rats traversing it. They had issued from the well which lay just within view to my right. Even then, while I gazed, they came up in troops, hurriedly, with ravenous eyes, allured by the scent of the meat. From this it required much effort and attention to scare them away.

It might have been half an hour, perhaps even an hour, (for I could take but imperfect note of time) before I again cast my eyes upward. What I then saw confounded and amazed me. The sweep of the pendulum had increased in extent by nearly a yard. As a natural consequence its velocity was also much greater. But what mainly disturbed me was the idea that it had perceptibly *descended.* I now observed—with what horror it is needless to say—that its nether extremity was formed of a crescent of glittering steel, about a foot in length from horn to horn; the horns upward, and the under edge evidently as keen as that of a razor. Like a razor also, it seemed massy and heavy, tapering from the edge into a solid and broad structure above. It was appended to a weighty rod of brass, and the whole *hissed* as it swung through the air.

I could no longer doubt the doom prepared for me by monkish ingenuity in torture. My cognizance of the pit had become known to the inquisitorial agents—*the pit,* whose horrors had been destined for so bold a recusant as myself—*the pit,* typical of hell, and regarded by rumor as the Ultima Thule of all their punishments. The plunge into this pit I had avoided by the merest of accidents, and I knew that surprise, or entrapment into torment, formed an important portion of all the grotesquerie of these dungeon deaths. Having failed to fall, it was no part of the demon plan to hurl me into the abyss; and thus (there being no alternative) a different and a milder destruction awaited me. Milder! I half smiled in my agony as I thought of such application of such a term.

What boots it to tell of the long, long hours of horror more than mortal, during which I counted the rushing oscillations of the steel! Inch by inch—line by line—with a descent only appreciable at intervals that seemed ages—down and still down it came! Days passed—it might have been that many days passed—ere it swept so closely over me as to fan me with its acrid breath. The odor of the sharp steel forced itself into my nostrils. I prayed—I wearied heaven with my prayer for its more speedy descent. I grew frantically mad, and struggled to force myself upward against the sweep of the fearful scimitar. And then I fell suddenly calm, and lay smiling at the glittering death, as a child at some rare bauble.

There was another interval of utter insensibility; it was brief; for, upon again lapsing into life, there had been no perceptible descent in the pendulum. But it might have been long—for I knew there were demons who took note of my swoon, and who could have arrested the vibration at pleasure. Upon my recovery, too, I felt very—oh, inexpressibly sick and weak, as if through long inanition. Even amid the agonies of that period, the human nature craved food. With painful effort I outstretched my left arm as far as my bonds permitted, and took possession of the small remnant which had been spared me by the rats. As I put a portion of it within my lips, there rushed to my mind a half formed thought of joy—of hope. Yet what business had *I* with hope? It was, as I say, a half formed thought—man has many such which are never completed. I felt that it was of joy—of hope; but I felt also that it had perished in its formation. In vain I struggled to perfect—to regain it. Long suffering had nearly annihilated all my ordinary powers of mind. I was an imbecile—an idiot.

The vibration of the pendulum was at right angles to my length. I saw that the crescent was designed to cross the region of the heart. It would fray the serge of my robe—it would return and repeat its operations—again—and again. Notwithstanding its terrifically wide sweep (some thirty feet or more) and the hissing vigor of its descent, sufficient to sunder these very walls of iron, still the fraying of my robe would be all that, for several minutes, it would accomplish. And at this thought I paused. I dared not go further than this reflection. I dwelt upon it with a pertinacity of attention—as if, in so dwelling, I could arrest *here* the descent of the steel. I forced myself to ponder upon the sound of the crescent as it should pass across the garment—upon the peculiar thrilling sensation which the friction of cloth produces on the nerves. I pondered upon all this frivolity until my teeth were on edge.

Down—steadily down it crept. I took a frenzied pleasure in contrasting its downward with its lateral velocity. To the right—to the left—far and wide—with the shriek of a damned spirit; to my heart with the stealthy pace of the tiger! I alternately laughed and howled, as the one or the other idea grew predominant.

Down—certainly, relentlessly down! It vibrated within three inches of my bosom! I struggled violently—furiously—to free my left arm. This was free only from the elbow to the hand. I could reach the latter, from the platter beside me, to my mouth, with great effort, but no farther. Could I have broken the fastenings above the elbow, I would have seized and attempted to arrest the pendulum. I might as well have attempted to arrest an avalanche!

Down—still unceasingly—still inevitably down! I gasped and struggled at each vibration. I shrunk convulsively at its every sweep. My eyes followed its outward or upward whirls with the eagerness of the most unmeaning despair; they closed themselves spasmodically at the descent, although death would have been a relief, oh! how unspeakable! Still I quivered in every nerve to think how slight a sinking of the machinery would precipitate that keen, glistening axe upon my bosom. It was *hope* that prompted the nerve to quiver—the frame to shrink. It was *hope*—the hope that triumphs on the rack—that whispers to the death-condemned even in the dungeons of the Inquisition.

I saw that some ten or twelve vibrations would bring the steel in actual contact with my robe—and with this observation there suddenly came over my spirit all the keen, collected calmness of despair. For the first time during many hours—or perhaps days—I *thought*. It now occurred to me, that the bandage, or surcingle, which enveloped me, was *unique*. I was tied by no separate cord. The first stroke of the razor-like crescent athwart any portion of the band would so detach it that it might be unwound from my person by means of my left hand. But how fearful, in that case, the proximity of the steel! The result of the slightest struggle, how deadly! Was it likely, moreover, that the minions of the torturer had not foreseen and provided for this possibility! Was it probable that the bandage crossed my bosom in the track of the pendulum? Dreading to find my faint, and, as it seemed, my last hope frustrated, I so far elevated my head as to obtain a distinct view of my breast. The surcingle enveloped my limbs and body close in all directions—*save in the path of the destroying crescent.*

Scarcely had I dropped my head back into its original position, when there flashed upon my mind what I cannot better describe than as the unformed half of that idea of deliverance to which I have previously alluded, and of which a moiety only floated inderminately through my brain when I raised food to my burning lips. The whole thought was now present—feeble, scarcely sane, scarcely definite—but still entire. I proceeded at once, with the nervous energy of despair, to attempt its execution.

For many hours the immediate vicinity of the low framework upon which I lay had been literally swarming with rats. They were wild, bold, ravenous; their red eyes glaring upon me as if they waited but for motionlessness on my part to make me their prey. "To what food," I thought, "have they been accustomed in the well?"

They had devoured, in spite of all my efforts to prevent them, all but a small remnant of the contents of the dish. I had fallen into an habitual see-saw or wave of the hand about the platter. and, at length, the unconscious uniformity of the movement deprived it of effect. In their voracity, the vermin frequently fastened their sharp fangs in my fingers. With the particles of the oily and spicy viand which now remained, I thoroughly rubbed the bandage wherever I could reach it; then, raising my hand from the floor, I lay breathlessly still.

At first, the ravenous animals were startled and terrified at the change—at the cessation of movement. They shrank alarmedly back; many sought the well. But this was only for a moment. I had not counted in vain upon their voracity. Observing that I remained without motion, one or two of the boldest leaped upon the framework, and smelt at the surcingle. This seemed the signal for a general rush. Forth from the well they hurried in fresh troops. They clung to the wood—they overran it, and leaped in hundreds upon my person. The measured movement of the pendulum disturbed them not at all. Avoiding its strokes, they busied themselves with the anointed bandage. They pressed—they swarmed upon me in ever accumulating heaps. They writhed upon my throat; their cold lips sought my own; I was half stifled by their thronging pressure; disgust, for which the world has no name, swelled my bosom, and chilled, with a heavy clamminess, my heart. Yet one minute, and I felt that the struggle would be over. Plainly I perceived the loosening of the bandage. I knew that in more than one place it must be already severed. With a more than human resolution I lay *still*.

Nor had I erred in my calculations—nor had I endured in vain. I at length felt that I was *free*. The surcingle hung in ribands from my body. But the stroke of the pendulum already pressed upon my bosom. It had divided the serge of the robe. It had cut through the linen beneath. Twice again it swung, and a sharp sense of pain shot through every nerve. But the moment of escape had arrived. At a wave of my hand my deliverers hurried tumultuously away. With a steady movement—cautious, sidelong, shrinking, and slow—I slid from the embrace of the bandage and beyond the reach of the scimitar. For the moment, at least, *I was free*.

Free!—and in the grasp of the Inquisition! I had scarcely stepped from my wooden bed of horror upon the stone floor of the prison, when the motion of the hellish machine ceased, and I beheld it drawn up, by some invisible force, through the ceiling. This was a lesson which I took desperately to heart. My every motion was undoubtedly watched. Free!—I had but escaped death in one form of agony, to be delivered unto worse than death in some other. With that thought I rolled my eyes nervously around on the barriers of iron that hemmed me in. Something unusual—some change which, at first, I could not appreciate distinctly—it was obvious, had taken place in the apartment. For many minutes of a dreamy and trembling abstraction, I busied myself in vain, unconnected conjecture. During this period, I became aware, for the first time, of the origin of the sulphurous light which illumined the cell. It proceeded from a fissure, about half an inch in width, extending entirely around the prison at the base of the walls, which thus appeared, and were, completely separated from the floor. I endeavored, but of course in vain, to look through the aperture.

As I arose from the attempt, the mystery of the alteration in the chamber broke at once upon my understanding. I have observed that, although the outlines of the figures upon the walls were sufficiently distinct, yet the colours seemed blurred and indefinite. These colors had now assumed, and were momentarily assuming, a startling and most intense brilliancy, that gave to the spectral and fiendish portraitures an aspect that might have thrilled even firmer nerves than my own. Demon eyes, of a wild and ghastly vivacity, glared upon me in a thousand directions, where none had been visible before, and gleamed with the lurid lustre of a fire that I could not force my imagination to regard as unreal.

Unreal!—Even while I breathed there came to my nostrils the breath of the vapor of heated iron! A suffocating odour pervaded the prison! A deeper glow settled each moment in the eyes that glared at my agonies! A richer tint of crimson diffused itself over the pictured horrors of blood. I panted! I gasped for breath! There could be no doubt of the design of my tormentors—oh! most unrelenting! oh! most demoniac of men! I shrank from the glowing metal to the centre of the cell. Amid the thought of the fiery destruction that impended, the idea of the coolness of the well came over my soul like balm. I rushed to its deadly brink. I threw my straining vision below. The glare from the enkindled roof illumined its inmost recesses. Yet, for a wild moment, did my spirit refuse to comprehend the meaning of what I saw. At length it forced—it wrestled its way into my soul—it burned itself in upon my shuddering reason. Oh! for a voice to speak!—oh! horror!—oh! any horror but this! With a shriek, I rushed from the margin, and buried my face in my hands—weeping bitterly.

The heat rapidly increased, and once again I looked up, shuddering as with a fit of the ague. There had been a second change in the cell—and now the change was obviously in the *form*. As before, it was in vain that I at first endeavoured to appreciate or understand what was taking place. But not long was I left in doubt. The Inquisitorial vengeance had been hurried by my two-fold escape, and there was to be no more dallying with the King of Terrors. The room had been square. I saw that two of its iron angles were now acute—two, consequently, obtuse. The fearful difference quickly increased with a low rumbling or moaning sound. In an instant the apartment had shifted its form into that of a lozenge. But the alteration stopped not here—I neither hoped nor desired it to stop. I could have clasped the red walls to my bosom as a garment of eternal peace. "Death," I said, "any death but that of the pit!" Fool! might I not have known that *into the pit* it was the object of the burning iron to urge me? Could I resist its glow? or, if even that, could I withstand its pressure? And now, flatter and flatter grew the lozenge, with a rapidity that left me no time for contemplation. Its centre, and of course, its greatest width, came just over the yawning gulf. I shrank back—but the closing walls pressed me resistlessly onward. At length for my seared and writhing body there was no longer an inch of foothold on the firm floor of the prison. I struggled no more, but the agony of my soul found vent in one loud, long, and final scream of despair. I felt that I tottered upon the brink—I averted my eyes—

There was a discordant hum of human voices! There was a loud blast as of many trumpets! There was a harsh grating as of a thousand thunders! The fiery walls rushed back! An outstretched-arm caught my own as I fell, fainting, into the abyss. It was that of General Lasalle. The French army had entered Toledo. The Inquisition was in the hands of its enemies.

THE MAN OF THE CROWD*

Ce grand malheur, de ne pouvoir être seul.

La Bruyère

IT WAS well said of a certain German book that *"es lässt sich nicht lesen"*—it does not permit itself to be read. There are some secrets which do not permit themselves to be told. Men die nightly in their beds, wringing the hands of ghostly confessors, and looking them piteously in the eyes—die with despair of heart and convulsion of throat, on account of the hideousness of mysteries which will not *suffer themselves* to be revealed. Now and then, alas, the conscience of man takes up a burden so heavy in horror that it can be thrown down only into the grave. And thus the essence of all crime is undivulged.

Not long ago, about the closing in of an evening in autumn, I sat at the large bow window of the D—— Coffee-House in London. For some months I had been ill in health, but was now convalescent, and, with returning strength, found myself in one of those happy moods which are so precisely the converse of *ennui*—moods of the keenest appetency, when the film from the mental vision departs—the ἀχλὺς ἣ πρὶν ἐπῆεν—and the intellect, electrified, surpasses as greatly its every-day condition, as does the vivid yet candid reason of Leibnitz, the mad and flimsy rhetoric of Gorgias. Merely to breathe was enjoyment; and I derived positive pleasure even from many of the legitimate sources of pain. I felt a calm but inquisitive interest in every thing. With a cigar in

* *Burton's Gentleman's Magazine,* December, 1840; 1845. Text corrected by J. L. Graham copy.

my mouth and a newspaper in my lap, I had been amusing myself for the greater part of the afternoon, now in poring over advertisements, now in observing the promiscuous company in the room, and now in peering through the smoky panes into the street.

This latter is one of the principal thoroughfares of the city, and had been very much crowded during the whole day. But, as the darkness came on, the throng momently increased; and, by the time the lamps were well lighted, two dense and continuous tides of population were rushing past the door. At this particular period of the evening I had never before been in a similar situation, and the tumultuous sea of human heads filled me, therefore, with a delicious novelty of emotion. I gave up, at length, all care of things within the hotel, and became absorbed in contemplation of the scene without.

At first my observations took an abstract and generalizing turn. I looked at the passengers in masses, and thought of them in their aggregate relations. Soon, however, I descended to details, and regarded with minute interest the innumerable varieties of figure, dress, air, gait, visage, and expression of countenance.

By far the greater number of those who went by had a satisfied business-like demeanor, and seemed to be thinking only of making their way through the press. Their brows were knit, and their eyes rolled quickly; when pushed against by fellow-wayfarers they evinced no symptom of impatience, but adjusted their clothes and hurried on. Others, still a numerous class, were restless in their movements, had flushed faces, and talked and gesticulated to themselves, as if feeling in solitude on account of the very denseness of the company around. When impeded in their progress, these people suddenly ceased muttering, but redoubled their gesticulations, and awaited, with an absent and overdone smile upon the lips, the course of the persons impeding them. If jostled, they bowed profusely to the jostlers, and appeared overwhelmed with confusion.—There was nothing very distinctive about these two large classes beyond what I have noted. Their habiliments belonged to that order which is pointedly termed the decent. They were undoubtedly noblemen, merchants, attorneys, tradesmen, stock-jobbers—the Eupatrids and the common-places of society—men of leisure and men actively engaged in affairs of their own—conducting business upon their own responsibility. They did not greatly excite my attention.

The tribe of clerks was an obvious one; and here I discerned two remarkable divisions. There were the junior clerks of flash houses—young gentlemen with tight coats, bright boots, well-oiled hair, and supercilious lips. Setting aside a certain dapperness of carriage, which may be termed *deskism* for want of a better word, the manner of these persons seemed to me an exact fac-simile of what had been the perfection of *bon ton* about twelve or eighteen months before. They wore the cast-off graces of the gentry;—and this, I believe, involves the best definition of the class.

The division of the upper clerks of staunch firms, or of the "steady old fellows," it was not possible to mistake. These were known by their coats and pantaloons of black or brown, made to sit comfortably, with white cravats and waistcoats, broad solid-looking shoes, and thick hose or gaiters.—They had all slightly bald heads, from which the right ears, long used to pen-holding, had an odd habit of standing off on end. I observed that they always removed or settled their hats with both hands, and wore watches, with short gold chains of a substantial and ancient pattern. Theirs was the affectation of respectability;—if indeed there be an affectation so honorable.

There were many individuals of dashing appearance, whom I easily understood as belonging to the race of swell pick-pockets, with which all great cities are infested. I watched these gentry with much inquisitiveness, and found it difficult to imagine how they should ever be mistaken for gentlemen by gentlemen themselves. Their voluminousness of wristband, with an air of excessive frankness, should betray them at once.

The gamblers, of whom I descried not a few, were still more easily recognisable. They wore every variety of dress, from that of the desperate thimble-rig bully, with velvet waistcoat, fancy neckerchief, gilt chains, and filigreed buttons, to that of the scrupulously inornate clergyman than which nothing could be less liable to suspicion. Still all were distinguished by a certain sodden swarthiness of complexion, a filmy dimness of eye, and pallor and compression of lip. There were two other traits, moreover, by which I could always detect them;—a guarded lowness of tone in conversation, and a more than ordinary extension of the thumb in a direction at right angles with the fingers.—Very often, in company with these sharpers, I observed an order of men somewhat different in habits, but still birds of a kindred feather. They may be defined as the gentlemen who live by their wits. They seem to prey upon the public in two battalions—that of the dandies and that of the military men. Of the first grade the leading features are long locks and smiles; of the second, frogged coats and frowns.

Descending in the scale of what is termed gentility, I found darker and deeper themes for speculation. I saw Jew peddlers, with hawk eyes flashing from countenances whose every other feature wore only an expression of abject humility; sturdy professional street beggars scowling upon mendicants of a better stamp, whom despair alone had driven forth into the night for charity; feeble and ghastly invalids, upon whom death had placed a sure hand, and who sidled and tottered through the mob, looking every one beseechingly in the face, as if in search of some chance consolation, some lost hope; modest young girls returning from long and late labor to a cheerless home, and shrinking more tearfully than indignantly from the glances of ruffians, whose direct contact, even, could not be avoided; women of the town of all kinds and of all ages—the unequivocal beauty in the prime of her womanhood, putting one in mind of the statue in Lucian, with the surface of Parian marble, and the interior filled with filth—the loathsome and utterly lost leper in rags—the wrinkled, bejewelled and paint-begrimed beldame, making a last effort at youth—the mere child of immature form, yet, from long association, an adept in the dreadful coquetries of her trade, and burning with a rabid ambition to be ranked the equal of her elders in vice; drunkards innumerable and indescribable—some in shreds and patches, reeling, inarticulate, with bruised visage and lack-lustre eyes—some in whole although filthy garments, with a slightly unsteady swagger, thick sensual lips, and hearty-looking rubicund faces—others clothed in materials which had once been good, and which even now were scrupulously well brushed—men who walked with a more than naturally firm and springy step, but whose countenances were fearfully pale, whose eyes were hideously wild and red, and who clutched with quivering fingers, as they strode through the crowd, at every object which came within their reach; beside these, pie-men, porters, coal-heavers, sweeps; organ-grinders, monkey-exhibitors and ballad-mongers, those who vended with those who sang; ragged artizans and exhausted laborers of every description, and all full of a noisy and inordinate vivacity which jarred discordantly upon the ear, and gave an aching sensation to the eye.

As the night deepened, so deepened to me the interest of the scene; for not only did the general character of the crowd materially alter (its gentler features retiring in the gradual withdrawal of the more orderly portion of the people, and its harsher ones coming out into bolder relief, as the late hour brought forth every species of infamy from its den,) but the rays of the gas-lamps, feeble at first in their struggle with the dying day, had now at length gained ascendancy, and threw over every thing a fitful and garish lustre. All was dark yet splendid—as that ebony to which has been likened the style of Tertullian.

The wild effects of the light enchained me to an examination of individual faces; and although the rapidity with which the world of light flitted before the window, prevented me from casting more than a glance upon each visage, still it seemed that, in my then peculiar mental state, I could frequently read, even in that brief interval of a glance, the history of long years.

With my brow to the glass, I was thus occupied in scrutinizing the mob, when suddenly there came into view a countenance (that of a decrepid old man, some sixty-five or seventy years of age,)—a countenance which at once arrested and absorbed my whole attention, on account of the absolute idiosyncrasy of its expression. Any thing even remotely resembling that expression I had never seen before. I well remember that my first thought, upon beholding it, was that Retszch, had he viewed it, would have greatly preferred it to his own pictural incarnations of the fiend. As I endeavored, during the brief minute of my original survey, to form some analysis of the meaning conveyed, there arose confusedly and paradoxically within my mind, the ideas of vast mental power, of caution, of penuriousness, of avarice, of coolness, of malice, of blood-thirstiness, of triumph, of merriment, of excessive terror, of intense—of supreme despair. I felt singularly aroused, startled, fascinated. "How wild a history," I said to myself, "is written within that bosom!" Then came a craving desire to keep the man in view—to know more of him. Hurriedly putting on an overcoat, and seizing my hat and cane, I made my way into the street, and pushed through the crowd in the direction which I had seen him take; for he had already disappeared. With some little difficulty I at length came within sight of him, approached, and followed him closely, yet cautiously, so as not to attract his attention.

I had now a good opportunity of examining his person. He was short in stature, very thin, and apparently very feeble. His clothes, generally, were filthy and ragged; but as he came, now and then, within the strong glare of a lamp, I perceived that his linen, although dirty, was of beautiful texture; and my vision deceived me, or, through a rent in a closely-buttoned and evidently second-handed *roquelaire* which enveloped him, I caught a glimpse both of a diamond and of a dagger. These observations heightened my curiosity, and I resolved to follow the stranger whithersoever he should go.

It was now fully night-fall, and a thick humid fog hung over the city, soon ending in a settled and heavy rain. This change of weather had an odd effect upon the crowd, the whole of which was at once put into new commotion, and overshadowed by a world of umbrellas. The waver, the jostle, and the hum increased in a tenfold degree. For my own part I did not much regard the rain—the lurking of an old fever in my system rendering the moisture somewhat too dangerously pleasant. Tying a handkerchief about my mouth, I kept on. For half an hour the old man held his way with difficulty along the great thoroughfare; and I here walked close at his elbow through fear of losing sight of him. Never once turning his head to look back, he did not observe me. By and bye he passed into a cross street, which, although densely filled with people, was not quite so much thronged as the main one he had quitted. Here a change in his demeanor became evident. He walked more slowly and with less object than before—more hesitatingly. He crossed and re-crossed the way repeatedly, without apparent aim; and the press was still so thick, that, at every such movement, I was obliged to follow him closely. The street was a narrow and long one, and his course lay within it for nearly an hour, during which the passengers had gradually diminished to about that number which is ordinarily seen at noon on Broadway near the park—so vast a difference is there between a London populace and that of the most frequented American city. A second turn brought us into a square, brilliantly lighted, and overflowing with life. The old manner of the stranger re-appeared. His chin fell upon his breast, while his eyes rolled wildly from under his knit brows, in every direction, upon those who hemmed him in. He urged his way steadily and perseveringly. I was surprised, however, to find, upon his having made the circuit of the square, that he turned and retraced his steps. Still more was I astonished to see him repeat the same walk several times—once nearly detecting me as he came round with a sudden movement.

In this exercise he spent another hour, at the end of which we met with far less interruption from passengers than at first. The rain fell fast; the air grew cool; and the people were retiring to their homes. With a gesture of impatience, the wanderer passed into a by-street comparatively deserted. Down this, some quarter of a mile long, he rushed with an activity I could not have dreamed of seeing in one so aged, and which put me to much trouble in pursuit. A few minutes brought us to a large and busy bazaar, with the localities of which the stranger appeared well acquainted, and where his original demeanor again became apparent, as he forced his way to and fro, without aim, among the host of buyers and sellers.

During the hour and a half, or thereabouts, which we passed in this place, it required much caution on my part to keep him within reach without attracting his observation. Luckily I wore a pair of caoutchouc over-shoes, and could move about in perfect silence. At no moment did he see that I watched him. He entered shop after shop, priced nothing, spoke no word, and looked at all objects with a wild and vacant stare. I was now utterly amazed at his behaviour, and firmly resolved that we should not part until I had satisfied myself in some measure respecting him.

A loud-toned clock struck eleven, and the company were fast deserting the bazaar. A shop-keeper, in putting up a shutter, jostled the old man, and at the instant I saw a strong shudder come over his frame. He hurried into the street, looked anxiously around him for an instant, and then ran with incredible swiftness through many crooked and people-less lanes, until we emerged once more upon the great thoroughfare whence we had started—the street of the D—— Hotel. It no longer wore, however, the same aspect. It was still brilliant with gas; but the rain fell fiercely, and there were few persons to be seen. The stranger grew pale. He walked moodily some paces up the once populous avenue, then, with a heavy sigh, turned in the direction of the river, and, plunging through a great variety of devious ways, came out, at length, in view of one of the principal theatres. It was about being closed, and the audience were thronging from the doors. I saw the old man gasp as if for breath while he threw himself amid the crowd; but I thought that the intense agony of his countenance had, in some measure, abated. His head again fell upon his breast; he appeared as I had seen him at first. I observed that he now took the course in which had gone the greater number of the audience—but, upon the whole, I was at a loss to comprehend the waywardness of his actions.

As he proceeded, the company grew more scattered, and his old uneasiness and vacillation were resumed. For some time he followed closely a party of some ten or twelve roisterers; but from this number one by one dropped off, until three only remained together, in a narrow and gloomy lane little frequented. The stranger paused, and, for a moment, seemed lost in thought; then, with every mark of agitation, pursued rapidly a route which brought us to the verge of the city, amid regions very different from those we had hitherto traversed. It was the most noisome quarter of London, where every thing wore the worst impress of the most deplorable poverty, and of the most desperate crime. By the dim light of an accidental lamp, tall, antique, worm-eaten, wooden tenements were seen tottering to their fall, in directions so many and capricious that scarce the semblance of a passage was discernible between them. The paving-stones lay at random, displaced from their beds by the rankly growing grass. Horrible filth festered in the dammed-up gutters. The whole atmosphere teemed with desolation. Yet, as we proceeded, the sounds of human life revived by sure degrees, and at length large bands of the most abandoned of a London populace were seen reeling to and fro. The spirits of the old man again flickered up, as a lamp which is near its death-hour. Once more he strode onward with elastic tread. Suddenly a corner was turned, a blaze of light burst upon our sight, and we stood before one of the huge suburban temples of Intemperance—one of the palaces of the fiend, Gin.

It was now nearly day-break; but a number of wretched inebriates still pressed in and out of the flaunting entrance. With a half shriek of joy the old man forced a passage within, resumed at once his original bearing, and stalked backward and forward, without apparent object, among the throng. He had not been thus long occupied, however, before a rush to the doors gave token that the host was closing them for the night. It was something even more intense than despair that I then observed upon the countenance of the singular being whom I had watched so pertinaciously. Yet he did not hesitate in his career, but, with a mad energy, retraced his steps at once, to the heart of the mighty London. Long and swiftly he fled, while I followed him in the wildest amazement, resolute not to abandon a scrutiny in which I now felt an interest all-absorbing. The sun arose while we proceeded, and, when we had once again reached that most thronged mart of the populous town, the street of the D—— Hotel, it presented an appearance of human bustle and activity scarcely inferior to what I had seen on the evening before. And here, long, amid the momently increasing confusion, did I persist in my pursuit of the stranger. But, as usual, he walked to and fro, and during the day did not pass from out the turmoil of that street. And, as the shades of the second evening came on, I grew wearied unto death, and, stopping fully in front of the wanderer, gazed at him steadfastly in the face. He noticed me not, but resumed his solemn walk, while I, ceasing to follow, remained absorbed in contemplation. "This old man," I said at length, "is the type and the genius of deep crime. He refuses to be alone. *He is the man of the crowd.* It will be in vain to follow; for I shall learn no more of him, nor of his deeds. The worst heart of the world is a grosser book than the 'Hortulus Animæ,' * and perhaps it is but one of the great mercies of God that *'es lässt sich nicht lesen.'* "

* The *Hortulus Animæ cum Oratiunculis Aliquibus Superadditis* of Grünninger.

THE IMP OF THE PERVERSE*

IN THE consideration of the faculties and impulses—of the *prima mobilia* of the human soul, the phrenologists have failed to make room for a propensity which, although obviously existing as a radical, primitive, irreducible sentiment, has been equally overlooked by all the moralists who have preceded them. In the pure arrogance of the reason, we have all overlooked it. We have suffered its existence to escape our senses, solely through want of belief—of faith;—whether it be faith in Revelation, or faith in the Kabbala. The idea of it has never occurred to us, simply because of its supererogation. We saw no *need* of the impulse—for the propensity. We could not perceive its necessity. We could not understand, that is to say, we could not have understood, had the notion of this *primum mobile* ever obtruded itself;—we could not have understood in what manner it might be made to further the objects of humanity, either temporal or eternal. It cannot be denied that phrenology, and in great measure, all metaphysicianism have been concocted *à priori*. The intellectual or logical man, rather than the understanding or observant man, set himself to imagine designs—to dictate purposes to God. Having thus fathomed to his satisfaction the intentions of Jehovah, out of these intentions he built his innumerable systems of mind. In the matter of phrenology, for example, we first determined, naturally enough, that it was the design of the Deity that man should eat. We then assigned to man an organ of alimentiveness, and this organ is the scourge with which the Deity compels man, will-I nill-I, into eating. Secondly, having settled it to be God's will that man

* *Graham's Magazine*, July, 1845; *The Mayflower*, 1845.

should continue his species, we discovered an organ of amativeness, forthwith. And so with combativeness, with ideality, with causality, with constructiveness,—so, in short, with every organ, whether representing a propensity, a moral sentiment, or a faculty of the pure intellect. And in these arrangements of the *principia* of human action, the Spurzheimites, whether right or wrong, in part, or upon the whole, have but followed, in principle, the footsteps of their predecessors; deducing and establishing every thing from the preconceived destiny of man, and upon the ground of the objects of his Creator.

It would have been wiser, it would have been safer to classify, (if classify we must,) upon the basis of what man usually or occasionally did, and was always occasionally doing, rather than upon the basis of what we took it for granted the Deity intended him to do. If we cannot comprehend God in his visible works, how then in his inconceivable thoughts, that call the works into being! If we cannot understand him in his objective creatures, how then in his substantive moods and phases of creation?

Induction, *à posteriori,* would have brought phrenology to admit, as an innate and primitive principle of human action, a paradoxical something, which we may call *perverseness,* for want of a more characteristic term. In the sense I intend, it is, in fact, a *mobile* without motive, a motive not *motivirt.* Through its promptings we act without comprehensible object; or, if this shall be understood as a contradiction in terms, we may so far modify the proposition as to say, that through its promptings we act, for the reason that we should *not.* In theory, no reason can be more unreasonable; but, in fact, there is none more strong. With certain minds, under certain conditions, it becomes absolutely irresistible. I am not more certain that I breathe, than that the assurance of the wrong or error of any action is often the one unconquerable *force* which impels us, and alone impels us to its prosecution. Nor will this overwhelming tendency to do wrong for the wrong's sake, admit of analysis, or resolution into ulterior elements. It is a radical, a primitive impulse—elementary. It will be said, I am aware, that when we persist in acts because we feel we should *not* persist in them, our conduct is but a modification of that which ordinarily springs from the *combativeness* of phrenology. But a glance will show the fallacy of this idea. The phrenological combativeness has for its essence, the necessity of self-defence. It is our safeguard against injury. Its principle regards our well-being; and thus the desire to be well, is excited simultaneously with its development. It follows, that the desire to be well must be excited simultaneously with any principle which shall be merely a modification of combativeness, but in the case of that something which I term *perverseness,* the desire to be well is not only not aroused, but a strongly antagonistical sentiment exists.

An appeal to one's own heart is, after all, the best reply to the sophistry just noticed. No one who trustingly consults and thoroughly questions his own soul, will be disposed to deny the entire radicalness of the propensity in question. It is not more incomprehensible than distinctive. There lives no man who at some period has not been tormented, for example, by an earnest desire to tantalize a listener by circumlocution. The speaker is aware that he displeases; he has every intention to please; he is usually curt, precise, and clear; the most laconic and luminous language is struggling for utterance upon his tongue; it is only with difficulty that he restrains himself from giving it flow; he dreads and deprecates the anger of him whom he addresses; yet, the thought strikes him, that by certain involutions and parentheses, this anger may be engendered. That single thought is enough. The impulse increases to a wish, the wish to a desire, the desire to an uncontrollable longing, and the longing, (to the deep regret and mortification of the speaker, and in defiance of all consequences,) is indulged.

We have a task before us which must be speedily performed. We know that it will be ruinous to make delay. The most important crisis of our life calls, trumpet-tongued, for immediate energy and action. We glow, we are consumed with eagerness to commence the work, with the anticipation of whose glorious result our whole souls are on fire. It must, it shall be undertaken to-day, and yet we put it off until to-morrow; and why? There is no answer, except that we feel *perverse,* using the word with no comprehension of the principle. To-morrow arrives, and with it a more impatient anxiety to do our duty, but with this very increase of anxiety arrives, also, a nameless, a positively fearful, because unfathomable, craving for delay. This craving gathers strength as the moments fly. The last hour for action is at hand. We tremble with the violence of the conflict within us,—of the definite with the indefinite—of the substance with the shadow. But, if the contest have proceeded thus far, it is the shadow which prevails,—we struggle in vain. The clock strikes, and is the knell of our welfare. At the same time, it is the chanticleer-note to the ghost that has so long overawed us. It flies—it disappears—we are free. The old energy returns. We will labor *now*. Alas, it is *too late!*

We stand upon the brink of a precipice. We peer into the abyss—we grow sick and dizzy. Our first impulse is to shrink from the danger. Unaccountably we remain. By slow degrees our sickness, and dizziness, and horror, become merged in a cloud of unnameable feeling. By gradations, still more imperceptible, this cloud assumes shape, as did the vapor from the bottle out of which arose the genius in the Arabian Nights. But out of this *our* cloud upon the precipice's edge, there grows into palpability, a shape, far more terrible than any genius, or any demon of a tale, and yet it is but a thought, although a fearful one, and one which chills the very marrow of our bones with the fierceness of the delight of its horror. It is merely the idea of what would be our sensations during the sweeping precipitancy of a fall from such a height. And this fall—this rushing annihilation—for the very reason that it involves that one most ghastly and loathsome of all the most ghastly and loathsome images of death and suffering which have ever presented themselves to our imagination—for this very cause do we now the most vividly desire it. And because our reason violently deters us from the brink, *therefore,* do we the most impetuously approach it. There is no passion in nature so demoniacally impatient, as that of him who shuddering upon the edge of a precipice, thus meditates a plunge. To indulge for a moment, in any attempt at *thought,* is to be inevitably lost; for reflection but urges us to forbear, and *therefore* it is, I say, that we *cannot.* If there be no friendly arm to check us, or if we fail in a sudden effort to prostrate ourselves backward from the abyss, we plunge, and are destroyed.

Examine these and similar actions as we will, we shall find them resulting solely from the spirit of the *Perverse.* We perpetrate them merely because we feel that we should *not.* Beyond or behind this, there is no intelligible principle; and we might, indeed, deem this perverseness a direct instigation of the arch-fiend, were it not occasionally known to operate in furtherance of good.

I have said thus much, that in some measure I may answer your question—that I may explain to you why I am here—that I may assign to you something that shall have at least the faint aspect of a cause for my wearing these fetters, and for my tenanting this cell of the condemned. Had I not been thus prolix, you might either have misunderstood me altogether, or, with the rabble, have fancied me mad. As it is, you will easily perceive that I am one of the many uncounted victims of the Imp of the Perverse.

It is impossible that any deed could have been wrought with a more thorough deliberation. For weeks, for months, I pondered upon the means of the murder. I rejected a thousand schemes, because their accomplishment involved a *chance* of detection. At length, in reading some French memoirs, I found an account of a nearly fatal illness that occurred to Madame Pilau, through the agency of a candle accidentally poisoned. The idea struck my fancy at once. I knew my victim's habit of reading in bed. I knew, too, that his apartment was narrow and ill-ventilated. But I need not vex you with impertinent details. I need not describe the easy artifices by which I substituted, in his bed-room candle-stand, a wax-light of my own making, for the one which I there found. The next morning he was discovered dead in his bed, and the coroner's verdict was,—"Death by the visitation of God."

Having inherited his estate, all went well with me for years. The idea of detection never once entered my brain. Of the remains of the fatal taper, I had myself carefully disposed. I had left no shadow of a clue by which it would be possible to convict, or even to suspect, me of the crime. It is inconceivable how rich a sentiment of satisfaction arose in my bosom as I reflected upon my absolute security. For a very long period of time, I was accustomed to revel in this sentiment. It afforded me more real delight than all the mere worldly advantages accruing from my sin. But there arrived at length an epoch, from which the pleasurable feeling grew, by scarcely perceptible gradations, into a haunting and harassing thought. It harassed because it haunted. I could scarcely get rid of it for an instant. It is quite a common thing to be thus annoyed with the ringing in our ears, or rather in our memories, of the burthen of some ordinary song, or some unimpressive snatches from an opera. Nor will we be the less tormented if the song in itself be good, or the opera air meritorious. In this manner, at last, I would perpetually catch myself pondering upon my security, and repeating, in a low under-tone, the phrase, "I am safe."

One day, whilst sauntering along the streets, I arrested myself in the act of murmuring, half aloud, these customary syllables. In a fit of petulance, I re-modelled them thus:—"I am safe—I am safe—yes—if I be not fool enough to make open confession!"

No sooner had I spoken these words, than I felt an icy chill creep to my heart. I had had some experience in these fits of perversity, (whose nature I have been at some trouble to explain,) and I remembered well that in no instance, I had successfully resisted their attacks. And now my own casual self-suggestion, that I might possibly be fool enough to confess the murder of which I had been guilty, confronted me, as if the very ghost of him whom I had murdered—and beckoned me on to death.

At first, I made an effort to shake off this nightmare of the soul. I walked vigorously—faster—still faster—at length I ran.

I felt a maddening desire to shriek aloud. Every succeeding wave of thought overwhelmed me with new terror, for, alas! I well, too well, understood that to *think,* in my situation, was to be lost. I still quickened my pace. I bounded like a madman through the crowded thoroughfares. At length, the populace took the alarm, and pursued me. I felt *then* the consummation of my fate. Could I have torn out my tongue, I would have done it—but a rough voice resounded in my ears—a rougher grasp seized me by the shoulder. I turned—I gasped for breath. For a moment, I experienced all the pangs of suffocation; I became blind, and deaf, and giddy; and then, some invisible fiend, I thought, struck me with his broad palm upon the back. The long-imprisoned secret burst forth from my soul.

They say that I spoke with a distinct enunciation, but with marked emphasis and passionate hurry, as if in dread of interruption before concluding the brief but pregnant sentences that consigned me to the hangman and to hell.

Having related all that was necessary for the fullest judicial conviction, I fell prostrate in a swoon.

But why shall I say more? To-day I wear these chains, and am *here!* To-morrow I shall be fetterless!—*but where?*

THE PURLOINED LETTER*

Nil sapientiæ odiosius acumine nimio. *Seneca*

At Paris, just after dark one gusty evening in the autumn of 18—, I was enjoying the twofold luxury of meditation and a meerschaum, in company with my friend C. Auguste Dupin, in his little back library, or book-closet, *au troisième, No. 33 Rue Dunôt, Faubourg St. Germain.* For one hour at least we had maintained a profound silence; while each, to any casual observer, might have seemed intently and exclusively occupied with the curling eddies of smoke that oppressed the atmosphere of the chamber. For myself, however, I was mentally discussing certain topics which had formed matter for conversation between us at an earlier period of the evening; I mean the affair of the Rue Morgue, and the mystery attending the murder of Marie Rogêt. I looked upon it, therefore, as something of a coincidence, when the door of our apartment was thrown open and admitted our old acquaintance, Monsieur G——, the Prefect of the Parisian police.

We gave him a hearty welcome; for there was nearly half as much of the entertaining as of the contemptible about the man, and we had not seen him for several years. We had been sitting in the dark, and Dupin now arose for the purpose of lighting a lamp, but sat down again, without doing so, upon G.'s saying that he had called to consult us, or rather to ask the opinion of my friend, about some official business which had occasioned a great deal of trouble.

"If it is any point requiring reflection," observed Dupin, as

* *The Gift,* 1845.—Text corrected by J. L. Graham copy.

he forbore to enkindle the wick, "we shall examine it to better purpose in the dark."

"That is another of your odd notions," said the Prefect, who had a fashion of calling every thing "odd" that was beyond his comprehension, and thus lived amid an absolute legion of "oddities."

"Very true," said Dupin, as he supplied his visiter with a pipe, and rolled towards him a comfortable chair.

"And what is the difficulty now?" I asked. "Nothing more in the assassination way, I hope?"

"Oh no; nothing of that nature. The fact is, the business is *very* simple indeed, and I make no doubt that we can manage it sufficiently well ourselves; but then I thought Dupin would like to hear the details of it, because it is so excessively *odd.*"

"Simple and odd," said Dupin.

"Why, yes; and not exactly that either. The fact is, we have all been a good deal puzzled because the affair *is* so simple, and yet baffles us altogether."

"Perhaps it is the very simplicity of the thing which puts you at fault," said my friend.

"What nonsense you *do* talk!" replied the Prefect, laughing heartily.

"Perhaps the mystery is a little *too* plain," said Dupin.

"Oh, good heavens! who ever heard of such an idea?"

"A little *too* self-evident."

"Ha! ha! ha!—ha! ha! ha!—ho! ho! ho!"—roared our visiter, profoundly amused, "oh, Dupin, you will be the death of me yet!"

"And what, after-all, *is* the matter on hand?" I asked.

"Why, I will tell you," replied the Prefect, as he gave a long, steady, and contemplative puff, and settled himself in his chair. "I will tell you in a few words; but, before I begin, let me caution you that this is an affair demanding the greatest secrecy, and that I should most probably lose the position I now hold, were it known that I confided it to any one."

"Proceed," said I.

"Or not," said Dupin.

"Well, then; I have received personal information, from a very high quarter, that a certain document of the last importance, has been purloined from the royal apartments. The individual who purloined it is known; this beyond a doubt; he was seen to take it. It is known, also, that it still remains in his possession."

"How is this known?" asked Dupin.

"It is clearly inferred," replied the Prefect, "from the nature of the document, and from the non-appearance of certain results which would at once arise from its passing *out* of the robber's possession;—that is to say, from his employing it as he must design in the end to employ it."

"Be a little more explicit," I said.

"Well, I may venture so far as to say that the paper gives its holder a certain power in a certain quarter where such power is immensely valuable." The Prefect was fond of the cant of diplomacy.

"Still I do not quite understand," said Dupin.

"No? Well; the disclosure of the document to a third person, who shall be nameless, would bring in question the honor of a personage of most exalted station; and this fact gives the holder of the document an ascendancy over the illustrious personage whose honor and peace are so jeopardized."

"But this ascendancy," I interposed, "would depend upon the robber's knowledge of the loser's knowledge of the robber. Who would dare—"

"The thief," said G., "is the Minister D——, who dares all things, those unbecoming as well as those becoming a man. The method of the theft was not less ingenious than bold. The document in question—a letter, to be frank—had been received by the personage robbed while alone in the royal *boudoir*. During its perusal she was suddenly interrupted by the entrance of the other exalted personage from whom especially it was her wish to conceal it. After a hurried and vain endeavor to thrust it in a drawer, she was forced to place it, open it was, upon a table. The address, however, was uppermost, and, the contents thus unexposed, the letter escaped notice. At this juncture enters the Minister D——. His lynx eye immediately perceives the paper, recognizes the handwriting of the address, observes the confusion of the personage addressed, and fathoms her secret. After some business transactions, hurried through in his ordinary manner, he produces a letter somewhat similar to the one in question, opens it, pretends to read it, and then places it in close juxtaposition to the other. Again he converses, for some fifteen minutes, upon the public affairs. At length, in taking leave, he takes also from the table the letter to which he had no claim. Its rightful owner saw, but, of course, dared not call attention to the act, in the presence of the third personage who stood at her elbow. The minister decamped; leaving his own letter—one of no importance—upon the table."

"Here, then," said Dupin to me, "you have precisely what you demand to make the ascendancy complete—the robber's knowledge of the loser's knowledge of the robber."

"Yes," replied the Prefect; "and the power thus attained has, for some months past, been wielded, for political purposes, to a very dangerous extent. The personage robbed is more thoroughly convinced, every day, of the necessity of reclaiming her letter. But this, of course, cannot be done openly. In fine, driven to despair, she has committed the matter to me."

"Than whom," said Dupin, amid a perfect whirlwind of smoke, "no more sagacious agent could, I suppose, be desired, or even imagined."

"You flatter me," replied the Prefect; "but it is possible that some such opinion may have been entertained."

"It is clear," said I, "as you observe, that the letter is still in the possession of the minister; since it is this possession, and not any employment of the letter, which bestows the power. With the employment the power departs."

"True," said G.; "and upon this conviction I proceeded. My first care was to make thorough search of the minister's hotel; and here my chief embarrassment lay in the necessity of searching without his knowledge. Beyond all things, I have been warned of the danger which would result from giving him reason to suspect our design."

"But," said I, "you are quite *au fait* in these investigations. The Parisian police have done this thing often before."

"O yes; and for this reason I did not despair. The habits of the minister gave me, too, a great advantage. He is frequently absent from home all night. His servants are by no means numerous. They sleep at a distance from their master's apartment, and, being chiefly Neapolitans, are readily made drunk. I have keys, as you know, with which I can open any chamber or cabinet in Paris. For three months a night has not passed, during the greater part of which I have not been engaged, personally, in ransacking the D—— Hôtel. My honor is interested, and, to mention a great secret, the reward is enormous. So I did not abandon the search until I had become fully satisfied that the thief is a more astute man than myself. I fancy that I have investigated every nook and corner of the premises in which it is possible that the paper can be concealed."

"But is it not possible," I suggested, "that although the letter may be in possession of the minister, as it unquestionably is, he may have concealed it elsewhere than upon his own premises?"

"This is barely possible," said Dupin. "The present peculiar condition of affairs at court, and especially of those intrigues in which D—— is known to be involved, would render the instant availability of the document—its susceptibility of being produced at a moment's notice—a point of nearly equal importance with its possession."

"Its susceptibility of being produced?" said I.

"That is to say, of being *destroyed*," said Dupin.

"True," I observed; "the paper is clearly then upon the premises. As for its being upon the person of the minister, we may consider that as out of the question."

"Entirely," said the Prefect. "He has been twice waylaid, as if by foot-pads, and his person rigorously searched under my own inspection."

"You might have spared yourself this trouble," said Dupin. "D——, I presume, is not altogether a fool, and, if not, must have anticipated these waylayings, as a matter of course."

"Not *altogether* a fool," said G., "but then he is a poet, which I take to be only one remove from a fool."

"True," said Dupin, after a long and thoughtful whiff from his meerschaum, "although I have been guilty of certain doggerel myself."

"Suppose you detail," said I, "the particulars of your search."

"Why the fact is, we took our time, and we searched *every where*. I have had long experience in these affairs. I took the entire building, room by room; devoting the nights of a whole week to each. We examined, first, the furniture of each apartment. We opened every possible drawer; and I presume you know that, to a properly trained police agent, such a thing as a *secret* drawer is impossible. Any man is a dolt who permits a 'secret' drawer to escape him in a search of this kind. The thing is *so* plain. There is a certain amount of bulk—of space—to be accounted for in every cabinet. Then we have accurate rules. The fiftieth part of a line could not escape us. After the cabinets we took the chairs. The cushions we probed with the fine long needles you have seen me employ. From the tables we removed the tops."

"Why so?"

"Sometimes the top of a table, or other similarly arranged piece of furniture, is removed by the person wishing to conceal an article; then the leg is excavated, the article deposited within the cavity, and the top replaced. The bottoms and tops of bed-posts are employed in the same way."

"But could not the cavity be detected by sounding?" I asked.

"By no means, if, when the article is deposited, a sufficient wadding of cotton be placed around it. Besides, in our case, we were obliged to proceed without noise."

"But you could not have removed—you could not have taken to pieces *all* articles of furniture in which it would have been possible to make a deposit in the manner you mention. A letter may be compressed into a thin spiral roll, not differing much in shape or bulk from a large knitting-needle, and in this form it might be inserted into the rung of a chair, for example. You did not take to pieces all the chairs?"

"Certainly not; but we did better—we examined the rungs of every chair in the hotel, and, indeed the jointings of every description of furniture, by the aid of a most powerful microscope. Had there been any traces of recent disturbance we should not have failed to detect it instantly. A single grain of gimlet-dust, for example, would have been as obvious as an apple. Any disorder in the glueing—any unusual gaping in the joints—would have sufficed to insure detection."

"I presume you looked to the mirrors, between the boards and the plates, and you probed the beds and the bed-clothes, as well as the curtains and carpets."

"That of course; and when we had absolutely completed every particle of the furniture in this way, then we examined the house itself. We divided its entire surface into compartments, which we numbered, so that none might be missed; then we scrutinized each individual square inch throughout the premises, including the two houses immediately adjoining, with the microscope as before."

"The two houses adjoining!" I exclaimed; "you must have had a great deal of trouble."

"We had; but the reward offered is prodigious."

"You include the *grounds* about the houses?"

"All the grounds are paved with brick. They gave us comparatively little trouble. We examined the moss between the bricks, and found it undisturbed."

"You looked among D——'s papers, of course, and into the books of the library?"

"Certainly; we opened every package and parcel; we not

only opened every book, but we turned over every leaf in each volume, not contenting ourselves with a mere shake, according to the fashion of some of our police officers. We also measured the thickness of every book-*cover*, with the most accurate admeasurement, and applied to each the most jealous scrutiny of the microscope. Had any of the bindings been recently meddled with, it would have been utterly impossible that the fact should have escaped observation. Some five or six volumes, just from the hands of the binder, we carefully probed, longitudinally, with the needles."

"You explored the floors beneath the carpets?"

"Beyond doubt. We removed every carpet, and examined the boards with the microscope."

"And the paper on the walls?"

"Yes."

"You looked into the cellars?"

"We did."

"Then," I said; "you have been making a miscalculation, and the letter is *not* upon the premises, as you suppose."

"I fear you are right there," said the Prefect. "And now, Dupin, what would you advise me to do?"

"To make a thorough re-search of the premises."

"That is absolutely needless," replied G——. "I am not more sure that I breathe than I am that the letter is not at the hotel."

"I have no better advice to give you," said Dupin. "You have, of course, an accurate description of the letter?"

"Oh, yes!"—And here the Prefect, producing a memorandum-book, proceeded to read aloud a minute account of the internal, and especially of the external, appearance of the missing document. Soon after finishing the perusal of this description, he took his departure, more entirely depressed in spirits than I had ever known the good gentleman before.

In about a month afterward he paid us another visit, and found us occupied very nearly as before. He took a pipe and a chair and entered into some ordinary conversation. At length I said;—

"Well, but G——, what of the purloined letter? I presume you have at last made up your mind that there is no such thing as overreaching the Minister?"

"Confound him, say I—yes; I made the re-examination, however, as Dupin suggested—but it was all labor lost, as I knew it would be."

"How much was the reward offered, did you say?" asked Dupin.

"Why, a very great deal—a *very* liberal reward—I don't like to say how much, precisely; but one thing I *will* say, that I wouldn't mind giving my individual check for fifty thousand francs to any one who could obtain me that letter. The fact is, it is becoming of more and more importance every day; and the reward has been lately doubled. If it were trebled, however, I could do no more than I have done."

"Why, yes," said Dupin, drawlingly, between the whiffs of his meerschaum, "I really—think, G——, you have not exerted yourself—to the utmost in this matter. You might—do a little more, I think, eh?"

"How?—in what way?"

"Why—puff, puff—you might—puff, puff—employ counsel in the matter, eh?—puff, puff, puff. Do you remember the story they tell of Abernethy?"

"No; hang Abernethy!"

"To be sure! hang him and welcome. But, once upon a time, a certain rich miser conceived the design of spunging upon this Abernethy for a medical opinion. Getting up, for this purpose, an ordinary conversation in a private company, he insinuated his case to the physician, as that of an imaginary individual.

" 'We will suppose,' said the miser, 'that his symptoms are such and such; now, doctor, what would *you* have directed him to take?'

" 'Take!' said Abernethy, 'why, take *advice,* to be sure.' "

"But," said the Prefect, a little discomposed, "*I* am *perfectly* willing to take advice, and to pay for it. I would *really* give fifty thousand francs to any one who would aid me in the matter."

"In that case," replied Dupin, opening a drawer, and producing a check-book, "you may as well fill me up a check for the amount mentioned. When you have signed it, I will hand you the letter."

I was astounded. The Prefect appeared absolutely thunderstricken. For some minutes he remained speechless and motionless, looking incredulously at my friend with open mouth, and eyes that seemed starting from their sockets; then, apparently recovering himself in some measure, he seized a pen, and after several pauses and vacant stares, finally filled up and signed a check for fifty thousand francs, and handed it across the table to Dupin. The latter examined it carefully and deposited it in his pocket-book; then, unlocking an *escritoire,* took thence a letter and gave it to the Prefect. This functionary grasped it in a perfect agony of joy, opened it with a trembling hand, cast a rapid glance at its contents, and then, scrambling and struggling to the door, rushed at length unceremoniously from the room and from the house, without having uttered a syllable since Dupin had requested him to fill up the check.

When he had gone, my friend entered into some explanations.

"The Parisian police," he said, "are exceedingly able in their way. They are persevering, ingenious, cunning, and thoroughly versed in the knowledge which their duties seem chiefly to demand. Thus, when G—— detailed to us his mode of searching the premises at the Hôtel D——, I felt entire confidence in his having made a satisfactory investigation—so far as his labors extended."

"So far as his labors extended?" said I.

"Yes," said Dupin. "The measures adopted were not only the best of their kind, but carried out to absolute perfection. Had the letter been deposited within the range of their search, these fellows would, beyond a question, have found it."

I merely laughed—but he seemed quite serious in all that he said.

"The measures, then," he continued, "were good in their kind, and well executed; their defect lay in their being inapplicable to the case, and to the man. A certain set of highly ingenious resources are, with the Prefect, a sort of Proscrustean bed, to which he forcibly adapts his designs. But he perpetually errs by being too deep or too shallow, for the matter in hand; and many a schoolboy is a better reasoner than he. I knew one about eight years of age, whose success at guessing in the game of 'even and odd' attracted universal admiration. This game is simple, and is played with marbles. One player holds in his hand a number of these toys, and demands of another whether that number is even or odd. If the guess is right, the guesser wins one; if wrong, he loses one. The boy to whom I allude won all the marbles of the school. Of course he had some principle of guessing; and this lay in mere observation and admeasurement of the astuteness of his opponents. For example, an arrant simpleton is his opponent, and, holding up his closed hand, asks, 'Are they even or odd?' Our schoolboy replies, 'Odd,' and loses; but upon the second trial he wins, for he then says to himself, 'The simpleton had them even upon the first trial, and his amount of cunning is just sufficient to make him have them odd upon the second; I will therefore guess odd;'—he guesses odd, and wins. Now, with a simpleton a degree above the first, he would have reasoned thus: 'This fellow finds that in the first instance I guessed odd, and, in the second, he will propose to himself upon the first impulse, a simple variation from even to odd, as did the first simpleton; but then a second thought will suggest that this is too simple a variation, and finally he will decide upon putting it even as before. I will therefore guess even;'—he guesses even, and wins. Now this mode of reasoning in the schoolboy, whom his fellows termed 'lucky,'—what, in its last analysis, is it?"

"It is merely," I said, "an identification of the reasoner's intellect with that of his opponent."

"It is," said Dupin; "and, upon inquiring of the boy by what means he effected the *thorough* identification in which his success consisted, I received answer as follows: 'When I wish to find out how wise, or how stupid, or how good, or how wicked is any one, or what are his thoughts at the moment, I fashion the expression of my face, as accurately as possible, in accordance with the expression of his, and then wait to see what thoughts or sentiments arise in my mind or heart, as if to match or correspond with the expression.' This response of the schoolboy lies at the bottom of all the spurious profundity which has been attributed to Rochefoucault, to La Bougive, to Machiavelli, and to Campanella."

"And the identification," I said, "of the reasoner's intellect with that of his opponent, depends, if I understand you aright, upon the accuracy with which the opponent's intellect is admeasured."

"For its practical value it depends upon this," replied Dupin; "and the Prefect and his cohort fail so frequently, first, by default of this identification, and, secondly, by ill-admeasurement, or rather through non-admeasurement, of the intellect with which they are engaged. They consider only their *own* ideas of ingenuity; and, in searching for anything hidden, advert only to the modes in which *they* would have hidden it. They are right in this much—that their own ingenuity is a faithful representative of that of *the mass;* but when the cunning of the individual felon is diverse in character from their own, the felon foils them, of course. This always happens when it is above their own, and very usually when it is below. They have no variation of principle in their investigations; at best, when urged by some unusual emergency—by some extraordinary reward—they extend or exaggerate their old modes of *practice,* without touching their principles. What, for example, in this case of D——, has been done to vary the principle of action? What is all this boring, and probing, and sounding, and scrutinizing with the microscope, and dividing the surface of the building into registered square inches—what is it all but an exaggeration *of the application* of the one principle or set of principles of search, which are based upon the one set of notions regarding human ingenuity, to which the Prefect, in the long routine of his duty, has been accustomed? Do you not see he has taken it for granted that *all* men proceed to conceal a letter,—not exactly in a gimlet-hole bored in a chair-leg—but, at least, in *some* out-of-the-way hole or corner suggested by the same tenor of thought which would urge a man to secrete a letter in a gimlet-hole bored in a chair-leg? And do you not see also, that such *recherchés* nooks for concealment are adapted only for ordinary occasions, and would be adopted only by ordinary intellects; for, in all cases of concealment, a disposal of the article concealed—a disposal of it in this *recherché* manner,—is, in the very first instance, presumable and presumed; and thus its discovery depends, not at all upon the acumen, but altogether upon the mere care, patience, and determination of the seekers; and where the case is of importance—or, what amounts to the same thing in the policial eyes, when the reward is of magnitude,—the qualities in question have *never* been known to fail. You will now understand what I meant in suggesting that, had the purloined letter been hidden anywhere within the limits of the Prefect's examination—in other words, had the principle of its concealment been comprehended within the principles of the Prefect—its discovery would have been a matter altogether beyond question. This functionary, however, has been thoroughly mystified; and the remote source of his defeat lies in the supposition that the Minister is a fool, because he has acquired renown as a poet. All fools are poets; this the Prefect *feels;* and he is merely guilty of a *non distributio medii* in thence inferring that all poets are fools."

"But is this really the poet?" I asked. "There are two brothers, I know; and both have attained reputation in letters. The Minister I believe has written learnedly on the Differential Calculus. He is a mathematician, and no poet."

"You are mistaken; I know him well; he is both. As poet

and mathematician, he would reason well; as mere mathematician, he could not have reasoned at all, and thus would have been at the mercy of the Prefect."

"You surprise me," I said, "by these opinions, which have been contradicted by the voice of the world. You do not mean to set at naught the well-digested idea of centuries. The mathematical reason has long been regarded as *the* reason *par excellence.*"

"'*Il y a à parier,*'" replied Dupin, quoting from Chamfort, "'*que toute idée publique, toute convention reçue, est une sottise, car elle a convenue au plus grand nombre.*' The mathematicians, I grant you, have done their best to promulgate the popular error to which you allude, and which is none the less an error for its promulgation as truth. With an art worthy a better cause, for example, they have insinuated the term 'analysis' into application to algebra. The French are the originators of this particular deception; but if a term is of any importance—if words derive any value from applicability—then 'analysis' conveys 'algebra' about as much as, in Latin, '*ambitus*' implies 'ambition,' '*religio*' 'religion,' or '*homines honesti,*' a set of *honorable* men."

"You have a quarrel on hand, I see," said I, "with some of the algebraists of Paris; but proceed."

"I dispute the availability, and thus the value, of that reason which is cultivated in any especial form other than the abstractly logical. I dispute, in particular, the reason educed by mathematical study. The mathematics are the science of form and quantity; mathematical reasoning is merely logic applied to observation upon form and quantity. The great error lies in supposing that even the truths of what is called *pure* algebra, are abstract or general truths. And this error is so egregious that I am confounded at the universality with which it has been received. Mathematical axioms are *not* axioms of general truth. What is true of *relation* —of form and quantity—is often grossly false in regard to morals, for example. In this latter science it is very usually *un*true that the aggregated parts are equal to the whole. In chemistry also the axiom fails. In the consideration of motive it fails; for two motives, each of a given value, have not, necessarily, a value when united, equal to the sum of their values apart. There are numerous other mathematical truths which are only truths within the limits of *relation*. But the mathematician argues from his *finite truths*, through habit, as if they were of an absolutely general applicability—as the world indeed imagines them to be. Bryant, in his very learned 'Mythology,' mentions an analogous source of error, when he says that 'although the Pagan fables are not believed, yet we forget ourselves continually, and make inferences from them as existing realities.' With the algebraists, however, who are Pagans themselves, the 'Pagan fables' *are* believed, and the inferences are made, not so much through lapse of memory as through an unaccountable addling of the brains. In short, I never yet encountered the mere mathematician who would be trusted out of equal roots, or one who did not clandestinely hold it as a point of his faith that $x^2 + px$ was absolutely and unconditionally equal to q. Say to one of these gentlemen, by way of experiment, if you please, that you believe occasions may occur where $x^2 + px$ is *not* altogether equal to q, and, having made him understand what you mean, get out of his reach as speedily as convenient, for, beyond doubt, he will endeavor to knock you down.

"I mean to say," continued Dupin, while I merely laughed at his last observations, "that if the Minister had been no more than a mathematician, the Prefect would have been under no necessity of giving me this check. I knew him, however, as both mathematician and poet, and my measures were adapted to his capacity, with reference to the circumstances by which he was surrounded. I knew him as a courtier, too, and as a bold *intriguant*. Such a man, I considered, could not fail to be aware of the ordinary policial modes of action. He could not have failed to anticipate—and events have proved that he did not fail to anticipate—the waylayings to which he was subjected. He must have foreseen, I reflected, the secret investigations of his premises. His frequent absences from home at night, which were hailed by the Prefect as certain aids to his success, I regarded only as *ruses,* to afford opportunity for thorough search to the police, and thus the sooner to impress them with the conviction to which G——, in fact, did finally arrive—the conviction that the letter was not upon the premises. I felt, also, that the whole train of thought, which I was at some pains in detailing to you just now, concerning the invariable principle of policial action in searches for articles concealed—I felt that this whole train of thought would necessarily pass through the mind of the Minister. It would imperatively lead him to despise all the ordinary *nooks* of concealment. *He* could not, I reflected, be so weak as not to see that the most intricate and remote recess of his hotel would be as open as his commonest closets to the eyes, to the probes, to the gimlets, and to the microscopes of the Prefect. I saw, in fine, that he would be driven, as a matter of course, to *simplicity,* if not deliberately induced to it as a matter of choice. You will remember, perhaps, how desperately the Prefect laughed when I suggested, upon our first interview, that it was just possible this mystery troubled him so much on account of its being so *very* self-evident."

"Yes," said I, "I remember his merriment well. I really thought he would have fallen into convulsions."

"The material world," continued Dupin, "abounds with very strict analogies to the immaterial; and thus some color of truth has been given to the rhetorical dogma, that metaphor, or simile, may be made to strengthen an argument as well as to embellish a description. The principle of the *vis inertiæ,* for example, seems to be identical in physics and metaphysics. It is not more true in the former, that a large body is with more difficulty set in motion than a smaller one, and that its subsequent *momentum* is commensurate with this difficulty, than it is, in the latter, that intellects of the vaster capacity, while more forcible, more constant, and more eventful in their movements than those of inferior grade, are yet the less readily moved, and more embarrassed and full of hesitation in the first few steps of their progress. Again: have you ever noticed which of the street signs, over the shop doors, are the most attractive of attention?"

"I have never given the matter a thought," I said.

"There is a game of puzzles," he resumed, "which is played upon a map. One party playing requires another to find a given word—the name of town, river, state or empire—any word, in short, upon the motley and perplexed surface of the chart. A novice in the game generally seeks to embarrass his opponents by giving them the most minutely lettered names; but the adept selects such words as stretch, in large characters, from one end of the chart to the other. These, like the over-largely lettered signs and placards of the street, escape observation by dint of being excessively obvious; and here the physical oversight is precisely analogous with the moral inapprehension by which the intellect suffers to pass unnoticed those considerations which are too obtrusively and too palpably self-evident. But this is a point, it appears, somewhat above or beneath the understanding of the Prefect. He never once thought it probable, or possible, that the minister had deposited the letter immediately beneath the nose of the whole world, by way of best preventing any portion of that world from perceiving it.

"But the more I reflected upon the daring, dashing, and discriminating ingenuity of D——; upon the fact that the document must always have been *at hand,* if he intended to use it to good purpose; and upon the decisive evidence, obtained by the Prefect, that it was not hidden within the limits of that dignitary's ordinary search—the more satisfied I became that, to conceal this letter, the Minister had resorted to the comprehensive and sagacious expedient of not attempting to conceal it at all.

"Full of these ideas, I prepared myself with a pair of green spectacles, and called one fine morning, quite by accident, at the Ministerial hotel. I found D—— at home, yawning, lounging, and dawdling, as usual, and pretending to be in the last extremity of *ennui.* He is, perhaps, the most really energetic human being now alive—but that is only when nobody sees him.

"To be even with him, I complained of my weak eyes, and lamented the necessity of the spectacles, under cover of which I cautiously and thoroughly surveyed the whole apartment, while seemingly intent only upon the conversation of my host.

"I paid especial attention to a large writing-table near which he sat, and upon which lay confusedly, some miscellaneous letters and other papers, with one or two musical instruments and a few books. Here, however, after a long and very deliberate scrutiny, I saw nothing to excite particular suspicion.

"At length my eyes, in going the circuit of the room, fell upon a trumpery filigree card-rack of pasteboard, that hung dangling by a dirty blue ribbon, from a little brass knob just beneath the middle of the mantel-piece. In this rack, which had three or four compartments, were five or six visiting cards and a solitary letter. This last was much soiled and crumpled. It was torn nearly in two, across the middle—as if a design, in the first instance, to tear it entirely up as worthless, had been altered, or stayed, in the second. It had a large black seal, bearing the D—— cipher *very* conspicuously, and was addressed, in a diminutive female hand, to D——, the minister, himself. It was thrust carelessly, and even, as it seemed, contemptuously, into one of the upper divisions of the rack.

"No sooner had I glanced at this letter than I concluded it to be that of which I was in search. To be sure, it was, to all appearance, radically different from the one of which the Prefect had read us so minute a description. Here the seal was large and black, with the D—— cipher; there it was small and red, with the ducal arms of the S—— family. Here, the address, to the Minister, was diminutive and feminine; there the superscription, to a certain royal personage, was markedly bold and decided; the size alone formed a point of correspondence. But, then, the *radicalness* of these differences, which was excessive; the dirt; the soiled and torn condition of the paper, so inconsistent with the *true* methodical habits of D——, and so suggestive of a design to delude the beholder into an idea of the worthlessness of the document;—these things, together with the hyperobtrusive situation of this document, full in the view of every visiter, and thus exactly in accordance with the conclusions to which I had previously arrived; these things, I say, were strongly corroborative of suspicion, in one who came with the intention to suspect.

"I protracted my visit as long as possible, and, while I maintained a most animated discussion with the Minister, upon a topic which I knew well had never failed to interest and excite him, I kept my attention really riveted upon the letter. In this examination, I committed to memory its external appearance and arrangement in the rack; and also fell, at length, upon a discovery which set at rest whatever trivial doubt I might have entertained. In scrutinizing the edges of the paper, I observed them to be more *chafed* than seemed necessary. They presented the *broken* appearance which is manifested when a stiff paper, having been once folded and pressed with a folder, is refolded in a reversed direction, in the same creases or edges which had formed the original fold. This discovery was sufficient. It was clear to me that the letter had been turned, as a glove, inside out, re-directed, and re-sealed. I bade the Minister good morning, and took my departure at once, leaving a gold snuff-box upon the table.

"The next morning I called for the snuff-box, when we resumed, quite eagerly, the conversation of the preceding day. While thus engaged, however, a loud report, as if of a pistol, was heard immediately beneath the windows of the hotel, and was succeeded by a series of fearful screams, and the shoutings of a mob. D—— rushed to a casement, threw it open, and looked out. In the meantime I stepped to the card-rack, took the letter, put it in my pocket, and replaced it by a *fac-simile,* (so far as regards externals) which I had carefully prepared at my lodgings; imitating the D—— cipher, very readily, by means of a seal formed of bread.

"The disturbance in the street had been occasioned by the frantic behavior of a man with a musket. He had fired it among a crowd of women and children. It proved, however, to have been without ball, and the fellow was suffered to go his way as a lunatic or a drunkard. When he had gone, D—— came from the window, whither I had followed him immediately upon securing the object in view. Soon afterward I bade him farewell. The pretended lunatic was a man in my own pay."

"But what purpose had you," I asked, "in replacing the letter by a *fac-simile?* Would it not have been better, at the first visit, to have seized it openly, and departed?"

"D——," replied Dupin, "is a desperate man, and a man of nerve. His hotel, too, is not without attendants devoted to his interests. Had I made the wild attempt you suggest, I might never have left the Ministerial presence alive. The good people of Paris might have heard of me no more. But I had an object apart from these considerations. You know my political prepossessions. In this matter, I act as a partisan of the lady concerned. For eighteen months the Minister has had her in his power. She has now him in hers; since, being unaware that the letter is not in his possession, he will proceed with his exactions as if it was. Thus will he inevitably commit himself, at once, to his political destruction. His downfall, too, will not be more precipitate than awkward. It is all very well to talk about the *facilis descensus Averni;* but in all kinds of climbing, as Catalani said of singing, it is far more easy to get up than to come down. In the present instance I have no sympathy—at least no pity—for him who descends. He is that *monstrum horrendum,* an unprincipled man of genius. I confess, however, that I should like very well to know the precise character of his thoughts, when, being defied by her whom the Prefect terms 'a certain personage,' he is reduced to opening the letter which I left for him in the card-rack."

"How? did you put any thing particular in it?"

"Why—it did not seem altogether right to leave the interior blank—that would have been insulting. D——, at Vienna once, did me an evil turn, which I told him, quite good-humoredly, that I should remember. So, as I knew he would feel some curiosity in regard to the identity of the person who had outwitted him,

I thought it a pity not to give him a clew. He is well acquainted with my MS., and I just copied into the middle of the blank sheet the words—

——Un dessein si funeste,
S'il n'est digne d'Atrée, est digne de Thyeste.

They are to be found in Crébillon's 'Atrée.' "

THE CASK OF AMONTILLADO*

THE thousand injuries of Fortunato I had borne as I best could, but when he ventured upon insult I vowed revenge. You, who so well know the nature of my soul, will not suppose, however, that I gave utterance to a threat. *At length* I would be avenged; this was a point definitely settled—but the very definitiveness with which it was resolved precluded the idea of risk. I must not only punish but punish with impunity. A wrong is unredressed when retribution overtakes its redresser. It is equally unredressed when the avenger fails to make himself felt as such to him who has done the wrong.

It must be understood that neither by word nor deed had I given Fortunato cause to doubt my good will. I continued, as was my wont, to smile in his face, and he did not perceive that my smile *now* was at the thought of his immolation.

He had a weak point—this Fortunato—although in other regards he was a man to be respected and even feared. He prided himself on his connoisseurship in wine. Few Italians have the true virtuoso spirit. For the most part their enthusiasm is adopted to suit the time and opportunity, to practise imposture upon the British and Austrian *millionnaires*. In painting and gemmary, Fortunato, like his countrymen, was a quack, but in the matter of old wines he was sincere. In this respect I did not differ from him materially;—I was skilful in the Italian vintages myself, and bought largely whenever I could.

It was about dusk, one evening during the supreme madness of the carnival season, that I encountered my friend. He accosted

* *Godey's Lady's Book,* November, 1846.

me with excessive warmth, for he had been drinking much. The man wore motley. He had on a tight-fitting parti-striped dress, and his head was surmounted by the conical cap and bells. I was so pleased to see him that I thought I should never have done wringing his hand.

I said to him—"My dear Fortunato, you are luckily met. How remarkably well you are looking to-day. But I have received a pipe of what passes for Amontillado, and I have my doubts."

"How?" said he. "Amontillado? A pipe? Impossible! And in the middle of the carnival!"

"I have my doubts," I replied; "and I was silly enough to pay the full Amontillado price without consulting you in the matter. You were not to be found, and I was fearful of losing a bargain."

"Amontillado!"

"I have my doubts."

"Amontillado!"

"And I must satisfy them."

"Amontillado!"

"As you are engaged, I am on my way to Luchresi. If any one has a critical turn, it is he. He will tell me——"

"Luchresi cannot tell Amontillado from Sherry."

"And yet some fools will have it that his taste is a match for your own."

"Come, let us go."

"Whither?"

"To your vaults."

"My friend, no; I will not impose upon your good nature. I perceive you have an engagement. Luchresi——"

"I have no engagement;—come."

"My friend, no. It is not the engagement, but the severe cold with which I perceive you are afflicted. The vaults are insufferably damp. They are encrusted with nitre."

"Let us go, nevertheless. The cold is merely nothing. Amontillado! You have been imposed upon. And as for Luchresi, he cannot distinguish Sherry from Amontillado."

Thus speaking, Fortunato possessed himself of my arm; and putting on a mask of black silk and drawing a *roquelaire* closely about my person, I suffered him to hurry me to my palazzo.

There were no attendants at home; they had absconded to make merry in honour of the time. I had told them that I should not return until the morning, and had given them explicit orders not to stir from the house. These orders were sufficient, I well knew, to insure their immediate disappearance, one and all, as soon as my back was turned.

I took from their sconces two flambeaux, and giving one to Fortunato, bowed him through several suites of rooms to the arch way that led into the vaults. I passed down a long and winding staircase, requesting him to be cautious as he followed. We came at length to the foot of the descent, and stood together on the damp ground of the catacombs of the Montresors.

The gait of my friend was unsteady, and the bells upon his cap jingled as he strode.

"The pipe?" said he.

"It is farther on," said I; "but observe the white web-work which gleams from these cavern walls."

He turned towards me, and looked into my eyes with two filmy orbs that distilled the rheum of intoxication.

"Nitre?" he asked, at length.

"Nitre," I replied. "How long have you had that cough?"

"Ugh! ugh! ugh!—ugh! ugh! ugh!—ugh! ugh! ugh!—ugh! ugh! ugh!—ugh! ugh! ugh!"

My poor friend found it impossible to reply for many minutes.

"It is nothing," he said, at last.

"Come," I said, with decision, "we will go back; your health is precious. You are rich, respected, admired, beloved; you are happy, as once I was. You are a man to be missed. For me it is no matter. We will go back; you will be ill, and I cannot be responsible. Besides, there is Luchresi——"

"Enough," he said; "the cough is a mere nothing; it will not kill me. I shall not die of a cough."

"True—true," I replied; "and, indeed, I had no intention of alarming you unnecessarily—but you should use all proper caution. A draught of this Medoc will defend us from the damps."

Here I knocked off the neck of a bottle which I drew from a long row of its fellows that lay upon the mould.

"Drink," I said, presenting him the wine.

He raised it to his lips with a leer. He paused and nodded to me familiarly, while his bells jingled.

"I drink," he said, "to the buried that repose around us."

"And I to your long life."

He again took my arm, and we proceeded.

"These vaults," he said, "are extensive."

"The Montresors," I replied, "were a great and numerous family."

"I forget your arms."

"A huge human foot d'or, in a field azure; the foot crushes a serpent rampant whose fangs are imbedded in the heel."

"And the motto?"

"Nemo me impune lacessit."

"Good!" he said.

The wine sparkled in his eyes and the bells jingled. My own fancy grew warm with the Medoc. We had passed through long walls of piled skeletons, with casks and puncheons intermingling, into the inmost recesses of the catacombs. I paused again, and this time I made bold to seize Fortunato by an arm above the elbow.

"The nitre!" I said; "see, it increases. It hangs like moss upon the vaults. We are below the river's bed. The drops of moisture trickle among the bones. Come, we will go back ere it is too late. Your cough——"

"It is nothing," he said; "let us go on. But first, another draught of the Medoc."

I broke and reached him a flagon of De Grâve. He emptied it at a breath. His eyes flashed with a fierce light. He laughed and threw the bottle upward with a gesticulation I did not understand.

I looked at him in surprise. He repeated the movement—a grotesque one.

"You do not comprehend?" he said.

"Not I," I replied.

"Then you are not of the brotherhood."

"How?"

"You are not of the masons."

"Yes, yes," I said; "yes, yes."

"You? Impossible! A mason?"

"A mason," I replied.

"A sign," he said, "a sign."

"It is this," I answered, producing from beneath the folds of my *roquelaire* a trowel.

"You jest," he exclaimed, recoiling a few paces. "But let us proceed to the Amontillado."

"Be it so," I said, replacing the tool beneath the cloak and again offering him my arm. He leaned upon it heavily. We continued our route in search of the Amontillado. We passed through a range of low arches, descended, passed on, and descending again, arrived at a deep crypt, in which the foulness of the air caused our flambeaux rather to glow than flame.

At the most remote end of the crypt there appeared another less spacious. Its walls had been lined with human remains, piled to the vault overhead, in the fashion of the great catacombs of Paris. Three sides of this interior crypt were still ornamented in this manner. From the fourth the bones had been thrown down, and lay promiscuously upon the earth, forming at one point a mound of some size. Within the wall thus exposed by the displacing of the bones, we perceived a still interior crypt or recess, in depth about four feet, in width three, in height six or seven. It seemed to have been constructed for no especial use within itself, but formed merely the interval between two of the colossal supports of the roof of the catacombs, and was backed by one of their circumscribing walls of solid granite.

It was in vain that Fortunato, uplifting his dull torch, endeavoured to pry into the depth of the recess. Its termination the feeble light did not enable us to see.

"Proceed," I said; "herein is the Amontillado. As for Luchresi——"

"He is an ignoramus," interrupted my friend, as he stepped unsteadily forward, while I followed immediately at his heels. In an instant he had reached the extremity of the niche, and finding his progress arrested by the rock, stood stupidly bewildered. A moment more and I had fettered him to the granite. In its surface were two iron staples, distant from each other about two feet, horizontally. From one of these depended a short chain, from the other a padlock. Throwing the links about his waist, it was but the work of a few seconds to secure it. He was too much astounded to resist. Withdrawing the key I stepped back from the recess.

"Pass your hand," I said, "over the wall; you cannot help feeling the nitre. Indeed it is *very* damp. Once more let me *implore* you to return. No? Then I must positively leave you. But I must first render you all the little attentions in my power."

"The Amontillado!" ejaculated my friend, not yet recovered from his astonishment.

"True," I replied; the "Amontillado."

As I said these words I busied myself among the pile of bones of which I have before spoken. Throwing them aside, I soon uncovered a quantity of building stone and mortar. With these materials and with the aid of my trowel, I began vigorously to wall up the entrance of the niche.

I had scarcely laid the first tier of the masonry when I discovered that the intoxication of Fortunato had in a great measure worn off. The earliest indication I had of this was a low moaning cry from the depth of the recess. It was *not* the cry of a drunken man. There was then a long and obstinate silence. I laid the second tier, and the third, and the fourth; and then I heard the furious vibrations of the chain. The noise lasted for several minutes, during which, that I might hearken to it with the more satisfaction, I ceased my labours and sat down upon the bones. When at last the clanking subsided, I resumed the trowel, and finished without interruption the fifth, the sixth, and the seventh tier. The wall was now nearly upon a level with my breast. I again paused, and holding the flambeaux over the mason-work, threw a few feeble rays upon the figure within.

A succession of loud and shrill screams, bursting suddenly from the throat of the chained form, seemed to thrust me violently back. For a brief moment I hesitated, I trembled. Unsheathing my rapier, I began to grope with it about the recess; but the thought of an instant reassured me. I placed my hand upon the solid fabric of the catacombs, and felt satisfied. I reapproached the wall. I replied to the yells of him who clamoured. I re-echoed, I aided, I surpassed them in volume and in strength. I did this, and the clamourer grew still.

It was now midnight, and my task was drawing to a close. I had completed the eighth, the ninth and the tenth tier. I had finished a portion of the last and the eleventh; there remained but a single stone to be fitted and plastered in. I struggled with its weight; I placed it partially in its destined position. But now there came from out the niche a low laugh that erected the hairs upon my head. It was succeeded by a sad voice, which I had difficulty in recognizing as that of the noble Fortunato. The voice said—

"Ha! ha! ha!—he! he! he!—a very good joke, indeed—an excellent jest. We will have many a rich laugh about it at the palazzo—he! he! he!—over our wine—he! he! he!"

"The Amontillado!" I said.

"He! he! he!—he! he! he!—yes, the Amontillado. But is it not getting late? Will not they be awaiting us at the palazzo, the Lady Fortunato and the rest? Let us be gone."

"Yes," I said, "let us be gone."

"For the love of God, Montresor!"

"Yes," I said, "for the love of God!"

But to these words I hearkened in vain for a reply. I grew impatient. I called aloud—

"Fortunato!"

No answer. I called again—

"Fortunato!"

No answer still. I thrust a torch through the remaining aperture and let it fall within. There came forth in return only a jingling of the bells. My heart grew sick; on account of the dampness of the catacombs. I hastened to make an end of my labour. I forced the last stone into its position; I plastered it up. Against the new masonry I re-erected the old rampart of bones. For the half of a century no mortal has disturbed them. *In pace requiescat!*

THE MASQUE OF THE RED DEATH*

THE "Red Death" had long devastated the country. No pestilence had ever been so fatal, or so hideous. Blood was its Avatar and its seal—the redness and the horror of blood. There were sharp pains, and sudden dizziness, and then profuse bleeding at the pores, with dissolution. The scarlet stains upon the body and especially upon the face of the victim, were the pest ban which shut him out from the aid and from the sympathy of his fellowmen. And the whole seizure, progress and termination of the disease, were the incidents of half an hour.

But the Prince Prospero was happy and dauntless and sagacious. When his dominions were half depopulated, he summoned to his presence a thousand hale and light-hearted friends from among the knights and dames of his court, and with these retired to the deep seclusion of one of his castellated abbeys. This was an extensive and magnificent structure, the creation of the prince's own eccentric yet august taste. A strong and lofty wall girdled it in. This wall had gates of iron. The courtiers, having entered, brought furnaces and massy hammers and welded the bolts. They resolved to leave means neither of ingress or egress to the sudden impulses of despair or frenzy from within. The abbey was amply provisioned. With such precautions the courtiers might bid defiance to contagion. The external world could take care of itself. In the meantime it was folly to grieve, or to think. The prince had provided all the appliances of pleasure. There were buffoons, there were improvisatori, there were ballet-dancers, there were musicians, there was Beauty, there was wine. All these and security were within. Without was the "Red Death."

* *Graham's Magazine,* May, 1842; *Broadway Journal,* II. 2.

It was toward the close of the fifth or sixth month of his seclusion, and while the pestilence raged most furiously abroad, that the Prince Prospero entertained his thousand friends at a masked ball of the most unusual magnificence.

It was a voluptuous scene, that masquerade. But first let me tell of the rooms in which it was held. There were seven—an imperial suite. In many palaces, however, such suites form a long and straight vista, while the folding doors slide back nearly to the walls on either hand, so that the view of the whole extent is scarcely impeded. Here the case was very different; as might have been expected from the duke's love of the *bizarre*. The apartments were so irregularly disposed that the vision embraced but little more than one at a time. There was a sharp turn at every twenty or thirty yards, and at each turn a novel effect. To the right and left, in the middle of each wall, a tall and narrow Gothic window looked out upon a closed corridor which pursued the windings of the suite. These windows were of stained glass whose color varied in accordance with the prevailing hue of the decorations of the chamber into which it opened. That at the eastern extremity was hung, for example, in blue—and vividly blue were its windows. The second chamber was purple in its ornaments and tapestries, and here the panes were purple. The third was green throughout, and so were the casements. The fourth was furnished and lighted with orange—the fifth with white—the sixth with violet. The seventh apartment was closely shrouded in black velvet tapestries that hung all over the ceiling and down the walls, falling in heavy folds upon a carpet of the same material and hue. But in this chamber only, the color of the windows failed to correspond with the decorations. The panes here were scarlet—a deep blood color. Now in no one of the seven apartments was there any lamp or candelabrum, amid the profusion of golden ornaments that lay scattered to and fro or depended from the roof. There was no light of any kind emanating from lamp or candle within the suite of chambers. But in the corridors that followed the suite, there stood, opposite to each window a heavy tripod, bearing a brazier of fire, that projected its rays through the tinted glass and so glaringly illumined the room. And thus were produced a multitude of gaudy and fantastic appearances. But in the western or black chamber the effect of the fire-light that streamed upon the dark hangings through the blood-tinted panes, was ghastly in the extreme, and produced so wild a look upon the countenances of those who entered, that there were few of the company bold enough to set foot within its precincts at all.

It was in this apartment, also, that there stood against the western wall, a gigantic clock of ebony. Its pendulum swung to and fro with a dull, heavy, monotonous clang; and when the minute-hand made the circuit of the face, and the hour was to be stricken, there came from the brazen lungs of the clock a sound which was clear and loud and deep and exceedingly musical, but of so peculiar a note and emphasis that, at each lapse of an hour, the musicians of the orchestra were constrained to pause, momentarily, in their performance, to hearken to the sound; and thus the waltzers perforce ceased their evolutions; and there was a brief disconcert of the whole gay company; and, while the chimes of the clock yet rang, it was observed that the giddiest grew pale, and the more aged and sedate passed their hands over their brows as if in confused revery or meditation. But when the echoes had fully ceased, a light laughter at once pervaded the assembly; the musicians looked at each other and smiled as if at their own nervousness and folly, and made whispering vows, each to the other, that the next chiming of the clock should produce in them no similar emotion; and then, after the lapse of sixty minutes. (which embrace three thousand and six hundred seconds of the Time that flies,) there came yet another chiming of the clock, and then were the same disconcert and tremulousness and meditation as before.

But, in spite of these things, it was a gay and magnificent revel. The tastes of the duke were peculiar. He had a fine eye for colors and effects. He disregarded the *decora* of mere fashion. His plans were bold and fiery, and his conceptions glowed with bar-

baric lustre. There are some who would have thought him mad. His followers felt that he was not. It was necessary to hear and see and touch him to be *sure* that he was not.

He had directed, in great part, the moveable embellishments of the seven chambers, upon occasion of this great *fête;* and it was his own guiding taste which had given character to the masqueraders. Be sure they were grotesque. There were much glare and glitter and piquancy and phantasm—much of what has been since seen in "Hernani." There were arabesque figures with unsuited limbs and appointments. There were delirious fancies such as the madman fashions. There were much of the beautiful, much of the wanton, much of the *bizarre,* something of the terrible, and not a little of that which might have excited disgust. To and fro in the seven chambers there stalked, in fact, a multitude of dreams. And these—the dreams—writhed in and about, taking hue from the rooms, and causing the wild music of the orchestra to seem as the echo of their steps. And, anon, there strikes the ebony clock which stands in the hall of the velvet. And then, for a moment, all is still, and all is silent save the voice of the clock. The dreams are stiff-frozen as they stand. But the echoes of the chime die away—they have endured but an instant—and a light, half-subdued laughter floats after them as they depart. And now again the music swells, and the dreams live, and writhe to and fro more merrily than ever, taking hue from the many-tinted windows through which stream the rays from the tripods. But to the chamber which lies most westwardly of the seven, there are now none of the maskers who venture; for the night is waning away; and there flows a ruddier light through the blood-colored panes; and the blackness of the sable drapery appals; and to him whose foot falls upon the sable carpet, there comes from the near clock of ebony a muffled peal more solemnly emphatic than any which reaches *their* ears who indulge in the more remote gaieties of the other apartments.

But these other apartments were densely crowded, and in them beat feverishly the heart of life. And the revel went whirlingly on, until at length there commenced the sounding of midnight upon the clock. And then the music ceased, as I have told; and the evolutions of the waltzers were quieted; and there was an uneasy cessation of all things as before. But now there were twelve strokes to be sounded by the bell of the clock; and thus it happened, perhaps, that more of thought crept, with more of time, into the meditations of the thoughtful among those who revelled. And thus, too, it happened, perhaps, that before the last echoes of the last chime had utterly sunk into silence, there were many individuals in the crowd who had found leisure to become aware of the presence of a masked figure which had arrested the attention of no single individual before. And the rumor of this new presence having spread itself whisperingly around, there arose at length from the whole company a buzz, or murmur, expressive of disapprobation and surprise—then, finally, of terror, of horror, and of disgust.

In an assembly of phantasms such as I have painted, it may well be supposed that no ordinary appearance could have excited such sensation. In truth the masquerade license of the night was nearly unlimited; but the figure in question had out-Heroded Herod, and gone beyond the bounds of even the prince's indefinite decorum. There are chords in the hearts of the most reckless which cannot be touched without emotion. Even with the utterly lost, to whom life and death are equally jests, there are matters of which no jest can be made. The whole company, indeed, seemed now deeply to feel that in the costume and bearing of the stranger neither wit nor propriety existed. The figure was tall and gaunt, and shrouded from head to foot in the habiliments of the grave. The mask which concealed the visage was made so nearly to resemble the countenance of a stiffened corpse that the closest scrutiny must have had difficulty in detecting the cheat. And yet all this might have been endured, if not approved, by the mad revellers around. But the mummer had gone so far as to assume the type of the Red Death. His vesture was dabbled in *blood*—

and his broad brow, with all the features of the face, was besprinkled with the scarlet horror.

When the eyes of Prince Prospero fell upon this spectral image (which with a slow and solemn movement, as if more fully to sustain its *rôle,* stalked to and fro among the waltzers) he was seen to be convulsed, in the first moment with a strong shudder either of terror or distaste; but, in the next, his brow reddened with rage.

"Who dares?" he demanded hoarsely of the courtiers who stood near him—"who dares insult us with this blasphemous mockery? Seize him and unmask him—that we may know whom we have to hang at sunrise, from the battlements!"

It was in the eastern or blue chamber in which stood the Prince Prospero as he uttered these words. They rang throughout the seven rooms loudly and clearly—for the prince was a bold and robust man, and the music had become hushed at the waving of his hand.

It was in the blue room where stood the prince, with a group of pale courtiers by his side. At first, as he spoke, there was a slight rushing movement of this group in the direction of the intruder, who at the moment was also near at hand, and now, with deliberate and stately step, made closer approach to the speaker. But from a certain nameless awe with which the mad assumptions of the mummer had inspired the whole party, there were found none who put forth hand to seize him; so that, unimpeded, he passed within a yard of the prince's person; and, while the vast assembly, as if with one impulse, shrank from the centres of the rooms to the walls, he made his way uninterruptedly, but with the same solemn and measured step which had distinguished him from the first, through the blue chamber to the purple—through the purple to the green—through the green to the orange—through this again to the white—and even thence to the violet, ere a decided movement had been made to arrest him. It was then, however, that the Prince Prospero, maddening with rage and the shame of his own momentary cowardice, rushed hurriedly through the six chambers, while none followed him on account of a deadly terror that had seized upon all. He bore aloft a drawn dagger, and had approached, in rapid impetuosity, to within three or four feet of the retreating figure, when the latter, having attained the extremity of the velvet apartment, turned suddenly and confronted his pursuer. There was a sharp cry—and the dagger dropped gleaming upon the sable carpet, upon which, instantly afterwards, fell prostrate in death the Prince Prospero. Then, summoning the wild courage of despair, a throng of the revellers at once threw themselves into the black apartment, and, seizing the mummer, whose tall figure stood erect and motionless within the shadow of the ebony clock, gasped in unutterable horror at finding the grave-cerements and corpse-like mask which they handled with so violent a rudeness, untenanted by any tangible form.

And now was acknowledged the presence of the Red Death. He had come like a thief in the night. And one by one dropped the revellers in the blood-bedewed halls of their revel, and died each in the despairing posture of his fall. And the life of the ebony clock went out with that of the last of the gay. And the flames of the tripods expired. And Darkness and Decay and the Red Death held illimitable dominion over all.

A DESCENT INTO THE MAELSTRÖM*

The ways of God in Nature, as in Providence, are not as *our* ways; nor are the models that we frame any way commensurate to the vastness, profundity, and unsearchableness of His works, *which have a depth in them greater than the well of Democritus.*

Joseph Glanville

We had now reached the summit of the loftiest crag. For some minutes the old man seemed too much exhausted to speak.

"Not long ago," said he at length, "and I could have guided you on this route as well as the youngest of my sons; but, about three years past, there happened to me an event such as never happened before to mortal man—or at least such as no man ever survived to tell of—and the six hours of deadly terror which I then endured have broken me up body and soul. You suppose me a *very* old man—but I am not. It took less than a single day to change these hairs from a jetty black to white, to weaken my limbs, and to unstring my nerves, so that I tremble at the least exertion, and am frightened at a shadow. Do you know I can scarcely look over this little cliff without getting giddy?"

The "little cliff," upon whose edge he had so carelessly thrown himself down to rest that the weightier portion of his body hung over it, while he was only kept from falling by the tenure of his elbow on its extreme and slippery edge—this "little cliff" arose, a sheer unobstructed precipice of black shining rock, some

* *Graham's Magazine,* May 1841; 1845.—Text corrected by J. L. Graham copy.

fifteen or sixteen hundred feet from the world of crags beneath us. Nothing would have tempted me to be within half a dozen yards of its brink. In truth so deeply was I excited by the perilous position of my companion, that I fell at full length upon the ground, clung to the shrubs around me, and dared not even glance upward at the sky—while I struggled in vain to divest myself of the idea that the very foundations of the mountain were in danger from the fury of the winds. It was long before I could reason myself into sufficient courage to sit up and look out into the distance.

"You must get over these fancies," said the guide, "for I have brought you here that you might have the best possible view of the scene of that event I mentioned—and to tell you the whole story with the spot just under your eye."

"We are now," he continued, in that particularizing manner which distinguished him—"we are now close upon the Norwegian coast—in the sixty-eighth degree of latitude—in the great province of Nordland—and in the dreary district of Lofoden. The mountain upon whose top we sit is Helseggen, the Cloudy. Now raise yourself up a little higher—hold on to the grass if you feel giddy—so—and look out, beyond the belt of vapor beneath us, into the sea."

I looked dizzily, and beheld a wide expanse of ocean, whose waters wore so inky a hue as to bring at once to my mind the Nubian geographer's account of the *Mare Tenebrarum.* A panorama more deplorably desolate no human imagination can conceive. To the right and left, as far as the eye could reach, there lay outstretched, like ramparts of the world, lines of horridly black and beetling cliff, whose character of gloom was but the more forcibly illustrated by the surf which reared high up against it its white and ghastly crest, howling and shrieking for ever. Just opposite the promontory upon whose apex we were placed, and at a distance of some five or six miles out at sea, there was visible a small, bleak-looking island; or, more properly, its position was discernible through the wilderness of surge in which it was enveloped. About two miles nearer the land, arose another of smaller size, hideously craggy and barren, and encompassed at various intervals by a cluster of dark rocks.

The appearance of the ocean, in the space between the more distant island and the shore, had something very unusual about it. Although, at the time, so strong a gale was blowing landward that a brig in the remote offing lay to under a double-reefed try-sail, and constantly plunged her whole hull out of sight, still there was here nothing like a regular swell, but only a short, quick, angry cross dashing of water in every direction—as well in the teeth of the wind as otherwise. Of foam there was little except in the immediate vicinity of the rocks.

"The island in the distance," resumed the old man, "is called by the Norwegians Vurrgh. The one midway is Moskoe. That a mile to the northward is Ambaaren. Yonder are Iflesen, Hoeyholm, Keildholm, Suarven, and Buckholm. Further off—between Moskoe and Vurrgh—are Otterholm, Flimen, Sandflesen, and Skarholm. These are the true names of the places—but why it has been thought necessary to name them at all, is more than either you or I can understand. Do you hear any thing? Do you see any change in the water?"

We had now been about ten minutes upon the top of Helseggen, to which we had ascended from the interior of Lofoden, so that we had caught no glimpse of the sea until it had burst upon us from the summit. As the old man spoke, I became aware of a loud and gradually increasing sound, like the moaning of a vast herd of buffaloes upon an American prairie; and at the same moment I perceived that what seamen term the *chopping* character of the ocean beneath us, was rapidly changing into a current which set to the eastward. Even while I gazed, this current acquired a monstrous velocity. Each moment added to its speed—to its headlong impetuosity. In five minutes the whole sea, as far as Vurrgh, was lashed into ungovernable fury; but it was between Moskoe and the coast that the main uproar held its sway. Here the vast bed of the waters, seamed and scarred into a thousand conflicting channels, burst suddenly into phrensied convulsion—heaving, boiling, hissing—gyrating in gigantic and innumerable vortices, and all whirling and plunging on to the eastward with a rapidity which water never elsewhere assumes, except in precipitous descents.

In a few minutes more, there came over the scene another radical alteration. The general surface grew somewhat more smooth, and the whirlpools, one by one, disappeared, while prodigious streaks of foam became apparent where none had been seen before. These streaks, at length, spreading out to a great distance, and entering into combination, took unto themselves the gyratory motion of the subsided vortices, and seemed to form the germ of another more vast. Suddenly—very suddenly—this assumed a distinct and definite existence, in a circle of more than half a mile in diameter. The edge of the whirl was represented by a broad belt of gleaming spray; but no particle of this slipped into the mouth of the terrific funnel, whose interior, as far as the eye could fathom it, was a smooth, shining, and jet-black wall of water, inclined to the horizon at an angle of some forty-five degrees, speeding dizzily round and round with a swaying and sweltering motion, and sending forth to the winds an appalling voice, half shriek, half roar, such as not even the mighty cataract of Niagara ever lifts up in its agony to Heaven.

The mountain trembled to its very base, and the rock rocked. I threw myself upon my face, and clung to the scant herbage in an excess of nervous agitation.

"This," said I at length, to the old man—"this *can* be nothing else than the great whirlpool of the Maelström."

"So it is sometimes termed," said he. "We Norwegians call it the Moskoe-ström, from the island of Moskoe in the midway."

The ordinary account of this vortex had by no means prepared me for what I saw. That of Jonas Ramus, which is perhaps the most circumstantial of any, cannot impart the faintest conception either of the magnificence, or of the horror of the scene—or of the wild bewildering sense of *the novel* which confounds the beholder. I am not sure from what point of view the writer in question surveyed it, nor at what time; but it could neither have been from the summit of Helseggen, nor during a storm. There are some passages of his description, nevertheless, which may be quoted for their details, although their effect is exceedingly feeble in conveying an impression of the spectacle.

"Between Lofoden and Moskoe," he says, "the depth of the water is between thirty-six and forty fathoms; but on the other side, toward Ver (Vurrgh) this depth decreases so as not to afford a convenient passage for a vessel, without the risk of splitting on the rocks, which happens even in the calmest weather. When it is flood, the stream runs up the country between Lofoden and Moskoe with a boisterous rapidity; but the roar of its impetuous ebb to the sea is scarce equalled by the loudest and most dreadful cataracts; the noise being heard several leagues off, and the vortices or pits are of such an extent and depth, that if a ship comes within its attraction, it is inevitably absorbed and carried down to the bottom, and there beat to pieces against the rocks; and when the water relaxes, the fragments thereof are thrown up again. But these intervals of tranquillity are only at the turn of the ebb and flood, and in calm weather, and last but a quarter of an hour, its violence gradually returning. When the stream is most boisterous, and its fury heightened by a storm, it is dangerous to come within a Norway mile of it. Boats, yachts, and ships have been carried away by not guarding against it before they were within its reach. It likewise happens frequently, that whales come too near the stream, and are overpowered by its violence; and then it is impossible to describe their howlings and bellowings in their fruitless struggles to disengage themselves. A bear once, attempting to swim from Lofoden to Moskoe, was caught by the stream and borne down, while he roared terribly, so as to be heard on shore. Large stocks of firs and pine trees, after being absorbed by the current, rise again broken and torn to such a degree as if bristles grew upon them. This plainly shows the bottom to consist of craggy rocks, among which they are whirled to and fro. This stream is regulated by the flux and reflux of the sea—it being constantly high and low water every six hours. In the year 1645, early in the morning of Sexagesima Sunday, it raged with such noise and impetuosity that the very stones of the houses on the coast fell to the ground."

In regard to the depth of the water, I could not see how this could have been ascertained at all in the immediate vicinity of the vortex. The "forty fathoms" must have reference only to portions of the channel close upon the shore either of Moskoe or Lofoden. The depth in the centre of the Moskoe-ström must be unmeasurably greater; and no better proof of this fact is necessary than can be obtained from even the sidelong glance into the abyss of the whirl which may be had from the highest crag of Helseggen. Looking down from this pinnacle upon the howling Phlegethon below, I could not help smiling at the simplicity with which the honest Jonas Ramus records, as a matter difficult of belief, the anecdotes of the whales and the bears, for it appeared to me, in fact, a self-evident thing, that the largest ships of the line in existence, coming within the influence of that deadly attraction, could resist it as little as a feather the hurricane, and must disappear bodily and at once.

The attempts to account for the phenomenon—some of which, I remember, seemed to me sufficiently plausible in perusal—now wore a very different and unsatisfactory aspect. The idea generally received is that this, as well as three smaller vortices among the Feroe islands, "have no other cause than the collision of waves rising and falling, at flux and reflux, against a ridge of rocks and shelves, which confines the water so that it precipitates itself like a cataract; and thus the higher the flood rises, the deeper must the fall be, and the natural result of all is a whirlpool or vortex, the prodigious suction of which is sufficiently known by lesser experiments."—These are the words of the Encyclopædia Britannica. Kircher and others imagine that in the centre of the channel of the maelström is an abyss penetrating the globe, and issuing in some very remote part—the Gulf of Bothnia being somewhat decidedly named in one instance. This opinion, idle in itself, was the one to which, as I gazed, my imagination most readily assented; and, mentioning it to the guide, I was rather surprised to hear him say that, although it was the view almost universally entertained of the subject by the Norwegians, it nevertheless was not his own. As to the former notion he confessed his inability to comprehend it; and here I agreed with him—for, however conclusive on paper, it becomes altogether unintelligible, and even absurd, amid the thunder of the abyss.

"You have had a good look at the whirl now," said the old man, "and if you will creep round this crag, so as to get in its lee, and deaden the roar of the water, I will tell you a story that will convince you I ought to know something of the Moskoe-ström."

I placed myself as desired, and he proceeded.

"Myself and my two brothers once owned a schooner-rigged smack of about seventy tons burthen, with which we were in the habit of fishing among the islands beyond Moskoe, nearly to Vurrgh. In all violent eddies at sea there is good fishing, at proper opportunities, if one has only the courage to attempt it; but among the whole of the Lofoden coastmen, we three were the only ones who made a regular business of going out to the islands, as I tell you. The usual grounds are a great way lower down to the southward. There fish can be got at all hours, without much risk, and therefore these places are preferred. The choice spots over here among the rocks, however, not only yield the finest variety, but in far greater abundance; so that we often got in a single day, what the more timid of the craft could not scrape together in a week. In fact, we made it a matter of desperate speculation—the risk of life standing instead of labor, and courage answering for capital.

"We kept the smack in a cove about five miles higher up the coast than this; and it was our practice, in fine weather, to take advantage of the fifteen minutes' slack to push across the main channel of the Moskoe-ström, far above the pool, and then drop down upon anchorage somewhere near Otterholm, or Sandflesen, where the eddies are not so violent as elsewhere. Here we used to remain until nearly time for slack-water again, when we weighed and made for home. We never set out upon this expedition without a steady side wind for going and coming—one that we felt sure would not fail us before our return—and we seldom made a miscalculation upon this point. Twice, during six years, we were forced to stay all night at anchor on account of a dead calm, which is a rare thing indeed just about here; and once we had to remain on the grounds nearly a week, starving to death, owing to a gale which blew up shortly after our arrival, and made the channel too boisterous to be thought of. Upon this occasion we should have been driven out to sea in spite of everything, (for the whirlpools threw us round and round so violently, that, at length, we fouled our anchor and dragged it) if it had not been that we drifted into one of the innumerable cross currents—here to-day and gone to-morrow—which drove us under the lee of Flimen, where, by good luck, we brought up.

"I could not tell you the twentieth part of the difficulties we encountered 'on the ground'—it is a bad spot to be in, even in good weather—but we make shift always to run the gauntlet of the Moskoe-ström itself without accident; although at times my heart has been in my mouth when we happened to be a minute or so behind or before the slack. The wind sometimes was not as strong as we thought it at starting, and then we made rather less way than we could wish, while the current rendered the smack unmanageable. My eldest brother had a son eighteen years old, and I had two stout boys of my own. These would have been of great assistance at such times, in using the sweeps, as well as afterward in fishing—but, somehow, although we ran the risk ourselves, we had not the heart to let the young ones get into the danger—for, after all said and done, it *was* a horrible danger, and that is the truth.

"It is now within a few days of three years since what I am going to tell you occurred. It was on the tenth of July, 18—, a day which the people of this part of the world will never forget—

for it was one in which blew the most terrible hurricane that ever came out of the heavens. And yet all the morning, and indeed until late in the afternoon, there was a gentle and steady breeze from the south-west, while the sun shone brightly, so that the oldest seaman among us could not have foreseen what was to follow.

"The three of us—my two brothers and myself—had crossed over to the islands about two o'clock P.M., and soon nearly loaded the smack with fine fish, which, we all remarked, were more plenty that day than we had ever known them. It was just seven, *by my watch,* when we weighed and started for home, so as to make the worst of the Ström at slack water, which we knew would be at eight.

"We set out with a fresh wind on our starboard quarter, and for some time spanked along at a great rate, never dreaming of danger, for indeed we saw not the slightest reason to apprehend it. All at once we were taken aback by a breeze from over Helseggen. This was most unusual—something that had never happened to us before—and I began to feel a little uneasy, without exactly knowing why. We put the boat on the wind, but could make no headway at all for the eddies, and I was upon the point of proposing to return to the anchorage, when, looking astern, we saw the whole horizon covered with a singular copper-colored cloud that rose with the most amazing velocity.

"In the meantime the breeze that had headed us off fell away and we were dead becalmed, drifting about in every direction. This state of things, however, did not last long enough to give us time to think about it. In less than a minute the storm was upon us—in less than two the sky was entirely overcast—and what with this and the driving spray, it became suddenly so dark that we could not see each other in the smack.

"Such a hurricane as then blew it is folly to attempt describing. The oldest seaman in Norway never experienced any thing like it. We had let our sails go by the run before it cleverly took us; but, at the first puff, both our masts went by the board as if they had been sawed off—the mainmast taking with it my youngest brother, who had lashed himself to it for safety.

"Our boat was the lightest feather of a thing that ever sat upon water. It had a complete flush deck, with only a small hatch near the bow, and this hatch it had always been our custom to batten down when about to cross the Ström, by way of precaution against the chopping seas. But for this circumstance we should have foundered at once—for we lay entirely buried for some moments. How my elder brother escaped destruction I cannot say, for I never had an opportunity of ascertaining. For my part, as soon as I had let the foresail run, I threw myself flat on deck, with my feet against the narrow gunwale of the bow, and with my hands grasping a ring-bolt near the foot of the foremast. It was mere instinct that prompted me to do this—which was undoubtedly the very best thing I could have done—for I was too much flurried to think.

"For some moments we were completely deluged, as I say, and all this time I held my breath, and clung to the bolt. When I could stand it no longer I raised myself upon my knees, still keeping hold with my hands, and thus got my head clear. Presently our little boat gave herself a shake, just as a dog does in coming out of the water, and thus rid herself, in some measure, of the seas. I was now trying to get the better of the stupor that had come over me, and to collect my senses so as to see what was to be done, when I felt somebody grasp my arm. It was my elder brother, and my heart leaped for joy, for I had made sure that he was overboard—but the next moment all this joy was turned into horror—for he put his mouth close to my ear, and screamed out the word *'Moskoe-ström!'*

"No one ever will know what my feelings were at that moment. I shook from head to foot as if I had had the most violent fit of the ague. I knew what he meant by that one word well enough—I knew what he wished to make me understand. With the wind that now drove us on, we were bound for the whirl of the Ström, and nothing could save us!

"You perceive that in crossing the Ström *channel,* we always went a long way up above the whirl, even in the calmest weather, and then had to wait and watch carefully for the slack—but now we were driving right upon the pool itself, and in such a hurricane as this! 'To be sure,' I thought, 'we shall get there just about the slack—there is some little hope in that'—but in the next moment I cursed myself for being so great a fool as to dream of hope at all. I knew very well that we were doomed, had we been ten times a ninety-gun ship.

"By this time the first fury of the tempest had spent itself, or perhaps we did not feel it so much, as we scudded before it, but at all events the seas, which at first had been kept down by the wind, and lay flat and frothing, now got up into absolute mountains. A singular change, too, had come over the heavens. Around in every direction it was still as black as pitch, but nearly overhead there burst out, all at once, a circular rift of clear sky—as clear as I ever saw—and of a deep bright blue—and through it there blazed forth the full moon with a lustre that I never before knew her to wear. She lit up every thing about us with the greatest distinctness—but, oh God, what a scene it was to light up!

"I now made one or two attempts to speak to my brother—but in some manner which I could not understand, the din had so increased that I could not make him hear a single word, although I screamed at the top of my voice in his ear. Presently he shook his head, looking as pale as death, and held up one of his fingers, as if to say *'listen!'*

"At first I could not make out what he meant—but soon a hideous thought flashed upon me. I dragged my watch from its fob. It was not going. I glanced at its face by the moonlight, and then burst into tears as I flung it far away into the ocean. *It had run down at seven o'clock! We were behind the time of the slack, and the whirl of the Ström was in full fury!*

"When a boat is well built, properly trimmed, and not deep laden, the waves in a strong gale, when she is going large, seem always to slip from beneath her—which appears strange to a landsman—and this is what is called *riding,* in sea phrase.

"Well, so far we had ridden the swells very cleverly; but presently a gigantic sea happened to take us right under the counter, and bore us with it as it rose—up—up—as if into the sky. I would not have believed that any wave could rise so high. And then down we came with a sweep, a slide, and a plunge that made me feel sick and dizzy, as if I was falling from some lofty mountain-top in a dream. But while we were up I had thrown a quick glance around—and that one glance was all sufficient. I saw our exact position in an instant. The Moskoe-ström whirlpool was about a quarter of a mile dead ahead—but no more like the every-day Moskoe-ström than the whirl, as you now see it, is like a mill-race. If I had not known where we were, and what we had to expect, I should not have recognised the place at all. As it was, I involuntarily closed my eyes in horror. The lids clenched themselves together as if in a spasm.

"It could not have been more than two minutes afterwards until we suddenly felt the waves subside, and were enveloped in foam. The boat made a sharp half turn to larboard, and then shot off in its new direction like a thunderbolt. At the same moment the roaring noise of the water was completely drowned in a kind of shrill shriek—such a sound as you might imagine given out by the water-pipes of many thousand steam-vessels letting off their steam all together. We were now in the belt of surf that always surrounds the whirl; and I thought, of course, that another moment would plunge us into the abyss—down which we could only see indistinctly on account of the amazing velocity with which we were borne along. The boat did not seem to sink into the water at all, but to skim like an air-bubble upon the surface of the surge. Her starboard side was next the whirl, and on the larboard arose the world of ocean we had left. It stood like a huge writhing wall between us and the horizon.

"It may appear strange, but now, when we were in the very jaws of the gulf, I felt more composed than when we were only approaching it. Having made up my mind to hope no more, I got rid of a great deal of that terror which unmanned me at first. I supposed it was despair that strung my nerves.

"It may look like boasting—but what I tell you is truth—I began to reflect how magnificent a thing it was to die in such a manner, and how foolish it was in me to think of so paltry a consideration as my own individual life, in view of so wonderful a manifestation of God's power. I do believe that I blushed with shame when this idea crossed my mind. After a little while I became possessed with the keenest curiosity about the whirl itself. I positively felt a *wish* to explore its depths, even at the sacrifice I was going to make; and my principal grief was that I should never to able to tell my old companions on shore about the mysteries I should see. These, no doubt, were singular fancies to occupy a man's mind in such extremity—and I have often thought since, that the revolutions of the boat around the pool might have rendered me a little light-headed.

"There was another circumstance which tended to restore my self-possession; and this was the cessation of the wind, which could not reach us in our present situation—for, as you saw for yourself, the belt of the surf is considerably lower than the general bed of the ocean, and this latter now towered above us, a high, black, mountainous ridge. If you have never been at sea in a heavy gale, you can form no idea of the confusion of mind occasioned by the wind and spray together. They blind, deafen, and strangle you, and take away all power of action or reflection. But we were now, in a great measure, rid of these annoyances—just as death-condemned felons in prison are allowed petty indulgences, forbidden them while their doom is yet uncertain.

"How often we made the circuit of the belt it is impossible to say. We careered round and round for perhaps an hour, flying rather than floating, getting gradually more and more into the middle of the surge, and then nearer and nearer to its horrible inner edge. All this time I had never let go of the ring-bolt. My brother was at the stern, holding on to a large empty water-cask which had been securely lashed under the coop of the counter, and was the only thing on deck that had not been swept overboard when the gale first took us. As we approached the brink of the pit he let go his hold upon this, and made for the ring, from which, in the agony of his terror, he endeavored to force my hands, as it was not large enough to afford us both a secure grasp. I never felt deeper grief than when I saw him attempt this act—although I knew he was a madman when he did it—a raving maniac through sheer fright. I did not care, however, to contest the point with him. I knew it could make no difference whether either of us held on at all; so I let him have the bolt, and went astern to the cask. This there was no great difficulty in doing; for the smack flew round steadily enough, and upon an even keel—only swaying to and fro with the immense sweeps and swelters of the whirl. Scarcely had I secured myself in my new position, when we gave a wild lurch to starboard, and rushed headlong into the abyss. I muttered a hurried prayer to God, and thought all was over.

"As I felt the sickening sweep of the descent, I had instinctively tightened my hold upon the barrel, and closed my eyes. For some seconds I dared not open them—while I expected instant destruction, and wondered that I was not already in my death-struggles with the water. But moment after moment elapsed. I still lived. The sense of falling had ceased; and the motion of the vessel seemed much as it had been before while in the belt of foam, with the exception that she now lay more along. I took courage and looked once again upon the scene.

"Never shall I forget the sensation of awe, horror, and admiration with which I gazed about me. The boat appeared to be hanging, as if by magic, midway down, upon the interior surface of a funnel vast in circumference, prodigious in depth, and whose perfectly smooth sides might have been mistaken for ebony, but for the bewildering rapidity with which they spun around, and for the gleaming and ghastly radiance they shot forth, as the rays of the full moon, from that circular rift amid the clouds which I have already described, streamed in a flood of golden glory along the black walls, and far away down into the inmost recesses of the abyss.

"At first I was too much confused to observe any thing accurately. The general burst of terrific grandeur was all that I beheld. When I recovered myself a little, however, my gaze fell instinctively downward. In this direction I was able to obtain an unobstructed view, from the manner in which the smack hung on the inclined surface of the pool. She was quite upon an even keel—that is to say, her deck lay in a plane parallel with that of the water—but this latter sloped at an angle of more than forty-five degrees, so that we seemed to be lying upon our beam-ends. I could not help observing, nevertheless, that I had scarcely more difficulty in maintaining my hold and footing in this situation, than if we had been upon a dead level; and this, I suppose, was owing to the speed at which we revolved.

"The rays of the moon seemed to search the very bottom of the profound gulf; but still I could make out nothing distinctly, on account of a thick mist in which every thing there was enveloped, and over which there hung a magnificent rainbow, like that narrow and tottering bridge which Musselmen say is the only pathway between Time and Eternity. This mist, or spray, was no doubt occasioned by the clashing of the great walls of the funnel, as they all met together at the bottom—but the yell that went up to the Heavens from out of that mist I dare not attempt to describe.

"Our first slide into the abyss itself, from the belt of foam above, had carried us to a great distance down the slope; but our farther descent was by no means proportionate. Round and round we swept—not with any uniform movement—but in dizzying swings and jerks, that sent us sometimes only a few hundred feet—sometimes nearly the complete circuit of the whirl. Our progress downward, at each revolution, was slow, but very perceptible.

"Looking about me upon the wide waste of liquid ebony on which we were thus borne, I perceived that our boat was not the only object in the embrace of the whirl. Both above and below us were visible fragments of vessels, large masses of building timber and trunks of trees, with many smaller articles, such as pieces of house furniture, broken boxes, barrels and staves. I have already described the unnatural curiosity which had taken the place of my original terrors. It appeared to grow upon me as I drew nearer and nearer to my dreadful doom. I now began to watch, with a strange interest, the numerous things that floated in our company. I *must* have been delirious—for I even sought *amusement* in speculating upon the relative velocities of their several descents toward the foam below. 'This fir tree,' I found myself at one time saying, 'will certainly be the next thing that takes the awful plunge and disappears,'—and then I was disappointed to find that the wreck of a Dutch merchant ship overtook it and went down before. At length, after making several guesses of this nature, and being deceived in all—this fact—the fact of my invariable miscalculation, set me upon a train of reflection that made my limbs again tremble, and my heart beat heavily once more.

"It was not a new terror that thus affected me, but the dawn of a more exciting *hope*. This hope arose partly from memory, and partly from present observation. I called to mind the great variety of buoyant matter that strewed the coast of Lofoden, having been absorbed and then thrown forth by the Moskoe-ström. By far the greater number of the articles were shattered in the most extraordinary way—so chafed and roughened as to have the appearance of being stuck full of splinters—but then I distinctly recollected that there were *some* of them which were not disfigured at all. Now I could not account for this difference except by supposing that the roughened fragments were the only ones which had been *completely absorbed*—that the others had entered the whirl at so late a period of the tide, or, from some reason, had descended so slowly after entering, that they did not reach the bottom before the turn of the flood came, or of the ebb, as the case might be. I conceived it possible, in either instance, that they might thus be whirled up again to the level of the ocean, without undergoing the fate of those which had been drawn in more early or absorbed more rapidly. I made, also, three important observations. The first was, that as a general rule, the larger the bodies were, the more rapid their descent;—the second, that, between two masses of equal extent, the one spherical, and the other *of any other shape,* the superiority in speed of descent was with the sphere;—the third, that, between two masses of equal size, the one cylindrical, and the other of any other shape, the cylinder was absorbed the more slowly. Since my escape, I have had several conversations on this subject with an old school-master of the district; and it was from him that I learned the use of the words 'cylinder' and 'sphere.' He explained to me—although I have forgotten the explanation—how what I observed was, in fact, the natural consequence of the forms of the floating fragments—and showed me how it happened that a cylinder, swimming in a vortex, offered more resistance to its suction, and was drawn in with greater difficulty than an equally bulky body, of any form whatever.*

"There was one startling circumstance which went a great way in enforcing these observations, and rendering me anxious to turn them to account, and this was that, at every revolution, we passed something like a barrel, or else the broken yard or the mast of a vessel, while many of these things, which had been on our level when I first opened my eyes upon the wonders of the whirlpool, were now high up above us, and seemed to have moved but little from their original station.

"I no longer hesitated what to do. I resolved to lash myself securely to the water-cask upon which I now held, to cut it loose from the counter, and to throw myself with it into the water. I attracted my brother's attention by signs, pointed to the floating barrels that came near us, and did every thing in my power to make him understand what I was about to do. I thought at length that he comprehended my design—but, whether this was the case or not, he shook his head despairingly, and refused to move from his station by the ring-bolt. It was impossible to force him; the emergency admitted of no delay; and so, with a bitter struggle, I

* See Archimedes, *De Incidentibus in Fluido,* lib. 2.

resigned him to his fate, fastened myself to the cask by means of the lashings which secured it to the counter, and precipitated myself with it into the sea, without another moment's hesitation.

"The result was precisely what I had hoped it might be. As it is myself who now tell you this tale—as you see that I *did* escape—and as you are already in possession of the mode in which this escape was effected, and must therefore anticipate all that I have farther to say—I will bring my story quickly to conclusion. It might have been an hour, or thereabout, after my quitting the smack, when, having descended to a vast distance beneath me, it made three or four wild gyrations in rapid succession, and, bearing my loved brother with it, plunged headlong, at once and forever, into the chaos of foam below. The barrel to which I was attached sunk very little farther than half the distance between the bottom of the gulf and the spot at which I leaped overboard, before a great change took place in the character of the whirlpool. The slope of the sides of the vast funnel became momently less and less steep. The gyrations of the whirl grew, gradually, less and less violent. By degrees, the froth and the rainbow disappeared, and the bottom of the gulf seemed slowly to uprise. The sky was clear, the winds had gone down, and the full moon was setting radiantly in the west, when I found myself on the surface of the ocean, in full view of the shores of Lofoden, and above the spot where the pool of the Moskoe-ström *had been*. It was the hour of the slack—but the sea still heaved in mountainous waves from the effects of the hurricane. I was borne violently into the channel of the Ström, and in a few minutes, was hurried down the coast into the 'grounds' of the fishermen. A boat picked me up—exhausted from fatigue—and (now that the danger was removed) speechless from the memory of its horror. Those who drew me on board were my old mates and daily companions—but they knew me no more than they would have known a traveller from the spirit-land. My hair, which had been raven black the day before, was as white as you see it now. They say too that the whole expression of my countenance had changed. I told them my story—they did not believe it. I now tell it to *you*—and I can scarcely expect you to put more faith in it than did the merry fishermen of Lofoden."

NARRATIVE OF A. GORDON PYM

INTRODUCTORY NOTE

Upon my return to the United States a few months ago, after the extraordinary series of adventure in the South Seas and elsewhere, of which an account is given in the following pages, accident threw me into the society of several gentlemen in Richmond, Va., who felt deep interest in all matters relating to the regions I had visited, and who were constantly urging it upon me, as a duty, to give my narrative to the public. I had several reasons, however, for declining to do so, some of which were of a nature altogether private, and concern no person but myself; others not so much so. One consideration which deterred me was, that having kept no journal during a greater portion of the time in which I was absent, I feared I should not be able to write, from mere memory, a statement so minute and connected as to have the *appearance* of that truth it would really possess, barring only the natural and unavoidable exaggeration to which all of us are prone when detailing events which have had powerful influence in exciting the imaginative faculties. Another reason was, that the incidents to be narrated were of a nature so positively marvellous that, unsupported as my assertions must necessarily be (except by the evidence of a single individual, and he a half-breed Indian), I could only hope for belief among my family, and those of my friends who have had reason, through life, to put faith in my veracity—the probability being that the public at large would regard what I should put forth as merely an impudent and ingenious fiction. A distrust in my own abilities as a writer was, nevertheless, one of the principal causes which prevented me from complying with the suggestions of my advisers.

Among those gentlemen in Virginia who expressed the greatest interest in my statement, more particularly in regard to that portion of it which related to the Antarctic Ocean, was Mr. Poe, lately editor of the *Southern*

Literary Messenger, a monthly magazine, published by Mr. Thomas W. White, in the city of Richmond. He strongly advised me, among others, to prepare at once a full account of what I had seen and undergone, and trust to the shrewdness and common-sense of the public—insisting, with great plausibility, that however roughly, as regards mere authorship, my book should be got up, its very uncouthness, if there were any, would give it all the better chance of being received as truth.

Notwithstanding this representation, I did not make up my mind to do as he suggested. He afterward proposed (finding that I would not stir in the matter) that I should allow him to draw up, in his own words, a narrative of the earlier portion of my adventures, from facts afforded by myself, publishing it in the *Southern Messenger under the garb of fiction.* To this, perceiving no objection, I consented, stipulating only that my real name should be retained. Two numbers of the pretended fiction appeared, consequently, in the *Messenger* for January and February (1837), and, in order that it might certainly be regarded as fiction, the name of Mr. Poe was affixed to the articles in the table of contents of the magazine.

The manner in which this *ruse* was received has induced me at length to undertake a regular compilation and publication of the adventures in question; for I found that, in spite of the air of fable which had been so ingeniously thrown around that portion of my statement which appeared in the *Messenger* (without altering or distorting a single fact), the public were still not at all disposed to receive it as fable, and several letters were sent to Mr. P.'s address, distinctly expressing a conviction to the contrary. I thence concluded that the facts of my narrative would prove of such a nature as to carry with them sufficient evidence of their own authenticity, and that I had consequently little to fear on the score of popular incredulity.

This *exposé* being made, it will be seen at once how much of what follows I claim to be my own writing; and it will also be understood that no fact is misrepresented in the first few pages which were written by Mr. Poe. Even to those readers who have not seen the *Messenger,* it will be unnecessary to point out where his portion ends and my own commences; the difference in point of style will be readily perceived.

A. G. PYM

New York, July, 1838.

NARRATIVE OF A. GORDON PYM

CHAPTER I

MY NAME is Arthur Gordon Pym. My father was a respectable trader in sea-stores at Nantucket, where I was born. My maternal grandfather was an attorney in good practice. He was fortunate in everything, and had speculated very successfully in stocks of the Edgarton New-Bank, as it was formerly called. By these and other means he had managed to lay by a tolerable sum of money. He was more attached to myself, I believe, than to any other person in the world, and I expected to inherit the most of his property at his death. He sent me, at six years of age, to the school of old Mr. Ricketts, a gentleman with only one arm, and of eccentric manners—he is well known to almost every person who has visited New Bedford. I stayed at his school until I was sixteen, when I left him for Mr. E. Ronald's academy on the hill. Here I became intimate with the son of Mr. Barnard, a sea captain, who generally sailed in the employ of Lloyd and Vredenburgh—Mr. Barnard is also very well known in New Bedford, and has many relations, I am certain, in Edgarton. His son was named Augustus, and he was nearly two years older than myself. He had been on a whaling voyage with his father in the John Donaldson, and was always talking to me of his adventures in the South Pacific Ocean. I used frequently to go home with him, and remain all day, and sometimes all night. We occupied the same bed, and he would be sure to keep me awake until almost light, telling me stories of the natives of the Island of Tinian, and other places he had visited in his travels. At last I could not help being interested in what he said, and by degrees I felt the greatest desire to go to sea. I owned a sail-boat called the Ariel, and worth about seventy-five dollars. She had a half deck or cuddy, and was rigged sloop-fashion—I forget her tonnage, but she would hold ten persons without much crowding. In this boat we were in the habit of going on some of the maddest freaks in the world; and, when I now think of them, it appears to me a thousand wonders that I am alive to-day.

I will relate one of these adventures by way of introduction to a longer and more momentous narrative. One night there was a party at Mr. Barnard's, and both Augustus and myself were not a little intoxicated toward the close of it. As usual, in such cases, I took part of his bed in preference to going home. He went to sleep, as I thought, very quietly (it being near one when the party broke up), and without saying a word on his favourite topic. It might have been half an hour from the time of our getting in bed, and I was just about falling into a doze, when he suddenly started up, and swore with a terrible oath that he would not go to sleep for any Arthur Pym in Christendom, when there was so glorious a breeze from the southwest. I never was so astonished in my life, not knowing what he intended, and thinking that the wines and liquors he had drunk had set him entirely beside himself. He proceeded to talk very coolly, however, saying he knew that I supposed him intoxicated, but that he was never more sober in his life. He was only tired, he added, of lying in bed on such a fine night like a dog, and was determined to get up and dress, and go out on a frolic with the boat. I can hardly tell what possessed me, but the words were no sooner out of his mouth than I felt a thrill of the greatest excitement and pleasure, and thought his mad idea one of the most delightful and most reasonable things in the world. It was blowing almost a gale, and the weather was very cold—it being late in October. I sprang out of bed, nevertheless, in a kind of ecstasy, and told him I was quite as brave as himself, and quite as tired as he was of lying in bed like a dog, and quite as ready for any fun or frolic as any Augustus Barnard in Nantucket.

We lost no time in getting on our clothes and hurrying down

to the boat. She was lying at the old decayed wharf by the lumber-yard of Pankey & Co., and almost thumping her sides out against the rough logs. Augustus got into her and bailed her, for she was nearly half full of water. This being done, we hoisted jib and mainsail, kept full, and started boldly out to sea.

The wind, as I before said, blew freshly from the south-west. The night was very clear and cold. Augustus had taken the helm, and I stationed myself by the mast, on the deck of the cuddy. We flew along at a great rate—neither of us having said a word since casting loose from the wharf. I now asked my companion what course he intended to steer, and what time he thought it probable we should get back. He whistled for a few minutes, and then said crustily: "*I* am going to sea—*you* may go home if you think proper." Turning my eyes upon him, I perceived at once that, in spite of his assumed *nonchalance,* he was greatly agitated. I could see him distinctly by the light of the moon—his face was paler than any marble, and his hand shook so excessively that he could scarcely retain hold of the tiller. I found that something had gone wrong, and became seriously alarmed. At this period I knew little about the management of a boat, and was now depending entirely upon the nautical skill of my friend. The wind, too, had suddenly increased, and we were fast getting out of the lee of the land—still I was ashamed to betray any trepidation, and for almost half an hour maintained a resolute silence. I could stand it no longer, however, and spoke to Augustus about the propriety of turning back. As before, it was nearly a minute before he made answer, or took any notice of my suggestion. "By-and-by," said he at length—"time enough—home by-and-by." I had expected such a reply, but there was something in the tone of these words which filled me with an indescribable feeling of dread. I again looked at the speaker attentively. His lips were perfectly livid, and his knees shook so violently together that he seemed scarcely able to stand. "For God's sake, Augustus," I screamed, now heartily frightened, "what ails you?—what is the matter?—what *are* you going to do?" "Matter!" he stammered, in the greatest apparent surprise, letting go the tiller at the same moment, and falling forward into the bottom of the boat—"matter—why, nothing is the—matter—going home—d—d—don't you see?" The whole truth now flashed upon me. I flew to him and raised him up. He was drunk—beastly drunk—he could no longer either stand, speak, or see. His eyes were perfectly glazed; and as I let him go in the extremity of my despair, he rolled like a mere log into the bilge-water, from which I had lifted him. It was evident that, during the evening, he had drunk far more than I suspected, and that his conduct in bed had been the result of a highly-concentrated state of intoxication—a state which, like madness, frequently enables the victim to imitate the outward demeanour of one in perfect possession of his senses. The coolness of the night air, however, had had its usual effect—the mental energy began to yield before its influence—and the confused perception which he no doubt then had of his perilous situation had assisted in hastening the catastrophe. He was now thoroughly insensible, and there was no probability that he would be otherwise for many hours.

It is hardly possible to conceive the extremity of my terror. The fumes of the wine lately taken had evaporated, leaving me doubly timid and irresolute. I knew that I was altogether incapable of managing the boat, and that a fierce wind and strong ebb-tide were hurrying us to destruction. A storm was evidently gathering behind us; we had neither compass nor provisions; and it was clear that, if we held our present course, we should be out of sight of land before daybreak. These thoughts, with a crowd of others equally fearful, flashed through my mind with a bewildering rapidity, and for some moments paralyzed me beyond the possibility of making any exertion. The boat was going through the water at a terrible rate—full before the wind—no reef in either jib or mainsail—running her bows completely under the foam. It was a thousand wonders she did not broach to—Augustus having let go the tiller, as I said before, and I being too much agitated to think of taking it myself. By good luck, however, she kept steady, and gradually I recovered some degree of presence of mind. Still the wind was increasing fearfully; and whenever we rose from a plunge forward. the sea behind fell combing over our counter, and deluged us with water. I was so utterly benumbed, too, in every limb, as to be nearly unconscious of sensation. At length I summoned up the resolution of despair, and rushing to the mainsail, let it go by the run. As might have been expected, it flew over the bows, and, getting drenched with water, carried away the mast short off by the board. This latter accident alone saved me from instant destruction. Under the jib only, I now boomed along before the wind, shipping heavy seas occasionally, but relieved from the terror of immediate death. I took the helm, and breathed with greater freedom, as I found that there yet remained to us a chance of ultimate escape. Augustus still lay senseless in the bottom of the boat; and as there was imminent danger of his drowning (the water being nearly a foot deep just where he fell), I contrived to raise him partially up, and keep him in a sitting position, by passing a rope round his waist, and lashing it to a ringbolt in the deck of the cuddy. Having thus arranged everything as well as I could in my chilled and agitated condition, I recommended myself to God, and made up my mind to bear whatever might happen with all the fortitude in my power.

Hardly had I come to this resolution, when, suddenly, a loud and long scream or yell, as if from the throats of a thousand demons, seemed to pervade the whole atmosphere around and above the boat. Never while I live shall I forget the intense agony of terror I experienced at that moment. My hair stood erect on my head—I felt the blood congealing in my veins—my heart ceased utterly to beat, and without having once raised my eyes to learn the source of my alarm, I tumbled headlong and insensible upon the body of my fallen companion.

I found myself, upon reviving, in the cabin of a large whaling-ship (the Penguin) bound to Nantucket. Several persons were standing over me, and Augustus, paler than death, was busily occupied in chafing my hands. Upon seeing me open my eyes, his exclamations of gratitude and joy excited alternate laughter and tears from the rough-looking personages who were present. The mystery of our being in existence was now soon explained. We had been run down by the whaling-ship, which was close hauled, beating up to Nantucket with every sail she could venture to set, and consequently running almost at right angles to our own course. Several men were on the look-out forward, but did not perceive our boat until it was an impossibility to avoid coming in contact—their shouts of warning upon seeing us were what so terribly alarmed me. The huge ship, I was told, rode immediately over us with as much ease as our own little vessel would have passed over a feather, and without the least perceptible impediment to her progress. Not a scream arose from the deck of the victim—there was a slight grating sound to be heard mingling with the roar of wind and water, as the frail bark which was swallowed up rubbed for a moment along the keel of her destroyer—but this was all. Thinking our boat (which it will be remembered was dismasted) some mere shell cut adrift as useless, the captain (Captain E. T. V. Block of New London) was for proceeding on his course without troubling himself further about the matter. Luckily, there were two of the look-out who swore positively to having seen some person at our helm, and represented the possibility of yet saving him. A discussion ensued, when Block grew angry, and, after a while, said that "it was no business of his to be eternally watching for egg-shells; that the ship should *not* put about for any such nonsense; and if there was a man run down, it was nobody's fault but his own—he might drown and be d—d," or some language to that effect. Henderson, the first mate, now took the matter up, being justly indignant, as well as the whole ship's crew, at a speech evincing such a degree of heartless atrocity. He spoke plainly, seeing himself upheld by the men, told the captain he considered him a fit subject for the gallows, and that he would disobey his orders if he were hanged for it the moment he set his foot on shore. He strode aft, jostling Block (who turned very pale and made no answer) on one side, and seizing the helm, gave the word, in a firm voice, *Hard-a-lee!* The men flew to their posts, and the ship went cleverly about. All this had occupied nearly five minutes, and it was supposed to be hardly within the bounds of possibility that any individual could be saved—allowing any to have been on board the boat. Yet, as the reader has seen, both Augustus and myself were rescued; and our deliverance seemed to have been brought about by two of those almost inconceivable pieces of good fortune which are attributed by the wise and pious to the special interference of Providence.

While the ship was yet in stays, the mate lowered the jolly-boat and jumped into her with the very two men, I believe, who spoke up as having seen me at the helm. They had just left the lee of the vessel (the moon still shining brightly) when she made a long and heavy roll to windward, and Henderson, at the same moment, starting up in his seat, bawled out to his crew to *back water*. He would say nothing else—repeating his cry impatiently, *back water! back water!* The men put back as speedily as possible; but by this time the ship had gone round, and gotten fully under headway, although all hands on board were making great exertions to take in sail. In despite of the danger of the attempt, the mate clung to the main-chains as soon as they came within his reach. Another huge lurch now brought the starboard side of the vessel out of the water neatly as far as her keel, when the cause of his anxiety was rendered obvious enough. The body of a man was seen to be affixed in the most singular manner to the smooth and shining bottom (the Penguin was coppered and copper-fastened), and beating violently against it with every movement of the hull. After several ineffectual efforts, made during the lurches of the ship, and at the imminent risk of swamping the boat, I was finally disengaged from my perilous situation and taken on board—for the body proved to be my own. It appeared that one of the timber-bolts having started and broken a passage through the copper, it had arrested my progress as I passed under the ship, and fastened me in so extraordinary a manner to her bottom. The head of the bolt had made its way through the collar of the green baize jacket I had on, and through the back part of my neck, forcing itself out between two sinews and just below the right ear. I was immediately put to bed—although life seemed to be totally extinct. There was no surgeon on board. The captain, however, treated me with every attention—to make amends, I presume, in the eyes of his crew, for his atrocious behaviour in the previous portion of the adventure.

In the meantime, Henderson had again put off from the ship, although the wind was now blowing almost a hurricane. He had not been gone many minutes when he fell in with some fragments of our boat, and shortly afterward one of the men with him asserted that he could distinguish a cry for help at intervals amid the roaring of the tempest. This induced the hardy seamen to persevere in their search for more than half an hour, although repeated signals to return were made them by Captain Block, and although every moment on the water in so frail a boat was fraught to them with the most imminent and deadly peril. Indeed, it is nearly impossible to conceive how the small jolly they were in could have escaped destruction for a single instant. She was built, however, for the whaling service, and was fitted, as I have since had reason to believe, with air-boxes, in the manner of some life-boats used on the coast of Wales.

After searching in vain for about the period of time just mentioned, it was determined to get back to the ship. They had scarcely made this resolve when a feeble cry arose from a dark object that floated rapidly by. They pursued and soon overtook it. It proved to be the entire deck of the Ariel's cuddy. Augustus was struggling near it, apparently in the last agonies. Upon getting hold of him it was found that he was attached by a rope to the floating timber. This rope, it will be remembered, I had myself tied round his waist, and made fast to a ringbolt, for the purpose of keeping him in an upright position, and my so doing, it appeared, had been ultimately the means of preserving his life. The Ariel was slightly put together, and in going down her frame naturally went to pieces; the deck of the cuddy, as might have been expected, was lifted, by the force of the water rushing in, entirely from the main timbers, and floated (with other fragments, no doubt) to the surface—Augustus was buoyed up with it, and thus escaped a terrible death.

It was more than an hour after being taken on board the Penguin before he could give any account of himself, or be made to comprehend the nature of the accident which had befallen our boat. At length he became thoroughly aroused, and spoke much of his sensations while in the water. Upon his first attaining any degree of consciousness, he found himself beneath the surface, whirling round and round with inconceivable rapidity, and with a rope wound in three or four folds tightly about his neck. In an instant afterward he felt himself going rapidly upward, when, his head striking violently against a hard substance, he again relapsed into insensibility. Upon once more reviving he was in fuller possession of his reason—this was still, however, in the greatest degree clouded and confused. He now knew that some accident had occurred, and that he was in the water, although his mouth was above the surface, and he could breathe with some freedom. Possibly, at this period the deck was drifting rapidly before the wind, and drawing him after it as he floated upon his back. Of course, as long as he could have retained this position, it would have been nearly impossible that he should be drowned. Presently a surge threw him directly athwart the deck; and this post he endeavoured to maintain, screaming at intervals for help. Just before he was discovered by Mr. Henderson, he had been obliged to relax his hold through exhaustion, and, falling into the sea, had given himself up for lost. During the whole period of his struggles he had not the faintest recollection of the Ariel, nor of any matters in connection with the source of his disaster. A vague feeling of terror and despair had taken entire possession of his faculties. When he was finally picked up, every power of his mind had failed him; and, as before said, it was nearly an hour after getting on board the Penguin before he became fully aware of his condition. In regard to myself—I was resuscitated from a state bordering very nearly upon death (and after every other means had been tried in vain for three hours and a half) by vigorous friction with flannels bathed in hot oil—a proceeding suggested by Augustus. The wound in my neck, although of an ugly appearance, proved of little real consequence, and I soon recovered from its effects.

The Penguin got into port about nine o'clock in the morning, after encountering one of the severest gales ever experienced off Nantucket. Both Augustus and myself managed to appear at Mr. Barnard's in time for breakfast—which, luckily, was somewhat late, owing to the party over night. I suppose all at the table were too much fatigued themselves to notice our jaded appearance—of course, it would not have borne a very rigid scrutiny. Schoolboys, however, can accomplish wonders in the way of deception, and I verily believe not one of our friends in Nantucket had the slightest suspicion that the terrible story told by some sailors in town of their having run down a vessel at sea and drowned some thirty or forty poor devils, had reference either to the Ariel, my companion, or myself. We two have since very frequently talked the matter over—but never without a shudder. In one of our conversations Augustus frankly confessed to me, that in his whole life he had at no time experienced so excruciating a sense of dismay, as when on board our little boat he first discovered the extent of his intoxication, and felt himself sinking beneath its influence.

CHAPTER II

In no affairs of mere prejudice, *pro* or *con*, do we deduce inferences with entire certainty even from the most simple data. It might be supposed that a catastrophe such as I have just related would have effectually cooled my incipient passion for the sea. On the contrary, I never experienced a more ardent longing for the wild adventures incident to the life of a navigator than within a week after our miraculous deliverance. This short period proved amply long enough to erase from my memory the shadows, and bring out in vivid light all the pleasurably exciting points of colour, all the picturesqueness of the late perilous accident. My conversations with Augustus grew daily more frequent and more intensely full of interest. He had a manner of relating his stories of the ocean (more than one half of which I now suspect to have been sheer fabrications) well adapted to have weight with one of my enthusiastic temperament, and somewhat gloomy although glowing imagination. It is strange, too, that he most strongly enlisted my feelings in behalf of the life of a seaman, when he depicted his more terrible moments of suffering and despair. For the bright side of the painting I had a limited sympathy. My visions were of shipwreck and famine; of death or captivity among barbarian hordes; of a lifetime dragged out in sorrow and tears, upon some gray and desolate rock, in an ocean unapproachable and unknown. Such visions or desires—for they amounted to desires—are common, I have since been assured, to the whole numerous race of the melancholy among men—at the time of which I speak I regarded them only as prophetic glimpses of a destiny which I felt myself in a measure bound to fulfil. Augustus thoroughly entered into my state of mind. It is probable, indeed, that our intimate communion had resulted in a partial interchange of character.

About eighteen months after the period of the Ariel's disaster, the firm of Lloyd and Vredenburgh (a house connected in some manner with the Messieurs Enberby, I believe, of Liverpool) were engaged in repairing and fitting out the brig Grampus for a whaling voyage. She was an old hulk, and scarcely seaworthy when all was done to her that could be done. I hardly know why she was chosen in preference to other and good vessels belonging to the same owners—but so it was. Mr. Barnard was appointed to command her, and Augustus was going with him. While the brig was getting ready, he frequently urged upon me the excellency of the opportunity now offered for indulging my desire of travel. He found me by no means an unwilling listener—yet the matter could not be so easily arranged. My father made no direct opposition; but my mother went into hysterics at the bare mention of the design; and, more than all, my grandfather, from whom I expected much, vowed to cut me off with a shilling if I should ever broach the subject to him again. These difficulties, however, so far from abating my desire, only added fuel to the flame. I determined to go at all hazards; and, having made known my intention to Augustus, we set about arranging a plan by which it might be accomplished. In the meantime I forbore speaking to any of my relations in regard to the voyage, and, as I busied myself ostensibly with my usual studies, it was supposed that I had abandoned the design. I have since frequently examined my conduct on this occasion with sentiments of displeasure as well as of surprise. The intense hypocrisy I made use of for the furtherance of my project—an hypocrisy pervading every word and action of my life for so long a period of time—could only have been rendered tolerable to myself by the wild and burning expectation with which I looked forward to the fulfilment of my long-cherished visions of travel.

In pursuance of my scheme of deception, I was necessarily obliged to leave much to the management of Augustus, who was employed for the greater part of every day on board the Grampus, attending to some arrangements for his father in the cabin and cabin hold. At night, however, we were sure to have a conference and talk over our hopes. After nearly a month passed in this manner, without our hitting upon any plan we thought likely to succeed, he told me at last that he had determined upon everything necessary. I had a relation living in New Bedford, a Mr. Ross, at whose house I was in the habit of spending occasionally two or three weeks at a time. The brig was to sail about the middle of June (June, 1827), and it was agreed that, a day or two before her putting to sea, my father was to receive a note, as usual, from Mr. Ross, asking me to come over and spend a fortnight with Robert and Emmet (his sons). Augustus charged himself with the inditing of this note and getting it delivered. Having set out, as supposed, for New Bedford, I was then to report myself to my companion, who would contrive a hiding-place for me in the Grampus. This hiding-place, he assured me, would be rendered sufficiently comfortable for a residence of many days, during which I was not to make my appearance. When the brig had proceeded so far on her course as to make any turning back a matter out of question, I should then, he said, be formally installed in all the comforts of the cabin; and as to his father, he would only laugh heartily at the joke. Vessels enough would be met with by which a letter might be sent home explaining the adventure to my parents.

The middle of June at length arrived, and everything had been matured. The note was written and delivered, and on a Monday morning I left the house for the New Bedford packet, as supposed. I went, however, straight to Augustus, who was waiting for me at the corner of a street. It had been our original plan that I should keep out of the way until dark, and then slip on board the brig; but, as there was now a thick fog in our favour, it was agreed to lose no time in secreting me. Augustus led the way to the wharf, and I followed at a little distance, enveloped in a thick seaman's cloak, which he had brought with him, so that my person might not be easily recognized. Just as we turned the second corner, after passing Mr. Edmund's well, who should appear, standing right in front of me, and looking me full in the face, but old Mr. Peterson, my grandfather. "Why, bless my soul, Gordon," said he, after a long pause, "why, why,—*whose* dirty cloak is that you have on?" "Sir!" I replied, assuming, as well as I could, in the exigency of the moment, an air of offended surprise, and talking in the gruffest of all imaginable tones—"sir! you are a sum'mat mistaken; my name, in the first place, bee'nt nothing at all like Goddin, and I'd want you for to know better, you blackguard, than to call my new obercoat a darty one." For my life I could hardly refrain from screaming with laughter at the odd manner in which the old gentleman received this handsome rebuke. He started back two or three steps, turned first pale and then excessively red, threw up his spectacles, then, putting them down, ran full tilt at me, with his umbrella uplifted. He stopped short, however, in his career, as if struck with a sudden recollection; and presently, turning round, hobbled off down the street, shaking all the while with rage, and muttering between his teeth: "Won't do —new glasses—thought it was Gordon—d——d good-for-nothing salt water Long Tom."

After this narrow escape we proceeded with greater caution, and arrived at our point of destination in safety. There were only one or two of the hands on board, and these were busy forward, doing something to the forecastle combings. Captain Barnard, we knew very well, was engaged at Lloyd and Vredenburgh's, and would remain there until late in the evening, so we had little to apprehend on his account. Augustus went first up the vessel's side, and in a short while I followed him, without being noticed by the men at work. We proceeded at once into the cabin, and found no person there. It was fitted up in the most comfortable style—a thing somewhat unusual in a whaling-vessel. There were four very excellent state-rooms, with wide and convenient berths. There was also a large stove, I took notice, and a remarkably thick and valuable carpet covering the floor of both the cabin and state-rooms. The ceiling was full seven feet high, and, in short, everything appeared of a more roomy and agreeable nature than I had anticipated. Augustus, however, would allow me but little time for observation, insisting upon the necessity of my concealing myself as soon as possible. He led the way into his own state-room, which was on the starboard side of the brig, and next to the bulkheads. Upon entering, he closed the door and bolted it. I thought I had never seen a nicer little room than the one in which I now found myself. It was about ten feet long, and had only one berth, which, as I said before, was wide and convenient. In that portion of the closet nearest the bulkheads there was a space of four feet square, containing a table, a chair, and a set of hanging shelves full of books, chiefly books of voyages and travels. There were many other little comforts in the room, among which I ought not to forget a kind of safe or refrigerator, in which Augustus pointed out to me a host of delicacies, both in the eating and drinking department.

He now pressed with his knuckles upon a certain spot of the carpet in one corner of the space just mentioned, letting me know that a portion of the flooring, about sixteen inches square, had been neatly cut out and again adjusted. As he pressed, this portion rose up at one end sufficiently to allow the passage of his finger beneath. In this manner he raised the mouth of the trap (to which the carpet was still fastened by tacks), and I found that it led into the after hold. He next lit a small taper by means of a phosphorus match, and, placing the light in a dark lantern, descended with it through the opening, bidding me follow. I did so, and he then pulled the cover upon the hole, by means of a nail driven into the under side—the carpet, of course, resuming its original position on the floor of the state-room, and all traces of the aperture being concealed.

The taper gave out so feeble a ray that it was with the greatest difficulty I could grope my way through the confused mass of lumber among which I now found myself. By degrees, however, my eyes became accustomed to the gloom, and I proceeded with less trouble, holding on to the skirts of my friend's coat. He brought me, at length, after creeping and winding through innumerable narrow passages, to an iron-bound box, such as is used sometimes for packing fine earthenware. It was nearly four feet high, and full six long, but very narrow. Two large empty oil-casks lay on the top of it, and above these, again, a vast quantity of straw matting, piled up as high as the floor of the cabin. In every other direction around was wedged as closely as possible, even up to the ceiling, a complete chaos of almost every species of ship-furniture, together with a heterogeneous medley of crates, hampers, barrels, and bales, so that it seemed a matter no less than miraculous that we had discovered any passage at all to the box. I afterward found that Augustus had purposely arranged the stowage in this hold with a view to affording me a thorough concealment, having had only one assistant in the labor, a man not going out in the brig.

My companion now showed me that one of the ends of the box could be removed at pleasure. He slipped it aside and displayed the interior, at which I was excessively amused. A mattress from one of the cabin berths covered the whole of its bottom, and it contained almost every article of mere comfort which could be crowded into so small a space, allowing me, at the same time, sufficient room for my accommodation, either in a sitting position or lying at full length. Among other things, there were some books, pen, ink, and paper, three blankets, a large jug full of water, a keg of sea-biscuit, three or four immense Bologna sausages, an enormous ham, a cold leg of roast mutton, and half a dozen bottles of cordials and liqueurs. I proceeded immediately to take possession of my little apartment, and this with feelings of higher satisfaction, I am sure, than any monarch ever experienced upon entering a new palace. Augustus now pointed out to me the method of fastening the open end of the box, and then, holding the taper close to the deck, showed me a piece of dark whipcord lying along it. This, he said, extended from my hiding-place throughout all the necessary windings among the lumber, to a nail which was driven into the deck of the hold, immediately beneath the trap-door leading into his state-room. By means of this cord I should be enabled readily to trace my way out without his guidance, provided any unlooked-for accident should render such a step necessary. He now took his departure, leaving with me the lantern, together with a copious supply of tapers and phosphorus, and promising to pay me a visit as often as he could contrive to do so without observation. This was on the seventeenth of June.

I remained three days and nights (as nearly as I could guess) in my hiding-place without getting out of it at all, except twice for the purpose of stretching my limbs by standing erect between two crates just opposite the opening. During the whole period I saw nothing of Augustus; but this occasioned me little uneasiness, as I knew the brig was expected to put to sea every hour, and in the bustle he would not easily find opportunities of coming down to me. At length I heard the trap open and shut, and presently he called in a low voice, asking if all was well, and if there was anything I wanted. "Nothing," I replied; "I am as comfortable as can be; when will the brig sail?" "She will be under weigh in less than half an hour," he answered. "I came to let you know, and for fear you should be uneasy at my absence. I shall not have a chance of coming down again for some time—perhaps for three or four days more. All is going on right above-board. After I go up and close the trap, do you creep along by the whipcord to where the nail is driven in. You will find my watch there—it may be useful to you, as you have no daylight to keep time by. I suppose you can't tell how long you have been buried—only three days—this is the twentieth. I would bring the watch to your box, but am afraid of being missed." With this he went up.

In about an hour after he had gone I distinctly felt the brig in motion, and congratulated myself upon having at length fairly commenced a voyage. Satisfied with this idea, I determined to make my mind as easy as possible, and await the course of events until I should be permitted to exchange the box for the more roomy, although hardly more comfortable, accommodations of the cabin. My first care was to get the watch. Leaving the taper burning, I groped along in the dark, following the cord through windings innumerable, in some of which I discovered that, after toiling a long distance, I was brought back within a foot or two of a former position. At length I reached the nail, and securing the object of my journey, returned with it in safety. I now looked over the books which had been so thoughtfully provided, and selected the expedition of Lewis and Clark to the mouth of the Columbia. With this I amused myself for some time, when, growing sleepy, I extinguished the light with great care, and soon fell into a sound slumber.

Upon awaking I felt strangely confused in mind, and some time elapsed before I could bring to recollection all the various circumstances of my situation. By degrees, however, I remembered all. Striking a light, I looked at the watch; but it was run down, and there were, consequently, no means of determining how long I slept. My limbs were greatly cramped, and I was forced to relieve them by standing between the crates. Presently feeling an almost ravenous appetite, I bethought myself of the cold mutton, some of which I had eaten just before going to sleep, and found excellent. What was my astonishment in discovering it to be in a state of absolute putrefaction! This circumstance occasioned me great disquietude; for, connecting it with the disorder of mind I experienced upon awaking, I began to suppose that I must have slept for an inordinately long period of time. The close atmosphere of the hold might have something to do with this, and might, in the end, be productive of the most serious results. My head ached excessively; I fancied that I drew every breath with difficulty; and, in short, I was oppressed with a multitude of gloomy feelings. Still I could not venture to make any disturbance by opening the trap or otherwise, and, having wound up the watch, contented myself as well as possible.

Throughout the whole of the next tedious twenty-four hours no person came to my relief, and I could not help accusing Augustus of the grossest inattention. What alarmed me chiefly was, that the water in my jug was reduced to about half a pint, and I was suffering much from thirst, having eaten freely of the Bologna sausages after the loss of my mutton. I became very uneasy, and could no longer take any interest in my books. I was overpowered, too, with a desire to sleep, yet trembled at the thought of indulging it, lest there might exist some pernicious influence, like that of burning charcoal, in the confined air of the hold. In the meantime the roll of the brig told me that we were far in the main ocean, and a dull humming sound, which reached my ears as if from an immense distance, convinced me no ordinary gale was blowing. I could not imagine a reason for the absence of Augustus. We were surely far enough advanced on our voyage to allow of my going up. Some accident might have happened to him—but I could think of none which would account for his suffering me to remain so long a prisoner, except, indeed, his having suddenly died or fallen overboard, and upon this idea I could not dwell with any degree of patience. It was possible that we had been baffled by head-winds, and were still in the near vicinity of Nantucket. This notion, however, I was forced to abandon; for such being the case, the brig must have frequently gone about; and I was entirely satisfied, from her continual inclination to the larboard, that she had been sailing all along with a steady breeze on her starboard quarter. Besides, granting that we were still in the neighbourhood of the island, why should not Augustus have visited me and informed me of the circumstance? Pondering in this manner upon the difficulties of my solitary and cheerless condition, I resolved to wait yet another twenty-four hours, when, if no relief were obtained, I would make my way to the trap, and endeavour either to hold a parley with my friend, or get at least a little fresh air through the opening, and a further supply of water from the state-room. While occupied with this thought, however, I fell, in spite of every exertion to the contrary, into a state of profound sleep, or rather stupor. My dreams were of the most terrific description. Every species of calamity and horror befell me. Among other miseries I was smothered to death between huge pillows, by demons of the most ghastly and ferocious aspect. Immense serpents held me in their embrace, and looked earnestly in my face with their fearfully shining eyes. Then deserts, limitless, and of the most forlorn and awe-inspiring character, spread themselves out before me. Immensely tall trunks of trees, gray and leafless, rose up in endless succession as far as the eye could reach. Their root were concealed in wide-spreading morasses, whose dreary water lay intensely black, still, and altogether terrible, beneath. And the strange trees seemed endowed with a human vitality, and, waving to and fro their skeleton arms, were crying to the silent waters for mercy, in the shrill and piercing accents of the most accute agony and despair. The scene changed; and I stood, naked and alone, amid the burning sand-plains of

Zahara. At my feet lay crouched a fierce lion of the tropics. Suddenly his wild eyes opened and fell upon me. With a convulsive bound he sprang to his feet, and laid bare his horrible teeth. In another instant there burst from his red throat a roar like the thunder of the firmament, and I fell impetuously to the earth. Stifling in a paroxysm of terror, I at last found myself partially awake. My dream, then, was not all a dream. Now, at least, I was in possession of my senses. The paws of some huge and real monster were pressing heavily upon my bosom—his hot breath was in my ear—and his white and ghastly fangs were gleaming upon me through the gloom.

Had a thousand lives hung upon the movement of a limb or the utterance of a syllable, I could have neither stirred nor spoken. The beast, whatever it was, retained his position without attempting any immediate violence, while I lay in an utterly helpless, and, I fancied, a dying condition beneath him. I felt that my powers of body and mind were fast leaving me—in a word, that I was perishing, and perishing of sheer fright. My brain swam—I grew deadly sick—my vision failed—even the glaring eyeballs above me grew dim. Making a last strong effort, I at length breathed a faint ejaculation to God, and resigned myself to die. The sound of my voice seemed to arouse all the latent fury of the animal. He precipitated himself at full length upon my body; but what was my astonishment, when, with a long and low whine, he commenced licking my face and hands with the greatest eagerness, and with the most extravagant demonstration of affection and joy! I was bewildered, utterly lost in amazement—but I could not forget the peculiar whine of my Newfoundland dog Tiger, and the odd manner of his caresses I well knew. It was he. I experienced a sudden rush of blood to my temples—a giddy and overpowering sense of deliverance and reanimation. I rose hurriedly from the mattress upon which I had been lying, and, throwing myself upon the neck of my faithful follower and friend, relieved the long oppression of my bosom in a flood of the most passionate tears.

As upon a former occasion, my conceptions were in a state of the greatest indistinctness and confusion after leaving the mattress. For a long time I found it nearly impossible to connect any ideas—but, by very slow degrees, my thinking faculties returned, and I again called to memory the several incidents of my condition. For the presence of Tiger I tried in vain to account; and after busying myself with a thousand different conjectures respecting him, was forced to content myself with rejoicing that he was with me to share my dreary solitude, and render me comfort by his caresses. Most people love their dogs—but for Tiger I had an affection far more ardent than common; and never, certainly, did any creature more truly deserve it. For seven years he had been my inseparable companion, and in a multitude of instances had given evidence of all the noble qualities for which we value the animal. I had rescued him, when a puppy, from the clutches of a malignant little villain in Nantucket, who was leading him, with a rope around his neck, to the water; and the grown dog repaid the obligation, about three years afterward, by saving me from the bludgeon of a street robber.

Getting now hold of the watch, I found, upon applying it to my ear, that it had again run down; but at this I was not at all surprised, being convinced, from the peculiar state of my feelings, that I had slept, as before, for a very long period of time; how long, it was of course impossible to say. I was burning up with fever, and my thirst was almost intolerable. I felt about the box for my little remaining supply of water, for I had no light, the taper having burnt to the socket of the lantern, and the phosphorus-box not coming readily to hand. Upon finding the jug, however, I discovered it to be empty—Tiger, no doubt, having been tempted to drink it, as well as to devour the remnant of mutton, the bone of which lay, well picked, by the opening of the box. The spoiled meat I could well spare, but my heart sank as I thought of the water. I was feeble in the extreme, so much so that I shook all over, as with an ague, at the slightest movement or exertion. To add to my troubles, the brig was pitching and rolling with great violence, and the oil-casks which lay upon my box were in momentary danger of falling down, so as to block up the only way of ingress or egress. I felt, also, terrible sufferings from seasickness. These considerations determined me to make my way, at all hazards, to the trap, and obtain immediate relief, before I should be incapacitated from doing so altogether. Having come to this resolve, I again felt about for the phosphorus-box and tapers. The former I found after some little trouble; but, not discovering the tapers as soon as I had expected (for I remembered very nearly the spot in which I had placed them), I gave up the search for the present, and bidding Tiger lie quiet, began at once my journey towards the trap.

In this attempt my great feebleness became more than ever apparent. It was with the utmost difficulty I could crawl along at all, and very frequently my limbs sank suddenly from beneath me; when, falling prostrate on my face, I would remain for some minutes in a state bordering on insensibility. Still I struggled forward by slow degrees, dreading every moment that I should swoon amid the narrow and intricate windings of the lumber, in which event I had nothing but death to expect as the result. At length, upon making a push forward with all the energy I could command, I struck my forehead violently against the sharp corner of an iron-bound crate. The accident only stunned me for a few moments; but I found, to my inexpressible grief, that the quick and violent roll of the vessel had thrown the crate entirely across my path, so as effectually to block up the passage. With my utmost exertions I could not move it a single inch from its position, it being closely wedged in among the surrounding boxes and ship-furniture. It became necessary, therefore, enfeebled as I was, either to leave the guidance of the whipcord and seek out a new passage, or to climb over the obstacle, and resume the path on the other side. The former alternative presented too many difficulties and dangers to be thought of without a shudder. In my present weak state of both mind and body, I should infallibly lose my way if I attempted it, and perish miserably amid the dismal and disgusting labyrinths of the hold. I proceeded, therefore, without hesitation, to summon up all my remaining strength and fortitude, and endeavour, as I best might, to clamber over the crate.

Upon standing erect, with this end in view, I found the undertaking even a more serious task than my fears had led me to imagine. On each side of the narrow passage arose a complete wall of various heavy lumber, which the least blunder on my part might be the means of bringing down upon my head; or, if this accident did not occur, the path might be effectually blocked up against my return by the descending mass, as it was in front by the obstacle there. The crate itself was a long and unwieldy box, upon which no foothold could be obtained. In vain I attempted, by every means in my power, to reach the top, with the hope of being thus enabled to draw myself up. Had I succeeded in reaching it, it is certain that my strength would have proved utterly inadequate to the task of getting over, and it was better in every respect that I failed. At length, in a desperate effort to force the crate from its ground, I felt a strong vibration in the side next me. I thrust my hand eagerly to the edge of the planks, and found that a very large one was loose. With my pocket-knife, which luckily, I had with me, I succeeded after great labour, in prying it entirely off; and getting through the aperture, discovered, to my exceeding joy, that there were no boards on the opposite side —in other words, that the top was wanting, it being the bottom through which I had forced my way. I now met with no important difficulty in proceeding along the line until I finally reached the nail. With a beating heart I stood erect, and with a gentle touch pressed against the cover of the trap. It did not rise as soon as I had expected, and I pressed it with somewhat more determination, still dreading lest some other person than Augustus might be in his state-room. The door, however, to my astonishment, remained steady, and I became somewhat uneasy, for I knew that it had formerly required little or no effort to remove it. I pushed it strongly—it was nevertheless firm: with all my strength—it still did not give way: with rage, with fury, with despair—it set at defiance my utmost efforts; and it was evident, from the unyielding nature of the resistance, that the hole had either been discovered and effectually nailed up, or that some immense weight had been placed upon it, which it was useless to think of removing.

My sensations were those of extreme horror and dismay. In vain I attempted to reason on the probable cause of my being thus entombed. I could summon up no connected chain of reflection, and, sinking on the floor, gave way, unresistingly, to the most gloomy imaginings, in which the dreadful deaths of thirst, famine, suffocation, and premature interment, crowded upon me as the prominent disasters to be encountered. At length there returned to me some portion of presence of mind. I arose, and felt with my fingers for the seams or cracks of the aperture. Having found them, I examined them closely to ascertain if they emitted any light from the state-room; but none was visible. I then forced the pen-blade of my knife through them, until I met with some hard obstacle. Scraping against it, I discovered it to be a solid mass of iron, which, from its peculiar wavy feel as I passed the blade along it, I concluded to be a chain-cable. The only course now left me was to retrace my way to the box, and there either yield to my sad fate, or try so to tranquillize my mind as to admit of my arranging some plan of escape. I immediately set about the attempt, and succeeded, after innumerable difficulties, in getting back. As I sank, utterly exhausted, upon the mattress, Tiger threw himself at full length by my side, and seemed as if desirous, by his caresses, of consoling me in my troubles, and urging me to bear them with fortitude.

The singularity of his behaviour at length forcibly arrested my attention. After licking my face and hands for some minutes, he would suddenly cease doing so, and utter a low whine. Upon reaching out my hand towards him, I then invariably found him lying on his back, with his paws uplifted. This conduct, so frequently repeated, appeared strange, and I could in no manner account for it. As the dog seemed distressed, I concluded that he had received some injury; and, taking his paws in my hands, I examined them one by one, but found no sign of any hurt. I then supposed him hungry, and gave him a large piece of ham, which he devoured with avidity—afterward, however, resuming his extraordinary manœuvres. I now imagined that he was suffering, like myself, the torments of thirst, and was about adopting this conclusion as the true one, when the idea occurred to me that I had as yet only examined his paws, and that there might possibly be a wound upon some portion of his body or head. The latter I felt carefully over, but found nothing. On passing my hand, however, along his back, I perceived a slight erection of the hair extending completely across it. Probing this with my finger, I discovered a string, and tracing it up, found that it encircled the whole body. Upon a closer scrutiny, I came across a small slip of what had the feeling of letter paper, through which the string had been fastened in such a manner as to bring it immediately beneath the left shoulder of the animal.

CHAPTER III

THE thought instantly occurred to me that the paper was a note from Augustus, and that some unaccountable accident having happened to prevent his relieving me from my dungeon, he had devised this method of acquainting me with the true state of affairs. Trembling with eagerness, I now commenced another search for my phosphorus matches and tapers. I had a confused recollection of having put them carefully away just before falling asleep; and, indeed, previously to my last journey to the trap, I had been able to remember the exact spot where I had deposited them. But now I endeavoured in vain to call it to mind, and busied myself for a full hour in a fruitless and vexatious search for the missing articles; never, surely, was there a more tantalizing state of anxiety and suspense. At length, while groping about, with my head close to the ballast, near the opening of the box, and outside of it, I perceived a faint glimmering of light in the direction of the steerage. Greatly surprised, I endeavoured to make my way towards it, as it appeared to be but a few feet from my position. Scarcely had I moved with this intention, when I lost sight of the glimmer entirely, and, before I could bring it into view again, was obliged to feel along by the box until I had exactly resumed my original situation. Now, moving my head with caution to and fro, I found that, by proceeding slowly, with great care, in an opposite direction to that in which I had at first started, I was enabled to draw near the light, still keeping it in view. Presently I came directly upon it (having squeezed my way through innumerable narrow windings), and found that it proceeded from some fragments of my matches lying in an empty barrel turned upon its side. I was wondering how they came in such a place, when my hand fell upon two or three pieces of taperwax, which had been evidently mumbled by the dog. I concluded at once that he had devoured the whole of my supply of candles, and I felt hopeless of being ever able to read the note of Augustus. The small remnants of the wax were so smashed up among other rubbish in the barrel, that I despaired of deriving any service from them, and left them as they were. The phosphorus, of which there was only a speck or two, I gathered up as well as I could, and returned with it, after much difficulty, to my box, where Tiger had all the while remained.

What to do next I could not tell. The hold was so intensely dark that I could not see my hand, however close I would hold it to my face. The white slip of paper could barely be discerned, and not even that when I looked at it directly; by turning the exterior portions of the retina toward it—that is to say, by surveying it slightly askance, I found that it became in some measure perceptible. Thus the gloom of my prison may be imagined, and the note of my friend, if indeed it were a note from him, seemed only likely to throw me into further trouble, by disquieting to no purpose my already enfeebled and agitated mind. In vain I revolved in my brain a multitude of absurd expedients for procuring light—such expedients precisely as a man in the perturbed sleep occasioned by opium would be apt to fall upon for a similar purpose—each and all of which appear by turns to the dreamer the most reasonable and the most preposterous of conceptions, just as the reasoning or imaginative faculties flicker, alternately, one above the other. At last an idea occurred to me which seemed rational, and which gave me cause to wonder, very justly, that I had not entertained it before. I placed the slip of paper on the back of a book, and, collecting the fragments of the phosphorus matches which I had brought from the barrel, laid them together upon the paper. I then, with the palm of my hand, rubbed the whole over quickly, yet steadily. A clear light diffused itself immediately throughout the whole surface; and had there been any writing upon it, I should not have experienced the least difficulty, I am sure, in reading it. Not a syllable was there, however—nothing but a dreary and unsatisfactory blank; the illumination died away in a few seconds, and my heart died away within me as it went.

I have before stated more than once that my intellect, for some period prior to this, had been in a condition nearly bordering on idiocy. There were, to be sure, momentary intervals of perfect sanity, and, now and then, even of energy, but these were few. It must be remembered that I had been, for many days certainly, inhaling the almost pestilential atmosphere of a close hole in a whaling vessel, and for a long portion of that time but scantily supplied with water. For the last fourteen or fifteen hours I had none—nor had I slept during that time. Salt provisions of the most exciting kind had been my chief, and, indeed, since the loss of the mutton, my only supply of food, with the exception of the sea-biscuit; and these latter were utterly useless to me, as they were too dry and hard to be swallowed in the swollen and parched condition of my throat. I was now in a high state of fever, and in every respect exceedingly ill. This will account for the fact that many miserable hours of despondency elapsed after my last adventure with the phosphorus, before the thought suggested itself that I had examined only one side of the paper. I shall not attempt to describe my feelings of rage (for I believe I was more angry than anything else) when the egregious oversight I had committed flashed suddenly upon my perception. The blunder itself would have been unimportant, had not my own folly and impetuosity rendered it otherwise—in my disappointment at not finding some words upon the slip, I had childishly torn it in pieces and thrown it away, it was impossible to say where.

From the worst part of this dilemma I was relieved by the sagacity of Tiger. Having got, after a long search, a small piece of the note, I put it to the dog's nose, and endeavoured to make him understand that he must bring me the rest of it. To my astonishment (for I had taught him none of the usual tricks for which his breed are famous), he seemed to enter at once into my meaning, and, rummaging about for a few moments, soon found another considerable portion. Bringing me this, he paused a while, and, rubbing his nose against my hand, appeared to be waiting for my approval of what he had done. I patted him on the head, when he immediately made off again. It was now some minutes before he came back—but when he did come, he brought with him a large slip, which proved to be all the paper missing—it having been torn, it seems, only into three pieces. Luckily, I had no trouble in finding what few fragments of the phosphorus were left—being guided by the indistinct glow one or two of the particles still emitted. My difficulties had taught me the necessity of caution, and I now took time to reflect upon what I was about to do. It was very probable, I considered, that some words were written upon that side of the paper which had not been examined—but which side was that? Fitting the pieces together gave me no clue in this respect, although it assured me that the words (if there were any) would be found all on one side, and connected in a proper manner, as written. There was the greater necessity of ascertaining the point in question beyond a doubt, as the phosphorus remaining would be altogether insufficient for a third attempt, should I fail in the one I was now about to make. I placed the paper on a book as before, and sat for some minutes thoughtfully revolving the matter over in my mind. At last I thought it barely possible that the written side might have some unevenness on its surface, which a delicate sense of feeling might enable me to detect. I determined to make the experiment, and passed my finger very carefully over the side which first presented itself—nothing, however, was perceptible, and I turned the paper, adjusting it on the book. I now again carried my forefinger cautiously along, when I was aware of an exceedingly slight, but still discernible glow, which followed as it proceeded. This, I knew, must arise from some very minute remaining particles of the phosphorus with which I had covered the paper in my previous attempt. The other, or under side, then, was that on which lay the writing, if writing there should finally prove to be. Again I turned the note, and went to work as I had previously done. Having rubbed in the phosphorus, a brilliancy ensued as before—but this time several lines of MS. in a large hand, and apparently in red ink, became distinctly visible. The glimmer, although sufficiently bright, was but momentary. Still, had I not been too greatly excited, there would have been ample time enough for me to peruse the whole three sentences before me—for I saw there were three. In my anxiety, however, to read all at once, I succeeded only in reading the seven concluding words, which thus appeared —*"blood—your life depends upon lying close."*

Had I been able to ascertain the entire contents of the note —the full meaning of the admonition which my friend had thus attempted to convey, that admonition, even although it should have revealed a story of disaster the most unspeakable, could not, I am firmly convinced, have imbued my mind with one tithe of the harrowing and yet indefinable horror with which I was inspired by the fragmentary warning thus received. And *"blood,"* too, that word of all words—so rife at all times with mystery, and suffering, and terror—how trebly full of import did it now appear —how chilly and heavily (disjointed, as it thus was, from any foregoing words to qualify or render it distinct) did its vague syllables fall, amid the deep gloom of my prison, into the innermost recesses of my soul!

Augustus had, undoubtedly, good reasons for wishing me to remain concealed, and I formed a thousand surmises as to what they could be—but I could think of nothing affording a satisfactory solution of the mystery. Just after returning from my last journey to the trap, and before my attention had been otherwise directed by the singular conduct of Tiger, I had come to the resolution of making myself heard at all events by those on board, or, if I could not succeed in this directly, of trying to cut my way through the orlop deck. The half certainty which I felt of being able to accomplish one of these two purposes in the last emergency, had given me courage (which I should not otherwise have had) to endure the evils of my situation. The few words I had been able to read, however, had cut me off from these final resources, and I now, for the first time, felt all the misery of my fate. In a paroxysm of despair I threw myself again upon the mattress, where, for about the period of a day and night, I lay in a kind of stupor, relieved only by momentary intervals of reason and recollection.

At length I once more arose, and busied myself in reflection upon the horrors which encompassed me. For another twenty-four hours it was barely possible that I might exist without water—for a longer time I could not do so. During the first portion of my imprisonment I had made free use of the cordials with which Augustus had supplied me, but they only served to excite fever, without in the least degree assuaging my thirst. I had now only about a gill left, and this was of a species of strong peach liqueur at which my stomach revolted. The sausages were entirely consumed; of the ham nothing remained but a small piece of the skin; and all the biscuit, except a few fragments of one, had been eaten by Tiger. To add to my troubles, I found that my headache was increasing momentarily, and with it the species of delirium which had distressed me more or less since my first falling asleep. For some hours past it had been with the greatest difficulty I could breathe at all, and now each attempt at so doing was attended with the most distressing spasmodic action of the chest. But there was still another and very different source of disquietude, and one, indeed, whose harassing terrors had been the chief means of arousing me to exertion from my stupor on the mattress. It arose from the demeanour of the dog.

I first observed an alteration in his conduct while rubbing in the phosphorus on the paper in my last attempt. As I rubbed, he ran his nose against my hand with a slight snarl; but I was too greatly excited at the time to pay much attention to the circumstance. Soon afterward, it will be remembered, I threw myself on the mattress, and fell into a species of lethargy. Presently I became aware of a singular hissing sound close at my ears, and discovered it to proceed from Tiger, who was panting and wheezing in a state of the greatest apparent excitement, his eyeballs flashing fiercely through the gloom. I spoke to him, when he replied with a low growl, and then remained quiet. Presently I relapsed into my stupor, from which I was again awakened in a similar manner. This was repeated three or four times, until finally his behaviour inspired me with so great a degree of fear, that I became fully aroused. He was now lying close by the door of the box, snarling fearfully, although in a kind of undertone, and grinding his teeth as if strongly convulsed. I had no doubt whatever that the want of water or the confined atmosphere of the hold had driven him mad, and I was at a loss what course to pursue. I could not endure the thought of killing him, yet it seemed absolutely necessary for my own safety. I could distinctly perceive his eyes fastened upon me with an expression of the most deadly animosity, and I expected every instant that he would attack me. At last I could endure my terrible situation no longer, and determined to make my way from the box at all hazards, and dispatch him, if his opposition should render it necessary for me to do so. To get out, I had to pass directly over his body, and he already seemed to anticipate my design—raising himself upon his fore-legs (as I perceived by the altered position of his eyes), and displayed the whole of his white fangs, which were easily discernible. I took the remains of the ham-skin, and the bottle containing the liqueur, and secured them about my person, together with a large carving knife which Augustus had left me—then, folding my cloak around me as closely as possible, I made a movement toward the mouth of the box. No sooner did I do this, than the dog sprang with a loud growl towards my throat. The whole weight of his body struck me on the right shoulder, and I fell violently to the left, while the enraged animal passed entirely over me. I had fallen upon my knees, with my head buried among the blankets, and these protected me from a second furious assault, during which I felt the sharp teeth pressing vigorously upon the woollen which enveloped my neck—yet, luckily, without being able to penetrate all the folds. I was now beneath the dog, and a few moments would place me completely in his power. Despair gave me strength, and I rose boldly up, shaking him from me by main force, and dragging with me the blankets from the mattress. These I now threw over him, and before he could extricate himself, I had got through the door and closed it effectually against his pursuit. In this struggle, however, I had been forced to drop the morsel of ham-skin, and I now found my whole stock of provisions reduced to a single gill of liqueur. As this reflection crossed my mind, I felt myself actuated by one of those fits of perverseness which might be supposed to influence a spoiled child in similar circumstances, and, raising the bottle to my lips, I drained it to the last drop, and dashed it furiously upon the floor.

Scarcely had the echo of the crash died away, when I heard my name pronounced in an eager but subdued voice, issuing from the direction of the steerage. So unexpected was anything of the kind, and so intense was the emotion excited within me by the sound, that I endeavoured in vain to reply. My powers of speech totally failed, and, in an agony of terror lest my friend should conclude me dead, and return without attempting to reach me, I stood up between the crates near the door of the box. trembling convulsively, and gasping and struggling for utterance. Had a thousand words depended upon a syllable, I could not have spoken it. There was a slight movement now audible among the lumber somewhere forward of my station. The sound presently grew less distinct, then again less so, and still less. Shall I ever forget my feelings at this moment? He was going—my friend—my companion, from whom I had a right to expect so much—he was going—he would abandon me—he was gone! He would leave me to perish miserably, to expire in the most horrible and loathsome of dungeons—and one word, one little syllable would save me—yet that single syllable I could not utter! I felt, I am sure, more than ten thousand times the agonies of death itself. My brain reeled, and I fell, deadly sick, against the end of the box.

As I fell, the carving-knife was shaken out from the waistband of my pantaloons, and dropped with a rattling sound to the floor. Never did any strain of the richest melody come so sweetly to my ears! With the intensest anxiety I listened to ascertain the effect of the noise upon Augustus—for I knew that the person who called my name could be no one but himself. All was silent for some moments. At length I again heard the word *"Arthur!"* repeated in a low tone, and one full of hesitation. Reviving hope loosened at once my powers of speech, and I now screamed—at the top of my voice, *"Augustus! oh, Augustus!"* "Hush—for God's sake be silent!" he replied, in a voice trembling with agitation; "I will be with you immediately—as soon as I can make my way through the hold." For a long time I heard him moving among the lumber, and every moment seemed to me an age. At length I felt his hand upon my shoulder, and he placed at the same moment a bottle of water to my lips. Those only who have been suddenly redeemed from the jaws of the tomb, or who have known the insufferable torments of thirst under circumstances as aggravated as those which encompassed me in my dreary prison, can form any idea of the unutterable transports which that one long draught of the richest of all physical luxuries afforded.

When I had in some degree satisfied my thirst, Augustus produced from his pocket three or four cold boiled potatoes, which I devoured with the greatest avidity. He had brought with him a light in a dark lantern, and the grateful rays afforded me scarcely less comfort than the food and drink. But I was impatient to learn the cause of his protracted absence, and he proceeded to recount what had happened on board during my incarceration.

CHAPTER IV

THE brig put to sea, as I had supposed, in about an hour after he had left the watch. This was on the twentieth of June. It will be remembered that I had then been in the hold for three days; and, during this period, there was so constant a bustle on board, and so much running to and fro, especially in the cabin and staterooms, that he had had no chance of visiting me without the risk of having the secret of the trap discovered. When at length he did come, I had assured him that I was doing as well as possible; and, therefore, for the two next days he felt but little uneasiness on my account—still, however, watching an opportunity of going down. It was not *until the fourth day* that he found one. Several times during this interval he had made up his mind to let his father know of the adventure, and have me come up at once; but we were still within reaching distance of Nantucket, and it was doubtful, from some expressions which had escaped Captain Barnard, whether he would not immediately put back if he discovered me to be on board. Besides, upon thinking the matter over, Augustus, so he told me, could not imagine that I was in immediate want, or that I would hesitate, in such case, to make myself heard at the trap. When, therefore he considered everything, he concluded to let me stay until he could meet with an opportunity of visiting me unobserved. This, as I said before, did not occur until the fourth day after his bringing me the watch, and the seventh since I had first entered the hold. He then went down without taking with him any water or provisions, intending in the first place merely to call my attention, and get me to come from the box to the trap—when he would go up to the state-room and thence hand me down a supply. When he descended for this purpose he found that I was asleep, for it seems that I was snoring very loudly. From all the calculations I can make on the subject, this must have been the slumber into which I fell just after my return from the trap with the watch, and which, consequently, must have lasted *for more than three entire days and nights* at the very least. Latterly, I have had reason, both from my own experience and the assurance of others, to be acquainted with the strong soporific effects of the stench arising from old fish-oil when closely confined; and when I think of the condition of the hold in which I was imprisoned, and the long period during which the brig had been used as a whaling vessel, I am more inclined to wonder that I awoke at all, after once falling asleep, than that I should have slept uninterruptedly for the period specified above.

Augustus called to me at first in a low voice and without closing the trap—but I made him no reply. He then shut the trap, and spoke to me in a louder, and finally in a very loud tone—still I continued to snore. He was now at a loss what to do. It would take him some time to make his way through the lumber to my box, and in the mean while his absence would be noticed by Captain Barnard, who had occasion for his services every minute, in arranging and copying papers connected with the business of the voyage. He determined, therefore, upon reflection, to ascend, and await another opportunity of visiting me. He was the more easily induced to this resolve, as my slumber appeared to be of the most tranquil nature, and he could not suppose that I had undergone any inconvenience from my incarceration. He had just made up his mind on these points when his attention was arrested by an unusual bustle, the sound of which proceeded apparently from the cabin. He sprang through the trap as quickly as possible, closed it, and threw open the door of his state-room. No sooner had he put his foot over the threshold than a pistol flashed in his face, and he was knocked down, at the same moment, by a blow from a handspike.

A strong hand held him on the cabin floor, with a tight grasp upon his throat—still he was able to see what was going on around him. His father was tied hand and foot, and lying along the steps of the companion-way with his head down, and a deep wound in the forehead, from which the blood was flowing in a continued stream. He spoke not a word, and was apparently dying. Over him stood the first mate, eyeing him with an expression of fiendish derision, and deliberately searching his pockets, from which he presently drew forth a large wallet and a chronometer. Seven of the crew (among whom was the cook, a negro) were rummaging the state-rooms on the larboard for arms, where they soon equipped themselves with muskets and ammunition. Besides Augustus and Captain Barnard, there were nine men altogether in the cabin, and these among the most ruffianly of the brig's company. The villains now went upon deck, taking my friend with them, after having secured his arms behind his back. They proceeded straight to the forecastle, which was fastened down—two of the mutineers standing by it with axes—two also at the main hatch. The mate called out in a loud voice: "Do you hear there below? tumble up with you—one by one—now, mark that—and no grumbling!" It was some minutes before anyone appeared: —at last an Englishman, who had shipped as a raw hand, came up, weeping piteously, and entreating the mate, in the most humble manner, to spare his life. The only reply was a blow on the forehead from an axe. The poor fellow fell to the deck, without a groan, and the black cook lifted him up in his arms as he would a child, and tossed him deliberately into the sea. Hearing the blow and the plunge of the body, the men below could now be induced to venture on deck neither by threats nor promises, until a proposition was made to smoke them out. A general rush then ensued, and for a moment it seemed possible that the brig might be retaken. The mutineers, however, succeeded at last in closing the forecastle effectually before more than six of their opponents could get up. These six, finding themselves so greatly outnumbered and without arms, submitted after a brief struggle. The mate gave them fair words—no doubt with a view of inducing those below to yield, for they had no difficulty in hearing all that was said on deck. The result proved his sagacity, no less than his diabolical villainy. All in the forecastle presently signified their intention of submitting, and, ascending one by one, were pinioned and then thrown on their backs, together with the first six—there being, in all of the crew who were not concerned in the mutiny, twenty-seven.

A scene of the most horrible butchery ensued. The bound seamen were dragged to the gangway. Here the cook stood with an axe, striking each victim on the head as he was forced over the side of the vessel by the other mutineers. In this manner twenty-two perished, and Augustus had given himself up for lost, expecting every moment his own turn to come next. But it seemed that the villains were now either weary, or in some measure disgusted with their bloody labour; for the four remaining prisoners, together with my friend, who had been thrown on the deck with the rest, were respited while the mate sent below for rum, and the whole murderous party held a drunken carouse, which lasted until sunset. They now fell to disputing in regard to the fate of the survivors, who lay not more than four paces off, and could distinguish every word said. Upon some of the mutineers the liquor appeared to have a softening effect, for several voices were heard in favor of releasing the captives altogether, on condition of joining the mutiny and sharing the profits. The black cook, however, (who in all respects was a perfect demon, and who seemed to exert as much influence, if not more, than the mate himself), would listen to no proposition of the kind, and rose repeatedly for the purpose of resuming his work at the gangway. Fortunately he was so far overcome by intoxication as to be easily restrained by the less blood-thirsty of the party, among whom was a line-manager, who went by the name of Dirk Peters. This man was the son of an Indian woman of the tribe of Upsarokas, who live among the fastnesses of the Black Hills near the source of the Missouri. His father was a fur-trader, I believe, or at least connected in some manner with the Indian trading-posts on Lewis river. Peters himself was one of the most ferocious-looking men I ever beheld. He was short in stature, not more than four feet eight inches high—but his limbs were of Herculean mould. His hands, especially, were so enormously thick and broad as hardly to retain a human shape. His arms, as well as legs, were *bowed* in the most singular manner, and appeared to possess no flexibility whatever. His head was equally deformed, being of immense size, with an indentation on the crown (like that on the head of most negroes), and entirely bald. To conceal this latter deficiency, which did not proceed from old age, he usually wore a wig formed of any hair-like material which presented itself—occasionally the skin of a Spanish dog or American grizzly bear. At the time spoken of he had on a portion of one of these bear-skins; and it added no little to the natural ferocity of his countenance, which betook of the Upsaroka character. The mouth extended nearly from ear to ear; the lips were thin, and seemed, like some other portions of his frame, to be devoid of natural pliancy, so that the ruling expression never varied under the influence of any emotion whatever. This ruling expression may be conceived when it is considered that the teeth were exceedingly long and protruding, and never even partially covered, in any instance, by the lips. To pass this man with a casual glance, one might imagine him to be convulsed with laughter; but a second look would induce a shuddering acknowledgment, that if such an expression were indicative of merriment, the merriment must be that of a demon. Of this singular being many anecdotes were prevalent among the seafaring men of Nantucket. These anecdotes went to prove his prodigious strength when under excitement, and some of them had given rise to a doubt of his sanity. But on board the Grampus, it seems, he was regarded at the time of the mutiny, with feelings more of derision than of any thing else. I have been thus particular in speaking of

Dirk Peters, because, ferocious as he appeared, he proved the main instrument in preserving the life of Augustus, and because I shall have frequent occasion to mention him hereafter in the course of my narrative—a narrative, let me here say, which, in its later portions, will be found to include incidents of a nature so entirely out of the range of human experience, and for this reason so far beyond the limits of human credulity, that I proceed in utter hopelessness of obtaining credence for all that I shall tell, yet confidently trusting in time and progressing science to verify some of the most important and most improbable of my statements.

After much indecision and two or three violent quarrels, it was determined at last that all the prisoners (with the exception of Augustus, whom Peters insisted in a jocular manner upon keeping as his clerk) should be set adrift in one of the smallest whaleboats. The mate went down into the cabin to see if Captain Barnard was still living—for, it will be remembered, he was left below when the mutineers came up. Presently the two made their appearance, the captain pale as death, but somewhat recovered from the effects of his wound. He spoke to the men in a voice hardly articulate, entreated them not to set him adrift, but to return to their duty, and promising to land them wherever they chose, and to take no steps for bringing them to justice. He might as well have spoken to the winds. Two of the ruffians seized him by the arms and hurled him over the brig's side into the boat, which had been lowered while the mate went below. The four men who were lying on the deck were then untied and ordered to follow, which they did without attempting any resistance—Augustus being still left in his painful position, although he struggled and prayed only for the poor satisfaction of being permitted to bid his father farewell. A handful of sea-biscuits and a jug of water were now handed down; but neither mast, sail, oar, nor compass. The boat was towed astern for a few minutes, during which the mutineers held another consultation—it was then finally cut adrift. By this time night had come on—there were neither moon nor stars visible—and a short and ugly sea was running, although there was no great deal of wind. The boat was instantly out of sight, and little hope could be entertained for the unfortunate sufferers who were in it. This event happened, however, in latitude 35° 30′ north, longitude 61° 20′ west, and consequently at no very great distance from the Bermuda Islands. Augustus therefore endeavoured to console himself with the idea that the boat might either succeed in reaching the land, or come sufficiently near to be fallen in with by vessels off the coast.

All sail was now put upon the brig, and she continued her original course to the southwest—the mutineers being bent upon some piratical expedition, in which, from all that could be understood, a ship was to be intercepted on her way from the Cape Verd Islands to Porto Rico. No attention was paid to Augustus, who was untied and suffered to go about anywhere forward of the cabin companion-way. Dirk Peters treated him with some degree of kindness, and on one occasion saved him from the brutality of the cook. His situation was still one of the most precarious, as the men were continually intoxicated, and there was no relying upon their continued good-humour or carelessness in regard to himself. His anxiety on my account he represented, however, as the most distressing result of his condition; and, indeed, I had never reason to doubt the sincerity of his friendship. More than once he had resolved to acquaint the mutineers with the secret of my being on board, but was restrained from so doing, partly through recollection of the atrocities he had already beheld, and partly through a hope of being able soon to bring me relief. For the latter purpose he was constantly on the watch; but, in spite of the most constant vigilance, three days elapsed after the boat was cut adrift before any chance occurred. At length, on the night of the third day, there came on a heavy blow from the eastward, and all hands were called up to take in sail. During the confusion which ensued, he made his way below unobserved, and into the state-room. What was his grief and horror in discovering that the latter had been rendered a place of deposit for a variety of sea-stores and ship furniture, and that several fathoms of old chain-cable, which had been stowed away beneath the companion-ladder, had been dragged thence to make room for a chest, and were now lying immediately upon the trap! To remove it without discovery was impossible, and he returned on deck as quickly as he could. As he came up the mate seized him by the throat, and demanding what he had been doing in the cabin, was about flinging him over the larboard bulwark, when his life was again preserved through the interference of Dirk Peters. Augustus was now put in handcuffs (of which there were several pairs on board), and his feet lashed tightly together. He was then taken into the steerage, and thrown into a lower berth next to the forecastle bulkheads, with the assurance that he should never put his foot on deck again "until the brig was no longer a brig." This was the expression of the cook, who threw him into the berth—it is hardly possible to say what precise meaning was intended by the phrase. The whole affair, however, proved the ultimate means of my relief, as will presently appear.

CHAPTER V

FOR some minutes after the cook had left the forecastle, Augustus abandoned himself to despair, never hoping to leave the berth alive. He now came to the resolution of acquainting the first of the men who should come down with my situation, thinking it better to let me take my chance with the mutineers than perish of thirst in the hold—for it had been ten days since I was first imprisoned, and my jug of water was not a plentiful supply even for four. As he was thinking on this subject, the idea came all at once into his head that it might be possible to communicate with me by way of the main hold. In any other circumstances, the difficulty and hazard of the undertaking would have prevented him from attempting it; but now he had, at all events, little prospect of life, and consequently little to lose—he bent his whole mind, therefore, upon the task.

His handcuffs were the first consideration. At first he saw no method of removing them, and feared that he should thus be baffled in the very outset; but, upon a closer scrutiny, he discovered that the irons could be slipped off and on at pleasure, with very little effort or inconvenience, merely by squeezing his hands through them,—this species of manacle being altogether ineffectual in confining young persons, in whom the smaller bones readily yield to pressure. He now untied his feet, and, leaving the cord in such a manner that it could easily be readjusted in the event of any person's coming down, proceeded to examine the bulkhead where it joined the berth. The partition here was of soft pine board, an inch thick, and he saw that he should have little trouble in cutting his way through. A voice was now heard at the forecastle companion-way, and he had just time to put his right hand into its handcuff (the left had not been removed), and to draw the rope in a slipknot around his ankle, when Dirk Peters came below, followed by Tiger, who immediately leaped into the berth and lay down. The dog had been brought on board by Augustus, who knew my attachment to the animal, and thought it would give me pleasure to have him with me during the voyage. He went up to our house for him immediately after first taking me into the hold, but did not think of mentioning the circumstance upon his bringing the watch. Since the mutiny, Augustus had not seen him before his appearance with Dirk Peters, and had given him up for lost, supposing him to have been thrown overboard by some of the malignant villains belonging to the mate's gang. It appeared afterward that he had crawled into a hole beneath a whale-boat, from which, not having room to turn round, he could not extricate himself. Peters at last let him out, and with a species of good feeling which my friend knew well how to appreciate, had now brought him to him in the forecastle as a companion, leaving at the same time some salt junk and potatoes, with a can of water: he then went on deck, promising to come down with something more to eat on the next day.

When he had gone, Augustus freed both hands from the manacles and unfastened his feet. He then turned down the head of the mattress on which he had been lying, and with his penknife (for the ruffians had not thought it worth while to search him) commenced cutting vigorously across one of the partition planks, as closely as possible to the floor of the berth. He chose to cut here, because, if suddenly interrupted, he would be able to conceal what had been done by letting the head of the mattress fall into its proper position. For the remainder of the day, however, no disturbance occurred, and by night he had completely divided the plank. It should here be observed that none of the crew occupied the forecastle as a sleeping-place, living altogether in the cabin since the mutiny, drinking the wines, and feasting on the sea-stores of Captain Barnard, and giving no more heed than was absolutely necessary to the navigation of the brig. These circumstances proved fortunate both for myself and Augustus; for, had matters been otherwise, he would have found it impossible to reach me. As it was, he proceeded with confidence in his design. It was near daybreak, however, before he completed the second division of the board (which was about a foot above the first cut), thus making an aperture quite large enough to admit his passage through with facility to the main orlop deck. Having got here, he made his way with but little trouble to the lower main hatch, although in so doing he had to scramble over tiers of oil-casks piled nearly as high as the upper deck, there being barely room enough left for his body. Upon reaching the hatch he found that Tiger had followed him below, squeezing between two rows of the casks. It was now too late, however, to attempt getting to me before dawn, as the chief difficulty lay in passing through the close stowage in the lower hold. He therefore resolved to return, and wait till the next night. With this design, he proceeded to loosen the hatch, so that he might have as little detention as possible when he should come again. No sooner had he loosened it than Tiger sprang eagerly to the small opening produced, snuffed for a moment, and then uttered a long whine, scratching at the same time, as if anxious to remove the covering with his paws. There could be no doubt, from his behaviour, that he was aware of my being in the hold, and Augustus thought it possible that he would be able to get to me if he put him down. He now hit upon the expedient of sending the note, as it was especially desirable that I should make no attempt at forcing my way out, at least under existing circumstances, and there could be no certainty of his getting to me himself on the morrow as he intended. After events proved how fortunate it was that the idea occurred to him as it did: for, had it not been for the receipt of the note, I should undoubtedly have fallen upon some plan, however desperate, of alarming the crew, and both our lives would most probably have been sacrificed in consequence.

Having concluded to write, the difficulty was now to procure the materials for so doing. An old toothpick was soon made into a pen; and this by means of feeling altogether, for the between-decks were as dark as pitch. Paper enough was obtained from the back of a letter—a duplicate of the forged letter from Mr. Ross. This had been the original draught; but the handwriting not being sufficiently well imitated, Augustus had written another, thrusting the first, by good fortune, into his coat-pocket, where it was now most opportunely discovered. Ink alone was thus wanting, and a substitute was immediately found for this by means of a slight incision with the penknife on the back of a finger just above the nail—a copious flow of blood ensuing, as usual, from wounds in that vicinity. The note was now written, as well as it could be in the dark and under the circumstances. It briefly explained that a mutiny had taken place; that Captain Barnard was set adrift; and that I might expect immediate relief as far as provisions were concerned, but must not venture upon making any disturbance. It concluded with these words: *"I have scrawled this with blood—your life depends upon lying close."*

This slip of paper being tied upon the dog, he was now put

down the hatchway, and Augustus made the best of his way back to the forecastle, where he found no reason to believe that any of the crew had been in his absence. To conceal the hole in the partition, he drove his knife in just above it, and hung up a pea-jacket which he found in the berth. His handcuffs were then replaced, and also the rope around his ankles.

These arrangements were scarcely completed when Dirk Peters came below, very drunk, but in excellent humour, and bringing with him my friend's allowance of provision for the day. This consisted of a dozen large Irish potatoes roasted, and a pitcher of water. He sat for some time on a chest by the berth, and talked freely about the mate, and the general concerns of the brig. His demeanour was exceedingly capricious, and even grotesque. At one time Augustus was much alarmed by his odd conduct. At last, however, he went on deck, muttering a promise to bring his prisoner a good dinner on the morrow. During the day two of the crew (harpooners) came down, accompanied by the cook, all three in nearly the last stage of intoxication. Like Peters, they made no scruple of talking unreservedly about their plans. It appeared that they were much divided among themselves as to their ultimate course, agreeing in no point except the attack on the ship from the Cape Verd Islands, with which they were in hourly expectation of meeting. As far as could be ascertained, the mutiny had not been brought about altogether for the sake of booty; a private pique of the chief mate's against Captain Barnard having been the main instigation. There now seemed to be two principal factions among the crew—one headed by the mate, the other by the cook. The former party were for seizing the first suitable vessel which should present itself, and equipping it at some of the West India Islands for a piratical cruise. The latter division, however, which was the stronger, and included Dirk Peters among its partisans, was bent upon pursuing the course originally laid out for the brig into the South Pacific; there either to take whale, or act otherwise, as circumstances should suggest. The representations of Peters, who had frequently visited these regions, had great weight, apparently, with the mutineers, wavering, as they were, between half-engendered notions of profit and pleasure. He dwelt on the world of novelty and amusement to be found among the innumerable islands of the Pacific, on the perfect security and freedom from all restraint to be enjoyed, but, more particularly, on the deliciousness of the climate, on the abundant means of good living, and on the voluptuous beauty of the women. As yet, nothing had been absolutely determined upon; but the pictures of the hybrid line-manager were taking strong hold upon the ardent imaginations of the seamen, and there was every probability that his intentions would be finally carried into effect.

The three men went away in about an hour, and no one else entered the forecastle all day. Augustus lay quiet until nearly night. He then freed himself from the rope and irons, and prepared for his attempt. A bottle was found in one of the berths, and this he filled with water from the pitcher left by Peters, storing his pockets at the same time with cold potatoes. To his great joy he also came across a lantern, with a small piece of tallow candle in it. This he could light at any moment, as he had in his possession a box of phosphorus matches. When it was quite dark, he got through the hole in the bulkhead, having taken the precaution to arrange the bedclothes in the berth so as to convey the idea of a person covered up. When through, he hung up the pea-jacket on his knife, as before, to conceal the aperture—this manœuvre being easily effected, as he did not readjust the piece of plank taken out until afterward. He was now on the main orlop deck, and proceeded to make his way, as before, between the upper deck and the oil-casks to the main hatchway. Having reached this, he lit the piece of candle, and descended, groping with extreme difficulty among the compact stowage of the hold. In a few moments he became alarmed at the insufferable stench and the closeness of the atmosphere. He could not think it possible that I had survived my confinement for so long a period breathing so oppressive an air. He called my name repeatedly, but I made him no reply, and his apprehensions seemed thus to be confirmed. The brig was rolling violently, and there was so much noise in consequence, that it was useless to listen for any weak sound, such as those of my breathing or snoring. He threw open the lantern, and held it as high as possible, whenever an opportunity occurred, in order that, by observing the light, I might, if alive, be aware that succour was approaching. Still nothing was heard from me, and the supposition of my death began to assume the character of certainty. He determined, nevertheless, to force a passage, if possible, to the box, and at least ascertain beyond a doubt the truth of his surmises. He pushed on for some time in a most pitiable state of anxiety, until, at length, he found the pathway utterly blocked up, and that there was no possibility of making any farther way by the course in which he had set out. Overcome now by his feelings, he threw himself among the lumber in despair, and wept like a child. It was at this period that he heard the crash occasioned by the bottle which I had thrown down. Fortunate, indeed, was it that the incident occurred—for, upon this incident, trivial as it appears, the thread of my destiny depended. Many years elapsed, however, before I was aware of this fact. A natural shame and regret for his weakness and indecision prevented Augustus from confiding to me at once what a more intimate and unreserved communion afterward induced him to reveal. Upon finding his further progress in the hold impeded by obstacles which he could not overcome, he had resolved to abandon his attempt at reaching me, and return at once to the forecastle. Before condemning him entirely on this head, the harassing circumstances which embarrassed him should be taken into consideration. The night was fast wearing away, and his absence from the forecastle might be discovered; and, indeed, would necessarily be so, if he should fail to get back to the berth by daybreak. His candle was expiring in the socket, and there would be the greatest difficulty in retracing his way to the hatchway in the dark. It must be allowed, too, that he had every good reason to believe me dead; in which event no benefit could result to me from his reaching the box, and a world of danger would be encountered to no purpose by himself. He had repeatedly called, and I had made him no answer. I had been now eleven days and nights with no more water than that contained in the jug which he had left with me—a supply which it was not at all probable I had hoarded in the beginning of my confinement, as I had every cause to expect a speedy release. The atmosphere of the hold, too, must have appeared to him, coming from the comparatively open air of the steerage, of a nature absolutely poisonous, and by far more intolerable than it had seemed to me upon my first taking up my quarters in the box—the hatchways at that time having been constantly open for many months previous. Add to these considerations that of the scene of bloodshed and terror so lately witnessed by my friend; his confinement, privations, and narrow escapes from death; together with the frail and equivocal tenure by which he still existed—circumstances all so well calculated to prostrate every energy of mind—and the reader will be easily brought, as I have been, to regard his apparent falling off in friendship and in faith with sentiments rather of sorrow than of anger.

The crash of the bottle was distinctly heard, yet Augustus was not sure that it proceeded from the hold. The doubt, however, was sufficient inducement to persevere. He clambered up nearly to the orlop deck by means of the stowage, and then, watching for a lull in the pitchings of the vessel, he called out to me in as loud a tone as he could command—regardless, for the moment, of being overheard by the crew. It will be remembered that on this occasion the voice reached me, but I was so entirely overcome by violent agitation as to be incapable of reply. Confident, now, that his worst apprehensions were well founded, he descended, with a view of getting back to the forecastle without loss of time. In his haste some small boxes were thrown down, the noise occasioned by which I heard, as will be recollected. He had made considerable progress on his return when the fall of the knife again caused him to hesitate. He retraced his steps immediately, and, clambering up the stowage a second time, called out my name, loudly as before, having watched for a lull. This time I found voice to answer. Overjoyed at discovering me to be still alive, he now resolved to brave every difficulty and danger in reaching me. Having extricated himself as quickly as possible from the labyrinth of lumber by which he was hemmed in, he at length struck into an opening which promised better, and finally, after a series of struggles, arrived at the box in a state of utter exhaustion.

CHAPTER VI

THE leading particulars of this narration were all that Augustus communicated to me while we remained near the box. It was not until afterward that he entered fully into all the details. He was apprehensive of being missed, and I was wild with impatience to leave my detested place of confinement. We resolved to make our way at once to the hole in the bulkhead, near which I was to remain for the present, while he went through to reconnoitre. To leave Tiger in the box was what neither of us could endure to think of; yet, how to act otherwise was the question. He now seemed to be perfectly quiet, and we could not even distinguish the sound of his breathing upon applying our ears closely to the box. I was convinced that he was dead, and determined to open the door. We found him lying at full length, apparently in a deep stupor, yet still alive. No time was to be lost, yet I could not bring myself to abandon an animal who had now been twice instrumental in saving my life, without some attempt at preserving him. We therefore dragged him along with us as well as we could, although with the greatest difficulty and fatigue; Augustus, during part of the time, being forced to clamber over the impediments in our way with the huge dog in his arms—a feat to which the feebleness of my frame rendered me totally inadequate. At length we succeeded in reaching the hole, when Augustus got through, and Tiger was pushed in afterward. All was found to be safe, and we did not fail to return sincere thanks to God for our deliverance from the imminent danger we had escaped. For the present, it was agreed that I should remain near the opening, through which my companion could readily supply me with a part of his daily provision, and where I could have the advantages of breathing an atmosphere comparatively pure.

In explanation of some portions of this narrative, wherein I have spoken of the stowage of the brig, and which may appear ambiguous to some of my readers who may have seen a proper or regular stowage, I must here state that the manner in which this most important duty had been performed on board the Grampus was a most shameful piece of neglect on the part of Captain Barnard, who was by no means as careful or as experienced a seaman as the hazardous nature of the service on which he was employed would seem necessarily to demand. A proper stowage cannot be accomplished in a careless manner, and many most disastrous accidents, even within the limits of my own experience, have arisen from neglect or ignorance in this particular. Coasting vessels, in the frequent hurry and bustle attendant upon taking in or discharging cargo, are the most liable to mishap from the want of a proper attention to stowage. The great point is to allow no possibility of the cargo or ballast's shifting position even in the most violent rollings of the vessel. With this end, great attention must be paid, not only to the bulk taken in, but to the nature of the bulk, and whether there be a full or only a partial cargo. In most kinds of freight the stowage is accomplished by means of a screw. Thus, in a load of tobacco or flour, the whole is screwed so tightly into the hold of the vessel that the barrels or hogsheads, upon discharging, are found to be completely flattened, and take some time to regain their original shape. This screwing, however, is resorted to principally with a view of obtaining more room in the hold; for in a *full* load of any such commodities as flour or tobacco, there can be no danger of any shifting whatever, at least none from which inconvenience can result. There have been instances, indeed, where this method of screwing has resulted in the most lamentable consequences, arising from a cause altogether distinct from the danger attendant upon a shifting of cargo. A load of cotton, for example, tightly screwed while in certain conditions, has been known, through the expansion of its bulk, to rend a vessel asunder at sea. There can be no doubt, either, that the same result would ensue in the case of tobacco, while undergoing its usual course of fermentation, were it not for the interstices consequent upon the rotundity of the hogsheads.

It is when a partial cargo is received that danger is chiefly to be apprehended from shifting, and that precaution should be always taken to guard against such misfortune. Only those who have encountered a violent gale of wind, or, rather, who have experienced the rolling of a vessel in a sudden calm after the gale, can form an idea of the tremendous force of the plunges, and of the consequent terrible impetus given to all loose articles in the vessel. It is then that the necessity of a cautious stowage, when there is a partial cargo, becomes obvious. When lying to (especially with a small head sail), a vessel which is not properly modelled in the bows is frequently thrown upon her beam-ends; this occurring even every fifteen or twenty minutes upon an average, yet without any serious consequences resulting, *provided there be a proper stowage.* If this, however, has not been strictly attended to, in the first of these heavy lurches the whole of the cargo tumbles over to the side of the vessel which lies upon the water, and, being thus prevented from regaining her equilibrium, as she would otherwise necessarily do, she is certain to fill in a few seconds and go down. It is not too much to say that at least one-half of the instances in which vessels have foundered in heavy gales at sea may be attributed to a shifting of cargo or of ballast.

When a partial cargo of any kind is taken on board, the whole, after being first stowed as compactly as may be, should be covered with a layer of stout shifting-boards, extending completely across the vessel. Upon these boards strong temporary stanchions should be erected, reaching to the timbers above, and thus securing everything in its place. In cargoes consisting of grain, or any similar matter, additional precautions are requisite. A hold filled entirely with grain upon leaving port will be found not more than three fourths full upon reaching its destination—this, too, although the freight, when measured bushel by bushel by the consignee, will overrun by a vast deal (on account of the swelling of the grain) the quantity consigned. This result is occasioned by *settling* during the voyage, and is the more perceptible in proportion to the roughness of the weather experienced. If grain loosely thrown in a vessel, then, is ever so well secured by shifting-boards and stanchions, it will be liable to shift in a long passage so greatly as to bring about the most distressing calamities. To prevent these, every method should be employed before leaving port to *settle* the cargo as much as possible; and for this there are many contrivances, among which may be mentioned the driving of wedges into the grain. Even after all this is done, and unusual pains taken to secure the shifting boards, no seaman who knows what he is about will feel altogether secure in a gale of any violence with a cargo of grain on board, and, least of all, with a partial cargo. Yet there are hundreds of our coasting vessels, and, it is likely, many more from the ports of Europe, which sail daily with partial cargoes, even of the most dangerous species, and without any precautions whatever. The wonder is that no more accidents occur than do actually happen. A lamentable instance of this heedlessness occurred to my knowledge in the case of Captain Joel Rice of the schooner Firefly, which sailed from Richmond, Virgina, to Madeira, with a cargo of corn, in the year 1825. The captain had gone many voyages without serious accident, although he was in the habit of paying no attention whatever to his stowage, more than to secure it in the ordinary manner. He had never before sailed with a cargo of grain, and on this occasion had the corn thrown on board loosely, when it did not much more than half fill the vessel. For the first portion of the voyage he met with nothing more than light breezes; but when within a day's sail of Madeira there came on a strong gale from the N. N. E. which forced him to lie to. He brought the schooner to the wind under a double-reefed foresail alone, when she rode as well as any vessel could be expected to do, and shipped not a drop of water. Towards night the gale somewhat abated, and she rolled with more unsteadiness than before, but still did very well, until a heavy lurch threw her upon her beam-ends to starboard. The corn was then heard to shift bodily, the force of the movement bursting open the main hatchway. The vessel went down like a shot. This happened within hail of a small sloop from Madeira, which picked up one of the crew (the only person saved), and which rode out the gale in perfect security, as indeed a jolly-boat might have done under proper management.

The stowage on board the Grampus was most clumsily done, if stowage that could be called which was little better than a promiscuous huddling together of oil-casks* and ship furniture. I have already spoken of the condition of articles in the hold. On the orlop deck there was space enough for my body (as I have stated) between the oil-casks and the upper deck; a space was left open around the main hatchway; and several other large spaces were left in the stowage. Near the hole cut through the bulkhead by Augustus there was room enough for an entire cask, and in this space I found myself comfortably situated for the present.

By the time my friend had got safely into the berth, and readjusted his handcuffs and the rope, it was broad daylight. We had made a narrow escape indeed; for scarcely had he arranged all matters, when the mate came below with Dirk Peters and the cook. They talked for some time about the vessel from the Cape Verds, and seemed to be excessively anxious for her appearance. At length the cook came to the berth in which Augustus was lying, and seated himself in it near the head. I could see and hear everything from my hiding-place, for the piece cut out had not been put back, and I was in momentary expectation that the negro would fall against the pea-jacket, which was hung up to conceal

* Whaling vessels are usually fitted with iron oil-tanks—why the Grampus was not I have never been able to ascertain.

the aperture, in which case all would have been discovered, and our lives would, no doubt, have been instantly sacrificed. Our good fortune prevailed, however; and although he frequently touched it as the vessel rolled, he never pressed against it sufficiently to bring about a discovery. The bottom of the jacket had been carefully fastened to the bulkhead, so that the hole might not be seen by its swinging to one side. All this time Tiger was lying in the foot of the berth, and appeared to have recovered in some measure his faculties, for I could see him occasionally open his eyes and draw a long breath.

After a few minutes the mate and cook went above, leaving Dirk Peters behind, who, as soon as they were gone, came and sat himself down in the place just occupied by the mate. He began to talk very sociably with Augustus, and we could now see that the greater part of his apparent intoxication, while the two others were with him, was a feint. He answered all my companion's questions with perfect freedom; told him that he had no doubt of his father's having been picked up, as there were no less than five sail in sight just before sundown on the day he was cut adrift; and used other language of a consolatory nature, which occasioned me no less surprise than pleasure. Indeed, I began to entertain hopes, that through the instrumentality of Peters we might be finally enabled to regain possession of the brig, and this idea I mentioned to Augustus as soon as I found an opportunity. He thought the matter possible, but urged the necessity of the greatest caution in making the attempt, as the conduct of the hybrid appeared to be instigated by the most arbitrary caprice alone; and, indeed, it was difficult to say if he was at any moment of sound mind. Peters went upon deck in about an hour, and did not return again until noon, when he brought Augustus a plentiful supply of junk beef and pudding. Of this, when we were left alone, I partook heartily, without returning through the hole. No one else came down into the forecastle during the day, and at night I got into Augustus's berth, where I slept soundly and sweetly until nearly daybreak, when he awakened me upon hearing a stir upon deck and I regained my hiding-place as quickly as possible. When the day was fully broke, we found that Tiger had recovered his strength almost entirely, and gave no indications of hydrophobia, drinking a little water that was offered him with great apparent eagerness. During the day he regained all his former vigour and appetite. His strange conduct had been brought on, no doubt, by the deleterious quality of the air of the hold, and had no connection with canine madness. I could not sufficiently rejoice that I had persisted in bringing him with me from the box. This day was the thirtieth of June, and the thirteenth since the Grampus made sail from Nantucket.

On the second of July the mate came below, drunk as usual, and in an excessively good-humour. He came to Augustus's berth, and, giving him a slap on the back, asked him if he thought he could behave himself if he let him loose, and whether he would promise not to be going into the cabin again. To this, of course, my friend answered in the affirmative, when the ruffian set him at liberty, after making him drink from a flask of rum which he drew from his coat-pocket. Both now went on deck, and I did not see Augustus for about three hours. He then came below with the good news that he had obtained permission to go about the brig as he pleased anywhere forward of the mainmast, and that he had been ordered to sleep, as usual, in the forecastle. He brought me, too, a good dinner, and a plentiful supply of water. The brig was still cruising for the vessel from the Cape Verds, and a sail was now in sight, which was thought to be the one in question. As the events of the ensuing eight days were of little importance, and had no direct bearing upon the main incidents of my narrative, I will here throw them into the form of a journal, as I do not wish to omit them altogether.

July 3d. Augustus furnished me with three blankets, with which I contrived a comfortable bed in my hiding-place. No one came below, except my companion, during the day. Tiger took his station in the berth just by the aperture, and slept heavily, as if not yet entirely recovered from the effects of his sickness. Towards night a flaw of wind struck the brig before sail could be taken in, and very nearly capsized her. The puff died away immediately, however, and no damage was done beyond the splitting of the foretopsail. Dirk Peters treated Augustus all this day with great kindness, and entered into a long conversation with him respecting the Pacific Ocean, and the islands he had visited in that region. He asked him whether he would not like to go with the mutineers on a kind of exploring and pleasure voyage in those quarters, and said that the men were gradually coming over to the mate's views. To this Augustus thought it best to reply that he would be glad to go on such an adventure, since nothing better could be done, and that anything was preferable to a piratical life.

July 4th. The vessel in sight proved to be a small brig from Liverpool, and was allowed to pass unmolested. Augustus spent most of his time on deck, with a view of obtaining all the information in his power respecting the intentions of the mutineers. They had frequent and violent quarrels among themselves, in one of which a harpooner, Jim Bonner, was thrown overboard. The party of the mate was gaining ground. Jim Bonner belonged to the cook's gang, of which Peters was a partisan.

July 5th. About daybreak there came on a stiff breeze from the west, which at noon freshened into a gale, so that the brig could carry nothing more than her trysail and foresail. In taking in the foretopsail, Simms, one of the common hands, and belonging also to the cook's gang, fell overboard, being very much in liquor, and was drowned—no attempt being made to save him. The whole number of persons on board was now thirteen, to wit: Dirk Peters; Seymour, the black cook; —— Jones; —— Greely; Hartman Rogers, and William Allen, of the cook's party; the mate, whose name I never learned; Absalom Hicks; —— Wilson; John Hunt; and Richard Parker, of the mate's party;—besides Augustus and myself.

July 6th. The gale lasted all this day, blowing in heavy squalls, accompanied with rain. The brig took in a good deal of water through her seams, and one of the pumps was kept continually going, Augustus being forced to take his turn. Just at twilight a large ship passed close by us, without having been discovered until within hail. The ship was supposed to be the one for which the mutineers were on the look-out. The mate hailed her, but the reply was drowned in the roaring of the gale. At eleven, a sea was shipped amid-ships, which tore away a great portion of the larboard bulwarks, and did some other slight damage. Towards morning the weather moderated, and at sunrise there was very little wind.

July 7th. There was a heavy swell running all this day, during which the brig, being light, rolled excessively, and many articles broke loose in the hold, as I could hear distinctly from my hiding-place. I suffered a great deal from sea-sickness. Peters had a long conversation this day with Augustus, and told him that two of his gang, Greely and Allen, had gone over to the mate, and were resolved to turn pirates. He put several questions to Augustus which he did not then exactly understand. During a part of this evening the leak gained upon the vessel; and little could be done to remedy it, as it was occasioned by the brig's straining, and taking in the water through her seams. A sail was thrummed, and got under the bows, which aided us in some measure, so that we began to gain upon the leak.

July 8th. A light breeze sprang up at sunrise from the eastward when the mate headed the brig to the southwest, with the intention of making some of the West India islands, in pursuance of his piratical designs. No opposition was made by Peters or the cook; at least none in the hearing of Augustus. All idea of taking the vessel from the Cape Verds was abandoned. The leak was now easily kept under by one pump going every three quarters of an hour. The sail was drawn from beneath the bows. Spoke two small schooners during the day.

July 9th. Fine weather. All hands employed in repairing bulwarks. Peters had again a long conversation with Augustus, and spoke more plainly than he had done heretofore. He said nothing should induce him to come into the mate's views, and even hinted his intention of taking the brig out of his hands. He asked my friend if he could depend upon his aid in such case, to which Augustus said, "Yes," without hesitation. Peters then said he would sound the others of his party upon the subject, and went away. During the remainder of the day Augustus had no opportunity of speaking with him privately.

CHAPTER VII

JULY 10TH. Spoke a brig from Rio, bound to Norfolk. Weather hazy, with a light baffling wind from the eastward. To-day Hartman Rogers died, having been attacked on the eighth with spasms after drinking a glass of grog. This man was of the cook's party, and one upon whom Peters placed his main reliance. He told Augustus that he believed the mate had poisoned him, and that he expected, if he did not be on the lookout, his own turn would come shortly. There were now only himself, Jones, and the cook belonging to his own gang—on the other side there were five. He had spoken to Jones about taking the command from the mate; but the project having been coolly received, he had been deterred from pressing the matter any further, or from saying anything to the cook. It was well, as it happened, that he was so prudent, for in the afternoon the cook expressed his determination of siding with the mate, and went over formally to that party; while Jones took an opportunity of quarrelling with Peters, and hinted that he would let the mate know of the plan in agitation. There was now, evidently, no time to be lost, and Peters expressed his determination of attempting to take the vessel at all hazards, provided Augustus would lend him his aid. My friend at once assured him of his willingness to enter into any plan for that purpose, and, thinking the opportunity a favourable one, made known the fact of my being on board. At this the hybrid was not more astonished than delighted, as he had no reliance whatever upon Jones, whom he already considered as belonging to the party of the mate. They went below immediately, when Augustus called to me by name, and Peters and myself were soon made acquainted. It was agreed that we should attempt to retake the vessel upon the first good opportunity, leaving Jones altogether out of our councils. In the event of success, we were to run the brig into the first port that offered, and deliver her up. The desertion of his party had frustrated Peters's design of going into the Pacific—an adventure which could not be accomplished without a crew, and he depended upon either getting acquitted upon trial, on the score of insanity (which he solemnly averred had actuated him in lending his aid to the mutiny), or upon obtaining a pardon, if found guilty, through the representations of Augustus and myself. Our deliberations were interrupted for the present by the cry of, "All hands take in sail," and Peters and Augustus ran up on deck.

As usual, the crew were nearly all drunk; and, before sail could be properly taken in, a violent squall laid the brig on her beam-ends. By keeping her away, however, she righted, having shipped a good deal of water. Scarcely was everything secure, when another squall took the vessel, and immediately afterward another—no damage being done. There was every appearance of a gale of wind, which, indeed, shortly came on, with great fury, from the northward and westward. All was made as snug as possible, and we laid to, as usual, under a close-reefed foresail. As night drew on, the wind increased in violence, with a remarkably heavy sea. Peters now came into the forecastle with Augustus, and we resumed our deliberations.

We agreed that no opportunity could be more favourable than the present for carrying our design into effect, as an attempt at such a moment would never be anticipated. As the brig was snugly laid to, there would be no necessity of manœuvring her until good weather, when, if we succeeded in our attempt, we might liberate one, or perhaps two of the men, to aid us in taking her into port. The main difficulty was the great disproportion in our forces. There were only three of us, and in the cabin there were nine. All the arms on board, too, were in their possession, with the exception of a pair of small pistols which Peters had concealed about his person, and the large seaman's knife which he always wore in the waistband of his pantaloons. From certain indications, too—such, for example, as there being no such thing as an axe or a handspike lying in their customary places—we began to fear that the mate had his suspicions, at least in regard to Peters, and that he would let slip no opportunity of getting rid of him. It was clear, indeed, that what we should determine to do could not be done too soon. Still the odds were too much against us to allow of our proceeding without the greatest caution.

Peters proposed that he should go up on deck, and enter into conversation with the watch (Allen), when he would be able to throw him into the sea without trouble, and without making any disturbance, by seizing a good opportunity; that Augustus and myself should then come up, and endeavour to provide ourselves with some kind of weapons from the deck; and that we should then make a rush together, and secure the companion-way before any opposition could be offered. I objected to this, because I could not believe that the mate (who was a cunning fellow in all matters which did not affect his superstitious prejudices) would suffer himself to be so easily entrapped. The very fact of there being a watch on deck at all was sufficient proof that he was upon the alert—it not being usual, except in vessels where discipline is most rigidly enforced, to station a watch on deck when a vessel is lying to in a gale of wind. As I address myself principally, if not altogether, to persons who have never been to sea, it may be as well to state the exact condition of a vessel under such circumstances. Lying to, or, in sea-parlance, "laying to," is a measure resorted to for various purposes, and effected in various manners. In moderate weather it is frequently done with a view of merely bringing the vessel to a standstill, to wait for another vessel, or any similar object. If the vessel which lies to is under full sail, the manœuvre is usually accomplished by throwing round some portion of her sails so as to let the wind take them aback, when she becomes stationary. But we are now speaking of lying to in a gale of wind. This is done when the wind is ahead, and too violent to admit of carrying sail without danger of capsizing; and sometimes even when the wind is fair, but the sea too heavy for the vessel to be put before it. If a vessel be suffered to scud before the wind in a very heavy sea, much damage is usually done her by the shipping of water over her stern, and sometimes by the violent plunges she makes forward. This manœuvre, then, is seldom resorted to in such case, unless through necessity. When the vessel is in a leaky condition, she is often put before the wind even in the heaviest seas; for, when lying to, her seams are sure to be greatly opened by her violent straining, and it is not so much the case when scudding. Often, too, it becomes necessary to scud a vessel, either when the blast is so exceedingly furious as to tear in pieces the sail which is employed with a view of bringing her head to the wind, or when, through the false modelling of the frame or other causes, this main object cannot be effected.

Vessels in a gale of wind are laid to in different manners, according to their peculiar construction. Some lie to best under a foresail, and this, I believe, is the sail most usually employed. Large square-rigged vessels have sails for the express purpose, called storm-staysails. But the jib is occasionally employed by itself—sometimes the jib and foresail, or a double-reefed foresail, and not unfrequently the after-sails, are made use of. Foretopsails are very often found to answer the purpose better than any other species of sail. The Grampus was generally laid to under a close-reefed foresail.

When a vessel is to be laid to, her head is brought up to the wind just so nearly as to fill the sail under which she lies when hauled flat aft, that is, when brought diagonally across the vessel. This being done, the bows point within a few degrees of the direction from which the wind issues, and the windward bow of course receives the shock of the waves. In this situation a good vessel will ride out a very heavy gale of wind without shipping a drop of water, and without any further attention being requisite on the part of the crew. The helm is usually lashed down, but this is altogether unnecessary (except on account of the noise it makes when loose), for the rudder has no effect upon the vessel when lying to. Indeed, the helm had far better be left loose than lashed very fast, for the rudder is apt to be torn off by heavy seas if there be no room for the helm to play. As long as the sail holds, a well-modelled vessel will maintain her situation, and ride every sea, as if instinct with life and reason. If the violence of the wind, however, should tear the sail into pieces (a feat which it requires a perfect hurricane to accomplish under ordinary circumstances), there is then imminent danger. The vessel falls off from the wind, and, coming broadside to the sea, is completely at its mercy: the only resource in this case is to put her quietly before the wind, letting her scud until some other sail can be set. Some vessels will lie to under no sail whatever, but such are not to be trusted at sea.

But to return from this digression. It had never been customary with the mate to have any watch on deck when lying to in a gale of wind, and the fact that he had now one, coupled with the circumstance of the missing axes and handspikes, fully convinced us that the crew were too well on the watch to be taken by surprise in the manner Peters had suggested. Something, however, was to be done, and that with as little delay as practicable, for there could be no doubt that a suspicion having been once entertained against Peters, he would be sacrificed upon the earliest occasion, and one would certainly be either found or made upon the breaking of the gale.

Augustus now suggested that if Peters could contrive to remove, under any pretext, the piece of chain-cable which lay over the trap in the state-room, we might possibly be able to come upon them unawares by means of the hold; but a little reflection convinced us that the vessel rolled and pitched too violently for any attempt of that nature.

By good fortune I at length hit upon the idea of working upon the superstitious terrors and guilty conscience of the mate. It will be remembered that one of the crew, Hartman Rogers, had died during the morning, having been attacked two days before with spasms after drinking some spirits and water. Peters had expressed to us his opinion that this man had been poisoned by the mate, and for this belief he had reasons, so he said, which were incontrovertible, but which he could not be prevailed upon to explain to us—this wayward refusal being only in keeping with other points of his singular character. But whether or not he had any better grounds for suspecting the mate than we had ourselves, we were easily led to fall in with his suspicion, and determined to act accordingly.

Rogers had died about eleven in the forenoon, in violent convulsions; and the corpse presented in a few minutes after death one of the most horrid and loathsome spectacles I ever remember to have seen. The stomach was swollen immensely, like that of a man who has been drowned and lain under water for many weeks. The hands were in the same condition, while the face was shrunken, shrivelled, and of a chalky whiteness, except where relieved by two or three glaring red blotches, like those occasioned by the erysipelas: one of these blotches extended diagonally across the face, completely covering up an eye as if with a band of red velvet. In this disgusting condition the body had been brought up from the cabin at noon to be thrown overboard, when the mate getting a glimpse of it (for he now saw it for the first time), and being either touched with remorse for his crime or struck with terror at so horrible a sight, ordered the men to sew the body up in its hammock, and allow it the usual rites of sea-burial. Having given these directions he went below, as if to avoid any further sight of his victim. While preparations were making to obey his orders, the gale came on with great fury, and the design was abandoned for the present. The corpse, left to itself, was washed into the larboard scuppers, where it still lay at the time of which I speak, floundering about with the furious lurches of the brig.

Having arranged our plan, we set about putting it in execution as speedily as possible. Peters went upon deck, and, as he had anticipated, was immediately accosted by Allen, who appeared to be stationed more as a watch upon the forecastle than for any other purpose. The fate of this villain, however, was speedily and silently decided; for Peters, approaching him in a careless manner, as if about to address him, seized him by the throat, and, before he could utter a single cry, tossed him over the bulwarks. He then called to us, and we came up. Our first precaution was to look about for something with which to arm ourselves, and in doing this we had to proceed with great care, for it was impossible to stand on deck an instant without holding fast, and violent seas broke over the vessel at every plunge forward. It was indispensable, too, that we should be quick in our operations, for every minute we expected the mate to be up to set the pumps going, as it was evident the brig must be taking in water very fast. After searching about for some time, we could find nothing more fit for our purpose than the two pump-handles, one of which Augustus took, and I the other. Having secured these, we stripped off the shirt of the corpse and dropped the body overboard. Peters and myself then went below, leaving Augustus to watch upon deck, where he took his station just where Allen had been placed, and with his back to the cabin companion-way, so that, if any one of the mate's gang should come up, he might suppose it was the watch.

As soon as I got below I commenced disguising myself so as to represent the corpse of Rogers. The shirt which we had taken from the body aided us very much, for it was of singular form and character, and easily recognizable—a kind of smock, which the deceased wore over his other clothing. It was a blue stockinett, with large white stripes running across. Having put this on, I proceeded to equip myself with a false stomach, in imitation of the horrible deformity of the swollen corpse. This was soon effected by means of stuffing with some bedclothes. I then gave the same appearance to my hands by drawing on a pair of white woollen mittens, and filling them in with any kind of rags that offered themselves. Peters then arranged my face, first rubbing it well over with white chalk, and afterward blotching it with blood, which he took from a cut in his finger. The streak across the eye was not forgotten, and presented a most shocking appearance.

CHAPTER VIII

As I viewed myself in a fragment of looking-glass which hung up in the cabin, and by the dim light of a kind of battle-lantern, I was so impressed with a sense of vague awe at my appearance, and at the recollection of the terrific reality which I was thus representing, that I was seized with a violent tremour, and could scarcely summon resolution to go on with my part. It was necessary, however, to act with decision, and Peters and myself went upon deck.

We there found everything safe, and, keeping close to the bulwarks, the three of us crept to the cabin companion-way. It was only partially closed, precautions having been taken to prevent its being suddenly pushed to from without, by means of placing billets of wood on the upper step so as to interfere with the shutting. We found no difficulty in getting a full view of the interior of the cabin through the cracks where the hinges were placed. It now proved to have been very fortunate for us that we had not attempted to take them by surprise, for they were evidently on the alert. Only one was asleep, and he lying just at the foot of the companion-ladder, with a musket by his side. The rest were seated on several mattresses, which had been taken from the berths and thrown on the floor. They were engaged in earnest conversation; and although they had been carousing, as appeared from two empty jugs, with some tin tumblers which lay about, they were not as much intoxicated as usual. All had knives, one or two of them pistols, and a great many muskets were lying in a berth close at hand.

We listened to their conversation for some time before we could make up our minds how to act, having as yet resolved on nothing determinate, except that we would attempt to paralyze their exertions, when we should attack them, by means of the apparition of Rogers. They were discussing their piratical plans, in which all we could hear distinctly was, that they would unite with the crew of a schooner Hornet, and, if possible, get the schooner herself into their possession preparatory to some attempt on a large scale, the particulars of which could not be made out by either of us.

One of the men spoke of Peters, when the mate replied to him in a low voice which could not be distinguished, and afterward added more loudly, that "he could not understand his being so much forward with the captain's brat in the forecastle, and he thought the sooner both of them were overboard the better." To this no answer was made, but we could easily perceive that the hint was well received by the whole party, and more particularly by Jones. At this period I was excessively agitated, the more so as I could see that neither Augustus nor Peters could determine how to act. I made up my mind, however, to sell my life as dearly as possible, and not to suffer myself to be overcome by any feelings of trepidation.

The tremendous noise made by the roaring of the wind in the rigging, and the washing of the sea over the deck, prevented us from hearing what was said, except during momentary lulls. In one of these, we all distinctly heard the mate tell one of the men to "go forward, and order the d—d lubbers to come into the cabin," where he could have an eye upon them, for he wanted no such secret doings on board the brig. It was well for us that the pitching of the vessel at this moment was so violent as to prevent this order from being carried into instant execution. The cook got up from his mattress to go for us, when a tremendous lurch, which I thought would carry away the masts, threw him headlong against one of the larboard state-room doors, bursting it open, and creating a good deal of other confusion. Luckily, neither of our party was thrown from his position, and we had time to make a precipitate retreat to the forecastle, and arrange a hurried plan of action before the messenger made his appearance, or rather before he put his head out of the companion-hatch, for he did not come on deck. From this station he could not notice the absence of Allen, and he accordingly bawled out, as if to him, repeating the orders of the mate. Peters cried out, "Ay, ay," in a disguised voice, and the cook immediately went below, without entertaining a suspicion that all was not right.

My two companions now proceeded boldly aft and down into the cabin, Peters closing the door after him in the same manner he had found it. The mate received them with feigned cordiality, and told Augustus that, since he had behaved himself so well of late, he might take up his quarters in the cabin and be one of them for the future. He then poured him out a tumbler half full of rum, and made him drink it. All this I saw and heard, for I followed my friends to the cabin as soon as the door was shut, and took up my old point of observation. I had brought with me the two pump-handles, one of which I secured near the companion-way, to be ready for use when required.

I now steadied myself as well as possible so as to have a good view of all that was passing within, and endeavoured to nerve myself to the task of descending among the mutineers when Peters should make a signal to me as agreed upon. Presently he contrived to turn the conversation upon the bloody deeds of the mutiny, and by degrees led the men to talk of the thousand superstitions which are so universally current among seamen. I could not make out all that was said, but I could plainly see the effects of the conversation in the countenances of those present. The mate was evidently much agitated and presently, when some one mentioned the terrific appearance of Rogers's corpse, I thought he was upon the point of swooning. Peters now asked him if he did not think it would be better to have the body thrown overboard at once as it was too horrible a sight to see it floundering about in the scuppers. At this the villain absolutely gasped for breath, and turned his head slowly round upon his companions, as if imploring some one to go up and perform the task. No one, however, stirred, and it was quite evident that the whole party were wound up to the highest pitch of nervous excitement. Peters now made me the signal. I immediately threw open the door of the companion-way, and, descending, without uttering a syllable, stood erect in the midst of the party.

The intense effect produced by this sudden apparition is not at all to be wondered at when the various circumstances are taken into consideration. Usually, in cases of a similar nature, there is left in the mind of the spectator some glimmering of doubt as to the reality of the vision before his eyes; a degree of hope, however feeble, that he is the victim of chicanery, and that the apparition is not actually a visitant from the world of shadows. It is not too much to say that such remnants of doubt have been at the bottom of almost every such visitation, and that the appalling horror which has sometimes been brought about, is to be attributed, even in the cases most in point, and where most suffering has been experienced, more to a kind of anticipative horror, lest the apparition *might possibly be* real, than to an unwavering belief in its reality. But, in the present instance, it will be seen immediately, that in the minds of the mutineers there was not even the shadow of a basis upon which to rest a doubt that the apparition of Rogers was indeed a revivification of his disgusting corpse, or at least its spiritual image. The isolated situation of the brig, with its entire inaccessibility on account of the gale, confined the apparently possible means of deception within such narrow and definite limits, that they must have thought themselves enabled to survey them all at a glance. They had now been at sea twenty-four days, without holding more than a speaking communication with any vessel whatever. The whole of the crew, too, at least all whom they had the most remote reason for suspecting to be on board, were assembled in the cabin, with the exception of Allen, the watch; and his gigantic stature (he was six feet six inches high) was too familiar in their eyes to permit the notion that he was the apparition before them to enter their minds even for an instant. Add to these considerations the awe-inspiring nature of the tempest, and that of the conversation brought about by Peters; the deep impression which the loathsomeness of the actual corpse had made in the morning upon the imaginations of the men; the excellence of the imitation in my person, and the uncertain and wavering light in which they held me, as the glare of the cabin lantern, swinging violently to and fro, fell dubiously and fitfully upon my figure, and there will be no reason to wonder that the deception had even more than the entire effect which we had anticipated. The mate sprang up from the mattress on which he was lying, and, without uttering a syllable, fell back, stone dead, upon the cabin floor, and was hurled to the leeward like a log by a heavy roll of the brig. Of the remaining seven, there were but three who had at first any degree of presence of mind. The four others sat for some time rooted apparently to the floor, the most pitiable objects of horror and utter despair my eyes ever encountered. The only opposition we experienced at all was from the cook, John Hunt, and Richard Parker; but they made but a feeble and irresolute defence. The two former were shot instantly by Peters, and I felled Parker with a blow on the head from the pump-handle which I had brought with me. In the mean time Augustus seized one of the muskets lying on the floor and shot another mutineer (—— Wilson) through the breast. There were now but three remaining; but by this time they had become aroused from their lethargy, and perhaps began to see that a deception had been practised upon them, for they fought with great resolution and fury, and, but for the immense muscular strength of Peters, might have ultimately got the better of us. These three men were —— Jones, —— Greely, and Absalom Hicks. Jones had thrown Augustus on the floor, stabbed him in several places along the right arm, and would no doubt have soon dispatched him (as neither Peters nor myself could immediately get rid of our own antagonists), had it not been for the timely aid of a friend, upon whose assistance we surely had never depended. This friend was no other than Tiger. With a low growl, he bounded into the cabin, at a most critical moment for Augustus, and throwing himself upon Jones, pinned him to the floor in an instant. My friend, however, was now too much injured to render us any aid whatever, and I was so encumbered with my disguise that I could do but little. The dog would not leave his hold upon the throat of Jones —Peters, nevertheless, was far more than a match for the two men who remained, and would, no doubt, have dispatched them sooner, had it not been for the narrow space in which he had to act, and the tremendous lurches of the vessel. Presently he was enabled to get hold of a heavy stool, several of which lay about the floor. With this he beat out the brains of Greely as he was in the act of discharging a musket at me, and immediately afterward a roll of the brig throwing him in contact with Hicks, he seized him by the throat, and, by dint of sheer strength, strangled him instantaneously. Thus, in far less time than I had taken to tell it, we found ourselves masters of the brig.

The only person of our opponents who was left alive was Richard Parker. This man, it will be remembered, I had knocked down with a blow from the pump-handle at the commencement of the attack. He now lay motionless by the door of the shattered state-room; but, upon Peters touching him with his foot, he spoke, and entreated for mercy. His head was only slightly cut, and otherwise he had received no injury, having been merely stunned by the blow. He now got up, and, for the present, we secured his hands behind his back. The dog was still growling over Jones; but, upon examination, we found him completely dead, the blood issuing in a stream from a deep wound in the throat, inflicted, no doubt, by the sharp teeth of the animal.

It was now about one o'clock in the morning, and the wind was still blowing tremendously. The brig evidently laboured much more than usual, and it became absolutely necessary that something should be done with a view of easing her in some measure. At almost every roll to leeward she shipped a sea, several of which came partially down into the cabin during our scuffle, the hatchway having been left open by myself when I descended. The entire range of bulwarks to larboard had been swept away, as well as the caboose, together with the jollyboat from the counter. The creaking and working of the mainmast, too, gave indication that it was nearly sprung. To make room for more stowage in the after hold, the heel of this mast had been stepped between decks (a very reprehensible practice, occasionally restorted to by ignorant ship-builders), so that it was in imminent danger of working from its step. But, to crown all our difficulties, we plumbed the well, and found no less than seven feet of water.

Leaving the bodies of the crew lying in the cabin, we got to work immediately at the pumps—Parker, of course, being set at liberty to assist us in the labour. Augustus's arm was bound up as well as we could effect it, and he did what he could, but that was not much. However, we found that we could just manage to keep the leak from gaining upon us by having one pump constantly going. As there were only four of us, this was severe labour; but we endeavoured to keep up our spirits, and looked anxiously for daybreak, when we hoped to lighten the brig by cutting away the mainmast.

In this manner we passed a night of terrible anxiety and fatigue, and, when the day at length broke, the gale had neither abated in the least, nor were there any signs of its abating. We now dragged the bodies on deck and threw them overboard. Our next care was to get rid of the mainmast. The necessary preparations having been made, Peters cut away at the mast (having found axes in the cabin), while the rest of us stood by the stays and lanyards. As the brig gave a tremendous lee-lurch, the word was given to cut away the weather-lanyards, which being done, the whole mass of wood and rigging plunged into the sea, clear of the brig, and without doing any material injury. We now found that the vessel did not labour quite as much as before, but our situation was still exceedingly precarious, and, in spite of the utmost exertions, we could not gain upon the leak without the aid of both pumps. The little assistance which Augustus could render us was not really of any importance. To add to our distress, a heavy sea, striking the brig to the windward, threw her off several points from the wind, and, before she could regain her position, another broke completely over her, and hurled her full upon her beam-ends. The ballast now shifted in a mass to leeward (the stowage had been knocking about perfectly at random for some time), and for a few moments we thought nothing could save us from capsizing. Presently, however, we partially righted; but the ballast still retaining its place to larboard, we lay so much along that it was useless to think of working the pumps, which indeed we could not have done much longer in any case, as our hands were entirely raw with the excessive labour we had undergone, and were bleeding in the most horrible manner.

Contrary to Parker's advice, we now proceeded to cut away the foremast, and at length accomplished it after much difficulty, owing to the position in which we lay. In going overboard the wreck took with it the bowsprit, and left us a complete hulk.

So far we had had reason to rejoice in the escape of our longboat, which had received no damage from any of the huge seas which had come on board. But we had not long to congratulate ourselves; for the foremast having gone, and, of course, the foresail with it, by which the brig had been steadied, every sea now made a complete breach over us, and in five minutes our deck was swept from stem to stern, the longboat and starboard bulwarks torn off, and even the windlass shattered into fragments. It was, indeed, hardly possible for us to be in a more pitiable condition.

At noon there seemed to be some slight appearance of the gale's abating, but in this we were sadly disappointed, for it only lulled for a few minutes to blow with redoubled fury. About four in the afternoon it was utterly impossible to stand up against the violence of the blast; and, as the night closed in upon us, I had not a shadow of hope that the vessel would hold together until morning.

By midnight we had settled very deep in the water, which was now up to the orlop deck. The rudder went soon afterward, the sea which tore it away lifting the after portion of the brig entirely from the water, against which she thumped in her descent with such a concussion as would be occasioned by going ashore. We had all calculated that the rudder would hold its own to the last, as it was unusually strong, being rigged as I have never seen one rigged either before or since. Down its main timber there ran a succession of stout iron hooks, and others in the same manner down the stern-post. Through these hooks there extended a very thick wrought-iron rod, the rudder being thus held to the stern-post, and swinging freely on the rod. The tremendous force of the sea which tore it off may be estimated by the fact, that the hooks in the stern-post, which ran entirely through it, being clinched on the inside, were drawn every one of them completely out of the solid wood.

We had scarcely time to draw breath after the violence of this shock, when one of the most tremendous waves I had then ever known broke right on board of us, sweeping the companion-way clear off, bursting in the hatchways, and filling every inch of the vessel with water.

CHAPTER IX

LUCKILY, just before night, all four of us had lashed ourselves firmly to the fragments of the windlass, lying in this manner as flat upon the deck as possible. This precaution alone saved us from destruction. As it was we were all more or less stunned by the immense weight of water which tumbled upon us, and which did not roll from above us until we were nearly exhausted. As soon as I could recover breath, I called aloud to my companions. Augustus alone replied, saying, "It is all over with us, and may God have mercy upon our souls." By-and-by both the others were enabled to speak, when they exhorted us to take courage, as there was still hope; it being impossible, from the nature of the cargo, that the brig could go down, and there being every chance that the gale would blow over by the morning. These words inspired me with new life; for, strange as it may seem, although it was obvious that a vessel with a cargo of empty oil-casks would not sink, I had been hitherto so confused in mind as to have overlooked this consideration altogether; and the danger which I had for some time regarded as the most imminent was that of foundering. As hope revived within me, I made use of every opportunity to strengthen the lashings which held me to the remains of the windlass, and in this occupation I soon discovered that my companions were also busy. The night was as dark as it could possibly be, and the horrible shrieking din and confusion which surrounded us it is useless to attempt describing. Our deck lay level with the sea, or rather we were encircled with a towering ridge of foam, a portion of which swept over us every instant. It is not too much to say that our heads were not fairly out of water more than one second in three. Although we lay close together, no one of us could see the other, or, indeed, any portion of the brig itself, upon which we were so tempestuously hurled about. At intervals we called one to the other, thus endeavouring to keep alive hope, and render consolation and encouragement to such of us as stood most in need of it. The feeble condition of Augustus made him an object of solicitude with us all; and as, from the lacerated condition of his right arm, it must have been impossible for him to secure his lashings with any degree of firmness, we were in momentary expectation of finding that he had gone overboard—yet to render him aid was a thing altogether out of the question. Fortunately, his station was more secure than that of any of the rest of us; for the upper part of his body lying just beneath a portion of the shattered windlass, the seas, as they tumbled in upon him, were greatly broken in their violence. In any other situation than this (into which he had been accidentally thrown after having lashed himself in a very exposed spot) he must inevitably have perished before morning. Owing to the brig's lying so much along, we were all less liable to be washed off than otherwise would have been the case. The heel, as I have before stated, was to larboard, about one half of the deck being constantly under water. The seas, therefore, which struck us to starboard were much broken by the vessel's side, only reaching us in fragments as we lay flat on our faces; while those which came from larboard, being what are called back-water seas, and obtaining little hold upon us on account of our posture, had not sufficient force to drag us from our fastenings.

In this frightful situation we lay until the day broke so as to show us more fully the horrors which surrounded us. The brig was a mere log, rolling about at the mercy of every wave; the gale was upon the increase, if anything, blowing indeed a complete hurricane, and there appeared to us no earthy prospect of deliverance. For several hours we held on in silence, expecting every moment that our lashings would either give way, that the remains of the windlass would go by the board, or that some of the huge seas, which roared in every direction around us and above us, would drive the hulk so far beneath the water that we should be drowned before it could regain the surface. By the mercy of God, however, we were preserved from these imminent dangers, and about midday were cheered by the light of the blessed sun. Shortly afterward we could perceive a sensible diminution in the force of the wind, when, now for the first time since the latter part of the evening before, Augustus spoke, asking Peters, who lay closest to him, if he thought there was any possibility of our being saved. As no reply was at first made to this question, we all concluded that the hybrid had been drowned where he lay; but presently, to our great joy, he spoke, although very feebly, saying that he was in great pain, being so cut by the tightness of his lashings across the stomach, that he must either find means of loosening them or perish, as it was impossible that he could endure his misery much longer. This occasioned us great distress, as it was altogether useless to think of aiding him in any manner while the sea continued washing over us as it did. We exhorted him to bear his sufferings with fortitude, and promised to seize the first opportunity which should offer itself to relieve him. He replied that it would soon be too late; that it would be all over with him before we could help him; and then, after moaning for some minutes, lay silent, when we concluded that he had perished.

As the evening drew on, the sea had fallen so much that scarcely more than one wave broke over the hulk from windward in the course of five minutes, and the wind had abated a great deal, although still blowing a severe gale. I had not heard any of my companions speak for hours, and now called to Augustus. He replied, although very feebly, so that I could not distinguish what he said. I then spoke to Peters and to Parker, neither of whom returned any answer.

Shortly after this period I fell into a state of partial insensibility, during which the most pleasing images floated in my imagination; such as green trees, waving meadows of ripe grain, processions of dancing girls, troops of cavalry, and other phantasies. I now remembered that, in all which passed before my mind's eye, *motion* was a predominant idea. Thus, I never fancied any stationary object, such as a house, a mountain, or anything of that kind; but windmills, ships, large birds, balloons, people on horseback, carriages driving furiously, and similar moving objects, presented themselves in endless succession. When I recovered from this state, the sun was, as near as I could guess, an hour high. I had the greatest difficulty in bringing to recollection the various circumstances connected with my situation, and for some time remained firmly convinced that I was still in the hold of the brig, near the box, and that the body of Parker was that of Tiger.

When I at length completely came to my senses, I found that the wind blew no more than a moderate breeze, and that the sea was comparatively calm; so much so that it only washed over the brig amidships. My left arm had broken loose from its lashings, and was much cut about the elbow; my right was entirely benumbed, and the hand and wrist swollen prodigiously by the pressure of the rope, which had worked from the shoulder downward. I was also in great pain from another rope which went about my waist, and had been drawn to an insufferable degree of tightness. Looking round upon my companions, I saw that Peters still lived, although a thick line was pulled so forcibly around his loins as to give him the appearance of being cut nearly in two; as I stirred, he made a feeble motion to me with his hand, pointing to the rope. Augustus gave no indication of life whatever, and was bent nearly double across a splinter of the windlass. Parker spoke to me when he saw me moving, and asked me if I had not sufficient strength to release him from his situation; saying, that if I would summon up what spirits I could, and contrive to untie him, we might yet save our lives; but that otherwise we must all perish. I told him to take courage, and I would endeavour to free him. Feeling in my pantaloons' pocket, I got hold of my penknife, and, after several ineffectual attempts, at length succeeded in opening it. I then, with my left hand, managed to free my right from its fastenings, and afterward cut the other ropes which held me. Upon attempting, however, to move from my position, I found that my legs failed me altogether, and that I could not get up; neither could I move my right arm in any direction. Upon mentioning this to Parker, he advised me to lie quiet for a few minutes, holding on to the windlass with my left hand, so as to allow time for the blood to circulate. Doing this, the numbness presently began to die away so that I could move first one of my legs, and then the other; and, shortly afterward I regained the partial use of my right arm. I now crawled with great caution towards Parker, without getting on my legs, and soon cut loose all the lashings about him, when, after a short delay, he also recovered the partial use of his limbs. We now lost no time in getting loose the rope from Peters. It had cut a deep gash through the waistband of his woollen pantaloons, and through two shirts, and made its way into his groin, from which the blood flowed out copiously as we removed the cordage. No sooner had we removed it, however, than he spoke, and seemed to experience instant relief—being able to move with much greater ease than either Parker or myself—this was no doubt owing to the discharge of blood.

We had little hope that Augustus would recover, as he evinced no signs of life; but, upon getting to him, we discovered that he had merely swooned from loss of blood, the bandages we had placed around his wounded arm having been torn off by the water; none of the ropes which held him to the windlass were drawn sufficiently tight to occasion his death. Having relieved him from the fastenings, and got him clear of the broken wood about the windlass, we secured him in a dry place to windward, with his head somewhat lower than his body, and all three of us busied ourselves in chafing his limbs. In about half an hour he came to himself, although it was not until the next morning that he gave signs of recognizing any of us, or had sufficient strength to speak. By the time we had thus got clear of our lashings it was quite dark, and it began to cloud up, so that we were again in the greatest agony lest it should come on to blow hard, in which event nothing could have saved us from perishing, exhausted as we were. By good fortune it continued very moderate during the night, the sea subsiding every minute, which gave us great hopes of ultimate preservation. A gentle breeze still blew from the N.W., but the weather was not at all cold. Augustus was lashed carefully to windward in such a manner as to prevent him from slipping overboard with the rolls of the vessel, as he was still too weak to hold on at all. For ourselves there was no such necessity. We sat close together, supporting each other with the aid of the broken ropes about the windlass, and devising methods of escape from our frightful situation. We derived much comfort from taking off our clothes and wringing the water from them. When we put them on after this, they felt remarkably warm and pleasant, and served to invigorate us in no little degree. We helped Augustus off with his, and wrung them for him, when he experienced the same comfort.

Our chief sufferings were now those of hunger and thirst, and when we looked forward to the means of relief in this respect, our hearts sunk within us, and we were induced to regret that we had escaped the less dreadful perils of the sea. We endeavoured, however, to console ourselves with the hope of being speedily picked up by some vessel, and encouraged each other to bear with fortitude the evils that might happen.

The morning of the fourteenth at length dawned, and the weather still continued clear and pleasant, with a steady but very light breeze from the N.W. The sea was now quite smooth and as, from some cause which we could not determine, the brig did not lie so much along as she had done before, the deck was comparatively dry, and we could move about with freedom. We had now been better than three entire days and nights without either food or drink, and it became absolutely necessary that we should make an attempt to get up something from below. As the brig was completely full of water, we went to this work despondingly, and with but little expectation of being able to obtain anything. We made a kind of drag by driving some nails which we broke out from the remains of the companion-hatch into two pieces of wood. Tying these across each other, and fastening them to the end of a rope, we threw them into the cabin, and dragged them to and fro, in the faint hope of being thus able to entangle some article which might be of use to us for food, or which might at least render us assistance in getting it. We spent the greater part of the morning in this labour without effect, fishing up nothing more than a few bedclothes, which were readily caught by the nails. Indeed, our contrivance was so very clumsy that any greater success was hardly to be anticipated.

We now tried the forecastle, but equally in vain, and were upon the brink of despair, when Peters proposed that we should fasten a rope to his body, and let him make an attempt to get up something by diving into the cabin. This proposition we hailed with all the delight which reviving hope could inspire. He proceeded immediately to strip off his clothes with the exception of his pantaloons; and a strong rope was then carefully fastened around his middle, being brought up over his shoulders in such a manner that there was no possibility of its slipping. The undertaking was one of great difficulty and danger; for, as we could hardly expect to find much, if any, provision in the cabin itself, it was necessary that the diver, after letting himself down, should make a turn to the right, and proceed under water a distance of ten or twelve feet, in a narrow passage, to the storeroom, and return, without drawing breath.

Everything being ready, Peters now descended into the cabin, going down the companion-ladder until the water reached his chin. He then plunged in, head first, turning to the right as he plunged, and endeavouring to make his way to the storeroom. In this first attempt, however, he was altogether unsuccessful. In less than half a minute after his going down we felt the rope jerked violently (the signal we had agreed upon when he desired to be drawn up). We accordingly drew him up instantly, but so incautiously as to bruise him badly against the ladder. He had brought nothing with him, and had been unable to penetrate more than a very little way into the passage, owing to the constant exertions he found it necessary to make in order to keep himself from floating up against the deck. Upon getting out he was very much exhausted, and had to rest full fifteen minutes before he could again venture to descend.

The second attempt met with even worse success; for he remained so long under water without giving the signal, that, becoming alarmed for his safety, we drew him out without it, and found that he was almost at the last gasp, having, as he said, repeatedly jerked at the rope without our feeling it. This was probably owing to a portion of it having become entangled in the balustrade at the foot of the ladder. This balustrade was, indeed, so much in the way, that we determined to remove it, if possible, before proceeding with our design. As we had no means of getting it away except by main force, we all descended into the water as far as we could on the ladder, and giving a pull against it with our united strength, succeeded in breaking it down.

The third attempt was equally unsuccessful with the two first, and it now became evident that nothing could be done in this manner without the aid of some weight with which the diver might steady himself, and keep to the floor of the cabin while making his search. For a long time we looked about in vain for something which might answer this purpose; but at length, to our great joy, we discovered one of the weather-forechains so loose that we had not the least difficulty in wrenching it off. Having fastened this securely to one of his ankles Peters now made his fourth descent into the cabin, and this time succeeded in making his way to the door of the steward's room. To his inexpressible grief, however, he found it locked, and was obliged to return without effecting an entrance, as, with the greatest exertion, he could remain under water not more, at the utmost extent, than a single minute. Our affairs now looked gloomy indeed, and neither Augustus nor myself could refrain from bursting into tears, as we thought of the host of difficulties which encompassed us, and the slight probability which existed of our finally making an escape. But this weakness was not of long duration. Throwing ourselves on our knees to God, we implored His aid in the many dangers which beset us; and arose with renewed hope and vigour to think what could yet be done by mortal means towards accomplishing our deliverance.

CHAPTER X

SHORTLY afterward an incident occurred which I am induced to look upon as more intensely productive of emotion, as far more replete with the extremes first of delight and then of horror, than even any of the thousand chances which afterward befell me in nine long years, crowded with events of the most startling and, in many cases, of the most unconceived and unconceivable character. We were lying on the deck near the companion-way, and debating the possibility of yet making our way into the storeroom, when, looking toward Augustus, who lay fronting myself, I perceived that he had become all at once deadly pale, and that his lips were quivering in the most singular and unaccountable manner. Greatly alarmed, I spoke to him, but he made me no reply, and I was beginning to think that he was suddenly taken ill, when I took notice of his eyes, which were glaring apparently at some object behind me. I turned my head, and shall never forget the ecstatic joy which thrilled through every particle of my frame, when I perceived a large brig bearing down upon us, and not more than a couple of miles off. I sprung to my feet as if a musket bullet had suddenly struck me to the heart; and, stretching out my arms in the direction of the vessel, stood in this manner, motionless, and unable to articulate a syllable. Peters and Parker were equally affected, although in different ways. The former danced about the deck like a madman, uttering the most extravagant rodomontades, intermingled with howls and imprecations, while the latter burst into tears, and continued for many minutes weeping like a child.

The vessel in sight was a large hermaphrodite brig, of a Dutch build, and painted black, with a tawdry gilt figurehead. She had evidently seen a good deal of rough weather, and, we supposed, had suffered much in the gale which had proved so disastrous to ourselves; for her foretopmast was gone, and some of her starboard bulwarks. When we first saw her, she was, as I have already said, about two miles off and to windward, bearing down upon us. The breeze was very gentle, and what astonished us chiefly was, that she had no other sails set than her foresail and mainsail, with a flying jib—of course she came down but slowly, and our impatience amounted nearly to phrensy. The awkward manner in which she steered, too, was remarked by all of us, even excited as we were. She yawed about so considerably, that once or twice we thought it impossible she could see us, or imagined that, having seen us, and discovered no person on board, she was about to tack and make off in another direction. Upon each of these occasions we screamed and shouted at the top of our voices, when the stranger would appear to change for a moment her intention, and again hold on towards us—this singular conduct being repeated two or three times, so that at last we could think of no other manner of accounting for it than by supposing the helmsman to be in liquor.

No person was seen upon her decks until she arrived within

about a quarter of a mile of us. We then saw three seamen, whom by their dress we took to be Hollanders. Two of these were lying on some old sails near the forecastle, and the third, who appeared to be looking at us with great curiosity, was leaning over the starboard bow near the bowsprit. This last was a stout and tall man, with a very dark skin. He seemed by his manner to be encouraging us to have patience, nodding to us in a cheerful although rather odd way, and smiling constantly, so as to display a set of the most brilliantly white teeth. As his vessel drew nearer, we saw a red flannel cap which he had on fall from his head into the water; but of this he took little or no notice, continuing his odd smiles and gesticulations. I relate these things and circumstances minutely, and I relate them, it must be understood, precisely as they *appeared* to us.

The brig came on slowly, and now more steadily than before, and—I cannot speak calmly of this event—our hearts leaped up wildly within us, and we poured out our whole souls in shouts and thanksgiving to God for the complete, unexpected, and glorious deliverance that was so palpably at hand. Of a sudden, and all at once, there came wafted over the ocean from the strange vessel (which was now close upon us) a smell, a stench, such as the whole world has no name for—no conception of—hellish—utterly suffocating—insufferable, inconceivable. I gasped for breath, and turning to my companions, perceived that they were paler than marble. But we had now no time left for question or surmise—the brig was within fifty feet of us, and it seemed to be her intention to run under our counter, that we might board her without her putting out a boat. We rushed aft, when, suddenly, a wide yaw threw her off full five or six points from the course she had been running, and, as she passed under our stern at the distance of about twenty feet, we had a full view of her decks. Shall I ever forget the triple horror of that spectacle? Twenty-five or thirty human bodies, among whom were several females, lay scattered about between the counter and the galley in the last and most loathsome state of putrefaction. We plainly saw that not a soul lived in that fated vessel! Yet we could not help shouting to the dead for help! Yes, long and loudly did we beg, in the agony of the moment, that those silent and disgusting images would stay for us, would not abandon us to become like them, would receive us among their goodly company! We were raving with horror and despair—thoroughly mad through the anguish of our grievous disappointment.

As our first loud yell of terror broke forth, it was replied to by something, from near the bowsprit of the stranger, so closely resembling the scream of a human voice that the nicest ear might have been startled and deceived. At this instant another sudden yaw brought the region of the forecastle for a moment into view, and we beheld at once the origin of the sound. We saw the tall stout figure still leaning on the bulwark, and still nodding his head to and fro, but his face was now turned from us so that we could not behold it. His arms were extended over the rail, and the palms of his hands fell outward. His knees were lodged upon a stout rope, tightly stretched, and reaching from the heel of the bowsprit to a cathead. On his back, from which a portion of the shirt had been torn, leaving it bare, there sat a huge seagull, busily gorging itself with the horrible flesh, its bill and talons deep buried, and its white plumage spattered all over with blood. As the brig moved further round so as to bring us close in view, the bird, with much apparent difficulty, drew out its crimsoned head, and, after eying us for a moment as if stupefied, arose lazily from the body upon which it had been feasting, and, flying directly above our deck, hovered there a while with a portion of clotted and liver-like substance in its beak. The horrid morsel dropped at length with a sullen splash immediately at the feet of Parker. May God forgive me, but now, for the first time, there flashed through my mind a thought, a thought which I will not mention, and I felt myself making a step towards the ensanguined spot. I looked upward, and the eyes of Augustus met my own with a degree of intense and eager meaning which immediately brought me to my senses. I sprang forward quickly, and, with a deep shudder, threw the frightful thing into the sea.

The body from which it had been taken, resting as it did upon the rope, had been easily swayed to and fro by the exertions of the carnivorous bird, and it was this motion which had at first impressed us with the belief of its being alive. As the gull relieved it of its weight, it swung round and fell partially over, so that the face was fully discovered. Never, surely, was any object so terribly full of awe! The eyes were gone, and the whole flesh around the mouth, leaving the teeth utterly naked. This, then, was the smile which had cheered us on to hope! this the—but I forbear. The brig, as I have already told, passed under our stern, and made its way slowly but steadily to leeward. With her and with her terrible crew went all our gay visions of deliverance and joy. Deliberately as she went by, we might possibly have found means of boarding her, had not our sudden disappointment, and the appalling nature of the discovery which accompanied it, laid entirely prostrate every active faculty of mind and body. We had seen and felt, but we could neither think nor act, until, alas, too late. How much our intellects had been weakened by this incident may be estimated by the fact, that when the vessel had proceeded so far that we could perceive no more than the half of her hull, the proposition was seriously entertained of attempting to overtake her by swimming!

I have, since this period, vainly endeavoured to obtain some clew to the hideous uncertainty which enveloped the fate of the stranger. Her build and general appearance, as I have before stated, led us to the belief that she was a Dutch trader, and the dresses of the crew also sustained this opinion. We might have easily seen the name upon her stern, and, indeed, taken other observations, which would have guided us in making out her character; but the intense excitement of the moment blinded us to everything of that nature. From the saffron-like hue of such of the corpses as were not entirely decayed, we concluded that the whole of her company had perished by the yellow fever, or some other virulent disease of the same fearful kind. If such were the case (and I know not what else to imagine), death, to judge from the positions of the bodies, must have come upon them in a manner awfully sudden and overwhelming, in a way totally distinct from that which generally characterizes even the most deadly pestilences with which mankind are acquainted. It is possible, indeed, that poison, accidentally introduced into some of their sea-stores, may have brought about the disaster; or that the eating some unknown venomous species of fish, or other marine animal, or oceanic bird, might have induced it—but it is utterly useless to form conjectures where all is involved, and will, no doubt, remain for ever involved, in the most appalling and unfathomable mystery.

CHAPTER XI

WE SPENT the remainder of the day in a condition of stupid lethargy, gazing after the retreating vessel until the darkness, hiding her from our sight, recalled us in some measure to our senses. The pangs of hunger and thirst then returned, absorbing all other cares and considerations. Nothing, however, could be done until the morning, and, securing ourselves as well as possible, we endeavoured to snatch a little repose. In this I succeeded beyond my expectations, sleeping until my companions, who had not been so fortunate, aroused me at daybreak to renew our attempts at getting up provision from the hull.

It was now a dead calm, with the sea as smooth as I have ever known it—the weather warm and pleasant. The brig was out of sight. We commenced our operations by wrenching off, with some trouble, another of the forechains; and having fastened both to Peters's feet, he again made an endeavour to reach the door of the store-room, thinking it possible that he might be able to force it open, provided he could get at it in sufficient time; and this he hoped to do, as the hulk lay much more steadily than before.

He succeeded very quickly in reaching the door, when, loosening one of the chains from his ankle, he made every exertion to force a passage with it, but in vain, the framework of the room being far stronger than was anticipated. He was quite exhausted with his long stay under water, and it became absolutely necessary that some other one of us should take his place. For this service Parker immediately volunteered; but, after making three ineffectual efforts, found that he could never even succeed in getting near the door. The condition of Augustus's wounded arm rendered it useless for him to attempt going down, as he would be unable to force the room open should he reach it, and it accordingly now devolved upon me to exert myself for our common deliverance.

Peters had left one of the chains in the passage, and I found, upon plunging in, that I had not sufficient balance to keep me firmly down. I determined, therefore, to attempt no more, in my first effort, than merely to recover the other chain. In groping along the floor of the passage for this I felt a hard substance, which I immediately grasped, not having time to ascertain what it was, but returning and ascending instantly to the surface. The prize proved to be a bottle, and our joy may be conceived when I say that it was found to be full of Port wine. Giving thanks to God for this timely and cheering assistance, we immediately drew the cork with my penknife, and, each taking a moderate sup, felt the most indescribable comfort from the warmth, strength, and spirits with which it inspired us. We then carefully recorked the bottle, and, by means of a handkerchief, swung it in such a manner that there was no possibility of its getting broken.

Having rested a while after this fortunate discovery, I again descended, and now recovered the chain, with which I instantly came up. I then fastened it on and went down for the third time, when I became fully satisfied that no exertions whatever, in that situation, would enable me to force open the door of the storeroom. I therefore returned in despair.

There seemed now to be no longer any room for hope, and I could perceive in the countenances of my companions that they had made up their minds to perish. The wine had evidently produced in them a species of delirium, which, perhaps, I had been prevented from feeling by the immersion I had undergone since drinking it. They talked incoherently, and about matters unconnected with our condition, Peters repeatedly asking me questions about Nantucket. Augustus, too, I remember, approached me with a serious air, and requested me to lend him a pocket-comb, as his hair was full of fish-scales, and he wished to get them out before going on shore. Parker appeared somewhat less affected, and urged me to dive at random into the cabin, and bring up any article which might come to hand. To this I consented, and, in the first attempt, after staying under a fell minute, brought up a small leather trunk belonging to Captain Barnard. This was immediately opened in the faint hope that it might contain something to eat or drink. We found nothing, however, except a box of razors and two linen shirts. I now went down again, and returned without any success. As my head came above water I heard a crash on deck, and, upon getting up, saw that my companions had ungratefully taken advantage of my absence to drink the remainder of the wine, having let the bottle fall in the endeavour to replace it before I saw them. I remonstrated with them on the heartlessness of their conduct, when Augustus burst into tears. The other two endeavoured to laugh the matter off as a joke, but I hope never again to behold laughter of such a species: the distortion of countenance was absolutely frightful. Indeed, it was apparent that the stimulus, in the empty state of their stomachs, had taken instant and violent effect, and that they were all exceedingly intoxicated. With great difficulty I prevailed upon them to lie down, when they fell very soon into a heavy slumber, accompanied with loud stertorous breathing.

I now found myself, as it were, alone in the brig, and my reflections, to be sure, were of the most fearful and gloomy nature. No prospect offered itself to my view but a lingering death by famine, or, at the best, by being overwhelmed in the first gale which should spring up, for in our present exhausted condition we could have no hope of living through another.

The gnawing hunger which I now experienced was nearly insupportable, and I felt myself capable of going to any lengths in order to appease it. With my knife I cut off a small portion of the leather trunk, and endeavoured to eat it, but found it utterly impossible to swallow a single morsel, although I fancied that some little alleviation of my suffering was obtained by chewing small pieces of it and spitting them out. Towards night my companions awoke, one by one, each in an indescribable state of weakness and horror, brought on by the wine, whose fumes had now evaporated. They shook as if with a violent ague, and uttered the most lamentable cries for water. Their condition affected me in the most lively degree, at the same time causing me to rejoice in the fortunate train of circumstances which had prevented me from indulging in the wine, and consequently from sharing their melancholy and most distressing sensations. Their conduct, however, gave me great uneasiness and alarm; for it was evident that, unless some favourable change took place, they could afford me no assistance in providing for our common safety. I had not yet abandoned all idea of being able to get up something from below; but the attempt could not possibly be resumed until some one of them was sufficiently master of himself to aid me by holding the end of the rope while I went down. Parker appeared to be somewhat more in possession of his senses than the others, and I endeavoured, by every means in my power, to arouse him. Thinking that a plunge in the sea-water might have a beneficial effect, I contrived to fasten the end of a rope around his body, and then, leading him to the companion-way (he remaining quite passive all the while), pushed him in, and immediately drew him out. I had good reason to congratulate myself upon having made this experiment; for he appeared much revived and invigorated, and, upon getting out, asked me, in a rational manner, why I had so served him. Having explained my object, he expressed himself indebted to me, and said that he felt greatly better from the immersion, afterward conversing sensibly upon our situation. We then resolved to treat Augustus and Peters in the same way, which we immediately did, when they both experienced much benefit from the shock. This idea of sudden immersion had been suggested to me by reading in some medical work the good effect of the shower-bath in a case where the patient was suffering from *mania a potu.*

Finding that I could now trust my companions to hold the end of the rope, I again made three or four plunges into the cabin, although it was now quite dark, and a gentle but long swell from the northward rendered the hulk somewhat unsteady. In the course of these attempts I succeeded in bringing up two case-knives, a three-gallon jug empty, and a blanket, but nothing which could serve us for food. I continued my efforts, after getting these articles, until I was completely exhausted, but brought up nothing else. During the night Parker and Peters occupied themselves by turns in the same manner; but nothing coming to hand, we now gave up this attempt in despair, concluding that we were exhausting ourselves in vain.

We passed the remainder of this night in a state of the most intense mental and bodily anguish that can possibly be imagined. The morning of the sixteenth at length dawned, and we looked eagerly around the horizon for relief, but to no purpose. The sea was still smooth, with only a long swell from the northward, as on yesterday. This was the sixth day since we had tasted either food or drink, with the exception of the bottle of Port wine, and it was clear that we could hold out but a very little while longer unless something could be obtained. I never saw before, nor wish to see again, human beings so utterly emaciated as Peters and Augustus. Had I met them on shore in their present condition I should not have had the slightest suspicion that I had ever beheld them.

Their countenances were totally changed in character, so that I could not bring myself to believe them really the same individuals with whom I had been in company but a few days before. Parker, although sadly reduced, and so feeble that he could not raise his head from his bosom, was not so far gone as the other two. He suffered with great patience, making no complaint, and endeavouring to inspire us with hope in every manner he could devise. For myself, although at the commencement of the voyage I had been in bad health, and was at all times of a delicate constitution, I suffered less than any of us, being much less reduced in frame, and retaining my powers of mind in a surprising degree, while the rest were completely prostrated in intellect, and seemed to be brought to a species of second childhood, generally simpering in their expressions, with idiotic smiles, and uttering the most absurd platitudes. At intervals, however, they would appear to revive suddenly, as if inspired all at once with a consciousness of their condition, when they would spring upon their feet in a momentary flash of vigour, and speak, for a short period, of their prospects, in a manner altogether rational, although full of the most intense despair. It is possible, however, that my companions may have entertained the same opinion of their own condition as I did of mine, and that I may have unwittingly been guilty of the same extravagances and imbecilities as themselves—this is a matter which cannot be determined.

About noon Parker declared that he saw land off the larboard quarter, and it was with the utmost difficulty I could restrain him from plunging into the sea with the view of swimming towards it. Peters and Augustus took little notice of what he said, being apparently wrapped up in moody contemplation. Upon looking in the direction pointed out, I could not perceive the faintest appearance of the shore—indeed, I was too well aware that we were far from any land to indulge in a hope of that nature. It was a long time, nevertheless, before I could convince Parker of his mistake. He then burst into a flood of tears, weeping like a child, with loud cries and sobs, for two or three hours, when, becoming exhausted, he fell asleep.

Peters and Augustus now made several ineffectual efforts to swallow portions of the leather. I advised them to chew it and spit it out; but they were too excessively debilitated to be able to follow my advice. I continued to chew pieces of it at intervals, and found some relief from so doing; my chief distress was for water, and I was only prevented from taking a draught from the sea by remembering the horrible consequences which thus have resulted to others who were similarly situated with ourselves.

The day wore on in this manner, when I suddenly discovered a sail to the eastward, and on our larboard bow. She appeared to be a large ship, and was coming nearly athwart us, being probably twelve or fifteen miles distant. None of my companions had as yet discovered her, and I forbore to tell them of her for the present, lest we might again be disappointed of relief. At length, upon her getting nearer, I saw distinctly that she was heading immediately for us, with her light sails filled. I could now contain myself no longer, and pointed her out to my fellow-sufferers. They immediately sprang to their feet, again indulging in the most extravagant demonstrations of joy, weeping, laughing in an idiotic manner, jumping, stamping upon the deck, tearing their hair, and praying and cursing by turns. I was so affected by their conduct, as well as by what I now considered a sure prospect of deliverance, that I could not refrain from joining in with their madness, and gave way to the impulses of my gratitude and ecstasy by lying and rolling on the deck, clapping my hands, shouting, and other similar acts, until I was suddenly called to my recollection, and once more to the extreme of human misery and despair, by perceiving the ship all at once with her stern fully presented towards us, and steering in a direction nearly opposite to that in which I had at first perceived her.

It was some time before I could induce my poor companions to believe that this sad reverse in our prospects had actually taken place. They replied to all my assertions with a stare and a gesture implying that they were not to be deceived by such misrepresentations. The conduct of Augustus most sensibly affected me. In spite of all I could say or do to the contrary, he persisted in saying that the ship was rapidly nearing us, and in making preparations to go on board of her. Some sea-weed floating by the brig, he maintained that it was the ship's boat, and endeavoured to throw himself upon it, howling and shrieking in the most heart-rending manner, when I forcibly restrained him from thus casting himself into the sea.

Having become in some degree pacified, we continued to watch the ship until we finally lost sight of her, the weather becoming hazy, with a light breeze springing up. As soon as she was entirely gone, Parker turned suddenly towards me with an expression of countenance which made me shudder. There was about him an air of self-possession which I had not noticed in him until now, and before he opened his lips my heart told me what he would say. He proposed, in a few words, that one of us should die to preserve the existence of the others.

CHAPTER XII

I HAD, for some time past, dwelt upon the prospect of our being reduced to this last horrible extremity, and had secretly made up my mind to suffer death in any shape or under any circumstances rather than resort to such a course. Nor was this resolution in any degree weakened by the present intensity of hunger under which I laboured. The proposition had not been heard by either Peters or Augustus. I therefore took Parker aside; and mentally praying to God for power to dissuade him from the horrible purpose he entertained, I expostulated with him for a long time, and in the most supplicating manner, begging him in the name of everything which he held sacred, and urging him by every species of argument which the extremity of the case suggested, to abandon the idea, and not to mention it to either of the other two.

He heard all I said without attempting to controvert any of my arguments, and I had begun to hope that he would be prevailed upon to do as I desired. But when I had ceased speaking, he said that he knew very well all I had said was true, and that to resort to such a course was the most horrible alternative which could enter into the mind of man; but that he had now held out as long as human nature could be sustained; that it was unnecessary for all to perish, when, by the death of one, it was possible, and even probable, that the rest might be finally preserved; adding that I might save myself the trouble of trying to turn him from his purpose, his mind having been thoroughly made up on the subject even before the appearance of the ship, and that only her heaving in sight had prevented him from mentioning his intention at an earlier period.

I now begged him, if he would not be prevailed upon to abandon his design, at least to defer it for another day, when some vessel might come to our relief; again reiterating every argument I could devise, and which I thought likely to have influence with one of his rough nature. He said, in reply, that he had not spoken until the very last possible moment; that he could exist no longer without sustenance of some kind, and that therefore in another day his suggestion would be too late, as regarded himself at least.

Finding that he was not to be moved by anything I could say in a mild tone, I now assumed a different demeanour, and told him that he must be aware I had suffered less than any of us from our calamities; that my health and strength, consequently, were at that moment far better than his own, or than that either of Peters or Augustus; in short, that I was in a condition to have my own way by force if I found it necessary; and that if he attempted in any manner to acquaint the others with his bloody and cannibal designs, I would not hesitate to throw him into the sea. Upon this he immediately seized me by the throat, and drawing a knife, made several ineffectual efforts to stab me in the stomach; an atrocity which his excessive debility alone prevented him from accomplishing. In the meantime, being roused to a high pitch of anger, I forced him to the vessel's side, with the full intention of throwing him overboard. He was saved from this fate, however, by the interference of Peters, who now approached and separated us, asking the cause of the disturbance. This Parker told before I could find means in any manner to prevent him.

The effect of his words was even more terrible than what I had anticipated. Both Augustus and Peters, who, it seems, had long secretly entertained the same fearful idea which Parker had been merely the first to broach, joined with him in his design and insisted upon its immediately being carried into effect. I had calculated that one at least of the two former would be found still possessed of sufficient strength of mind to side with myself in resisting any attempt to execute so dreadful a purpose; and, with the aid of either one of them, I had no fear of being able to prevent its accomplishment. Being disappointed in this expectation, it became absolutely necessary that I should attend to my own safety, as a further resistance on my part might possibly be considered by men in their frightful condition a sufficient excuse for refusing me fair play in the tragedy that I knew would speedily be enacted.

I now told them I was willing to submit to the proposal, merely requesting a delay of about one hour, in order that the fog which had gathered around us might have an opportunity of lifting, when it was possible that the ship we had seen might be again in sight. After great difficulty I obtained from them a promise to wait thus long; and, as I had anticipated (a breeze rapidly coming in), the fog lifted before the hour had expired, when, no vessel appearing in sight, we prepared to draw lots.

It is with extreme reluctance that I dwell upon the appalling scene which ensued; a scene which, with its minutest details, no after events have been able to efface in the slightest degree from my memory, and whose stern recollection will embitter every future moment of my existence. Let me run over this portion of my narrative with as much haste as the nature of the events to be spoken of will permit. The only method we could devise for the terrific lottery, in which we were to take each a chance, was that of drawing straws. Small splinters of wood were made to answer our purpose, and it was agreed that I should be the holder. I retired to one end of the hulk, while my poor companions silently took up their station in the other with their backs turned towards me. The bitterest anxiety which I endured at any period of this fearful drama was while I occupied myself in the arrangement of the lots. There are few conditions into which man can possibly fall where he will not feel a deep interest in the preservation of his existence; an interest momentarily increasing with the frailness of the tenure by which that existence may be held. But now that the silent, definite, and stern nature of the business in which I was engaged (so different from the tumultuous dangers of the storm or the gradually approaching horrors of famine) allowed me to reflect on the few chances I had of escaping the most appalling of deaths—a death for the most appalling of purposes—every particle of that energy which had so long buoyed me up departed like feathers before the wind, leaving me a helpless prey to the most abject and pitiable terror. I could not, at first, even summon up sufficient strength to tear and fit together the small splinters of wood, my fingers absolutely refusing their office, and my knees knocking violently against each other. My mind ran over rapidly a thousand absurd projects by which to avoid becoming a partner in the awful speculation. I thought of falling on my knees to my companions, and entreating them to let me escape this necessity; of suddenly rushing upon them, and, by putting one of them to death, of rendering the decision by lot useless—in short, of everything but of going through with the matter I had in hand. At last, after wasting a long time in this imbecile conduct, I was recalled to my senses by the voice of Parker, who urged me to relieve them at once from the terrible anxiety they were enduring. Even then I could not bring myself to arrange the splinters upon the spot, but thought over every species of finesse by which I could trick some one of my fellow-sufferers to draw the short straw, as it had been agreed that whoever drew the shortest of four splinters from my hand was to die for the preservation of the rest. Before any one condemn me for this apparent heartlessness, let him be placed in a situation precisely similar to my own.

At length delay was no longer possible, and, with a heart almost bursting from my bosom, I advanced to the region of the forecastle, where my companions were awaiting me. I held out my hand with the splinters, and Peters immediately drew. He was free—*his,* at least, was not the shortest; and there was now another chance against my escape. I summoned up all my strength, and passed the lots to Augustus. He also drew immediately, and he also was free; and now, whether I should live or die, the chances were no more than precisely even. At this moment all the fierceness of the tiger possessed my bosom, and I felt towards my poor fellow-creature, Parker, the most intense, the most diabolical hatred. But the feeling did not last; and, at length, with a convulsive shudder and closed eyes, I held out the two remaining splinters towards him. It was full five minutes before he could summon resolution to draw, during which period of heart-rending suspense I never once opened my eyes. Presently one of the two lots was quickly drawn from my hand. The decision was then over, yet I knew not whether it was for me or against me. No one spoke, and still I dared not satisfy myself by looking at the splinter I held. Peters at length took me by the hand, and I forced myself to look up, when I immediately saw by the countenance of Parker that I was safe, and that he it was who had been doomed to suffer. Gasping for breath, I fell senseless to the deck.

I recovered from my swoon in time to behold the consummation of the tragedy in the death of him who had been chiefly instrumental in bringing it about. He made no resistance whatever, and was stabbed in the back by Peters, when he fell instantly dead. I must not dwell upon the fearful repast which immediately ensued. Such things may be imagined, but words have no power to impress the mind with the exquisite horror of their reality. Let it suffice to say that, having in some measure appeased the raging thirst which consumed us by the blood of the victim, and having by common consent taken off the hands, feet, and head, throwing them together with the entrails, into the sea, we devoured the rest of the body, piecemeal, during the four ever memorable days of the seventeenth, eighteenth, nineteenth, and twentieth of the month.

On the nineteenth, there coming on a smart shower which lasted fifteen or twenty minutes, we contrived to catch some water by means of a sheet which had been fished up from the cabin by our drag just after the gale. The quantity we took in all did not amount to more than half a gallon; but even this scanty allowance supplied us with comparative strength and hope.

On the twenty-first we were again reduced to the last necessity. The weather still remained warm and pleasant, with occasional fogs and light breezes, most usually from N. to W.

On the twenty-second, as we were sitting close huddled together, gloomily revolving over our lamentable condition, there flashed through my mind all at once an idea which inspired me with a bright gleam of hope. I remembered that, when the foremast had been cut away, Peters, being in the windward chains, passed one of the axes into my hand, requesting me to put it, if possible, in a place of security, and that a few minutes before the last heavy sea struck the brig and filled her I had taken this axe into the forecastle and laid it in one of the larboard berths. I now thought it possible that, by getting at this axe, we might cut through the deck over the store-room, and thus readily supply ourselves with provisions.

When I communicated this project to my companions, they uttered a feeble shout of joy, and we all proceeded forthwith to the forecastle. The difficulty of descending here was greater than that of going down in the cabin, the opening being much smaller, for it will be remembered that the whole framework about the cabin companion-hatch had been carried away, whereas the forecastle-way, being a simple hatch of only about three feet square, had remained uninjured. I did not hesitate, however, to attempt the descent; and a rope being fastened round my body as before, I plunged boldly in, feet foremost, made my way quickly to the berth, and, at the first attempt brought up the axe. It was hailed with the most ecstatic joy and triumph, and the ease with which it had been obtained was regarded as an omen of our ultimate preservation.

We now commenced cutting at the deck with all the energy of rekindled hope, Peters and myself taking the axe by turns, Augustus's wounded arm not permitting him to aid us in any degree. As we were still so feeble as to be scarcely able to stand unsupported, and could consequently work but a minute or two without resting, it soon became evident that many long hours would be requisite to accomplish our task—that is, to cut an opening sufficiently large to admit of a free access to the store-room. This consideration, however, did not discourage us; and, working all night by the light of the moon, we succeeded in effecting our purpose by daybreak on the morning of the twenty-third.

Peters now volunteered to go down; and, having made all arrangements as before, he descended, and soon returned, bringing up with him a small jar, which, to our great joy, proved to be full of olives. Having shared these among us, and devoured them with the greatest avidity, we proceeded to let him down again. This time he succeeded beyond our utmost expectations, returning instantly with a large ham and a bottle of Madeira wine. Of the latter we each took a moderate sup, having learned by experience the pernicious consequences of indulging too freely. The ham, except about two pounds near the bone, was not in a condition to be eaten, having been entirely spoiled by the salt water. The sound part was divided among us. Peters and Augustus, not being able to restrain their appetite, swallowed theirs upon the instant; but I was more cautious, and ate but a small portion of mine, dreading the thirst which I knew would ensue.

We now rested a while from our labours, which had been intoler ably severe.

By noon, feeling somewhat strengthened and refreshed, we again renewed our attempt at getting up provisions, Peters and myself going down alternately, and always with more or less success, until sundown. During this interval we had the good fortune to bring up, altogether, four more small jars of olives, another ham, a carboy containing nearly three gallons of excellent Cape Madeira wine, and, what gave us still more delight, a small tortoise of the Gallipago breed, several of which had been taken on board by Captain Barnard, as the Grampus was leaving port, from the schooner Mary Pitts, just returned from a sealing voyage in the Pacific.

In a subsequent portion of this narrative I shall have frequent occasion to mention this species of tortoise. It is found principally, as most of my readers may know, in the group of islands called the Gallipagos, which, indeed, derive their name from the animal—the Spanish word Gallipago meaning a freshwater terrapin. From the peculiarity of their shape and action they have been sometimes called elephant tortoise. They are frequently found of an enormous size. I have myself seen several which would weigh from twelve to fifteen hundred pounds, although I do not remember that any navigator speaks of having seen them weighing more than eight hundred. Their appearance is singular, and even disgusting. Their steps are very slow, measured, and heavy, their bodies being carried about a foot from the ground. Their neck is long, and exceedingly slender; from eighteen inches to two feet is a very common length, and I killed one, where the distance from the shoulder to the extremity of the of the head was no less than three feet ten inches. The head has a striking resemblance to that of a serpent. They can exist without food for an almost incredible length of time, instances having been known where they have been thrown into the hold of a vessel and lain two years without nourishment of any kind—being as fat, and, in every respect, in as good order at the expiration of the time as when they were first put in. In one particular these extraordinary animals bear a resemblance to the dromedary, or camel of the desert. In a bag at the root of the neck they carry with them a constant supply of water. In some instances, upon killing them after a full year's deprivation of all nourishment, as much as three gallons of perfectly sweet and fresh water have been found in their bags. Their food is chiefly wild parsley and celery, with purslane, sea-kelp, and prickly-pears, upon which latter vegetable they thrive wonderfully, a great quantity of it being usually found on the hill-sides near the shore wherever the animal itself is discovered. They are excellent and highly nutritious food, and have, no doubt, been the means of preserving the lives of thousands of seamen employed in the whale-fishery and other pursuits in the Pacific.

The one which we had the good fortune to bring up from the storeroom was not of a large size, weighing probably sixty-five or seventy pounds. It was a female, and in excellent condition, being exceedingly fat, and having more than a quart of limpid and sweet water in its bag. This was indeed a treasure; and, falling on our knees with one accord, we returned fervent thanks to God for so seasonable a relief.

We had great difficulty in getting the animal up through the opening, as its struggles were fierce and its strength prodigious. It was upon the point of making its escape from Peters's grasp, and slipping back into the water, when Augustus, throwing a rope with a slip-knot around its throat, held it up in this manner until I jumped into the hole by the side of Peters, and assisted him in lifting it out.

The water we drew carefully from the bag into the jug, which, it will be remembered, had been brought up before from the cabin. Having done this, we broke off the neck of a bottle so as to form, with the cork, a kind of glass, holding not quite half a gill. We then each drank one of these measures full, and resolved to limit ourselves to this quantity per day as long as it should hold out.

During the last two or three days, the weather having been

dry and pleasant, the bedding we had obtained from the cabin, as well as our clothing, had become thoroughly dry, so that we passed this night (that of the twenty-third) in comparative comfort, enjoying a tranquil repose, after having supped plentifully on olives and ham, with a small allowance of the wine. Being afraid of losing some of our stores overboard during the night, in the event of a breeze springing up, we secured them as well as possible with cordage to the fragments of the windlass. Our tortoise, which we were anxious to preserve alive as long as we could, we threw on its back, and otherwise carefully fastened.

CHAPTER XIII

JULY 24TH. This morning saw us wonderfully recruited in spirits and strength. Notwithstanding the perilous situation in which we were still placed, ignorant of our position, although certainly at a great distance from land, without more food than would last us for a fortnight even with great care, almost entirely without water, and floating about at the mercy of every wind and wave on the merest wreck in the world, still the infinitely more terrible distresses and dangers from which we had so lately and so providentially been delivered caused us to regard what we now endured as but little more than an ordinary evil—so strictly comparative is either good or ill.

At sunrise we were preparing to renew our attempts at getting up something from the storeroom, when, a smart shower coming on, with some lightning, we turned our attention to the catching of water by means of the sheet we had used before for this purpose. We had no other means of collecting the rain than by holding the sheet spread out with one of the forechain-plates in the middle of it. The water, thus conducted to the centre, was drained through into our jug. We had nearly filled it in this manner, when, a heavy squall coming on from the northward, obliged us to desist, as the hulk began once more to roll so violently that we could no longer keep our feet. We now went forward, and, lashing ourselves securely to the remnant of the windlass as before, awaited the event with far more calmness than could have been anticipated or would have been imagined possible under the circumstances. At noon the wind had freshened into a two-reef breeze, and by night into a stiff gale, accompanied with a tremendously heavy swell. Experience having taught us, however, the best method of arranging our lashings, we weathered this dreary night in tolerable security, although thoroughly drenched at almost every instant by the sea, and in momentary dread of being washed off. Fortunately, the weather was so warm as to render the water rather grateful than otherwise.

July 25th. This morning the gale had diminished to a mere ten-knot breeze, and the sea had gone down with it so considerably that we were able to keep ourselves dry upon the deck. To our great grief, however, we found that two jars of our olives, as well as the whole of our ham, had been washed overboard, in spite of the careful manner in which they had been fastened. We determined not to kill the tortoise as yet, and contented ourselves for the present with a breakfast on a few of the olives, and a measure of water each, which latter we mixed, half and half, with wine, finding great relief and strength from the mixture, without the distressing intoxication which had ensued upon drinking the Port. The sea was still far too rough for the renewal of our efforts at getting up provision from the storeroom. Several articles, of no importance to us in our present situation, floated up through the opening during the day, and were immediately washed overboard. We also now observed that the hulk lay more along than ever, so that we could not stand an instant without lashing ourselves. On this account we passed a gloomy and uncomfortable day. At noon the sun appeared to be nearly vertical, and we had no doubt that we had been driven down by the long succession of northward and northwesterly winds into the near vicinity of the equator. Towards evening saw several sharks, and were somewhat alarmed by the audacious manner in which an enormously large one approached us. At one time, a lurch throwing the deck very far beneath the water, the monster actually swam in upon us, floundering for some moments just over the companion-hatch, and striking Peters violently with his tail. A heavy sea at length hurled him overboard, much to our relief. In moderate weather we might have easily captured him.

July 26th. This morning, the wind having greatly abated, and the sea not being very rough, we determined to renew our exertions in the storeroom. After a great deal of hard labour during the whole day, we found that nothing further was to be expected from this quarter, the partitions of the room having been stove during the night, and its contents swept into the hold. This discovery, as may be supposed, filled us with despair.

July 27th. The sea nearly smooth, with a light wind, and still from the northward and westward. The sun coming out hotly in the afternoon, we occupied ourselves in drying our clothes. Found great relief from thirst, and much comfort otherwise, by bathing in the sea; in this, however, we were forced to use great caution, being afraid of sharks, several of which were seen swimming around the brig during the day.

July 28th. Good weather still. The brig now began to lie along so alarmingly that we feared she would eventually roll bottom up. Prepared ourselves as well as we could for this emergency, lashing our tortoise, water-jug, and two remaining jars of olives as far as possible over to the windward, placing them outside the hull, below the main-chains. The sea very smooth all day, with little or no wind.

July 29th. A continuance of the same weather. Augustus's wounded arm began to evince symptoms of mortification. He complained of drowsiness and excessive thirst, but no acute pain. Nothing could be done for his relief beyond rubbing his wounds with a little of the vinegar from the olives, and from this no benefit seemed to be experienced. We did everything in our power for his comfort, and trebled his allowance of water.

July 30th. An excessively hot day, with no wind. An enormous shark kept close by the hulk during the whole of the fore-noon. We made several unsuccessful attempts to capture him by means of a noose. Augustus much worse, and evidently sinking as much from want of proper nourishment as from the effect of his wounds. He constantly prayed to be released from his sufferings, wishing for nothing but death. This evening we ate the last of our olives, and found the water in our jug so putrid that we could not swallow it at all without the addition of wine. Determined to kill our tortoise in the morning.

July 31st. After a night of excessive anxiety and fatigue, owing to the position of the hulk, we set about killing and cutting up our tortoise. It proved to be much smaller than we had supposed, although in good condition—the whole meat about him not amounting to more than ten pounds. With a view of preserving a portion of this as long as possible, we cut it into fine pieces, and filled with them our three remaining olive-jars and the wine-bottle (all of which had been kept), pouring in afterward the vinegar from the olives. In this manner we put away about three pounds of the tortoise, intending not to touch it until we had consumed the rest. We concluded to restrict ourselves to about four ounces of the meat per day; the whole would thus last us thirteen days. A brisk shower, with severe thunder and lightning, came on about dusk, but lasted so short a time that we only succeeded in catching about half a pint of water. The whole of this, by common consent, was given to Augustus, who now appeared to be in the last extremity. He drank the water from the sheet as we caught it (we holding it above him as he lay so as to let it run into his mouth), for we had now nothing left capable of holding water, unless we had chosen to empty out our wine from the carboy, or the stale water from the jug. Either of these expedients would have been resorted to had the shower lasted.

The sufferer seemed to derive but little benefit from the draught. His arm was completely black from the wrist to the shoulder, and his feet were like ice. We expected every moment to see him breathe his last. He was frightfully emaciated; so much so that, although he weighed a hundred and twenty-seven pounds upon his leaving Nantucket, he now did not weigh more than *forty or fifty at the farthest.* His eyes were sunk far in his head, being scarcely perceptible, and the skin of his cheeks hung so loosely as to prevent his masticating any food, or even swallowing any liquid, without great difficulty.

August 1st. A continuance of the same calm weather, with an oppressively hot sun. Suffered exceedingly from thirst, the water in the jug being absolutely putrid and swarming with vermin. We contrived, nevertheless, to swallow a portion of it by mixing it with wine—our thirst, however, was but little abated. We found more relief by bathing in the sea, but could not avail ourselves of this expedient except at long intervals, on acount of the continual presence of sharks. We now saw clearly that Augustus could not be saved; that he was evidently dying. We could do nothing to relieve his sufferings, which appeared to be great. About twelve o'clock he expired in strong convulsions, and without having spoken for several hours. His death filled us with the most gloomy forebodings, and had so great an effect upon our spirits that we sat motionless by the corpse during the whole day, and never addressed each other except in a whisper. It was not until some time after dark that we took courage to get up and throw the body overboard. It was then loathsome beyond expression, and so far decayed that, as Peters attempted to lift it, an entire leg came off in his grasp. As the mass of putrefaction slipped over the vessel's side into the water, the glare of phosphoric light with which it was surrounded plainly discovered to us seven or eight large sharks, the clashing of whose horrible teeth, as their prey was torn to pieces among them, might have been heard at the distance of a mile. We shrunk within ourselves in the extremity of horror at the sound.

August 2d. The same fearfully calm and hot weather. The dawn found us in a state of pitiable dejection as well as bodily exhaustion. The water in the jug was now absolutely useless, being a thick gelatinous mass; nothing but frightful-looking worms mingled with slime. We threw it out, and washed the jug well in the sea, afterward pouring a little vinegar in it from our bottles of pickled tortoise. Our thirst could now scarcely be endured, and we tried in vain to relieve it by wine, which seemed only to add fuel to the flame, and excited us to a high degree of intoxication. We afterward endeavoured to relieve our sufferings by mixing the wine with sea-water; but this instantly brought about the most violent retchings, so that we never again attempted it. During the whole day we anxiously sought an opportunity of bathing, but to no purpose; for the hulk was now entirely besieged on all sides with sharks—no doubt the identical monsters who had devoured our poor companion on the evening before, and who were in momentary expectation of another similar feast. This circumstance occasioned us the most bitter regret, and filled us with the most depressing and melancholy forebodings. We had experienced indescribable relief in bathing, and to have this resource cut off in so frightful a manner was more than we could bear. Nor, indeed, were we altogether free from the apprehension of immediate danger, for the least slip or false movement would have thrown us at once within reach of those voracious fish, who frequently thrust themselves directly upon us, swimming up to leeward. No shouts or exertions on our part seemed to alarm them. Even when one of the largest was struck with an axe by Peters and much wounded, he persisted in his attempts to push in where we were. A cloud came up at dusk, but, to our extreme anguish, passed over without discharging itself. It is quite impossible to conceive our sufferings from thirst at this period. We passed a sleepless night, both on this account and through dread of the sharks.

August 3d. No prospect of relief, and the brig lying still more and more along, so that now we could not maintain a footing upon deck at all. Busied ourselves in securing our wine and tortoise-meat, so that we might not lose them in the event of our rolling over. Got out two stout spikes from the forechains, and, by means of the axe, drove them into the hull to windward within a couple of feet of the water; this not being very far from the keel, as we were nearly upon our beam-ends. To these spikes we now lashed our provisions, as being more secure than their former position beneath the chains. Suffered great agony from thirst during the whole day—no chance of bathing on account of the sharks, which never left us for a moment. Found it impossible to sleep.

August 4th. A little before daybreak we perceived that the hulk was heeling over, and aroused ourselves to prevent being thrown off by the movement. At first the roll was slow and gradual, and we contrived to clamber over to windward very well, having taken the precaution to leave ropes hanging from the spikes we had driven in for the provision. But we had not calculated sufficiently upon the acceleration of the impetus; for, presently the heel became too violent to allow of our keeping pace with it; and, before either of us knew what was to happen, we found ourselves hurled furiously into the sea, and struggling several fathoms beneath the surface, with the huge hull immediately above us.

In going under the water I had been obliged to let go my hold upon the rope; and finding that I was completely beneath the vessel, and my strength nearly exhausted, I scarcely made a struggle for life, and resigned myself, in a few seconds, to die. But here again I was deceived, not having taken into consideration the natural rebound of the hull to windward. The whirl of the water upward, which the vessel occasioned in rolling partially back, brought me to the surface still more violently than I had been plunged beneath. Upon coming up I found myself about twenty yards from the hulk, as near as I could judge. She was lying keel up, rocking furiously from side to side, and the sea in all directions around was much agitated, and full of strong whirlpools. I could see nothing of Peters. An oil-cask was floating within a few feet of me, and various other articles from the brig were scattered about.

My principal terror was now on account of the sharks, which I knew to be in my vicinity. In order to deter these, if possible, from approaching me, I splashed the water vigorously with both hands and feet as I swam toward the hulk, creating a body of foam. I have no doubt that to this expedient, simple as it was, I was indebted for my preservation; for the sea all round the brig, just before her rolling over, was so crowded with these monsters, that I must have been, and really was, in actual contact with some of them during my progress. By great good fortune, however, I reached the side of the vessel in safety, although so utterly weakened by the violent exertion I had used that I should never have been able to get upon it but for the timely assistance of Peters, who now, to my great joy, made his appearance (having scrambled up to the keel from the opposite side of the hull), and threw me the end of a rope—one of those which had been attached to the spikes.

Having barely escaped this danger, our attention was now directed to the dreadful imminency of another—that of absolute starvation. Our whole stock of provision had been swept overboard in spite of all our care in securing it; and seeing no longer the remotest possibility of obtaining more, we gave way both of us to despair, weeping aloud like children, and neither of us attempting to offer consolation to the other. Such weakness can scarcely be conceived, and to those who have never been similarly situated will, no doubt, appear unnatural; but it must be remembered that our intellects were so entirely disordered by the long course of privation and terror to which we had been subjected, that we could not justly be considered, at that period, in the light of rational beings. In subsequent perils, nearly as great, if not greater, I bore up with fortitude against all the evils of my situation, and Peters, it will be seen, evinced a stoical philosophy nearly as incredible as his present childlike supineness and imbecility—the mental condition made the difference.

The overturning of the brig, even with the consequent loss of the wine and turtle, would not, in fact, have rendered our situation more deplorable than before, except for the disappearance of the bedclothes by which we had been hitherto enabled to catch rain-water, and of the jug in which we had kept it when caught;

for we found the whole bottom, from within two or three feet of the bends as far as the keel, together with the keel itself, *thickly covered with large barnacles, which proved to be excellent and highly nutritious food.* Thus, in two important respects, the accident we had so greatly dreaded proved a benefit rather than an injury; it had opened to us a supply of provisions which we could not have exhausted, using it moderately, in a month; and it had greatly contributed to our comfort as regards position, we being much more at our ease, and in infinitely less danger, than before.

The difficulty, however, of now obtaining water blinded us to all the benefits of the change in our condition. That we might be ready to avail ourselves, as far as possible, of any shower which might fall, we took off our shirts, to make use of them as we had of the sheets—not hoping, of course, to get more in this way, even under the most favourable circumstances, than half a gill at a time. No signs of a cloud appeared during the day, and the agonies of our thirst were nearly intolerable. At night, Peters obtained about an hour's disturbed sleep, but my intense sufferings would not permit me to close my eyes for a single moment.

August 5th. To-day, a gentle breeze springing up carried us through a vast quantity of seaweed, among which we were so fortunate as to find eleven small crabs, which afforded us several delicious meals. Their shells being quite soft, we ate them entire, and found that they irritated our thirst far less than the barnacles. Seeing no trace of sharks among the seaweed, we also ventured to bathe, and remained in the water for four or five hours, during which we experienced a very sensible diminution of our thirst. Were greatly refreshed, and spent the night somewhat more comfortably than before, both of us snatching a little sleep.

August 6th. This day we were blessed by a brisk and continual rain, lasting from about noon until after dark. Bitterly did we now regret the loss of our jug and carboy; for, in spite of the little means we had of catching the water, we might have filled one, if not both of them. As it was, we contrived to satisfy the cravings of thirst by suffering the shirts to become saturated, and then wringing them so as to let the grateful fluid trickle into our mouths. In this occupation we passed the entire day.

August 7th. Just at daybreak we both at the same instant descried a sail to the eastward, and *evidently coming towards us!* We hailed the glorious sight with a long, although feeble shout of rapture; and began instantly to make every signal in our power, by flaring the shirts in the air, leaping as high as our weak condition would permit, and even by hallooing with all the strength of our lungs, although the vessel could not have been less than fifteen miles distant. However, she still continued to near our hulk, and we felt that, if she but held her present course, she must eventually come so close as to perceive us. In about an hour after we first discovered her, we could clearly see the people on her decks. She was a long, low, and rakish-looking topsail schooner, with a black ball in her foretopsail, and had, apparently, a full crew. We now became alarmed, for we could hardly imagine it possible that she did not observe us, and were apprehensive that she meant to leave us to perish as we were—an act of fiendish barbarity, which, however incredible it may appear, has been repeatedly perpetrated at sea, under circumstances very nearly similar, and by beings who were regarded as belonging to the human species.*

* The case of the brig Polly, of Boston, is one so much in point, and her fate, in many respects, so remarkably similar to our own, that I cannot forbear alluding to it here. This vessel, of one hundred and thirty tons burden, sailed from Boston, with a cargo of lumber and provisions, for Santa Croix, on the 12th of December, 1811, under the command of Captain Casneau. There were eight souls on board besides the captain—the mate, four seamen, and the cook, together with a Mr. Hunt, and a negro girl belonging to him. On the fifteenth, having cleared the shoal of Georges, she sprung a leak in a gale of wind from the southeast, and was finally capsized; but, the masts going by the board, she afterward righted. They remained in this situation, without fire, and with very little provision, for the period of *one hundred and ninety-one days* (from December the fifteenth to June the twentieth), when Captain Casneau and Samuel Badger, the only survivors, were taken off the wreck by the Fame, of Hull, Captain Featherstone, bound home from Rio Janeiro. When picked up, they were in latitude 28° N., longitude 13° W., *having drifted above two thousand miles!* On the ninth

In this instance, however, by the mercy of God, we were destined to be most happily deceived; for, presently we were aware of a sudden commotion on the deck of the stranger, who immediately afterward ran up a British flag, and, hauling her wind, bore up directly upon us. In half an hour more we found ourselves in her cabin. She proved to be the Jane Guy, of Liverpool, Captain Guy, bound on a sealing and trading voyage to the South Seas and Pacific.

CHAPTER XIV

THE Jane Guy was a fine-looking topsail schooner of a hundred and eighty tons burden. She was unusually sharp in the bows, and on a wind, in moderate weather, the fastest sailer I have ever seen. Her qualities, however, as a rough sea-boat, were not so good, and her draught of water was by far too great for the trade to which she was destined. For this peculiar service, a larger vessel, and one of a light proportionate draught, is desirable—say a vessel of from three to three hundred and fifty tons. She should be bark-rigged, and in other respects of a different construction from the usual South Sea ships. It is absolutely necessary that she should be well armed. She should have, say ten or twelve twelve-pound carronades, and two or three long twelves, with brass blunderbusses, and water-tight arm-chests for each top. Her anchors and cables should be of far greater strength than is required for

---

of July the Fame fell in with the brig Dromeo, Captain Perkins, who landed the two sufferers in Kennebeck. The narrative from which we gather these details ends in the following words:

"It is natural to inquire how they could float such a vast distance, upon the most frequented part of the Atlantic and not be discovered all this time. *They were passed by more than a dozen sail, one of which came so nigh them that they could distinctly see the people on deck and on the rigging looking at them; but, to the inexpressible disappointment of the starving and freezing men, they stifled the dictates of compassion, hoisted sail, and cruelly abandoned them to their fate.*"

any other species of trade, and, above all, her crew should be numerous and efficient; not less, for such a vessel as I have described, than fifty or sixty able-bodied men. The Jane Guy had a crew of thirty-five, all able seamen, besides the captain and mate, but she was not altogether as well armed or otherwise equipped, as a navigator acquainted with the difficulties and dangers of the trade could have desired.

Captain Guy was a gentleman of great urbanity of manner, and of considerable experience in the southern traffic, to which he had devoted the greater portion of his life. He was deficient, however, in energy, and consequently, in that spirit of enterprise which is here so absolutely requisite. He was part owner of the vessel in which he sailed, and was invested with discretionary powers to cruise in the South Seas for any cargo which might come most readily to hand. He had on board, as usual in such voyages, beads, looking-glasses, tinder-works, axes, hatchets, saws, adzes, planes, chisels, gouges, gimlets, files, spokeshaves, rasps, hammers, nails, knives, scissors, razors, needles, thread, crockery-ware, calico, trinkets, and other similar articles.

The schooner sailed from Liverpool on the tenth of July, crossed the Tropic of Cancer on the twenty-fifth, in longitude twenty degrees west, and reached Sal, one of the Cape Verd Islands, on the twenty-ninth, where she took in salt and other necessaries for the voyage. On the third of August, she left the Cape Verds and steered southwest, stretching over towards the coast of Brazil, so as to cross the equator between the meridians of twenty-eight and thirty degrees west longitude. This is the course usually taken by vessels bound from Europe to the Cape of Good Hope, or by that route to the East Indies. By proceeding thus they avoid the calms and strong contrary currents which continually prevail on the coast of Guinea, while in the end, it is found to be the shortest track, as westerly winds are never wanting afterward by which to reach the Cape. It was Captain Guy's intention to make his first stoppage at Kerguelen's Land—I hardly know for what reason. On the day we were picked up the schooner was off Cape St. Roque, in longitude thirty-one degrees W.; so that, when found, we had drifted probably, from north to south, ***not** less than five-and-twenty degrees!*

On board the Jane Guy we were treated with all the kindness our distressed situation demanded. In about a fortnight, during which time we continued steering to the southeast, with gentle breezes and fine weather, both Peters and myself recovered entirely from the effects of our late privation and dreadful suffering, and we began to remember what had passed rather as a frightful dream from which we had been happily awakened, than as events which had taken place in sober and naked reality. I have since found that this species of partial oblivion is usually brought about by sudden transition, whether from joy to sorrow or from sorrow to joy—the degree of forgetfulness being proportioned to the degree of difference in the exchange. Thus, in my own case, I now feel it impossible to realize the full extent of the misery which I endured during the days spent upon the hulk. The incidents are remembered, but not the feelings which the incidents elicited at the time of their occurrence. I only know, that when they did occur, I *then* thought human nature could sustain nothing more of agony.

We continued our voyage for some weeks without any incidents of greater moment than the occasional meeting with whaling-ships, and more frequently with the black or right whale, so called in contradistinction to the spermaceti. These, however, were chiefly found south of the twenty-fifth parallel. On the sixteenth of September, being in the vicinity of the Cape of Good Hope, the schooner encountered her first gale of any violence since leaving Liverpool. In this neighbourhood, but more frequently to the south and east of the promontory (we were to the westward), navigators have often to contend with storms from the northward which rage with great fury. They always bring with them a heavy sea, and one of their most dangerous features is the instantaneous chopping round of the wind, an occurrence almost certain to take place during the greatest force of the gale. A perfect hurricane will be blowing at one moment from the northward or northeast, and in the next not a breath of wind will be felt in that direction, while from the southwest it will come out all at once with a violence almost inconceivable. A bright spot to the southward is the sure forerunner of the change, and vessels are thus enabled to take the proper precautions.

It was about six in the morning when the blow came on with a white squall, and, as usual, from the northward. By eight it had increased very much, and brought down upon us one of the most tremendous seas I had then ever beheld. Everything had been made as snug as possible, but the schooner laboured excessively, and gave evidence of her bad qualities as a seaboat, pitching her forecastle under at every plunge, and with the greatest difficulty struggling up from one wave before she was buried in another. Just before sunset the bright spot for which we had been on the lookout made its appearance in the southwest, and in an hour afterward we perceived the little head-sail we carried flapping listlessly against the mast. In two minutes more, in spite of every preparation, we were hurled on our beam-ends as if by magic, and a perfect wilderness of foam made a clear breach over us as we lay. The blow from the southwest, however, luckily proved to be nothing more than a squall, and we had the good fortune to right the vessel without the loss of a spar. A heavy cross sea gave us great trouble for a few hours after this, but towards morning we found ourselves in nearly as good condition as before the gale. Captain Guy considered that he had made an escape little less than miraculous.

On the thirteenth of October we came in sight of Prince Edward's Island, in latitude 46° 53′ S., longitude 37° 46′ E. Two days afterward we found ourselves near Possession Island, and presently passed the islands of Crozet, in latitude 42° 59′ S., longitude 48° E. On the eighteenth we made Kerguelen's or Desolation Island, in the Southern Indian Ocean, and came to anchor in Christmas Harbour, having four fathoms of water.

This island, or rather group of islands, bears southeast from the Cape of Good Hope, and is distant therefrom nearly eight hundred leagues. It was first discovered in 1772, by the Baron de Kergulen, or Kerguelen, a Frenchman, who, thinking the land to form a portion of an extensive southern continent, carried home information to that effect, which produced much excitement at the time. The government, taking the matter up, sent the baron back in the following year for the purpose of giving his new discovery a critical examination, when the mistake was discovered. In 1777, Captain Cook fell in with the same group, and gave to the principal one the name of Desolation Island, a title which it certainly well deserves. Upon approaching the land, however, the navigator might be induced to suppose otherwise, as the sides of most of the hills, from September to March, are clothed with very brilliant verdure. This deceitful appearance is caused by a small plant resembling saxifrage, which is abundant, growing in large patches on a species of crumbling moss. Besides this plant there is scarcely a sign of vegetation on the island, if we except some coarse rank grass near the harbour, some lichen, and a shrub which bears resemblance to a cabbage shooting into seed, and which has a bitter and acrid taste.

The face of the country is hilly, although none of the hills can be called lofty. Their tops are perpetually covered with snow. There are several harbours, of which Christmas Harbour is the most convenient. It is the first to be met with on the northeast side of the island after passing Cape François, which forms the northern shore, and, by its peculiar shape, serves to distinguish the harbour. Its projecting point terminates in a high rock, through which is a large hole, forming a natural arch. The entrance is in latitude 48° 40′ S., longitude 69° 6′ E. Passing in here, good anchorage may be found under the shelter of several small islands, which form a sufficient protection from all easterly winds. Proceeding on eastwardly from this anchorage you come to Wasp Bay, at the head of the harbour. This is a small basin, completely landlocked, into which you can go with four fathoms, and find anchorage in from ten to three, hard clay bottom. A ship might lie here with her best bower ahead all the year round without risk. To the westward, at the head of Wasp Bay, is a small stream of excellent water, easily procured.

Some seal of the fur and hair species are still to be found on Kerguelen's Island, and sea-elephants abound. The feathered tribes are discovered in great numbers. Penguins are very plenty, and of these there are four different kinds. The royal penguin, so called from its size and beautiful plumage, is the largest. The upper part of the body is usually gray, sometimes of a lilac tint; the under portion of the purest white imaginable. The head is of a glossy and most brilliant black, the feet also. The chief beauty of the plumage, however, consists in two broad stripes of a gold color, which pass along from the head to the breast. The bill is long, and either pink or bright scarlet. These birds walk erect, with a stately carriage. They carry their heads high with their wings drooping like two arms, and, as their tails project from their body in a line with the legs, the resemblance to a human figure is very striking, and would be apt to deceive the spectator at a casual glance or in the gloom of the evening. The royal penguins which we met with on Kerguelen's Land were rather larger than a goose. The other kinds are the maccaroni, the jackass, and the rookery penguin. These are much smaller, less beautiful in plumage, and different in other respects.

Besides the penguin many other birds are here to be found, among which may be mentioned seahens, blue petrel, teal, ducks, Port Egmont hens, shags, Cape pigeons, the nelly, sea-swallows, terns, sea-gulls, Mother Carey's chickens, Mother Carey's geese, or the great petrel, and, lastly, the albatross.

The great petrel is as large as the common albatross, and is carnivorous. It is frequently called the break-bones, or osprey petrel. They are not at all shy, and, when properly cooked, are palatable food. In flying they sometimes sail very close to the surface of the water, with the wings expanded, without appearing to move them in the least degree, or make any exertion with them whatever.

The albatross is one of the largest and fiercest of the South Sea birds. It is of the gull species, and takes its prey on the wing, never coming on land except for the purpose of breeding. Between this bird and the penguin the most singular friendship exists. Their nests are constructed with great uniformity upon a plan concerted between the two species—that of the albatross being placed in the centre of a little square formed by the nests of four penguins. Navigators have agreed in calling an assemblage of such encampments *a rookery*. These rookeries have been often described, but as my readers may not all have seen these descriptions, and as I shall have occasion hereafter to speak of the penguin and albatross, it will not be amiss to say something here of their mode of building and living.

When the season for incubation arrives, the birds assemble in vast numbers, and for some days appear to be deliberating upon the proper course to be pursued. At length they proceed to action. A level piece of ground is selected, of suitable extent, usually comprising three or four acres, and situated as near the sea as possible, being still beyond its reach. The spot is chosen with reference to its evenness of surface, and that is preferred which is the least encumbered with stones. This matter being arranged, the birds proceed, with one accord, and actuated apparently by one mind, to trace out, with mathematical accuracy, either a square or other parallelogram, as may best suit the nature of the ground, and of just sufficient size to accommodate easily all the birds assembled, and no more—in this particular seeming determined upon preventing the access of future stragglers who have not participated in the labour of the encampment. One side of the place thus marked out runs parallel with the water's edge, and is left open for ingress or egress.

Having defined the limits of the rookery, the colony now begin to clear it of every species of rubbish, picking up stone by stone, and carrying them outside of the lines, and close by them, so as to form a wall on the three inland sides. Just within this wall a perfectly level and smooth walk is formed, from six to eight feet wide, and extending around the encampment—thus serving the purpose of a general promenade.

The next process is to partition out the whole area into small squares exactly equal in size. This is done by forming narrow paths, very smooth, and crossing each other at right angles throughout the entire extent of the rookery. At each intersection of these paths the nest of an albatross is constructed, and a penguin's nest in the centre of each square—thus every penguin is surrounded by four albatrosses, and each albatross by a like number of penguins. The penguin's nest consists of a hole in the earth, very shallow, being only just of sufficient depth to keep her single egg from rolling. The albatross is somewhat less simple in her arrangements, erecting a hillock about a foot high and two in diameter. This is made of earth, sea-weed, and shells. On its summit she builds her nest.

The birds take especial care never to leave their nests unoccupied for an instant during the period of incubation, or, indeed, until the young progeny are sufficiently strong to take care of themselves. While the male is absent at sea in search of food, the female remains on duty, and it is only upon the return of her partner that she ventures abroad. The eggs are never left uncovered at all—while one bird leaves the nest the other nestling in by its side. This precaution is rendered necessary by the thievish propensities prevalent in the rookery, the inhabitants making no scruple to purloin each other's eggs at every good opportunity.

Although there are some rookeries in which the penguin and albatross are the sole population, yet in most of them a variety of oceanic birds are to be met with, enjoying all the privileges of citizenship, and scattering their nests here and there, wherever they can find room, never interfering, however, with the stations of the larger species. The appearance of such encampments, when seen from a distance, is exceedingly singular. The whole atmosphere just above the settlement is darkened with the immense number of the albatross (mingled with the smaller tribes) which are continually hovering over it, either going to the ocean or returning home. At the same time a crowd of penguins are to be observed, some passing to and fro in the narrow alleys, and some marching with the military strut so peculiar to them, around the general promenade-ground which encircles the rookery. In short, survey it as we will, nothing can be more astonishing than the spirit of reflection evinced by these feathered beings, and nothing surely can be better calculated to elicit reflection in every well-regulated human intellect.

On the morning after our arrival in Christmas Harbour the chief mate, Mr. Patterson, took the boats, and (although it was somewhat early in the season) went in search of seal, leaving the captain and a young relation of his on a point of barren land to the westward, they having some business, whose nature I could not ascertain, to transact in the interior of the island. Captain Guy took with him a bottle, in which was a sealed letter, and made his way from the point on which he was set on shore towards one of the highest peaks in the place. It is probable that his design was to leave the letter on that height for some vessel which he expected to come after him. As soon as we lost sight of him we proceeded (Peters and myself being in the mate's boat) on our cruise around the coast, looking for seal. In this business we were occupied about three weeks, examining with great care every nook and corner, not only of Kerguelen's Land, but of the several small islands in the vicinity. Our labours, however, were not crowned with any important success. We saw a great many fur seal, but they were exceedingly shy, and with the greatest exertions, we could only procure three hundred and fifty skins in all. Sea elephants were abundant, especially on the western coast of the mainland, but of these we killed only twenty, and this with great difficulty. On the smaller islands we discovered a good many of the hair seal, but did not molest them. We returned to the schooner on the eleventh, where we found Captain Guy and his nephew, who gave a very bad account of the interior, representing it as one of the most dreary and utterly barren countries in the world. They had remained two nights on the island, owing to some misunderstanding, on the part of the second mate, in regard to the sending a jollyboat from the schooner to take them off.

CHAPTER XV

ON THE twelfth we made sail from Christmas Harbour, retracing our way to the westward, and leaving Marion's Island, one of Crozet's group, on the larboard. We afterward passed Prince Edward's Island, leaving it also on our left; then, steering more to the northward, made, in fifteen days, the islands of Tristan d'Acunha, in latitude 37° 8′ S., longitude 12° 8′ W.

This group, now so well known, and which consists of three circular islands, was first discovered by the Portuguese, and was visited afterward by the Dutch in 1643, and by the French in 1767. The three islands together form a triangle, and are distant from each other about ten miles, there being fine open passages between. The land in all of them is very high, especially in Tristan d'Acunha, properly so called. This is the largest of the group, being fifteen miles in circumference, and so elevated that it can be seen in clear weather at the distance of eighty or ninety miles. A part of the land towards the north rises more than a thousand feet perpendicularly from the sea. A tableland at this height extends back nearly to the centre of the island, and from this tableland arises a lofty cone like that of Teneriffe. The lower half of this cone is clothed with trees of good size, but the upper region is barren rock, usually hidden among the clouds, and covered with snow during the greater part of the year. There are no shoals or other dangers about the island, the shores being remarkably bold and the water deep. On the northwestern coast is a bay, with a beach of black sand, where a landing with boats can be easily effected, provided there be a southerly wind. Plenty of excellent water may here be readily procured; also cod, and other fish, may be taken with hook and line.

The next island in point of size, and the most westwardly of the group, is that called the Inaccessible. Its precise situation is 37° 17′ S. latitude, longitude 12° 24′ W. It is seven or eight miles in circumference, and on all sides presents a forbidding and precipitous aspect. Its top is perfectly flat, and the whole region is sterile, nothing growing upon it except a few stunted shrubs.

Nightingale Island, the smallest and most southerly, is in latitude 37° 26′ S., longitude 12° 12′ W. Off its southern extremity is a high ledge of rocky islets; a few also of a similar appearance are seen to the northeast. The ground is irregular and sterile, and a deep valley partially separates it.

The shores of these islands abound, in the proper season, with sea lions, sea elephants, the hair and fur seal, together with a great variety of oceanic birds. Whales are also plenty in their vicinity. Owing to the ease with which these various animals were here formerly taken, the group has been much visited since its discovery. The Dutch and French frequented it at a very early period. In 1790, Captain Patten, of the ship Industry, of Philadelphia, made Tristan d'Acunha, where he remained seven months (from August, 1790, to April, 1791) for the purpose of collecting sealskins. In this time he gathered no less than five thousand six hundred, and says that he would have had no difficulty in loading a large ship with oil in three weeks. Upon his arrival he found no quadrupeds, with the exception of a few wild goats—the island now abounds with all our most valuable domestic animals, which have been introduced by subsequent navigators.

I believe it was not long after Captain Patten's visit that Captain Colquhoun, of the American brig Betsey, touched at the largest of the islands for the purpose of refreshment. He planted onions, potatoes, cabbages, and a great many other vegetables, an abundance of all which are now to be met with.

In 1811, a Captain Heywood, in the Nereus, visited Tristan. He found there three Americans, who were residing upon the island to prepare sealskins and oil. One ot these men was named Jonathan Lambert, and he called himself the sovereign of the country. He had cleared and cultivated about sixty acres of land,

and turned his attention to raising the coffee-plant and sugar-cane, with which he had been furnished by the American Minister at Rio de Janeiro. This settlement, however, was finally abandoned, and in 1817 the islands were taken possession of by the British Government, who sent a detachment for that purpose from the Cape of Good Hope. They did not, however, retain them long; but, upon the evacuation of the country as a British possession, two or three English families took up their residence there independently of the Government. On the twenty-fifth of March, 1824, the Berwick, Captain Jeffrey, from London to Van Diemen's Land, arrived at the place, where they found an Englishman of the name of Glass, formerly a corporal in the British artillery. He claimed to be supreme governor of the islands, and had under his control twenty-one men and three women. He gave a very favourable account of the salubrity of the climate and of the productiveness of the soil. The population occupied themselves chiefly in collecting sealskins and sea-elephant oil, with which they traded to the Cape of Good Hope, Glass owning a small schooner. At the period of our arrival the governor was still a resident, but his little community had multiplied, there being fifty-six persons upon Tristan, besides a smaller settlement of seven on Nightingale Island. We had no difficulty in procuring almost every kind of refreshment which we required—sheep, hogs, bullocks, rabbits, poultry, goats, fish in great variety, and vegetables were abundant. Having come to anchor close in with the large island, in eighteen fathoms, we took all we wanted on board very conveniently. Captain Guy also purchased of Glass five hundred sealskins and some ivory. We remained here a week, during which the prevailing winds were from the northward and westward, and the weather somewhat hazy. On the fifth of November we made sail to the southward and westward, with the intention of having a thorough search for a group of islands called the Auroras, respecting whose existence a great diversity of opinion has existed.

These islands are said to have been discovered as early as 1762, by the commander of the ship Aurora. In 1790, Captain

Manuel de Oyarvido, in the ship Princess, belonging to the Royal Philippine Company, sailed, as he asserts, directly among them. In 1794, the Spanish corvette Atrevida went with the determination of ascertaining their precise situation, and, in a paper published by the Royal Hydrographical Society of Madrid in the year 1809, the following language is used respecting this expedition: "The corvette Atrevida practised, in their immediate vicinity, from the twenty-first to the twenty-seventh of January, all the necessary observations, and measured by chronometers the difference of longitude between these islands and the port of Soledad in the Manilas. The islands are three; they are very nearly in the same meridian; the centre one is rather low, and the other two may be seen at nine leagues' distance." The observations made on board the Atrevida give the following results as the precise situation of each island. The most northern is in latitude 52° 37′ 24″ S., longitude 47° 43′ 15″ W.; the middle one in latitude 53° 2′ 40″ S., longitude 47° 55′ 15″ W.; and the most southern in latitude 53° 15′ 22″ S., longitude 47° 57′ 15″ W.

On the twenty-seventh of January 1820, Captain James Weddell, of the British navy, sailed from Staten Island also in search of the Auroras. He reports that, having made the most diligent search and passed not only immediately over the spots indicated by the commander of the Atrevida, but in every direction throughout the vicinity of these spots, he could discover no indication of land. These conflicting statements have induced other navigators to look out for the islands; and, strange to say, while some have sailed through every inch of sea where they are supposed to lie without finding them, there have been not a few who declare positively that they have seen them; and even been close in with their shores. It was Captain Guy's intention to make every exertion within his power to settle the question so oddly in dispute.*

* Among the vessels which at various times have professed to meet with the Auroras may be mentioned the ship San Miguel, in 1769; the ship Aurora, in 1774; the brig Pearl, in 1779; and the ship Dolores, in 1790. They all agree in giving the mean latitude fifty-three degrees south.

We kept on our course, between the south and west, with variable weather, until the twentieth of the month, when we found ourselves on the debated ground, being in latitude 53° 15′ S., longitude 47° 58′ W.—that is to say, very nearly upon the spot indicated as the situation of the most southern of the group. Not perceiving any sign of land, we continued to the westward in the parallel of fifty-three degrees south, as far as the meridian of fifty degrees west. We then stood to the north as far as the parallel of fifty-two degrees south, when we turned to the eastward, and kept our parallel by double altitudes, morning and evening, and meridian altitudes of the planets and moon. Having thus gone eastwardly to the meridian of the western coast of Georgia, we kept that meridian until we were in the latitude from which we set out. We then took diagonal courses throughout the entire extent of sea circumscribed, keeping a lookout constantly at the masthead, and repeating our examination with the greatest care for a period of three weeks, during which the weather was remarkably pleasant and fair, with no haze whatsoever. Of course we were thoroughly satisfied that, whatever islands might have existed in this vicinity at any former period, no vestige of them remained at the present day. Since my return home I find that the same ground was traced over, with equal care, in 1822, by Captain Johnson, of the American schooner Henry, and by Captain Morrell, in the American schooner Wasp—in both cases with the same result as in our own.

CHAPTER XVI

IT HAD been Captain Guy's original intention, after satisfying himself about the Auroras, to proceed through the Strait of Magellan, and up along the western coast of Patagonia; but information received at Tristan d'Acunha induced him to steer to the southward, in the hope of falling in with some small islands said to lie about the parallel of 60° S., longitude 41° 20′ W. In the event of his not discovering these lands, he designed, should the season prove favourable, to push on toward the pole. Accordingly, on the twelfth of December, we made sail in that direction. On the eighteenth we found ourselves about the station indicated by Glass, and cruised for three days in that neighbourhood without finding any traces of the islands he had mentioned. On the twenty-first, the weather being unusually pleasant, we again made sail to the southward, with the resolution of penetrating in that course as far as possible. Before entering upon this portion of my narrative, it may be as well, for the information of those readers who have paid little attention to the progress of discovery in these regions, to give some brief account of the very few attempts at reaching the southern pole which have hitherto been made.

That of Captain Cook was the first of which we have any distinct account. In 1772 he sailed to the south in the Resolution, accompanied by Lieutenant Furneaux in the Adventure. In December he found himself as far as the fifty-eighth parallel of south latitude, and in longitude 26° 57′ E. Here he met with narrow fields of ice, about eight or ten inches thick, and running northwest and southeast. This ice was in large cakes, and usually it was packed so closely that the vessel had great difficulty in forcing a passage. At this period Captain Cook supposed, from the vast number of birds to be seen, and from other indications, that he was in the near vicinity of land. He kept on to the southward, the weather being exceedingly cold, until he reached the sixty-fourth parallel, in longitude 38° 14′ E. Here he had mild weather, with gentle breezes, for five days, the thermometer being at thirty-six. In January, 1773, the vessels crossed the Antarctic circle, but did not succeed in penetrating much farther; for, upon reaching latitude 67° 15′, they found all farther progress impeded by an immense body of ice, extending all along the southern horizon as far as the eye could reach. This ice was of every variety—and some large floes of it, miles in extent, formed a compact mass, rising eighteen or twenty feet above the water. It being late in the season, and no hope entertained of rounding these obstructions, Captain Cook now reluctantly turned to the northward.

In the November following he renewed his search in the Antarctic. In latitude 59° 40′ he met with a strong current setting to the southward. In December, when the vessels were in latitude 67° 31′, longitude 142° 54′ W., the cold was excessive, with heavy gales and fog. Here also birds were abundant: the albatross, the penguin, and the petrel especially. In latitude 70° 23′ some large islands of ice were encountered, and shortly afterward the clouds to the southward were observed to be of a snowy whiteness, indicating the vicinity of field ice. In latitude 71° 10′, longitude 106° 54′ W., the navigators were stopped, as before, by an immense frozen expanse, which filled the whole area of the southern horizon. The northern edge of this expanse was ragged and broken, so firmly wedged together as to be utterly impassable, and extending about a mile to the southward. Behind it the frozen surface was comparatively smooth for some distance, until terminated in the extreme background by gigantic ranges of ice mountains, the one towering above the other. Captain Cook concluded that this vast field reached the southern pole or was joined to a continent. Mr. J. N. Reynolds, whose great exertions and perseverance have at length succeeded in getting set on foot a national expedition, partly for the purpose of exploring these regions, thus speaks of the attempt of the Resolution: "We are not surprised that Captain Cook was unable to go beyond 71° 10′, but we are astonished that he did attain that point on the meridian of 106° 54′ west longitude. Palmer's Land lies south of the Shetland, latitude sixty-four degrees, and tends to the southward and westward farther than any navigator has yet penetrated. Cook was standing for this land when his progress was arrested by the ice; which, we apprehend, must always be the case in that point, and so early in the season as the sixth of January—and we should not be surprised if a portion of the icy mountains described was attached to the main body of Palmer's Land, or to some other portions of land lying farther to the southward and westward."

In 1803, Captains Kreutzenstern and Lisiausky were dispatched by Alexander of Russia for the purpose of circumnavigating the globe. In endeavouring to get south, they made no farther than 59° 58′, in longitude 70° 15′ W. They here met with strong currents setting eastwardly. Whales were abundant, but they saw no ice. In regard to this voyage, Mr. Reynolds observes that, if Kreutzenstern had arrived where he did earlier in the season, he must have encountered ice—it was March when he reached the latitude specified. The winds prevailing, as they do, from the southward and westward, had carried the floes, aided by currents, into that icy region bounded on the north by Georgia, east by Sandwich Land and the South Orkneys, and west by the South Shetland islands.

In 1822, Captain James Weddell, of the British navy, with two very small vessels, penetrated farther to the south than any previous navigator, and this too, without encountering extraordinary difficulties. He states that although he was frequently hemmed in by ice *before* reaching the seventy-second parallel, yet, upon attaining it, not a particle was to be discovered, and that, upon arriving at the latitude of 74° 15′, no fields, and only three islands of ice were visible. It is somewhat remarkable that, although vast flocks of birds were seen, and other usual indications of land, and although, south of the Shetlands, unknown coasts were observed from the masthead tending southwardly, Weddell discourages the idea of land existing in the polar regions of the south.

On the 11th of January, 1823, Captain Benjamin Morrell, of the American schooner Wasp, sailed from Kerguelen's Land with a view of penetrating as far south as possible. On the first of February he found himself in latitude 64° 52′ S., longitude 118° 27′ E. The following passage is extracted from his journal of that date: "The wind soon freshened to an eleven-knot breeze, and we embraced this opportunity of making to the west; being however convinced that the farther we went south beyond latitude sixty-four degrees, the less ice was to be apprehended, we steered a little to the southward, until we crossed the Antarctic circle, and were in latitude 69° 15′ E. In this latitude there was *no field ice*, and very few ice islands in sight."

Under the date of March fourteenth I find also this entry: "The sea was now entirely free of field ice, and there were not more than a dozen ice islands in sight. At the same time the temperature of the air and water was at least thirteen degrees higher (more mild) than we had ever found it between the parallels of sixty and sixty-two south. We are now in latitude 70° 14′ S., and the temperature of the air was forty-seven, and that of the water forty-four. In this situation I found the variation to be 14° 27′ easterly, per azimuth. . . . I have several times passed within the Antarctic circle, on different meridians, and have uniformly found the temperature, both of the air and water, to become more and more mild the farther I advanced beyond the sixty-fifth degree of south latitude, and that the variation decreases in the same proportion. While north of this latitude, say between sixty and sixty-five south, we frequently had great difficulty in finding a passage for the vessel between the immense and almost innumerable ice islands, some of which were from one to two miles in circumference, and more than five hundred feet above the surface of the water."

Being nearly destitute of fuel and water, and without proper instruments, it being also late in the season, Captain Morrell was now obliged to put back, without attempting any farther progress to the westward, although an entirely open sea lay before him. He expresses the opinion that, had not these overruling considerations obliged him to retreat, he could have penetrated, if not to the pole itself, at least to the eighty-fifth parallel. I have given his ideas respecting these matters somewhat at length, that the reader may have an opportunity of seeing how far they were borne out by my own subsequent experience.

In 1831, Captain Briscoe, in the employ of the Messieurs Enderby, whale-ship owners of London, sailed in the brig Lively for the South Seas, accompanied by the cutter Tula. On the twenty-eighth of February, being in latitude 66° 30′ S., longitude 47° 13′ E., he descried land, and "clearly discovered through the snow the black peaks of a range of mountains running E. S. E." He remained in this neighbourhood during the whole of the following month, but was unable to approach the coast nearer than within ten leagues, owing to the boisterous state of the weather.

Finding it impossible to make further discovery during this season, he returned northward to winter in Van Diemen's Land.

In the beginning of 1832 he again proceeded southwardly, and on the fourth of February land was seen to the southeast in latitude 67° 15′, longitude 69° 29′ W. This was soon found to be an island near the headland of the country he had first discovered. On the twenty-first of the month he succeeded in landing on the latter, and took possession of it in the name of William IV., calling it Adelaide's Island, in honour of the English queen. These particulars being made known to the Royal Geographical Society of London, the conclusion was drawn by that body "that there is a continuous tract of land extending from 47° 30′ E. to 69° 29′ W. longitude, running the parallel of from sixty-six to sixty-seven degrees south latitude." In respect to this conclusion Mr. Reynolds observes, "In the correctness of it we by no means concur; nor do the discoveries of Briscoe warrant any such inference. It was within these limits that Weddell proceeded south on a meridian to the east of Georgia, Sandwich Land, and the South Orkney and Shetland islands." My own experience will be found to testify most directly to the falsity of the conclusion arrived at by the society.

These are the principal attempts which have been made at penetrating to a high southern latitude, and it will now be seen that there remained, previous to the voyage of the Jane, nearly three hundred degrees of longitude in which the Antarctic circle had not been crossed at all. Of course a wide field lay before us for discovery, and it was with feelings of most intense interest that I heard Captain Guy express his resolution of pushing boldly to the southward.

CHAPTER XVII

WE KEPT our course southwardly for four days after giving up the search for Glass's islands, without meeting with any ice at all. On the twenty-sixth, at noon, we were in latitude 63° 23′ S., longitude 41° 25′ W. We now saw several large ice islands, and a floe of field ice, not, however, of any great extent. The winds generally blew from the southeast, or the northeast, but were very light. Whenever we had a westerly wind, which was seldom, it was invariably attended with a rain squall. Every day we had more or less snow. The thermometer, on the twenty-seventh stood at thirty-five.

January 1, 1828. This day we found ourselves completely hemmed in by the ice, and our prospects looked cheerless indeed. A strong gale blew, during the whole forenoon, from the northeast, and drove large cakes of the drift against the rudder and counter with such violence that we all trembled for the consequences. Toward evening, the gale still blowing with fury, a large field in front separated, and we were enabled, by carrying a press of sail, to force a passage through the smaller flakes into some open water beyond. As we approached this space we took in sail by degrees, and having at length got clear, lay to under a single reefed foresail.

January 2d. We had now tolerably pleasant weather. At noon we found ourselves in latitude 69° 10′ S., longitude 42° 20′ W., having crossed the Antarctic circle. Very little ice was to be seen to the southward, although large fields of it lay behind us. This day we rigged some sounding gear, using a large iron pot capable of holding twenty gallons, and a line of two hundred fathoms. We found the current setting to the north, about a quarter of a mile per hour. The temperature of the air was now about thirty-three. Here we found the variation to be 14° 28′ easterly, per azimuth.

January 5th. We had still held on to the southward without any very great impediments. On this morning, however, being in latitude 73° 15′ E., longitude 42° 10′ W., we were again brought to a stand by an immense expanse of firm ice. We saw, nevertheless, much open water to the southward, and felt no doubt of being able to reach it eventually. Standing to the eastward along the edge of the floe, we at length came to a passage of about a mile in width, through which we warped our way by sundown. The sea in which we now were was thickly covered with ice islands, but had no field ice, and we pushed on boldly as before. The cold did not seem to increase, although we had snow very frequently, and now and then hail squalls of great violence. Immense flocks of the albatross flew over the schooner this day, going from southeast to northwest.

January 7th. The sea still remained pretty well open, so that we had no difficulty in holding on our course. To the westward we saw some icebergs of incredible size, and in the afternoon passed very near one whose summit could not have been less than four hundred fathoms from the surface of the ocean. Its girth was probably, at the base, three quarters of a league, and several streams of water were running from crevices in its sides. We remained in sight of this island two days, and then only lost it in a fog.

January 10th. Early this morning we had the misfortune to lose a man overboard. He was an American, named Peter Vredenburgh, a native of New York, and was one of the most valuable hands on board the schooner. In going over the bows his foot slipped, and he fell between two cakes of ice, never rising again. At noon of this day we were in latitude 78° 30′, longitude 40° 15′ W. The cold was now excessive, and we had hail squalls continually from the northward and eastward. In this direction also we saw several more immense icebergs, and the whole horizon to the eastward appeared to be blocked up with field ice, rising in tiers, one mass above the other. Some driftwood floated by during the evening, and a great quantity of birds flew over, among which were nellies, petrels, albatrosses, and a large bird of a brilliant blue plumage. The variation here, per azimuth, was less than it had been previously to our passing the Antarctic circle.

January 12th. Our passage to the south again looked doubtful, as nothing was to be seen in the direction of the pole but one apparently limitless floe, backed by absolute mountains of ragged ice, one precipice of which arose frowningly above the other. We stood to the westward until the fourteenth, in the hope of finding an entrance.

January 14th. This morning we reached the western extremity of the field which had impeded us, and, weathering it, came to an open sea, without a particle of ice. Upon sounding with two hundred fathoms, we here found a current setting southwardly at the rate of half a mile per hour. The temperature of the air was forty-seven, that of the water thirty-four. We now sailed to the southward without meeting any interruption of moment until the sixteenth, when, at noon, we were in latitude 81° 21′, longitude 42° W. We here again sounded, and found a current setting still southwardly, and at the rate of three-quarters of a mile per hour. The variation per azimuth had diminished, and the temperature of the air was mild and pleasant, the thermometer being as high as fifty-one. At this period not a particle of ice was to be discovered. All hands on board now felt certain of attaining the pole.

January 17th. This day was full of incidents. Innumerable flights of birds flew over us from the southward, and several were shot from the deck; one of them, a species of pelican, proved to be excellent eating. About midday a small floe of ice was seen from the masthead off the larboard bow, and upon it there appeared to be some large animal. As the weather was good and nearly calm, Captain Guy ordered out two of the boats to see what it was. Dirk Peters and myself accompanied the mate in the larger boat. Upon coming up with the floe, we perceived that it was in possession of a gigantic creature of the race of the Arctic bear, but far exceeding in size the largest of these animals. Being well armed, we made no scruple of attacking it at once. Several shots were fired in quick succession, the most of which took effect, apparently, in the head and body. Nothing discouraged, however, the monster threw himself from the ice, and swam, with open jaws, to the boat in which were Peters and myself. Owing to the confusion which ensued among us at this unexpected turn of the adventure, no person was ready immediately with a second shot, and the bear had actually succeeded in getting half his vast bulk across our gunwale, and seizing one of the men by the small of his back, before any efficient means were taken to repel him. In this extremity nothing but the promptness and agility of Peters saved us from destruction. Leaping upon the back of the huge beast, he plunged the blade of a knife behind the neck, reaching the spinal marrow at a blow. The brute tumbled into the sea lifeless, and without a struggle, rolling over Peters as he fell. The latter soon recovered himself, and a rope being thrown him, he secured the carcass before entering the boat. We then returned in triumph to the schooner, towing our trophy behind us. This bear, upon admeasurement, proved to be full fifteen feet in his greatest length. His wool was perfectly white, and very coarse, curling tightly. The eyes were of a blood red, and larger than those of the Arctic bear; the snout also more rounded, rather resembling the snout of the bull-dog. The meat was tender, but excessively rank and fishy, although the men devoured it with avidity, and declared it excellent eating.

Scarcely had we got our prize alongside, when the man at the masthead gave the joyful shout of *"land on the starboard bow!"* All hands were now upon the alert, and, a breeze springing up very opportunely from the northward and eastward, we were soon close in with the coast. It proved to be a low rocky islet, of about a league in circumference, and altogether destitute of vegetation, if we except a species of prickly pear. In approaching it from the northward, a singular ledge of rock is seen projecting into the sea, and bearing a strong resemblance to corded bales of cotton. Around this ledge to the westward is a small bay, at the bottom of which our boats effected a convenient landing.

It did not take us long to explore every portion of the island, but, with one exception, we found nothing worthy of our observation. In the southern extremity, we picked up near the shore, half buried in a pile of loose stones, a piece of wood, which seemed to have formed the prow of a canoe. There had been evidently some attempt at carving upon it, and Captain Guy fancied that he made out the figure of a tortoise, but the resemblance did not strike me very forcibly. Besides this prow, if such it were, we found no other token that any living creature had ever been here before. Around the coast we discovered occasional small floes of ice—but these were very few. The exact situation of this islet (to which Captain Guy gave the name of Bennet's Islet, in honor of his partner in the ownership of the schooner) is 82° 50′ S. latitude, 42° 20′ W. longitude.

We had now advanced to the southward more than eight degrees farther than any previous navigators, and the sea still lay perfectly open before us. We found, too, that the variation uniformly decreased as we proceeded, and, what was still more surprising, that the temperature of the air, and latterly of the water, became milder. The weather might even be called pleasant, and we had a steady but very gentle breeze always from some northern point of the compass. The sky was usually clear, with now and then a slight appearance of thin vapour in the southern horizon—this, however, was invariably of brief duration. Two difficulties alone presented themselves to our view; we were getting short of fuel, and symptoms of scurvy had occurred among several of the crew. These considerations began to impress upon Captain Guy the necessity of returning, and he spoke of it frequently. For my own part, confident as I was of soon arriving at land of some description upon the course we were pursuing, and having every reason to believe, from present appearances, that we should not find it the sterile soil met with in the higher Arctic latitudes, I warmly pressed upon him the expediency of persevering, at least for a few days longer, in the direction we were now holding. So tempting an opportunity of solving the great problem in regard to an Antarctic continent had never yet been afforded to man, and I confess that I felt myself bursting with indignation at the timid and ill-timed suggestions of our commander. I believe, indeed, that what I could not refrain from saying to him on this head had the effect of inducing him to push on. While, therefore, I cannot but lament the most unfortunate and bloody events which immediately arose from my advice, I must still be allowed to feel some degree of gratification at having been instrumental, however remotely, in opening to the eye of science one of the most intensely exciting secrets which has ever engrossed its attention.

CHAPTER XVIII

JANUARY 18TH. This morning* we continued to the southward, with the same pleasant weather as before. The sea was entirely smooth, the air tolerably warm and from the northeast, the temperature of the water fifty-three. We now again got our sounding-gear in order, and, with a hundred and fifty fathoms of line, found the current setting towards the pole at the rate of a mile an hour. This constant tendency to the southward, both in the wind and current, caused some degree of speculation, and even of alarm, in different quarters of the schooner, and I saw distinctly that no little impression had been made upon the mind of Captain Guy. He was exceedingly sensitive to ridicule, however, and I finally succeeded in laughing him out of his apprehensions. The variation was now very trivial. In the course of the day we saw several large whales of the right species, and innumerable flights of the albatross passed over the vessel. We also picked up a bush, full of red berries, like those of the hawthorn, and the carcass of a singular-looking land-animal. It was three feet in length, and but six inches in height, with four very short legs, the feet armed with long claws of a brilliant scarlet, and resembling coral in substance. The body was covered with a straight silky hair, perfectly white.

* The terms *morning* and *evening*, which I have made use of to avoid confusion in my narrative, as far as possible, must not, of course, be taken in their ordinary sense. For a long time past we had had no night at all, the daylight being continual. The dates throughout are according to nautical time, and the bearings must be understood as per compass. I would also remark, in this place, that I cannot, in the first portion of what is here written, pretend to strict accuracy in respect to dates, or latitudes and longitudes, having kept no regular journal until after the period of which this first portion treats. In many instances I have relied altogether upon memory.

The tail was peaked like that of a rat, and about a foot and a half long. The head resembled a cat's with the exception of the ears—these were flapped like the ears of a dog. The *teeth* were of the same brilliant scarlet as the claws.

January 19th. To-day, being in latitude 83° 20′, longitude 43° 5′ W. (the sea being of an extraordinarily dark colour), we again saw land from the masthead, and, upon a closer scrutiny, found it to be one of a group of very large islands. The shore was precipitous, and the interior seemed to be well wooded, a circumstance which occasioned us great joy. In about four hours from our first discovering the land we came to anchor in ten fathoms, sandy bottom, a league from the coast, as a high surf, with strong ripples here and there, rendered a nearer approach of doubtful expediency. The two largest boats were now ordered out, and a party, well armed (among whom were Peters and myself), proceeded to look for an opening in the reef which appeared to encircle the island. After searching about for some time, we discovered an inlet, which we were entering, when we saw four large canoes put off from the shore, filled with men who seemed to be well armed. We waited for them to come up, and as they moved with great rapidity, they were soon within hail. Captain Guy now held up a white handkerchief on the blade of an oar, when the strangers made a full stop, and commenced a loud jabbering all at once, intermingled with occasional shouts, in which we could distinguish the word *Anamoo-moo!* and *Lama-Lama!* They continued this for at least half an hour, during which we had a good opportunity of observing their appearance.

In the four canoes, which might have been fifty feet long and five broad, there were a hundred and ten savages in all. They were about the ordinary stature of Europeans, but of a more musuclar and brawny frame. Their complexion a jet black, with thick and long woolly hair. They were clothed in skins of an unknown black animal, shaggy and silky, and made to fit the body with some degree of skill, the hair being inside, except where turned out about the neck, wrists, and ankles. Their arms consisted principally of clubs, of a dark, and apparently very heavy wood. Some spears, however, were observed among them, headed with flint, and a few slings. The bottoms of the canoes were full of black stones about the size of a large egg.

When they had concluded their harangue (for it was clear they intended their jabbering for such), one of them who seemed to be the chief stood up in the prow of his canoe, and made signs for us to bring our boats alongside of him. This hint we pretended not to understand, thinking it the wiser plan to maintain, if possible, the interval between us, as their number more than quadrupled our own. Finding this to be the case, the chief ordered the three other canoes to hold back, while he advanced towards us with his own. As soon as he came up with us he leaped on board the largest of our boats, and seated himself by the side of Captain Guy, pointing at the same time to the schooner, and repeating the words *Anamoo-moo!* and *Lama-Lama!* We now put back to the vessel, the four canoes following at a little distance.

Upon getting alongside the chief evinced symptoms of extreme surprise and delight, clapping his hands, slapping his thighs and breast, and laughing obstreperously. His followers behind joined in his merriment, and for some minutes the din was so excessive as to be absolutely deafening. Quiet being at length restored, Captain Guy ordered the boats to be hoisted up, as a necessary precaution, and gave the chief (whose name we soon found to be *Too-wit*) to understand that we could admit no more than twenty of his men on deck at one time. With this arrangement he appeared perfectly satisfied, and gave some directions to the canoes, when one of them approached, the rest remaining about fifty yards off. Twenty of the savages now got on board, and proceeded to ramble over every part of the deck, and scramble about among the rigging, making themselves much at home, and examining every article with great inquisitiveness.

It was quite evident that they had never before seen any of the white race—from whose complexion, indeed, they appeared to recoil. They believed the Jane to be a living creature, and seemed to be afraid of hurting it with the points of their spears, carefully turning them up. Our crew were much amused with the conduct of Too-wit in one instance. The cook was splitting some wood near the galley, and, by accident, struck his axe into the deck, making a gash of considerable depth. The chief immediately ran up, and pushing the cook on one side rather roughly, commenced a half whine, half howl, strongly indicative of sympathy in what he considered the sufferings of the schooner, patting and smoothing the gash with his hand, and washing it from a bucket of sea-water which stood by. This was a degree of ignorance for which we were not prepared, and for my part I could not help thinking some of it affected.

When the visitors had satisfied, as well as they could, their curiosity in regard to our upper works, they were admitted below, when their amazement exceeded all bounds. Their astonishment now appeared to be far too deep for words, for they roamed about in silence, broken only by low ejaculations. The arms afforded them much food for speculation, and they were suffered to handle and examine them at leisure. I do not believe that they had the least suspicion of their actual use, but rather took them for idols, seeing the care we had of them, and the attention with which we watched their movements while handling them. At the great guns their wonder was redoubled. They approached them with every mark of the profoundest reverence and awe, but forbore to examine them minutely. There were two large mirrors in the cabin, and here was the acme of their amazement. Too-wit was the first to approach them, and he had got in the middle of the cabin, with his face to one and his back to the other, before he fairly perceived them. Upon raising his eyes and seeing his reflected self in the glass, I thought the savage would go mad; but, upon turning short round to make a retreat, and beholding himself a second time in the opposite direction, I was afraid he would expire upon the spot. No persuasion could prevail upon him to take another look; but, throwing himself upon the floor, with his face buried in his hands, he remained thus until we were obliged to drag him upon deck.

The whole of the savages were admitted on board in this manner, twenty at a time, Too-wit being suffered to remain during the entire period. We saw no disposition to thievery among them, nor did we miss a single article after their departure. Throughout the whole of their visit they evinced the most friendly manner. There were, however, some points in their demeanour which we found it impossible to understand: for example, we could not get them to approach several very harmless objects—such as the schooner's sails, an egg, an open book, or a pan of flour. We endeavoured to ascertain if they had among them any articles which might be turned to account in the way of traffic, but found great difficulty in being comprehended. We made out, nevertheless, what greatly astonished us, that the islands abounded in the large tortoise of the Gallipagos, one of which we saw in the canoe of Too-wit. We saw also some *bêche de mer* in the hands of one of the savages, who was greedily devouring it in its natural state. These anomalies, for they were such when considered in regard to the latitude, induced Captain Guy to wish for a thorough investigation of the country, in the hope of making a profitable speculation in his discovery. For my own part, anxious as I was to know something more of these islands, I was still more earnestly bent on prosecuting the voyage to the southward without delay. We had now fine weather, but there was no telling how long it would last; and being already in the eighty-fourth parallel, with an open sea before us, a current setting strongly to the southward, and the wind fair, I could not listen with any patience to a proposition of stopping longer than was absolutely necessary for the health of the crew and the taking on board a proper supply of fuel and fresh provisions. I represented to the captain that we might easily make this group on our return, and winter here in the event of being blocked up by the ice. He at length came into my views (for in some way, hardly known to myself, I had acquired much influence over him), and it was finally resolved that, even in the event of our finding *bêche de mer,* we should only stay here a week to recruit, and then push on to the southward while we might. Accordingly we made every necessary preparation, and, under the guidance of Too-wit, got the Jane through the reef in safety, coming to anchor about a mile from the shore, in an excellent bay completely landlocked, on the southeastern coast of the main island, and in ten fathoms of water, black sandy bottom. At the head of this bay there were three fine springs (we were told) of good water, and we saw abundance of wood in the vicinity. The four canoes followed us in, keeping, however, at a respectful distance. Too-wit himself remained on board, and, upon dropping our anchor, invited us to accompany him on shore, and visit his village in the interior. To this Captain Guy consented; and ten savages being left on board as hostages, a party of us, twelve in all, got in readiness to attend the chief. We took care to be well armed, yet without evincing any distrust. The schooner had her guns run out, her boarding-nettings up, and every other proper precaution was taken to guard against surprise. Directions were left with the chief mate to admit no person on board during our absence, and, in the event of our not appearing in twelve hours, to send the cutter, with a swivel, around the island in search of us.

At every step we took inland the conviction forced itself upon us that we were in a country differing essentially from any hitherto visited by civilised men. We saw nothing with which we had been formerly conversant. The trees resembled no growth of either the torrid, the temperate, or the northern frigid zones, and were altogether unlike those of the lower southern latitudes we had already traversed. The very rocks were novel in their mass, their colour, and their stratification; and the streams themselves, utterly incredible as it may appear, had so little in common with those of other climates, that we were scrupulous of tasting them, and, indeed, had difficulty in bringing ourselves to believe that their qualities were purely those of nature. At a small brook which crossed our path (the first we had reached) Too-wit and his attendants halted to drink. On account of the singular character of the water, we refused to taste it, supposing it to be polluted; and it was not until some time afterward we came to understand that such was the appearance of the streams throughout the whole group. I am at a loss to give a distinct idea of the nature of this liquid, and cannot do so without many words. Although it flowed with rapidity in all declivities where common water would do so, yet never, except when falling in a cascade, had it the customary appearance of *limpidity*. It was, nevertheless, in point of fact, as perfectly limpid as any limestone water in existence, the difference being only in appearance. At first sight, and especially in cases where little declivity was found, it bore resemblance, as regards consistency, to a thick infusion of gum arabic in common water. But this was only the least remarkable of its extraordinary qualities. It was *not* colourless, nor was it of any one uniform colour—presenting to the eye, as it flowed, every possible shade of purple, like the hues of a changeable silk. This variation in shade was produced in a manner which excited as profound astonishment in the minds of our party as the mirror had done in the case of Too-wit. Upon collecting a basinful, and allowing it to settle thoroughly, we perceived that the whole mass of liquid was made up of a number of distinct veins, each of a distinct hue; that these veins did not commingle; and that their cohesion was perfect in regard to their own particles among themselves, and imperfect in regard to neighbouring veins. Upon passing the blade of a knife athwart the veins, the water closed over it immediately, as with us, and also, in withdrawing it, all traces of the passage of the knife were instantly obliterated. If, however,the blade was passed down accurately between the two veins, a perfect separation was effected, which the power of cohesion did not immediately rectify. The phenomena of this water formed the first definite link in that vast chain of apparent miracles with which I was destined to be at length encircled.

CHAPTER XIX

WE WERE nearly three hours in reaching the village, it being more than nine miles in the interior, and the path lying through a rugged country. As we passed along, the party of Too-wit (the whole hundred and ten savages of the canoes) was momentarily strengthened by smaller detachments, of from two to six or seven, which joined us, as if by accident, at different turns of the road. There appeared so much of system in this that I could not help feeling distrust, and I spoke to Captain Guy of my apprehensions. It was now too late, however, to recede, and we concluded that our best security lay in evincing a perfect confidence in the good faith of Too-wit. We accordingly went on, keeping a wary eye upon the manœuvres of the savages, and not permitting them to divide our numbers by pushing in between. In this way, passing through a precipitous ravine, we at length reached what we were told was the only collection of habitations upon the island. As we came in sight of them, the chief set up a shout, and frequently repeated the word *Klock-klock,* which we supposed to be the name of the village, or perhaps the generic name for villages.

The dwellings were of the most miserable description imaginable, and, unlike those of even the lowest of the savage races with which mankind are acquainted, were of no uniform plan. Some of them (and these we found belonged to the *Wampoos* or *Yampoos,* the great men of the land) consisted of a tree cut down at about four feet from the root, with a large black skin thrown over it, and hanging in loose folds upon the ground. Under this the savage nestled. Others were formed by means of rough limbs of trees, with the withered foliage upon them, made to recline, at an angle of forty-five degrees, against a bank of clay, heaped up, without regular form, to the height of five or six feet. Others, again, were mere holes dug in the earth perpendicularly, and covered over with similar branches, these being removed when the tenant was about to enter, and pulled on again when he had entered. A few were built among the forked limbs of trees as they stood, the upper limbs being partially cut through, so as to bend over upon the lower, thus forming thicker shelter from the weather. The greater number, however, consisted of small shallow caverns, apparently scratched in the face of a precipitous ledge of dark stone, resembling fuller's earth, with which three sides of the village were bounded. At the door of each of these primitive caverns was a small rock, which the tenant carefully placed before the entrance upon leaving his residence, for what purpose I could not ascertain, as the stone itself was never of sufficient size to close up more than a third of the opening.

This village, if it were worthy of the name, lay in a valley of some depth, and could only be approached from the southward, the precipitous ledge of which I have already spoken cutting off all access in other directions. Through the middle of the valley ran a brawling stream of the same magical-looking water which has been described. We saw several strange animals about the dwellings, all appearing to be thoroughly domesticated. The largest of these creatures resembled our common hog in the structure of the body and snout; the tail, however, was bushy, and the legs slender as those of the antelope. Its motion was exceedingly awkward and indecisive, and we never saw it attempt to run. We noticed also several animals very similar in appearance, but of a greater length of body, and covered with a black wool. There were a great variety of tame fowls running about, and these seemed to constitute the chief food of the natives. To our astonishment we saw black albatross among these birds in a state of entire domestication, going to sea periodically for food, but always returning to the village as a home, and using the southern shore in the vicinity as a place of incubation. There they were joined by their friends the pelicans as usual, but these latter never followed them to the dwellings of the savages. Among the other kinds of tame fowls were ducks, differing very little from the canvas-back of our own country, black gannets, and a large bird not unlike the buzzard in appearance, but not carnivorous. Of fish there seemed to be a great abundance. We saw, during our visit, a quantity of dried salmon, rock cod, blue dolphins, mackerel, blackfish, skate, conger eels, elephant-fish, mullets, soles, parrotfish, leather-jackets, gurnards, hake, flounders, paracutas, and innumerable other varieties. We noticed, too, that most of them were similar to the fish about the group of the Lord Auckland islands, in a latitude as low as fifty-one degrees south. The Gallipago tortoise was also very plentiful. We saw but few wild animals, and none of a large size, or of a species with which we were familiar. One or two serpents of a formidable aspect crossed our path, but the natives paid them little attention, and we concluded that they were not venomous.

As we approached the village with Too-wit and his party, a vast crowd of the people rushed out to meet us, with loud shouts, among which we could only distinguish the everlasting *Anamoo-moo!* and *Lama-Lama!* We were much surprised at perceiving that, with one or two exceptions, these new comers were entirely naked, the skins being used only by the men of the canoes. All the weapons of the country seemed also to be in the possession of the latter, for there was no appearance of any among the villagers. There were a great many women and children, the former not altogether wanting in what might be termed personal beauty. They were straight, tall, and well formed, with a grace and freedom of carriage not to be found in civilized society. Their lips, however, like those of the men, were thick and clumsy, so that, even when laughing, the teeth were never disclosed. Their hair was of a finer texture than that of the males. Among these naked villagers there might have been ten or twelve who were clothed, like the party of Too-wit, in dresses of black skin, and armed with lances and heavy clubs. These appeared to have great influence among the rest, and were always addressed by the title *Wampoo.* These, too, were the tenants of the black skin palaces. That of Too-wit was situated in the centre of the village, and was much larger and somewhat better constructed than others of its kind. The tree which formed its support was cut off at a distance of twelve feet or thereabout from the root, and there were several branches left just below the cut, these serving to extend the covering, and in this way prevent its flapping about the trunk. The covering, too, which consisted of four very large skins fastened together with wooden skewers, was secured at the bottom with pegs driven through it and into the ground. The floor was strewed with a quantity of dry leaves by way of carpet.

To this hut we were conducted with great solemnity, and as many of the natives crowded in after us as possible. Too-wit seated himself on the leaves, and made signs that we should follow his example. This we did, and presently found ourselves in a situation peculiarly uncomfortable, if not indeed critical. We were on the ground, twelve in number, with the savages, as many as forty, sitting on their hams so closely around us that, if any disturbance had arisen, we should have found it impossible to make use of our arms, or indeed to have risen on our feet. The pressure was not only inside the tent, but outside, where probably was every individual on the whole island, the crowd being prevented from trampling us to death only by the incessant exertions and vociferations of Too-wit. Our chief security lay, however, in the presence of Too-wit himself among us, and we resolved to stick by him closely, as the best chance of extricating ourselves from the dilemma, sacrificing him immediately upon the first appearance of hostile design.

After some trouble a certain degree of quiet was restored, when the chief addressed us in a speech of great length, and very nearly resembling the one delivered in the canoes, with the exception that the *Anamoo-moos!* were now somewhat more strenuously insisted upon than the *Lama-Lamas!* We listened in profound silence until the conclusion of his harangue, when Captain Guy replied by assuring the chief of his eternal friendship and good-will, concluding what he had to say by a present of several strings of blue beads and a knife. At the former the monarch, much to our surprise, turned up his nose with some expression of contempt; but the knife gave him the most unlimited satisfaction, and he immediately ordered dinner. This was handed into the tent over the heads of the attendants, and consisted of the palpitating entrails of a species of unknown animal, probably one of the slim-legged hogs which we had observed in our approach to the village. Seeing us at a loss how to proceed, he began, by way of setting us an example, to devour yard after yard of the enticing food, until we could positively stand it no longer, and evinced such manifest symptoms of rebellion of stomach as inspired his majesty with a degree of astonishment only inferior to that brought about by the looking-glasses. We declined, however, partaking of the delicacies before us, and endeavoured to make him understand that we had no appetite whatever, having just finished a hearty *déjeuner*.

When the monarch had made an end of his meal, we commenced a series of cross-questioning in every ingenious manner we could devise, with a view of discovering what were the chief productions of the country, and whether any of them might be turned to profit. At length he seemed to have some idea of our meaning, and offered to accompany us to a part of the coast where he assured us the *bêche de mer* (pointing to a specimen of that animal) was to be found in great abundance. We were glad of this early opportunity of escaping from the oppression of the crowd, and signified our eagerness to proceed. We now left the tent, and, accompanied by the whole population of the village, followed the chief to the southeastern extremity of the island, not far from the bay where our vessel lay at anchor. We waited here for about an hour, until the four canoes were brought round by some of the savages to our station. The whole of our party then getting into one of them, we were paddled along the edge of the reef before mentioned, and of another still farther out, where we saw a far greater quantity of *bêche de mer* than the oldest seaman among us had ever seen in those groups of the lower latitudes most celebrated for this article of commerce. We stayed near these reefs only long enough to satisfy ourselves that we could easily load a dozen vessels with the animal if necessary, when we were taken alongside the schooner, and parted with Too-wit, after obtaining from him a promise that he would bring us, in the course of twenty-four hours, as many of the canvas-back ducks and Gallipago tortoises as his canoes would hold. In the whole of this adventure we saw nothing in the demeanour of the natives calculated to create suspicion, with the single exception of the systematic manner in which their party was strengthened during our route from the schooner to the village.

CHAPTER XX

THE chief was as good as his word, and we were soon plentifully supplied with fresh provisions. We found the tortoises as fine as we had ever seen, and the ducks surpassed our best species of wild fowl, being exceedingly tender, juicy, and well-flavoured. Besides these, the savages brought us, upon our making them comprehend our wishes, a vast quantity of brown celery and scurvy grass, with a canoe-load of fresh fish and some dried. The celery was a treat indeed, and the scurvy grass proved of incalculable benefit in restoring those of our men who had shown symptoms of disease. In a very short time we had not a single person on the sick-list. We had also plenty of other kinds of fresh provisions, among which may be mentioned a species of shell-fish resembling the mussel in shape, but with the taste of an oyster. Shrimps, too, and prawns were abundant, and albatross and other birds' eggs with dark shells. We took in, too, a plentiful stock of the flesh of the hog which I have mentioned before. Most of the men found it a palatable food, but I thought it fishy and otherwise disagreeable. In return for these good things we presented the natives with blue beads, brass trinkets, nails, knives, and pieces of red cloth, they being fully delighted in the exchange. We established a regular market on shore, just under the guns of the schooner, where our barterings were carried on with every appearance of good faith, and a degree of order which their conduct at the village of *Klock-klock* had not led us to expect from the savages.

Matters went on thus very amicably for several days, during which parties of the natives were frequently on board the schooner, and parties of our men frequently on shore, making long excursions into the interior, and receiving no molestation whatever. Finding the ease with which the vessel might be loaded with *bêche de mer,* owing to the friendly disposition of the islanders, and the readiness with which they would render us assistance in collecting it, Captain Guy resolved to enter into negotiation with Too-wit for the erection of suitable houses in which to cure the article, and for the services of himself and tribe in gathering as much as possible, while he himself took advantage of the fine weather to prosecute his voyage to the southward. Upon mentioning this project to the chief he seemed very willing to enter into an agreement. A bargain was accordingly struck, perfectly satisfactory to both parties, by which it was arranged that, after making the necessary preparations such as laying off the proper grounds, erecting a portion of the buildings, and doing some other work in which the whole of our crew would be required, the schooner should proceed on her route, leaving three of her men on the island to superintend the fulfilment of the project, and instruct the natives in drying the *bêche de mer.* In regard to terms, these were made to depend upon the exertions of the savages in our absence. They were to receive a stipulated quantity of blue beads, knives, red cloth, and so forth, for every certain number of piculs of the *bêche de mer* which should be ready on our return.

A description of the nature of this important article of commerce, and the method of preparing it, may prove of some interest to my readers, and I can find no more suitable place than this for introducing an account of it. The following comprehensive notice of the substance is taken from a modern history of a voyage to the South Seas.

"It is that *mollusca* from the Indian Seas which is known to commerce by the French name *bouche de mer* (a nice morsel from the sea). If I am not much mistaken, the celebrated Cuvier calls it *gasteropoda pulmonifera.* It is abundantly gathered in the coasts of the Pacific islands, and gathered especially for the Chinese market, where it commands a great price, perhaps as much as their much-talked-of edible bird's nests, which are probably made up of the gelatinous matter picked up by a species of swallow from the body of these molluscæ. They have no shell, no legs, nor any prominent part, except an *absorbing* and an *excretory,* opposite organs; but, by their elastic wings, like caterpillars or worms, they creep in shallow waters, in which, when low, they can be seen by a kind of swallow, the sharp bill of which, inserted in the soft animal, draws a gummy and filamentous substance. which, by drying, can be wrought into the solid walls of their nest. Hence the name of *gasteropoda pulmonifera.*

"This mollusca is oblong, and of different sizes, from three to eighteen inches in length; and I have seen a few that were not less than two feet long. They were nearly round, a little flattish on one side, which lies next to the bottom of the sea; and they are from one to eight inches thick. They crawl up into shallow water at particular seasons of the year, probably for the purpose of gendering, as we often find them in pairs. It is when the sun has the most power on the water, rendering it tepid, that they approach the shore; and they often go up into places so shallow that, on the tide's receding, they are left dry, exposed to the heat of the sun. But they do not bring forth their young in shallow water, as we never see any of their progeny, and the full-grown ones are always observed coming in from deep water. They feed principally on that class of zoöphites which produce the coral.

"The *bêche de mer* is generally taken in three or four feet of water; after which they are brought on shore, and split at one end with a knife, the incision being one inch or more, according to the size of the mollusca. Through this opening the entrails are forced out by pressure, and they are much like those of any other small tenant of the deep. The article is then washed, and afterward boiled to a certain degree, which must not be too much or too little. They are then buried in the ground for four hours, then boiled again for a short time, after which they are dried, either by the fire or the sun. Those cured by the sun are worth the most; but where one picul (133⅓ lbs.) can be cured that way, I can cure thirty piculs by the fire. When once properly cured, they can be kept in a dry place for two or three years without any risk; but they should be examined once in every few months, say four times a year, to see if any dampness is likely to affect them.

"The Chinese, as before stated, consider *bêche de mer* a very great luxury, believing that it wonderfully strengthens and nourishes the system, and renews the exhausted system of the immoderate voluptuary. The first quality commands a high price in Canton, being worth ninety dollars a picul; the second quality, seventy-five dollars; the third, fifty dollars; the fourth, thirty dollars; the fifth, twenty dollars; the sixth, twelve dollars; the seventh, eight dollars; and the eighth, four dollars; small cargoes, however, will often bring more in Manila, Singapore, and Batavia."

An agreement having been thus entered into, we proceeded immediately to land everything necessary for preparing the buildings and clearing the ground. A large flat space near the eastern shore of the bay was selected, where there was plenty of both wood and water, and within a convenient distance of the principal reefs on which the *bêche de mer* was to be procured. We now all set to work in good earnest, and soon, to the great astonishment of the savages, had felled a sufficient number of trees for our purpose, getting them quickly in order for the framework of the houses, which in two or three days were so far under way that we could safely trust the rest of the work to the three men whom we intended to leave behind. These were John Carson, Alfred Harris, —— Peterson (all natives of London, I believe), who volunteered their services in this respect.

By the last of the month we had everything in readiness for departure. We had agreed, however, to pay a formal visit of leavestaking to the village, and Too-wit insisted so pertinaciously upon our keeping the promise, that we did not think it advisable to run the risk of offending him by a final refusal. I believe that not one of us had at this time the slightest suspicion of the good faith of the savages. They had uniformly behaved with the greatest decorum, aiding us with alacrity in our work, offering us their commodities, frequently without price, and never, in any instance, pilfering a single article, although the high value they set upon the goods we had with us was evident by the extravagant demonstrations of joy always manifested upon our making them a present. The women especially were most obliging in every respect, and, upon the whole, we should have been the most suspicious of human beings had we entertained a single thought of perfidy on the part of a people who treated us so well. A very short while sufficed to prove that this apparent kindness of disposition was only the result of a deeply-laid plan for our destruction, and that the islanders for whom we entertained such inordinate feelings of esteem, were among the most barbarous, subtle, and bloodthirsty wretches that ever contaminated the face of the globe.

It was on the first of February that we went on shore for the purpose of visiting the village. Although, as said before, we entertained not the slightest suspicion, still no proper precaution was neglected. Six men were left in the schooner with instructions to permit none of the savages to approach the vessel during our absence, under any pretence whatever, and to remain constantly on deck. The boarding-nettings were up, the guns double-shotted with grape and canister, and the swivels loaded with canisters of musket-balls. She lay, with her anchor apeak, about a mile from the shore, and no canoe could approach her in any direction without being distinctly seen and exposed to the full fire of our swivels immediately.

The six men being left on board, our shore-party consisted of thirty-two persons in all. We were armed to the teeth, having with us muskets, pistols, and cutlasses, besides, each had a long kind of seaman's knife, somewhat resembling the Bowie knife now so much used throughout our western and southern country. A hundred of the black-skin warriors met us at the landing for the purpose of accompanying us on our way. We noticed, however, with some surprise, that they were now entirely without arms; and, upon questioning Too-wit in relation to this circumstance, he merely answered that *Mattee non we pa pa si*—meaning that there was no need of arms where all were brothers. We took this in good part, and proceeded.

We had passed the spring and rivulet of which I before spoke, and were now entering upon a narrow gorge leading through the chain of soapstone hills among which the village was situated. This gorge was very rocky and uneven, so much so that it was with no little difficulty we scrambled through it on our first visit to Klock-klock. The whole length of the ravine might have been a mile and a half, or probably two miles. It wound in every possible direction through the hills (having apparently formed, at some remote period, the bed of a torrent), in no instance proceeding more than twenty yards without an abrupt turn. The sides of this dell would have averaged, I am sure, seventy or eighty feet in perpendicular altitude throughout the whole of their extent, and in some portions they arose to an astonishing height, overshadowing the pass so completely that but little of the light of day could penetrate. The general width was about forty feet, and occasionally it diminished so as not to allow the passage of more than five or six persons abreast. In short, there could be no place in the world better adapted for the consummation of an ambuscade, and it was no more than natural that we should look carefully to our arms as we entered upon it. When I now think of our egregious folly, the chief subject of astonishment seems to be, that we should have ever ventured, under any circumstances, so completely into the power of unknown savages as to permit them to march both before and behind us in our progress through this ravine. Yet such was the order we blindly took up, trusting foolishly to the force of our party, the unarmed condition of Too-wit and his men, the certain efficacy of our firearms (whose effect was yet a secret to the natives), and, more than all, to the long-sustained pretension of friendship kept up by these infamous wretches. Five or six of them went on before, as if to lead the way, ostentatiously busying themselves in removing the larger stones and rubbish from the path. Next came our own party. We walked closely together, taking care only to prevent separation. Behind followed the main body of the savages, observing unusual order and decorum.

Dirk Peters, a man named Wilson Allen, and myself were on the right of our companions, examining, as we went along, the singular stratification of the precipice which overhung us. A fissure in the soft rock attracted our attention. It was about wide enough for one person to enter without squeezing, and extended back into the hill some eighteen or twenty feet in a straight course, sloping afterward to the left. The height of the opening, as far as we could see into it from the main gorge, was perhaps sixty or seventy feet. There were one or two stunted shrubs growing from the crevices, bearing a species of filbert which I felt some curiosity to examine, and pushed in briskly for that purpose, gathering five or six of the nuts at a grasp, and then hastily retreating. As I turned, I found that Peters and Allen had followed me. I desired them to go back, as there was not room for two persons to pass, saying they should have some of my nuts. They accordingly turned, and were scrambling back, Allen being close to the mouth of the fissure, when I was suddenly aware of a concussion resembling nothing I had ever before experienced, and which impressed me with a vague conception, if indeed I then thought of anything, that the whole foundations of the solid globe were suddenly rent asunder, and that the day of universal dissolution was at hand.

CHAPTER XXI

As soon as I could collect my scattered senses, I found myself nearly suffocated, and grovelling in utter darkness among a quantity of loose earth, which was also falling upon me heavily in every direction, threatening to bury me entirely. Horribly alarmed at this idea, I struggled to gain my feet, and at last succeeded. I then remained motionless for some moments, endeavouring to conceive what had happened to me, and where I was. Presently I heard a deep groan just at my ear, and afterward the smothered voice of

Peters calling to me for aid in the name of God. I scrambled one or two paces forward, when I fell directly over the head and shoulders of my companion, who, I soon discovered, was buried in a loose mass of earth as far as his middle, and struggling desperately to free himself from the pressure. I tore the dirt from around him with all the energy I could command, and at length succeeded in getting him out.

As soon as we sufficiently recovered from our fright and surprise to be capable of conversing rationally, we both came to the conclusion that the walls of the fissure in which we had ventured had, by some convulsion of nature, or probably from their own weight, caved in overhead, and that we were consequently lost for ever, being thus entombed alive. For a long time we gave up supinely to the most intense agony and despair, such as cannot be adequately imagined by those who have never been in a similar situation. I firmly believed that no incident ever occurring in the course of human events is more adapted to inspire the supremeness of mental and bodily distress than a case like our own, of living inhumation. The blackness of darkness which envelops the victim, the terrific oppression of lungs, the stifling fumes from the damp earth, unite with the ghastly considerations that we are beyond the remotest confines of hope, and that such is the allotted portion of *the dead,* to carry into the human heart a degree of appalling awe and horror not to be tolerated—never to be conceived.

At length Peters proposed that we should endeavour to ascertain precisely the extent of our calamity, and grope about our prison; it being barely possible, he observed, that some opening might yet be left us for escape. I caught eagerly at this hope, and, arousing myself to exertion, attempted to force my way through the loose earth. Hardly had I advanced a single step before a glimmer of light became perceptible, enough to convince me that, at all events, we should not immediately perish for want of air. We now took some degree of heart, and encouraged each other to hope for the best. Having scrambled over a bank of rubbish which impeded our farther progress in the direction of the light, we found less difficulty in advancing, and also experienced some relief from the excessive oppression of lungs which had tormented us. Presently we were enabled to obtain a glimpse of the objects around, and discovered that we were near the extremity of the straight portion of the fissure, where it made a turn to the left. A few struggles more, and we reached the bend, when, to our inexpressible joy, there appeared a long seam or crack extending upward a vast distance, generally at an angle of about forty-five degrees, although sometimes much more precipitous. We could not see through the whole extent of this opening; but, as a good deal of light came down it, we had little doubt of finding at the top of it (if we could by any means reach the top) a clear passage into the open air.

I now called to mind that three of us had entered the fissure from the main gorge, and that our companion, Allen, was still missing; we determined at once to retrace our steps and look for him. After a long search, and much danger from the farther caving in of the earth above us, Peters at length cried out to me that he had hold of our companion's foot, and that his whole body was deeply buried beneath the rubbish beyond the possibility of extricating him. I soon found that what he said was too true, and that, of course, life had been long extinct. With sorrowful hearts, therefore, we left the corpse to its fate, and again made our way to the bend.

The breadth of the seam was barely sufficient to admit us, and, after one or too ineffectual efforts at getting up, we began once more to despair. I have before said that the chain of hills through which ran the main gorge was composed of a species of soft rock resembling soap-stone. The sides of the cleft we were now attempting to ascend were of the same material, and so excessively slippery, being wet, that we could get but little foothold upon them even in their least preciptious parts; in some places, where the ascent was nearly perpendicular, the difficulty was, of course, much aggravated; and, indeed, for some time we thought insurmountable. We took courage, however, from despair; and what, by dint of cutting steps in the soft stone with our Bowie knives, and swinging, at the risk of our lives, to small projecting points of a harder species of slaty rock which now and then protruded from the general mass, we at length reached a natural platform, from which was perceptible a patch of blue sky, at the extremity of a thickly-wooded ravine. Looking back now, with somewhat more leisure, at the passage through which we had thus far proceeded, we clearly saw from the appearance of its sides, that it was of late formation, and we concluded that the concussion, whatever it was, which had so unexpectedly overwhelmed us, had also, at the same moment, laid open this path for escape. Being quite exhausted with exertion, and, indeed, so weak that we were scarcely able to stand or articulate, Peters now proposed that we should endeavour to bring our companions to the rescue by firing the pistols which still remained in our girdles—the muskets as well as cutlasses had been lost among the loose earth at the bottom of the chasm. Subsequent events proved that, had we fired, we should have sorely repented it; but luckily a half suspicion of foul play had by this time arisen in my mind, and we forbore to let the savages know of our whereabouts.

After having reposed for about an hour, we pushed on slowly up the ravine, and had gone no great way before we heard a succession of tremendous yells. At length we reached what might be called the surface of the ground; for our path hitherto, since leaving the platform, had lain beneath an archway of high rock and foliage, at a vast distance overhead. With great caution we stole to a narrow opening, through which we had a clear sight of the surrounding country, when the whole dreadful secret of the concussion broke upon us in one moment and at one view.

The spot from which we looked was not far from the summit of the highest peak in the range of the soap-stone hills. The gorge in which our party of thirty-two had entered ran within fifty feet to the left of us. But, for at least one hundred yards, the channel or bed of this gorge was entirely filled up with the chaotic ruins of more than a million tons of earth and stone that had been artificially tumbled within it. The means by which the vast mass had been precipitated were not more simple than evident, for sure traces of the murderous work were yet remaining. In several spots along the top of the eastern side of the gorge (we were now on the western) might be seen stakes of wood driven into the earth. In these spots the earth had not given way; but throughout the whole extent of the face of the precipice from which the mass *had* fallen, it was clear, from marks left in the soil resembling those made by the drill of the rock-blaster, that stakes similar to those we saw standing had been inserted, at not more than a yard apart, for the length of perhaps three hundred feet, and ranging at about ten feet back from the edge of the gulf. Strong cords of grape vine were attached to the stakes still remaining on the hill, and it was evident that such cords had also been attached to each of the other stakes. I have already spoken of the singular stratification of these soap-stone hills; and the description just given of the narrow and deep fissure through which we effected our escape from inhumation will afford a further conception of its nature. This was such that almost every natural convulsion would be sure to split the soil into perpendicular layers or ridges running parallel with one another; and a very moderate exertion of art would be sufficient for effecting the same purpose. Of this stratification the savages had availed themselves to accomplish their treacherous ends. There can be no doubt that, by the continuous line of stakes, a partial rupture of the soil had been brought about, probably to the depth of one or two feet, when, by means of a savage pulling at the end of each of the cords (these cords being attached to the tops of the stakes, and extending back from the edge of the cliff), a vast leverage power was obtained, capable of hurling the whole face of the hill, upon a given signal, into the bosom of the abyss below. The fate of our poor companions was no longer a matter of uncertainty. We alone had escaped from the tempest of that overwhelming destruction. We were the only living white men upon the island.

CHAPTER XXII

OUR situation, as it now appeared, was scarcely less dreadful than when we had conceived ourselves entombed forever. We saw before us no prospect but that of being put to death by the savages, or of dragging out a miserable existence in captivity among them. We might, to be sure, conceal ourselves for a time from their observation among the fastnesses of the hills, and, as a final resort, in the chasm from which we had just issued; but we must either perish in the long Polar winter through cold and famine, or be ultimately discovered in our efforts to obtain relief.

The whole country around us seemed to be swarming with savages, crowds of whom, we now perceived, had come over from the islands to the southward on flat rafts, doubtless with a view of lending their aid in the capture and plunder of the Jane. The vessel still lay calmly at anchor in the bay, those on board being apparently quite unconscious of any danger awaiting them. How we longed at that moment to be with them! either to aid in effecting their escape, or to perish with them in attempting a defence. We saw no chance even of warning them of their danger without bringing immediate destruction upon our own heads, with but a remote hope of benefit to them. A pistol fired might suffice to appraise them that something wrong had occurred; but the report could not possibly inform them that their only prospect of safety lay in getting out of the harbour forthwith—it could not tell them that no principles of honour now bound them to remain, that their companions were no longer among the living. Upon hearing the discharge they could not be more thoroughly prepared to meet the foe, who were now getting ready to attack, than they already were, and always had been. No good, therefore, and infinite harm, would result from our firing, and, after mature deliberation, we forbore.

Our next thought was to attempt to rush toward the vessel, to seize one of the four canoes which lay at the head of the bay, and endeavour to force a passage on board. But the utter impossibility of succeeding in this desperate task soon became evident. The country, as I said before, was literally swarming with the natives, skulking among the bushes and recesses of the hills, so as not to be observed from the schooner. In our immediate vicinity especially, and blockading the sole path by which we could hope to attain the shore at the proper point, were stationed the whole party of the black-skin warriors, with Too-wit at their head, and apparently only waiting for some re-enforcement to commence his onset upon the Jane. The canoes, too, which lay at the head of the bay, were manned with savages, unarmed, it is true, but who undoubtedly had arms within reach. We were forced, therefore, however unwillingly, to remain in our place of concealment, mere spectators of the conflict which presently ensued.

In about half an hour we saw some sixty or seventy rafts, or flat-boats, with outriggers, filled with savages, and coming round the southern bight of the harbour. They appeared to have no arms except short clubs, and stones which lay in the bottom of the rafts. Immediately afterward another detachment, still larger, approached in an opposite direction, and with similar weapons. The four canoes, too, were now quickly filled with natives, starting up from the bushes at the head of the bay, and put off swiftly to join the other parties. Thus, in less time than I have taken to tell it, and as if by magic, the Jane saw herself surrounded by an immense multitude of desperadoes evidently bent upon capturing her at all hazards.

That they would succeed in so doing could not be doubted for an instant. The six men left in the vessel, however resolutely they might engage in her defence, were altogether unequal to the proper management of the guns, or in any manner to sustain a contest at such odds. I could hardly imagine that they would make resistance at all, but in this was deceived; for presently I saw them get springs upon the cable, and bring the vessel's starboard broadside to bear upon the canoes, which by this time were within pistol range, the rafts being nearly a quarter of a mile to windward. Owing to some cause unknown, but most probably to the agitation of our poor friends at seeing themselves in so hopeless a situation, the discharge was an entire failure. Not a canoe was hit or a single savage injured, the shot striking short and ricochetting over their heads. The only effect produced upon them was astonishment at the unexpected report and smoke, which was so excessive that for some moments I almost thought they would abandon their design entirely, and return to the shore. And this they would most likely have done had our men followed up their broadside by a discharge of small arms, in which, as the canoes were now so near at hand, they could not have failed in doing some execution, sufficient, at least, to deter this party from a farther advance, until they could have given the rafts also a broadside. But, in place of this, they left the canoe party to recover from their panic, and, by looking about them, to see that no injury had been sustained, while they flew to the larboard to get ready for the rafts.

The discharge to larboard produced the most terrible effect. The star and double-headed shot of the large guns cut seven or eight of the rafts completely asunder, and killed, perhaps, thirty or forty of the savages outright, while a hundred of them, at least, were thrown into the water, the most of them dreadfully wounded. The remainder, frightened out of their senses, commenced at once a precipitate retreat, not even waiting to pick up their maimed companions, who were swimming about in every direction, screaming and yelling for aid. This great success, however, came too late for the salvation of our devoted people. The canoe party were already on board the schooner to the number of more than a hundred and fifty, the most of them having succeeded in scrambling up the chains and over the boarding-nettings even before the matches had been applied to the larboard guns. Nothing now could withstand their brute rage. Our men were borne down at once, overwhelmed, trodden under foot, and absolutely torn to pieces in an instant.

Seeing this, the savages on the rafts got the better of their fears, and came up in shoals to the plunder. In five minutes the

Jane was a pitiable scene indeed of havoc and tumultuous outrage. The decks were split open and ripped up; the cordage, sails, and everything movable on deck demolished as if by magic; while, by dint of pushing at the stern, towing with the canoes, and hauling at the sides, as they swam in thousands around the vessel, the wretches finally forced her on shore (the cable having been slipped), and delivered her over to the good offices of Too-wit, who, during the whole of the engagement, had maintained, like a skilful general, his post of security and reconnoissance among the hills, but, now that the victory was completed to his satisfaction, condescended to scamper down with his warriors of the black skin, and become a partaker in the spoils.

Too-wit's descent left us at liberty to quit our hiding-place and reconnoitre the hill in the vicinity of the chasm. At about fifty yards from the mouth of it we saw a small spring of water, at which we slaked the burning thirst that now consumed us. Not far from the spring we discovered several of the filbert-bushes which I mentioned before. Upon tasting the nuts we found them palatable, and very nearly resembling in flavour the common English filbert. We collected our hats full immediately, deposited them within the ravine, and returned for more. While we were busily employed in gathering these, a rustling in the bushes alarmed us, and we were upon the point of stealing back to our covert, when a large black bird of the bittern species strugglingly and slowly arose above the shrubs. I was so much startled that I could do nothing, but Peters had sufficient presence of mind to run up to it before it could make its escape, and seize it by the neck. Its struggles and screams were tremendous, and we had thoughts of letting it go, lest the noise should alarm some of the savages who might be still lurking in the neighbourhood. A stab with a Bowie knife, however, at length brought it to the ground, and we dragged it into the ravine, congratulating ourselves that, at all events, we had thus obtained a supply of food enough to last us for a week.

We now went out again to look about us, and ventured a

considerable distance down the southern declivity of the hill, but met with nothing else which could serve us for food. We therefore collected a quantity of dry wood and returned, seeing one or two large parties of the natives on their way to the village, laden with the plunder of the vessel, and who, we were apprehensive, might discover us in passing beneath the hill.

Our next care was to render our place of concealment as secure as possible, and with this object, we arranged some brushwood over the aperture which I have before spoken of as the one through which we saw the patch of blue sky, on reaching the platform from the interior of the chasm. We left only a very small opening, just wide enough to admit of our seeing the bay, without the risk of being discovered from below. Having done this, we congratulated ourselves upon the security of the position; for we were now completely excluded from observation, as long as we chose to remain within the ravine itself, and not venture out upon the hill. We could perceive no traces of the savages having ever been within this hollow; but, indeed, when we came to reflect upon the probability that the fissure through which we attained it had been only just now created by the fall of the cliff opposite, and that no other way of attaining it could be perceived, we were not so much rejoiced at the thought of being secure from molestation as fearful lest there should be absolutely no means left us for descent. We resolved to explore the summit of the hill thoroughly, when a good opportunity should offer. In the mean time we watched the motions of the savages through our loophole.

They had already made a complete wreck of the vessel, and were now preparing to set her on fire. In a little while we saw the smoke ascending in huge volumes from her main hatchway, and, shortly afterward, a dense mass of flame burst up from the forecastle. The rigging, masts, and what remained of the sails caught immediately, and the fire spread rapidly along the decks. Still a great many of the savages retained their stations about her, hammering with large stones, axes, and cannon-balls at the bolts and other iron and copper work. On the beach, and in canoes and rafts, there were not less, altogether, in the immediate vicinity of the schooner, than ten thousand natives, besides the shoals of them who, laden with booty, were making their way inland and over to the neighbouring islands. We now anticipated a catastrophe, and were not disappointed. First of all there came a smart shock (which we felt as distinctly where we were as if we had been slightly galvanized), but unattended with any visible signs of an explosion. The savages were evidently startled, and paused for an instant from their labours and yellings. They were upon the point of recommencing, when suddenly a mass of smoke puffed up from the decks, resembling a black and heavy thunder-cloud—then, as if from its bowels, arose a tall stream of vivid fire to the height, apparently, of a quarter of a mile—then there came a sudden circular expansion of the flame—then the whole atmosphere was magically crowded, in a single instant, with a wild chaos of wood, and metal, and human limbs—and, lastly, came the concussion in its fullest fury, which hurled us impetuously from our feet, while the hills echoed and re-echoed the tumult, and a dense shower of the minutest fragments of the ruins tumbled headlong in every direction around us.

The havoc among the savages far exceeded our utmost expectation, and they had now, indeed, reaped the full and perfect fruits of their treachery. Perhaps a thousand perished by the explosion, while at least an equal number were desperately mangled. The whole surface of the bay was literally strewn with the struggling and drowning wretches, and on shore matters were even worse. They seemed utterly appalled by the suddenness and completeness of their discomfiture, and made no efforts at assisting one another. At length we observed a total change in their demeanour. From absolute stupor, they appeared to be, all at once, aroused to the highest pitch of excitement, and rushed wildly about, going to and from a certain point on the beach, with the strangest expressions of mingled horror, rage, and intense curiosity depicted on their countenances, and shouting, at the top of their voices, *"Tekeli-li! Tekeli-li!"*

Presently we saw a large body go off into the hills, whence they returned in a short time, carrying stakes of wood. These they brought to the station where the crowd was the thickest, which now separated so as to afford us a view of the object of all this excitement. We perceived something white lying upon the ground, but could not immediately make out what it was. At length we saw that it was the carcass of the strange animal with the scarlet teeth and claws which the schooner had picked up at sea on the eighteenth of January. Captain Guy had had the body preserved for the purpose of stuffing the skin and taking it to England. I remember he had given some directions about it just before our making the island, and it had been brought into the cabin and stowed away in one of the lockers. It had now been thrown on shore by the explosion; but why it had occasioned so much concern among the savages was more than we could comprehend. Although they crowded around the carcass at a little distance, none of them seemed willing to approach it closely. By-and-by the men with the stakes drove them in a circle around it, and, no sooner was this arrangement completed, than the whole of the vast assemblage rushed into the interior of the island, with loud screams of *"Tekeli-li! Tekeli-li!"*

CHAPTER XXIII

DURING the six or seven days immediately following we remained in our hiding-place upon the hill, going out only occasionally, and then with the greatest precaution, for water and filberts. We had made a kind of pent-house on the platform, furnishing it with a bed of dry leaves, and placing in it three large flat stones, which served us for both fire-place and table. We kindled a fire without difficulty by rubbing two pieces of dry wood together, the one soft, the other hard. The bird we had taken in such good season proved excellent eating, although somewhat tough. It was not an oceanic fowl, but a species of bittern, with jet black and grizzly plumage, and diminutive wings in proportion to its bulk. We afterward saw three of the same kind in the vicinity of the ravine, apparently seeking for the one we had captured; but, as they never alighted, we had no opportunity of catching them.

As long as this fowl lasted we suffered nothing from our situation, but it was now entirely consumed, and it became absolutely necessary that we should look out for provision. The filberts would not satisfy the cravings of hunger, afflicting us, too, with severe gripings of the bowels, and, if freely indulged in, with violent headache. We had seen several large tortoises near the seashore to the eastward of the hill, and perceived they might be easily taken, if we could get at them without the observation of the natives. It was resolved, therefore, to make an attempt at descending.

We commenced by going down the southern declivity, which seemed to offer the fewest difficulties, but had not proceeded a hundred yards before (as we had anticipated from appearances on the hill-top) our progress was entirely arrested by a branch of the gorge in which our companions had perished. We now passed along the edge of this for about a quarter of a mile, when we were again stopped by a precipice of immense depth, and, not being able to make our way along the brink of it, we were forced to retrace our steps by the main ravine.

We now pushed over to the eastward, but with precisely similar fortune. After an hour's scramble, at the risk of breaking our necks, we discovered that we had merely descended into a vast pit of black granite, with fine dust at the bottom, and whence the only egress was by the rugged path in which we had come down. Toiling again up this path, we now tried the northern edge of the hill. Here we were obliged to use the greatest possible caution in our manœuvres, as the least indiscretion would expose us to the full view of the savages in the village. We crawled along, therefore, on our hands and knees, and, occasionally, were even forced to throw ourselves at full length, dragging our bodies along by means of the shrubbery. In this careful manner we had proceeded but a little way, when we arrived at a chasm far deeper than any we had yet seen, and leading directly into the main gorge. Thus our fears were fully confirmed, and we found ourselves cut off entirely from access to the world below. Thoroughly exhausted by our exertions, we made the best of our way back to the platform, and, throwing ourselves upon the bed of leaves, slept sweetly and soundly for some hours.

For several days after this fruitless search we were occupied in exploring every part of the summit of the hill, in order to inform ourselves of its actual resources. We found that it would afford us no food, with the exception of the unwholesome filberts, and a rank species of scurvy grass, which grew in a little patch of not more than four rods square, and would be soon exhausted. On the fifteenth of February, as near as I can remember, there was not a blade of this left, and the nuts were growing scarce; our situation, therefore, could hardly be more lamentable.* On the sixteenth we again went round the walls of our prison, in hope of finding some avenue of escape, but to no purpose. We also descended the chasm in which we had been overwhelmed, with the faint expectation of discovering, through this channel, some opening to the main ravine. Here, too, we were disappointed, although we found and brought up with us a musket.

On the seventeenth we set out with the determination of examining more thoroughly the chasm of black granite into which we had made our way in the first search. We remembered that one of the fissures in the sides of this pit had been but partially looked into, and we were anxious to explore it, although with no expectation of discovering here any opening.

We found no great difficulty in reaching the bottom of the hollow as before, and were now sufficiently calm to survey it with some attention. It was, indeed, one of the most singular looking places imaginable, and we could scarcely bring ourselves to believe

* This day was rendered remarkable by our observing in the south several huge wreaths of the grayish vapour I have before spoken of.

it altogether the work of nature. The pit, from its eastern to its western extremity, was about five hundred yards in length, when all its windings were threaded; the distance from east to west in a straight line not being more (I should suppose, having no means of accurate examination) than forty or fifty yards. Upon first descending into the chasm, that is to say, for a hundred feet downward from the summit of the hill, the sides of the abyss bore little resemblance to each other, and, apparently, had at no time been connected, the one surface being of the soap-stone, and the other of marl, granulated with some metallic matter. The average breadth, or interval between the two cliffs, was probably here sixty feet, but there seemed to be no regularity of formation. Passing down, however, beyond the limit spoken of, the interval rapidly contracted, and the sides began to run parallel, although for some distance farther, they were still dissimilar in their material and form of surface. Upon arriving within fifty feet of the bottom, a perfect regularity commenced. The sides were now entirely uniform in substance, in colour, and in lateral direction, the material being a very black and shining granite, and the distance between the two sides, at all points, facing each other, exactly twenty yards. The precise formation of the chasm will be best understood by means of a delineation taken upon the spot; for I had luckily with me a pocket-book and pencil, which I preserved with great care through a long series of subsequent adventure, and to which I am indebted for memoranda of many subjects which would otherwise have been crowded from my remembrance.

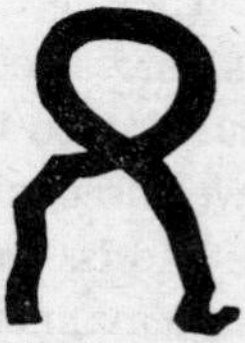

FIG. 1

This figure (see figure 1) gives the general outlines of the chasm, without the minor cavities in the sides, of which there were several, each cavity having a corresponding protuberance opposite. The bottom of the gulf was covered to the depth of three or four inches with a powder almost impalpable, beneath which we found a continuation of the black granite. To the right, at the lower extremity, will be noticed the appearance of a small opening; this is the fissure alluded to above, and to examine which more minutely than before was the object of our second visit. We now pushed into it with vigour, cutting away a quantity of brambles which impeded us, and removing a vast heap of sharp flints somewhat resembling arrowheads in shape. We were encouraged to persevere, however, by perceiving some little light proceeding from the farther end. We at length squeezed our way for about thirty feet,

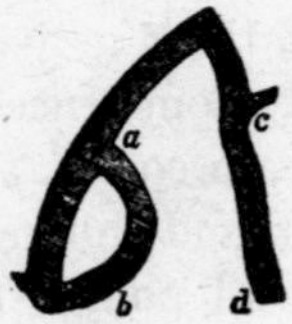

FIG. 2

and found that the aperture was a low and regularly-formed arch, having a bottom of the same impalpable powder as that in the main chasm. A strong light now broke upon us, and, turning a short bend, we found ourselves in another lofty chamber, similar to the one we had left in every respect but longitudinal form. Its general figure is here given. (See figure 2.)

The total length of this chasm, commencing at the opening *a* and proceeding round the curve *b* to the extremity *d*, is five hundred and fifty yards. At *c* we discovered a small aperture similar to the one through which we had issued from the other chasm, and this was choked up in the same manner with brambles and a quantity of the white arrowhead flints. We forced our way through it, finding it about forty feet long, and emerged into a third chasm.

This, too, was precisely like the first, except in its longitudinal shape, which was thus. (See figure 3.)

We found the entire length of the third chasm three hundred and twenty yards. At the point *a* was an opening about six feet wide, and extending fifteen feet into the rock, where it terminated

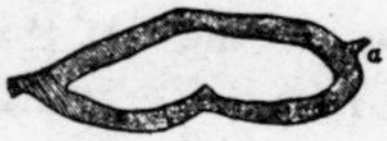

FIG. 3

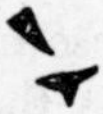

FIG. 5

in a bed of marl, there being no other chasm beyond, as we had expected. We were about leaving this fissure, into which very little light was admitted, when Peters called my attention to a range of singular looking indentures in the surface of the marl forming the termination of the *cul-de-sac*. With a very slight exertion of the imagination, the left, or most northern of these indentures might have been taken for the intentional, although rude, representation of a human figure standing erect, with out-stretched arm. The rest of them bore also some little resemblance to alphabetical characters, and Peters was willing, at all events, to adopt the idle opinion that they were really such. I convinced him of his error, finally, by directing his attention to the floor of the fissure, where, among the powder, we picked up, piece by piece, several large flakes of the marl, which had evidently been broken off by some convulsion from the surface where the indentures were found, and which had projecting points exactly fitting the indentures; thus proving them to have been the work of nature. Figure 4 presents an accurate copy of the whole.

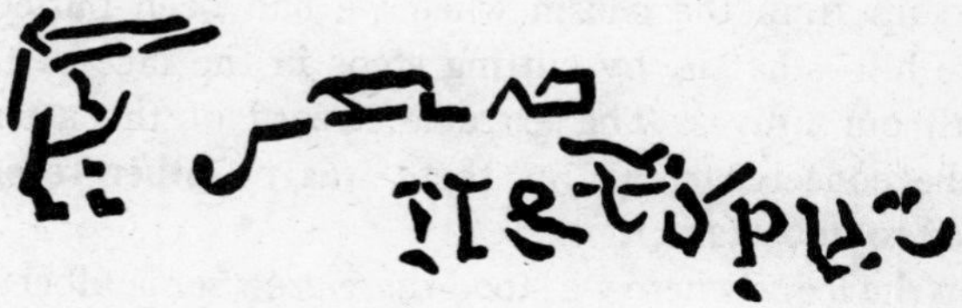

FIG. 4

After satisfying ourselves that these singular caverns afforded us no means of escape from our prison, we made our way back, dejected and dispirited, to the summit of the hill. Nothing worth mentioning occurred during the next twenty-four hours, except that, in examining the ground to the eastward of the third chasm, we found two triangular holes of great depth, and also with black granite sides. Into these holes we did not think it worth while to attempt descending, as they had the appearance of mere natural wells, without outlet. They were each about twenty yards in circumference, and their shape, as well as relative position in regard to the third chasm, is shown in figure 5.

CHAPTER XXIV

ON THE twentieth of the month, finding it altogether impossible to subsist any longer upon the filberts, the use of which occasioned us the most excruciating torment, we resolved to make a desperate attempt at descending the southern declivity of the hill. The face of the precipice was here of the softest species of soap-stone, although nearly perpendicular throughout its whole extent (a depth of a hundred and fifty feet at the least), and in many places even overarching. After a long search we discovered a narrow ledge about twenty feet below the brink of the gulf; upon this Peters contrived to leap, with what assistance I could render him by means of our pocket-handkerchiefs tied together. With somewhat more difficulty I also got down; and we then saw the possibility of descending the whole way by the process in which we had clambered up from the chasm when we had been buried by the fall of the hill—that is, by cutting steps in the face of the soapstone with our knives. The extreme hazard of the attempt can scarcely be conceived; but, as there was no other resource, we determined to undertake it.

Upon the ledge where we stood there grew some filbert-bushes; and to one of these we made fast an end of our rope of handkerchiefs. The other end being tied round Peters's waist, I lowered him down over the edge of the precipice until the handkerchiefs were stretched tight. He now proceeded to dig a deep hole in the soap-stone (as far in as eight or ten inches), sloping away the rock above to the height of a foot, or thereabout, so as to allow of his driving, with the butt of a pistol, a tolerably strong peg into the leveled surface. I then drew him up for about four feet, when he made a hole similar to the one below, driving in a peg as before, and having thus a resting-place for both feet and hands. I now unfastened the handkerchiefs from the bush, throwing him the end, which he tied to the peg in the uppermost hole, letting himself down gently to a station about three feet lower than he had yet been—that is, to the full extent of the handkerchiefs. Here he dug another hole, and drove another peg. He then drew himself up, so as to rest his feet in the hole just cut, taking hold with his hands upon the peg in the one above. It was now necessary to untie the handkerchiefs from the topmost peg, with the view of fastening them to the second; and here he found that an error had been committed in cutting the holes at so great a distance apart. However, after one or two unsuccessful and dangerous attempts at reaching the knot (having to hold on with his left hand while he laboured to undo the fastening with his right), he at length cut the string, leaving six inches of it affixed to the peg. Tying the handkerchiefs now to the second peg, he descended to a station below the third, taking care not to go too far down. By these means (means which I should never have conceived of myself, and for which we were indebted altogether to Peters's ingenuity and resolution) my companion finally succeeded, with the occasional aid of projections in the cliff, in reaching the bottom without accident.

It was some time before I could summon sufficient resolution to follow him; but I did at length attempt it. Peters had taken off his shirt before descending, and this, with my own, formed the rope necessary for the adventure. After throwing down the musket found in the chasm, I fastened this rope to the bushes, and let myself down rapidly, striving, by the vigour of my movements, to banish the trepidation which I could overcome in no other manner. This answered sufficiently well for the first four or five steps; but presently I found my imagination growing terribly excited by thoughts of the vast depths yet to be descended, and the precarious nature of the pegs and soap-stone holes which were my only support. It was in vain I endeavoured to banish these reflections, and to keep my eyes steadily bent upon the flat surface of the cliff before me. The more earnestly I struggled *not to think,* the more intensely vivid became my conceptions, and the more horribly distinct. At length arrived that crisis of fancy, so fearful in all similar cases, the crisis in which we begin to anticipate the feelings with which we *shall* fall—to picture to ourselves the sickness, and dizziness, and the last struggle, and the half swoon, and the final bitterness of the rushing and headlong descent. And now I found these fancies creating their own realities, and all imagined horrors crowding upon me in fact. I felt my knees strike violently together, while my fingers were gradually but certainly relaxing their grasp. There was a ringing in my ears, and I said, "This is my knell of death!" And now I was consumed with the irrepressible desire of looking below. I could not, I would not, confine my glances to the cliff; and, with a wild, indefinable emotion, half of horror, half of a relieved oppression, I threw my vision far down into the abyss. For one moment my fingers clutched convulsively upon their hold, while, with the movement, the faintest possible idea of ultimate escape wandered, like a shadow, through my mind—in the next my whole soul was pervaded with *a longing to fall;* a desire, a yearning, a passion utterly uncontrollable. I let go at once my grasp upon the peg, and, turning half round from the precipice, remained tottering for an instant against its naked face. But now there came a spinning of the brain; a shrill-sounding and phantom voice screamed within my ears; a dusky, fiendish, and filmy figure stood immediately beneath me; and, sighing, I sunk down with a bursting heart, and plunged within its arms.

I had swooned, and Peters had caught me as I fell. He had observed my proceedings from his station at the bottom of the cliff; and perceiving my imminent danger, had endeavoured to inspire me with courage by every suggestion he could devise; although my confusion of mind had been so great as to prevent my hearing what he said, or being conscious that he had even spoken to me at all. At length, seeing me totter, he hastened to ascend to my rescue, and arrived just in time for my preservation. Had I fallen with my full weight, the rope of linen would inevitably have snapped, and I should have been precipitated into the abyss; as it was, he contrived to let me down gently, so as to remain suspended without danger until animation returned. This was in about fifteen minutes. On recovery, my trepidation had entirely vanished; I felt a new being, and, with some little further aid from my companion, reached the bottom also in safety.

We now found ourselves not far from the ravine which had proved the tomb of our friends, and to the southward of the spot where the hill had fallen. The place was one of singular wildness, and its aspect brought to my mind the descriptions given by travellers of those dreary regions marking the site of degraded Babylon. Not to speak of the ruins of the disruptured cliff, which formed a chaotic barrier in the vista to the northward, the surface of the ground in every other direction was strewn with huge tumuli, apparently the wreck of some gigantic structures of art; although, in detail, no semblance of art could be detected. Scoria were abundant, and large shapeless blocks of the black granite, intermingled with others of marl,* and both granulated with metal. Of vegetation there were no traces whatsoever throughout the whole of the desolate area within sight. Several immense scorpions were seen, and various reptiles not elsewhere to be found in the high latitudes.

As food was our most immediate object, we resolved to make our way to the sea-coast, distant not more than half a mile, with

* The marl was also black; indeed, we noticed no light-colored substances of any kind upon the island.

a view of catching turtle, several of which we had observed from our place of concealment on the hill. We had proceeded some hundred yards, threading our route cautiously between the huge rocks and tumuli, when, upon turning a corner, five savages sprung upon us from a small cavern, felling Peters to the ground with a blow from a club. As he fell the whole party rushed upon him to secure their victim, leaving me time to recover from my astonishment. I still had the musket, but the barrel had received so much injury in being thrown from the precipice that I cast it aside as useless, preferring to trust my pistols, which had been carefully preserved in order. With these I advanced upon the assailants, firing one after the other in quick succession. Two savages fell, and one, who was in the act of thrusting a spear into Peters, sprung to his feet without accomplishing his purpose. My companion being thus released, we had no further difficulty. He had his pistols also, but prudently declined using them, confiding in his great personal strength, which far exceeded that of any person I have ever known. Seizing a club from one of the savages who had fallen, he dashed out the brains of the three who remained, killing each instantaneously with a single blow of the weapon, and leaving us completely masters of the field.

So rapidly had these events passed, that we could scarcely believe in their reality, and were standing over the bodies of the dead in a species of stupid contemplation, when we were brought to recollection by the sound of shouts in the distance. It was clear that the savages had been alarmed by the firing, and that we had little chance of avoiding discovery. To regain the cliff, it would be necessary to proceed in the direction of the shouts; and even should we succeed in arriving at its base, we should never be able to ascend it without being seen. Our situation was one of the greatest peril, and we were hesitating in which path to commence a flight, when one of the savages whom I had shot, and supposed dead, sprang briskly to his feet, and attempted to make his escape. We overtook him, however, before he had advanced many paces, and were about to put him to death, when Peters suggested that we might derive some benefit from forcing him to accompany us in our attempt to escape. We therefore dragged him with us, making him understand that we would shoot him if he offered resistance. In a few minutes he was perfectly submissive, and ran by our sides as we pushed in among the rocks, making for the seashore.

So far, the irregularities of the ground we had been traversing hid the sea, except at intervals, from our sight, and, when we first had it fairly in view, it was, perhaps, two hundred yards distant. As we emerged into the open beach we saw, to our great dismay, an immense crowd of the natives pouring from the village, and from all visible quarters of the island, making towards us with gesticulations of extreme fury, and howling like wild beasts. We were upon the point of turning upon our steps, and trying to secure a retreat among the fastnesses of the rougher ground, when I discovered the bows of two canoes projecting from behind a large rock which ran out into the water. Towards these we now ran with all speed, and, reaching them, found them unguarded, and without any other freight than three of the large Gallipago turtles and the usual supply of paddles for sixty rowers. We instantly took possession of one of them, and, forcing our captive on board, pushed out to sea with all the strength we could command.

We had not made, however, more than fifty yards from the shore before we became sufficiently calm to perceive the great oversight of which we had been guilty in leaving the other canoe in the power of the savages, who, by this time, were not more than twice as far from the beach as ourselves, and were rapidly advancing to the pursuit. No time was now to be lost. Our hope was, at best, a forlorn one, but we had none other. It was very doubtful whether, with the utmost exertion, we could get back in time to anticipate them in taking possession of the canoe; but yet there was a chance that we could. We might save ourselves if we succeeded, while not to make the attempt was to resign ourselves to inevitable butchery.

The canoe was modelled with the bow and stern alike, and, in place of turning it around, we merely changed our position in paddling. As soon as the savages perceived this they redoubled their yells, as well as their speed, and approached with inconceivable rapidity. We pulled, however, with all the energy of desperation, and arrived at the contested point before more than one of the natives had attained it. This man paid dearly for his superior agility, Peters shooting him through the head with a pistol as he approached the shore. The foremost among the rest of his party were probably some twenty or thirty paces distant as we seized upon the canoe. We at first endeavoured to pull her into the deep water, beyond the reach of the savages, but, finding her too firmly aground, and there being no time to spare, Peters, with one or two heavy strokes from the butt of the musket, succeeded in dashing out a large portion of the bow and of one side. We then pushed off. Two of the natives by this time had got hold of our boat, obstinately refusing to let go, until we were forced to dispatch them with our knives. We were now clear off, and making great way out to sea. The main body of the savages, upon reaching the broken canoe, set up the most tremendous yell of rage and disappointment conceivable. In truth, from everything I could see of these wretches, they appeared to be the most wicked, hypocritical, vindictive, bloodthirsty, and altogether fiendish race of men upon the face of the globe. It is clear we should have had no mercy had we fallen into their hands. They made a mad attempt at following us in the fractured canoe, but, finding it useless, again vented their rage in a series of hideous vociferations, and rushed up into the hills.

We were thus relieved from immediate danger, but our situation was still sufficiently gloomy. We knew that four canoes of the kind we had were at one time in the possession of the savages, and were not aware of the fact (afterward ascertained from our captive) that two of these had been blown to pieces in the explosion of the Jane Guy. We calculated, therefore, upon being yet pursued, as soon as our enemies could get round to the bay (distant about three miles) where the boats were usually laid up. Fearing this, we made every exertion to leave the island behind us, and went rapidly through the water, forcing the prisoner to take a paddle. In about half an hour, when we had gained, probably, five or six miles to the southward, a large fleet of the flat-bottomed canoes or rafts were seen to emerge from the bay evidently with the design of pursuit. Presently they put back, despairing to overtake us.

CHAPTER XXV

We now found ourselves in the wide and desolate Antarctic Ocean, in a latitude exceeding eighty-four degrees, in a frail canoe, and with no provision but the three turtles. The long Polar winter, too, could not be considered as far distant, and it became necessary that we should deliberate well upon the course to be pursued. There were six or seven islands in sight belonging to the same group, and distant from each other about five or six leagues; but upon neither of these had we any intention to venture. In coming from the northward in the Jane Guy we had been gradually leaving behind us the severest regions of ice—this, however little it may be in accordance with the generally received notions respecting the Antarctic, was a fact experience would not permit us to deny. To attempt, therefore, getting back, would be folly—especially at so late a period of the season. Only one course seemed to be left open for hope. We resolved to steer boldly to the southward, where there was at least a probability of discovering other lands, and more than a probability of finding a still milder climate.

So far we had found the Antarctic, like the Arctic Ocean, peculiarly free from violent storms or immoderately rough water; but our canoe was, at best, of frail structure, although large, and we set busily to work with a view of rendering her as safe as the limited means in our possession would admit. The body of the boat was of no better material than bark—the bark of a tree unknown. The ribs were of a tough osier, well adapted to the purpose for which it was used. We had fifty feet room from stem to stern, from four to six in breadth, and in depth throughout four feet and a half—the boats thus differing vastly in shape from those of any other inhabitants of the Southern Ocean with whom civilized nations are acquainted. We never did believe them the workmanship of the ignorant islanders who owned them; and some days after this period discovered, by questioning our captive, that they were in fact made by the natives of a group to the southwest of the country where we found them, having fallen accidentally into the hands of our barbarians. What we could do for the security of our boat was very little indeed. Several wide rents were discovered near both ends, and these we contrived to patch up with pieces of woollen jacket. With the help of the superfluous paddles, of which there were a great many, we erected a kind of framework about the bow, so as to break the force of any seas which might threaten to fill us in that quarter. We also set up two paddle-blades for masts, placing them opposite each other, one by each gunwale, thus saving the necessity of a yard. To these masts we attached a sail made of our shirts—doing this with some difficulty, as here we could get no assistance from our prisoner whatever, although he had been willing enough to labour in all the other operations. The sight of the linen seemed to affect him in a very singular manner. He could not be prevailed upon to touch it or go near it, shuddering when we attempted to force him, and shrieking out, *Tekeli-li.*

Having completed our arrangements in regard to the security of the canoe, we now set sail to the south southeast for the present, with the view of weathering the most southerly of the group in sight. This being done, we turned the bow full to the southward. The weather could by no means be considered disagreeable. We had a prevailing and very gentle wind from the northward, a smooth sea, and continual daylight. No ice whatever was to be seen; *nor did I ever see one particle of this after leaving the parallel of Bennett's Islet.* Indeed, the temperature of the water was here far too warm for its existence in any quantity. Having killed the largest of our tortoises, and obtained from him not only food but a copious supply of water, we continued on our course, without any incident of moment, for perhaps seven or eight days, during which period we must have proceeded a vast distance to the southward, as the wind blew constantly with us, and a very strong current set continually in the direction we were pursuing.

March 1.* Many unusual phenomena now indicated that we were entering upon a region of novelty and wonder. A high range of light gray vapour appeared constantly in the southern horizon, flaring up occasionally in lofty streaks, now darting from east to west, now from west to east, and again presenting a level and uniform summit—in short, having all the wild variations of the Aurora Borealis. The average height of this vapour, as apparent from our station, was about twenty-five degrees. The temperature of the sea seemed to be increasing momentarily, and there was a very perceptible alteration in its colour.

March 2. To-day, by repeated questioning of our captive, we came to the knowledge of many particulars in regard to the island of the massacre, its inhabitants, and customs—but with these how can I *now* detain the reader? I may say, however, that we learned there were eight islands in the group, that they were governed by a common king, named *Tsalemon* or *Psalemoun,* who resided in one of the smallest of the islands—that the black skins forming the dress of the warriors came from an animal of huge size to be found only in a valley near the court of the king—that the inhabitants of the group fabricated no other boats than the flat-bottomed rafts—the four canoes being all of the kind in their possession, and these having been obtained, by mere accident, from some large island in the southwest—that his own name was Nu-Nu—that he had no knowledge of Bennett's Islet—and that the appellation of the island we had left was Tsalal. The commencement of the words *Tsalemon* and *Tsalal* was given with a

* For obvious reasons I cannot pretend to strict accuracy in these dates. They are given principally with a view to perspicuity of narration, and as set down in my pencil memorandum.

prolonged hissing sound, which we found it impossible to imitate, even after repeated endeavours, and which was precisely the same with the note of the black bittern we had eaten up on the summit of the hill.

March 3. The heat of the water was now truly remarkable, and in colour was undergoing a rapid change, being no longer transparent, but of a milky consistency and hue. In our immediate vicinity it was usually smooth, never so rough as to endanger the canoe—but we were frequently surprised at perceiving, to our right and left, at different distances, sudden and extensive agitations of the surface—these, we at length noticed, were always preceded by wild flickerings in the region of the vapour to the southward.

March 4. To-day, with the view of widening our sail, the breeze from the northward dying away perceptibly, I took from my coat-pocket a white handkerchief. Nu-Nu was seated at my elbow, and the linen accidentally flaring in his face, he became violently affected with convulsions. These were succeeded by drowsiness and stupor, and low murmurings of *Tekeli-li! Tekeli-li!*

March 5. The wind had entirely ceased, but it was evident that we were still hurrying on to the southward, under the influence of a powerful current. And now, indeed, it would seem reasonable that we should experience some alarm at the turn events were taking—but we felt none. The countenance of Peters indicated nothing of this nature, although it wore at times an expression I could not fathom. The Polar winter appeared to be coming on—but coming without its terrors. I felt a *numbness* of body and mind—a dreaminess of sensation—but this was all.

March 6. The gray vapour had now arisen many more degrees above the horizon, and was gradually losing its grayness of tint. The heat of the water was extreme, even unpleasant to the touch, and its milky hue was more evident than ever. To-day a violent agitation of the water occurred very close to the canoe. It was attended, as usual, with a wild flaring up of the vapour at its summit, and a momentary division at its base. A fine white powder, resembling ashes—but certainly not such—fell over the canoe and over a large surface of the water, as the flickering died away among the vapour and the commotion subsided in the sea. Nu-Nu now threw himself on his face in the bottom of the boat, and no persuasions could induce him to arise.

March 7. This day we questioned Nu-Nu concerning the motives of his countrymen in destroying our companions; but he appeared to be too utterly overcome by terror to afford us any rational reply. He still obstinately lay in the bottom of the boat; and, upon our reiterating the questions as to the motive made use only of idiotic gesticulations, such as raising with his forefinger the upper lip, and displaying the teeth which lay beneath it. These were black. We had never before seen the teeth of an inhabitant of Tsalal.

March 8. To-day there floated by us one of the white animals whose appearance upon the beach at Tsalal had occasioned so wild a commotion among the savages. I would have picked it up, but there came over me a sudden listlessness, and I forbore. The heat of the water still increased, and the hand could no longer be endured within it. Peters spoke little, and I knew not what to think of his apathy. Nu-Nu breathed, and no more.

March 9. The whole ashy material fell now continually around us, and in vast quantities. The range of vapour to the southward had arisen prodigiously in the horizon, and began to assume more distinctness of form. I can liken it to nothing but a limitless cataract, rolling silently into the sea from some immense and far-distant rampart in the heaven. The gigantic curtain ranged along the whole extent of the southern horizon. It emitted no sound.

March 21. A sullen darkness now hovered above us—but from out the milky depths of the ocean a luminous glare arose, and stole up along the bulwarks of the boat. We were nearly overwhelmed by the white ashy shower which settled upon us and upon the canoe, but melted into the water as it fell. The summit of the cataract was utterly lost in the dimness and the distance.

Yet we were evidently approaching it with a hideous velocity. At intervals there were visible in it wide, yawning, but momentary rents, and from out these rents, within which was a chaos of flitting and indistinct images, there came rushing and mighty, but soundless winds, tearing up the enkindled ocean in their course.

March 22. The darkness had materially increased, relieved only by the glare of the water thrown back from the white curtain before us. Many gigantic and pallidly white birds flew continuously now from beyond the veil, and their scream was the eternal *Tekeli-li!* as they retreated from our vision. Hereupon Nu-Nu stirred in the bottom of the boat; but upon touching him, we found his spirit departed. And now we rushed into the embraces of the cataract, where a chasm threw itself open to receive us. But there arose in our pathway a shrouded human figure, very far larger in its proportions than any dweller among men. And the hue of the skin of the figure was of the perfect whiteness of the snow.

NOTE

The circumstances connected with the late sudden and distressing death of Mr. Pym are already well known to the public through the medium of the daily press. It is feared that the few remaining chapters which were to have completed his narrative, and which were retained by him, while the above were in type, for the purpose of revision, have been irrecoverably lost through the accident by which he perished himself. This, however, may prove not to be the case, and the papers, if ultimately found, will be given to the public.

No means have been left untried to remedy the deficiency. The gentleman whose name is mentioned in the preface, and who, from the statement there made, might be supposed able to fill the vacuum, has declined the task —this, for satisfactory reasons connected with the general inaccuracy of the details afforded him, and his disbelief in the entire truth of the latter portions of the narration. Peters, from whom some information might be expected, is still alive, and a resident of Illinois, but cannot be met with at present. He may hereafter be found, and will, no doubt, afford material for a conclusion of Mr. Pym's account.

The loss of two or three final chapters (for there were but two or three) is the more deeply to be regretted, as, it cannot be doubted, they contained matter relative to the Pole itself, or at least to regions in its very near proximity; and as, too, the statements of the author in relation to these regions may shortly be verified or contradicted by means of the governmental expedition now preparing for the Southern Ocean.

On one point in the narrative some remarks may well be offered; and it would afford the writer of this appendix much pleasure if what he may here observe should have a tendency to throw credit, in any degree, upon the very singular pages now published. We allude to the chasms found in the island of Tsalal, and to the whole of the figures upon pages 319, 320, and 321.

Mr. Pym has given the figures of the chasms without comment, and speaks decidedly of the *indentures* found at the extremity of the most easterly of these chasms as having but a fanciful resemblance to alphabetical characters, and, in short, as being positively *not such.* This assertion is made in a manner so simple, and sustained by a species of demonstration so conclusive, viz. (the fitting of the projections of the fragments found among the dust into the indentures upon the wall), that we are forced to believe the writer in earnest; and no reasonable reader should suppose otherwise. But as the facts in relation to *all* the figures are most singular (especially when taken in connection with statements made in the body of the narrative), it may be as well to say a word or two concerning them all—this, too, the more especially as the facts in question have, beyond doubt, escaped the attention of Mr. Poe.

Figure 1, then, figure 2, figure 3, and figure 5, when conjoined with one another in the precise order which the chasms themselves presented, and when deprived of the small lateral branches or arches (which, it will be remembered, served only as a means of communication between the main chambers, and were of totally distinct character), constitute an Ethiopian verbal root—the root 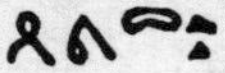 "To be shady,"—whence all the inflections of shadow or darkness.

In regard to the "left or most northwardly" of the indentures in figure 4, it is more than probable that the opinion of Peters was correct, and that the hieroglyphical appearance was really the work of art, and intended as the representation of a human form. The delineation is before the reader, and he may, or may not, preceive the resemblance suggested; but the rest of the indentures afford strong confirmation of Peters's idea. The upper range is evidently the Arabic verbal root 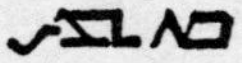 "To be white," whence all the inflections of brilliancy and whiteness. The lower range is not so immediately perspicuous. The characters are somewhat broken and disjointed; nevertheless, it cannot be doubted that, in their perfect state, they formed the full Egyptian word 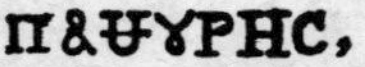 "The region of the south." It should be observed that these interpretations confirm the opinion of Peters in regard to the "most northwardly" of the figures. The arm is outstretched towards the south.

Conclusions such as these open a wide field for speculation and exciting conjecture. They should be regarded, perhaps, in connection with some of the most faintly-detailed incidents of the narrative; although in no visible manner is this chain of connection complete. Tekeli-li was the cry of the affrighted natives of Tsalal upon discovering the carcass of the *white* animal picked up at sea. This also was the shuddering exclamation of the captive Tsalalian upon encountering the *white* materials in possession of Mr. Pym. This also was the shriek of the swift-flying, *white,* and gigantic birds which issued from the vapoury *white* curtain of the South. Nothing *white* was to be found at Tsalal, and nothing otherwise in the subsequent voyage to the region beyond. It is not impossible that "Tsalal," the appellation of the island of the chasms, may be found, upon minute philological scrutiny, to betray either some alliance with the chasms themselves, or some reference to the Ethiopian characters so mysteriously written in their windings.

"I have graven it within the hills, and my vengeance upon the dust within the rock."

THE GOLD-BUG*

> **What ho! what ho! this fellow is dancing mad!**
> **He hath been bitten by the Tarantula.**
>
> ***All in the Wrong***

MANY years ago, I contracted an intimacy with a Mr. William Legrand. He was of an ancient Huguenot family, and had once been wealthy; but a series of misfortunes had reduced him to want. To avoid the mortification consequent upon his disasters, he left New Orleans, the city of his forefathers, and took up his residence at Sullivan's Island, near Charleston, South Carolina.

This island is a very singular one. It consists of little else than the sea sand, and is about three miles long. Its breadth at no point exceeds a quarter of a mile. It is separated from the mainland by a scarcely perceptible creek, oozing its way through a wilderness of reeds and slime, a favorite resort of the marsh-hen. The vegetation, as might be supposed, is scant, or at least dwarfish. No trees of any magnitude are to be seen. Near the western extremity, where Fort Moultrie stands, and where are some miserable frame buildings, tenanted, during summer, by the fugitives from Charleston dust and fever, may be found, indeed, the bristly palmetto; but the whole island, with the exception of this western point, and a line of hard, white beach on the seacoast, is covered with a dense undergrowth of the sweet myrtle so much prized by the horticulturists of England. The shrub here

*** Published in *Dollar Newspaper* (Philadelphia), *Sunday Courier*, and *Volunteer*, 1843.**

often attains the height of fifteen or twenty feet, and forms an almost impenetrable coppice, burthening the air with its fragrance.

In the inmost recesses of this coppice, not far from the eastern or more remote end of the island, Legrand had built himself a small hut, which he occupied when I first, by mere accident, made his acquaintance. This soon ripened into friendship—for there was much in the recluse to excite interest and esteem. I found him well educated, with unusual powers of mind, but infected with misanthropy, and subject to perverse moods of alternate enthusiasm and melancholy. He had with him many books, but rarely employed them. His chief amusements were gunning and fishing, or sauntering along the beach and through the myrtles, in quest of shells or entomological specimens—his collection of the latter might have been envied by a Swammerdamm. In these excursions he was usually accompanied by an old negro, called Jupiter, who had been manumitted before the reverses of the family, but who could be induced, neither by threats nor by promises, to abandon what he considered his right of attendance upon the footsteps of his young "Massa Will." It is not improbable that the relatives of Legrand, conceiving him to be somewhat unsettled in intellect, had contrived to instil this obstinacy into Jupiter, with a view to the supervision and guardianship of the wanderer.

The winters in the latitude of Sullivan's Island are seldom very severe, and in the fall of the year it is a rare event indeed when a fire is considered necessary. About the middle of October, 18—, there occurred, however, a day of remarkable chilliness. Just before sunset I scrambled my way through the evergreens to the hut of my friend, whom I had not visited for several weeks—my residence being, at that time, in Charleston, a distance of nine miles from the island, while the facilities of passage and repassage were very far behind those of the present day. Upon reaching the hut I rapped, as was my custom, and getting no reply, sought for the key where I knew it was secreted, unlocked the door, and went in. A fine fire was blazing upon the hearth. It was a novelty, and by no means an ungrateful one. I threw off an overcoat, took an arm-chair by the crackling logs, and awaited patiently the arrival of my hosts.

Soon after dark they arrived, and gave me a most cordial welcome. Jupiter, grinning from ear to ear, bustled about to prepare some marsh-hens for supper. Legrand was in one of his fits—how else shall I term them?—of enthusiasm. He had found an unknown bivalve, forming a new genus, and, more than this, he had hunted down and secured, with Jupiter's assistance, a *scarabæus* which he believed to be totally new, but in respect to which he wished to have my opinion on the morrow.

"And why not to-night?" I asked, rubbing my hands over the blaze, and wishing the whole tribe of *scarabæi* at the devil.

"Ah, if I had only known you were here!" said Legrand, "but it's so long since I saw you; and how could I foresee that you would pay me a visit this very night of all others? As I was coming home I met Lieutenant G——, from the fort, and, very foolishly, I lent him the bug; so it will be impossible for you to see it until the morning. Stay here to-night, and I will send Jup down for it at sunrise. It is the loveliest thing in creation!"

"What?—sunrise?"

"Nonsense! no!—the bug. It is of a brilliant gold color—about the size of a large hickory-nut—with two jet black spots near one extremity of the back, and another, somewhat longer, at the other. The *antennæ* are—"

"Dey aint *no* tin in him, Massa Will, I keep a tellin' on you," here interrupted Jupiter; "de bug is a goole-bug, solid, ebery bit of him, inside and all, sep him wing—neber feel half so hebby a bug in my life."

"Well, suppose it is, Jup," replied Legrand, somewhat more earnestly, it seemed to me, than the case demanded; "is that any reason for your letting the birds burn? The color"—here he turned to me—"is really almost enough to warrant Jupiter's idea. You never saw a more brilliant metallic lustre than the scales emit—but of this you cannot judge till tomorrow. In the meantime I can give you some idea of the shape." Saying this, he seated himself at a small table, on which were a pen and ink, but no paper. He looked for some in a drawer, but found none.

"Never mind," he said at length, "this will answer"; and he drew from his waistcoat pocket a scrap of what I took to be very dirty foolscap, and made upon it a rough drawing with the pen. While he did this, I retained my seat by the fire, for I was still chilly. When the design was complete, he handed it to me without rising. As I received it, a loud growl was heard, succeeded by a scratching at the door. Jupiter opened it, and a large Newfoundland, belonging to Legrand, rushed in, leaped upon my shoulders, and loaded me with caresses; for I had shown him much attention during previous visits. When his gambols were over, I looked at the paper, and, to speak the truth, found myself not a little puzzled at what my friend had depicted.

"Well!" I said, after contemplating it for some minutes, "this *is* a strange *scarabœus,* I must confess; new to me; never saw any thing like it before—unless it was a skull, or a death's-head, which it more nearly resembles than any thing else that has come under *my* observation."

"A death's-head!" echoed Legrand. "Oh—yes—well, it has something of that appearance upon paper, no doubt. The two upper black spots look like eyes, eh? and the longer one at the bottom like a mouth—and then the shape of the whole is oval."

"Perhaps so," said I; "but, Legrand, I fear you are no artist. I must wait until I see the beetle itself, if I am to form any idea of its personal appearance."

"Well, I don't know," said he, a little nettled, "I draw tolerably—*should* do it at least—have had good masters, and flatter myself that I am not quite a blockhead."

"But, my dear fellow, you are joking then," said I, "this is a very passable *skull*—indeed, I may say that it is a very *excellent* skull, according to the vulgar notions about such specimens of physiology—and your *scarabœus* must be the queerest *scarabœus* in the world if it resembles it. Why, we may get up a very thrilling bit of superstition upon this hint. I presume you will call the bug *scarabœus caput hominis,* or something of that kind—there are many similar titles in the Natural Histories. But where are the *antennœ* you spoke of?"

"The *antennœ!*" said Legrand, who seemed to be getting unaccountably warm upon the subject; "I am sure you must see the *antennœ*. I made them as distinct as they are in the original insect, and I presume that is sufficient."

"Well, well," I said, "perhaps you have—still I don't see them"; and I handed him the paper without additional remark, not wishing to ruffle his temper; but I was much surprised at the turn affairs had taken; his ill humor puzzled me—and, as for the drawing of the beetle, there were positively *no antennœ* visible, and the whole *did* bear a very close resemblance to the ordinary cuts of a death's-head.

He received the paper very peevishly, and was about to crumple it, apparently to throw it in the fire, when a casual glance at the design seemed suddenly to rivet his attention. In an instant his face grew violently red—in another as excessively pale. For some minutes he continued to scrutinize the drawing minutely where he sat. At length he arose, took a candle from the table, and proceeded to seat himself upon a sea-chest in the farthest corner of the room. Here again he made an anxious examination of the paper; turning it in all directions. He said nothing, however, and his conduct greatly astonished me; yet I thought it prudent not to exacerbate the growing moodiness of his temper by any comment. Presently he took from his coat-pocket a wallet, placed the paper carefully in it, and deposited both in a writing-desk, which he locked. He now grew more composed in his demeanor; but his original air of enthusiasm had quite disappeared. Yet he seemed not so much sulky as abstracted. As the evening wore away he became more and more absorbed in revery, from which no sallies of mine could arouse him. It had been my intention to pass the night at the hut, as I had frequently done before, but, seeing my host in this mood, I deemed it proper to take leave. He did not press me to remain, but, as I departed, he shook my hand with even more than his usual cordiality.

It was about a month after this (and during the interval I had seen nothing of Legrand) when I received a visit, at Charleston, from his man, Jupiter. I had never seen the good old negro look so dispirited, and I feared that some serious disaster had befallen my friend.

"Well, Jup," said I, "what is the matter now?—how is your master?"

"Why, to speak de troof, massa, him not so berry well as mought be."

"Not well! I am truly sorry to hear it. What does he complain of?"

"Dar! dat's it!—him neber 'plain of notin'—but him berry sick for all dat."

"*Very* sick, Jupiter!—why didn't you say so at once? Is he confined to bed?"

"No, dat he aint!—he aint 'fin'd nowhar—dat's just whar de shoe pinch—my mind is got to be berry hebby 'bout poor Massa Will."

"Jupiter, I should like to understand what it is you are talking about. You say your master is sick. Hasn't he told you what ails him?"

"Why, massa, 'taint worf while for to git mad about de matter—Massa Will say noffin at all aint de matter wid him—but den what make him go about looking dis here way, wid he head down and he soldiers up, and as white as a gose? And den he keep a syphon all de time—"

"Keeps a what, Jupiter?"

"Keeps a syphon wid de figgurs on de slate—de queerest figgurs I ebber did see. Ise gittin' to be skeered, I tell you. Hab for to keep mighty tight eye 'pon him 'noovers. Todder day he gib me slip 'fore de sun up and was gone de whole ob de blessed day. I had a big stick ready cut for to gib him deuced good beating when he did come—but Ise sich a fool dat I hadn't de heart arter all—he looked so berry poorly."

"Eh?—what?—ah yes!—upon the whole I think you had better not be too severe with the poor fellow—don't flog him, Jupiter—he can't very well stand it—but can you form no idea of what has occasioned this illness, or rather this change of conduct? Has any thing unpleasant happened since I saw you?"

"No, massa, dey aint bin noffin onpleasant *since* den—'twas *'fore* den I'm feared—'twas de berry day you was dare."

"How? what do you mean?"

"Why, massa, I mean de bug—dare now."

"The what?"

"De bug—I'm berry sartain dat Massa Will bin bit somewhere 'bout de head by dat goole-bug."

"And what cause have you, Jupiter, for such a supposition?"

"Claws enuff, massa, and mouff too. I nebber did see sich a deuced bug—he kick and he bite ebery ting what cum near him. Massa Will cotch him fuss, but had for to let him go 'gin mighty quick, I tell you—den was de time he must ha' got de bite. I didn't like de look ob de bug mouff, myself, nohow, so I wouldn't take hold ob him wid my finger, but I cotch him wid a piece ob paper dat I found. I rap him up in de paper and stuff a piece of it in he mouff—dat was de way."

"And you think, then, that your master was really bitten by the beetle, and that the bite made him sick?"

"I don't think noffin about it—I nose it. What make him dream 'bout de goole so much, if 'taint cause he bit by de goole-bug? Ise heerd 'bout dem goole-bugs 'fore dis."

"But how do you know he dreams about gold?"

"How I know? why, 'cause he talk about it in he sleep—dat's how I nose."

"Well, Jup, perhaps you are right; but to what fortunate circumstance am I to attribute the honor of a visit from you to-day?"

"What de matter, massa?"

"Did you bring any message from Mr. Legrand?"

"No, massa, I bring dis her pissel"; and here Jupiter handed me a note which ran thus:

"My Dear——

"Why have I not seen you for so long a time? I hope you have not been so foolish as to take offence at any little *brusquerie* of mine; but no, that is improbable.

"Since I saw you I have had great cause for anxiety. I have something to tell you, yet scarcely know how to tell it, or whether I should tell it at all.

"I have not been quite well for some days past, and poor old Jup annoys me, almost beyond endurance, by his well-meant attentions. Would you believe it?—he had prepared a huge stick, the other day, with which to chastise me for giving him the slip, and spending the day, *solus,* among the hills on the main land. I verily believe that my ill looks alone saved me a flogging.

"I have made no addition to my cabinet since we met.

"If you can, in any way, make it convenient, come over with Jupiter. *Do* come. I wish to see you *to-night,* upon business of importance. I assure you that it is of the *highest* importance.

"Ever yours,

"William Legrand"

There was something in the tone of this note which gave me great uneasiness. Its whole style differed materially from that of Legrand. What could he be dreaming of? What new crotchet possessed his excitable brain? What "business of the highest importance" could *he* possibly have to transact? Jupiter's account of him boded no good. I dreaded lest the continued pressure of misfortune had, at length, fairly unsettled the reason of my friend. Without a moment's hesitation, therefore, I prepared to accompany the negro.

Upon reaching the wharf, I noticed a scythe and three spades, all apparently new, lying in the bottom of the boat in which we were to embark.

"What is the meaning of all this, Jup?" I inquired.

"Him syfe, massa, and spade."

"Very true; but what are they doing here?"

"Him de syfe and de spade what Massa Will sis 'pon my buying for him in de town, and de debbil's own lot of money I had to gib for 'em."

"But what, in the name of all that is mysterious, is your 'Massa Will' going to do with scythes and spades?"

"Dat's more dan *I* know, and debbil take me if I don't b'lieve 'tis more dan he know too. But it's all cum ob de bug."

Finding that no satisfaction was to be obtained of Jupiter, whose whole intellect seemed to be absorbed by "de bug," I now stepped into the boat, and made sail. With a fair and strong breeze we soon ran into the little cove to the northward of Fort Moultrie, and a walk of some two miles brought us to the hut. It was about three in the afternoon when we arrived. Legrand had been waiting us in eager expectation. He grasped my hand with a nervous *empressement* which alarmed me and strengthened the suspicions already entertained. His countenance was pale even to ghastliness, and his deep-set eyes glared with unnatural lustre. After some inquiries respecting his health, I asked him, not knowing what better to say, if he had yet obtained the *scarabæus* from Lieutenant G——.

"Oh, yes," he replied, coloring violently, "I got it from him the next morning. Nothing should tempt me to part with that *scarabæus*. Do you know that Jupiter is quite right about it?"

"In what way?" I asked, with a sad foreboding at heart.

"In supposing it to be a bug of *real gold*." He said this with an air of profound seriousness, and I felt inexpressibly shocked.

"This bug is to make my fortune," he continued, with a triumphant smile; "to reinstate me in my family possessions. Is it any wonder, then, that I prize it? Since Fortune has thought fit to bestow it upon me, I have only to use it properly, and I shall arrive at the gold of which it is the index. Jupiter, bring me that *scarabœus!*"

"What! de bug, massa? I'd rudder not go fer trubble dat bug; you mus' git him for your own self." Hereupon Legrand arose, with a grave and stately air, and brought me the beetle from a glass case in which it was enclosed. It was a beautiful *scarabœus,* and, at that time, unknown to naturalists—of course a great prize in a scientific point of view. There were two round black spots near one extremity of the back, and a long one near the other. The scales were exceedingly hard and glossy, with all the appearance of burnished gold. The weight of the insect was very remarkable, and, taking all things into consideration, I could hardly blame Jupiter for his opinion respecting it; but what to make of Legrand's concordance with that opinion, I could not, for the life of me, tell.

"I sent for you," said he, in a grandiloquent tone, when I had completed my examination of the beetle, "I sent for you that I might have your counsel and assistance in furthering the views of Fate and of the bug—"

"My dear Legrand," I cried, interrupting him, "you are certainly unwell, and had better use some little precautions. You shall go to bed, and I will remain with you a few days, until you get over this. You are feverish and—"

"Feel my pulse," said he.

I felt it, and, to say the truth, found not the slightest indication of fever.

"But you may be ill and yet have no fever. Allow me this once to prescribe for you. In the first place go to bed. In the next—"

"You are mistaken," he interposed, "I am as well as I can expect to be under the excitement which I suffer. If you really wish me well, you will relieve this excitement."

"And how is this to be done?"

"Very easily. Jupiter and myself are going upon an expedition into the hills, upon the main land, and, in this expedition, we shall need the aid of some person in whom we can confide. You are the only one we can trust. Whether we succeed or fail, the excitement which you now perceive in me will be equally allayed."

"I am anxious to oblige you in any way," I replied; "but do you mean to say that this infernal beetle has any connection with your expedition into the hills?"

"It has."

"Then, Legrand, I can become a party to no such absurd proceeding."

"I am sorry—very sorry—for we shall have to try it by ourselves."

"Try it by yourselves! The man is surely mad!—but stay!—how long do you propose to be absent?"

"Probably all night. We shall start immediately, and be back, at all events, by sunrise."

"And will you promise me, upon your honor, that when this freak of yours is over, and the bug business (good God!) settled to your satisfaction, you will then return home and follow my advice implicitly, as that of your physician."

"Yes; I promise; and now let us be off, for we have no time to lose."

With a heavy heart I accompanied my friend. We started about four o'clock—Legrand, Jupiter, the dog, and myself. Jupiter had with him the scythe and spades—the whole of which he insisted upon carrying—more through fear, it seemed to me, of trusting either of the implements within reach of his master, than from any excess of industry or complaisance. His demeanor was dogged in the extreme, and "dat deuced bug" were the sole words which escaped his lips during the journey. For my own part, I had charge of a couple of dark lanterns, while Legrand contented himself with the *scarabæus,* which he carried attached to the end of a bit of whip-cord; twirling it to and fro, with the air of a conjuror, as he went. When I observed this last, plain evidence of my friend's aberration of mind, I could scarcely refrain from tears. I thought it best, however, to humor his fancy, at least for the present, or until I could adopt some more energetic measures with a chance of success. In the meantime I endeavored, but all in vain, to sound him in regard to the object of the expedition. Having succeeded in inducing me to accompany him, he seemed unwilling to hold conversation upon any topic of minor importance, and to all my questions vouchsafed no other reply than "we shall see!"

We crossed the creek at the head of the island by means of a skiff, and, ascending the high grounds on the shore of the main land, proceeded in a northwesterly direction, through a tract of country excessively wild and desolate, where no trace of a human footstep was to be seen. Legrand led the way with decision; pausing only for an instant, here and there, to consult what appeared to be certain landmarks of his own contrivance upon a former occasion.

In this manner we journed for about two hours, and the sun was just setting when we entered a region infinitely more dreary than any yet seen. It was a species of table-land, near the summit of an almost inaccessible hill, densely wooded from base to pinnacle, and interspersed with huge crags that appeared to lie loosely upon the soil, and in many cases were prevented from precipitating themselves into the valleys below, merely by the support of the trees against which they reclined. Deep ravines, in various directions, gave an air of still sterner solemnity to the scene.

The natural platform to which we had clambered was thickly overgrown with brambles, through which we soon discovered that it would have been impossible to force our way but for the scythe; and Jupiter, by direction of his master, proceeded to clear forth a path to the foot of an enormously tall tulip-tree, which stood, with some eight or ten oaks, upon the level, and far surpassed them all, and all other trees which I had then ever seen, in the beauty of its foliage and form, in the wide spread of its branches, and in the general majesty of its appearance. When we reached this tree, Legrand turned to Jupiter, and asked him if he thought he could climb it. The old man seemed a little staggered by the question, and for some moments made no reply. At length he approached the huge trunk, walked slowly around it, and examined it with minute attention. When he had completed his scrutiny, he merely said:

"Yes, massa, Jup climb any tree he ebber see in he life."

"Then up with you as soon as possible, for it will soon be too dark to see what we are about."

"How far mus' go up, massa?" inquired Jupiter.

"Get up the main trunk first, and then I will tell you which way to go—and here—stop! take this beetle with you."

"De bug, Massa Will!—de goole-bug!" cried the negro, drawing back in dismay—"what for mus' tote de bug way up de tree?—d—n if I do!"

"If you are afraid, Jup, a great big negro like you, to take hold of a harmless little dead beetle, why you can carry it up by this string—but, if you do not take it up with you in some way, I shall be under the necessity of breaking your head with this shovel."

"What de matter now, massa?" said Jup, evidently shamed into compliance; "always want for to raise fuss wid old nigger. Was only funnin anyhow. *Me* feered de bug! what I keer for de bug?" Here he took cautiously hold of the extreme end of the string, and, maintaining the insect as far from his person as circumstances would permit, prepared to ascend the tree.

In youth, the tulip-tree, or *Liriodendron Tulipiferum,* the most magnificent of American foresters, has a trunk peculiarly smooth, and often rises to a great height without lateral branches; but, in its riper age, the bark becomes gnarled and uneven, while many short limbs make their appearance on the stem. Thus the difficulty of ascension, in the present case, lay more in semblance than in reality. Embracing the huge cylinder, as closely as possible, with his arms and knees, seizing with his hands some projections, and resting his naked toes upon others, Jupiter, after one or two narrow escapes from falling, at length wriggled himself into the first great fork, and seemed to consider the whole business as virtually accomplished. The *risk* of the achievement was, in fact, now over, although the climber was some sixty or seventy feet from the ground.

"Which way mus' go now, Massa Will?" he asked.

"Keep up the largest branch—the one on this side," said Legrand. The negro obeyed him promptly, and apparently with but little trouble; ascending higher and higher, until no glimpse of his squat figure could be obtained through the dense foliage which enveloped it. Presently his voice was heard in a sort of halloo.

"How much fudder is got for go?"

"How high up are you?" asked Legrand.

"Ebber so fur," replied the negro; "can see de sky fru de top ob de tree."

"Never mind the sky, but attend to what I say. Look down the trunk and count the limbs below you on this side. How many limbs have you passed?"

"One, two, tree, four, fibe—I done pass fibe big limb, massa 'pon dis side."

"Then go one limb higher."

In a few minutes the voice was heard again, announcing that the seventh limb was attained.

"Now, Jup," cried Legrand, evidently much excited, "I want you to work your way out upon that limb as far as you can. If you see any thing strange let me know."

By this time what little doubt I might have entertained of my poor friend's insanity was put finally at rest. I had no alternative but to conclude him stricken with lunacy, and I became seriously anxious about getting him home. While I was pondering upon what was best to be done, Jupiter's voice was again heard.

"Mos' feerd for to venture 'pon dis limb berry far—'tis dead limb putty much all de way."

"Did you say it was a *dead* limb, Jupiter?" cried Legrand in a quavering voice.

"Yes, massa, him dead as de door-nail—done up for sartain —done departed dis here life."

"What in the name of heaven shall I do?" asked Legrand, seemingly in the greatest distress.

"Do!" said I, glad of an opportunity to interpose a word, "why come home and go to bed. Come now!—that's a fine fellow. It's getting late, and, besides, you remember your promise."

"Jupiter," cried he, without heeding me in the least, "do you hear me?"

"Yes, Massa Will, hear you ebber so plain."

"Try the wood well, then, with your knife, and see if you think it *very* rotten."

"Him rotten, massa, sure nuff," replied the negro in a few moments, "but not so berry rotten as mought be. Mought venture out leetle way 'pon de limb by myself, dat's true."

"By yourself!—what do you mean?"

"Why, I mean de bug. 'Tis *berry* hebby bug. Spose I drop him down fuss, and den de limb won't break wid just de weight ob one nigger."

"You infernal scoundrel!" cried Legrand, apparently much relieved, "what do you mean by telling me such nonsense as that? As sure as you drop that beetle I'll break your neck. Look here, Jupiter, do you hear me?"

"Yes, massa, needn't hollo at poor nigger dat style."

"Well! now listen!—if you will venture out on the limb as far as you think safe, and not let go the beetle, I'll make you a present of a silver dollar as soon as you get down."

"I'm gwine, Massa Will—deed I is," replied the negro very promptly—"mos' out to the eend now."

"Out to the end!" here fairly screamed Legrand; "**do you** say you are out to the end of that limb?"

"Soon be to de eend, massa—o-o-o-o-oh! Lor-gol-a-marcy! what *is* dis here pon de tree?"

"Well!" cried Legrand, highly delighted, "what is it?"

"Why taint noffin but a skull—somebody bin left him head up de tree, and de crows done gobble ebery bit ob de meat off."

"A skull, you say!—very well,—how is it fastened to the limb?—what holds it on?"

"Sure nuff, massa; mus' look. Why dis berry curous sarcumstance, 'pon my word—dare's a great big nail in de skull, what fastens ob it on to de tree."

"Well now, Jupiter, do exactly as I tell you—do you hear?"

"Yes, massa."

"Pay attention, then—find the left eye of the skull."

"Hum! hoo! dat's good! why dey aint no eye lef' at all."

"Curse your stupidity! do you know your right hand from your left?"

"Yes, I knows dat—know all bout dat—'tis my lef' hand what I chops de wood wid."

"To be sure! you are left-handed; and your left eye is on the same side as your left hand. Now, I suppose, you can find the left eye of the skull, or the place where the left eye has been. Have you found it?"

Here was a long pause. At length the negro asked:

"Is de lef' eye ob de skull 'pon de same side as de lef' hand ob de skull too?—cause de skull aint got not a bit ob a hand at all—nebber mind! I got de lef' eye now—here de lef' eye! what mus' do wid it?"

"Let the beetle drop through it, as far as the string will reach—but be careful and not let go your hold of the string."

"All dat done, Massa Will; mighty easy ting for to put the bug fru de hole—look out for him dare below!"

During this colloquy no portion of Jupiter's person could be seen; but the beetle, which he had suffered to descend, was now visible at the end of the string, and glistened, like a globe of burnished gold, in the last rays of the setting sun, some of which still faintly illumined the eminence upon which we stood. The *scarabæus* hung quite clear of any branches, and, if allowed to fall, would have fallen at our feet. Legrand immediately took the scythe, and cleared with it a circular space, three or four yards in diameter, just beneath the insect, and, having accomplished this, ordered Jupiter to let go the string and come down from the tree.

Driving a peg, with great nicety, into the ground, at the precise spot where the beetle fell, my friend now produced from his pocket a tape-measure. Fastening one end of this at that point of the trunk of the tree which was nearest the peg, he unrolled it till it reached the peg and thence further unrolled it, in the direction already established by the two points of the tree and the peg, for the distance of fifty feet—Jupiter clearing away the brambles with the scythe. At the spot thus attained a second peg was driven, and about this, as a centre, a rude circle, about four feet in diameter, described. Taking now a spade himself, and giving one to Jupiter and one to me, Legrand begged us to set about digging as quickly as possible.

To speak the truth, I had no especial relish for such amusement at any time, and, at that particular moment, would most willingly have declined it; for the night was coming on, and I felt much fatigued with the exercise already taken; but I saw no mode of escape, and was fearful of disturbing my poor friend's equanimity by a refusal. Could I have depended, indeed upon Jupiter's aid, I would have had no hesitation in attempting to get the lunatic home by force; but I was too well assured of the old negro's disposition, to hope that he would assist me, under any circumstances, in a personal contest with his master. I made no doubt that the latter had been infected with some of the innumerable Southern superstitions about money buried, and that his phantasy had received confirmation by the finding of the *scarabœus,* or, perhaps, by Jupiter's obstinacy in maintaining it to be "a bug of real gold." A mind disposed to lunacy would readily be led away by such suggestions—especially if chiming in with favorite preconceived ideas—and then I called to mind the poor fellow's speech about the beetle's being "the index of his fortune." Upon the whole, I was sadly vexed and puzzled, but, at length, I concluded to make a virtue of necessity—to dig with a good will, and thus the sooner to convince the visionary, by ocular demonstration, of the fallacy of the opinions he entertained.

The lanterns having been lit, we all fell to work with a zeal worthy a more rational cause; and, as the glare fell upon our persons and implements, I could not help thinking how picturesque a group we composed, and how strange and suspicious our labors must have appeared to any interloper who, by chance, might have stumbled upon our whereabouts.

We dug very steadily for two hours. Little was said; and our chief embarrassment lay in the yelpings of the dog, who took exceeding interest in our proceedings. He, at length, became so obstreperous that we grew fearful of his giving the alarm to some stragglers in the vicinity,—or, rather, this was the apprehension of Legrand;—for myself, I should have rejoiced at any interruption which might have enabled me to get the wanderer home. The noise was, at length, very effectually silenced by Jupiter, who, getting out of the hole with a dogged air of deliberation, tied the brute's mouth up with one of his suspenders, and then returned, with a grave chuckle, to his task.

When the time mentioned had expired, we had reached a depth of five feet, and yet no signs of any treasure became manifest. A general pause ensued, and I began to hope that the farce was at an end. Legrand, however, although evidently much disconcerted, wiped his brow thoughtfully and recommenced. We had excavated the entire circle of four feet diameter, and now we slightly enlarged the limit, and went to the farther depth of two feet. Still nothing appeared. The gold-seeker, whom I sincerely pitied, at length clambered from the pit, with the bitterest disappointment imprinted upon every feature, and proceeded, slowly and reluctantly, to put on his coat, which he had thrown off at the beginning of his labor. In the meantime I made no remark. Jupiter, at a signal from his master, began to gather up his tools.

This done, and the dog having been unmuzzled, we turned in profound silence toward home.

We had taken, perhaps, a dozen steps in this direction, when, with a loud oath, Legrand strode up to Jupiter, and seized him by the collar. The astonished negro opened his eyes and mouth to the fullest extent, let fall the spades, and fell upon his knees.

"You scoundrel!" said Legrand, hissing out the syllables from between his clenched teeth—"you infernal black villain!—speak, I tell you!—answer me this instant, without prevarication!—which—which is your left eye?"

"Oh, my golly, Massa Will! aint dis here my lef' eye for sartain?" roared the terrified Jupiter, placing his hand upon his *right* organ of vision, and holding it there with a desperate pertinacity, as if in immediate dread of his master's attempt at a gouge.

"I thought so!—I knew it! hurrah!" vociferated Legrand, letting the negro go and executing a series of curvets and caracols, much to the astonishment of his valet, who, arising from his knees, looked, mutely, from his master to myself, and then from myself to his master.

"Come! we must go back," said the latter, "the game's not up yet"; and he again led the way to the tulip-tree.

"Jupiter," said he, when we reached its foot, "come here! was the skull nailed to the limb with the face outward, or with the face to the limb?"

"De face was out, massa, so dat de crows could get at de eyes good, widout any trouble."

"Well, then, was it this eye or that through which you dropped the beetle?"—here Legrand touched each of Jupiter's eyes.

" 'Twas dis eye, massa—de lef' eye—jis as you tell me," and here it was his right eye that the negro indicated.

"That will do—we must try it again."

Here my friend, about whose madness I now saw, or fancied

that I saw, certain indications of method, removed the peg which marked the spot where the beetle fell, to a spot about three inches to the westward of its former position. Taking, now, the tape measure from the nearest point of the trunk to the peg, as before, and continuing the extension in a straight line to the distance of fifty feet, a spot was indicated, removed, by several yards, from the point at which we had been digging.

Around the new position a circle, somewhat larger than in the former instance, was now described, and we again set to work with the spade. I was dreadfully weary, but, scarcely understanding what had occasioned the change in my thoughts, I felt no longer any great aversion from the labor imposed. I had become most unaccountably interested—nay, even excited. Perhaps there was something, amid all the extravagant demeanor of Legrand—some air of forethought, or of deliberation, which impressed me. I dug eagerly, and now and then caught myself actually looking, with something that very much resembled expectation, for the fancied treasure, the vision of which had demented my unfortunate companion. At a period when such vagaries of thought most fully possessed me, and when we had been at work perhaps an hour and a half, we were again interrupted by the violent howlings of the dog. His uneasiness, in the first instance, had been, evidently, but the result of playfulness or caprice, but he now assumed a bitter and serious tone. Upon Jupiter's again attempting to muzzle him, he made furious resistance, and, leaping into the hole, tore up the mould frantically with his claws. In a few seconds he had uncovered a mass of human bones, forming two complete skeletons, intermingled with several buttons of metal, and what appeared to be the dust of decayed woollen. One or two strokes of a spade up-turned the blade of a large Spanish knife, and, as we dug farther, three or four loose pieces of gold and silver coin came to light.

At sight of these the joy of Jupiter could scarcely be restrained, but the countenance of his master wore an air of extreme disappointment. He urged us, however, to continue our exertions, and the words were hardly uttered when I stumbled and fell forward, having caught the toe of my boot in a large ring of iron that lay half buried in the loose earth.

We now worked in earnest, and never did I pass ten minutes of more intense excitement. During this interval we had fairly unearthed an oblong chest of wood, which, from its perfect preservation and wonderful hardness, had plainly been subjected to some mineralizing process—perhaps that of the bi-chloride of mercury. This box was three feet and a half long, three feet broad, and two and a half feet deep. It was firmly secured by bands of wrought iron, riveted, and forming a kind of open trellis-work over the whole. On each side of the chest, near the top, were three rings of iron—six in all—by means of which a firm hold could be obtained by six persons. Our utmost united endeavors served only to disturb the coffer very slightly in its bed. We at once saw the impossibility of removing so great a weight. Luckily, the sole fastenings of the lid consisted of two sliding bolts. These we drew back—trembling and panting with anxiety. In an instant, a treasure of incalculable value lay gleaming before us. As the rays of the lanterns fell within the pit, there flashed upward a glow and a glare, from a confused heap of gold and of jewels, that absolutely dazzled our eyes.

I shall not pretend to describe the feelings with which I gazed. Amazement was, of course, predominant. Legrand appeared exhausted with excitement, and spoke very few words. Jupiter's countenance wore, for some minutes, as deadly a pallor as it is possible, in the nature of things, for any negro's visage to assume. He seemed stupefied—thunderstricken. Presently he fell upon his knees in the pit, and burying his naked arms up to the elbows in gold, let them there remain, as if enjoying the luxury of a bath. At length, with a deep sigh, he exclaimed, as if in a soliloquy:

"And dis all cum ob de goole-bug! de putty goole-bug! the poor little goole-bug, what I boosed in dat sabage kind ob style! Aint you shamed ob yourself, nigger?—answer me dat!"

It became necessary, at last, that I should arouse both master and valet to the expediency of removing the treasure. It was growing late, and it behooved us to make exertion, that we might get every thing housed before daylight. It was difficult to say what should be done, and much time was spent in deliberation—so confused were the ideas of all. We, finally, lightened the box by removing two thirds of its contents, when we were enabled, with some trouble, to raise it from the hole. The articles taken out were deposited among the brambles, and the dog left to guard them, with strict orders from Jupiter neither, upon any pretence, to stir from the spot, nor to open his mouth until our return. We then hurriedly made for home with the chest; reaching the hut in safety, but after excessive toil, at one o'clock in the morning. Worn out as we were, it was not in human nature to do more immediately. We rested until two, and had supper; starting for the hills immediately afterward, armed with three stout sacks, which, by good luck, were upon the premises. A little before four we arrived at the pit, divided the remainder of the booty, as equally as might be, among us, and, leaving the holes unfilled, again set out for the hut, at which, for the second time, we deposited our golden burthens, just as the first faint streaks of the dawn gleamed from over the tree-tops in the East.

We were now thoroughly broken down; but the intense excitement of the time denied us repose. After an unquiet slumber of some three or four hours' duration, we arose, as if by preconcert, to make examination of our treasure.

The chest had been full to the brim, and we spent the whole day, and the greater part of the next night, in a scrutiny of its contents. There had been nothing like order or arrangement. Every thing had been heaped in promiscuously. Having assorted all with care, we found ourselves possessed of even vaster wealth than we had at first supposed. In coin there was rather more than four hundred and fifty thousand dollars—estimating the value of the pieces, as accurately as we could, by the tables of the period. There was not a particle of silver. All was gold of antique date and of great variety—French, Spanish, and German money, with a few English guineas, and some counters, of which we had never seen specimens before. There were several very large and heavy coins, so worn that we could make nothing of their inscriptions. There was no American money. The value of the jewels we found more difficulty in estimating. There were diamonds—some of them exceedingly large and fine—a hundred and ten in all, and not one of them small; eighteen rubies of remarkable brilliancy;—three hundred and ten emeralds, all very beautiful; and twenty-one sapphires, with an opal. These stones had all been broken from their settings and thrown loose in the chest. The settings themselves, which we picked out from among the other gold, appeared to have been beaten up with hammers, as if to prevent identification. Besides all this, there was a vast quantity of solid gold ornaments: nearly two hundred massive finger- and ear-rings; rich chains—thirty of these, if I remember; eighty-three very large and heavy crucifixes; five gold censers of great value; a prodigious golden punch-bowl, ornamented with richly chased vine-leaves and Bacchanalian figures; with two sword-handles exquisitely embossed, and many other smaller articles which I cannot recollect. The weight of these valuables exceeded three hundred and fifty pounds avoirdupois; and in this estimate I have not included one hundred and ninety-seven superb gold watches; three of the number being worth each five hundred dollars, if one. Many of them were very old, and as timekeepers valueless; the works having suffered, more or less, from corrosion—but all were richly jewelled and in cases of great worth. We estimated the entire contents of the chest, that night, at a million and a half of dollars; and upon the subsequent disposal of the trinkets and jewels (a few being retained for our own use), it was found that we had greatly undervalued the treasure.

When, at length, we had concluded our examination, and the intense excitement of the time had, in some measure, subsided,

Legrand, who saw that I was dying with impatience for a solution of this most extraordinary riddle, entered into a full detail of all the circumstances connected with it.

"You remember," said he, "the night when I handed you the rough sketch I had made of the *scarabœus*. You recollect also, that I became quite vexed at you for insisting that my drawing resembled a death's-head. When you first made this assertion I thought you were jesting; but afterward I called to mind the peculiar spots on the back of the insect, and admitted to myself that your remark had some little foundation in fact. Still, the sneer at my graphic powers irritated me—for I am considered a good artist—and, therefore, when you handed me the scrap of parchment, I was about to crumple it up and throw it angrily into the fire."

"The scrap of paper, you mean," said I.

"No; it had much of the appearance of paper, and at first I supposed it to be such, but when I came to draw upon it, I discovered it at once to be a piece of very thin parchment. It was quite dirty, you remember. Well, as I was in the very act of crumpling it up, my glance fell upon the sketch at which you had been looking, and you may imagine my astonishment when I perceived, in fact, the figure of a death's-head just where, it seemed to me, I had made the drawing of the beetle. For a moment I was too much amazed to think with accuracy. I knew that my design was very different in detail from this—although there was a certain similarity in general outline. Presently I took a candle, and seating myself at the other end of the room, proceeded to scrutinize the parchment more closely. Upon turning it over, I saw my own sketch upon the reverse, just as I had made it. My first idea, now, was mere surprise at the really remarkable similarity of outline—at the singular coincidence involved in the fact that, unknown to me, there should have been a skull upon the other side of the parchment, immediately beneath my figure of the *scarabœus*, and that this skull, not only in outline, but in size, should so closely resemble my drawing. I say the singularity of this coincidence absolutely stupefied me for a time. This is the usual effect of such coincidences. The mind struggles to establish a connection—a sequence of cause and effect—and, being unable to do so, suffers a species of temporary paralysis. But, when I recovered from this stupor, there dawned upon me gradually a conviction which startled me even far more than the coincidence. I began distinctly, positively, to remember that there had been *no* drawing upon the parchment when I made my sketch of the *scarabæus*. I became perfectly certain of this; for I recollected turning up first one side and then the other, in search of the cleanest spot. Had the skull been then there, of course I could not have failed to notice it. Here was indeed a mystery which I felt it impossible to explain; but, even at that early moment, there seemed to glimmer, faintly, within the most remote and secret chambers of my intellect, a glow-worm-like conception of that truth which last night's adventure brought to so magnificent a demonstration. I arose at once, and putting the parchment securely away, dismissed all further reflection until I should be alone.

"When you had gone, and when Jupiter was fast asleep, I betook myself to a more methodical investigation of the affair. In the first place I considered the manner in which the parchment had come into my possession. The spot where we discovered the *scarabæus* was on the coast of the main-land, about a mile eastward of the island, and but a short distance above high-water mark. Upon my taking hold of it, it gave me a sharp bite, which caused me to let it drop. Jupiter, with his accustomed caution, before seizing the insect, which had flown toward him, looked about him for a leaf, or something of that nature, by which to take hold of it. It was at this moment that his eyes, and mine also, fell upon the scrap of parchment, which I then supposed to be paper. It was lying half buried in the sand, a corner sticking up. Near the spot where we found it, I observed the remnants of the hull of what appeared to have been a ship's long-boat. The wreck seemed to have been there for a very great while; for the resemblance to boat timbers could scarcely be traced.

"Well, Jupiter picked up the parchment, wrapped the beetle in it, and gave it to me. Soon afterward we turned to go home, and on the way met Lieutenant G——. I showed him the insect, and he begged me to let him take it to the fort. Upon my consenting, he thrust it forthwith into his waistcoat pocket, without the parchment in which it had been wrapped, and which I had continued to hold in my hand during his inspection. Perhaps he dreaded my changing my mind, and thought it best to make sure of the prize at once—you know how enthusiastic he is on all subjects connected with Natural History. At the same time, without being conscious of it, I must have deposited the parchment in my own pocket.

"You remember that when I went to the table, for the purpose of making a sketch of the beetle, I found no paper where it was usually kept. I looked in the drawer, and found none there. I searched my pockets, hoping to find an old letter, when my hand fell upon the parchment. I thus detail the precise mode in which it came into my possession; for the circumstances impressed me with peculiar force.

"No doubt you will think me fanciful—but I had already established a kind of *connection*. I had put together two links of a great chain. There was a boat lying upon the sea-coast, and not far from the boat was a parchment—*not a paper*—with a skull depicted upon it. You will, of course, ask 'where is the connection?' I reply that the skull, or death's-head, is the well-known emblem of the pirate. The flag of the death's-head is hoisted in all engagements.

"I have said that the scrap was parchment, and not paper. Parchment is durable—almost imperishable. Matters of little moment are rarely consigned to parchment; since, for the mere ordinary purposes of drawing or writing, it is not nearly so well adapted as paper. This reflection suggested some meaning—some relevancy—in the death's-head. I did not fail to observe, also, the *form* of the parchment. Although one of its corners had been, by some accident, destroyed, it could be seen that the original form was oblong. It was just such a slip, indeed, as might have been chosen for a memorandum—for a record of something to be long remembered and carefully preserved."

"But," I interposed, "you say that the skull was ***not*** upon the parchment when you made the drawing of the beetle. How then do you trace any connection between the boat and the skull—since this latter, according to your own admission, must have been designed (God only knows how or by whom) as some period subsequent to your sketching the *scarabœus?*"

"Ah, hereupon turns the whole mystery; although the secret, at this point, I had comparatively little difficulty in solving. My steps were sure, and could afford a single result. I reasoned, for example, thus: When I drew the *scarabœus,* there was no skull apparent upon the parchment. When I had completed the drawing I gave it to you, and observed you narrowly until you returned it. *You,* therefore, did not design the skull, and no one else was present to do it. Then it was not done by human agency. And nevertheless it was done.

"At this stage of my reflections I endeavored to remember, and *did* remember, with entire distinctness, every incident which occurred about the period in question. The weather was chilly (oh, rare and happy accident!), and a fire was blazing upon the hearth. I was heated with exercise and sat near the table. You, however, had drawn a chair close to the chimney. Just as I placed the parchment in your hand, and as you were in the act of inspecting it, Wolf, the Newfoundland, entered, and leaped upon your shoulders. With your left hand you caressed him and kept him off, while your right, holding the parchment, was permitted to fall listlessly between your knees, and in close proximity to the fire. At one moment I thought the blaze had caught it, and was about to caution you, but, before I could speak, you had withdrawn it, and were engaged in its examination. When I considered all these particulars, I doubted not for a moment that ***heat*** had been the agent in bringing to light, upon the parchment, the skull which I saw designed upon it. You are well aware that chemical preparations exist, and have existed time out of mind, by means of which it is possible to write upon either paper or vellum, so that the characters shall become visible only when subjected to the action of fire. Zaffre, digested in *aqua regia,* and diluted with four times its weight of water, is sometimes employed; a green tint results. The regulus of cobalt, dissolved in spirit of nitre, gives a red. These colors disappear at longer or shorter intervals after the material written upon cools, but again become apparent upon the re-application of heat.

"I now scrutinized the death's-head with care. Its outer edges—the edges of the drawing nearest the edge of the vellum—were far more *distinct* than the others. It was clear that the action of the caloric had been imperfect or unequal. I immediately kindled a fire, and subjected every portion of the parchment to a glowing heat. At first, the only effect was the strengthening of the faint lines in the skull; but, upon persevering in the experiment, there became visible, at the corner of the slip, diagonally opposite to the spot in which the death's-head was delineated, the figure of what I at first supposed to be a goat. A closer scrutiny, however, satisfied me that it was intended for a kid."

"Ha! ha!" said I, "to be sure I have no right to laugh at you—a million and a half of money is too serious a matter for mirth—but you are not about to establish a third link in your chain—you will not find any especial connection between your pirates and a goat—pirates, you know, have nothing to do with goats; they appertain to the farming interest."

"But I have just said that the figure was *not* that of a goat."

"Well, a kid then—pretty much the same thing."

"Pretty much, but not altogether," said Legrand. "You may have heard of one *Captain* Kidd. I at once looked upon the figure of the animal as a kind of punning or hieroglyphical signature. I say signature; because its position upon the vellum suggested this idea. The death's-head at the corner diagonally opposite, had, in the same manner, the air of a stamp, or seal. But I was sorely put out by the absence of all else—of the body to my imagined instrument—of the text for my context."

"I presume you expected to find a letter between the stamp and the signature."

"Something of that kind. The fact is, I felt irresistibly impressed with a presentiment of some vast good fortune impending. I can scarcely say why. Perhaps, after all, it was rather a desire than an actual belief;—but do you know that Jupiter's silly words, about the bug being of solid gold, had a remarkable effect upon my fancy? And then the series of accidents and coincidences—these were so *very* extraordinary. Do you observe how mere an accident it was that these events should have occurred upon the *sole* day of all the year in which it has been, or may be sufficiently cool for fire, and that without the fire, or without the intervention of the dog at the percise moment in which he appeared, I should never have become aware of the death's-head, and so never the possessor of the treasure?"

"But proceed—I am all impatience."

"Well; you have heard, of course, the many stories current—the thousand vague rumors afloat about money buried, somewhere upon the Atlantic coast, by Kidd and his associates. These rumors must have had some foundation in fact. And that the rumors have existed so long and so continuous, could have resulted, it appeared to me, only from the circumstance of the buried treasure still *remaining* entombed. Had Kidd concealed his plunder for a time, and afterward reclaimed it, the rumors would scarcely have reached us in their present unvarying form. You will observe that the stories told are all about money-seekers, not about money-finders. Had the pirate recovered his money, there the affair would have dropped. It seemed to me that some accident—say the loss of a memorandum indicating its locality—had deprived him of the means of recovering it, and that this accident had become known to his followers, who otherwise might never have heard that treasure had been concealed at all, and who, busying themselves in vain, because unguided, attempts to regain it, had given first birth, and then universal currency, to the reports which are now so common. Have you ever heard of any important treasure being unearthed along the coast?"

"Never."

"But that Kidd's accumulations were immense, is well known. I took it for granted, therefore, that the earth still held them; and you will scarcely be surprised when I tell you that I felt a hope, nearly amounting to certainty, that the parchment so strangely found involved a lost record of the place of deposit."

"But how did you proceed?"

"I held the vellum again to the fire, after increasing the heat, but nothing appeared. I now thought it possible that the coating of dirt might have something to do with the failure: so I carefully rinsed the parchment by pouring warm water over it, and, having done this, I placed it in a tin pan, with the skull downward, and put the pan upon a furnace of lighted charcoal. In a few minutes, the pan having become thoroughly heated, I removed the slip, and, to my inexpressible joy, found it spotted, in several places, with what appeared to be figures arranged in lines. Again I placed it in the pan, and suffered it to remain another minute. Upon taking it off, the whole was just as you see it now."

Here Legrand, having re-heated the parchment, submitted it to my inspection. The following characters were rudely traced, in a red tint, between the death's-head and the goat:

"53‡‡†305))6*;4826)4‡.)4‡);806*;48†8¶60))85;1‡(;:‡*8†83
(88)5*†;46(;88*96*?;8)*‡(;485);5*†2:*‡(;4956*2(5*—4)8¶8
;4069285);)6†8)4‡‡;1(‡9;48081;8:8‡1;48†85;4)485†528806
81(‡9;48;(88;4(‡?34;48)4‡;161;:188;‡?;"

"But," said I, returning him the slip, "I am as much in the dark as ever. Were all the jewels of Golconda awaiting me upon my solution of this enigma, I am quite sure that I should be unable to earn them."

"And yet," said Legrand, "the solution is by no means so

difficult as you might be led to imagine from the first hasty inspection of the characters. These characters, as any one might readily guess, form a cipher—that is to say, they convey a meaning; but then from what is known of Kidd, I could not suppose him capable of constructing any of the more abstruse cryptographs. I made up my mind, at once, that this was of a simple species—such, however, as would appear, to the crude intellect of the sailor, absolutely insoluble without the key."

"And you really solved it?"

"Readily; I have solved others of an abstruseness ten thousand times greater. Circumstances, and a certain bias of mind, have led me to take interest in such riddles, and it may well be doubted whether human ingenuity can construct an enigma of the kind which human ingenuity may not, by proper application, resolve. In fact, having once established connected and legible characters, I scarcely gave a thought to the mere difficulty of developing their import.

"In the present case—indeed in all cases of secret writing—the first question regards the *language* of the cipher; for the principles of solution, so far, especially, as the more simple ciphers are concerned, depend upon, and are varied by, the genius of the particular idiom. In general, there is no alternative but experiment (directed by probabilities) of every tongue known to him who attempts the solution, until the true one be attained. But, with the cipher now before us all difficulty was removed by the signature. The pun upon the word 'Kidd' is appreciable in no other language than the English. But for this consideration I should have begun my attempts with the Spanish and French, as the tongues in which a secret of this kind would most naturally have been written by a pirate of the Spanish main. As it was, I assumed the cryptograph to be English.

"You observe there are no divisions between the words. Had there been divisions the task would have been comparatively easy. In such cases I should have commenced with a collation and analysis of the shorter words, and, had a word of a single letter occurred, as is most likely (*a* or *I,* for example), I should have considered the solution as assured. But, there being no division, my first step was to ascertain in the predominant letters, as well as the least frequent. Counting all, I constructed a table thus:

Of the character	8	there are	33.
	;	"	26.
	4	"	19.
	‡)	"	16.
	*	"	13.
	5	"	12.
	6	"	11.
	†1	"	8.
	0	"	6.
	92	"	5.
	:3	"	4.
	?	"	3.
	¶	"	2.
	—.	"	1.

"Now, in English, the letter which most frequently occurs is *e*. Afterward the succession runs thus: *a o i d h n r s t u y c f g l m w b k p q x z. E* predominates so remarkably, that an individual sentence of any length is rarely seen, in which it is not the prevailing character.

"Here, then, we have, in the very beginning, the groundwork for something more than a mere guess. The general use which may be made of the table is obvious—but, in this particular cipher, we shall only very partially require its aid. As our predominant character is 8, we will commence by assuming it as the *e* of the natural alphabet. To verify the supposition, let us observe if the 8 be seen often in couples—for *e* is doubled with great frequency in English—in such words, for example, as 'meet,' 'fleet,' 'speed,' 'seen,' 'been,' 'agree,' etc. In the present instance we see it doubled no less than five times, although the cryptograph is brief.

"Let us assume 8, then, as *e*. Now, of all *words* in the language, 'the' is most usual; let us see, therefore, whether there are not repetitions of any three characters, in the same order of collocation, the last of them being 8. If we discover repetitions of such letters, so arranged, they will most probably represent the word 'the.' Upon inspection, we find no less than seven such arrangements, the characters being; 48. We may, therefore, assume that ; represents *t,* 4 represents *h,* and 8 represents *e*—the last being now well confirmed. Thus a great step has been taken.

"But, having established a single word, we are enabled to establish a vastly important point; that is to say, several commencements and terminations of other words. Let us refer, for example, to the last instance but one, in which the combination ;48 occurs—not far from the end of the cipher. We know that the ; immediately ensuing is the commencement of a word, and, of the six characters succeeding this 'the,' we are cognizant of no less than five. Let us set these characters down, thus, by the letters we know them to represent, leaving a space for the unknown—

t eeth.

"Here we are enabled, at once, to discard the *'th,'* as forming no portion of the word commencing with the first *t;* since, by experiment of the entire alphabet for a letter adapted to the vacancy, we perceive that no word can be formed of which this *th* can be a part. We are thus narrowed into

t ee,

and, going through the alphabet, if necessary, as before, we arrive at the word 'tree,' as the sole possible reading. We thus gain another letter, *r,* represented by (, with the words 'the tree' in juxtaposition.

"Looking beyond these words, for a short distance, we again see the combination ;48, and employ it by way of *termination* to what immediately precedes. We have thus this arrangement:

the tree ;4(‡?34 the,

or, substituting the natural letters, where known, it reads thus:

the tree thr‡?3h the.

"Now, if, in place of the unknown characters, we leave blank spaces, or substitute dots, we read thus:

the tree thr...h the,

when the word *'through'* makes itself evident at once. But this discovery gives us three new letters, *o, u,* and *g,* represented by ‡, ?, and 3.

"Looking now, narrowly, through the cipher for combinations of known characters, we find, not very far from the beginning, this arrangement,

83(88, or egree,

which, plainly, is the conclusion of the word 'degree,' and gives us another letter, *d,* represented by †.

"Four letters beyond the word 'degree,' we perceive the combination

;46(;88.

"Translating the known characters, and representing the unknown by dots, as before, we read thus:

th.rtee,

an arrangement immediately suggestive of the word 'thirteen,' and again furnishing us with two new characters, *i* and *n,* represented by 6 and *.

"Referring, now, to the beginning of the cryptograph, we find the combination,

53‡‡†

"Translating as before, we obtain

.good,

which assures us that the first letter is *A,* and that the first two words are 'A good.'

"It is now time that we arrange our key, as far as discovered, in a tabular form, to avoid confusion. It will stand thus:

5	represents	a
†	"	d
8	"	e
3	"	g
4	"	h
6	"	i
*	"	n
‡	"	o
(	"	r
;	"	t
?	"	u

"We have, therefore, no less than eleven of the most important letters represented, and it will be unnecessary to proceed with the details of the solution. I have said enough to convince you that ciphers of this nature are readily soluble, and to give you some insight into the *rationale* of their development. But be assured that the specimen before us appertains to the very simplest species of cryptograph. It now only remains to give you the full translation of the characters upon the parchment, as unriddled. Here it is:

" 'A good glass in the bishop's hostel in the devil's seat forty-one degrees and thirteen minutes northeast and by north main branch seventh limb east side shoot from the left eye of the death's-head a bee-line from the tree through the shot fifty feet out.' "

"But," said I, "the enigma seems still in as bad a condition as ever. How is it possible to extort a meaning from all this jargon about 'devil's seats,' 'death's-heads,' and 'bishop's hostels'?"

"I confess," replied Legrand, "that the matter still wears a serious aspect, when regarded with a casual glance. My first endeavor was to divide the sentence into the natural division intended by the cryptographist."

"You mean, to punctuate it?"

"Something of that kind."

"But how was it possible to effect this?"

"I reflected that it had been a *point* with the writer to run his words together without division, so as to increase the difficulty of solution. Now, a not over-acute man, in pursuing such an object, would be nearly certain to overdo the matter. When, in the course of his composition, he arrived at a break in his subject which would naturally require a pause, or a point, he would be exceedingly apt to run his characters, at this place, more than usually close together. If you will observe the MS., in the present instance, you will easily detect five such cases of unusual crowding. Acting upon this hint, I made the division thus:

"'*A good glass in the bishop's hostel in the devil's seat—forty-one degrees and thirteen minutes—northeast and by north—main branch seventh limb east side—shoot from the left eye of the death's-head—a bee-line from the tree through the shot fifty feet out.*'"

"Even this division," said I, "leaves me still in the dark."

"It left me also in the dark," replied Legrand, "for a few days; during which I made diligent inquiry, in the neighborhood of Sullivan's Island, for any building which went by the name of the 'Bishop's Hotel'; for, of course, I dropped the obsolete word 'hostel.' Gaining no information on the subject, I was on the point of extending my sphere of search, and proceeding in a more systematic manner, when, one morning, it entered into my head, quite suddenly, that this 'Bishop's Hostel' might have some reference to an old family, of the name of Bessop, which, time out of mind, had held possession of an ancient manor-house, about four miles to the northward of the island. I accordingly went over to the plantation, and re-instituted my inquiries among the older negroes of the place. At length one of the most aged of the women said that she had heard of such a place as *Bessop's Castle*, and thought that she could guide me to it, but that it was not a castle, nor a tavern, but a high rock.

"I offered to pay her well for her trouble, and, after some demur, she consented to accompany me to the spot. We found it without much difficulty, when, dismissing her, I proceeded to examine the place. The 'castle' consisted of an irregular assemblage of cliffs and rocks—one of the latter being quite remarkable for its height as well as for its insulated and artificial appearance. I clambered to its apex, and then felt much at a loss as to what should be next done.

"While I was busied in reflection, my eyes fell upon a narrow ledge in the eastern face of the rock, perhaps a yard below the summit upon which I stood. This ledge projected about eighteen inches, and was not more than a foot wide, while a niche in the cliff just above it gave it a rude resemblance to one of the hollow-backed chairs used by our ancestors. I made no doubt that here was the 'devil's-seat' alluded to in the MS., and now I seemed to grasp the full secret of the riddle.

"The 'good glass,' I knew, could have reference to nothing but a telescope; for the word 'glass' is rarely employed in any other sense by seamen. Now here, I at once saw, was a telescope to be used, and a definite point of view, *admitting no variation,* from which to use it. Nor did I hesitate to believe that the phrases, 'forty-one degrees and thirteen minutes,' and 'northeast and by north,' were intended as directions for the levelling of the glass. Greatly excited by these discoveries, I hurried home, procured a telescope, and returned to the rock.

"I let myself down to the ledge, and found that it was impossible to retain a seat upon it except in one particular position. This fact confirmed my preconceived idea. I proceeded to use the glass. Of course, the 'forty-one degrees and thirteen minutes' could allude to nothing but elevation above the visible horizon, since the horizontal direction was clearly indicated by the words, 'northeast and by north.' This latter direction I at once established by means of a pocket-compass; then, pointing the glass as nearly at an angle of forty-one degrees of elevation as I could do it by guess, I moved it cautiously up or down, until my attention was arrested by a circular rift or opening in the foliage of a large tree that overtopped its fellows in the distance. In the centre of this rift I perceived a white spot, but could not, at first, distinguish what it was. Adjusting the focus of the telescope, I again looked, and now made it out to be a human skull.

"Upon this discovery I was so sanguine as to consider the enigma solved; for the phrase 'main branch, seventh limb, east side,' could refer only to the position of the skull upon the tree, while 'shoot from the left eye of the death's-head' admitted, also, of but one interpretation, in regard to a search for buried treasure. I perceived that the design was to drop a bullet from the left eye of the skull, and that a bee-line, or, in other words, a straight line, drawn from the nearest point of the trunk through 'the shot' (or the spot where the bullet fell), and thence extended to a distance of fifty feet, would indicate a definite point—and beneath this point I thought it at least *possible* that a deposit of value lay concealed."

"All this," I said, "is exceedingly clear, and, although ingenious, still simple and explicit. When you left the 'Bishop's Hotel,' what then?"

"Why, having carefully taken the bearings of the tree, I turned homeward. The instant that I left 'the devil's-seat,' however, the circular rift vanished; nor could I get a glimpse of it afterward, turn as I would. What seems to me the chief ingenuity in this whole business, is the fact (for repeated experiment has convinced me it *is* a fact) that the circular opening in question is visible from no other attainable point of view than that afforded by the narrow ledge upon the face of the rock.

"In this expedition to the 'Bishop's Hotel' I had been attended by Jupiter, who had, no doubt, observed, for some weeks past, the abstraction of my demeanor, and took especial care not to leave me alone. But, on the next day, getting up very early, I contrived to give him the slip, and went into the hills in search of the tree. After much toil I found it. When I came home at night my valet proposed to give me a flogging. With the rest of the adventure I believe you are as well acquainted as myself."

"I suppose," said I, "you missed the spot, in the first attempt at digging, through Jupiter's stupidity in letting the bug fall through the right instead of through the left eye of the skull."

"Precisely. This mistake made a difference of about two inches and a half in the 'shot'—that is to say, in the position of the peg nearest the tree; and had the treasure been *beneath* the 'shot,' the error would have been of little moment; but 'the shot,' together with the nearest point of the tree, were merely two points for the establishment of a line of direction; of course the error, however trivial in the beginning, increased as we proceeded with the line, and by the time we had gone fifty feet threw us quite off the scent. But for my deep-seated impressions that treasure was here somewhere actually buried, we might have had all our labor in vain."

"But your grandiloquence, and your conduct in swinging the beetle—how excessively odd! I was sure you were mad. And why did you insist upon letting fall the bug, instead of a bullet, from the skull?"

"Why, to be frank, I felt somewhat annoyed by your evident suspicions touching my sanity, and so resolved to punish you quietly, in my own way, by a little bit of sober mystification. For this reason I swung the beetle, and for this reason I let it fall from the tree. An observation of yours about its great weight suggested the latter idea."

"Yes, I perceive; and now there is only one point which puzzles me. What are we to make of the skeletons found in the hole?"

"That is a question I am no more able to answer than yourself. There seems, however, only one plausible way of accounting for them—and yet it is dreadful to believe in such atrocity as my suggestion would imply. It is clear that Kidd—if Kidd indeed secreted this treasure, which I doubt not—it is clear that he must have had assistance in the labor. But this labor concluded, he may have thought it expedient to remove all participants in his secret. Perhaps a couple of blows with a mattock were sufficient, while his coadjutors were busy in the pit; perhaps it required a dozen—who shall tell?"

BERENICE*

Dicebant mihi sodales, si sepulchrum amicæ visitarem, curas meas aliquar tulum fore levatas.

Ebn Zaiat

MISERY is manifold. The wretchedness of earth is multiform. Overreaching the wide horizon as the rainbow, its hues are as various as the hues of that arch—as distinct too, yet as intimately blended. Overreaching the wide horizon as the rainbow! How is it that from beauty I have derived a type of unloveliness?—from the covenant of peace, a simile of sorrow? But, as in ethics, evil is a consequence of good, so, in fact, out of joy is sorrow born. Either the memory of past bliss is the anguish of to-day, or the agonies which *are,* have their origin in the ecstasies which *might have been.*

My baptismal name is Egæus; that of my family I will not mention. Yet there are no towers in the land more time-honored than my gloomy, gray, hereditary halls. Our line has been called a race of visionaries; and in many striking particulars—in the character of the family mansion—in the frescos of the chief saloon—in the tapestries of the dormitories—in the chiselling of some buttresses in the armory—but more especially in the gallery of antique paintings—in the fashion of the library chamber—and, lastly, in the very peculiar nature of the library's contents—there is more than sufficient evidence to warrant the belief.

The recollections of my earliest years are connected with that

* Published in *Southern Literary Messenger,* 1835; *Broadway Journal,* 1845.

chamber, and with its volumes—of which latter I will say no more. Here died my mother. Herein was I born. But it is mere idleness to say that I had not lived before—that the soul has no previous existence. You deny it?—let us not argue the matter. Convinced myself, I seek not to convince. There is, however, a remembrance of aërial forms—of spiritual and meaning eyes—of sounds, musical yet sad; a remembrance which will not be excluded; a memory like a shadow—vague, variable, indefinite, unsteady; and like a shadow, too, in the impossibility of my getting rid of it while the sunlight of my reason shall exist.

In that chamber was I born. Thus awakening from the long night of what seemed, but was not, nonentity, at once into the very regions of fairy land—into a palace of imagination—into the wild dominions of monastic thought and erudition—it is not singular that I gazed around me with a startled and ardent eye—that I loitered away my boyhood in books, and dissipated my youth in revery; but it *is* singular, that as years rolled away, and the noon of manhood found me still in the mansion of my fathers—it *is* wonderful what a stagnation there fell upon the springs of my life—wonderful how total an inversion took place in the character of my commonest thought. The realities of the world affected me as visions, and as visions only, while the wild ideas of the land of dreams became, in turn, not the material of my every-day existence, but in very deed that existence utterly and solely in itself.

* * *

Berenice and I were cousins, and we grew up together in my paternal halls. Yet differently we grew—I, ill of health, and buried in gloom—she, agile, graceful, and overflowing with energy; hers the ramble on the hillside—mine, the studies of the cloister; I, living within my own heart, and addicted, body and soul, to the most intense and painful meditation—she, roaming carelessly through life, with no thought of the shadows in her path, or the silent flight of the raven-winged hours. Berenice!—I call upon her name—Berenice!—and from the gray ruins of memory a thousand tumultuous recollections are startled at the sound! Ah, vividly is her image before me now, as in the early days of her light-heartedness and joy! Oh, gorgeous yet fantastic beauty! Oh, sylph amid the shrubberies of Arnheim! Oh, Naiad among its fountains! And then—then all is mystery and terror, and a tale which should not be told. Disease—a fatal disease, fell like the simoon upon her frame; and even, while I gazed upon her, the spirit of change swept over her, pervading her mind, her habits, and her character, and, in a manner the most subtle and terrible, disturbing even the identity of her person! Alas! the destroyer came and went!—and the victim—where is she? I knew her not—or knew her no longer as Berenice!

Among the numerous train of maladies superinduced by that fatal and primary one which effected a revolution of so horrible a kind in the moral and physical being of my cousin, may be mentioned as the most distressing and obstinate in its nature, a species of epilepsy not unfrequently terminating in *trance* itself—trance very nearly resembling positive dissolution, and from which her manner of recovery was, in most instances, startingly abrupt. In the meantime, my own disease—for I have been told that I should call it by no other appellation—my own disease, then, grew rapidly upon me, and assumed finally a monomaniac character of a novel and extraordinary form—hourly and momently gaining vigor—and at length obtaining over me the most incomprehensible ascendency. This monomania, if I must so term it, consisted in a morbid irritability of those properties of the mind in metaphysical science termed the *attentive*. It is more than probable that I am not understood; but I fear, indeed, that it is in no manner possible to convey to the mind of the merely general reader, an adequate idea of that nervous *intensity of interest* with which, in my case, the powers of meditation (not to speak technically) busied and buried themselves, in the contemplation of even the most ordinary objects of the universe.

To muse for long unwearied hours, with my attention riveted to some frivolous device on the margin or in the typography of a book; to become absorbed, for the better part of a summer's day, in a quaint shadow falling aslant upon the tapestry or upon the floor; to lose myself, for an entire night, in watching the steady flame of a lamp, or the embers of a fire; to dream away whole days over the perfume of a flower; to repeat, monotonously, some common word, until the sound, by dint of frequent repetition, ceased to convey any idea whatever to the mind; to lose all sense of motion or physical existence, by means of absolute bodily quiescence long and obstinately persevered in: such were a few of the most common and least pernicious vagaries induced by a condition of the mental faculties, not, indeed, altogether unparalleled, but certainly bidding defiance to any thing like analysis or explanation.

Yet let me not be misapprehended. The undue, earnest, and morbid attention thus excited by objects in their own nature frivolous, must not be confounded in character with that ruminating propensity common to all mankind, and more especially indulged in by persons of ardent imagination. It was not even, as might be at first supposed, an extreme condition, or exaggeration of such propensity, but primarily and essentially distinct and different. In the one instance, the dreamer, or enthusiast, being interested by an object usually *not* frivolous, imperceptibly loses sight of this object in a wilderness of deductions and suggestions issuing therefrom, until, at the conclusion of a day-dream *often replete with luxury,* he finds the *incitamentum,* or first cause of his musings, entirely vanished and forgotten. In my case, the primary object was *invariably frivolous,* although assuming, through the medium of my distempered vision, a refracted and unreal importance. Few deductions, if any, were made; and those few pertinaciously returning in upon the original object as a centre. The meditations were *never* pleasurable; and at the termination of the revery, the first cause, so far from being out of sight, had attained that supernaturally exaggerated interest which was the prevailing feature of the disease. In a word, the powers of mind more particularly exercised were, with me, as I have said before, the *attentive,* and are, with the daydreamer, the *speculative.*

My books, at this epoch, if they did not actually serve to

irritate the disorder, partook, it will be perceived, largely, in their imaginative and inconsequential nature, of the characteristic qualities of the disorder itself. I well remember, among others, the treatise of the noble Italian, Cœlius Secundus Curio, *"De Amplitudine Beati Regni Dei"*; St. Austin's great work, "The City of God"; and Tertullian's *"De Carne Christi,"* in which the paradoxical sentence, *"Mortuus est Dei filius; credible est quia ineptum est; et sepultus resurrexit; certum est quia impossible est,"* occupied my undivided time, for many weeks of laborious and fruitless investigation.

Thus it will appear that, shaken from its balance only by trivial things, my reason bore resemblance to that ocean-crag spoken of by Ptolemy Hephestion, which steadily resisting the attacks of human violence, and the fiercer fury of the waters and the winds, trembled only to the touch of the flower called Asphodel. And although, to a careless thinker, it might appear a matter beyond doubt, that the alteration produced by her unhappy malady, in the *moral* condition of Berenice, would afford me many objects for the exercise of that intense and abnormal meditation whose nature I have been at some trouble in explaining, yet such was not in any degree the case. In the lucid intervals of my infirmity, her calamity, indeed, gave me pain, and, taking deeply to heart that total wreck of her fair and gentle life, I did not fail to ponder, frequently and bitterly, upon the wonder-working means by which so strange a revolution had been so suddenly brought to pass. But these reflections partook not of the idiosyncrasy of my disease, and were such as would have occurred, under similar circumstances, to the ordinary mass of mankind. True to its own character, my disorder revelled in the less important but more startling changes wrought in the *physical* frame of Berenice—in the singular and most appalling distortion of her personal identity.

During the brightest days of her unparalleled beauty, most surely I had never loved her. In the strange anomaly of my existence, feelings with me, *had never been* of the heart, and my passions *always were* of the mind. Through the gray of the early morning—among the trellised shadows of the forest at noonday—and in the silence of my library at night—she had flitted by my eyes, and I had seen her—not as the living and breathing Berenice, but as the Berenice of a dream; not as a being of the earth, earthy, but as the abstraction of such a being; not as a thing to admire, but to analyze; not as an object of love, but as the theme of the most abstruse although desultory speculation. And *now*—now I shuddered in her presence, and grew pale at her approach; yet, bitterly lamenting her fallen and desolate condition, I called to mind that she had loved me long, and, in an evil moment, I spoke to her of marriage.

And at length the period of our nuptials was approaching, when, upon an afternoon in the winter of the year—one of those unseasonably warm, calm, and misty days which are the nurse of the beautiful Halcyon,*—I sat (and sat, as I thought, alone) in the inner apartment of the library. But, uplifting my eyes, I saw that Berenice stood before me.

Was it my own excited imagination—or the misty influence of the atmosphere—or the uncertain twilight of the chamber—or the gray draperies which fell around her figure—that caused in it so vacillating and indistinct an outline? I could not tell. She spoke no word; and I—not for worlds could I have uttered a syllable. An icy chill ran through my frame; a sense of insufferable anxiety oppressed me; a consuming curiosity pervaded my soul; and, sinking back upon the chair, I remained for some time breathless and motionless, with my eyes riveted upon her person. Alas! its emaciation was excessive, and not one vestige of the former being lurked in any single line of the contour. My burning glances at length fell upon the face.

The forehead was high, and very pale, and singularly placid; and the once jetty hair fell partially over it, and overshadowed the hollow temples with innumerable ringlets, now of a vivid yellow, and jarring discordantly, in their fantastic character,

* For as Jove, during the winter season, gives twice seven days of warmth, men have called this clement and temperate time the nurse of the beautiful Halcyon.—*Simonides*.

with the reigning melancholy of the countenance. The eyes were lifeless, and lustreless, and seemingly pupilless, and I shrank involuntarily from their glassy stare to the contemplation of the thin and shrunken lips. They parted; and in a smile of peculiar meaning, *the teeth* of the changed Berenice disclosed themselves slowly to my view. Would to God that I had never beheld them, or that, having done so, I had died!

* * *

The shutting of a door disturbed me, and looking up, I found that my cousin had departed from the chamber. But from the disordered chamber of my brain, had not, alas! departed, and would not be driven away, the white and ghastly *spectrum* of the teeth. Not a speck on their surface—not a shade on their enamel—not an indenture in their edges—but what that brief period of her smile had sufficed to brand in upon my memory. I saw them *now* even more unequivocally than I beheld them *then*. The teeth!—the teeth!—they were here, and there, and everywhere, and visibly and palpably before me; long, narrow, and excessively white, with the pale lips writhing about them, as in the very moment of their first terrible development. Then came the full fury of my *monomania*, and I struggled in vain against its strange and irresistible influence. In the multiplied objects of the external world I had no thoughts but for the teeth. For these I longed with a frenzied desire. All other matters and all different interests became absorbed in their single contemplation. They—they alone were present to the mental eye, and they, in their sole individuality, became the essence of my mental life. I held them in every light. I turned them in every attitude. I surveyed their characteristics. I dwelt upon their peculiarities. I pondered upon their conformation. I mused upon the alteration in their nature. I shuddered as I assigned to them, in imagination, a sensitive and sentient power, and, even when unassisted by the lips, a capability of moral expression. Of Mademoiselle Salle it has been well said: *"Que tous ses pas étaient des sentiments,"* and of Berenice I more seriously believed *que tous ses dents étaient des idées. Des idées!*—ah, here was the idiotic thought that destroyed me! *Des idées!*—ah, *therefore* it was that I coveted them so madly! I felt that their possession could alone ever restore me to peace, in giving me back to reason.

And the evening closed in upon me thus—and then the darkness came, and tarried, and went—and the day again dawned—and the mists of a second night were now gathering around—and still I sat motionless in that solitary room—and still I sat buried in meditation—and still the *phantasma* of the teeth maintained its terrible ascendancy, as, with the most vivid and hideous distinctness, it floated about amid the changing lights and shadows of the chamber. At length there broke in upon my dreams a cry as of horror and dismay; and thereunto, after a pause, succeeded the sound of troubled voices, intermingled with many low moanings of sorrow or of pain. I arose from my seat, and throwing open one of the doors of the library, saw standing out in the antechamber a servant maiden, all in tears, who told me that Berenice was—no more! She had been seized with epilepsy in the early morning, and now, at the closing in of the night, the grave was ready for its tenant, and all the preparations for the burial were completed.

* * *

I found myself sitting in the library, and again sitting there alone. It seemed to me that I had newly awakened from a confused and exciting dream. I knew that it was now midnight, and I was well aware, that since the setting of the sun, Berenice had been interred. But of that dreary period which intervened I had no positive, at least no definite, comprehension. Yet its memory was replete with horror—horror more horrible from being vague, and terror more terrible from ambiguity. It was a fearful page in the record of my existence, written all over with dim, and hideous, and unintelligible recollections. I strived to decipher them, but in vain; while ever and anon, like the spirit of a departed sound, the shrill and piercing shriek of a female voice seemed to be ringing in my ears. I had done a deed—what was it? I asked myself the question aloud, and the whispering echoes of the chamber answered me—*"What was it?"*

On the table beside me burned a lamp, and near it lay a little box. It was of no remarkable character, and I had seen it frequently before, for it was the property of the family physician; but how came it *there,* upon my table, and why did I shudder in regarding it? These things were in no manner to be accounted for, and my eyes at length dropped to the open pages of a book, and to a sentence underscored therein. The words were the singular but simple ones of the poet Ebn Zaiat:—*"Dicebant mihi sodales si sepulchrum amicæ visitarem, curas meas aliquantulum fore levatas."* Why, then, as I perused them, did the hairs of my head erect themselves on end, and the blood of my body become congealed within my veins?

There came a light tap at the library door—and, pale as the tenant of a tomb, a menial entered upon tiptoe. His looks were wild with terror, and he spoke to me in a voice tremulous, husky, and very low. What said he?—some broken sentences I heard. He told of a wild cry disturbing the silence of the night—of the gathering together of the household—of a search in the direction of the sound; and then his tones grew thrillingly distinct as he whispered me of a violated grave—of a disfigured body enshrouded, yet still breathing—still palpitating—*still alive!*

He pointed to my garments; they were muddy and clotted with gore. I spoke not, and he took me gently by the hand: it was indented with the impress of human nails. He directed my attention to some object against the wall. I looked at it for some minutes: it was a spade. With a shriek I bounded to the table, and grasped the box that lay upon it. But I could not force it open; and, in my tremor, it slipped from my hands, and fell heavily, and burst into pieces; and from it, with a rattling sound, there rolled out some instruments of dental surgery, intermingled with thirty-two small, white, and ivory-looking substances that were scattered to and fro about the floor.

Matters of Taste

PHILOSOPHY OF FURNITURE*

IN THE internal decoration, if not in the external architecture of their residences, the English are supreme. The Italians have but little sentiment beyond marbles and colors. In France, *meliora probant, deteriora sequuntur*—the people are too much a race of gadabouts to maintain those household proprieties of which, indeed, they have a delicate appreciation, or at least the elements of a proper sense. The Chinese and most of the Eastern races have a warm but inappropriate fancy. The Scotch are *poor* decorists. The Dutch have, perhaps, an indeterminate idea that a curtain is not a cabbage. In Spain they are *all* curtains—a nation of hangmen. The Russians do not furnish. The Hottentots and Kickapoos are very well in their way. The Yankees alone are preposterous.

How this happens, it is not difficult to see. We have no aristocracy of blood, and having therefore as a natural, and indeed as an inevitable thing, fashioned for ourselves an aristocracy of dollars, the *display of wealth* has here to take the place and perform the office of the heraldic display in monarchial countries. By a transition readily understood, and which might have been as readily foreseen, we have been brought to merge in simple *show* our notions of taste itself.

To speak less abstractly. In England, for example, no mere parade of costly appurtenances would be so likely as with us, to create an impression of the beautiful in respect to the appurtenances themselves—or of taste as regards the proprietor:—this for the reason, first, that wealth is not, in England, the loftiest object of ambition as constituting a nobility; and secondly, that there,

* *Burton's Gentleman's Magazine,* May, 1840; *Broadway Journal,* I. 18

the true nobility of blood, confining itself within the strict limits of legitimate taste, rather avoids than affects that mere costliness in which a *parvenu* rivalry may at any time be successfully attempted.

The people *will* imitate the nobles, and the result is a thorough diffusion of the proper feeling. But in America, the coins current being the sole arms of the aristocracy, their display may be said, in general, to be the sole means of aristocratic distinction; and the populace, looking always upward for models, are insensibly led to confound the two entirely separate ideas of magnificence and beauty. In short, the cost of an article of furniture has at length come to be, with us, nearly the sole test of its merit in a decorative point of view—and this test, once established, has led the way to many analogous errors, readily traceable to the one primitive folly.

There could be nothing more directly offensive to the eye of an artist than the interior of what is termed in the United States—that is to say, in Appalachia—a well-furnished apartment. Its most usual defect is a want of keeping. We speak of the keeping of a room as we would of the keeping of a picture—for both the picture and the room are amenable to those undeviating principles which regulate all varieties of art; and very nearly the same laws by which we decide on the higher merits of a painting, suffice for decision on the adjustment of a chamber.

A want of keeping is observable sometimes in the character of the several pieces of furniture, but generally in their colours or modes of adaptation to use. *Very* often the eye is offended by their inartistical arrangement. Straight lines are too prevalent—too uninterruptedly continued—or clumsily interrupted at right angles. If curved lines occur, they are repeated into unpleasant uniformity. By undue precision, the appearance of many a fine apartment is utterly spoiled.

Curtains are rarely well disposed, or well chosen in respect to other decorations. With formal furniture, curtains are out of place; and an extensive volume of drapery of any kind is, under any circumstances, irreconcilable with good taste—the proper quantum, as well as the proper adjustment, depending upon the character of the general effect.

Carpets are better understood of late than of ancient days, but we still very frequently err in their patterns and colours. The soul of the apartment is the carpet. From it are deduced not only the hues but the forms of all objects incumbent. A judge at common law may be an ordinary man; a good judge of a carpet *must be* a genius. Yet we have heard discoursing of carpets, with the air *"d'un mouton qui rêve,"* fellows who should not and who could not be entrusted with the management of their own *moustaches.* Every one knows that a large floor *may* have a covering of large figures, and that a small one *must* have a covering of small—yet this is not all the knowledge in the world. As regards texture, the Saxony is alone admissible. Brussels is the preterpluperfect tense of fashion, and Turkey is taste in its dying agonies. Touching pattern—a carpet should *not* be bedizzened out like a Riccaree Indian—all red chalk, yellow ochre, and cock's feathers. In brief—distinct grounds, and vivid circular or cycloid figures, *of no meaning,* are here Median laws. The abomination of flowers, or representations of well-known objects of any kind, should not be endured within the limits of Christendom. Indeed, whether on carpets, or curtains, or tapestry, or ottoman coverings, all upholstery of this nature should be rigidly Arabesque. As for those antique floor-cloths still occasionally seen in the dwellings of the rabble—cloths of huge, sprawling, and radiating devices, stripe-interspersed, and glorious with all hues, among which no ground is intelligible—these are but the wicked invention of a race of time-servers and money-lovers—children of Baal and worshippers of Mammon—Benthams, who, to spare thought and economize fancy, first cruelly invented the Kaleidoscope, and then established joint-stock companies to twirl it by steam.

Glare is a leading error in the philosophy of American household decoration—an error easily recognised as deduced from the perversion of taste just specified. We are violently enamoured of gas and of glass. The former is totally inadmissible within doors. Its harsh and unsteady light offends. No one having both brains and eyes will use it. A mild, or what artists term a cool light, with its consequent warm shadows, will do wonders for even an ill-furnished apartment. Never was a more lovely thought than that of the astral lamp. We mean, of course, the astral lamp proper—the lamp of Argand, with its original plain ground-glass shade, and its tempered and uniform moonlight rays. The cut-glass shade is a weak invention of the enemy. The eagerness with which we have adopted it, partly on account of its *flashiness,* but principally on account of its *greater cost,* is a good commentary on the proposition with which we began. It is not too much to say, that the deliberate employer of a cut-glass shade, is either radically deficient in taste, or blindly subservient to the caprices of fashion. The light proceeding from one of these gaudy abominations is unequal, broken, and painful. It alone is sufficient to mar a world of good effect in the furniture subjected to its influence. Female loveliness, in especial, is more than one-half disenchanted beneath its evil eye.

In the matter of glass, generally, we proceed upon false principles. Its leading feature is *glitter*—and in that one word how much of all that is detestable do we express! Flickering, unquiet lights, are *sometimes* pleasing—to children and idiots always so—but in the embellishment of a room they should be scrupulously avoided. In truth, even strong *steady* lights are inadmissible. The huge and unmeaning glass chandeliers, prism-cut, gas-lighted, and without shade, which dangle in our most fashionable drawing-rooms, may be cited as the quintessence of all that is false in taste or preposterous in folly.

The rage for *glitter*—because its idea has become, as we before observed, confounded with that of magnificence in the abstract—has led us, also, to the exaggerated employment of mirrors. We line our dwellings with great British plates, and then imagine we have done a fine thing. Now the slightest thought will be sufficient to convince any one who has an eye at all, of the ill effect of numerous looking-glasses, and especially of large ones. Regarded apart from its reflection, the mirror presents a continuous, flat, colourless, unrelieved surface,—a thing always and obviously unpleasant. Considered as a reflector, it is potent in producing a monstrous and odious uniformity: and the evil is here aggravated, not in merely direct proportion with the augmentation of its sources, but in a ratio constantly increasing. In fact, a room with four or five mirrors arranged at random, is, for all purposes of artistic show, a room of no shape at all. If we add to this evil, the attendant glitter upon glitter, we have a perfect farrago of discordant and displeasing effects. The veriest bumpkin, on entering an apartment so bedizzened, would be instantly aware of something wrong, although he might be altogether unable to assign a cause for his dissatisfaction. But let the same person be led into a room tastefully furnished, and he would be startled into an exclamation of pleasure and surprise.

It is an evil growing out of our republican institutions, that here a man of large purse has usually a very little soul which he keeps in it. The corruption of taste is a portion or a pendant of the dollar-manufacture. As we grow rich, our ideas grow rusty. It is, therefore, not among *our* aristocracy that we must look (if at all, in Appalachia), for the spirituality of a British *boudoir*. But we have seen apartments in the tenure of Americans of modern means, which, in negative merit at least, might vie with any of the *or-molu'd* cabinets of our friends across the water. Even *now,* there is present to our mind's eye a small and not ostentatious chamber with whose decorations no fault can be found. The proprietor lies asleep on a sofa—the weather is cool—the time is near midnight: we will make a sketch of the room during his slumber.

It is oblong—some thirty feet in length and twenty-five in breadth—a shape affording the best (ordinary) opportunities for the adjustment of furniture. It has but one door—by no means a wide one—which is at one end of the parallelogram, and but two windows, which are at the other. These latter are large, reaching down to the floor—have deep recesses—and open on an Italian *veranda.* Their panes are of a crimson-tinted glass, set in rosewood framings, more massive than usual. They are curtained within the recess, by a thick silver tissue adapted to the shape of the window, and hanging loosely in small volumes. Without the recess are curtains of an exceedingly rich crimson silk, fringed with a deep network of gold, and lined with silver tissue, which is the material of the exterior blind. There are no cornices; but the folds of the whole fabric (which are sharp rather than massive, and have an airy appearance), issue from beneath a broad entablature of rich giltwork, which encircles the room at the junction of the ceiling and walls. The drapery is thrown open also, or closed, by means of a thick rope of gold loosely enveloping it, and resolving itself readily into a knot; no pins or other such devices are apparent. The colours of the curtains and their fringe—the tints of crimson and gold—appear everywhere in profusion, and determine the *character* of the room. The carpet—of Saxony material—is quite half an inch thick, and is of the same crimson ground, relieved simply by the appearance of a gold cord (like that festooning the curtains) slightly relieved above the surface of the *ground,* and thrown upon it in such a manner as to form a succession of short irregular curves—one occasionally overlaying the other. The walls are prepared with a glossy paper of a silver gray tint, spotted with small Arabesque devices of a fainter hue of the prevalent crimson. Many paintings relieve the expanse of the paper. These are chiefly landscapes of an imaginative cast—such as the fairy grottoes of Stanfield, or the lake of the Dismal Swamp of Chapman. There are, nevertheless, three or four female heads, of an ethereal beauty—portraits in the manner of Sully. The tone of each picture is warm, but dark. There are no "brilliant effects." *Repose* speaks in all. Not one is of small size. Diminutive paintings give that *spotty* look to a room, which is the blemish of so many a fine work of Art overtouched. The frames are broad but not deep, and richly carved, without being *dulled* or filigreed. They have the whole lustre of burnished gold. They lie flat on the walls, and do not hang off with cords. The designs themselves are often seen to better advantage in this latter position, but the general appearance of the chamber is injured. But one mirror—and this is not a very large one—is visible. In shape it is nearly circular—and it is hung so that a reflection of the person can be obtained from it in none of the ordinary sitting-places of the room. Two large low sofas of rosewood and crimson silk, gold-flowered, form the only seats, with the exception of two light conversation chairs, also of rose-wood. There is a pianoforte (rosewood, also), without cover, and thrown open. An octagonal table, formed altogether of the richest gold-threaded marble, is placed near one of the sofas. This is also without cover—the drapery of the curtains has been thought sufficient. Four large and gorgeous Sèvres vases, in which bloom a profusion of sweet and vivid flowers, occupy the slightly rounded angles of the room. A tall candelabrum, bearing a small antique lamp with highly perfumed oil, is standing near the head of my sleeping friend. Some light and graceful hanging shelves, with golden edges and crimson silk cords with gold tassels, sustain two or three hundred magnificently bound books. Beyond these things, there is no furniture, if we except an Argand lamp, with a plain crimson-tinted ground-glass shade, which depends from the lofty vaulted ceiling by a single slender gold chain, and throws a tranquil but magical radiance over all.

THE DOMAIN OF ARNHEIM*

The garden like a lady fair was cut,
  That lay as if she slumbered in delight,
And to the open skies her eyes did shut.
  The azure fields of Heaven were 'sembled right
  In a large round set with the flowers of light.
The flowers de luce and the round sparks of dew
That hung upon their azure leaves did shew
Like twinkling stars that sparkle in the evening blue.

Giles Fletcher

FROM his cradle to his grave a gale of prosperity bore my friend Ellison along. Nor do I use the word prosperity in its mere worldly sense. I mean it as synonymous with happiness. The person of whom I speak seemed born for the purpose of foreshadowing the doctrines of Turgot, Price, Priestley and Condorcet—of exemplifying by individual instance what has been deemed the chimera of the perfectionists. In the brief existence of Ellison I fancy that I have seen refuted the dogma, that in man's very nature lies some hidden principle, the antagonist of bliss. An anxious examination of his career has given me to understand that, in general, from the violation of a few simple laws of humanity arises the wretchedness of mankind—that as a species we have in our possession the as yet unwrought elements of content—and that, even now, in the present darkness and madness of all thought on the great question of the social condition, it is not impossible that

* *Columbian Magazine,* March, 1847. This piece afterwards incorporated *The Landscape Garden.*

man, the individual, under certain unusual and highly fortuitous conditions, may be happy.

With opinions such as these my young friend, too, was fully imbued; and thus it is worthy of observation that the uninterrupted enjoyment which distinguished his life was, in great measure, the result of preconcert. It is, indeed, evident that with less of the instinctive philosophy which, now and then, stands so well in the stead of experience, Mr. Ellison would have found himself precipitated, by the very extraordinary success of his life, into the common vortex of unhappiness which yawns for those of pre-eminent endowments. But it is by no means my object to pen an essay on happiness. The ideas of my friend may be summed up in a few words. He admitted but four elementary principles, or, more strictly, conditions, of bliss. That which he considered chief was (strange to say!) the simple and purely physical one of free exercise in the open air. "The health," he said, "attainable by other means is scarcely worth the name." He instanced the ecstasies of the fox-hunter, and pointed to the tillers of the earth, the only people who, as a class, can be fairly considered happier than others. His second condition was the love of woman. His third, and most difficult of realization, was the contempt of ambition. His fourth was an object of unceasing pursuit; and he held that, other things being equal, the extent of attainable happiness was in proportion to the spirituality of this object.

Ellison was remarkable in the continuous profusion of good gifts lavished upon him by fortune. In personal grace and beauty he exceeded all men. His intellect was of that order to which the acquisition of knowledge is less a labor than an intuition and a necessity. His family was one of the most illustrious of the empire. His bride was the loveliest and most devoted of women. His possessions had been always ample; but, on the attainment of his majority, it was discovered that one of those extraordinary freaks of fate had been played in his behalf which startle the whole social world amid which they occur, and seldom fail radically to alter the moral constitution of those who are their objects.

It appears that, about a hundred years before Mr. Ellison's coming of age, there had died, in a remote province, one Mr. Seabright Ellison. This gentleman had amassed a princely fortune, and, having no immediate connections, conceived the whim of suffering his wealth to accumulate for a century after his decease. Minutely and sagaciously directing the various modes of investment, he bequeathed the aggregate amount to the nearest of blood, bearing the name Ellison, who should be alive at the end of the hundred years. Many attempts had been made to set aside this singular bequest; their *ex post facto* character rendered them abortive; but the attention of a jealous government was aroused, and a legislative act finally obtained, forbidding all similar accumulations. This act, however, did not prevent young Ellison from entering into possession, on his twenty-first birth-day, as the heir of his ancestor Seabright, of a fortune of *four hundred and fifty millions of dollars*.*

When it had become known that such was the enormous wealth inherited, there were, of course, many speculations as to the mode of its disposal. The magnitude and the immediate availability of the sum bewildered all who thought on the topic. The possessor of any *appreciable* amount of money might have been imagined to perform any one of a thousand things. With riches merely surpassing those of any citizen, it would have been easy to suppose him engaging to supreme excess in the fashionable extravagances of his time—or busying himself with political intrigue—or aiming at ministerial power—or purchasing increase of

* An incident, similar in outline to the one here imagined, occurred, not very long ago, in England. The name of the fortunate heir was Thelluson. I first saw an account of this matter in the "Tour" of Prince Pückler-Muskau, who makes the sum inherited *ninety millions of pounds,* and justly observes that "in the contemplation of so vast a sum, and of the services to which it might be applied, there is something even of the sublime." To suit the views of this article I have followed the Prince's statement, although a grossly exaggerated one. The germ, and, in fact, the commencement of the present paper was published many years ago—previous to the issue of the first number of Sue's admirable *"Juif Errant,"* which may possibly have been suggested to him by Muskau's account.

nobility—or collecting large museums of *virtù*—or playing the munificent patron of letters, of science, of art—or endowing, and bestowing his name upon, extensive institutions of charity. But for the inconceivable wealth in the actual possession of the heir, these objects and all ordinary objects were felt to afford too limited a field. Recourse was had to figures, and these but sufficed to confound. It was seen that, even at three per cent., the annual income of the inheritance amounted to no less than thirteen millions and five hundred thousand dollars; which was one million and one hundred and twenty-five thousand per month; or thirty-six thousand nine hundred and eighty-six per day; or one thousand five hundred and forty-one per hour; or six and twenty dollars for every minute that flew. Thus the usual track of supposition was thoroughly broken up. Men knew not what to imagine. There were some who even conceived that Mr. Ellison would divest himself of at least one half of his fortune, as of utterly superfluous opulence—enriching whole troops of his relatives by division of his superabundance. To the nearest of these he did, in fact, abandon the very unusual wealth which was his own before the inheritance.

I was not surprised, however, to perceive that he had long made up his mind on a point which had occasioned so much discussion to his friends. Nor was I greatly astonished at the nature of his decision. In regard to individual charities he had satisfied his conscience. In the possibility of any improvement, properly so called, being effected by man himself in the general condition of man, he had (I am sorry to confess it) little faith. Upon the whole, whether happily or unhappily, he was thrown back, in very great measure, upon self.

In the widest and noblest sense he was a poet. He comprehended, moreover, the true character, the august aims, the supreme majesty and dignity of the poetic sentiment. The fullest, if not the sole proper satisfaction of this sentiment he instinctively felt to lie in the creation of novel forms of beauty. Some peculiarities, either in his early education, or in the nature of his intellect, had tinged with what is termed materialism all his ethical speculations; and it was this bias, perhaps, which led him to believe that the most advantageous at least, if not the sole legitimate field for the poetic exercise, lies in the creation of novel moods of purely *physical* loveliness. Thus it happened he became neither musician nor poet—if we use this latter term in its every-day acceptation. Or it might have been that he neglected to become either, merely in pursuance of his idea that in contempt of ambition is to be found one of the essential principles of happiness on earth. Is it not, indeed, possible that, while a high order of genius is necessarily ambitious, the highest is above that which is termed ambition? And may it not thus happen that many far greater than Milton have contentedly remained "mute and inglorious?" I believe that the world has never seen—and that, unless through some series of accidents goading the noblest order of mind into distasteful exertion, the world will never see—that full extent of triumphant execution, in the richer domains of art, of which the human nature is absolutely capable.

Ellison became neither musician nor poet; although no man lived more profoundly enamored of music and poetry. Under other circumstances than those which invested him, it is not impossible that he would have become a painter. Sculpture, although in its nature rigorously poetical, was too limited in its extent and consequences, to have occupied, at any time, much of his attention. And I have now mentioned all the provinces in which the common understanding of the poetic sentiment has declared it capable of expatiating. But Ellison maintained that the richest, the truest, and most natural, if not altogether the most extensive province, had been unaccountably neglected. No definition had spoken of the landscape-gardener as of the poet; yet it seemed to my friend that the creation of the landscape-garden offered to the proper Muse the most magnificent of opportunities. Here, indeed, was the fairest field for the display of imagination in the endless combining of forms of novel beauty; the elements to enter into combination being, by a vast superiority, the most glorious which the earth could afford. In the multiform and multicolor of the flower and the trees, he recognized the most direct and energetic efforts of Nature at physical loveliness. And in the direction or concentration of this effort—or, more properly, in its adaptation to the eyes which were to behold it on earth—he perceived that he should be employing the best means—laboring to the greatest advantage—in the fulfilment, not only of his own destiny as poet, but of the august purposes for which the Deity had implanted the poetic sentiment in man.

"Its adaptation to the eyes which were to behold it on earth." In his explanation of this phraseology, Mr. Ellison did much toward solving what has always seemed to me an enigma:—I mean the fact (which none but the ignorant dispute) that no such combination of scenery exists in nature as the painter of genius may produce. No such paradises are to be found in reality as have glowed on the canvas of Claude. In the most enchanting of natural landscapes, there will always be found a defect or an excess—many excesses and defects. While the component parts may defy, individually, the highest skill of the artist, the arrangement of these parts will always be susceptible of improvement. In short, no position can be attained on the wide surface of the *natural* earth, from which an artistical eye, looking steadily, will not find matter of offence in what is termed the "composition" of the landscape. And yet how unintelligible is this! In all other matters we are justly instructed to regard nature as supreme. With her details we shrink from competition. Who shall presume to imitate the colors of the tulip, or to improve the proportions of the lily of the valley? The criticism which says, of sculpture or portraiture, that here nature is to be exalted or idealized rather than imitated, is in error. No pictorial or sculptural combinations of points of human loveliness do more than approach the living and breathing beauty. In landscape alone is the principle of the critic true, and, having felt its truth here, it is but the headlong spirit of generalization which has led him to pronounce it true throughout all the domains of art. Having, I say, *felt* its truth here; for the feeling is no affectation or chimera. The mathematics afford no more absolute demonstrations than the sentiment of his art yields the artist. He not only believes, but positively knows, that such and such apparently arbitrary arrangements of matter constitute and alone constitute the true beauty. His reasons, however, have not yet been matured into expression. It remains for a more profound analysis than the world has yet seen, fully to investigate and express them. Nevertheless he is confirmed in his instinctive opinions by the voice of all his brethren. Let a "composition" be defective; let an emendation be wrought in its mere arrangement of form; let this emendation be submitted to every artist in the world; by each will its necessity be admitted. And even far more than this:—in remedy of the defective composition, each insulated member of the fraternity would have suggested the identical emendation.

I repeat that in landscape arrangements alone is the physical nature susceptible of exaltation, and that, therefore, her susceptibility of improvement at this one point, was a mystery I had been unable to solve. My own thoughts on the subject had rested in the idea that the primitive intention of nature would have so arranged the earth's surface as to have fulfilled at all points man's sense of perfection in the beautiful, the sublime, or the picturesque; but that this primitive intention had been frustrated by the known geological disturbances—disturbances of form and color-grouping, in the correction or allaying of which lies the soul of art. The force of this idea was much weakened, however, by the necessity which it involved of considering the disturbances abnormal and unadapted to any purpose. It was Ellison who suggested that they were prognostic of *death*. He thus explained: —Admit the earthly immortality of man to have been the first intention. We have then the primitive arrangement of the earth's surface adapted to his blissful estate, as not existent but designed. The disturbances were the preparations for his subsequently conceived deathful condition.

"Now," said my friend, "what we regard as exaltation of the

landscape may be really such, as respects only the moral or human *point of view.* Each alteration of the natural scenery may possibly effect a blemish in the picture, if we can suppose this picture viewed at large—in mass—from some point distant from the earth's surface, although not beyond the limits of its atmosphere. It is easily understood that what might improve a closely scrutinized detail, may at the same time injure a general or more distinctly observed effect. There *may* be a class of beings, human once, but now invisible to humanity, to whom, from afar, our disorder may seem order—our unpicturesqueness picturesque; in a word, the earth-angels, for whose scrutiny more especially than our own, and for whose death-refined appreciation of the beautiful, may have been set in array by God the wide landscape-gardens of the hemispheres."

In the course of discussion, my friend quoted some passages from a writer on landscape-gardening, who has been supposed to have well treated his theme:

"There are properly but two styles of landscape-gardening, the natural and the artificial. One seeks to recall the original beauty of the country, by adapting its means to the surrounding scenery; cultivating trees in harmony with the hills or plains of the neighboring land; detecting and bringing into practice those nice relations of size, proportion and color which, hid from the common observer, are revealed everywhere to the experienced student of nature. The result of the natural style of gardening, is seen rather in the absence of all defects and incongruities—in the prevalence of a healthy harmony and order—than in the creation of any special wonders or miracles. The artificial style has as many varieties as there are different tastes to gratify. It has a certain general relation to the various styles of building. There are the stately avenues and retirements of Versailles; Italian terraces; and a various mixed old English style, which bears some relation to the domestic Gothic or English Elizabethan architecture. Whatever may be said against the abuses of the artificial landscape-gardening, a mixture of pure art in the garden scene adds to it a great beauty. This is partly pleasing to the eye, by the show of order and design, and partly moral. A terrace, with an old moss-covered balustrade, calls up at once to the eye the fair forms that have passed there in other days. The slightest exhibition of art is an evidence of care and human interest."

"From what I have already observed," said Ellison, "you will understand that I reject the idea, here expressed, of recalling the original beauty of the country. The original beauty is never so great as that which may be introduced. Of course, everything depends on the selection of a spot with capabilities. What is said about detecting and bringing into practice nice relations of size, proportion, and color, is one of those mere vaguenesses of speech which serve to veil inaccuracy of thought. The phrase quoted may mean anything, or nothing, and guides in no degree. That the true result of the natural style of gardening is seen rather in the absence of all defects and incongruities than in the creation of any special wonders or miracles, is a proposition better suited to the grovelling apprehension of the herd than to the fervid dreams of the man of genius. The negative merit suggested appertains to that hobbling criticism which, in letters, would elevate Addison into apotheosis. In truth, while that virtue which consists in the mere avoidance of vice appeals directly to the understanding, and can thus be circumscribed in *rule,* the loftier virtue, which flames in creation, can be apprehended in its results alone. Rule applies but to the merits of denial—to the excellencies which refrain. Beyond these the critical art can but suggest. We may be instructed to build a "Cato," but we are in vain told *how* to conceive a Parthenon or an "Inferno." The thing done, however; the wonder. accomplished; and the capacity for apprehension becomes universal. The sophists of the negative school who, through inability to create, have scoffed at creation, are now found the loudest in applause. What, in its chrysalis condition of principle, affronted their demure reason, never fails, in its maturity of accomplishment, to extort admiration from their instinct of beauty.

"The author s observations on the artificial style," continued

Ellison, "are less objectionable. A mixture of pure art in a garden scene adds to it a great beauty. This is just; as also is the reference to the sense of human interest. The principle expressed is incontrovertible—but there *may* be something beyond it. There may be an object in keeping with the principle—an object unattainable by the means ordinarily possessed by individuals, yet which, if attained, would lend a charm to the landscape-garden far surpassing that which a sense of merely human interest could bestow. A poet, having very unusual pecuniary resources, might, while retaining the necessary idea of art, or culture, or, as our author expresses it, of interest, so imbue his designs at once with extent and novelty of beauty, as to convey the sentiment of spiritual interference. It will be seen that, in bringing about such result, he secures all the advantages of interest or *design,* while relieving his work of the harshness or technicality of the worldly *art*. In the most rugged of wildernesses—in the most savage of the scenes of pure nature—there is apparent the *art* of a creator; yet this art is apparent to reflection only; in no respect has it the obvious force of a feeling. Now let us suppose this sense of the Almighty design to be *one step depressed*—to be brought into something like harmony or consistency with the sense of human art—to form an intermedium between the two:—let us imagine, for example, a landscape whose combined vastness and definitiveness—whose united beauty, magnificence, and *strangeness,* shall convey the idea of care, or culture, or superintendence, on the part of beings superior, yet akin to humanity—then the sentiment of *interest* is preserved, while the art intervolved is made to assume the air of an intermediate or secondary nature—a nature which is not God, nor an emanation from God, but which still is nature in the sense of the handiwork of the angels that hover between man and God."

It was in devoting his enormous wealth to the embodiment of a vision such as this—in the free exercise in the open air ensured by the personal superintendence of his plans—in the unceasing object which these plans afforded—in the high spirituality of the object—in the contempt of ambition which it enabled him truly to feel—in the perennial springs with which it gratified, without possibility of satiating, that one master passion of his soul, the thirst for beauty; above all, it was in the sympathy of a woman, not unwomanly, whose loveliness and love enveloped his existence in the purple atmosphere of Paradise, that Ellison thought to find, *and found*, exemption from the ordinary cases of humanity, with a far greater amount of positive happiness than ever glowed in the rapt day-dreams of De Staël.

I despair of conveying to the reader any distinct conception of the marvels which my friend did actually accomplish. I wish to describe, but am disheartened by the difficulty of description, and hesitate between detail and generality. Perhaps the better course will be to unite the two in their extremes.

Mr. Ellison's first step regarded, of course, the choice of a locality; and scarcely had he commenced thinking on this point, when the luxuriant nature of the Pacific Islands arrested his attention. In fact, he had made up his mind for a voyage to the South Seas, when a night's reflection induced him to abandon the idea. "Were I misanthropic," he said, "such a *locale* would suit me. The thoroughness of its insulation and seclusion, and the difficulty of ingress and egress, would in such case be the charm of charms; but as yet I am not Timon. I wish the composure but not the depression of solitude. There must remain with me a certain control over the extent and duration of my repose. There will be frequent hours in which I shall need, too, the sympathy of the poetic in what I have done. Let me seek, then, a spot not far from a populous city—whose vicinity, also, will best enable me to execute my plans."

In search of a suitable place so situated, Ellison travelled for several years, and I was permitted to accompany him. A thousand spots with which I was enraptured he rejected without hesitation, for reasons which satisfied me, in the end, that he was right. We came at length to an elevated table-land of wonderful fertility and beauty, affording a panoramic prospect very little less in extent than that of Ætna, and, in Ellison's opinion as well as my own, surpassing the far-famed view from that mountain in all the true elements of the picturesque.

"I am aware," said the traveller, as he drew a sigh of deep delight after gazing on this scene, entranced, for nearly an hour, "I know that here, in my circumstances, nine-tenths of the most fastidious of men would rest content. This panorama is indeed glorious, and I should rejoice in it but for the excess of its glory. The taste of all the architects I have ever known leads them, for the sake of 'prospect,' to put up buildings on hill-tops. The error is obvious. Grandeur in any of its moods, but especially in that of extent, startles, excites—and then fatigues, depresses. For the occasional scene nothing can be better—for the constant view nothing worse. And, in the constant view, the most objectionable phase of grandeur is that of extent; the worst phase of extent, that of distance. It is at war with the sentiment and with the sense of *seclusion*—the sentiment and sense which we seek to humor in 'retiring to the country.' In looking from the summit of a mountain we cannot help feeling *abroad* in the world. The heart-sick avoid distant prospects as a pestilence."

It was not until toward the close of the fourth year of our search that we found a locality with which Ellison professed himself satisfied. It is, of course, needless to say *where* was the locality. The late death of my friend, in causing his domain to be thrown open to certain classes of visitors, has given to *Arnheim* a species of secret and subdued if not solemn celebrity, similar in kind, although infinitely superior in degree, to that which so long distinguished Fonthill.

The usual approach to Arnheim was by the river. The visitor left the city in the early morning. During the forenoon he passed between shores of a tranquil and domestic beauty, on which grazed innumerable sheep, their white fleeces spotting the vivid green of rolling meadows. By degrees the idea of cultivation subsided into that of merely pastoral care. This slowly became merged in a sense of retirement—this again in a consciousness of solitude. As the evening approached the channel grew more narrow; the banks more and more precipitous; and these latter were clothed in richer, more profuse, and more sombre foliage. The water increased in transparency. The stream took a thousand turns, so that at no moment could its gleaming surface be seen for a greater distance than a furlong. At every instant the vessel seemed imprisoned within an enchanted circle, having insuperable and impenetrable walls of foliage, a roof of ultra-marine satin, and *no* floor—the keel balancing itself with admirable nicety on that of a phantom bark which, by some accident having been turned upside down, floated in constant company with the substantial one, for the purpose of sustaining it. The channel now became a *gorge*—although the term is somewhat inapplicable, and I employ it merely because the language has no word which better represents the most striking—not the most distinctive—feature of the scene. The character of gorge was maintained only in the height and parallelism of the shores; it was lost altogether in their other traits. The walls of the ravine (through which the clear water still tranquilly flowed) arose to an elevation of a hundred and occasionally of a hundred and fifty feet, and inclined so much toward each other as, in a great measure, to shut out the light of day; while the long plume-like moss which depended densely from the intertwining shrubberies overhead, gave the whole chasm an air of funereal gloom. The windings became more frequent and intricate, and seemed often as if returning in upon themselves, so that the voyager had long lost all idea of direction. He was, moreover, enwrapt in an exquisite sense of the strange. The thought of nature still remained, but her character seemed to have undergone modification: there was a weird symmetry, a thrilling uniformity, a wizard propriety in these her works. Not a dead branch—not a withered leaf—not a stray pebble—not a patch of the brown earth was anywhere visible. The crystal water welled up against the clean granite, or the unblemished moss, with a sharpness of outline that delighted while it bewildered the eye.

Having threaded the mazes of this channel for some hours,

the gloom deepening every moment, a sharp and unexpected turn of the vessel brought it suddenly, as if dropped from heaven, into a circular basin of very considerable extent when compared with the width of the gorge. It was about two hundred yards in diameter, and girt in at all points but one—that immediately fronting the vessel as it entered—by hills equal in general height to the walls of the chasm, although of a thoroughly different character. Their sides sloped from the water's edge at an angle of some forty-five degrees, and they were clothed from base to summit—not a perceptible point escaping—in a drapery of the most gorgeous flower-blossoms; scarcely a green leaf being visible among the sea of odorous and fluctuating color. This basin was of great depth, but so transparent was the water that the bottom, which seemed to consist of a thick mass of small round alabaster pebbles, was distinctly visible by glimpses—that is to say, whenever the eye could permit itself *not* to see, far down in the inverted Heaven, the duplicate blooming of the hills. On these latter there were no trees, nor even shrubs of any size. The impressions wrought on the observer were those of richness, warmth, color, quietude, uniformity, softness, delicacy, daintiness, voluptuousness, and a miraculous extremeness of culture that suggested dreams of a new race of fairies, laborious, tasteful, magnificent and fastidious; but as the eye traced upward the myriad-tinted slope, from its sharp junction with the water to its vague termination amid the folds of overhanging cloud, it became, indeed, difficult not to fancy a panoramic cataract of rubies, sapphires, opals and golden onyxes, rolling silently out of the sky.

The visitor, shooting suddenly into this bay from out the gloom of the ravine, is delighted but astounded by the full orb of the declining sun, which he had supposed to be already far below the horizon, but which now confronts him, and forms the sole termination of an otherwise limitless vista seen through another chasm-like rift in the hills.

But here the voyager quits the vessel which has borne him so far, and descends into a light canoe of ivory, stained with arabesque devices in vivid scarlet, both within and without. The poop and beak of this boat arise high above the water, with sharp points, so that the general form is that of an irregular crescent. It lies on the surface of the bay with the proud grace of a swan. On its ermined floor reposes a single feathery paddle of satin-wood; but no oarsman or attendant is to be seen. The guest is bidden to be of good cheer—that the fates will take care of him. The larger vessel disappears, and he is left alone in the canoe, which lies apparently motionless in the middle of the lake. While he considers what course to pursue, however, he becomes aware of a gentle movement in the fairy bark. It slowly swings itself around until its prow points toward the sun. It advances with a gentle but gradually accelerated velocity, while the slight ripples it creates seem to break about the ivory side in divinest melody—seem to offer the only possible explanation of the soothing yet melancholy music for whose unseen origin the bewildered voyager looks around him in vain.

The canoe steadily proceeds, and the rocky gate of the vista is approached, so that its depths can be more distinctly seen. To the right arise a chain of lofty hills rudely and luxuriantly wooded. It is observed, however, that the trait of exquisite *cleanness* where the bank dips into the water, still prevails. There is not one token of the usual river *débris*. To the left the character of the scene is softer and more obviously artificial. Here the bank slopes upward from the stream in a very gentle ascent, forming a broad sward of grass of a texture resembling nothing so much as velvet, and of a brilliancy of green which would bear comparison with the tint of the purest emerald. This *plateau* varies in width from ten to three hundred yards; reaching from the river-bank to a wall, fifty feet high, which extends, in an infinity of curves, but following the general direction of the river, until lost in the distance to the westward. This wall is of one continuous rock, and has been formed by cutting perpendicularly the once rugged precipice of the stream's southern bank; but no trace of the labor has been suffered to remain. The chiselled stone has the hue of ages and is profusely overhung and overspread with the ivy, the coral honeysuckle, the eglantine, and the clematis. The uniformity of the top and bottom lines of the wall is fully relieved by occasional trees of gigantic height, growing singly or in small groups, both along the *plateau* and in the domain behind the wall, but in close proximity to it; so that frequent limbs (of the black walnut especially) reach over and dip their pendent extremities into the water. Farther back within the domain, the vision is impeded by an impenetrable screen of foliage.

These things are observed during the canoe's gradual approach to what I have called the gate of the vista. On drawing nearer to this, however, its chasm-like appearance vanishes; a new outlet from the bay is discovered to the left—in which direction the wall is also seen to sweep, still following the general course of the stream. Down this new opening the eye cannot penetrate very far; for the stream, accompanied by the wall, still bends to the left, until both are swallowed up by the leaves.

The boat, nevertheless, glides magically into the winding channel; and here the shore opposite the wall is found to resemble that opposite the wall in the straight vista. Lofty hills, rising occasionally into mountains, and covered with vegetation in wild luxuriance, still shut in the scene.

Floating gently onward, but with a velocity slightly augmented, the voyager, after many short turns, finds his progress apparently barred by a gigantic gate or rather door of burnished gold, elaborately carved and fretted, and reflecting the direct rays of the now fast-sinking sun with an effulgence that seems to wreathe the whole surrounding forest in flames. This gate is inserted in the lofty wall; which here appears to cross the river at right angles. In a few moments, however, it is seen that the main body of the water still sweeps in a gentle and extensive curve to the left, the wall following it as before, while a stream of considerable volume, diverging from the principal one, makes its way, with a slight ripple, under the door, and is thus hidden from sight. The canoe falls into the lesser channel and approaches the gate.

Its ponderous wings are slowly and musically expanded. The boat glides between them, and commences a rapid descent into a vast amphitheatre entirely begirt with purple mountains, whose bases are laved by a gleaming river throughout the full extent of their circuit. Meantime the whole Paradise of Arnheim bursts upon the view. There is a gush of entrancing melody; there is an oppressive sense of strange sweet odor;—there is a dream-like intermingling to the eye of tall slender Eastern trees—bosky shrubberies—flocks of golden and crimson birds—lily-fringed lakes—meadows of violets, tulips, poppies, hyacinths, and tuberoses—long intertangled lines of silver streamlets—and, upspringing confusedly from amid all, a mass of semi-Gothic, semi-Saracenic architecture, sustaining itself by miracle in mid-air, glittering in the red sunlight with a hundred oriels, minarets, and pinnacles; and seeming the phantom handiwork, conjointly, of the Sylphs, of the Fairies, of the Genii, and of the Gnomes.

BOSTON AND THE BOSTONIANS*

EDITORIAL MISCELLANY

WE TAKE the following paragraph from "The Sunday Times and Messenger" of October 26:

MR. POE'S POEM.—Mr. Poe was invited to deliver a poem before the Boston Lyceum, which he did to a large and distinguished audience. It was, to use the language of an intelligent hearer, "an elegant and classic production, based on the right principle; containing the essence of true poetry, mingled with a

* Text: *Broadway Journal,* Nov. 1, 1845.

gorgeous imagination, exquisite painting, every charm of metre, and graceful delivery." And yet the papers abused him, and the audience were fidgetty—made their exit one by one, and did not at all appreciate the efforts of a man of admitted ability, whom they had invited to deliver a poem before them. The poem was called the "Messenger Star." We presume Mr. Poe will not accept another invitation to recite poetry, original or selected, in that section of the Union.

Our excellent friend Major Noah has suffered himself to be cajoled by that most beguiling of all beguiling little divinities, Miss Walters, of "The Transcript." We have been looking all over her article, with the aid of a taper, to see if we could discover a single syllable of truth in it—and really blush to acknowledge that we cannot. The adorable creature has been telling a parcel of fibs about us, by way of revenge for something that we did to Mr. Longfellow (who admires her very much) and for calling her "a pretty little witch" into the bargain.

The facts of the case seem to be these:—We *were* invited to "deliver" (stand and deliver) a poem before the Boston Lyceum. As a matter of course, we accepted the invitation. The audience *was* "large and distinguished." Mr. Cushing preceded us with a very capital discourse: he was much applauded. On arising, we were most cordially received. We occupied some fifteen minutes with an apology for not "delivering," as is usual in such cases, a didactic poem: a didactic poem, in our opinion, being precisely no poem at all. After some farther words—still of apology—for the "indefinitiveness" and "general imbecility" of what we had to offer—all so unworthy a *Bostonian* audience—we commenced, and, with many interruptions of applause, concluded. Upon the whole the approbation was considerably more (the more the pity too) than that bestowed upon Mr. Cushing.

When we had made an end, the audience, of course, arose to depart—and about one-tenth of them, probably, had really departed, when Mr. Coffin, one of the managing committee, arrested those who remained, by the announcement that we had been requested to deliver "The Raven." We delivered "The Raven" forthwith—(without taking a receipt)—were very cordially applauded again—and this was the end of it—with the exception of the sad tale invented to suit her own purposes, by that amiable little enemy of ours, Miss Walters. We shall never call a woman a "pretty little witch" again, as long as we live.

We like Boston. We were born there—and perhaps it is just as well not to mention that we are heartily ashamed of the fact. The Bostonians are very well in their way. Their hotels are bad. Their pumpkin pies are delicious. Their poetry is not so good. Their common is no common thing—and the duck-pond might answer—if its answer could be heard for the frogs.

But with all these good qualities the Bostonians have no soul. They have always evinced towards us individually, the basest ingratitude for the services we rendered them in enlightening them about the originality of Mr. Longfellow. When we accepted, therefore, an invitation to "deliver" a poem in Boston—we accepted it simply and solely, because we had a curiosity to know how it felt to be publicly hissed—and because we wished to see what effect we would produce by a neat little *impromptu* speech in reply. Perhaps, however, we overrated our own importance, or the Bostonian want of common civility—which is not quite so manifest as one or two of their editors would wish the public to believe. We assure Major Noah that he is wrong. The Bostonians are well-bred—as *very* dull persons very generally are.

Still, with their vile ingratitude staring us in the eyes, it could scarcely be supposed that we would put ourselves to the trouble of composing for the Bostonians anything in the shape of an *original* poem. We did not. We had a poem (of about 500 lines) lying by us—one quite as good as new—one, at all events, that we considered would answer sufficiently well for an audience of Transcendentalists. *That* we gave them—it was the best that we had—for the price—and it *did* answer remarkably well. Its name was *not* "The Messenger Star"—who but Miss Walters would ever think of so delicious a little bit of invention as that? We had *no* name for it at all. The poem is what is occasionally called a "juvenile poem"—but the fact is, it is anything but juvenile now, for we wrote it, printed it, and published it, in book form, before we had fairly completed our tenth year. We read it *verbatim,* from a copy now in our possession, and which we shall be happy to show at any moment to any of our inquisitive friends.

We do not, ourselves, think the poem a remarkably good one:—it is not sufficiently transcendental. Still it did well enough for the Boston audience—who evinced characteristic discrimination in understanding, and especially applauding, all those knotty passages which we ourselves have not yet been able to understand.

As regards the anger of the "Boston Times" and one or two other asurdities—as regards, we say, the wrath of Achilles—we incurred it—or rather its manifestation—by letting some of our cat out of the bag a few hours sooner than we had intended. Over a bottle of champagne, that night, we confessed to Mess. Cushing, Whipple, Hudson, Field, and a few other natives who swear not altogether by the frog-pond—we confessed, we say, the soft impeachment of the hoax. *Et hinc illoe irae.* We should have waited a couple of days.

PROSPECTUS

OF

THE PENN MAGAZINE

A Monthly Literary Journal
To be Edited and Published in the City of Philadelphia
by Edgar A. Poe

To the Public.—Since resigning the conduct of the Southern Literary Messenger, at the commencement of its third year, I have had always in view the establishment of a Magazine which should retain some of the chief features of that Journal, abandoning or greatly modifying the rest. Delay, however, has been occasioned by a variety of causes, and not until now have I found myself at liberty to attempt the execution of the design.

I will be pardoned for speaking more directly of the Messenger. Having in it no proprietary right, my objects too being at variance in many respects with those of its very worthy owner, I found difficulty in stamping upon its pages that *individuality* which I believe essential to the full success of all similar publications. In regard to their permanent influence, it appears to me that a continuous, definite character, and a marked certainty of purpose, are desiderata of vital importance, and only attainable where one mind alone has the general direction of the undertaking. Experience has rendered obvious, what might indeed have been *a priori;* that in founding a Magazine of my own lies my sole chance of carrying out to completion whatever peculiar intentions I may have entertained.

To those who remember the early days of the Southern periodical in question it will be scarcely necessary to say that its main feature was a somewhat overdone causticity in its department of Critical Notices of new books. The Penn Magazine will retain this trait of severity in so much only as the calmest yet sternest sense of justice will permit. Some years since elapsed may have mellowed down the petulance without interfering with the rigor of the critic. Most surely they have not yet taught him to read through the medium of a publisher's will, nor convinced him that the interests of letters are unallied with the interests of truth. It shall be the first and chief purpose of the Magazine now proposed to become known as one where may be found at all times, and upon all subjects, an honest and fearless opinion. It shall be a leading object to assert in precept, and to maintain in practice the rights, while in effect it demonstrates the advantages, of an absolutely independent criticism—a criticism self-sustained; guiding itself only by the purest rules of Art; analyzing and urging these rules as it applies them; holding itself aloof from all personal bias; acknowledging no fear save that of outraging the right; yielding no point either to the vanity of the author, or to the assumptions of antique prejudice, or to the involute and anonymous cant of the Quarterlies, or to the arrogance of those organized *cliques* which, hanging like nightmares to American literature, manufacture, at the nod of our principal booksellers, a pseudo-public-opinion by wholesale. These are objects of which no man need be ashamed. They are purposes, moreover, whose novelty at least will give them interest. For assurance that I will fulfill them in the best spirit and to the very letter, I appeal with confidence to the many thousands of my friends, and especially of my Southern friends, who sustained me in the Messenger, where I had but a very partial opportunity of completing my own plans.

In respect to the other features of the Penn Magazine, a few words here will suffice. It will endeavour to support the general interests of the republic of letters, without reference to particular regions; regarding the world at large as the true audience of the author. Beyond the precincts of literature, properly so called, it will leave in better hands the task of instruction upon all matters of *very* grave moment. Its aim chiefly shall be to *please;* and this through means of versatility, originality, and pungency. It may be as well here to observe that nothing said in this Prospectus should be construed into a design of sullying the Magazine with any tincture of buffoonery, scurrillity, or profanity, which are the blemish of some of the most vigorous of the European prints. In all branches of the literary department, the best aid, from the highest and purest sources, is secured.

To the mechanical execution of the work the greatest attention will be given which such a matter can require. In this respect it is proposed to surpass, by very much, the ordinary Magazine style. The form will nearly resemble that of The Knickerbocker; the paper will be equal to that of The North American Review; the pictorial embellishments will be numerous, and by the leading artists of the country, but will be introduced only in the necessary illustration of the text.

The Penn Magazine will be published in Philadelphia, on the first of each month, and will form, half-yearly, a volume of about 500 pages. The price will be $5 per annum, payable in advance, or upon the receipt of the first number, which will be issued on the first of January, 1841. Letters addressed to the Editor and Proprietor,

Edgar A. Poe.

Criticism

THE POETIC PRINCIPLE*

I HOLD that a long poem does not exist. I maintain that the phrase, "a long poem," is simply a flat contradiction in terms.

I need scarcely observe that a poem deserves its title only inasmuch as it excites, by elevating the soul. The value of the poem is in the ratio of this elevating excitement. But all excitements are, through a psychal necessity, transient. That degree of excitement which would entitle a poem to be so called at all, cannot be sustained throughout a composition of any great length. After the lapse of half an hour, at the very utmost, it flags—fails—a revulsion ensues—and then the poem is, in effect, and in fact, no longer such.

There are, no doubt, many who have found difficulty in reconciling the critical dictum that the "Paradise Lost" is to be devoutly admired throughout, with the absolute impossibility of maintaining for it, during perusal, the amount of enthusiasm which that critical dictum would demand. This great work, in fact, is to be regarded as poetical, only when, losing sight of that vital requisite in all works of Art, Unity, we view it merely as a series of minor poems. If, to preserve its Unity—its totality of effect or impression—we read it (as would be necessary) at a single sitting, the result is but a constant alternation of excitement and depression. After a passage of what we feel to be true poetry, there follows, inevitably, a passage of platitude which no critical pre-judgment can force us to admire; but if upon completing the work, we read it again; omitting the first book—that is to say, commencing with the second—we shall be surprised at now

* Text: *Sartain's Union Magazine,* October, 1850.

finding that admirable which we before condemned—that damnable which we had previously so much admired. It follows from all this that the ultimate, aggregate, or absolute effect of even the best epic under the sun, is a nullity:—and this is precisely the fact.

In regard to the Iliad, we have, if not positive proof, at least very good reason, for believing it intended as a series of lyrics; but, granting the epic intention, I can say only that the work is based in an imperfect sense of Art. The modern epic is, of the supposititious ancient model, but an inconsiderate and blindfold imitation. But the day of these artistic anomalies is over. If, at any time, any very long poem *were* popular in reality, which I doubt, it is at least clear that no very long poem will ever be popular again.

* * *

On the other hand, it is clear that a poem may be improperly brief. Undue brevity degenerates into mere epigrammatism. A *very* short poem, while now and then producing a brilliant or vivid, never produces a profound or enduring effect. There must be the steady pressing down of the stamp upon the wax.

* * *

While the epic mania—while the idea that, to merit in poetry, prolixity is indispensable—has, for some years past, been gradually dying out of the public mind, by mere dint of its own absurdity, we find it succeeded by a heresy too palpably false to be long tolerated, but one which, in the brief period it has already endured, may be said to have accomplished more in the corruption of our Poetical Literature than all its other enemies combined. I allude to the heresy of *The Didactic*. It has been assumed, tacitly and avowedly, directly and indirectly, that the ultimate object of all Poetry is Truth. Every poem, it is said, should inculcate a moral; and by this moral is the poetical merit of the work to be adjudged. We Americans especially have patronised this happy idea; and we Bostonians, very especially, have developed it in full. We have taken it into our heads that to write a poem simply for the poem's sake, and to acknowledge such to have been our design, would be to confess ourselves radically wanting in the true Poetic dignity and force:—but the simple fact is, that, would we but permit ourselves to look into our own souls, we should immediately there discover that under the sun there neither exists nor *can* exist any work more thoroughly dignified—more supremely noble than this very poem—this poem *per se*—this poem which is a poem and nothing more—this poem written solely for the poem's sake.

With as deep a reverence for the True as ever inspired the bosom of man, I would, nevertheless, limit, in some measure, its modes of inculcation. I would limit to enforce them. I would not enfeeble them by dissipation. The demands of Truth are severe. She has no sympathy with the myrtles. All *that* which is so indispensable in Song, is precisely all *that* with which *she* has nothing whatever to do. It is but making her a flaunting paradox, to wreathe her in gems and flowers. In enforcing a truth, we need severity rather than efflorescence of language. We must be simple, precise, terse. We must be cool, calm, unimpassioned. In a word, we must be in that mood which, as nearly as possible, is the exact converse of the poetical. *He* must be blind indeed who does not perceive the radical and chasmal differences between the truthful and the poetical modes of inculcation. He must be theory-mad beyond redemption who, in spite of these differences, shall still persist in attempting to reconcile the obstinate oils and waters of Poetry and Truth.

Dividing the world of mind into its three most immediately obvious distinctions, we have the Pure Intellect, Taste, and the Moral Sense. I place Taste in the middle, because it is just this position which, in the mind, it occupies. It holds intimate relations with either extreme; but from the Moral Sense is separated by so faint a difference that Aristotle has not hesitated to place some of its operations among the virtues themselves. Nevertheless, we find the offices of the trio marked with a sufficient distinction. Just as the intellect concerns itself with Truth, so Taste informs us of the Beautiful while the Moral Sense is regardful of Duty. Of this latter, while Conscience teaches the obligation, and Reason the expediency, Taste contents herself with displaying the charms:—waging war upon Vice solely on the ground of her deformity—her disproportion—her animosity to the fitting, to the appropriate, to the harmonious—in a word, to Beauty.

An immortal instinct, deep within the spirit of man, is thus, plainly, a sense of the Beautiful. This it is which administers to his delight in the manifold forms, and sounds, and odours, and sentiments amid which he exists. And just as the lily is repeated in the lake, or the eyes of Amaryllis in the mirror, so is the mere oral or written repetition of these forms, and sounds, and colours, and odours, and sentiments, a duplicate source of delight. But this mere repetition is not poetry. He who shall simply sing, with however glowing enthusiasm, or with however vivid a truth of description, of the sights, and sounds, and odours, and colours, and sentiments, which greet *him* in common with all mankind—he, I say, has yet failed to prove his divine title. There is still a something in the distance which he has been unable to attain. We have still a thirst unquenchable, to allay which he has not shown us the crystal springs. This thirst belongs to the immortality of Man. It is at once a consequence and an indication of his perennial existence. It is the desire of the moth for the star. It is no mere appreciation of the Beauty before us—but a wild effort to reach the Beauty above. Inspired by an ecstatic prescience of the glories beyond the grave, we struggle, by multiform combinations among the things and thoughts of Time, to attain a portion of that Loveliness whose very elements, perhaps, appertain to eternity alone. And thus when by Poetry—or when by Music, the most entrancing of the Poetic moods—we find ourselves melted into tears—we weep then—not as the Abbate Gravina supposes—through excess of pleasure, but through a certain, petulant, impatient sorrow at our inability to grasp *now* wholly, here on earth, at once and for ever, those divine and rapturous joys, of which *through* the poem, or *through* the music, we attain to but brief and indeterminate glimpses.

The struggle to apprehend the supernal Loveliness—this struggle, on the part of souls fittingly constituted—has given to the world all *that* which it (the world) has ever been enabled at once to understand and *to feel* as poetic.

The Poetic Sentiment, of course, may develope itself in various modes—in Painting, in Sculpture, in Architecture, in the Dance—very especially in Music,—and very peculiarly, and with a wide field, in the composition of the Landscape Garden. Our present theme, however, has regard only to its manifestation in words. And here let me speak briefly on the topic of rhythm. Contenting myself with the certainty that Music, in its various modes of metre, rhythm, and rhyme, is of so vast a moment in Poetry as never to be wisely rejected—is so vitally important an adjunct, that he is simply silly who declines its assistance, I will not now pause to maintain its absolute essentiality. It is in Music, perhaps, that the soul most nearly attains the great end for which, when inspired by the Poetic Sentiment, it struggles—the creation of supernal Beauty. It *may* be, indeed, that here this sublime end is, now and then, attained *in fact*. We are often made to feel, with a shivering delight, that from an earthly harp are stricken notes which *cannot* have been unfamiliar to the angels. And thus there can be little doubt that in the union of Poetry with Music in its popular sense, we shall find the widest field for the Poetic development. The old Bards and Minnesingers had advantages which we do not possess—and Thomas Moore, singing his own songs, was, in the most legitimate manner, perfecting them as poems.

To recapitulate, then:—I would define, in brief, the Poetry of words as *The Rhythmical Creation of Beauty*. Its sole arbiter is Taste. With the Intellect or with the Conscience, it has only collateral relations. Unless incidentally, it has no concern whatever either with Duty or with Truth.

A few words, however, in explanation. *That* pleasure which

is at once the most pure, the most elevating, and the most intense, is derived, I maintain, from the contemplation of the Beautiful. In the contemplation of Beauty we alone find it possible to attain that pleasurable elevation, or excitement, *of the soul,* which we recognize as the Poetic Sentiment, and which is so easily distinguished from Truth, which is the satisfaction of the Reason, or from Passion, which is the excitement of the heart. I make Beauty, therefore—using the word as inclusive of the sublime—I make Beauty the province of the poem, simply because it is an obvious rule of Art that effects should be made to spring as directly as possible from their causes—no one as yet having been weak enough to deny that the peculiar elevation in question is at least *most readily* attainable in the poem. It by no means follows, however, that the incitements of Passion, or the precepts of Duty, or even the lessons of Truth, may not be introduced into a poem, and with advantage; for they may subserve, incidentally, in various ways, the general purposes of the work:—but the true artist will always contrive to tone them down in proper subjection to that *Beauty* which is the atmosphere and the real essence of the poem.

* * *

. . . While this [the poetic] Principle itself is, strictly and simply, the Human Aspiration for Supernal Beauty, the manifestation of the Principle is always found in *an elevating excitement of the Soul*—quite independent of that passion which is the intoxication of the Heart—or of that Truth which is the satisfaction of the Reason. For, in regard to Passion, alas! its tendency is to degrade rather than elevate the Soul. Love, on the contrary—Love—the true, the divine Eros—the Uranian, as distinguished from the Dionæan Venus—is unquestionably the purest and truest of all poetical themes. And in regard to Truth—if, to be sure, through the attainment of a truth, we are led to perceive a harmony where none was apparent before, we experience, at once, the true poetical effect—but this effect is referable to the harmony alone, and not in the least degree to the truth which merely served to render the harmony manifest.

THE PHILOSOPHY OF COMPOSITION*

* * *

LET us dismiss, as irrelevant to the poem, *per se,* the circumstance—or say the necessity—which, in the first place, gave rise to the intention of composing *a* poem that should suit at once the popular and the critical taste.

We commence, then, with this intention.

The initial consideration was that of extent. If any literary work is too long to be read at one sitting, we must be content to dispense with the immensely important effect derivable from unity of impression—for, if two sittings be required, the affairs of the world interfere, and every thing like totality is at once destroyed. But since, *ceteris paribus,* no poet can afford to dispense with *any thing* that may advance his design, it but remains to be seen whether there is, in extent, any advantage to counterbalance the loss of unity which attends it. Here I say no, at once. What we term a long poem, is, in fact, merely a succession of brief ones —that is to say, of brief poetical effects. It is needless to demonstrate that a poem is such, only inasmuch as it intensely excites, by elevating, the soul; and all intense excitements are, through a psychal necessity, brief. For this reason, at least one half of the "Paradise Lost" is essentially prose—a succession of poetical excitement interspersed, *inevitably,* with corresponding depressions—the whole being deprived, through the extremeness of its length, of the vastly important artistic element, totality, or unity, of effect.

It appears evident, then, that there is a distinct limit, as regards length, to all works of literary art—the limit of a single

* Text: *Graham's Magazine,* April, 1846.

sitting—and that, although in certain classes of prose composition, such as "Robinson Crusoe," (demanding no unity,) this limit may be advantageously overpassed, it can never properly be overpassed in a poem. Within this limit, the extent of a poem may be made to bear mathematical relation to its merit—in other words, to the excitement or elevation—again, in other words, to the degree of the true poetical effect which it is capable of inducing; for it is clear that the brevity must be in direct ratio of the intensity of the intended effect:—this, with one proviso—that a certain degree of duration is absolutely requisite for the production of any effect at all.

Holding in view these considerations, as well as that degree of excitement which I deemed not above the popular, while not below the critical, taste, I reached at once what I conceived the proper *length* for my intended poem—a length of about one hundred lines. It is, in fact, a hundred and eight.

My next thought concerned the choice of an impression, or effect, to be conveyed: and here I may as well observe that, throughout the construction, I kept steadily in view the design of rendering the work *universally* appreciable. I should be carried too far out of my immediate topic were I to demonstrate a point upon which I have repeatedly insisted, and which, with the poetical, stands not in the slightest need of demonstration—the point, I mean, that Beauty is the sole legitimate province of the poem. A few words, however, in elucidation of my real meaning, which some of my friends have evinced a disposition to misrepresent. That pleasure which is at once the most intense, the most elevating, and the most pure, is, I believe, found in the contemplation of the beautiful. When, indeed, men speak of Beauty, they mean, precisely, not a quality, as is supposed, but an effect—they refer, in short, just to that intense and pure elevation of *soul*—*not* of intellect, or of heart—upon which I have commented, and which is experienced in consequence of contemplating "the beautiful." Now I designate Beauty as the province of the poem, merely because it is an obvious rule of Art that effects should be made to spring from direct causes—that objects should be attained through means best adapted for their attainment—no one as yet having been weak enough to deny that the peculiar elevation alluded to is *most readily* attained in the poem. Now the object, Truth, or the satisfaction of the intellect, and the object Passion, or the exitement of the heart, are, although attainable, to a certain extent, in poetry, far more readily attainable in prose. Truth, in fact, demands a precision, and Passion a *homeliness* (the truly passionate will comprehend me) which are absolutely antagonistic to that Beauty which, I maintain, is the excitement, or pleasurable elevation, of the soul. It by no means follows from any thing here said, that passion, or even truth, may not be introduced, and even profitably introduced, into a poem—for they may serve in elucidation, or aid the general effect, as do discords in music, by contrast—but the true artist will always contrive, first, to tone them into proper subservience to the predominant aim, and, secondly, to enveil them, as far as possible, in that Beauty which is the atmosphere and the essence of the poem.

Regarding, then, Beauty as my province, my next question referred to the *tone* of its highest manifestation—and all experience has shown that this tone is one of *sadness*. Beauty of whatever kind, in its supreme development, invariably excites the sensitive soul to tears. Melancholy is thus the most legitimate of all the poetical tones.

The length, the province, and the tone, being thus determined, I betook myself to ordinary induction, with the view of obtaining some artistic piquancy which might serve me as a keynote in the construction of the poem—some pivot upon which the whole structure might turn. In carefully thinking over all the usual artistic effects—or more properly *points*, in the theatrical sense—I did not fail to perceive immediately that no one had been so universally employed as that of the *refrain*. The universality of its employment sufficed to assure me of its intrinsic value, and spared me the necessity of submitting it to analysis. I considered it, however, with regard to its susceptibility of improvements, and soon saw it to be in a primitive condition. As commonly used, the *refrain,* or burden, not only is limited to lyric verse, but depends for its impression upon the force of monotone—both in sound and thought. The pleasure is deduced solely from the sense of identity—of repetition. I resolved to diversify, and so heighten, the effect, by adhering, in general, to the monotone of sound, while I continually varied that of thought: that is to say, I determined to produce continuously novel effects, by the variation of *the application* of the *refrain*—the *refrain* itself remaining, for the most part, unvaried.

These points being settled, I next bethought me of the *nature* of my *refrain.* Since its application was to be repeatedly varied, it was clear that the *refrain* itself must be brief, for there would have been an insurmountable difficulty in frequent variations of application in any sentence of length. In proportion to the brevity of the sentence, would, of course, be the facility of the variation. This led me at once to a single word as the best *refrain.*

The question now arose as to the *character* of the word. Having made up my mind to a *refrain,* the division of the poem into stanzas was, of course, a corollary: the *refrain* forming the close of each stanza. That such a close, to have force, must be sonorous and susceptible of protracted emphasis, admitted no doubt: and these considerations inevitably led me to the long *o* as the most sonorous vowel, in connection with *r* as the most producible consonant.

The sound of the *refrain* being thus determined, it became necessary to select a word embodying this sound, and at the same time in the fullest possible keeping with that melancholy which I had pre-determined as the tone of the poem. In such a search it would have been absolutely impossible to overlook the word "Nevermore." In fact, it was the very first which presented itself.

The next *desideratum* was a pretext for the continuous use of the one word "nevermore." In observing the difficulty which I at once found in inventing a sufficiently plausible reason for its continuous repetition, I did not fail to perceive that this difficulty arose solely from the pre-assumption that the word was to be so continuously or monotonously spoken by a *human* being—I did not fail to perceive, in short, that the difficulty lay in the reconciliation of this monontony with the exercise of reason on the part of the creature repeating the word. Here, then, immediately arose the idea of a *non*-reasoning creature capable of speech; and, very naturally, a parrot, in the first instance, suggested itself, but was superseded forthwith by a Raven, as equally capable of speech, and infinitely more in keeping with the intended *tone.*

I had now gone so far as the conception of a Raven—the bird of ill omen—monotonously repeating the one word, "Nevermore," at the conclusion of each stanza, in a poem of melancholy tone, and in length about one hundred lines. Now, never losing sight of the object *supremeness,* or perfection, at all points, I asked myself—"Of all melancholy topics, what, according to the *universal* understanding of mankind, is the *most* melancholy?" Death—was the obvious reply. "And when," I said, "is this most melancholy of topics most poetical?" From what I have already explained at some length, the answer, here also, is obvious—"When it most closely allies itself to *Beauty:* the death, then, of a beautiful woman is, unquestionably, the most poetical topic in the world—and equally is it beyond doubt that the lips best suited for such topic are those of a bereaved lover."

I had now to combine the two ideas, of a lover lamenting his deceased mistress and a Raven continuously repeating the word "Nevermore."—I had to combine these, bearing in mind my design of varying, at every turn, the *application* of the word repeated; but the only intelligible mode of such combination is that of imagining the Raven employing the word in answer to the queries of the lover. And here it was that I saw at once the opportunity afforded for the effect on which I had been depending—that is to say, the effect of the *variation of application.* I saw that I could make the first query propounded by the lover—the first query to which the Raven should reply "Nevermore"—that I could make this first query a commonplace one—the second less so—the third still less, and so on—until at length the lover, startled from his original *nonchalance* by the melancholy character of the word itself—by its frequent repetition—and by a consideration of the ominous reputation of the fowl that uttered it—is at length excited to superstition, and wildly propounds queries of a far different character—queries whose solution he has passionately at heart—propounds them half in superstition and half in that species of despair which delights in self-torture—propounds them not altogether because he believes in the prophetic or demoniac character of the bird (which, reason assures him, is merely repeating a lesson learned by rote) but because he experiences a frenzied pleasure in so modeling his questions as to receive from the *expected* "Nevermore" the most delicious because the most intolerable of sorrow. Perceiving the opportunity thus afforded me—or, more strictly, thus forced upon me in the process of the construction—I first established in mind the climax, or concluding query—that query to which "Nevermore" should be in the last place an answer—that query in reply to which this word "Nevermore" should involve the uttermost conceivable amount of sorrow and despair.

Here then the poem may be said to have its beginning—at the end, where all works of art should begin—for it was here, at this point of my preconsiderations, that I first put pen to paper in the composition of the stanza:

> "Prophet," said I, "thing of evil! prophet still if bird or devil!
> By that heaven that bends above us—by that God we both adore
> Tell this soul with sorrow laden, if within the distant Aidenn,
> It shall clasp a sainted maiden whom the angels name Lenore—
> Clasp a rare and radiant maiden whom the angels name Lenore."
> Quoth the raven "Nevermore."

I composed this stanza, at this point, first that, by establishing the climax, I might the better vary and graduate, as regards seriousness and importance, the preceding queries of the lover—and, secondly, that I might definitely settle the rhythm, the metre, and the length and general arrangement of the stanza—as well as graduate the stanzas which were to precede, so that none of them might surpass this in rhythmical effect. Had I been able, in the subsequent composition, to construct more vigorous stanzas, I should, without scruple, have purposely enfeebled them, so as not to interfere with the climacteric effect.

And here I may as well say a few words of the versification. My first object (as usual) was originality. The extent to which this has been neglected, in versification, is one of the most unaccountable things in the world. Admitting that there is little possibility of variety in mere *rhythm,* it is still clear that the possible varieties of metre and stanza are absolutely infinite—and yet, *for centuries, no man, in verse, has ever done, or ever seemed to think of doing, an original thing.* The fact is, that originality (unless in minds of very unusual force) is by no means a matter, as some suppose, of impulse or intuition. In general, to be found, it must be elaborately sought, and although a positive merit of the highest class, demands in its attainment less of invention that negation.

Of course, I pretend to no originality in either the rhythm or metre of the "Raven." The former is trochaic—the latter is octameter acatalectic, alternating with heptameter catalectic repeated in the *refrain* of the fifth verse, and terminating with tetrameter catalectic. Less pedantically—the feet employed throughout (trochees) consist of a long syllable followed by a short: the first line of the stanza consists of eight of these feet—the second of seven and a half (in effect two-thirds)—the third of eight—the fourth of seven and a half—the fifth the same—the sixth three and a half. Now, each of these lines, taken individually, has been employed before, and what originality the "Raven" has, is in their *combination into stanza;* nothing even remotely approaching this combination has ever been attempted. The effect of this originality of combination is aided by other unusual, and some altogether novel effects, arising from an extension of the application of the principles of rhyme and alliteration.

The next point to be considered was the mode of bringing together the lover and the Raven—and the first branch of this consideration was the *locale*. For this the most natural suggestion might seem to be a forest, or the fields—but it has always appeared to me that a close *circumscription of space* is absolutely necessary to the effect of insulated incident:—it has the force of a frame to a picture. It has an indisputable moral power in keeping concentrated the attention, and, of course, must not be confounded with mere unity of place.

I determined, then, to place the lover in his chamber—in a chamber rendered sacred to him by memories of her who had frequented it. The room is represented as richly furnished—this in mere pursuance of the ideas I have already explained on the subject of Beauty, as the sole true poetical thesis.

The *locale* being thus determined, I had now to introduce the bird—and the thought of introducing him through the window, was inevitable. The idea of making the lover suppose, in the first instance, that the flapping of the wings of the bird against the shutter, is a "tapping" at the door, originated in a wish to increase, by prolonging, the reader's curiosity, and in a desire to admit the incidental effect arising from the lover's throwing open the door, finding all dark, and thence adopting the half-fancy that it was the spirit of his mistress that knocked.

I made the night tempestuous, first, to account for the Raven's seeking admission, and secondly, for the effect of contrast with the (physical) serenity within the chamber.

I made the bird alight on the bust of Pallas, also for the effect of contrast between the marble and the plumage—it being understood that the bust was absolutely *suggested* by the bird—the bust of *Pallas* being chosen, first, as most in keeping with the scholarship of the lover, and, secondly, for the sonorousness of the word, Pallas, itself.

About the middle of the poem, also, I have availed myself of the force of contrast, with a view of deepening the ultimate impression. For example, an air of the fantastic—approaching as nearly to the ludicrous as was admissible—is given to the Raven's entrance. He comes in "with many a flirt and flutter."

> Not the *least obeisance made he*—not a moment stopped or stayed he,
> *But with mien of lord or lady,* perched above my chamber door.

In the two stanzas which follow, the design is more obviously carried out:—

> Then this ebony bird beguiling my sad fancy into smiling
> By the *grave and stern decorum of the countenance it wore,*
> "Though thy *crest be shorn and shaven* thou," I said, "art sure no craven,
> Ghastly grim and ancient Raven wandering from the nightly shore—
> Tell me what thy lordly name is on the Night's Plutonian shore?"
> Quoth the Raven "Nevermore."
>
> Much I marvelled *this ungainly fowl* to hear discourse so plainly
> Though its answer little meaning—little relevancy bore;
> For we cannot help agreeing that no living human being
> *Ever yet was blessed with seeing bird above his chamber door—*
> *Bird or beast upon the sculptured bust above his chamber door,*
> With such name as "Nevermore."

The effect of the *dénouement* being thus provided for, I immediately drop the fantastic for a tone of the most profound seriousness:—this tone commencing in the stanza directly following the one last quoted, with the line,

> But the Raven, sitting lonely on that placid bust, spoke only, etc.

From this epoch the lover no longer jests—no longer sees any thing even of the fantastic in the Raven's demeanor. He speaks of him as a "grim, ungainly, ghastly, gaunt, and ominous bird of yore," and feels the "fiery eyes" burning into his "bosom's core." This revolution of thought, or fancy, on the lover's part, is intended to induce a similar one on the part of the reader—to bring the mind into a proper frame for the *dénouement*—which is now brought about as rapidly and as *directly* as possible.

With the *dénouement* proper—with the Raven's reply, "Nevermore," to the lover's final demand if he shall meet his mistress in another world—the poem, in its obvious phase, that of a simple narrative, may be said to have its completion. So far, everything is within the limits of the accountable—of the real. A raven, having learned by rote the single word "Nevermore," and having escaped from the custody of its owner, is driven at midnight, through the violence of a storm, to seek admission at a window from which a light still gleams—the chamber-window of a student, occupied half in poring over a volume, half in dreaming of a beloved mistress deceased. The casement being thrown open at the fluttering of the bird's wings, the bird itself perches on the most convenient seat out of the immediate reach of the student, who, amused by the incident and the oddity of the visitor's demeanor, demands of it, in jest and without looking for a reply, its name. The raven addressed, answers with its customary word, "Nevermore"—a word which finds immediate echo in the melancholy heart of the student, who, giving utterance aloud to certain thoughts suggested by the occasion, is again startled by the fowl's repetition of "Nevermore." The student now guesses the state of the case, but is impelled, as I have before explained, by the human thirst for self-torture, and in part by superstition, to propound such queries to the bird as will bring him, the lover, the most of the luxury of sorrow, through the anticipated answer "Nevermore." With the indulgence, to the extreme, of this self-torture, the narration, in what I have termed its first or obvious phase, has a natural termination, and so far there has been no overstepping of the limits of the real.

But in subjects so handled, however skilfully, or with however vivid an array of incident, there is always a certain hardness or nakedness, which repels the artistical eye. Two things are invariably required—first, some amount of complexity, or more properly, adaptation; and, secondly, some amount of suggestiveness—some under-current, however indefinite, of meaning. It is this latter, in especial, which imparts to a work of art so much of that *richness* (to borrow from colloquy a forcible term) which we are too fond of confounding with *the ideal.* It is the *excess* of the suggested meaning—it is the rendering this the upper instead of the under current of the theme—which turns into prose (and that of the very flattest kind) the so-called poetry of the so-called transcendentalists.

Holding these opinions, I added the two concluding stanzas of the poem—their suggestiveness being thus made to pervade all the narrative which has preceded them. The under-current of meaning is rendered first apparent in the lines—

"Take thy beak from out *my heart,* and take thy form from off my door!"
Quoth the Raven "Nevermore!"

It will be observed that the words, "from out my heart," involve the first metaphorical expression in the poem. They, with the answer, "Nevermore," dispose the mind to seek a moral in all that has been previously narrated. The reader begins now to regard the Raven as emblematical—but it is not until the very last line of the very last stanza, that the intention of making him emblematical of *Mournful and Never-ending Remembrance* is permitted distinctly to be seen:

And the Raven, never flitting, still is sitting, still is sitting,
On the pallid bust of Pallas just above my chamber door;
And his eyes have all the seeming of a demon's that is dreaming,
And the lamplight o'er him streaming throws his shadow on the floor;
And my soul *from out that shadow* that lies floating on the floor
Shall be lifted—nevermore.

MARGINALIA*

. . . Man's chief idiosyncrasy being reason, it follows that his savage condition—his condition of action *without* reason—is his *un*natural state. The more he reasons, the nearer he approaches the position to which this chief idiosyncrasy irresistibly impels him; and not until he attains this position with exactitude—not until his reason has exhausted itself for his improvement—not until he has stepped upon the highest pinnacle of civilization—will his *natural* state be ultimately reached, or thoroughly determined.

* * *

It is the curse of a certain order of mind, that it can never rest satisfied with the consciousness of its ability to do a thing. Still less is it content with doing it. It must both know and show how it was done.

* * *

To see distinctly the machinery—the wheels and pinions—of any work of Art is, unquestionably, of itself, a pleasure, but one which we are able to enjoy only just in proportion as we do *not* enjoy the legitimate effect designed by the artist:—and, in fact, it too often happens that to reflect analytically upon Art, is to reflect after the fashion of the mirrors in the temple of Smyrna, which represent the fairest images as deformed.

* * *

The more there are great excellences in a work, the less am I surprised at finding great demerits. When a book is said to have

* Text: *Democratic Review,* November, 1844.

many faults, nothing is decided, and I cannot tell, by this, whether it is excellent or execrable. It is said of another that it is without fault; if the account be just, the work *cannot* be excellent.—*Trublet.*

The "*cannot*" here is much too positive. The opinions of Trublet are wonderfully prevalent, but they are none the less demonstrably false. It is merely the *indolence* of genius which has given them currency. The truth seems to be that genius of the highest order lives in a state of perpetual vacillation between ambition and *the scorn of it.* The ambition of a great intellect is at best negative. It struggles—it labors—it creates—not because excellence is desirable, but because to be excelled where there exists a sense of the power to excel, is unendurable. Indeed I cannot help thinking that the *greatest* intellects (since these most clearly perceive the laughable absurdity of human ambition) remain contentedly "mute and inglorious." At all events, the *vacillation* of which I speak is the prominent feature of genius. Alternately inspired and depressed, its inequalities of mood are stamped upon its labors. This is the truth, generally—but it is a truth very different from the assertion involved in the "cannot" of Trublet. Give to genius a sufficiently enduring *motive,* and the result will be harmony, proportion, beauty, perfection—all, in this case, synonymous terms. Its supposed "inevitable" irregularities shall not be found:—for it is clear that the susceptibility to impressions of beauty—that susceptibility which is the most important element of genius—implies an equally exquisite sensitiveness and aversion to deformity. The motive—the *enduring* motive—has indeed, hitherto, fallen *rarely* to the lot of genius; but I could point to several compositions which, "without any fault," are yet "excellent"—supremely so. The world, too, is on the threshold of an epoch, wherein, with the aid of a calm philosophy, such compositions shall be ordinarily the work of that genius which is *true.* One of the first and most essential steps, in overpassing this threshold, will serve to kick out of the world's way this very idea of Trublet—this untenable and paradoxical idea of the incompatibility of genius with *art*.

* * *

About the "Antigone," as about all the ancient plays, there seems to me a certain *baldness,* the result of inexperience in art, but which pedantry would force us to believe the result of a studied and supremely artistic simplicity. Simplicity, indeed, is a very important feature in all true art—but *not* the simplicity which we see in the Greek drama. That of the Greek sculpture is everything that can be desired, because here the art in itself is simplicity in itself and its elements. The Greek sculptor chiselled his forms from what he saw before him every day, in a beauty nearer to perfection than any work of any Cleomenes in the world. But in the drama, the direct, straightforward, *un-German* Greek had no Nature so immediately presented from which to make copy. He did what he could—but I do not hesitate to say that that was exceedingly little worth. The profound sense of one or two tragic, or rather, melo-dramatic elements (such as the idea of inexorable Destiny)—this sense gleaming at intervals from out the darkness of the ancient stage, serves, in the very imperfection of its development, to show, not the dramatic ability, but the dramatic *in*ability of the ancients. In a word, the simple arts spring into perfection at their origin; the complex as inevitably demand the long and painfully progressive experience of ages. . . . The naked Senses sometimes see too little—but then *always* they see too much.

The *pure Imagination* chooses, from *either Beauty or Deformity,* only the most combinable things hitherto uncombined; the compound, as a general rule, partaking, in character, of beauty, or sublimity, in the ratio of the respective beauty or sublimity of the things combined—which are themselves still to be considered as atomic—that is to say, as previous combinations. But, as often analogously happens in physical chemistry, so not unfrequently does it occur in this chemistry of the intellect, that the admixture of two elements results in a something that has nothing of the qualities of one of them, or even nothing of the qualities of either. . . . Thus, the range of Imagination is unlimited. Its materials extend throughout the universe. Even out of deformities it fabricates that *Beauty* which is at once its sole object and its inevitable test. But, in general, the richness or force of the matters combined; the facility of discovering combinable novelties worth combining; and, especially, the absolute "chemical combination" of the completed mass—are the particulars to be regarded in our estimate of Imagination. It is this thorough harmony of an imaginative work which so often causes it to be undervalued by the thoughtless, through the character of *obviousness* which is superinduced. We are apt to find ourselves asking *why* it is that these combinations have never been imagined before.

How very commonly we hear it remarked, that such and such thoughts are beyond the compass of words! I do not believe that any thought, properly so called, is out of the reach of language. I fancy, rather, that where difficulty in expression is experienced, there is, in the intellect which experiences it, a want either of deliberateness or of method. For my own part, I have never had a thought which I could not set down in words, with even more distinctness than that with which I conceived it:—as I have before observed, the thought is logicalized by the effort at (written) expression.

There is, however, a class of fancies, of exquisite delicacy, which are *not* thoughts, and to which, *as yet*, I have found it absolutely impossible to adapt language. I use the word *fancies* at random, and merely because I must use *some* word; but the idea commonly attached to the term is not even remotely applicable to the shadows of shadows in question. They seem to me rather psychal than intellectual. They arise in the soul (alas, how rarely!) only at its epochs of most intense tranquillity—when the bodily and mental health are in perfection—and at those mere points of time where the confines of the waking world blend with those of the world of dreams. I am aware of these "fancies" only when I am upon the very brink of sleep, with the consciousness that I am so. I have satisfied myself that this condition exists but for an inappreciable *point* of time—yet it is crowded with these "shadows of shadows"; and for absolute *thought* there is demanded time's *endurance*. These "fancies" have in them a pleasurable ecstasy, as far beyond the most pleasurable of the world of wakefulness, or of dreams, as the Heaven of the Northman theology is beyond its Hell. I regard the visions, even as they arise, with an awe which, in some measure, moderates or tranquillizes the ecstasy—I so regard them, through a conviction (which seems a portion of the ecstasy itself) that this ecstasy, in itself, is of a character supernal to the Human Nature—is a glimpse of the spirit's outer world; and I arrive at this conclusion—if this term is at all applicable to instantaneous intuition—by a perception that the delight experienced has, as its element, but *the absoluteness of novelty*. I say the absoluteness—for in these fancies—let me now term them psychal impressions—there is really nothing even approximate in character to impressions ordinarily received. It is as if the five senses were supplanted by five myriad others alien to mortality.

Now, so entire is my faith in the *power of words,* that, at times, I have believed it impossible to embody even the evanescence of fancies such as I have attempted to describe. In experiments with this end in view, I have proceeded so far as, first, to control (when the bodily and mental health are good) the existence of the condition:—that is to say, I can now (unless when ill) be sure that the condition will supervene, if I so wish it, at the point of time already described: of its supervention, until lately, I could never be certain, even under the most favorable circumstances. I mean to say, merely, that now I can be sure, when all circumstances are favorable, of the supervention of the condition, and feel even the capacity of inducing or compelling it:—the favorable circumstances, however, are not the less rare—else had I compelled, already, the Heaven into the earth.

I have proceeded so far, secondly, as to prevent the lapse from *the point* of which I speak—the point of blending between wakefulness and sleep—as to prevent at will, I say, the lapse from this border-ground into the dominion of sleep. Not that I can *continue* the condition—not that I can render the point more than a point—but that I can startle myself from the point into wakefulness—and *thus transfer the point itself into the realm of Memory*—convey its impressions, or more properly their recollections, to a situation where (although still for a brief period) I can survey them with the eye of analysis.

For these reasons—that is to say, because I have been enabled to accomplish thus much—I do not altogether despair of embodying in words at least enough of the fancies in question to convey, to certain classes of intellect, a shadowy conception of their character.

In saying this I am not to be understood as supposing that the fancies, or psychal impressions, to which I allude, are confined to my individual self—are not, in a word, common to all mankind—for on this point it is quite impossible that I should form an opinion—but nothing can be more certain than that even a partial record of the impressions would startle the universal intellect of mankind, by the *supremeness of the novelty* of the material employed, and of its consequent suggestions. In a word—should I ever write a paper on this topic, the world will be compelled to acknowledge that, at last, I have done an original thing. . . . True passion is prosaic—homely. Any strong mental emotion stimulates *all* the mental faculties; thus grief the imagination:—but in proportion as the effect is strengthened, the cause surceases. The excited fancy triumphs—the grief is subdued—chastened,—is no longer grief. In this mood we are poetic, and it is clear that a poem now written will be poetic in the exact ratio of its dispassion. A passionate poem is a contradiction in terms. . . .

"What is Poetry?" notwithstanding Leigh Hunt's rigmarolic attempt at answering it, is a query that, with great care and deliberate agreement beforehand on the exact value of certain leading words, *may*, possibly, be settled to the partial satisfaction of a few analytical intellects, but which, in the existing condition of metaphysics, never *can* be settled to the satisfaction of the majority; for the question is purely metaphysical, and the whole science of metaphysics is at present a chaos, through the impossibility of fixing the meanings of the words which its very nature compels it to employ. But as regards versification, this difficulty is only partial; for although one-third of the topic may be considered metaphysical, and thus may be mooted at the fancy of this individual or of that, still the remaining two-thirds belong, undeniably, to the mathematics. The questions ordinarily discussed with so much gravity in regard to rhythm, metre, etc., are susceptible of positive adjustment by demonstration. Their laws are merely a portion of the Median laws of form and quantity—of relation. In respect, then, to any of these ordinary questions—these sillily moot points which so often arise in common criticism—the prosodist would speak as weakly in saying "this or that proposition is *probably* so and so, or *possibly* so and so," as would the mathematician in admitting that, in his humble opinion, or if he were not greatly mistaken, any two sides of a triangle were, together, greater than the third side. I must add, however, as some palliation of the discussions referred to, and of the objections so often urged with a sneer to "particular theories of versification binding no one but their inventor"—that there is really extant no such work as a Prosody *Raisonnée*.

The object of what we call *scansion* is the distinct marking of the rhythmical flow. Scansion with accents or perpendicular lines between the feet—that is to say scansion *by* the voice only—is scansion *to* the ear only; and all very good in its way. The written scansion addresses the ear through the eye. In either case the object is the distinct marking of the rhythmical, musical, or reading flow. There *can* be no other object and there is none. Of course, then, the scansion and the reading flow should go hand in hand. The former must agree with the latter. The former represents and expresses the latter; and is good or bad as it truly or falsely represents and expresses it. If by the written scansion of a line we are not enabled to perceive any rhythm or music in the line, then either the line is unrhythmical or the scansion false. . . . in a series of lines, if one line contains more syllables than the law of the verse demands, and if, nevertheless, this line is pronounced in the same time, upon the whole, as the rest of the lines, then this line suggests celerity—on account of the increased rapidity of enunciation required. Thus in the Greek Hexameter the dactylic lines—those most abounding in dactyls—serve best to convey the idea of rapid motion. The spondaic lines convey that of slowness.

. . . It is a gross mistake to suppose that the Greek dactylic line is "the model in this matter"—the matter of the English Alexandrine. The Greek dactylic line is of the same number of feet—bars—beats—pulsations—as the ordinary dactylic-spondaic lines among which it occurs. But the Alexandrine is longer by one foot—by one pulsation—than the pentameters among which it arises. For its pronunciation it demands *more time,* and therefore, *ceteris paribus,* it would well serve to convey the impression of length, or duration, and thus, indirectly, of slowness. I say *ceteris paribus*. But, by varying conditions, we can effect a total change in the impression conveyed. When the idea of slowness is conveyed by the Alexandrine, it is not conveyed by any slower enunciation of syllables—that is to say, it is not *directly* conveyed—but indirectly, through the idea of *length* in the whole line. Now, if we wish to convey, by means of an Alexandrine, the impression of velocity, we readily do so by giving rapidity to our enunciation of the syllables composing the several feet. To effect this, however, we must have *more* syllables, or we shall get through the whole line too quickly for the intended time. To get more syllables, all we have to do, is to use in place of iambuses what our prosodies call anapæsts.* Thus, in the line,

> Flies o'er the unbending corn and skims along the main,

the syllables *"the unbend"* form an anapæst and, demanding unusual rapidity of enunciation, in order that we may get them in the ordinary time of an iambus, serve to suggest celerity. By the elision of *e* in *the,* as is customary, the whole of the intended effect is lost; for *th'unbend* is nothing more than the usual iambus. In a word, whenever an Alexandrine expresses celerity, we shall find it to contain one or more anapæsts—the more anapæsts, the more decided the impression. But the tendency of the Alexandrine consisting merely of the usual iambuses, is to convey slowness—although it conveys this idea feebly, on account of conveying it indirectly. It follows, from what I have said, that the common pentameter, interspersed with anapæsts, would better convey celerity than the Alexandrine interspersed with them in a similar degree;—and it unquestionably does.

I have never yet seen an English heroic verse on the proper model of the Greek—although there have been innumerable attempts, among which those of Coleridge are, perhaps, the most absurd, next to those of Sir Philip Sidney and Longfellow. The author of "The Vision of Rubeta" has done better, and Percival better yet; but no one has seemed to suspect that the natural preponderance of spondaic words in the Latin and Greek must, in the English, be supplied by art—that is to say, by a careful

* I use the prosodial word "anapæst," merely because here I have no space to show . . . that the additional syllable introduced, does *not* make the foot an anapæst, or the equivalent of an anapæst, and that, if it did, it would spoil the line. On this topic, and on all topics connected with verse, there is not a prosody in existence which is not a mere jumble of the grossest error.

culling of the few spondaic words which the language affords—as, for example, here:

> Man is a | complex, | compound, | compost, | yet is he | God-born.

This, to all intents, is a Greek hexameter, but then its spondees are spondees, and not mere trochees. The verses of Coleridge and others are dissonant, for the simple reason that there is no equality in time between a trochee and a dactyl. When Sir Philip Sidney writes,

> So to the | woods Love | runnes as | well as | rides to the | palace,

he makes an heroic verse only to the eye; for "woods Love" is the only true spondee, "runs as," "well as," and "palace," have each the first syllable long and the second short—that is to say, they are all trochees, and occupy less time than the dactyls or spondee—hence the halting. Now, all this seems to be the simplest thing in the world, and the only wonder is how men professing to be scholars should attempt to engraft a verse, of which the spondee is an element, upon a stock which repels the spondee as antagonistical.

At Ermenonville, too, there is a striking instance of the Gallic rhythm with which a Frenchman regards the English verse. There Gerardin has the following inscription to the memory of Shenstone:

> This plain stone
> To William Shenstone.
> In his writings he displayed
> A mind natural;
> At Leasowes he laid
> Arcadian greens rural.

There are few Parisians, speaking English, who would find anything *particularly* the matter with this epitaph.

Few things have greater tendency than inversion, to render verse feeble and ineffective. In most cases where a line is spoken of as "forcible," the force may be referred to directness of expression. A vast majority of the passages which have become household through frequent quotation, owe their popularity either to this directness, or, in general, to the scorn of "poetic license." In short, as regards verbal construction, *the more prosaic* a poetical style is, the better. . . . What, in rhyme, first and principally pleases, may be referred to the human sense or appreciation of *equality*—the common element, as might be easily shown, of all the gratification we derive from music in its most extended sense —very especially in its modifications of metre and rhythm. We see, for example, a crystal, and are immediately interested by the equality between the sides and angles of one of its faces—but on bringing to view a second face, in all respects similar to our first, our pleasure seems to be *squared*—on bringing to view a third, it appears to be *cubed,* and so on: I have no doubt, indeed, that the delight experienced, if measurable, would be found to have exact mathematical relations, such, or nearly such, as I suggest—that is to say, as far as a certain point, beyond which there would be a decrease, in similar relations. Now here, as the ultimate result of analysis, we reach the sense of mere *equality,* or rather the human delight in this sense; and it was an instinct, rather than a clear comprehension of this delight as a principle, which, in the first instance, led the poet to attempt an increase of the effect arising from the mere similarity (that is to say equality) between two sounds—led him, I say, to attempt increasing this effect by making a secondary equalization, in placing the rhymes at equal distances—that is, at the ends of lines of equal length. In this manner, rhyme and the termination of the line grew connected in men's thoughts—grew into a conventionalism—the principle being lost sight of altogether. And it was simply because Pindaric verses had, before this epoch, existed—*i.e.,* verses of unequal length—that rhymes were subsequently found at unequal distances. It was for this reason solely, I say—for none more profound—rhyme had come to be regarded as of right appertaining to the end of verse—and here we complain that the matter has finally rested.

But it is clear that there was much more to be considered. So far, the sense of equality alone, entered the effect; or, if this equality was slightly varied, it was varied only through an accident—the accident of the existence of Pindaric metres. It will be seen that the rhymes were always anticipated. The eye, catching the end of a verse, whether long or short, expected, for the ear, a rhyme. The great element of unexpectedness was not dreamed of —that is to say, of novelty—of originality. "But," says Lord Bacon, (how justly!) "there is no exquisite beauty without some strangeness in the proportions." Take away this element of strangeness—of unexpectedness—of novelty—of originality—call it what we will—and all that is ethereal in loveliness is lost at once. We lose—we miss the unknown—the vague—the uncomprehended, because offered before we have time to examine and comprehend. We lose, in short, all that assimilates the beauty of earth with what we dream of the beauty of Heaven.

Perfection of rhyme is attainable only in the combination of the two elements, Equality and Unexpectedness. But as evil cannot exist without good, so unexpectedness must arise from expectedness. We do not contend for mere arbitrariness of rhyme. In the first place, we must have equi-distant or regularly recurring rhymes, to form the basis, expectedness, out of which arises the element, unexpectedness, by the introduction of rhymes, not arbitrarily, but with an eye to the greatest amount of unexpectedness. We should not introduce them, for example, at such points that the entire line is a multiple of the syllables preceding the points. When, for instance, I write—

> And the silken, sad, uncertain rustling of each purple curtain,

I produce more, to be sure, but not remarkably more than the ordinary effect of rhymes regularly recurring at the end of lines;

for the number of syllables in the whole verse is merely a multiple of the number of syllables preceding the rhyme introduced at the middle, and there is still left, therefore, a certain degree of expectedness. What there is of the element unexpectedness, is addressed, in fact, to the eye only—for the ear divides the verse into two ordinary lines, thus—

And the silken, sad, uncertain
Rustling of each purple curtain.

I obtain, however, the whole effect of unexpectedness, when I write—

Thrilled me, *filled* me with fantastic terrors never felt before.

There are few cases in which mere popularity should be considered a proper test of merit; but the case of song-writing is, I think, one of the few. In speaking of song-writing, I mean, of course, the composition of brief poems with an eye to their adaptation for music in the vulgar sense. In this ultimate destination of the song proper, lies its essence—its genius. It is the strict reference to music—it is the dependence upon modulated expression—which gives to this branch of letters a character altogether *unique,* and separates it, in great measure and in a manner not sufficiently considered, from ordinary literature; rendering it independent of merely ordinary proprieties; allowing it, and in fact demanding for it, a wide latitude of Law; absolutely, insisting upon a certain wild license and *indefinitiveness*—an indefinitiveness recognized by every musician who is not a mere fiddler, as an important point in the philosophy of his science—as the *soul,* indeed, of the sensations derivable from its practice—sensations which bewilder while they enthral—and which would *not* so enthral if they did not so bewilder.

* * *

That *indefinitiveness* which is, at least, *one* of the essentials of true music, must, of course, be kept in view by the song-writer;

while, by the critic, it should always be considered in his estimate of the *song*. It is, in the author, a consciousness—sometimes merely an instinctive appreciation, of this necessity for the indefinite, which imparts to all songs, rightly conceived, that free, affluent, and *hearty* manner, little scrupulous about niceties of phrase, which cannot be better expressed than by the hackneyed French word *abandonnement,* and which is so strikingly exemplified in both the serious and joyous ballads and carols of our old English progenitors. Wherever verse has been found most strictly married to music, this feature prevails.

There are moments when, even to the sober eye of Reason, the world of our sad humanity must assume the aspect of Hell; but the Imagination of Man is no Carathis, to explore with impunity its every cavern. Alas! the grim legion of sepulchral terrors can*not* be regarded as altogether fanciful; but like the Demons in whose company Afrasiab made his voyage down the Oxus, they must sleep, or they will devour us—they must be suffered to slumber, or we perish. . . . That individuals *have* so soared above the plane of their race, is scarcely to be questioned; but, in looking back through history for traces of their existence, we should pass over all biographies of "the good and the great," while we search carefully the slight records of wretches who died in prison, in Bedlam, or upon the gallows.

If any ambitious man have a fancy to revolutionize, at one effort, the universal world of human thought, human opinion, and human sentiment, the opportunity is his own—the road to immortal renown lies straight, open, and unencumbered before him. All that he has to do is write and publish a very little book. Its title should be simple—a few plain words—"My Heart Laid Bare." But—this little book must be *true to its title.*

Now, is it not very singular that, with the rabid thirst for notoriety which distinguishes so many of mankind—so many, too, who care not a fig what is thought of them after death, there should not be found one man having sufficient hardihood to write this little book? To *write,* I say. There are ten thousand men who, if the book were once written, would laugh at the notion of being disturbed by its publication during their life, and who could not even conceive *why* they should object to its being published after their death. But to write it—*there* is the rub. No man dare write it. No man ever will dare write it. No man *could* write it, even if he dared. The paper would shrivel and blaze at every touch of the fiery pen.

REVIEW OF NATHANIEL HAWTHORNE'S *TWICE-TOLD TALES**

THE PIECES in the volumes entitled "Twice-Told Tales," are now in their third republication, and, of course, are thrice-told. Moreover, they are by no means *all* tales, either in the ordinary or in the legitimate understanding of the term. Many of them are pure essays; for example, "Sights from a Steeple," "Sunday at Home," "Little Annie's Ramble," "A Rill from the Town Pump," "The Toll-Gatherer's Day," "The Haunted Mind," "The Sister Years," "Snow-Flakes," "Night Sketches," and "Foot-Prints on the Sea-Shore." I mention these matters chiefly on account of their discrepancy with that marked precision and finish by which the body of the work is distinguished.

Of the Essays just named, I must be content to speak in brief. They are each and all beautiful, without being characterized by the polish and adaptation so visible in the tales proper. A painter would at once note their leading or predominant feature, and style it *repose*. There is no attempt at effect. All is quiet, thoughtful, subdued. Yet this repose may exist simultaneously with high originality of thought; and Mr. Hawthorne has demonstrated the fact. At every turn we meet with novel combination; yet these combinations never surpass the limits of the quiet. We are soothed as we read; and with all is a calm astonishment that

* Revision published in *Godey's Lady's Book,* 1847, together with a review of *Mosses from an Old Manse;* original version published in *Graham's Lady's and Gentleman's Magazine,* 1842.

ideas so apparently obvious have never occurred or been presented to us before. Herein our author differs materially from Lamb or Hunt or Hazlitt—who, with vivid originality of manner and expression, have less of the true novelty of thought than is generally supposed, and whose originality, at best, has an uneasy and meretricious quaintness, replete with startling effects unfounded in nature, and inducing trains of reflection which lead to no satisfactory result. The Essays of Hawthorne have much of the character of Irving, with more of originality, and less of finish; while, compared with the Spectator, they have a vast superiority at all points. The Spectator, Mr. Irving, and Hawthorne have in common that tranquil and subdued manner which I have chosen to denominate *repose;* but, in the case of the two former, this repose is attained rather by the absence of novel combination, or of originality, than otherwise, and consists chiefly in the calm, quiet, unostentatious expression of commonplace thoughts, in an unambitious, unadulterated Saxon. In them, by strong effort, we are made to conceive the absence of all. In the essays before me the absence of effort is too obvious to be mistaken, and a strong undercurrent of *suggestion* runs continuously beneath the upper stream of the tranquil thesis. In short, these effusions of Mr. Hawthorne are the product of a truly imaginative intellect, restrained, and in some measure repressed, by fastidiousness of taste, by constitutional melancholy, and by indolence.

But it is of his tales that I desire principally to speak. The tale proper, in my opinion, affords unquestionably the fairest field for the exercise of the loftiest talent, which can be afforded by the wide domains of mere prose. Were I bidden to say how the highest genius could be most advantageously employed for the best display of its own powers, I should answer, without hesitation—in the composition of a rhymed poem, not to exceed in length what might be perused in an hour. Within this limit alone can the highest order of true poetry exist. I need only here say, upon this topic, that, in almost all classes of composition, the unity of effect or impression is a point of the greatest importance. It is clear, moreover, that this unity cannot be thoroughly preserved in productions whose perusal cannot be completed at one sitting. We may continue the reading of a prose composition, from the very nature of prose itself, much longer than we can persevere, to any good purpose, in the perusal of a poem. This latter, if truly fulfilling the demands of the poetic sentiment, induces an exaltation of the soul which cannot be long sustained. All high excitements are necessarily transient. Thus a long poem is a paradox. And, without unity of impression, the deepest effects cannot be brought about. Epics were the offspring of an imperfect sense of Art, and their reign is no more. A poem *too* brief may produce a vivid, but never an intense or enduring impression. Without a certain continuity of effort—without a certain duration of repetition or purpose—the soul is never deeply moved. There must be the dropping of the water upon the rock. De Béranger has wrought brilliant things—pungent and spirit-stirring—but, like all immassive bodies, they lack *momentum*, and thus fail to satisfy the poetic Sentiment. They sparkle and excite, but, from want of continuity, fail deeply to impress. Extreme brevity will degenerate into epigrammatism; but the sin of extreme length is more unpardonable. *In medio tutissimus ibis.*

Were I called upon, however, to designate that class of composition which, next to such a poem as I have suggested, should best fulfil the demands of high genius—should offer it the most advantageous field of exertion—I should unhesitatingly speak of the prose tale as Mr. Hawthorne has here exemplified it. I allude to the short prose narrative, requiring from a half-hour to one or two hours in its perusal. The ordinary novel is objectionable, from its length, for reasons already stated in substance. As it cannot be read at one sitting, it deprives itself, of course, of the immense force derivable from *totality.* Worldly interests intervening during the pauses of perusal, modify, annul, or counteract, in a greater or less degree, the impressions of the book. But simple cessation in reading would, of itself, be sufficient to destroy the true unity. In the brief tale, however, the author is enabled to carry out the fulness of his intention, be it what it may. During the hour of perusal the soul of the reader is at the writer's control. There are no external or extrinsic influences—resulting from weariness or interruption.

A skilful literary artist has constructed a tale. If wise, he has not fashioned his thoughts to accommodate his incidents; but having conceived, with deliberate care, a certain unique or single *effect* to be wrought out, he then invents such incidents—he then combines such events as may best aid him in establishing this preconceived effect. If his very initial sentence tend not to the outbringing of this effect, then he has failed in his first step. In the whole composition there should be no word written, of which the tendency, direct or indirect, is not to the one pre-established design. And by such means, with such care and skill, a picture is at length painted which leaves in the mind of him who contemplates it with a kindred art, a sense of the fullest satisfaction. The idea of the tale has been presented unblemished, because undisturbed; and this is an end unattainable by the novel. Undue brevity is just as exceptionable here as in the poem; but undue length is yet more to be avoided.

We have said that the tale has a point of superiority even over the poem. In fact, while the *rhythm* of this latter is an essential aid in the development of the poem's highest idea—the idea of the Beautiful—the artificialities of this rhythm are an inseparable bar to the development of all points of thought or expression which have their basis in *Truth*. But Truth is often, and in very great degree, the aim of the tale. Some of the finest tales are tales of ratiocination. Thus the field of this species of composition, if not in so elevated a region on the mountain of Mind, is a table-land of far vaster extent than the domain of the mere poem. Its products are never so rich, but infinitely more numerous, and more appreciable by the mass of mankind. The writer of the prose tale, in short, may bring to his theme a vast variety of modes or inflections of thought and expression—(the ratiocinative, for example, the sarcastic or the humorous) which are not only antagonistical to the nature of the poem, but absolutely forbidden by one of its most peculiar and indispensable adjuncts; we allude, of course, to rhythm. It may be added, here, *par parenthèse,* that the author who aims at the purely beautiful in a prose tale is laboring at a great disadvantage. For Beauty can be better treated in the poem. Not so with terror, or passion, or horror, or a multitude of such other points. And here it will be seen how full of prejudice are the usual animadversions against those *tales of effect,* many fine examples of which were found in the earlier numbers of Blackwood. The impressions produced were wrought in a legitimate sphere of action, and constituted a legitimate although sometimes an exaggerated interest. They were relished by every man of genius: although there were found many men of genius who condemned them without just ground. The true critic will but demand that the design intended be accomplished, to the fullest extent, by means most advantageously applicable.

We have very few American tales of real merit—we may say, indeed, none, with the exception of "The Tales of a Traveller" of Washington Irving, and these "Twice-Told Tales" of Mr. Hawthorne. Some of the pieces of Mr. John Neal abound in vigor and originality; but in general, his compositions of this class are excessively diffuse, extravagant, and indicative of an imperfect sentiment of Art. Articles at random are, now and then, met with in our periodicals which might be advantageously compared with the best effusions of the British Magazines; but, upon the whole, we are far behind our progenitors in this department of literature.

Of Mr. Hawthorne's Tales we would say, emphatically, that they belong to the highest region of Art—an Art subservient to genius of a very lofty order. We had supposed, with good reason for so supposing, that he had been thrust into his present position by one of the impudent *cliques* which beset our literature, and whose pretensions it is our full purpose to expose at the earliest opportunity; but we have been most agreeably mistaken. We know of few compositions which the critic can more honestly commend than these "Twice-Told Tales." As Americans, we feel proud of the book.

Mr. Hawthorne's distinctive trait is invention, creation, imagination, originality—a trait which, in the literature of fiction, is positively worth all the rest. But the nature of the originality, so far as regards its manifestation in letters, is but imperfectly understood. The inventive or original mind as frequently displays itself in novelty of *tone* as in novelty of matter. Mr. Hawthorne is original in *all* points.

It would be a matter of some difficulty to designate the best of these tales; we repeat that, without exception, they are beautiful. "Wakefield" is remarkable for the skill with which an old idea—a well-known incident—is worked up or discussed. A man of whims conceives the purpose of quitting his wife and residing *incognito,* for twenty years in her immediate neighborhood. Something of this kind actually happened in London. The force of Mr. Hawthorne's tale lies in the analysis of the motives which must or might have impelled the husband to such folly, in the first instance, with the possible causes of his perseverance. Upon this thesis a sketch of singular power has been constructed. "The Wedding Knell" is full of the boldest imagination—an imagination fully controlled by taste. The most captious critic could find no flaw in this production. "The Minister's Black Veil" is a masterly composition of which the sole defect is that to the rabble its exquisite skill will be *caviare*. The *obvious* meaning of this article will be found to smother its insinuated one. The *moral* put into the mouth of the dying minister will be supposed to convey the *true* import of the narrative; and that a crime of dark dye, (having reference to the "young lady") has been committed, is a point which only minds congenial with that of the author will perceive. "Mr. Higginbotham's Catastrophe" is vividly original and managed most dexterously. "Dr. Heidegger's Experiment" is exceedingly well imagined, and executed with surpassing ability. The artist breathes in every line of it. "The White Old Maid" is objectionable, even more than the "Minister's Black Veil," on the score of its mysticism. Even with the thoughtful and analytic, there will be much trouble in penetrating its entire import.

"The Hollow of the Three Hills" we would quote in full, had we space;—not as evincing higher talent than any of the other pieces, but as affording an excellent example of the author's peculiar ability. The subject is commonplace. A witch subjects the Distant and the Past to the view of a mourner. It has been the fashion to describe, in such cases, a mirror in which the images of the absent appear; or a cloud of smoke is made to arise, and thence the figures are gradually unfolded. Mr. Hawthorne has wonderfully heightened his effect by making the ear, in place of the eye, the medium by which the fantasy is conveyed. The head of the mourner is enveloped in the cloak of the witch, and within its magic folds there arise sounds which have an all-sufficient intelligence. Throughout this article also, the artist is conspicuous—not more in positive than in negative merits. Not only is all done that should be done, but (what perhaps is an end with more difficulty attained) there is nothing done which should not be. Every word *tells,* and there is not a word which does *not* tell.

In "Howe's Masquerade" we observe something which resembles a plagiarism—but which *may* be a very flattering coincidence of thought. We quote the passage in question.

> *With a dark flush of wrath* upon his brow they saw the general *draw his sword* and *advance to meet* the figure *in the cloak* before the latter had stepped one pace upon the floor. *"Villain, unmuffle yourself,"* cried he, "you pass no farther!" The figure, without blenching a hair's breadth from the sword which was pointed at his breast, made a solemn pause, and *lowered the cape of the cloak* from his face, yet not sufficiently for the spectators to catch a glimpse of it. But Sir William Howe had evidently seen enough. The sternness of his countenance gave place to a look of wild amazement, if not horror, while he recoiled several steps from the figure, *and let fall his sword upon the floor.*—See vol. 2, p. 20.

The idea here is, that the figure in the cloak is the phantom or reduplication of Sir William Howe; but in an article called "William Wilson," one of the "Tales of the Grotesque and Arabesque," we have not only the same idea, but the same idea similarly presented in several respects. We quote two paragraphs, which our readers may compare with what has been already given. We have italicized, above, the immediate particulars of resemblance.

> The brief moment in which I averted my eyes had been sufficient to produce, apparently, a material change in the arrangement at the upper or farther end of the room. A large mirror, it appeared to me, now stood where none had been perceptible before; and as I stepped up to it in extremity of terror, mine own image, but with features all pale and dabbled in blood, *advanced* with a feeble and tottering gait to meet me. Thus it appeared I say, but was not. It was Wilson, who then stood before me in the agonies of dissolution. Not a line in all the marked and singular lineaments of that face which was not even identically mine own. *His mask and cloak lay where he had thrown them, upon the floor.* Vol. 2, p. 336.

Here, it will be observed that, not only are the two general conceptions identical, but there are various *points* of similarity. In each case the figure seen is the wraith or duplication of the beholder. In each case the scene is a masquerade. In each case the figure is cloaked. In each, there is a quarrel—that is to say, angry words pass between the parties. In each the beholder is enraged. In each the cloak and sword fall upon the floor. The "villain, unmuffle yourself," of Mr. H. is precisely paralleled by a passage at page 56, of "William Wilson."

I must hasten to conclude this paper with a summary of Mr. Hawthorne's merits and demerits.

He is peculiar and *not* original—unless in those detailed fancies and detached thoughts which his want of general originality will deprive of the appreciation due to them, in preventing them from ever reaching the *public* eye. He is infinitely too fond of allegory, and can never hope for popularity so long as he persists in it. This he will not do, for allegory is at war with the whole tone of his nature, which disports itself never so well as when escaping from the mysticism of his Goodman Browns and White Old Maids into the hearty, genial, but still Indian-summer sunshine of his Wakefields and Little Annie's Rambles. Indeed, *his* spirit of "metaphor run-mad" is clearly imbibed from the phalanx and phalanstery atmosphere in which he has been so long struggling for breath. He has not half the material for the exclusiveness of authorship that he possesses for its universality. He has the purest style, the finest taste, the most available scholarship, the most delicate humor, the most touching pathos, the most radiant imagination, the most consummate ingenuity; and with these varied good qualities he has done *well* as a mystic. But is there any one of these qualities which should prevent his doing doubly as well in a career of honest, upright, sensible, prehensible and comprehensible things? Let him mend his pen, get a bottle of visible ink, come out from the Old Manse, cut Mr. Alcott, hang (if possible) the editor of "The Dial," and throw out of the window to the pigs all his odd numbers of "The North American Review."

Poetry

TO HELEN

Helen, thy beauty is to me
  Like those Nicean barks of yore,
That gently, o'er a perfumed sea,
  The weary, way-worn wanderer bore
  To his own native shore.

On desperate seas long wont to roam,
  Thy hyacinth hair, thy classic face,
Thy Naiad airs have brought me home
  To the glory that was Greece
And the grandeur that was Rome.

Lo! in yon brilliant window-niche
  How statue-like I see thee stand!
  The agate lamp within thy hand,
Ah! Psyche, from the regions which
  Are Holy Land!

LENORE

Ah, broken is the golden bowl! the spirit flown forever!
Let the bell toll!—a saintly soul floats on the Stygian river;
And, Guy De Vere, hast *thou* no tear?—weep now or never more!
See on yon drear and rigid bier low lies thy love, Lenore!
Come! let the burial rite be read—the funeral song be sung!—
An anthem for the queenliest dead that ever died so young—
A dirge for her the doubly dead in that she died so young.

"Wretches! ye loved her for her wealth and hated her for her pride,
And when she fell in feeble health, ye blessed her—that she died!
How *shall* the ritual, then, be read?—the requiem how be sung
By you—by yours, the evil eye,—by yours, the slanderous tongue
That did to death the innocence that died, and died so young?"

Peccavimus; but rave not thus! and let a Sabbath song
Go up to God so solemnly the dead may feel no wrong!
The sweet Lenore hath "gone before," with Hope, that flew beside,
Leaving thee wild for the dear child that should have been thy bride—
For her, the fair and *debonnaire,* that now so lowly lies,
The life upon her yellow hair but not within her eyes—
The life still there, upon her hair—the death upon her eyes.

Avaunt! to-night my heart is light. No dirge will I upraise,
But waft the angel on her flight with a pæan of old days!
Let *no* bell toll!—lest her sweet soul, amid its hallowed mirth,
Should catch the note, as it doth float up from the damnèd Earth.
To friends above, from fiends below, the indignant ghost is riven—
From Hell unto a high estate far up within the Heaven—
From grief and groan, to a golden throne, beside the King of Heaven."

SONNET—TO SCIENCE

Science! true daughter of Old Time thou art!
  Who alterest all things with thy peering eyes.
Why preyest thou thus upon the poet's heart,
  Vulture, whose wings are dull realities?
How should he love thee? or how deem thee wise?
  Who wouldst not leave him in his wandering
To seek for treasure in the jewelled skies,

Albeit he soared with an undaunted wing?
Hast thou not dragged Diana from her car?
And driven the Hamadryad from the wood
To seek a shelter in some happier star?
Hast thou not torn the Naiad from her flood,
The Elfin from the green grass, and from me
The summer dream beneath the tamarind tree?

TO ONE IN PARADISE

Thou wast that all to me, love,
For which my soul did pine—
A green isle in the sea, love,
A fountain and a shrine,
All wreathed with fairy fruits and flowers,
And all the flowers were mine.

Ah, dream too bright to last!
Ah, starry Hope! that didst arise
But to be overcast!
A voice from out the Future cries,
"On! on!"—but o'er the Past
(Dim gulf!) my spirit hovering lies
Mute, motionless, aghast!

For, alas! alas! with me
The light of Life is o'er!
No more—no more—no more—
(Such language holds the solemn sea
To the sands upon the shore)
Shall bloom the thunder-blasted tree,
Or the stricken eagle soar!

And all my days are trances,
And all my nightly dreams

Are where thy grey eye glances,
And where thy footstep gleams—
In what ethereal dances,
By what eternal streams.

ISRAFEL*

In Heaven a spirit doth dwell
"Whose heart-strings are a lute";
None sing so wildly well
As the angel Israfel,
And the giddy stars (so legends tell),
Ceasing their hymns, attend the spell
Of his voice, all mute.

Tottering above
In her highest noon,
The enamoured moon
Blushes with love,
While, to listen, the red levin
(With the rapid Pleiads, even,
Which were seven,)
Pauses in Heaven.

And they say (the starry choir
And the other listening things)
That Israfeli's fire
Is owing to that lyre
By which he sits and sings—
The trembling living wire
Of those unusual strings.

* And the angel Israfel, [whose heart-strings are a lute, and] who has the sweetest voice of all God's creatures.—KORAN.

But the skies that angel trod,
  Where deep thoughts are a duty,
Where Love's a grown-up God,
  Where the Houri glances are
Imbued with all the beauty
  Which we worship in a star.

Therefore, thou art not wrong,
  Israfeli, who despisest
An unimpassioned song;
To thee the laurels belong,
  Best bard, because the wisest!
Merrily live, and long!

The ecstasies above
  With thy burning measures suit—
Thy grief, thy joy, thy hate, thy love,
  With the fervour of thy lute—
  Well may the stars be mute!

Yes, Heaven is thine; but this
  Is a world of sweets and sours;
  Our flowers are merely—flowers,
And the shadow of thy perfect bliss
  Is the sunshine of ours.

If I could dwell
Where Israfel
  Hath dwelt, and he where I,
He might not sing so wildly well
  A mortal melody,
While a bolder note than this might swell
  From my lyre within the sky.

DREAM-LAND

By a route obscure and lonely,
Haunted by ill angels only,
Where an Eidolon, named NIGHT,
On a black throne reigns upright,
I have reached these lands but newly
From an ultimate dim Thule—
From a wild weird clime that lieth, sublime,
Out of SPACE—out of TIME.

Bottomless vales and boundless floods,
And chasms, and caves, and Titan woods,
With forms that no man can discover
For the tears that drip all over;
Mountains toppling evermore
Into seas without a shore;
Seas that restlessly aspire,
Surging, unto skies of fire;
Lakes that endlessly outspread
Their lone waters, lone and dead,—
Their still waters, still and chilly
With the snows of the lolling lilly.

By the lakes that thus outspread
Their lone waters, lone and dead,—
Their sad waters, sad and chilly
With the snows of the lolling lily,—
By the mountains—near the river
Murmuring lowly, murmuring ever,—
By the grey woods,—by the swamp
Where the toad and the newt encamp,—
By the dismal tarns and pools

Where dwell the Ghouls,—
By each spot the most unholy—
In each nook most melancholy,—
There the traveller meets, aghast,
Sheeted Memories of the Past—
Shrouded forms that start and sigh
As they pass the wanderer by—
White-robed forms of friends long given,
In agony, to the Earth—and Heaven.

For the heart whose woes are legion
'Tis a peaceful, soothing region—
For the spirit that walks in shadow
'Tis—oh, 'tis an Eldorado!
But the traveller, travelling through it,
May not—dare not openly view it;
Never its mysteries are exposed
To the weak human eye unclosed;
So wills its King, who hath forbid
The uplifting of the fringéd lid;
And thus the sad Soul that here passes
Beholds it but through darkened glasses.

By a route obscure and lonely,
Haunted by ill angels only,
Where an Eidolon, named NIGHT,
On a black throne reigns upright,
I have wandered home but newly
From this ultimate dim Thule.

THE BELLS

I

Hear the sledges with the bells—
Silver bells!
What a world of merriment their melody foretells!
How they tinkle, tinkle, tinkle,
In the icy air of night!
While the stars that oversprinkle
All the heavens, seem to twinkle
With a crystalline delight;
Keeping time, time, time,
In a sort of Runic rhyme,
To the tintinnabulation that so musically wells
From the bells, bells, bells, bells,
Bells, bells, bells—
From the jingling and the tinkling of the bells.

II

Hear the mellow wedding bells—
Golden bells!
What a world of happiness their harmony foretells!
Through the balmy air of night
How they ring out their delight!—
From the molten-golden notes,
And all in tune,
What a liquid ditty floats
To the turtle-dove that listens, while she gloats
On the moon!
Oh, from out the sounding cells,
What a gush of euphony voluminously wells!
How it swells!

How it dwells
On the Future!—how it tells
Of the rapture that impels
To the swinging and the ringing
Of the bells, bells, bells—
Of the bells, bells, bells, bells,
Bells, bells, bells—
To the rhyming and the chiming of the bells!

III

Hear the loud alarum bells—
Brazen bells!
What a tale of terror, now, their turbulency tells!
In the startled ear of night
How they scream out their affright!
Too much horrified to speak,
They can only shriek, shriek,
Out of tune,
In a clamorous appealing to the mercy of the fire,
In a mad expostulation with the deaf and frantic fire,
Leaping higher, higher, higher,
With a desperate desire,
And a resolute endeavor
Now—now to sit, or never,
By the side of the pale-faced moon.
Oh, the bells, bells, bells!
What a tale their terror tells
Of Despair!
How they clang, and clash, and roar!
What a horror they outpour
On the bosom of the palpitating air!
Yet the ear, it fully knows,
By the twanging
And the clanging,

How the danger ebbs and flows;
Yet the ear distinctly tells,
In the jangling
And the wrangling,
How the danger sinks and swells,
By the sinking or the swelling in the anger of the bells—
Of the bells,—
Of the bells, bells, bells, bells,
Bells, bells, bells—
In the clamor and the clangor of the bells!

IV

Hear the tolling of the bells—
Iron bells!
What a world of solemn thought their monody compels!
In the silence of the night,
How we shiver with affright
At the melancholy menace of their tone!
For every sound that floats
From the rust within their throats
Is a groan.
And the people—ah, the people—
They that dwell up in the steeple,
All alone,
And who tolling, tolling, tolling,
In that muffled monotone,
Feel a glory in so rolling
On the human heart a stone—
They are neither man nor woman—
They are neither brute nor human—
They are Ghouls:—
And their king it is who tolls:—
And he rolls, rolls, rolls,
Rolls

A pæan from the bells!
And his merry bosom swells
With the pæan of the bells!
And he dances, and he yells;
Keeping time, time, time,
In a sort of Runic rhyme,
To the pæan of the bells—
Of the bells:—
Keeping time, time, time,
In a sort of Runic rhyme,
To the throbbing of the bells—
Of the bells, bells, bells—
To the sobbing of the bells;
Keeping time, time, time,
As he knells, knells, knells,
In a happy Runic rhyme,
To the rolling of the bells—
Of the bells, bells, bells:—
To the tolling of the bells—
Of the bells, bells, bells, bells,
Bells, bells, bells—
To the moaning and the groaning of the bells.

THE RAVEN

Once upon a midnight dreary, while I pondered, weak and weary,
Over many quaint and curious volume of forgotten lore—
While I nodded, nearly napping, suddenly there came a tapping,
As of some one gently rapping, rapping at my chamber door.
" 'T is some visitor," I muttered, "tapping at my chamber door—
Only this and nothing more."

Ah, distinctly I remember it was in the bleak December;
And each separate dying ember wrought its ghost upon the floor.

Eagerly I wished the morrow;—vainly I had sought to borrow
From my books surcease of sorrow—sorrow for the lost Lenore—
For the rare and radiant maiden whom the angels name Lenore—
Nameless *here* for evermore.

And the silken, sad, uncertain rustling of each purple curtain
Thrilled me—filled me with fantastic terrors never felt before;
So that now, to still the beating of my heart, I stood repeating,
" 'T is some visitor entreating entrance at my chamber door—
Some late visitor entreating entrance at my chamber door;—
This it is and nothing more."

Presently my soul grew stronger; hesitating then no longer,
"Sir," said I, "or Madam, truly your forgiveness I implore;
But the fact is I was napping, and so gently you came rapping,
And so faintly you came tapping, tapping at my chamber door,
That I scarce was sure I heard you"—here I opened wide the door;—
Darkness there and nothing more.

Deep into that darkness peering, long I stood there wondering, fearing,
Doubting, dreaming dreams no mortal ever dared to dream before;
But the silence was unbroken, and the stillness gave no token,
And the only word there spoken was the whispered word, "Lenore"
This I whispered, and an echo murmured back the word, "Lenore?"
Merely this and nothing more.

Back into the chamber turning, all my soul within me burning,
Soon again I heard a tapping somewhat louder than before.
"Surely," said I, "surely that is something at my window lattice;
Let me see, then, what thereat is, and this mystery explore—

Let my heart be still a moment, and this mystery explore;—
'T is the wind and nothing more!"

Open here I flung the shutter, when, with many a flirt and flutter,
In there stepped a stately Raven of the saintly days of yore.
Not the least obeisance made he; not a minute stopped or stayed he;
But, with mien of lord or lady, perched above my chamber door—
Perched upon a bust of Pallas just above my chamber door—
Perched, and sat, and nothing more.

Then this ebony bird beguiling my sad fancy into smiling,
By the grave and stern decorum of the countenance it wore,
"Though thy crest be shorn and shaven, thou," I said, "art sure no craven,
Ghastly grim and ancient Raven wandering from the Nightly shore—
Tell me what thy lordly name is on the Night's Plutonian shore!"
Quoth the Raven, "Nevermore."

Much I marvelled this ungainly fowl to hear discourse so plainly,
Though its answer little meaning—little relevancy bore;
For we cannot help agreeing that no living human being
Ever yet was blessed with seeing bird above his chamber door—
Bird or beast upon the sculptured bust above his chamber door,
With such name as "Nevermore."

But the Raven, sitting lonely on that placid bust, spoke only
That one word, as if his soul in that one word he did outpour.
Nothing farther then he uttered—not a feather then he fluttered—
Till I scarcely more than muttered, "Other friends have flown before—
On the morrow *he* will leave me, as my Hopes have flown before."
Then the bird said, "Nevermore."

Startled at the stillness broken by reply so aptly spoken,
"Doubtless," said I, "what it utters is its only stock and store
Caught from some unhappy master whom unmerciful Disaster
Followed fast and followed faster till his songs one burden bore—
Till the dirges of his Hope that melancholy burden bore
Of 'Never—nevermore.' "

But the Raven still beguiling all my sad fancy into smiling,
Straight I wheeled a cushioned seat in front of bird and bust and door;
Then, upon the velvet sinking, I betook myself to linking
Fancy unto fancy, thinking what this ominous bird of yore—
What this grim, ungainly, ghastly, gaunt, and ominous bird of yore
Meant in croaking "Nevermore."

This I sat engaged in guessing, but no syllable expressing
To the fowl whose fiery eyes now burned into my bosom's core;
This and more I sat divining, with my head at ease reclining
On the cushion's velvet lining that the lamp-light gloated o'er,
But whose velvet-violet lining with the lamp-light gloating o'er,
She shall press, ah, nevermore!

Then, methought, the air grew denser, perfumed from an unseen censer
Swung by seraphim whose foot-falls tinkled on the tufted floor.
"Wretch," I cried, "thy God hath lent thee—by these angels he hath sent thee
Respite—respite and nepenthe from thy memories of Lenore;
Quaff, oh, quaff this kind nepenthe and forget this lost Lenore!"
Quoth the Raven, "Nevermore."

"Prophet!" said I, "thing of evil!—prophet still, if bird or devil!—
Whether Tempter sent, or whether tempest tossed thee here ashore,
Desolate, yet all undaunted, on this desert land enchanted—

On this home by Horror haunted—tell me truly, I implore—
Is there—*is* there balm in Gilead?—tell me—tell me, I implore!"
Quoth the Raven, "Nevermore."

"Prophet!" said I, "thing of evil!—prophet still, if bird or devil!
By that Heaven that bends above us—by that God we both adore—
Tell this soul with sorrow laden if, within the distant Aidenn,
It shall clasp a sainted maiden whom the angels name Lenore—
Clasp a rare and radiant maiden whom the angels name Lenore."
Quoth the Raven, "Nevermore."

"Be that word our sign of parting, bird or fiend!" I shrieked, upstarting—
"Get thee back into the tempest and the Night's Plutonian shore!
Leave no black plume as a token of that lie thy soul hath spoken!
Leave my loneliness unbroken!—quit the bust above my door!
Take thy beak from out my heart, and take thy form from off my door!"
Quoth the Raven, "Nevermore."

And the Raven, never flitting, still is sitting, *still* is sitting
On the pallid bust of Pallas just above my chamber door;
And his eyes have all the seeming of a demon's that is dreaming,
And the lamp-light o'er him streaming throws his shadow on the floor;
And my soul from out that shadow that lies floating on the floor
Shall be lifted—nevermore!

THE VALLEY OF UNREST

Once it smiled a silent dell
Where the people did not dwell;
They had gone unto the wars,

Trusting to the mild-eyed stars,
Nightly, from their azure towers,
To keep watch above the flowers,
In the midst of which all day
The red sun-light lazily lay.
Now each visitor shall confess
The sad valley's restlessness.
Nothing there is motionless—
Nothing save the airs that brood
Over the magic solitude.
Ah, by no wind are stirred those trees
That palpitate like the chill seas
Around the misty Hebrides!
Ah, by no wind those clouds are driven
That rustle through the unquiet Heaven
Uneasily, from morn till even,
Over the violets there that lie
In myriad types of the human eye—
Over the lilies there that wave
And weep above a nameless grave!
They wave:—from out their fragrant tops
Eternal dews come down in drops.
They weep:—from off their delicate stems
Perennial tears descend in gems.

THE CITY IN THE SEA

Lo! Death has reared himself a throne
In a strange city lying alone
Far down within the dim West,
Where the good and the bad and the worst and the best
Have gone to their eternal rest.
There shrines and palaces and towers

(Time-eaten towers that tremble not!)
Resemble nothing that is ours.
Around, by lifting winds forgot,
Resignedly beneath the sky
The melancholy waters lie.

No rays from the holy heaven come down
On the long night-time of that town;
But light from out the lurid sea
Streams up the turrets silently—
Gleams up the pinnacles far and free—
Up domes—up spires—up kingly halls—
Up fanes—up Babylon-like walls—
Up shadowy long-forgotten bowers
Of sculptured ivy and stone flowers—
Up many and many a marvellous shrine
Whose wreathéd friezes intertwine
The viol, the violet, and the vine.
Resignedly beneath the sky
The melancholy waters lie.
So blend the turrets and shadows there
That all seem pendulous in air,
While from a proud tower in the town
Death looks gigantically down.

There open fanes and gaping graves
Yawn level with the luminous waves;
But not the riches there that lie
In each idol's diamond eye—
Not the gaily-jewelled dead
Tempt the waters from their bed;
For no ripples curl, alas!
Along that wilderness of glass—
No swellings tell that winds may be

Upon some far-off happier sea—
No heavings hint that winds have been
On seas less hideously serene.

But lo, a stir is in the air!
The wave—there is a movement there!
As if the towers had thrust aside,
In slightly sinking, the dull tide—
As if their tops had feebly given
A void within the filmy Heaven.
The waves have now a redder glow—
The hours are breathing faint and low—
And when, amid no earthly moans,
Down, down that town shall settle hence,
Hell, rising from a thousand thrones,
Shall do it reverence.

ULALUME—A BALLAD

The skies they were ashen and sober;
  The leaves they were crispéd and sere—
  The leaves they were withering and sere;
It was night, in the lonesome October
  Of my most immemorial year:
It was hard by the dim lake of Auber,
  In the misty mid region of Weir—
It was down by the dank tarn of Auber,
  In the ghoul-haunted woodland of Weir.

Here once, through an alley Titanic,
  Of cypress, I roamed with my Soul—
  Of cypress, with Psyche, my Soul.
These were days when my heart was volcanic
  As the scoriac rivers that roll—

As the lavas that restlessly roll
Their sulphurous currents down Yaanek
In the ultimate climes of the Pole—
That groan as they roll down Mount Yaanek
In the realms of the Boreal Pole.

Our talk had been serious and sober,
But our thoughts they were palsied and sere—
Our memories were treacherous and sere;
For we knew not the month was October,
And we marked not the night of the year
(Ah, night of all nights in the year!)—
We noted not the dim lake of Auber
(Though once we had journey down here)—
Remembered not the dank tarn of Auber,
Nor the ghoul-haunted woodland of Weir.

And now, as the night was senescent
And star-dials pointed to morn—
As the star-dials hinted of morn—
At the end of our path a liquescent
And nebulous lustre was born,
Out of which a miraculous crescent
Arose with a duplicate horn—
Astarte's bediamonded crescent
Distinct with its duplicate horn.

And I said: "She is warmer than Dian;
She rolls through an ether of sighs—
She revels in a region of sighs.
She has seen that the tears are not dry on
These cheeks, where the worm never dies,
And has come past the stars of the Lion,
To point us the path to the skies—
To the Lethean peace of the skies—

Come up, in despite of the Lion,
  To shine on us with her bright eyes—
Come up through the lair of the Lion,
  With love in her luminous eyes."

But Psyche, uplifting her finger
  Said: "Sadly this star I mistrust—
  Her pallor I strangely mistrust:
Ah, hasten!—ah, let us not linger!
  Ah, fly!—let us fly!—for we must."
In terror she spoke, letting sink her
  Wings till they trailed in the dust—
In agony sobbed, letting sink her
  Plumes till they trailed in the dust—
  Till they sorrowfully trailed in the dust.

I replied: "This is nothing but dreaming:
  Let us on by this tremulous light!
  Let us bathe in this crystalline light!
Its Sibyllic splendor is beaming
  With Hope and in Beauty to-night!
  See!—it flickers up the sky through the night!
Ah, we safely may trust to its gleaming,
  And be sure it will lead us aright—
We safely may trust to a gleaming,
  That cannot but guide us aright,
  Since it flickers up to Heaven through the night."

Thus I pacified Psyche and kissed her,
  And tempted her out of her gloom—
  And conquered her scruples and gloom;
And we passed to the end of the vista,
  But were stopped by the door of a tomb—
  By the door of a legended tomb;
And I said: "What is written, sweet sister,

On the door of this legended tomb?"
She replied: "Ulalume—Ulalume!—
'Tis the vault of thy lost Ulalume!"

Then my heart it grew ashen and sober
As the leaves that were crispéd and sere—
As the leaves that were withering and sere;
And I cried: "It was surely October
On *this* very night of last year
That I journeyed—I journeyed down here!—
That I brought a dread burden down here—
On this night of all nights in the year,
Ah, what demon has tempted me here?
Well I know, now, this dim lake of Auber—
This misty mid region of Weir—
Well I know, now, this dank tarn of Auber,
This ghoul-haunted woodland of Weir."

Said we, then—the two, then: "Ah can it
Have been that woodlandish ghouls—
The pitiful, the merciful ghouls—
To bar up our way and to ban it
From the secret that lies in these wolds—
From the thing that lies hidden in these wolds—
Have drawn up the spectre of a planet
From the limbo of lunary souls—
This sinfully scintillant planet
From the Hell of the planetary souls?

ANNABEL LEE

It was many and many a year ago,
In a kingdom by the sea,
That a maiden there lived whom you may know

By the name of Annabel Lee;—
And this maiden she lived with no other thought
Than to love and be loved by me.

She was a child and *I* was a child,
In this kingdom by the sea,
But we loved with a love that was more than love—
I and my Annabel Lee—
With a love that the wingéd seraphs of Heaven
Coveted her and me.

And this was the reason that, long ago,
In this kingdom by the sea,
A wind blew out of a cloud, chilling
My beautiful Annabel Lee;
So that her highborn kinsman came
And bore her away from me,
To shut her up in a sepulchre
In this kingdom by the sea.

The angels, not half so happy in Heaven,
Went envying her and me:—
Yes! that was the reason (as all men know,
In this kingdom by the sea)
That the wind came out of the cloud, chilling
And killing my Annabel Lee.

But our love it was stronger by far than the love
Of those who were older than we—
Of many far wiser than we—
And neither the angels in Heaven above
Nor the demons down under the sea,
Can ever dissever my soul from the soul
Of the beautiful Annabel Lee:—

For the moon never beams without bringing me dreams
  Of the beautiful Annabel Lee;
And the stars never rise but I see the bright eyes
  Of the beautiful Annabel Lee;
And so, all the night-tide, I lie down by the side
Of my darling, my darling, my life and my bride,
  In her sepulchre there by the sea—
  In her tomb by the side of the sea.

ALONE

From childhood's hour I have not been
As others were—I have not seen
As others saw—I could not bring
My passions from a common spring—
From the same source I have not taken
My sorrow—I could not awaken
My heart to joy at the same tone—
And all I lov'd—*I* lov'd alone.
Then—in my childhood—in the dawn
Of a most stormy life—was drawn
From ev'ry depth of good and ill
The mystery which binds me still—
From the torrent, or the fountain—
From the red cliff of the mountain—
From the sun that round me roll'd
In its autumn tint of gold—
From the lightning in the sky
As it pass'd me flying by—
From the thunder, and the storm—
And the cloud that took the form
(When the rest of Heaven was blue)
Of a demon in my view.

THE SLEEPER

At midnight, in the month of June,
I stand beneath the mystic moon.
An opiate vapor, dewy, dim,
Exhales from out her golden rim,
And, softly dripping, drop by drop,
Upon the quiet mountain top,
Steals drowsily and musically
Into the universal valley.
The rosemary nods upon the grave;
The lily lolls upon the wave;
Wrapping the fog about its breast,
The ruin moulders into rest;
Looking like Lethe, see! the lake
A conscious slumber seems to take,
And would not, for the world, awake.
All Beauty sleeps!—and lo! where lies
(Her casement open to the skies)
Irene, with her Destinies!

Oh, lady bright! can it be right—
This window open to the night?
The wanton airs, from the tree-top,
Laughingly through the lattice drop—
The bodiless airs, a wizard rout,
Flit through thy chamber in and out,
And wave the curtain canopy
So fitfully—so carefully—
Above the closed and fringed lid
'Neath which thy slumb'ring soul lies hid,
That, o'er the floor and down the wall,
Like ghosts the shadows rise and fall!

Oh, lady dear, hast thou no fear?
Why and what art thou dreaming here?
Sure thou art come o'er far-off seas,
A wonder to these garden trees!
Strange is thy pallor! strange thy dress!
Strange, above all, thy length of tress,
And this all solemn silentness!

The lady sleeps! Oh, may her sleep,
Which is enduring, so be deep!
Heaven have her in its sacred keep!
This chamber changed for one more holy,
This bed for one more melancholy,
I pray to God that she may lie
Forever with unopened eye,
While the dim sheeted ghosts go by!

My love, she sleeps! Oh, may her sleep,
As it is lasting, so be deep!
Soft may the worms about her creep!
Far in the forest, dim and old,
For her may some tall vault unfold—
Some vault that oft hath flung its black
And winged panels fluttering back,
Triumphant, o'er the crested palls,
Of her grand family funerals—
Some sepulchre, remote, alone,
Against whose portal she hath thrown,
In childhood, many an idle stone—
Some tomb from out whose sounding door
She ne'er shall force an echo more,
Thrilling to think, poor child of sin!
It was the dead who groaned within.

A DREAM WITHIN A DREAM

Take this kiss upon the brow!
And, in parting from you now,
Thus much let me avow—
You are not wrong, who deem
That my days have been a dream;
Yet if hope has flown away
In a night, or in a day,
In a vision, or in none,
Is it therefore the less *gone?*
All that we see or seem
Is but a dream within a dream.

I stand amid the roar
Of a surf-tormented shore,
And I hold within my hand
Grains of the golden sand—
How few! yet how they creep
Through my fingers to the deep,
While I weep—while I weep!
O God! can I not grasp
Them with a tighter clasp?
O God! can I not save
One from the pitiless wave?
Is *all* that we see or seem
But a dream within a dream?

EUREKA

EUREKA

AN ESSAY ON

THE MATERIAL AND SPIRITUAL UNIVERSE

PREFACE

With very profound respect, this work is dedicated to Alexander Von Humboldt.

To the few who love me and whom I love—to those who feel rather than to those who think—to the dreamers and those who put faith in dreams as in the only realities—I offer this Book of Truths, not in its character of Truth-Teller, but for the Beauty that abounds in its Truth; constituting it true. To these I present the composition as an Art-Product alone:—let us say as a Romance; or, if I be not urging too lofty a claim, as a Poem.

What I here propound is true:—therefore it cannot die:—or, if by any means it be now trodden down so that it die, it will "rise again to the Life Everlasting."

Nevertheless it is as a Poem only that I wish this work to be judged after I am dead.

E. A. P.

IT IS with humility really unassumed—it is with a sentiment even of awe—that I pen the opening sentence of this work: for of all conceivable subjects I approach the reader with the most solemn—the most comprehensive—the most difficult—the most august.

What terms shall I find sufficiently simple in their sublimity—sufficiently sublime in their simplicity—for the mere enunciation of my theme?

I design to speak of the *Physical, Metaphysical and Mathe-*

matical—of the Material and Spiritual Universe:—of its Essence, its Origin, its Creation, its Present Condition and its Destiny. I shall be so rash, moreover, as to challenge the conclusions, and thus, in effect, to question the sagacity, of many of the greatest and most justly reverenced of men.

In the beginning, let me as distinctly as possible announce—not the theorem which I hope to demonstrate—for, whatever the mathematicians may assert, there is, in this world at least, *no such thing* as demonstration—but the ruling idea which, throughout this volume, I shall be continually endeavoring to suggest.

My general proposition, then, is this:—*In the Original Unity of the First Thing lies the Secondary Cause of All Things, with the Germ of their Inevitable Annihilation.*

In illustration of this idea, I propose to take such a survey of the Universe that the mind may be able really to receive and to perceive an individual impression.

He who from the top of Ætna casts his eyes leisurely around is affected chiefly by the *extent* and *diversity* of the scene. Only by a rapid whirling on his heel could he hope to comprehend the panorama in the sublimity of its *oneness.* But as, on the summit of Aetna, *no* man has thought of whirling on his heel, so no man has ever taken into his brain the full uniqueness of the prospect; and so, again, whatever considerations lie involved in this uniqueness, have as yet no practical existence for mankind.

I do not know a treatise in which a survey of the *Universe*—using the word in its most comprehensive and only legitimate acceptation—is taken at all:—and it may be as well here to mention that by the term "Universe," wherever employed without qualification in this essay, I mean to designate *the utmost conceivable expanse of space, with all things, spiritual and material, that can be imagined to exist within the compass of that expanse.*

In speaking of what is *ordinarily* implied by the expression, "Universe," I shall take a phrase of limitation—"the Universe of stars." Why this distinction is considered necessary, will be seen in the sequel.

But even of treatises on the really limited, although always assumed as the *un*limited, Universe of *stars,* I know none in which a survey, even of this limited Universe, is so taken as to warrant deductions from its *individuality*. The nearest approach to such a work is made in the "Cosmos" of Alexander Von Humboldt. He presents the subject, however, *not* in its individuality but in its generality. His theme, in its last result, is the law of *each* portion of the merely physical Universe, as this law is related to the laws of *every other* portion of this merely physical Universe. His design is simply synœretical. In a word, he discusses the universality of material relation, and discloses to the eye of Philosophy whatever inferences have hitherto lain hidden *behind* this universality. But however admirable be the succinctness with which he has treated each particular point of his topic, the mere multiplicity of these points occasions, necessarily, an amount of detail, and thus an involution of idea, which preclude all *individuality* of impression.

It seems to me that, in aiming at this latter effect, and, through it, at the consequences—the conclusions—the suggestions—the speculations—or, if nothing better offer itself, the mere guesses which may result from it—we require something like a mental gyration on the heel. We need so rapid a revolution of all things about the central point of sight that, while the minutiæ vanish altogether, even the more conspicuous objects become blended into one. Among the vanishing minutiae, in a survey of this kind, would be all exclusively terrestrial matters. The Earth would be considered in its planetary relations alone. A man, in this view, becomes mankind; mankind a member of the cosmical family of Intelligences.

And now, before proceeding to our subject proper, let me beg the reader's attention to an extract or two from a somewhat remarkable letter, which appears to have been found corked in a bottle and floating on the *Mare Tenebrarum*—an ocean well described by the Nubian geographer, Ptolemy Hephestion, but little frequented in modern days unless by the Transcendentalists and some other divers for crotchets. The date of this letter, I confess, surprises me even more particularly than its contents; for it seems to have been written in the year *two* thousand eight hundred and forty-eight. As for the passages I am about to transcribe, they, I fancy, will speak for themselves.

"Do you know, my dear friend," says the writer, addressing, no doubt, a contemporary—"Do you know that it is scarcely more than eight or nine hundred years ago since the metaphysicians first consented to relieve the people of the singular fancy that there exist *but two practicable roads to Truth?* Believe it if you can! It appears, however, that long, long ago, in the night of Time, there lived a Turkish philosopher called Aries and surnamed Tottle." [Here, possibly, the letter-writer means Aristotle; the best names are wretchedly corrupted in two or three thousand years.] "The fame of this great man depended mainly upon his demonstration that sneezing is a natural provision, by means of which over-profound thinkers are enabled to expel superfluous ideas through the nose; but he obtained a scarcely less valuable celebrity as the founder, or at all events as the principal propagator, of what was termed the *de*ductive or *à priori* philosophy. He started with what he maintained to be axioms, or self-evident truths:—and the now well-understood fact that *no* truths are *self*-evident, really does not make in the slightest degree against his speculations:—it was sufficient for his purpose that the truths in question were evident at all. From axioms he proceeded, logically, to results. His most illustrious disciples were one Tuclid, a geometrician," [meaning Euclid] "and one Kant, a Dutchman, the originator of that species of Transcendentalism which, with the change merely of a C for a K, now bears his peculiar name.

"Well, Aries Tottle flourished supreme, until the advent of one Hog, surnamed 'the Ettrick shepherd,' who preached an entirely different system, which he called the *à posteriori* or *in*ductive. His plan referred altogether to sensation. He proceeded by observing, analyzing, and classifying facts—*instantiæ Naturæ,* as they were somewhat affectedly called—and arranging them into general laws. In a word, while the mode of Aries rested on *noumena,* that of Hog depended on *phenomena;* and so great was the admiration excited by this latter system that, at its first introduction, Aries fell into general disrepute. Finally, however, he recovered ground, and was permitted to divide the empire of Philosophy with his more modern rival:—the savans contenting themselves with proscribing all *other* competitors, past, present, and to come; putting an end to all controversy on the topic by the promulgation of a Median law, to the effect that the Aristotelian and Baconian roads are, and of right ought to be, the sole possible avenues to knowledge:—'Baconian,' you must know, my dear friend," adds the letter-writer at this point, "was an adjective invented as equivalent to Hog-ian, and at the same time more dignified and euphonious.

"Now I do assure you most positively"—proceeds the epistle —"that I represent these matters fairly; and you can easily understand how restrictions so absurd on their very face must have operated, in those days, to retard the progress of true Science, which makes its most important advances—as all History will show—by seemingly intuitive *leaps.* These ancient ideas confined investigation to crawling; and I need not suggest to you that crawling, among varieties of locomotion, is a very capital thing of its kind;—but because the tortoise is sure of foot, for this reason must we clip the wings of the eagles? For many centuries, so great was the infatuation, about Hog especially, that a virtual stop was put to all thinking, properly so called. No man dared utter a truth for which he felt himself indebted to his soul alone. It mattered not whether the truth was even demonstrably such; for the dogmatizing philosophers of that epoch regarded only *the road* by which it professed to have been attained. The end, with them, was a point of no moment, whatever:—'the means!' they vociferated —'let us look at the means!'—and if, on scrutiny of the means, it was found to come neither under the category Hog, nor under the category Aries (which means ram), why then the savans went no farther, but, calling the thinker a fool and branding him a 'theorist,' would never, thenceforward, have any thing to do either with *him* or with his truths.

"Now, my dear friend," continues the letter-writer, "it cannot be maintained that by the crawling system, exclusively adopted, men would arrive at the maximum amount of truth, even in any long series of ages; for the repression of imagination was an evil not to be counterbalanced even by *absolute* certainty in the snail processes. But their certainty was very far from absolute. The error of our progenitors was quite analogous with that of the wiseacre who fancies he must necessarily see an object the more distinctly, the more closely he holds it to his eyes. They blinded themselves, too, with the impalpable, titillating Scotch snuff of *detail;* and thus the boasted facts of the Hog-ites were by no means always facts—a point of little importance but for the assumption that they always *were*. The vital taint, however, in Baconianism—its most lamentable fount of error—lay in its tendency to throw power and consideration into the hands of merely perceptive men—of those inter-Tritonic minnows, the microscopical savans—the diggers and pedlers of minute *facts,* for the most part in physical science—facts all of which they retailed at the same price upon the highway; their value depending, it was supposed, simply upon the *fact of their fact,* without reference to their applicability or inapplicability in the development of those ultimate and only legitimate facts, called Law.

"Than the persons"—the letter goes on to say—"than the persons thus suddenly elevated by the Hog-ian philosophy into a station for which they were unfitted—thus transferred from the sculleries into the parlors of Science—from its pantries into its pulpits—than these individuals a more intolerant—a more intolerable set of bigots and tyrants never existed on the face of the earth. Their creed, their text and their sermon were, alike, the one word '*fact*'—but, for the most part, even of this one word, they knew not even the meaning. On those who ventured to *disturb* their facts with the view of putting them in order and to use, the disciples of Hog had no mercy whatever. All attempts at generalization were met at once by the words 'theoretical,' 'theory,' 'theorist'—all *thought,* to be brief, was properly resented as a personal affront to themselves. Cultivating the natural sciences to the exclusion of Metaphysics, the Mathematics, and Logic, many of these Bacon-engendered philosophers—one-idead, one-sided, and lame of a leg—were more wretchedly helpless—more miserably ignorant, in view of all the comprehensible objects of knowledge, than the veriest unlettered hind who proves that he knows something at least, in admitting that he knows absolutely nothing.

"Nor had our forefathers any better right to talk about *certainty,* when pursuing, in blind confidence, the *à priori* path of axioms, or of the Ram. At innumerable points this path was scarcely as straight as a ram's-horn. The simple truth is, that the Aristotelians erected their castles upon a basis far less reliable than air; *for no such things as axioms ever existed or can possibly exist at all.* This they must have been very blind, indeed, not to see, or at least to suspect; for, even in their own day, many of their long-admitted 'axioms' had been abandoned:—'*ex nihilo nihil fit,*' for example, and a 'thing cannot act where it is not,' and 'there cannot be antipodes,' and 'darkness cannot proceed from light.' These and numerous similar propositions formerly accepted, without hesitation, as axioms, or undeniable truths, were, even at the period of which I speak, seen to be altogether untenable:—how absurd in these people, then, to persist in relying upon a basis, as immutable, whose mutability had become so repeatedly manifest!

"But, even through evidence afforded by themselves against themselves, it is easy to convict these *à priori* reasoners of the grossest unreason—it is easy to show the futility—the impalpability of their axioms in general. I have now lying before me"—it will be observed that we still proceed with the letter—"I have now lying before me a book printed about a thousand years ago. Pundit assures me that it is decidedly the cleverest ancient work on its topic, which is 'Logic.' The author, who was much esteemed in his day, was one Miller or Mill; and we find it recorded of him, as a point of some importance, that he rode a mill-horse whom he called Jeremy Bentham:—but let us glance at the volume itself.

"Ah!—'Ability or inability to conceive,' says Mr. Mill, very properly, 'is *in no case* to be received as a criterion of axiomatic truth.' Now, that this is a palpable truism, no one in his senses will deny. *Not* to admit the proposition, is to insinuate a charge of variability in Truth itself, whose very title is a synonym of the Steadfast. If ability to conceive be taken as a criterion of Truth, then a truth to *David* Hume would very seldom be a truth to *Joe;* and ninety-nine hundredths of what is undeniable in Heaven, would be demonstrable falsity upon Earth. The proposition of Mr. Mill, then, is sustained. I will not grant it to be an *axiom;* and this merely because I am showing that *no* axioms exist; but, with a distinction which could not have been cavilled at even by Mr. Mill himself, I am ready to grant that, *if* an axiom *there be,* then the proposition of which we speak has the fullest right to be considered an axiom—that no *more* absolute axiom *is*—and, consequently, that any subsequent proposition which shall conflict with this one primarily advanced, must be either a falsity in itself—that is to say no axiom—or, if admitted axiomatic, must at once neutralize both itself and its predecessor.

"And now, by the logic of their own propounder, let us proceed to test any one of the axioms propounded. Let us give Mr. Mill the fairest of play. We will bring the point to no ordinary issue. We will select for investigation no common-place axiom—no axiom of what, not the less preposterously because only impliedly, he terms his secondary class—as if a positive truth by definition could be either more or less positively a truth:—we will select, I say, no axiom of an unquestionability so questionable as is to be found in Euclid. We will not talk, for example, about such propositions as that two straight lines cannot enclose a space, or that the whole is greater than any one of its parts. We will afford the logician *every* advantage. We will come at once to a proposition which he regards as the acme of the unquestionable—as the quintessence of axiomatic undeniability. Here it is:—'Contradictions cannot *both* be true—that is, cannot cöexist in nature.' Here Mr. Mill means, for instance,—and I give the most forcible instance conceivable—that a tree must be either a tree or *not* a tree—that it cannot be at the same time a tree *and* not a tree: all which is quite reasonable of itself, and will answer remarkably well as an axiom, until we bring it into collation with an axiom insisted upon a few pages before—in other words—words which I have previously employed—until we test it by the logic of its own propounder. 'A tree,' Mr. Mill asserts, 'must be either a tree or *not* a tree.' Very well:—and now let me ask him, *why*. To this little query there is but one response:—I defy any man living to invent a second. The sole answer is this:—'Because we find it *impossible to conceive* that a tree can be anything else than a tree or not a tree.' This, I repeat, is Mr. Mill's sole answer:—he will not *pretend* to suggest another; and yet, by his own showing, his answer is clearly no answer at all—for has he not already required us to admit, *as an axiom,* that ability or inability to conceive is *in no case* to be taken as a criterion of axiomatic truth? Thus all—absolutely *all* his argumentation is at sea without a rudder. Let it not be urged that an exception from the general rule is to be made, in cases where the 'impossibility to conceive' is so peculiarly great as when we are called upon to conceive a tree *both* a tree and *not* a tree. Let no attempt, I say, be made at urging this sotticism; for, in the first place, there are no *degrees* of 'impossibility,' and thus no one impossible conception can be *more* peculiarly impossible than another impossible conception:—in the second place, Mr. Mill himself—no doubt after thorough deliberation, has most distinctly, and most rationally, excluded all opportunity for exception, by the emphasis of his proposition, that, *in no case,* is ability or inability to conceive, to be taken as a criterion of axiomatic truth:—in the third place, even were exceptions admissible at all, it remains to be shown how any exception is admissible *here.* That a tree can be both a tree and not a tree, is an idea which the angels, or the devils, *may* entertain, and which no doubt many an earthly Bedlamite, or Trancendentalist, *does.*

"Now I do not quarrel with these ancients," continues the letter-writer, "*so much* on account of the transparent frivolity of their logic—which, to be plain, was baseless, worthless and fantastic altogether—as on account of their pompous and infatuate proscription of all *other* roads to Truth than the two narrow and crooked paths—the one of creeping and the other of crawling—to which, in their ignorant perversity, they have dared to confine the Soul—the Soul which loves nothing so well as to soar in those regions of illimitable intuition which are utterly incognizant of '*path.*'

"By the bye, my dear friend, is it not an evidence of the mental slavery entailed upon those bigoted people by their Hogs and Rams, that in spite of the eternal prating of their savans about *roads* to Truth, none of them fell, even by accident, into what we now so distinctly perceive to be the broadest, the straightest and most available of all mere roads—the great thoroughfare—the majestic highway of the *Consistent?* Is it not wonderful that they should have failed to deduce from the works of God the vitally momentous consideration that *a perfect consistency can be nothing but an absolute truth?* How plain—how rapid our progress since the late announcement of this proposition! By its means, investigation has been taken out of the hands of the ground-moles, and given as a duty, rather than as a task, to the true—to the *only* true thinkers—to the generally-educated men of ardent imagination. These latter—our Keplers—our Laplaces—'speculate'—'theorize'—these are the terms—can you not fancy the shout of scorn with which they would be received by our progenitors, were it possible for them to be looking over my shoulders as I write? The Keplers, I repeat, speculate—theorize—and their theories are merely corrected—reduced—sifted—cleared, little by little, of their chaff of inconsistency—until at length there stands apparent and unencumbered *Consistency*—a consistency which the most stolid admit—because it *is* a consistency—to be an absolute and unquestionable *Truth.*

"I have often thought, my friend, that it must have puzzled

these dogmaticians of a thousand years ago, to determine, even, by which of their two boasted roads it is that the cryptographist attains the solution of the more complicated cyphers—or by which of them Champollion guided mankind to those important and innumerable truths which, for so many centuries, have lain entombed amid the phonetical hieroglyphics of Egypt. In especial, would it not have given these bigots some trouble to determine by which of their two roads was reached the most momentous and sublime of *all* their truths—the truth—the fact of *gravitation?* Newton deduced it from the laws of Kepler. Kepler admitted that these laws he *guessed*—these laws whose investigation disclosed to the greatest of British astronomers that principle, the basis of all (existing) physical principle, in going behind which we enter at once the nebulous kingdom of Metaphysics. Yes!—these vital laws Kepler *guessed*—that is to say, he *imagined* them. Had he been asked to point out either the *de*ductive or *in*ductive route by which he attained them, his reply might have been—'I know nothing about *routes*—but I *do* know the machinery of the Universe. Here it is. I grasped it with *my soul*—I reached it through mere dint of *intuition*. Alas, poor ignorant old man! Could not any metaphysician have told him that what he called 'intuition' was but the conviction resulting from *de*ductions or *in*ductions of which the processes were so shadowy as to have escaped his consciousness, eluded his reason, or bidden defiance to his capacity of expression? How great a pity it is that some 'moral philosopher' had not enlightened him about all this! How it would have comforted him on his death-bed to know that, instead of having gone intuitively and thus unbecomingly, he had, in fact, proceeded decorously and legitimately—that is to say Hog-ishly, or at least Ram-ishly—into the vast halls where lay gleaming, untended, and hitherto untouched by mortal hand—unseen by mortal eye—the imperishable and priceless secrets of the Universe!

"Yes, Kepler was essentially a *theorist;* but this title, *now* of so much sanctity, was, in those ancient days, a designation of supreme contempt. It is only *now* that men begin to appreciate that divine old man—to sympathize with the prophetical and poetical rhapsody of his ever memorable words. For *my* part," continues the unknown correspondent, "I glow with a sacred fire when I even think of them, and feel that I shall never grow weary of their repetition:—in concluding this letter, let me have the real pleasure of transcribing them once again:—'*I care not whether my work be read now or by posterity. I can afford to wait a century for readers when God himself has waited six thousand years for an observer. I triumph. I have stolen the golden secret of the Egyptians. I will indulge my sacred fury.*' "

Here end my quotations from this very unaccountable and, perhaps, somewhat impertinent epistle; and perhaps it would be folly to comment, in any respect, upon the chimerical, not to say revolutionary, fancies of the writer—whoever he is—fancies so radically at war with the well-considered and well-settled opinions of this age. Let us proceed, then, to our legitimate thesis, *The Universe.*

This thesis admits a choice between two modes of discussion:—We may *a*scend or *de*scend. Beginning at our own point of view—at the Earth on which we stand—we may pass to the other planets of our system—thence to the Sun—thence to our system considered collectively—and thence, through other systems, indefinitely outwards; or, commencing on high at some point as definite as we can make it or conceive it, we may come down to the habitation of Man. Usually—that is to say, in ordinary essays on Astronomy, the first of these two modes is, with certain reservation, adopted:—this for the obvious reason that astronomical *facts*, merely, and principles, being the object, that object is best fulfilled in stepping from the known because proximate, gradually onward to the point where all certitude becomes lost in the remote. For my present purpose, however,—that of enabling the mind to take in, as if from afar and at one glance, a distant conception of the *individual* Universe—it is clear that a descent to small from great—to the outskirts from the centre (if we could establish a centre)—to the end from the beginning (if we could fancy a beginning) would be the preferable course, but for the difficulty, if not impossibility, of presenting, in this course, to the unastronomical, a picture at all comprehensible in regard to such considerations as are involved in *quantity*—that is to say, in number, magnitude and distance.

Now, distinctness—intelligibility, at all points, is a primary feature in my general design. On important topics it is better to be a good deal prolix than even a very little obscure. But abstruseness is a quality appertaining to no subject *per se*. All are alike, in facility of comprehension, to him who approaches them by properly graduated steps. It is merely because a stepping-stone, here and there, is heedlessly left unsupplied in our road to Differential Calculus, that this latter is not altogether as simple a thing as a sonnet by Mr. Solomon Seesaw.

By way of admitting, then, no *chance* for misapprehension, I think it advisable to proceed as if even the more obvious facts of Astronomy were unknown to the reader. In combining the two modes of discussion to which I have referred, I propose to avail myself of the advantages peculiar to each—and very especially of the *iteration in detail* which will be unavoidable as a consequence of the plan. Commencing with a descent, I shall reserve for the return upwards those indispensable considerations of *quantity* to which allusion has already been made.

Let us begin, then, at once, with that merest of words, "Infinity." This, like "God," "spirit," and some other expressions of which the equivalents exist in all languages, is by no means the expression of an idea, but of an effort at one. It stands for the possible attempt at an impossible conception. Man needed a term by which to point out the *direction* of this effort—the cloud behind which lay, forever invisible, the *object* of this attempt. A word, in fine, was demanded, by means of which one human being might put himself in relation at once with another human being and with a certain *tendency* of the human intellect. Out of this demand arose the word, "Infinity;" which is thus the representative but of the *thought of a thought.*

As regards *that* infinity now considered—the infinity of space—we often hear it said that "its idea is admitted by the mind—is acquiesced in—is entertained—on account of the greater difficulty which attends the conception of a limit." But this is merely one of those *phrases* by which even profound thinkers, time out of mind, have occasionally taken pleasure in deceiving *themselves.* The quibble lies concealed in the word "Difficulty." "The mind," we are told, "entertains the idea of *limitless,* through the greater *difficulty* which it finds in entertaining that of *limited,* space." Now, were the proposition but fairly *put,* its absurdity would become transparent at once. Clearly, there is no mere *difficulty* in the case. The assertion intended, if presented *according* to its intention, and without sophistry, would run thus:—"The mind admits the idea of limitless, through the greater *impossibility* of entertaining that of limited, space."

It must be immediately seen that this is not a question of two statements between whose respective credibilities—or of two arguments between whose respective validities—the *reason* is called upon to decide:—it is a matter of two conceptions, directly conflicting, and each avowedly impossible, one of which the *intellect* is supposed to be capable of entertaining, on account of the greater *impossibility* of entertaining the other. The choice is *not* made between two difficulties; it is merely *fancied* to be made between two impossibilities. Now of the former, there *are* degrees, —but of the latter, none:—just as our impertinent letter-writer has already suggested. A task *may* be more or less difficult; but it is either possible or not possible:—there are no gradations. It *might* be more *difficult* to overthrow the Andes than an ant-hill; but it *can* be no more *impossible* to annihilate the matter of the one than the matter of the other. A man may jump ten feet with less *difficulty* than he can jump twenty, but the *impossibility* of his leaping to the moon is not a wit less than that of his leaping to the dog-star.

Since all this is undeniable: since the choice of mind is to be made between *impossibilities* of conception: since one impossibility cannot be greater than another: and since, thus, one cannot be preferred to another: the philosophers who not only maintain, on the grounds mentioned, man's *idea* of infinity but, on account of such supposititious idea, *infinity itself*—are plainly engaged in demonstrating one impossible thing to be possible by showing how it is that some one other thing—is impossible too. This, it will be said, is nonsense; and perhaps it is:—indeed I think it very capital nonsense, but forego all claim to it as nonsense of mine.

The readiest mode, however, of displaying the fallacy of the philosophical argument on this question, is by simply adverting to a *fact* respecting it which has been hitherto quite overlooked—the fact that the argument alluded to both proves and disproves its own proposition. "The mind is impelled," say the theologians and others, "to admit a *First Cause,* by the superior difficulty it experiences in conceiving cause beyond cause without end." The quibble, as before, lies in the word "difficulty"—but *here* what is it employed to sustain? A First Cause. And what is a First Cause? An ultimate termination of causes. And what is an ultimate termination of causes. Finity—the Finite. Thus the one quibble, in two processes, by God knows how many philosophers, is made to support now Finity and now Infinity; could it not be brought to support something besides? As for the quibbles—*they,* at least, are insupportable. But—to dismiss them:—what they prove in the one case is the identical nothing which they demonstrate in the other.

Of course, no one will suppose that I here contend for the absolute impossibility of *that* which we attempt to convey in the word "Infinity." My purpose is but to show the folly of endeavoring to prove Infinity itself, or even our conception of it, by any such blundering ratiocination as that which is ordinarily employed.

Nevertheless, as an individual, I may be permitted to say that I *cannot* conceive Infinity, and am convinced that no human being can. A mind not thoroughly self-conscious—not accustomed to the introspective analysis of its own operations, will, it is true, often deceive itself by supposing that it *has* entertained the conception of which we speak. In the effort to entertain it, we proceed step beyond step—we fancy point still beyond point; and so long as we *continue* the effort, it may be said, in fact, that we are *tending* to the formation of the idea designed; while the strength of the impression that we actually form or have formed it, is in the ratio of the period during which we keep up the mental endeavor. But it is in the act of discontinuing the endeavor—of fulfilling (as we think) the idea—of putting the finishing stroke (as we suppose) to the conception—that we overthrow at once the whole fabric of our fancy by resting upon some one ultimate and therefore, definite point. This fact, however, we fail to perceive, on account of the absolute coincidence, in time, between the settling down upon the ultimate point and the act of cessation in thinking.—In attempting, on the other hand, to frame the idea of a *limited* space, we merely converse the processes which involve the impossibility.

We *believe* in a God. We may or may not *believe* in finite or in infinite space; but our belief, in such cases, is more properly designated as *faith,* and is a matter quite distinct from that belief proper—from that *intellectual* belief—which presupposes the mental conception.

The fact is, that, upon the enunciation of any one of that class of terms to which "Infinity" belongs—the class representing *thoughts of thought*—he who has a right to say that he thinks *at all,* feels himself called upon, *not* to entertain a conception, but simply to direct his mental vision toward some given point, in the intellectual firmament, where lies a nebula never to be resolved.

To solve it, indeed, he makes no effort; for with a rapid instinct he comprehends, not only the impossibility, but, as regards all human purposes, the *inessentiality,* of its solution. He perceives that the Deity has not *designed* it to be solved. He sees, at once, that it lies *out* of the brain of man, and even *how,* if not exactly *why,* it lies out of it. There *are* people, I am aware, who, busying themselves in attempts at the unattainable, acquire very easily, by dint of the jargon they emit, among those thinkers-that-they-think with whom darkness and depth are synonymous, a kind of cuttle-fish reputation for profundity; but the finest quality of Thought is its self-cognizance; and, with some little equivocation, it may be said that no fog of the mind can well be greater than that which, extending to the very boundaries of the mental domain, shuts out even these boundaries themselves from comprehension.

It will now be understood that, in using the phrase, "Infinity of Space," I make no call upon the reader to entertain the impossibile conception of an *absolute* infinity. I refer simply to the *"utmost conceivable expanse"* of space—a shadowy and fluctuating domain, now shrinking, now swelling, in accordance with the vacillating energies of the imagination.

Hitherto, the Universe of stars has always been considered as coincident with the Universe proper, as I have defined it in the commencement of this Discourse. It has been always either directly or indirectly assumed—at least since the dawn of intelligible Astronomy—that, were it possible for us to attain any given point in space, we should still find, on all sides of us, an interminable succession of stars. This was the untenable idea of Pascal when making perhaps the most successful attempt ever made, at periphrasing the conception for which we struggle in the word "Universe." "It is a sphere," he says, "of which the centre is everywhere, the circumference, nowhere." But although his intended definition is, in fact, *no* definition of the Universe of *stars,* we may accept it, with some mental reservation, as a definition (rigorous enough for all practical purposes) of the Universe *proper*—that is to say, of the Universe of *space*. This latter, then, let us regard as *"a sphere of which the centre is everywhere, the circumference nowhere."* In fact, while we find it impossible to fancy an *end* to space, we have no difficulty in picturing to ourselves any one of an infinity of *beginnings*.

As our starting point, then, let us adopt the *Godhead*. Of this Godhead, *in itself*, he alone is not imbecile—he alone is not impious who propounds——nothing. *"Nous ne connaissons rien,"* says the Baron de Bielfeld—*"Nous ne connaissons rien de la nature ou de l'essence de Dieu:—pour savoir ce qu'il est, il faut être Dieu même."*—"We know absolutely *nothing* of the nature or essence of God:—in order to comprehend what he is, we should have to be God ourselves."

"We should have to be God ourselves!"—With a phrase so startling as this yet ringing in my ears, I nevertheless venture to demand if this our present ignorance of the Deity is an ignorance to which the soul is *everlastingly* condemned.

By *Him*, however—*now*, at least, the Incomprehensible—by Him—assuming him as a *Spirit*—that is to say, as *not Matter*—a distinction which, for all intelligible purposes, will stand well instead of a definition—by Him, then, existing as Spirit, let us content ourselves, to-night, with supposing to have been *created*, or made out of Nothing, by dint of his Volition—at some point of Space which we will take as a centre—at some period into which we do not pretend to inquire, but at all events immensely remote—by Him, then again, let us suppose to have been created——*what?* This is a vitally momentous epoch in our considerations. *What* is it that we are justified—that alone we are justified in supposing to have been, primarily and solely, *created?*

We have attained a point where only *Intuition* can aid us:—but now let me recur to the idea which I have already suggested as that alone which we can properly entertain of intuition. It is but *the conviction arising from those inductions or deductions of which the processes are so shadowy as to escape our consciousness, elude our reason, or defy our capacity of expression.* With this understanding, I now assert—that an intuition altogether irresistible, although inexpressible, forces me to the conclusion that what God originally created—that that Matter which, by dint of his Volition, he first made from his Spirit, or from Nihility, *could* have been nothing but Matter in its utmost conceivable state of——what?—of *Simplicity?*

This will be found the sole absolute *assumption* of my Discourse. I use the word "assumption" in its ordinary sense; yet I maintain that even this my primary proposition, is very, very far indeed, from being really a mere assumption. Nothing was ever more certainly—no human conclusion was ever, in fact, more regularly—more rigorously *de*duced:—but, alas! the processes lie out of the human analysis—at all events are beyond the utterance of the human tongue.

Let us now endeavor to conceive what Matter must be, when, or if, in its absolute extreme of *Simplicity*. Here the Reason flies at once to Imparticularity—to a particle—to *one* particle—a particle of *one* kind—of *one* character—of *one* nature—of *one size*—of one form—a particle, therefore, "*without* form and void"—a particle positively a particle at all points—a particle absolutely unique, individual, undivided, and not indivisible only because He who *created* it, by dint of his Will, can by an infinitely less energetic exercise of the same Will, as a matter of course, divide it.

Oneness, then, is all that I predicate of the originally created Matter; but I propose to show that this *Oneness is a principle abundantly sufficient to account for the constitution, the existing phœnomena and the plainly inevitable annihilation of at least the material Universe.*

The willing into being the primordial particle, has completed the act, or more properly the *conception* of Creation. We now proceed to the ultimate purpose for which we are to suppose the Particle created—that is to say, the ultimate purpose so far as our considerations *yet* enable us to see it—the constitution of the Universe from it, the Particle.

This constitution has been effected by *forcing* the originally and therefore normally *One* into the abnormal condition of *Many*. An action of this character implies reäction. A diffusion from Unity, under the conditions, involves a tendency to return into Unity—a tendency ineradicable until satisfied. But on these points I will speak more fully hereafter.

The assumption of absolute Unity in the primordial Particle includes that of infinite divisibility. Let us conceive the Particle, then, to be only not totally exhausted by diffusion into Space. From the one Particle, as a centre, let us suppose to be irradiated spherically—in all directions—to immeasurable but still to definite distances in the previously vacant space—a certain inexpressibly great yet limited number of unimaginably yet not infinitely minute atoms.

Now, of these atoms, thus diffused, or upon diffusion, what conditions are we permitted—not to assume, but to infer, from consideration as well of their source as of the character of the design apparent in their diffusion? *Unity* being their source, and *difference from Unity* the character of the design manifested in their diffusion, we are warranted in supposing this character to be at least *generally* preserved throughout the design, and to form a portion of the design itself:—that is to say, we shall be warranted in conceiving continual differences at all points from the uniquity and simplicity of the origin. But, for these reasons, shall we be justified in imagining the atoms heterogeneous, dissimilar, unequal, and inequidistant? More explicitly—are we to consider no two atoms as, at their diffusion, of the same nature, or of the same form, or of the same size?—and, after fulfilment of their diffusion into Space, is absolute inequidistance, each from each, to be understood of all of them? In such arrangement, under such conditions, we most easily and immediately comprehend the subsequent most feasible carrying out to completion of any such design as that which I have suggested—the design of variety out of unity—diversity out of sameness—heterogeneity out of homogeneity—complexity out of simplicity—in a word, the utmost possible multiplicity of *relation* out of the emphatically irrelative *One*. Undoubtedly, therefore, we *should* be warranted in assuming all that has been mentioned, but for the reflection, first, that supererogation is not presumable of any Divine Act; and, secondly, that the object supposed in view, appears as feasible when some of the conditions in question are dispensed with, in the beginning, as when all are understood immediately to exist. I mean to say that some are involved in the rest, or so instantaneous a consequence of them as to make the distinction inappreciable. Difference of *size,* for example, will at once be brought about through the tendency of one atom to a second, in preference to a third, on account of particular inequidistance; which is to be comprehended as *particular inequidistances between centres of quantity, in neighboring atoms of different form*—a matter not at all interfering with the generally-equable distribution of the atoms. Difference of *kind,* too, is easily conceived to be merely a result of differences in size and form, taken more or less conjointly:—in fact, since the *Unity* of the Particle Proper implies absolute homogeneity, we cannot imagine the atoms, at their diffusion, differing in kind, without imagining, at the same time, a special exercise of the Divine Will, at the emission of each atom, for the purpose of effecting, in each, a change of its essential nature:—so fantastic an idea is the less to be indulged, as the object proposed is seen to be thoroughly attainable without such minute and elaborate interposition. We perceive, therefore, upon the whole, that it would be supererogatory, and consequently unphilosophical, to predicate of the atoms, in view of their purposes, any thing more than *difference of form* at their dispersion, with particular inequidistance after it—all other differences arising at once out of these, in the very first processes of mass-constitution: —We thus establish the Universe on a purely *geometrical* basis. Of course, it is by no means necessary to assume absolute difference, even of form, among *all* the atoms irradiated—any more than absolute particular inequidistance of each from each. We are required to conceive merely that no *neighboring* atoms are of similar form—no atoms which can ever approximate, until their inevitable reunition at the end.

Although the immediate and perpetual *tendency* of the disunited atoms to return into their normal Unity, is implied, as I have said, in their abnormal diffusion; still it is clear that this tendency will be without consequence—a tendency and no more —until the diffusive energy, in ceasing to be exerted, shall leave *it,* the tendency, free to seek its satisfaction. The Divine Act, however, being considered as determinate, and discontinued on fulfilment of the diffusion, we understand, at once, a *rëaction*— in other words, a *satisfiable* tendency of the disunited atoms to return into *One.*

But the diffusive energy being withdrawn, and the rëaction having commenced in furtherance of the ultimate design—*that of the utmost possible Relation*—this design is now in danger of being frustrated, in detail, by reason of that very tendency to return which is to effect its accomplishment in general. *Multiplicity* is the object; but there is nothing to prevent proximate atoms, from lapsing *at once,* through the now satisfiable tendency —*before* the fulfilment of any ends proposed in multiplicity—into absolute oneness among themselves:—there is nothing to impede the aggregation of various *unique* masses, at various points of space:—in other words, nothing to interfere with the accumulation of various masses, each absolutely One.

For the effectual and thorough completion of the general design, we thus see the necessity for a repulsion of limited capacity—a separative *something* which, on withdrawal of the diffusive Volition, shall at the same time allow the approach, and forbid the junction, of the atoms; suffering them infinitely to approximate, while denying them positive contact; in a word, having the power—*up to a certain epoch*—of preventing their *coalition,* but no ability to interfere with their *coalescence* in any respect *or degree.* The repulsion, already considered as so peculiarly limited in other regards, must be understood, let me repeat, as having power to prevent absolute coalition, *only up to a certain epoch.* Unless we are to conceive that the appetite for Unity among the atoms is doomed to be satisfied *never;*—unless we are to conceive that what had a beginning is to have no end—a conception which cannot *really* be entertained, however much we may talk or dream of entertaining it—we are forced to conclude that the repulsive influence imagined, will, finally—under pressure of the *Unitendency collectively* applied, but never and in no degree *until,* on fulfilment of the Divine purposes, such collective application shall be naturally made—yield to a force which, at that ultimate epoch, shall be the superior force precisely to the extent required, and thus permit the universal subsidence into the inevitable, because original and therefore normal, *One.*—The conditions here to be reconciled are difficult indeed:—we cannot even comprehend the possibility of their conciliation;—nevertheless, the apparent impossibility is brilliantly suggestive.

That the repulsive something actually exists, *we see.* Man neither employs, nor knows, a force sufficient to bring two atoms into contact. This is but the well-established·proposition of the impenetrability of matter. All Experiment proves—all Philosophy admits it. The *design* of the repulsion—the necessity for its existence—I have endeavored to show; but from all attempt at investigating its nature have religiously abstained; this on account of an intuitive conviction that the principle at issue is strictly spiritual—lies in a recess impervious to our present understanding—lies involved in a consideration of what now—in our human state—is *not* to be considered—in a consideration of *Spirit in itself..* I feel, in a word, that here the God has interposed, and here only, because here and here only the knot demanded the interposition of the God.

In fact, while the tendency of the diffused atoms to return into Unity, will be recognized, at once, as the principle of the Newtonian Gravity, what I have spoken of as a repulsive influence prescribing limits to the (immediate) satisfaction of the tendency, will be understood as *that* which we have been in the practice of designating now as heat, now as magnetism, now as *electricity;* displaying our ignorance of its awful character in the vacillation of the phraseology with which we endeavor to circumscribe it.

Calling it, merely for the moment, electricity, we know that all experimental analysis of electricity has given, as an ultimate result, the principle, or seeming principle, *heterogeneity. Only* where things differ is electricity apparent; and it is presumable that they *never* differ where it is not developed at least, if not apparent. Now, this result is in the fullest keeping with that which I have reached unempirically. The design of the repulsive influence I have maintained to be that of preventing immediate Unity among the diffused atoms; and these atoms are represented as different each from each. *Difference* is their character—their essentiality—just as *no-difference* was the essentiality of their course. When we say, then, that an attempt to bring any two of these atoms together would induce an effort, on the part of the repulsive influence, to prevent the contact, we may as well use the strictly convertible sentence that an attempt to bring together any two differences will result in a development of electricity. All existing bodies, of coursc, are composed of these atoms in proximate contact, and are therefore to be considered as mere assemblages of more or fewer differences; and the resistance made by the repulsive spirit, on bringing together any two such assemblages, would be in the ratio of the two sums of the differences in each:—an expression which, when reduced, is equivalent to this: —*The amount of electricity developed on the approximation of two bodies, is proportional to the difference between the respective sums of the atoms of which the bodies are composed.* That *no* two bodies are absolutely alike, is a simple corollary from all that has been here said. Electricity, therefore, existing always, is *developed* whenever *any* bodies, but *manifested* only when bodies of appreciable difference, are brought into approximation.

To electricity—so, for the present, continuing to call it—we *may* not be wrong in referring the various physical appearances of light, heat and magnetism; but far less shall we be liable to err in attributing to this strictly spiritual principle the more important phænomena of vitality, consciousness and *Thought*. On this topic, however, I need pause *here* merely to suggest that these phænomena, whether observed generally or in detail, seem to proceed *at least in the ratio of the heterogeneous.*

Discarding now the two equivocal terms, "gravitation" and "electricity," let us adopt the more definite expressions, *"attraction"* and *"repulsion."* The former is the body; the latter the soul: the one is the material; the other the spiritual, principle of the Universe. *No other principles exist. All* phænomena are referable to one, or to the other, or to both combined. So rigorously is this the case—so thoroughly demonstrable is it that attraction and repulsion are the *sole* properties through which we perceive the Universe—in other words, by which Matter is manifested to Mind—that, for all merely argumentative purposes, we are fully justified in assuming that matter *exists* only as attraction and repulsion—that attraction and repulsion *are* matter:—there being no conceivable case in which we may not employ the term "matter" and the terms "attraction" and "repulsion," taken together, as equivalent, and therefore convertible, expressions in Logic.

I said, just now, that what I have described as the tendency of the diffused atoms to return into their original unity, would be understood as the principle of the Newtonian law of gravity; and, in fact, there can be but little difficulty in such an understanding, if we look at the Newtonian gravity in a merely general view, as a force impelling matter to seek matter; that is to say, when we pay no attention to the known *modus operandi* of the Newtonian force. The general coincidence satisfies us; but, upon looking closely, we see, in detail, much that appears *in*coincident, and much in regard to which no coincidence, at least, is established. For example; the Newtonian gravity, when we think of it in certain moods, does *not* seem to be a tendency to *oneness* at all, but rather a tendency of all bodies in all directions—a phrase apparently expressive of a tendency to diffusion. Here, then, is an *in*coincidence. Again; when we reflect on the mathematical *law* governing the Newtonian tendency, we see clearly that no coincidence has been made good, in respect of the *modus operandi,* at least, between gravitation as known to exist and that seemingly simple and direct tendency which I have assumed.

In fact, I have attained a point at which it will be advisable to strengthen my position by reversing my processes. So far, we have gone on *à priori,* from an abstract consideration of *Simplicity,* as that quality most likely to have characterized the original action of God. Let us now see whether the established facts of the Newtonian Gravitation may not afford us, *à posteriori,* some legitimate inductions.

What does the Newtonian law declare?—That all bodies attract each other with forces proportional to their quantities of matter inversely proportional to the squares of their distances. Purposely, I have given, in the first place, the vulgar version of the law; and I confess that in this, as in most other vulgar versions of great truths, we find little of a suggestive character. Let us now adopt a more philosophical phraseology:—*Every atom, of every body, attracts every other atom, both of its own and of every other body, with a force which varies inversely as the squares of the distances between the attracting and attracted atom.*—Here, indeed, a flood of suggestion bursts upon the mind.

But let us see distinctly what it was that Newton *proved*—according to the grossly irrational definitions of *proof* prescribed by the metaphysical schools. He was forced to content himself with showing how thoroughly the motions of an imaginary Universe, composed of attracting and attracted atoms obedient to the law he announced, coincide with those of the actually existing Universe so far as it comes under our observation. This was the amount of his *demonstration*—that is to say, this was the amount of it, according to the conventional cant of the "philosophies." His successes added proof multiplied by proof—such proof as a sound intellect admits—but the *demonstration* of the law itself, persist the metaphysicians, had not been strengthened in any degree. *"Ocular, physical* proof," however, of attraction, here upon Earth, in accordance with the Newtonian theory, was, at length, much to the satisfaction of some intellectual grovellers, afforded. This proof arose collaterally and incidentally (as nearly all important truths have arisen) out of an attempt to ascertain the mean density of the Earth. In the famous Maskelyne, Cavendish and Bailly experiments for this purpose, the attraction of the mass of a mountain was seen, felt, measured, and found to be mathematically consistent with the immortal theory of the British astronomer.

But in spite of this confirmation of that which needed none —in spite of the so-called corroboration of the "theory" by the so-called "ocular and physical proof"—in spite of the *character* of this corroboration—the ideas which even really philosophical men cannot help imbibing of gravity—and, especially, the ideas of it which ordinary men get and contentedly maintain, are *seen* to have been derived, for the most part, from a consideration of the principle as they find it developed—*merely in the planet upon which they stand.*

Now, to what does so partial a consideration tend—to what species of error does it give rise? On the Earth we *see* and *feel,* only that gravity impels all bodies towards the *centre* of the Earth. No man in the common walks of life could be *made* to see or feel anything else—could be made to perceive that anything, anywhere, has a perpetual, gravitating tendency in any *other* direction than to the centre of the Earth; yet (with an exception hereafter to be specified) it is a fact that every earthly thing (not to speak now of every heavenly thing) has a tendency not *only* to the Earth's centre but in every conceivable direction besides.

Now, although the philosophic cannot be said to *err with* the vulgar in this matter, they nevertheless permit themselves to be influenced, without knowing it, by the *sentiment* of the vulgar idea. "Although the Pagan fables are not believed," says Bryant, in his very erudite "Mythology," "yet we forget ourselves continually and make inferences from them as from existing realities." I mean to assert that the merely *sensitive perception* of gravity as we experience it on Earth, beguiles mankind into the fancy of *concentralization* or *especiality* respecting it—has been continually biasing towards this fancy even the mightiest intellects—perpetually, although imperceptibly, leading them away from the real characteristics of the principle; thus preventing them, up to this date, from ever getting a glimpse of that vital truth which lies in a diametrically opposite direction—behind the principle's *essential* characteristics—those, *not* of concentralization or especiality—but of *universality* and *diffusion.* This "vital truth" is *Unity* as the *source* of the Phenomenon.

Let me now repeat the definition of gravity:—*Every atom, of every body, attracts every other atom, both of its own and of every other body,* with a force which varies inversely as the squares of the distances of the attracting and attracted atom.

Here let the reader pause with me, for a moment, in contemplation of the miraculous—of the ineffable—of the altogether unimaginable complexity of relation involved in the fact that *each atom attracts every other atom*—involved merely in this fact of the attraction, without reference to the law or mode in which the attraction is manifested—involved *merely* in the fact that each atom attracts every other atom *at all,* in a wilderness of atoms so numerous that those which go to the composition of a cannon-ball, exceed, probably, in mere point of number, all the stars which go to the constitution of the Universe.

Had we discovered, simply, that each atom tended to some one favorite point—to some especially attractive atom—we should still have fallen upon a discovery which, in itself, would have sufficed to overwhelm the mind:—but what is it that we are actually called upon to comprehend? That each atom attracts—sympathizes with the most delicate movements of every other atom, and with each and with all at the same time, and forever, and according to a determinate law of which the complexity, even considered by itself solely, is utterly beyond the grasp of the imagination of man. If I propose to ascertain the influence of one mote in a sunbeam upon its neighboring mote, I cannot accomplish my purpose without first counting and weighing all the atoms in the Universe and defining the precise positions of all at one particular moment. If I venture to displace, by even the billionth part of an inch, the microscopical speck of dust which lies now upon the point of my finger, what is the character of that act upon which I have adventured? I have done a deed which shakes the Moon in her path, which causes the Sun to be no longer the Sun, and which alters forever the destiny of the multitudinous myriads of stars that roll and glow in the majestic presence of their Creator.

These ideas—conceptions such as *these*—unthought-like thoughts—soul-reveries rather than conclusions or even considerations of the intellect:—ideas, I repeat, such as these, are such as we can alone hope profitably to entertain in any effort at grasping the great principle, *Attraction.*

But now,—*with* such ideas—with such a *vision* of the marvellous complexity of Attraction fairly in his mind—let any person competent of thought on such topics as these, set himself to the task of imagining a *principle* for the phænomena observed—a condition from which they sprang.

Does not so evident a brotherhood among the atoms point to a common parentage? Does not a sympathy so omniprevalent, so ineradicable, and so thoroughly irrespective, suggest a common paternity as its source? Does not one extreme impel the reason to the other? Does not the infinite of division refer to the utterness of individuality? Does not the entireness of the complex hint at the perfection of the simple? It is *not* that the atoms, as we see them, are divided or that they are complex in their relations—but that they are inconceivably divided and unutterably complex:—it is the extremeness of the conditions to which I now allude, rather than to the conditions themselves. In a word, not because the atoms were, at some remote epoch of time, even *more than together*—is it not because originally, and therefore normally, they were *One*—that now, in all circumstances—at all points—in all directions—by all modes of approach—in all relations and through all conditions—they struggle *back* to this absolutely, this irrelatively, this unconditionally *one?*

Some person may here demand:—"Why—since it is to the *One* that the atoms struggle back—do we not find and define Attraction 'a merely general tendency to a centre?'—why, in especial, do not *your* atoms—the atoms which you describe as having been irradiated from a centre—proceed at once, rectilinearly, back to the central point of their origin?"

I reply that *they do;* as will be distinctly shown; but that the cause of their so doing is quite irrespective of the centre *as such.* They all tend rectilinearly towards a centre, because of the sphereicity with which they have been irradiated into space. Each atom, forming one of a generally uniform globe of atoms, finds more atoms in the direction of the centre, of course, than in any other, and in that direction, therefore, is impelled—but is *not* thus impelled because the centre is *the point of its origin.* It is not to any *point* that the atoms are allied. It is not any *locality,* either in the concrete or in the abstract, to which I suppose them bound. Nothing like *location* was conceived as their origin. Their source lies in the principle, *Unity. This* is their lost parent. *This* they seek always—immediately—in all directions—wherever it is even partially to be found; thus appeasing, in some measure, the ineradicable tendency, while on the way to its absolute satisfaction in the end. It follows from all this, that any principle which shall be adequate to account for the *law,* or *modus operandi,* of the attractive force in general, will account for this law in particular:—that is to say, any principle which will show why the atoms should tend to their *general centre of irradiation* with forces inversely proportional to the squares of the distances will be admitted as satisfactorily accounting, at the same time, for the tendency, according to the same law, of these atoms each to each; —*for* the tendency to the centre *is* merely the tendency each to each, and not any tendency to a centre as such.—Thus it will be seen, also, that the establishment of my propositions would involve no *necessity* of modification in the terms of the Newtonian definition of Gravity, which declares that each atom attracts each other atom and so forth, and declares this merely; but (always under the supposition that what I propose be, in the end, admitted) it seems clear that some error might occasionally be avoided, in the future processes of Science, were a more ample phraseology adopted:—for instance:—"Each atom tends to every other atom &c., with a force &c.: *the general result being a tendency of all, with a similar force, to a general centre.*"

The reversal of our processes has thus brought us to an identical result; but, while in the one process *intuition* was the starting-point, in the other it was the goal. In commencing the former journey I could only say that, with an irresistible intuition, I *felt* Simplicity to have been made the characteristic of the original action of God:—in ending the letter I can only declare that with an irresistible intuition, I perceive Unity to have been the source of the observed phænomena of the Newtonian gravitation. Thus, according to the schools, I *prove* nothing. So be it:—I design but to suggest—and to *convince* through the suggestion. I am proudly aware that there exist many of the most profound and cautiously discriminative human intellects which cannot *help* being abundantly content with my—suggestions. To these intellects—as to my own—there is no mathematical demonstration which *could* bring the least additional *true proof* of the great *Truth* which I have advanced—*the truth of Original Unity as the source—as the principle of the Universal Phœnomena.* For my part I am not sure that I speak and see—I am not so sure that my heart beats and that my soul lives:—of the rising of to-morrow's sun—a probability that as yet lies in the Future—I do not pretend to be one thousandth part as sure—as I am of the irretrievably by-gone *Fact* that All Things and All Thoughts of Things, with all their ineffable Multiplicity of Relation, sprang at once into being from the primordial and irrelative *One.*

Referring to the Newtonian Gravity, Dr. Nichol, the eloquent author of "The Architecture of the Heavens," says:—"In truth we have no reason to suppose this great Law, as now revealed, to be the ultimate or simplest, and therefore the universal and all-comprehensive, form of a great Ordinance. The mode in which its intensity diminishes with the element of distance, has not the aspect of an ultimate *principle;* which always assumes the simplicity and self-evidence of those axioms which constitute the basis of Geometry."

Now, it is quite true that "ultimate principles," in the common understanding of the words, always assume the simplicity of geometrical axioms—(as for "self-evidence," there is no such thing)—but these principles are clearly *not* "ultimate;" in other terms what we are in the habit of calling principles are no principles, properly speaking—since there can be but one *principle,* the Volition of God. We have no right to assume, then, from what we observe in rules that we choose foolishly to name "principles," anything at all in respect to the characteristics of a principle proper. The "ultimate principles" of which Dr. Nichol speaks as having geometrical simplicity, may and do have this geometrical turn, as being part and parcel of a vast geometrical system, and thus a system of simplicity itself—in which, nevertheless, the *truly* ultimate principle is, *as we know,* the consummation of the complex—that is to say, of the unintelligible—for is it not the Spiritual Capacity of God?

I quoted Dr. Nichol's remark, however, not so much to question its philosophy, as by way of calling attention to the fact that, while all men have admitted *some* principle as existing behind the Law of Gravity, no attempt has been yet made to point out what this principle in particular *is:*—if we except, perhaps, occasional fantastic efforts at referring it to Magnetism, or Mesmerism, or Swedenborgianism, or Transcendentalism, or some other equally delicious *ism* of the same species, and invariably patronized by one and the same species of people. The great mind of Newton, while boldly grasping the Law itself, shrank from the principle of the Law. The more fluent and comprehensive at least, if not the more patient and profound, sagacity of Laplace, had not the courage to attack it. But hesitation on the part of these two astronomers it is, perhaps, not so very difficult to understand. They, as well as all the first class of mathematicians, were mathematicians *solely*:—their intellect at least had a firmly-pronounced mathematico-physical tone. What lay not distinctly within the domain of Physics, or of Mathematics, seemed to them either Non-Entity or Shadow. Nevertheless, we may well wonder that Leibnitz, who was a marked exception to the general rule in these respects, and whose mental temperament was a singular admixture of the mathematical with the physico-metaphysical, did not at once investigate and establish the point at issue. Either Newton or Laplace, seeking a principle and discovering none *physical*, would have rested contentedly in the conclusion that there was absolutely none; but it is almost impossible to fancy, of Leibnitz, that, having exhausted in his search the physical dominions, he would not have stepped at once, boldly and hopefully, amid his old familiar haunts in the kingdom of Metaphysics. Here, indeed, it is clear that he *must* have adventured in search of the treasure:—that he did not find it after all, was, perhaps, because his fairy guide, imagination, was not sufficiently well-grown, or well-educated, to direct him aright.

I observed, just now, that, in fact, there had been certain vague attempts at referring Gravity to some very uncertain *isms*. These attempts, however, although considered bold and justly so considered, looked no farther than to the generality—the merest generality—of the Newtonian Law. Its *modus operandi* has never, to my knowledge, been approached in the way of an effort at explanation. It is, therefore, with no unwarranted fear of being taken for a madman at the outset, and before I can bring my propositions fairly to the eye of those who alone are competent to decide upon them, that I here declare the *modus operandi* of the Law of Gravity to be an exceedingly simple and perfectly explicable thing—that is to say, when we make our advances towards it in just gradations and in the true direction—when we regard it from the proper point of view.

Whether we reach the idea of absolute *Unity* as the source of All Things, from a consideration of Simplicity as the most probable characteristic of the original action of God;—whether we arrive at it from an inspection of the universality of relation in the gravitating phænomena;—or whether we attain it as a result of the mutual corroboration afforded by both processes;—still, the idea itself, if entertained at all, is entertained in inseparable connection with another idea—that of the condition of the Universe of stars as we *now* perceive it—that is to say, a condition of immeasurable *diffusion* through space. Now a connection between these two ideas—unity and diffusion—cannot be established unless through the entertainment of a third idea—that of *irradiation.* Absolute Unity being taken as a centre, then the existing Universe of stars is the result of *irradiation* from that centre.

Now, the laws of irradiation are *known.* They are part and parcel of the *sphere.* They belong to the class of *indisputable geometrical properties.* We say of them, "they are true—they are evident." To demand *why* they are true, would be to demand why the axioms are true upon which their demonstration is based. *Nothing* is demonstrable, strictly speaking; but *if* anything *be,* then the properties—the laws in question are demonstrated.

But these laws—what do they declare? Irradiation—how—by what steps does it proceed outwardly from a centre?

From a *luminous* centre, *Light* issues by irradiation; and the quantities of light received upon any given plane, supposed to be shifting its position so as to be now nearer the centre and now farther from it, will be diminished in the same proportion as the squares of the distances of the plane from the luminous body, are increased; and will be increased in the same proportion as these squares are diminished.

The expression of the law may be thus generalized:—the number of light-particles (or, if the phrase be preferred, the number of light-impressions) received upon the shifting plane, will be *inversely* proportional with the squares of the distances of the plane. Generalizing yet again, we may say that the diffusion—

the scattering—the irradiation, in a word—is *directly* proportional with the squares of the distances.

For example: at the distance B, from the luminous centre A, a certain number of particles are so diffused as to occupy the surface B. Then at double the distance—that is to say, at C—they will be so much farther diffused as to occupy four such surfaces:—at treble the distance, or at D, they will be so much farther separated as to occupy nine such surfaces;—while, at quadruple the distance, or at E, they will have become so scattered as to spread themselves over sixteen such surfaces—and so on forever.

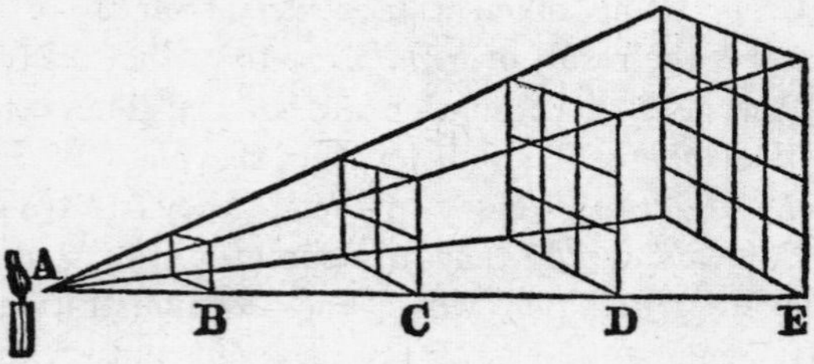

In saying, generally, that the irradiation proceeds in direct proportion with the squares of the distances, we use the term irradiation to express *the degree of the diffusion* as we proceed outwardly from the centre. Conversing the idea, and employing the word "concentralization" to express *the degree of the drawing together* as we come back toward the centre from an outward position, we may say that concentralization proceeds *inversely* as the squares of the distances. In other words, we have reached the conclusion that, on the hypothesis that matter was originally irradiated from a centre and is now returning to it, the concentralization, in the return, proceeds *exactly as we know the force of gravitation to proceed.*

Now here, if we could be permitted to assume that concentralization exactly represented the *force of the tendency to the centre*—that the one was exactly proportional to the other, and that the two proceeded together—we should have shown all that is required. The sole difficulty existing, then, is to establish a direct proportion between "concentralization" and the *force* of concentralization; and this is done, of course, if we establish such proportion between "irradiation" and the *force* of irradiation.

A very slight inspection of the Heavens assures us that the stars have a certain general uniformity, equability, or equidistance, of distribution through that region of space in which, collectively, and in a roughly globular form, they are situated:—this species of very general, rather than absolute, equability, being in full keeping with my deduction of inequidistance, within certain limits, among the originally diffused atoms, as a corollary from the evident design of infinite complexity of relation out of irrelation. I started, it will be remembered, with the idea of a generally uniform but particularly *un*uniform distribution of the atoms;—an idea, I repeat, which an inspection of the stars, as they exist, confirms.

But even in the merely general equability of distribution, as regards the atoms, there appears a difficulty which, no doubt, has already suggested itself to those among my readers who have borne in mind that I suppose this equability of distribution effected through *irradiation from a centre*. The very first glance at the idea, irradiation, forces us to the entertainment of the hitherto unseparated and seemingly inseparable idea of agglomeration about a centre, with dispersion as we recede from it—the idea, in a word, of *in*equability of distribution in respect to the matter irradiated.

Now, I have elsewhere observed that it is by just such difficulties as the one now in question—such roughnesses—such peculiarities—such protuberances above the plane of the ordinary—that Reason feels her way, if at all, in her search for the True. By the difficulty—the "peculiarity"—now presented, I leap at once to *the* secret—a secret which I might never have attained *but* for the peculiarity and the inferences which, *in its mere character of peculiarity,* it affords me.

The process of thought, at this point, may be thus roughly sketched:—I say to myself—"Unity, as I have explained it, is a truth—I feel it. Diffusion is a truth—I see it. Irradiation, by which alone these two truths are reconciled, is a consequent truth—I perceive it. *Equability* of diffusion, first deduced *à priori* and then corroborated by the inspection of phænomena, is also a truth—I fully admit it. So far all is clear around me:—there are no clouds behind which *the* secret—the great secret of the gravitating *modus operandi*—can possibly lie hidden;—but this secret lies *hereabouts,* most assuredly; and *were* there but a cloud in view, I should be driven to suspicion of that cloud." And now, just as I say this, there actually comes a cloud into view. This cloud is the seeming impossibility of reconciling my truth, *irradiation,* which my truth, *equability of diffusion.* I say now:—"Behind this *seeming* impossibility is to be found what I desire." I do not say *"real* impossibility;" for invincible faith in my truths assures me that it is a mere difficulty after all—but I go on to say, with unflinching confidence, that, *when* this *difficulty* shall be solved, we shall find, *wrapped up in the process of solution,* the key to the secret at which we aim. Moreover—I *feel* that we shall discover *but one* possible solution of the difficulty; this for the reason that, were there two, one would be supererogatory—would be fruitless—would be empty—would contain no key—since no duplicate key can be needed to any secret of Nature.

And now, let us see:—Our usual notions of irradiation—in fact, *all* our distinct notions of it—are caught merely from the process as we see it exemplified in *Light.* Here there is a *continuous* outpouring of *ray-streams,* and *with a force which we have at least no right to suppose varies at all.* Now, in any such irradiation *as this*—continuous and of unvarying force—the regions nearer the centre must *inevitably* be always more crowded with the irradiated matter than the regions more remote. But I have assumed *no* such irradiation *as this*. I assumed no *continuous* irradiation; and for the simple reason that such an assumption would have involved, first, the necessity of entertaining a conception which I have shown no man *can* entertain, and which (as I will more fully explain hereafter) all observation of the firmament refutes—the conception of the absolute infinity of the Universe of stars—and would have involved, secondly, the impossibility of understanding a rëaction—that is, gravitation—as existing now—since, while an act is continued, no rëaction, of course, can take place. My assumption, then, or rather my inevitable deduction from just premises—was that of a *determinate* irradiation—one finally *dis*continued.

Let me now describe the sole possible mode in which it is conceivable that matter could have been diffused through space, so as to fulfil the conditions at once of irradiation and of generally equable distribution.

For convenience of illustration, let us imagine, in the first place, a hollow sphere of glass, or of anything else, occupying the space throughout which the universal matter is to be thus equally diffused, by means of irradiation, from the absolute, irrelative, unconditional particle, placed in the centre of the sphere.

Now, a certain exertion of the diffusive power (presumed to be the Divine Volition)—in other words, a certain *force*—whose measure is the quantity of matter—that is to say, the number of atoms—emitted; emits, by irradiation, this certain number of atoms; forcing them in all directions outwardly from the centre—their proximity to each other diminishing as they proceed—until, finally, they are distributed, loosely, over the interior surface of the sphere.

When these atoms have attained this position, or while proceeding to attain it, a second and inferior exercise of the same force—or a second and inferior force of the same character—emits, in the same manner—that is to say, by irradiation as before—a second stratum of atoms which proceeds to deposit itself upon the first; the number of atoms, in this case as in the former, being of course the measure of the force which emitted them; in other words the force being precisely adapted to the purpose it effects —the force and the number of atoms sent out by the force, being *directly proportional.*

When this second stratum has reached its destined position —or while approaching it—a third still inferior exertion of the force, or a third inferior force of a similar character—the number of atoms emitted being in *all* cases the measure of the force—proceeds to deposit a third stratum upon the second:—and so on, until these concentric strata, growing gradually less and less, come down at length to the central point; and the diffusive matter, simultaneously with the diffusive force, is exhausted.

We have now the sphere filled, through means of irradiation, with atoms equably diffused. The two necessary conditions—those of irradiation and of equable diffusion—are satisfied; and by the *sole* process in which the possibility of their simultaneous satisfaction is conceivable. For this reason, I confidently expect to find, lurking in the present condition of the atoms as distributed throughout the sphere, the secret of which I am in search—the all-important principle of the *modus operandi* of the Newtonian law. Let us examine, then, the actual condition of the atoms.

They lie in a series of concentric strata. They are equably diffused throughout the sphere. They have been irradiated into these states.

The atoms being *equably* distributed, the greater the superficial extent of any of these concentric strata, or spheres, the more atoms will lie upon it. In other words, the number of atoms lying upon the surface of any one of the concentric spheres, is directly proportional with the extent of that surface.

*But, in any series of concentric sphères, the surfaces are directly proportional with the squares of the distances from the centre.**

Therefore the number of atoms in any stratum is directly

* Succinctly—The surfaces of spheres are as the squares of their radii.

proportional with the square of that stratum's distance from the centre.

But the number of atoms in any stratum is the measure of the force which emitted that stratum—that is to say, is *directly proportional* with the force.

Therefore the force which irradiated any stratum is directly proportional with the square of that stratum's distance from the centre:—or, generally,

The force of the irradiation has been directly proportional with the squares of the distances.

Now, Rëaction, as far as we know any thing of it, is Action conversed. The *general* principle of Gravity being, in the first place, understood as the rëaction of an act—as the expression of a desire on the part of Matter, while existing in a state of diffusion, to return into the Unity whence it was diffused; and, in the second place, the mind being called upon to determine the *character* of the desire—the manner in which it would, naturally, be manifested; in other words, being called upon to conceive a probable law, or *modus operandi,* for the return; could not well help arriving at the conclusion that this law of return would be precisely the converse of the law of departure. That such would be the case, any one, at least, would be abundantly justified in taking for granted, until such time as some person should suggest something like a plausible reason why it should *not* be the case—until such period as a law of return shall be imagined which the intellect can consider as preferable.

Matter, then, irradiated into space with a force varying as the squares of the distances, might, *à priori,* be supposed to return towards its centre of irradiation with a force varying *inversel* as the squares of the distances: and I have already shown that any principle which will explain why the atoms should tend, according to any law, to the general centre, must be admitted as satisfactorily explaining, at the same time, why, according to the same law, they should tend each to each. For, in fact, the tendency to the general centre is not to a centre as such, but because of its being a point in tending towards which each atom tends most directly to its real and essential centre, *Unity*—the absolute and final Union of all.

The consideration here involved presents to my own mind no embarrassment whatever—but this fact does not blind me to the possibility of its being obscure to those who may have been less in the habit of dealing with abstractions:—and, upon the whole, it may be as well to look at the matter from one or two other points of view.

The absolute, irrelative particle primarily created by the Volition of God, must have been in a condition of positive *normality,* or rightfulness—for wrongfulness implies *relation.* Right is positive; wrong is negative—is merely the negation of right; as cold is the negation of heat—darkness of light. That a thing may be wrong, it is necessary that there be some other thing in *relation* to which it *is* wrong—some condition which it fails to satisfy; some law which it violates; some being whom it aggrieves. If there be no such being, law, or condition, in respect to which the thing is wrong—and, still more especially, if no beings, laws, or conditions exist at all—then the thing can*not* be wrong and consequently must be *right.* Any deviation from normality involves a tendency to return to it. A difference from the normal—from the right—from the just—can be understood as effected only by the overcoming a difficulty; and if the force which overcomes the difficulty be not infinitely continued, the ineradicable tendency to return will at length be permitted to act for its own satisfaction. Upon withdrawal of the force, the tendency acts. This is the principle of rëaction as the inevitable consequence of finite action. Employing a phraseology of which the seeming affectation will be pardoned for its expressiveness, we may say that Rëaction is the return from the condition of *as it is and ought not to be* into the condition of *as it was, originally, and therefore ought to be:*—and let me add here that the *absolute* force of Rëaction would no doubt be always found in direct proportion with the reality—the truth—the absoluteness—of the *originality*—if ever it were possible to measure this latter:—and, consequently, the greatest of all conceivable rëactions must be that produced by the tendency which we now discuss—the tendency to return into the *absolutely original*—into the *supremely* primitive. Gravity, then, *must be the strongest of forces*—an idea reached *à priori* and abundantly confirmed by induction. What use I make of the idea, will be seen in the sequel.

The atoms, now, having been diffused from their normal condition of Unity, seek to return to——what? Not to any particular *point,* certainly; for it is clear that if, upon the diffusion, the whole Universe of matter had been projected, collectively, to a distance from the point of irradiation, the atomic tendency to the general centre of the sphere would not have been disturbed in the least:—the atoms would not have sought the point *in absolute space* from which they were originally impelled. It is merely the *condition,* and not the point or locality at which this condition took its rise, that these atoms seek to re-establish;—it is merely *that condition which is their normality,* that they desire. "But they seek a centre," it will be said, "and a centre is a point." True; but they seek this point not in its character of point—(for, were the whole sphere moved from its position, they would seek, equally, the centre; and the centre *then* would be a *new* point)—but because it so happens, on account of the form in which they collectively exist—(that of the sphere)—that only *through* the point in question—the sphere's centre—they can attain their true object, Unity. In the direction of the centre each atom perceives more atoms than in any other direction. Each atom is impelled towards the centre because along the straight line joining it and the centre and passing on to the circumference beyond, there lie a greater number of atoms than along any other straight line—a greater number of objects that seek it, the individual atom—a greater number of tendencies to Unity—a greater number of satisfactions for its own tendency to Unity—in a word, because in the direction of the centre lies the utmost possibility of satisfaction, generally, for its own individual appetite. To be brief, the *condition,* Unity, is all that is really sought; and if the atoms *seem* to seek the centre of the sphere, it is only impliedly, through implication—because such centre happens to imply, to include, or to involve, the only essential centre, Unity. But *on account of* this implication of involution, there is no possibility of practically separating the tendency to Unity in the abstract, from the tendency to the concrete centre. Thus the tendency of the atoms to the general centre *is,* to all practical intents and for all logical purposes, the tendency each to each; and the tendency each to each *is* the tendency to the centre; and the one tendency may be assumed *as* the other; whatever will apply to the one must be thoroughly applicable to the other; and, in conclusion, whatever principle will satisfactorily explain the one, cannot be questioned as an explanation of the other.

In looking carefully around me for a rational objection to what I have advanced, I am able to discover *nothing;*—but of that class of objections usually urged by the doubters for Doubt's sake, I very readily perceive *three;* and proceed to dispose of them in order.

It may be said, first: "That the proof that the force of irradiation (in the case described) is directly proportional to the squares of the distances, depends upon an unwarranted assumption—that of the number of atoms in each stratum being the measure of the force with which they are emitted."

I reply, not only that I am warranted in such assumption, but that I should be utterly *un*warranted in any other. What I assume is, simply, that an effect is the measure of its cause—that every exercise of the Divine Will will be proportional to that which demands the exertion—that the means of Ominipotence, or of Omniscience, will be exactly adapted to its purposes. Neither can a deficiency nor an excess of cause bring to pass any effect. Had the force which irradiated any stratum to its position, been either more or less than was needed for the purpose—that is to say, not *directly proportional* to the purpose—then to its position that stratum could not have been irradiated. Had the force which, with a view to general equability of distribution, emitted the proper number of atoms for each stratum, been not *directly proportional* to the number, then the number would *not* have been the number demanded for the equable distribution.

The second supposable objection is somewhat better entitled to an answer.

It is an admitted principle in Dynamics that every body, on receiving an impulse, or disposition to move, will move onward in a straight line, in the direction imparted by the impelling force, until deflected, or stopped, by some other force. How then, it may be asked, is my first or external stratum of atoms to be understood as discontinuing their movement at the circumference of the imaginary glass sphere, when no second force, of more than an imaginary character, appears, to account for the discontinuance?

I reply that the objection, in this case, actually does arise out of "an unwarranted assumption"—on the part of the objector—the assumption of a principle, in Dynamics, at an epoch when *no* "principles," in *anything*, exist:—I use the word "principle," of course, in the objector's understanding of the word.

"In the beginning" we can admit—indeed we can comprehend—but one *First Cause*—the truly ultimate *Principle*—the Volition of God. The primary *act*—that of Irradiation from Unity—must have been independent of all that which the world now calls "principle"—because all that we so designate is but a consequence of the rëaction of that primary act:—I say *"primary"* act; for the creation of the absolute material particle is more properly to be regarded as a *conception* than as an *"act"* in the ordinary meaning of the term. Thus, we must regard the primary act as an act for the establishment of what we now call "principles." But this primary act itself is to be considered as *continuous Volition*. The Thought of God is to be understood as originating the Diffusion—as proceeding with it—as regulating it—and, finally, as being withdrawn from it upon its completion. *Then* commences Rëaction, and through Rëaction, "Principle," as we employ the word. It will be advisable, however, to limit the application of this word to the two *immediate* results of the discontinuance of the Divine Volition—that is, to the two agents, *Attraction* and *Repulsion.* Every other Natural agent depends, either more or less immediately, upon these two, and therefore would be more conveniently designated as *sub*-principle.

It may be objected, thirdly, that, in general, the peculiar mode of distribution which I have suggested for the atoms, is "an hypothesis and nothing more."

Now, I am aware that the word hypothesis is a ponderous sledge-hammer, grasped immediately, if not lifted, by all very diminutive thinkers, upon the first appearance of any proposition wearing, in any particular, the garb of *a theory.* But "hypothesis" cannot be wielded *here* to any good purpose, even by those who succeed in lifting it—little men or great.

I maintain, first, that *only* in the mode described is it conceivable that Matter could have been diffused so as to fulfil at once the conditions of irradiation and of generally equable distribution. I maintain, secondly, that these conditions themselves have been imposed upon me, as necessities, in a train of ratiocination *as rigorously logical as that which establishes any demonstration in Euclid;* and I maintain, thirdly, that even if the charge of "hypothesis" were as fully sustained as it is, in fact, unsustained and untenable, still the validity and indisputability of my result would not, even in the slightest particular, be disturbed.

To explain:—The Newtonian Gravity—a law of Nature—a law whose existence as such no one out of Bedlam questions—a law whose admission as such enables us to account for nine-tenths of the Universal phænomena—a law which, merely because it does so enable us to account for these phænomena, we are perfectly willing, without reference to any other considerations, to admit, and cannot help admitting, as a law—a law, nevertheless, of which neither the principle nor the *modus operandi* of the principle, has ever yet been traced by the human analysis—a law, in short, which, neither in its detail nor in its generality, has been found susceptible of explanation *at all*—is at length seen to be at every point thoroughly explicable, provided we only yield our assent to——what? To an hypothesis? Why *if* an hypothesis—if the merest hypothesis—if an hypothesis for whose assumption—as in the case of that *pure* hypothesis the Newtonian law itself—no shadow of *à priori* reason could be assigned—if an hypothesis, even so absolute as all this implies, would enable us to perceive a principle for the Newtonian law—would enable us to understand as satisfied, conditions so miraculously—so ineffably complex and seemingly irreconcileable as those involved in the relations of which Gravity tells us,—what rational being *could* so expose his fatuity as to call even this absolute hypothesis an hypothesis any longer—unless, indeed, he were to persist in so calling it, with the understanding that he did so, simply for the sake of consistency *in words?*

But what is the true state of our present case? What is *the fact?* Not only that it is *not* an hypothesis which we are required *to adopt,* in order to admit the principle at issue explained, but that it *is* a logical conclusion which we are requested *not* to adopt if we can avoid it—which we are simply invited to *deny if we can:* —a conclusion of so accurate a logicality that to dispute it would be the effort—to doubt its validity beyond our power:—a conclusion from which we see no mode of escape, turn as we will; a result which confronts us either at the end of an *in*ductive journey from the phænomena of the very Law discussed, or at the close of a *de*ductive career from the most rigorously simple of all conceivable assumptions—*the assumption, in a word, of Simplicity itself.*

And if here, for the mere sake of cavilling, it be urged, that although my starting-point is, as I assert, the assumption of absolute Simplicity, yet Simplicity, considered merely in itself, is no axiom; and that only deductions from axioms are indisputable —it is thus that I reply:—

Every other science than Logic is the science of certain concrete relations. Arithmetic, for example, is the science of the relations of number—Geometry, of the relations of form—Mathematics in general, of the relations of quantity in general—of whatever can be increased or diminished. Logic, however, is the science of Relation in the abstract—of absolute Relation—of Relation considered solely in itself. An axiom in any particular science other than Logic is, thus, merely a proposition announcing certain concrete relations which seem to be too obvious for dispute—as when we say, for instance, that the whole is greater than its part;—and, thus again, the principle of the *Logical* axiom—in other words, of an axiom in the abstract—is, simply, *obviousness of relation*. Now, it is clear, not only that what is obvious to one mind may not be obvious to another, but that what is obvious to one mind at one epoch, may be anything but obvious, at another epoch, to the same mind. It is clear, moreover, that what, to-day, is obvious even to the majority of mankind, or to the majority of the best intellects of mankind, may to-morrow be, to either majority, more or less obvious, or in no respect obvious at all. It is seen, then, that the *axiomatic principle* itself is susceptible of variation, and of course that axioms are susceptible of similar change. Being mutable, the "truths" which grow out of them are necessarily mutable too; or, in other words, are never to be positively depended upon as truths at all—since Truth and Immutability are one.

It will now be readily understood that no axiomatic idea—no idea founded in the fluctuating principle, obviousness of relation—can possibly be so secure—so reliable a basis for any structure erected by the Reason, as *that* idea—(whatever it is, wherever we can find it, or *if* it be practicable to find it anywhere)—which is *ir*relative altogether—which not only presents to the understanding *no obviousness* of relation, either greater or less, to be considered, but subjects the intellect, not in the slightest degree, to the necessity of even looking at *any relation at all*. If such an idea be not what we too heedlessly term "an axiom," it is at least preferable, as a Logical basis, to any axiom ever propounded, or to all imaginable axioms combined:—and such, precisely, is the idea with which my deductive process, so thoroughly corroborated by induction, commences. My *particle proper* is but *absolute Irrelation.* To sum up what has been advanced:—As a starting point I have taken it for granted, simply, that the Beginning had nothing behind it or before it—that it was a Beginning in fact—that it was a beginning and nothing different from a beginning—in short, that this Beginning was—*that which it was.* If this be a "mere assumption" then a "mere assumption" let it be.

To conclude this branch of the subject:—I am fully warranted in announcing that *the Law which we have been in the habit of calling Gravity exists on account of Matter's having been irradiated, at its origin, atomically, into a limited* * *sphere of Space, from one, individual, unconditional, irrelative, and absolute Particle Proper, by the sole process in which it was possible to satisfy, at the same time, the two conditions, irradiation, and generally-equable distribution throughout the sphere—that is to say, by a force varying in direct proportion with the squares of the distances between the irradiated atoms, respectively, and the Particular centre of Irradiation.*

I have already given my reasons for presuming Matter to have been diffused by a determinate rather than by a continuous or infinitely continued force. Supposing a continuous force, we should be unable, in the first place, to comprehend a rëaction at all; and we should be required, in the second place, to entertain the impossible conception of an infinite extension of Matter. Not to dwell upon the impossibility of the conception, the infinite extension of Matter is an idea which, if not positively disproved, is at least not in any respect warranted by telescopic observation of the stars—a point to be explained more fully hereafter; and this empirical reason for believing in the original finity of Matter is unempirically confirmed. For example:—Admitting, for the moment, the possibility of understanding Space *filled* with the

* "Limited sphere"—A sphere is *necessarily* limited. I prefer tautology to a chance of misconception.

irradiated atoms—that is to say, admitting, as well as we can, for argument's sake, that the succession of the irradiated atoms had absolutely *no end*—then it is abundantly clear that, even when the Volition of God had been withdrawn from them, and thus the tendency to return into Unity permitted (abstractly) to be satisfied, this permission would have been nugatory and invalid—practically valueless and of no effect whatever. No Rëaction could have taken place; no movement toward Unity could have been made; no Law of Gravity could have obtained.

To explain:—Grant the *abstract* tendency of any one atom to any one other as the inevitable result of diffusion from the normal Unity:—or, what is the same thing, admit any given atom as *proposing* to move in any given direction—it is clear that, since there is an *infinity* of atoms on all sides of the atom proposing to move, it never can actually move toward the satisfaction of its tendency in the direction given, on account of a precisely equal and counter-balancing tendency in the direction diametrically opposite. In other words, exactly as many tendencies to Unity are behind the hesitating atom as before it; for it is a mere sotticism to say that one infinite line is longer or shorter than another infinite line, or that one infinite number is greater or less than another number that is infinite. Thus the atom in question must remain stationary forever. Under the impossible circumstances which we have been merely endeavoring to conceive for argument's sake, there could have been no aggregation of Matter—no stars—no worlds—nothing but a perpetually atomic and inconsequential Universe. In fact, view it as we will, the whole idea of unlimited Matter is not only untenable, but impossible and preposterous.

With the understanding of a *sphere* of atoms, however, we perceive, at once, a *satisfiable* tendency to union. The general result of the tendency each to each, being a tendency of all to the centre, the *general* process of condensation, or approximation, commences immediately, by a common and simultaneous movement, on withdrawal of the Divine Volition; the *individual* approximations, or coalescences—*not* cöalitions—of atom with atom, being subject to almost infinite variations of time, degree, and condition, on account of the excessive multiplicity of relation, arising from the differences of form assumed as characterizing the atoms at the moment of their quitting the Particle Proper; as well as from the subsequent particular inequidistance, each from each.

What I wish to impress upon the reader is the certainty of there arising, at once, (on withdrawal of the diffusive force, or Divine Volition,) out of the condition of the atoms as described, at innumerable points throughout the Universal sphere, innumerable agglomerations, characterized by innumerable specific differences of form, size, essential nature, and distance each from each. The development of Repulsion (Electricity) must have commenced, of course, with the very earliest particular efforts at Unity, and must have proceeded constantly in the ratio of Coalescence—that is to say, *in that of Condensation,* or, again, of Heterogeneity.

Thus the two Principles Proper, *Attraction* and *Repulsion*—the Material and the Spiritual—accompany each other, in the strictest fellowship, forever. Thus *The Body and The Soul walk hand in hand.*

If now, in fancy, we select *any one* of the agglomerations considered as in their primary stages throughout the Universal sphere, and suppose this incipient agglomeration to be taking place at that point where the centre of our Sun exists—or rather where it *did* exist originally; for the Sun is perpetually shifting his position—we shall find ourselves met, and borne onward for a time at least, by the most magnificent of theories—by the Nebular Cosmogony of Laplace:—although "Cosmogony" is far too comprehensive a term for what he really discusses—which is the constitution of our solar system alone—of one among the myriad of similar systems which make up the Universe Proper—that Universal sphere—that all-inclusive and absolute *Kosmos* which forms the subject of my present Discourse.

Confining himself to an *obviously limited* region—that of our solar system with its comparatively immediate vicinity—and *merely* assuming—that is to say, assuming without any basis whatever, either deductive or inductive—*much* of what I have been just endeavoring to place upon a more stable basis than assumption; assuming, for example, matter as diffused (without pretending to account for the diffusion) throughout, and somewhat beyond, the space occupied by our system—diffused in a state of heterogeneous nebulosity and obedient to that omniprevalent law of Gravity at whose principle he ventured to make no guess; assuming all this (which is quite true, although he had no logical right to its assumption) Laplace has shown, dynamically and mathematically, that the results in such case necessarily ensuing, are those and those alone which we find manifested in the actually existing condition of the system itself.

To explain:—Let us conceive *that* particular agglomeration of which we have just spoken—the one at the point designated by our Sun's centre—to have so far proceeded that a vast quantity of nebulous matter has here assumed a roughly globular form; its centre being, of course, coincident with what is now, or rather was originally, the centre of our Sun; and its periphery extending out beyond the orbit of Neptune, the most remote of our planets: —in other words, let us suppose the diameter of this rough sphere to be some 6000 millions of miles. For ages, this mass of matter has been undergoing condensation, until at length it has become reduced into the bulk we imagine; having proceeded gradually, of course, from its atomic and imperceptible state, into what we understand of visible, palpable, or otherwise appreciable nebulosity.

Now, the condition of this mass implies a rotation about an imaginary axis—a rotation which, commencing with the absolute incipiency of the aggregation, has been ever since acquiring velocity. The very first two atoms which met, approaching each other from points not diametrically opposite, would, in rushing partially past each other, form a nucleus for the rotary movement described. How this would increase in velocity, is readily seen. The two atoms are joined by others:—an aggregation is formed. The mass continues to rotate while condensing. But any atom at the circumference has, of course, a more rapid motion than one nearer the centre. The outer atom, however, with its superior velocity, approaches the centre; carrying this superior velocity with it as it goes. Thus every atom, proceeding inwardly, and finally attaching itself to the condensed centre, adds something to the original velocity of that centre—that is to say, increases the rotary movement of the mass.

Let us now suppose this mass so far condensed that it occupies *precisely* the space circumscribed by the orbit of Neptune, and that the velocity with which the surface of the mass moves, in the general rotation, is precisely that velocity with which Neptune now revolves about the Sun. At this epoch, then, we are to understand that the constantly increasing centrifugal force, having gotten the better of the non-increasing centripetal, loosened and separated the exterior and least condensed stratum, or a few of the exterior and least condensed strata, at the equator of the sphere, where the tangential velocity predominated; so that these strata formed about the main body an independent ring encircling the equatorial regions;—just as the exterior portion thrown off, by excessive velocity of rotation, from a grindstone, would form a ring about the grindstone, but for the solidity of the superficial material: were this caoutchouc, or anything similar in consistency precisely the phænomenon I describe would be presented.

The ring thus whirled from the nebulous mass, *revolved,* of course, *as* a separate ring, with just that velocity with which, while the surface of the mass, it *rotated.* In the meantime, condensation still proceeding, the interval between the discharged ring and the main body continued to increase, until the former was left at a vast distance from the latter.

Now, admitting the ring to have possessed, by some seemingly accidental arrangement of its heterogeneous materials, a constitution nearly uniform, then this ring, *as* such, would never have ceased revolving about its primary; but, as might have been anticipated, there appears to have been enough irregularity in the disposition of the materials, to make them cluster about centres of superior solidity; and thus the annular form was destroyed.* No doubt, the band was soon broken up into several portions, and one of these portions, predominating in mass, absorbed the others into itself; the whole settling, spherically, into a planet. That this latter, *as* a planet, continued the revolutionary movement which characterized it while a ring, is sufficiently clear; and that it took upon itself, also, an additional movement in its new condition of sphere, is readily explained. The ring being understood as yet unbroken, we see that its exterior, while the whole revolves about the parent body, moves more rapidly than its interior. When the rupture occurred, then, some portion in each fragment must have been moving with greater velocity than the others. The superior movement prevailing, must have whirled each fragment round—that is to say, have caused it to rotate; and the direction of the rotation must, of course, have been the direction of the revolution whence it arose. *All* the fragments having become subject to the rotation described, must, in coalescing, have imparted it to the one planet constituted by their coalescence.—This planet was Neptune. Its material continuing to undergo condensation, and the centrifugal force generated in its rotation getting, at length, the better of the centripetal, as before in the case of the parent orb, a ring was whirled also from the equatorial surface of this planet: this ring, having been ununiform in its constitution, was broken up, and its several fragments, being absorbed by the most massive, were collectively spherified into a moon. Subsequently, the operation was repeated, and a

* Laplace assumed his nebulosity heterogeneous, merely that he might be thus enabled to account for the breaking up of the rings; for had the nebulosity been homogeneous, they would not have broken. I reach the same result—heterogeneity of the secondary masses immediately resulting from the atoms—purely from an *à priori* consideration of their general design—*Relation.*

second moon was the result. We thus account for the planet Neptune, with the two satellites which accompany him.

In throwing off a ring from its equator, the Sun re-established that equilibrium between its centripetal and centrifugal forces which had been disturbed in the process of condensation; but, as this condensation still proceeded, the equilibrium was again immediately disturbed, through the increase of rotation. By the time the mass had so far shrunk that it occupied a spherical space just that circumscribed by the orbit of Uranus, we are to understand that the centrifugal force had so far obtained the ascendency that new relief was needed: a second equatorial band was, consequently, thrown off, which, proving ununiform, was broken up, as before in the case of Neptune; the fragments settling into the planet Uranus; the velocity of whose actual revolution about the Sun indicates, of course, the rotary speed of that Sun's equatorial surface at the moment of the separation. Uranus, adopting a rotation from the collective rotations of the fragments composing it, as previously explained, now threw off ring after ring; each of which, becoming broken up, settled into a moon:—three moons, at different epochs, having been formed, in this manner, by the rupture and general spherification of as many distinct ununiform rings.

By the time the Sun had shrunk until it occupied a space just that circumscribed by the orbit of Saturn, the balance, we are to suppose, between its centripetal and centrifugal forces had again become so far disturbed, through increase of rotary velocity, the result of condensation, that a third effort at equilibrium became necessary; and an annular band was therefore whirled off, as twice before; which, on rupture through ununiformity, became consolidated into the planet Saturn. This latter threw off, in the first place, seven uniform bands, which, on rupture, were spherified respectively into as many moons; but, subsequently, it appears to have discharged, at three distinct but not very distant epochs, three rings whose equability of constitution was, by apparent accident, so considerable as to present no occasion for their rupture; thus they continue to revolve as rings. I use the phrase "*apparent* accident;" for of accident in the ordinary sense there was, of course, nothing:—the term is properly applied only to the result of indistinguishable or not immediately traceable *law*.

Shrinking still farther, until it occupied just the space circumscribed by the orbit of Jupiter, the Sun now found need of farther effort to restore the counterbalance of its two forces, continually disarranged in the still continued increase of rotation. Jupiter, accordingly, was now thrown off; passing from the annular to the planetary condition; and, on attaining this latter, threw off in its turn, at four different epochs, four rings, which finally resolved themselves into so many moons.

Still shrinking, until its sphere occupied just the space defined by the orbit of the Asteroids, the Sun now discarded a ring which appears to have had *eight* centres of superior solidity, and, on breaking up, to have separated into eight fragments no one of which so far predominated in mass as to absorb the others. All therefore, as distinct although comparatively small planets, proceeded to revolve in orbits whose distances, each from each, may be considered as in some degree the measure of the force which drove them asunder:—all the orbits, nevertheless, being so closely coincident as to admit of our calling them *one*, in view of the other planetary orbits.

Continuing to shrink, the Sun, on becoming so small as just to fill the orbit of Mars, now discharged this planet—of course by the process repeatedly described. Having no moon, however, Mars could have thrown off no ring. In fact, an epoch had now arrived in the career of the parent body, the centre of the system. The *de*crease of its nebulosity, which is the *in*crease of its density, and which again is the *de*crease of its condensation, out of which latter arose the constant disturbance of equilibrium—must, by this period, have attained a point at which the efforts for restoration would have been more and more ineffectual just in proportion as they were less frequently needed. Thus the processes of which we have been speaking would everywhere show signs of exhaustion—in the planets, first, and secondly, in the original mass. We must not fall into the error of supposing the decrease of interval observed among the planets as we approach the Sun, to be in any respect indicative of an increase of frequency in the periods at which they were discarded. Exactly the converse is to be understood. The longest interval of time must have occurred between the discharges of the two interior; the shortest, between those of the two exterior, planets. The decrease of the interval of space is, nevertheless, the measure of the density, and thus inversely of the condensation, of the Sun, throughout the processes detailed.

Having shrunk, however, so far as to fill only the orbit of our Earth, the parent sphere whirled from itself still one other body—the Earth—in a condition so nebulous as to admit of this body's discarding, in its turn, yet another, which is our Moon;—but here terminated the lunar formations.

Finally, subsiding to the orbits first of Venus and then of Mercury, the Sun discarded these two interior planets; neither of which has given birth to any moon.

Thus from his original bulk—or, to speak more accurately, from the condition in which we first considered him—from a partially spherified nebular mass, *certainly* much more than 5,600 millions of miles in diameter—the great central orb and origin of our solar-planetary-lunar system, has gradually descended, by condensation, in obedience to the law of Gravity, to a globe only 882,000 miles in diameter; but it by no means follows, either that its condensation is yet complete, or that it may not still possess the capacity of whirling from itself another planet.

I have here given—in outline of course, but still with all the detail necessary for distinctness—a view of the Nebular Theory as its author himself conceived it. From whatever point we regard it, we shall find it *beautifully true*. It is by far too beautiful, indeed, *not* to possess Truth as its essentiality—and here I am very profoundly serious in what I say. In the revolution of the satellites of Uranus, there does appear something seemingly inconsistent with the assumptions of Laplace; but that *one* inconsistency can invalidate a theory constructed from a million of intricate consistencies, is a fancy fit only for the fantastic. In prophesying, confidently, that the apparent anomaly to which I refer, will, sooner or later, be found one of the strongest possible corroborations of the general hypothesis, I pretend to no especial spirit of divination. It is a matter which the only difficulty seems *not* to foresee.*

The bodies whirled off in the processes described, would exchange, it has been seen, the superficial *rotation* of the orbs whence they originated, for a *revolution* of equal velocity about these orbs as distant centres; and the revolution thus engendered must proceed, so long as the centripetal force, or that with which the discarded body gravitates toward its parent, is neither greater nor less than that by which it was discarded; that is, than the centrifugal, or, far more properly, than the tangential, velocity. From the unity, however, of the origin of these two forces, we might have expected to find them as they are found—the one accurately counterbalancing the other. It has been shown, indeed, that the act of whirling-off is, in every case, merely an act for the preservation of the counterbalance.

After referring, however, the centripetal force to the omniprevalent law of Gravity, it has been the fashion with astronomical treatises, to seek beyond the limits of mere Nature—that is to say, of *Secondary* Cause—a solution of the phænomenon of tangential velocity. This latter they attribute directly to a *First* Cause—to God. The force which carries a stellar body around its primary they assert to have originated in an impulse given immediately by the finger—this is the childish phraseology employed—by the finger of Deity itself. In this view, the planets, fully formed, are conceived to have been hurled from the Divine hand,

* I am prepared to show that the anomalous revolution of the satellites of Uranus is a simply perspective anomaly arising from the inclination of the axis of the planet.

to a position in the vicinity of the suns, with an impetus mathematically adapted to the masses, or attractive capacities, of the suns themselves. An idea so grossly unphilosophical, although so supinely adopted, could have arisen only from the difficulty of otherwise accounting for the absolutely accurate adaptation, each to each, of two forces so seemingly independent, one of the other, as are the gravitating and tangential. But it should be remembered that, for a long time, the coincidence between the moon's rotation and her sidereal revolution—two matters seemingly far more independent than those now considered—was looked upon as positively miraculous; and there was a strong disposition, even among astronomers, to attribute the marvel to the direct and continual agency of God—who, in this case, it was said, had found it necessary to interpose, specially, among his general laws, a set of subsidiary regulations, for the purpose of forever concealing from mortal eyes the glories, or perhaps the horrors, of the other side of the Moon—of that mysterious hemisphere which has always avoided, and must perpetually avoid, the telescopic scrutiny of mankind. The advance of Science, however, soon demonstrated—what to the philosophical instinct needed *no* demonstration—that the one movement is but a portion—something more, even, than a consequence—of the other.

For my part, I have no patience with fantasies at once so timorous, so idle, and so awkward. They belong to the veriest *cowardice* of thought. That Nature and the God of Nature are distinct, no thinking being can long doubt. By the former we imply merely the laws of the latter. But with the very idea of God, omnipotent, omniscient, we entertain, also, the idea of *the infallibility* of his laws. With Him there being neither Past nor Future—with Him all being *Now*—do we not insult him in supposing his laws so contrived as not to provide for every possible contingency?—or, rather, what idea *can* we have of *any* possible contingency, except that it is at once a result and a manifestation of his laws? He who, divesting himself of prejudice, shall have the rare courage to think absolutely for himself, cannot fail to arrive, in the end, at the condensation of *laws* into *Law—cannot* fail of reaching the conclusion that *each law of Nature is dependent at all points upon all other laws,* and that all are but consequences of one primary exercise of the Divine Volition. Such is the principle of the Cosmogony which, with all necessary deference, I here venture to suggest and to maintain.

In this view, it will be seen that, dismissing as frivolous, and even impious, the fancy of the tangential force having been imparted to the planets immediately by "the finger of God," I consider this force as originating in the rotation of the stars:—this rotation as brought about by the in-rushing of the primary atoms, towards their respective centres of aggregation:—this in-rushing as the consequence of the law of Gravity:—this law as but the mode in which is necessarily manifested the tendency of the atoms to return into imparticularity:—this tendency to return as but the inevitable rëaction of the first and most sublime of Acts—that act by which a God, self-existing and alone existing, became all things at once, through dint of his volition, while all things were thus constituted a portion of God.

The radical assumptions of this Discourse suggest to me, and in fact imply, certain important *modifications* of the Nebular Theory as given by Laplace. The efforts of the repulsive power I have considered as made for the purpose of preventing contact among the atoms, and thus as made in the ratio of the approach to contact—that is to say, in the ratio of condensation.* In other words, *Electricity,* with its involute phænomena, heat, light and magnetism, is to be understood as proceeding as condensation proceeds, and, of course, inversely as destiny proceeds, or the *cessation to condense*. Thus the Sun, in the process of its aggregation, must soon, in developing repulsion, have become excessively heated—perhaps incandescent: and we can perceive how the operation of discarding its rings must have been materially assisted by the slight incrustation of its surface consequent on cooling. Any common experiment shows us how readily a crust

* See page 475.

of the character suggested, is separated, through heterogeneity, from the interior mass. But, on every successive rejection of the crust, the new surface would appear incandescent as before; and the period at which it would again become so far incrusted as to be readily loosened and discharged, may well be imagined as exactly coincident with that at which a new effort would be needed, by the whole mass, to restore the equilibrium of its two forces, disarranged through condensation. In other words:—by the time the electric influence (Repulsion) has prepared the surface for rejection, we are to understand that the gravitating influence (Attraction) is precisely ready to reject it. Here, then, as everywhere, *the Body and the Soul walk hand in hand.*

These ideas are empirically confirmed at all points. Since condensation can never, in any body, be considered as absolutely at an end, we are warranted in anticipating that, whenever we have an opportunity of testing the matter, we shall find indications of resident luminosity in *all* the stellar bodies—moons and planets as well as suns. That our Moon is strongly self-luminous, we see at her every total eclipse, when, if not so, she would disappear. On the dark part of the satellite, too, during her phases, we often observe flashes like our own Auroras; and that these latter, with our various other so-called electrical phænomena, without reference to any more steady radiance, must give our Earth a certain appearance of luminosity to an inhabitant of the Moon, is quite evident. In fact, we should regard all the phænomena referred to, as mere manifestations, in different moods and degrees, of the Earth's feebly-continued condensation.

If my views are tenable, we should be prepared to find the newer planets—that is to say, those nearer the Sun—more luminous than those older and more remote:—and the extreme brilliancy of Venus (on whose dark portions, during her phases, the Auroras are frequently visible) does not seem to be altogether accounted for by her mere proximity to the central orb. She is no doubt vividly self-luminous, although less so than Mercury: while the luminosity of Neptune may be comparatively nothing.

Admitting what I have urged, it is clear that, from the moment of the Sun's discarding a ring, there must be a continuous diminution both of his heat and light, on account of the continuous incrustation of his surface; and that a period would arrive—the period immediately previous to a new discharge—when a *very material* decrease of both light and heat, must become apparent. Now, we know that tokens of such changes are distinctly recognisable. On the Melville islands—to adduce merely one out of a hundred examples—we find traces of *ultra-tropical* vegetation—of plants that never could have flourished without immensely more light and heat than are at present afforded by our Sun to any portion of the surface of the Earth. Is such vegetation referable to an epoch immediately subsequent to the whirling-off of Venus? At this epoch must have occurred to us our greatest access of solar influence; and, in fact, this influence must then have attained its maximum:—leaving out of view, of course, the period when the Earth itself was discarded—the period of its mere organization.

Again:—we know that there exist *non-luminous suns*—that is to say, suns whose existence we determine through the movements of others, but whose luminosity is not sufficient to impress us. Are these suns invisible merely on account of the length of time elapsed since their discharge of a planet? And yet again:—may we not—at least in certain cases—account for the sudden appearances of suns where none had been previously suspected, by the hypothesis that, having rolled with incrusted surfaces throughout the few thousand years of our astronomical history, each of these suns, in whirling off a new secondary, has at length been enabled to display the glories of its still incandescent interior?—To the well-ascertained fact of the proportional increase of heat as we descend into the Earth, I need of course, do nothing more than refer:—it comes in the strongest possible corroboration of all that I have said on the topic now at issue.

In speaking, not long ago, of the repulsive or electrical influence, I remarked that "the important phænomena of vitality, consciousness, and thought, whether we observe them generally or in detail, seem to proceed *at least in the ratio of the heterogeneous."* * I mentioned, too, that I would recur to the suggestion: —and this is the proper point at which to do so. Looking at the matter, first, in detail, we perceive that not merely the *manifestation* of vitality, but its importance, consequences, and elevation of character, keep pace, very closely, with the heterogeneity, or complexity, of the animal structure. Looking at the question, now, in its generality, and referring to the first movements of the atoms towards mass-constitution, we find that heterogeneousness, brought about directly through condensation, is proportional with it forever. We thus reach the proposition that *the importance of the development of the terrestrial vitality proceeds equably with the terrestrial condensation.*

Now this is in precise accordance with what we know of the succession of animals on the Earth. As it has proceeded in its condensation, superior and still superior races have appeared. Is it impossible that the successive geological revolutions which have attended, at least, if not immediately caused, these successive elevations of vitalic character—is it improbable that these revolutions have themselves been produced by the successive planetary discharges from the Sun—in other words, by the successive variations in the solar influence on the Earth? Were this idea tenable, we should not be unwarranted in the fancy that the discharge of yet a new planet, interior to Mercury, may give rise to yet a new modification of the terrestrial surface—a modification from which may spring a race both materially and spiritually superior to Man. These thoughts impress me with all the force of truth—but I throw them out, of course, merely in their obvious character of suggestion.

The Nebular Theory of Laplace has lately received far more confirmation than it needed, at the hands of the philosopher, Compte. These two have thus together shown—*not,* to be sure, that matter at any period actually existed as described, in a state

* Page 448.

of nebular diffusion, but that, admitting it so to have existed throughout the space and much beyond the space now occupied by our solar system, *and to have commenced a movement towards a centre*—it must gradually have assumed the various forms and motions which are now seen, in that system, to obtain. A demonstration such as this—a dynamical and mathematical demonstration, as far as demonstration can be—unquestionable and unquestioned—unless, indeed, by that unprofitable and disreputable tribe, the professional questioners—the mere madmen who deny the Newtonian law of Gravity on which the results of the French mathematicians are based—a demonstration, I say, such as this, would to most intellects be conclusive—and I confess that it is so to mine—of the validity of the nebular hypothesis upon which the demonstration depends.

That the demonstration does not *prove* the hypothesis, according to the common understanding of the word "proof," I admit, of course. To show that certain existing results—that certain established facts—may be, even mathematically, accounted for by the assumption of a certain hypothesis, is by no means to establish the hypothesis itself. In other words:—to show that, certain data being given, a certain existing result might, or even *must,* have ensued, will fail to prove that this result *did* ensue, *from the data,* until such time as it shall be also shown that there are, *and can be,* no other data from which the result in question might *equally* have ensued. But, in the case now discussed, although all must admit the deficiency of what we are in the habit of terming "proof," still there are many intellects, and those of the loftiest order, to which *no* proof could bring one iota of additional *conviction.* Without going into details which might impinge upon the Cloud-Land of Metaphysics, I may as well here observe, that the force of conviction, in cases such as this, will always, with the right-thinking, be proportional to the amount of *complexity* intervening between the hypothesis and the result. To be less abstract:—The greatness of the complexity found existing among cosmical conditions, by rendering great in the same proportion the difficulty of accounting for all these conditions, *at once,* strengthens, also in the same proportion, our faith in that hypothesis which does, in such manner, satisfactorily account for them:—and as *no* complexity can well be conceived greater than that of the astronomical conditions, so no conviction can be stronger—to *my* mind at least—than that with which I am impressed by an hypothesis that not only reconciles these conditions, with mathematical accuracy, and reduces them into a consistent and intelligible whole, but is, at the same time, the *sole* hypothesis by means of which the human intellect has been ever enabled to account for them *at all.*

A most unfounded opinion has been latterly current in gossiping and even in scientific circles—the opinion that the so-called Nebular Cosmogony has been overthrown. This fancy has arisen from the report of late observations made, among what hitherto have been termed the "nebulæ," through the large telescope of Cincinnati, and the world-renowned instrument of Lord Rosse. Certain spots in the firmament which presented, even to the most powerful of the old telescopes, the appearance of nebulosity, or haze, had been regarded for a long time as confirming the theory of Laplace. They were looked upon as stars in that very process of condensation which I have been attempting to describe. Thus it was supposed that we "had ocular evidence"—an evidence, by the way, which has always been found very questionable—of the truth of the hypothesis; and, although certain telescopic improvements, every now and then, enabled us to perceive that a spot, here and there, which we had been classing among the nebulæ, was, in fact, but a cluster of stars deriving its nebular character only from its immensity of distance—still it was thought that no doubt could exist as to the actual nebulosity of numerous other masses, the strong-holds of the nebulists, bidding defiance to every effort at segregation. Of these latter the most interesting was the great "nebulæ" in the constellation Orion:—but this, with innumerable other miscalled "nebulæ," when viewed through the magnificent modern telescopes, has become resolved into a simple collection of stars. Now this fact has been very generally understood as conclusive against the Nebular Hypothesis of Laplace; and, on announcement of the discoveries in question, the most enthusiastic defender and most eloquent popularizer of the theory, Dr. Nichol, went so far as to "admit the necessity of abandoning" an idea which had formed the material of his most praiseworthy book.*

Many of my readers will no doubt be inclined to say that the result of these new investigations *has* at least a strong *tendency* to overthrow the hypothesis; while some of them, more thoughtful, will suggest that, although the theory is by no means disproved through the segregation of the particular "nebulæ" alluded to, still a *failure* to segregate them, with such telescopes, might well have been understood as a triumphant *corroboration* of the theory:—and this latter class will be surprised, perhaps, to hear me say that even with *them* I disagree. If the propositions of this Discourse have been comprehended, it will be seen that, in my view, a failure to segregate the "nebulæ" would have tended to the refutation, rather than to the confirmation, of the Nebular Hypothesis.

Let me explain:—The Newtonian Law of Gravity we may, of course, assume as demonstrated. This law, it will be remembered, I have referred to the rëaction of the first Divine Act—to the rëaction of an exercise of the Divine Volition temporarily overcoming a difficulty. This difficulty is that of forcing the normal into the abnormal—of impelling that whose originality, and therefore whose rightful condition, was *One*, to take upon itself the wrongful condition of *Many*. It is only by conceiving this

* *Views of the Architecture of the Heavens.* A letter, purporting to be from Dr. Nichol to a friend in America, went the rounds of our newspapers, about two years ago, I think, admitting "the necessity" to which I refer. In a subsequent Lecture, however, Dr. N. appears in some manner to have gotten the better of the necessity, and does not quite *renounce* the theory, although he seems to wish that he could sneer at it as "a purely hypothetical one." What else was the Law of Gravity before the Maskelyne experiments? and who questioned the Law of Gravity, even then?

difficulty as *temporarily* overcome, that we can comprehend a rëaction. There could have been no reaction had the act been infinitely continued. So long as the act *lasted,* no reaction, of course, could commence; in other words, no *gravitation* could take place —for we have considered the one as but the manifestation of the other. But gravitation *has* taken place; therefore the act of Creation has ceased: and gravitation has long ago taken place; therefore the act of Creation has long ago ceased. We can no more expect, then, to observe *the primary processes* of Creation; and to those primary processes the condition of nebulosity has already been explained to belong.

Through what we know of the propagation of light, we have direct proof that the more remote of the stars have existed, under the forms in which we now see them, for an inconceivable number of years. So far back *at least,* then, as the period when these stars underwent condensation, must have been the epoch at which the mass-constitutive processes began. That we may conceive these processes, then, as still going on in the case of certain "nebulæ," while in all other cases we find them thoroughly at an end, we are forced into assumptions for which we have really *no* basis whatever—we have to thrust in, again, upon the revolting Reason, the blasphemous idea of special interposition—we have to suppose that, in the particular instances of these "nebulæ," an unerring God found it necessary to introduce certain supplementary regulations—certain improvements of the general law—certain re-touchings and emendations, in a word, which had the effect of deferring the completion of these individual stars for centuries of centuries beyond the æra during which all the other stellar bodies had time, not only to be fully constituted, but to grow hoary with an unspeakable old age.

Of course, it will be immediately objected that since the light by which we recognise the nebulæ now, must be merely that which left their surfaces a vast number of years ago, the processes at present observed, or supposed to be observed, are, in fact, *not* processes now actually going on, but the phantoms of processes completed long in the Past—just as I maintain all these mass-constitutive processes *must* have been.

To this I reply that neither is the now-observed condition of the condensed stars their actual condition, but a condition completed long in the past; so that my argument drawn from the *relative* condition of the stars and the "nebulæ," is in no manner disturbed. Moreover, those who maintain the existence of nebulæ, do *not* refer the nebulosity to extreme distance; they declare it a real and not merely a perspective nebulosity. That we may conceive, indeed, a nebular mass as visible at all, we must conceive it as *very near us* in comparison with the condensed stars brought into view by the modern telescopes. In maintaining the appearances in question, then, to be really nebulous, we maintain their comparative vicinity to our point of view. Thus, their condition, as we see them now, must be referred to an epoch *far less remote* than that to which we may refer the now-observed condition of at least the majority of the stars.—In a word, should Astronomy ever demonstrate a "nebula," in the sense at present intended, I should consider the Nebular Cosmogony—*not,* indeed, as corroborated by the demonstration—but as thereby irretrievably overthrown.

By way, however, of rendering unto Cæsar *no more* than the things that are Cæsar's, let me here remark that the assumption of the hypothesis which led him to so glorious a result, seems to have been suggested to Laplace in great measure by a misconception—by the very misconception of which we have just been speaking—by the generally prevalent misunderstanding of the character of the nebulæ, so mis-named. These he supposed to be, in reality, what their designation implies. The fact is, this great man had, very properly, an inferior faith in his own merely *perceptive* powers. In respect, therefore, to the actual existence of nebulæ—an existence so confidently maintained by his telescopic contemporaries—he depended less upon what he saw than upon what he heard.

It will be seen that the only valid objections to his theory, are those made to its hypothesis *as* such—to what suggested it—not to what it suggests; to its propositions rather than to its results. His most unwarranted assumption was that of giving the atoms a movement towards a centre, in the very face of his evident understanding that these atoms, in unlimited succession, extended throughout the Universal space. I have already shown that, under such circumstances, there could have occurred no movement at all; and Laplace, consequently, assumed one on no more philosophical ground than that something of the kind was necessary for the establishment of what he intended to establish.

His original idea seems to have been a compound of the true Epicurean atoms with the false nebulæ of his contemporaries; and thus his theory presents us with the singular anomaly of absolute truth deduced, as a mathematical result, from a hybrid datum of ancient imagination intertangled with modern inacumen. Laplace's real strength lay, in fact, in an almost miraculous mathematical instinct:—on this he relied; and in no instance did it fail or deceive him:—in the case of the Nebular Cosmogony, it led him, blindfolded, through a labyrinth of Error, into one of the most luminous and stupendous temples of Truth.

Let us now fancy, for the moment, that the ring first thrown off by the Sun—that is to say, the ring whose breaking-up constituted Neptune—did not, in fact, break up until the throwing-off of the ring out of which Uranus arose; that this latter ring, again, remained perfect until the discharge of that out of which sprang Saturn; that this latter, again, remained entire until the discharge of that from which originated Jupiter—and so on. Let us imagine, in a word, that no dissolution occurred among the rings until the final rejection of that which gave birth to Mercury. We thus paint to the eye of the mind a series of cöexistent concentric circles; and looking as well at *them* as at the processes by which, according to Laplace's hypothesis, they were constructed, we perceive at once a very singular analogy with the atomic strata and the process of the original irradiation as I have described it. Is it impossible that, on measuring the *forces*, respectively, by which each successive planetary circle was thrown off—that is to say, on measuring the successive excesses of rotation over gravitation which occasioned the successive discharges—we should find the analogy in question more decidedly confirmed? *Is it improbable that we should discover these forces to have varied—as in the original radiation—proportionally to the squares of the distances?*

Our solar system, consisting, in chief, of one sun, with sixteen planets certainly, and possibly a few more, revolving about it at various distances, and attended by seventeen moons assuredly, but *very* probably by several others—is now ,to be considered as *an example* of the innumerable agglomerations which proceeded to take place throughout the Universal Sphere of atoms on withdrawal of the Divine Volition. I mean to say that our solar system is to be understood as affording a *generic instance* of these agglomerations, or, more correctly, of the ulterior conditions at which they arrived. If we keep our attention fixed on the idea of *the utmost possible Relation* as the Omnipotent design, and on the precautions taken to accomplish it through difference of form, among the original atoms, and particular inequidistance, we shall find it impossible to suppose for a moment that even any two of the incipient agglomerations reached precisely the same result in the end. We shall rather be inclined to think that *no two* stellar bodies in the Universe—whether suns, planets or moons—are particularly, while *all* are generally, similar. Still less, then, can we imagine any two *assemblages* of such bodies—any two "systems"—as having more than a general resemblance.* Our telescopes, at this point, thoroughly confirm our deductions. Taking our own solar system, then, as merely a loose or general type of all, we have so far proceeded in our subject as to survey the Universe under the aspect of a spherical space, throughout

* It is not *impossible* that some unlooked-for optical improvement may disclose to us, among innumerable varieties of systems, a luminous sun, encircled by luminous and non-luminous rings, within and without and between which, revolve luminous and non-luminous planets, attended by moons having moons—and even these latter again having moons.

which, dispersed with merely general equability, exist a number of but generally similar *systems.*

Let us now, expanding our conceptions, look upon each of these systems as in itself an atom; which in fact it is, when we consider it as but one of the countless myriads of systems which constitute the Universe. Regarding all, then, as but colossal atoms, each with the same ineradicable tendency to Unity which characterizes the actual atoms of which it consists—we enter at once upon a new order of aggregations. The smaller systems, in the vicinity of a larger one, would, inevitably, be drawn into still closer vicinity. A thousand would assemble here; a million there —perhaps here, again, even a billion—leaving, thus, immeasurable vacancies in space. And if, now, it be demanded why, in the case of these systems—of these merely Titanic atoms—I speak, simply, of an "assemblage," and not, as in the case of the actual atoms, of a more or less consolidated agglomeration:—if it be asked, for instance, why I do not carry what I suggest to its legitimate conclusion, and describe, at once, these assemblages of system-atoms as rushing to consolidation in spheres—as each becoming condensed into one magnificent sun—my reply is that μέλλοντα ταῦτα—I am but pausing, for a moment, on the awful threshold of *the Future.* For the present, calling these assemblages "clusters," we see them in the incipient stages of their consolidation. Their *absolute* consolidation is *to come.*

We have now reached a point from which we behold the Universe as a spherical space, interspersed, *unequably,* with *clusters.* It will be noticed that I here prefer the adverb "unequably" to the phrase "with a merely general equability," employed before. It is evident, in fact, that the equability of distribution will diminish in the ratio of the agglomerative processes—that is to say, as the things distributed diminish in number. Thus the increase of *in*equability—an increase which must continue until, sooner or later, an epoch will arrive at which the largest agglomeration will absorb all the others—should be viewed as, simply, a corroborative indication of the *tendency to One.*

And here, at length, it seems proper to inquire whether the ascertained *facts* of Astronomy confirm the general arrangement which I have thus, deductively, assigned to the Heavens. Thoroughly, they *do*. Telescopic observation, guided by the laws of perspective, enables us to understand that the perceptible Universe exists as *a cluster of clusters, irregularly disposed.*

The "clusters" of which this Universal *"cluster of clusters"* consists, are merely what we have been in the practice of designating "nebulæ"—and, of these "nebulæ," *one* is of paramount interest to mankind. I allude to the Galaxy, or Milky Way. This interests us, first and most obviously, on account of its great superiority in apparent size, not only to any one other cluster in the firmament, but to all the other clusters taken together. The largest of these latter occupies a mere point, comparatively, and is distinctly seen only with the aid of a telescope. The Galaxy sweeps throughout the Heaven and is brilliantly visible to the naked eye. But it interests man chiefly, although less immediately, on account of its being his home; the home of the Earth on which he exists; the home of the Sun about which this Earth revolves; the home of that "system" of orbs of which the Sun is the centre and primary—the Earth one of sixteen secondaries, or planets—the Moon one of seventeen tertiaries, or satellites. The Galaxy, let me repeat, is but one of the *clusters* which I have been describing—but one of the miscalled "nebulæ" revealed to us—by the telescope alone, sometimes—as faint hazy spots in various quarters of the sky. We have no reason to suppose the Milky Way *really* more extensive than the least of these "nebulæ." Its vast superiority in size is but an apparent superiority arising from our position in regard to it—that is to say, from our position in its midst. However strange the assertion may at first appear to those unversed in Astronomy, still the astronomer himself has no hesitation in asserting that we are *in the midst* of that inconceivable host of stars—of suns—of systems—which constitute the Galaxy. Moreover, not only have *we*—not only has *our* Sun a right to claim the Galaxy as its own especial cluster, but, with slight reservation, it may be said that all the distinctly visible stars of the firmament—all the stars visible to the naked eye—have equally a right to claim it as *their* own.

There has been a great deal of misconception in respect to the *shape* of the Galaxy; which, in nearly all our astronomical treatises, is said to resemble that of a capital Y. The cluster in question has, in reality, a certain general—*very* general resemblance to the planet Saturn, with its encompassing triple ring. Instead of the solid orb of that planet, however, we must picture to ourselves a lenticular star-island, or collection of stars; our Sun lying excentrically—near the shore of the island—on that side of it which is nearest the constellation of the Cross and farthest from that of Cassiopeia. The surrounding ring, where it approaches our position, has in it a longitudinal *gash,* which does, in fact, cause *the ring, in our vicinity,* to assume, loosely, the appearance of a capital Y.

We must not fall into the error, however, of conceiving the somewhat indefinite girdle as at all *remote,* comparatively speaking, from the also indefinite lenticular cluster which it surrounds; and thus, for mere purpose of explanation, we may speak of our Sun as actually situated at that point of the Y where its three component lines unite; and, conceiving this letter to be of a certain solidity—of a certain thickness, very trivial in comparison with its length—we may even speak of our position as *in the middle* of this thickness. Fancying ourselves thus placed, we shall no longer find difficulty in accounting for the phænomena presented—which are perspective altogether. When we look upward or downward—that is to say, when we cast our eyes in the direction of the letter's *thickness*—we look through fewer stars than when we cast them in the direction of its *length,* or *along* either of the three component lines. Of course, in the former case, the stars appear scattered—in the latter, crowded.—To reverse this explanation:—An inhabitant of the Earth, when looking, as we commonly express ourselves, *at* the Galaxy, is then beholding it in some of the directions of its length—is looking *along* the lines of the Y—but when, looking out into the general Heaven, he turns his eyes *from* the Galaxy, he is then surveying it in the direction of the letter's thickness; and on this account the stars seem to him scattered; while, in fact, they are as close together, on an average, as in the mass of the cluster. *No* consideration could be better adapted to convey an idea of this cluster's stupendous extent.

If, with a telescope of high space-penetrating power, we carefully inspect the firmament, we shall become aware of a *belt of clusters*—of what we have hitherto called "nebulæ"—a *band,* of varying breadth, stretching from horizon to horizon, at right angles to the general course of the Milky Way. This band is the ultimate *cluster of clusters.* This belt is *The Universe.* Our Galaxy is but one, and perhaps one of the most inconsiderable, of the clusters which go to the constitution of this ultimate, Universal *belt* or band. The appearance of this cluster of clusters, to our eyes, *as* a belt or band, is altogether a perspective phænomenon of the same character as that which causes us to behold our own individual and roughly-spherical cluster, the Galaxy, under guise also of a belt, traversing the Heavens at right angles to the Universal one. The shape of the all-inclusive cluster is, of course *generally,* that of each individual cluster which it includes. Just as the scattered stars which, on looking *from* the Galaxy, we see in the general sky are, in fact, but a portion of that Galaxy itself, and as closely intermingled with it as any of the telescopic points in what seems the densest portion of its mass—so are the scattered "nebulæ" which, on casting our eyes *from* the Universal *belt,* we perceive at all points of the firmament—so, I say, are these scattered "nebulæ" to be understood as only perspectively scattered, and as part and parcel of the one supreme and Universal *sphere.*

No astronomical fallacy is more untenable, and none has been more pertinaciously adhered to, than that of the absolute *illimitation* of the Universe of Stars. The reasons for limitation, as I have already assigned them, *à priori,* seem to me unanswerable; but, not to speak of these, *observation* assures us that there is, in numerous directions around us, certainly, if not in all, a positive limit—or, at the very least, affords us no basis whatever for thinking otherwise. Were the succession of stars endless, then the background of the sky would present us an uniform luminosity, like that displayed by the Galaxy—*since there could be absolutely no point, in all that background, at which would not exist a star.* The only mode, therefore, in which, under such a state of affairs, we could comprehend the *voids* which our telescopes find in innumerable directions, would be by supposing the distance of the invisible background so immense that no ray from it has yet been able to reach us at all. That this *may* be so, who shall venture to deny? I maintain, simply, that we have not even the shadow of a reason for believing that it *is* so.

When speaking of the vulgar propensity to regard all bodies on the Earth as tending merely to the Earth's centre, I observed that, "with certain exceptions to be specified hereafter, every body on the Earth tended not only to the Earth's centre, but in every conceivable direction besides." * The "exceptions" refer to those frequent gaps in the Heavens, where our utmost scrutiny can detect not only no stellar bodies, but no indications of their existence:—where yawning chasms, blacker than Erebus, seem to afford us glimpses, through the boundary walls of the Universe of Stars, into the illimitable Universe of Vacancy, beyond. Now as any body, existing on the Earth, chances to pass, either through its own movement or the Earth's, into a line with any one of these voids, or cosmical abysses, it clearly is no longer attracted *in the direction of that void,* and for the moment, consequently, is "heavier" than at any period, either after or before. Independently of the consideration of these voids, however, and looking only at the generally unequable distribution of the stars, we see that the absolute tendency of bodies on the Earth to the Earth's centre, is in a state of perpetual variation.

We comprehend, then, the insulation of our Universe. We

* Page 462.

perceive the isolation of *that*—of *all* that which we grasp with the senses. We know that there exists one *cluster of clusters*—a collection around which, on all sides, extend the immeasurable wildernesses of a Space *to all human perception* untenanted. But *because* upon the confines of this Universe of Stars we are compelled to pause, through want of farther evidence from the senses, is it right to conclude that, in fact, there *is* no material point beyond that which we have thus been permitted to attain? Have we, or have we not, an analogical right to the inference that this perceptible Universe—that this cluster of clusters—is but one of *a series* of clusters of clusters, the rest of which are invisible through distance—through the diffusion of their light being so excessive, ere it reaches us, as not to produce upon our retinas a light-impression—or from there being no such emanation as light at all, in these unspeakably distant worlds—or, lastly, from the mere interval being so vast, that the electric tidings of their presence in Space, have not yet—through the lapsing myriads of years—been enabled to traverse that interval?

Have we any right to inferences—have we any ground whatever for visions such as these? If we have a right to them in *any* degree, we have a right to their infinite extension.

The human brain has obviously a leaning to the *"Infinite,"* and fondles the phantom of the idea. It seems to long with a passionate fervor for this impossible conception, with the hope of intellectually believing it when conceived. What is general among the whole race of Man, of course no individual of that race can be warranted in considering abnormal; nevertheless, there *may* be a class of superior intelligences, to whom the human bias alluded to may wear all the character of monomania.

My question, however, remains unanswered:—Have we any right to infer—let us say, rather, to imagine—an interminable succession of the "clusters of clusters," or of "Universes" more or less similar?

I reply that the "right," in a case such as this, depends absolutely upon the hardihood of that imagination which ventures to claim the right. Let me declare, only, that, as an individual, I myself feel impelled to *fancy*—without daring to call it more—that there *does* exist a *limitless* succession of Universes, more or less similar to that of which we have cognizance—to that of which *alone* we shall ever have cognizance—at the very least until the return of our own particular Universe into Unity. *If* such clusters of clusters exist, however—*and they do*—it is abundantly clear that, having had no part in our origin, they have no portion in our laws. They neither attract us, nor we them. Their material—their spirit is not ours—is not that which obtains in any part of our Universe. They could not impress our senses or our souls. Among them and us—considering all, for the moment, collectively—there are no influences in common. Each exists, apart and independently, *in the bosom of its proper and particular God.*

In the conduct of this Discourse, I am aiming less at physical than at metaphysical order. The clearness with which even material phænomena are presented to the understanding, depends very little, I have long since learned to perceive, upon a merely natural, and almost altogether upon a moral, arrangement. If then I seem to step somewhat too discursively from point to point of my topic, let me suggest that I do so in the hope of thus the better keeping unbroken that chain of *graduated impression* by which alone the intellect of Man can expect to encompass the grandeurs of which I speak, and, in their majestic totality, to comprehend them.

So far, our attention has been directed, almost exclusively, to a general and relative grouping of the stellar bodies in space. Of specification there has been little; and whatever ideas of *quantity* have been conveyed—that is to say, of number, magnitude, and distance—have been conveyed incidentally and by way of preparation for more definitive conceptions. These latter let us now attempt to entertain.

Our solar system, as has been already mentioned, consists, in chief, of one sun and sixteen planets certainly, but in all probability a few others, revolving around it as a centre, and attended by seventeen moons of which we know, with possibly several more of which as yet we know nothing. These various bodies are not true spheres, but oblate spheroids—spheres flattened at the poles of the imaginary axes about which they rotate:—the flattening being a consequence of the rotation. Neither is the Sun absolutely the centre of the system; for this Sun itself, with all the planets, revolves about a perpetually shifting point of space, which is the system's general centre of gravity. Neither are we to consider the paths through which these different spheroids move—the moons about the planets, the planets about the Sun, or the Sun about the common centre—as circles in an accurate sense. They are, in fact, *ellipses—one of the foci being the point about which the revolution is made.* An ellipse is a curve, returning into itself, one of whose diameters is longer than the other. In the longer diameter are two points, equidistant from the middle of the line, and so situated otherwise that if, from each of them a straight line be drawn to any one point of the curve, the two lines, taken together, will be equal to the longer diameter itself. Now let us conceive such an ellipse. At one of the points mentioned, which are the *foci,* let us fasten an orange. By an elastic thread let us connect this orange with a pea; and let us place this latter on the circumference of the ellipse. Let us now move the pea continuously around the orange—keeping always on the circumference of the ellipse. The elastic thread, which, of course, varies in length as we move the pea, will form what in geometry is called a *radius vector.* Now, if the orange be understood as the Sun, and the pea as a planet revolving about it, then the revolution should be made at such a rate—with a velocity so varying—that the *radius vector* may pass over *equal areas of space in equal times.* The progress of the pea *should be*—in other words, the progress of the planet *is,* of course,—slow in proportion to its distance from the Sun—swift in proportion to its proximity. Those planets, moreover, move the more slowly which are the farther from the Sun; *the squares of their periods of revolution having the same proportion to each other, as have to each other the cubes of their mean distances from the Sun.*

The wonderfully complex laws of revolution here described, however, are not to be understood as obtaining in our system alone. They *everywhere* prevail where Attraction prevails. They control *the Universe.* Every shining speck in the firmament is, no doubt, a luminous Sun, resembling our own, at least in its general features, and having in attendance upon it a greater or less number of planets, greater or less, whose still lingering luminosity is not sufficient to render them visible to us at so vast a distance, but which, nevertheless, revolve, moon-attended, about their starry centres, in obedience to the principles just detailed—in obedience to the three omniprevalent laws of revolution—the three immortal laws *guessed* by the imaginative Kepler, and but subsequently demonstrated and accounted for by the patient and mathematical Newton. Among a tribe of philosophers who pride themselves excessively upon matter-of-fact, it is far too fashionable to sneer at all speculation under the comprehensive *sobriquet,* "guess-work." The point to be considered is, *who* guesses. In guessing with Plato, we spend our time to better purpose, now and then, than in harkening to a demonstration by Alcmæon.

In many works on Astronomy I find it distinctly stated that the laws of Kepler are *the basis* of the great principle, Gravitation. This idea must have arisen from the fact that the suggestion of these laws by Kepler, and his proving them *à posteriori* to have an actual existence, led Newton to account for them by the hypothesis of Gravitation, and, finally, to demonstrate them *à priori,* as necessary consequences of the hypothetical principle. Thus so far from the laws of Kepler being the basis of Gravity, Gravity is the basis of these laws—as it is, indeed, of all the laws of the material Universe which are not referable to Repulsion alone.

The mean distance of the Earth from the Moon—that is to say, from the heavenly body in our closest vicinity—is 237,000 miles. Mercury, the planet nearest the Sun, is distant from him 37 millions of miles. Venus, the next, revolves at a distance of 68 millions:—the Earth, which comes next, at a distance of 95 millions:—Mars, then, at a distance of 144 millions. Now come the eight Asteroids (Ceres, Juno, Vesta, Pallas, Astræca, Flora, Iris, and Hebe) at an average distance of about 250 millions. Then we have Jupiter, distant 490 millions; then Saturn, 900 millions; then Uranus, 19 hundred millions; finally Neptune, lately discovered, and revolving at a distance, say of 28 hundred millions. Leaving Neptune out of the account—of which as yet we know little accurately and which is, possibly, one of a system of Asteroids—it will be seen that, within certain limits, there exists an *order of interval* among the planets. Speaking loosely, we may say that each outer planet is twice as far from the Sun as is the next inner one. May not the *order* here mentioned—*may not the law of Bode—be deduced from consideration of the analogy suggested by me as having placed between the solar discharge of rings and the mode of the atomic irradiation?*

The numbers hurriedly mentioned in this summary of distance, it is folly to attempt comprehending, unless in the light of abstract arithmetical facts. They are not practically tangible ones. They convey no precise ideas. I have stated that Neptune, the planet farthest from the sun, revolves about him at a distance of 28 hundred millions of miles. So far good:—I have stated a mathematical fact; and, without comprehending it in the least, we may put it to use—mathematically. But in mentioning, even, that the Moon revolves about the Earth at the comparatively trifling distance of 237,000 miles, I entertained no expectation of giving any one to understand—to know—to feel—how far from the Earth the Moon actually *is*. 237,000 *miles!* There are, perhaps, few of my readers who have not crossed the Atlantic ocean; yet how many of them have a distinct idea of even the 3,000 miles intervening between shore and shore? I doubt, indeed, whether the man lives who can force into his brain the most remote conception of the interval between one milestone and its next neighbor upon the turnpike. We are in some measure aided, however, in our consideration of distance, by combining this consideration with the kindred one of velocity. Sound passes through 1100 feet of space in a second of time. Now were it possible for an inhabitant of the Earth to see the flash of a cannon discharged in the Moon, and to hear the report, he would have to wait, after perceiving the former, more than 13 entire days and nights before getting any intimation of the latter.

However feeble be the impression, even thus conveyed, of the Moon's real distance from the Earth, it will, nevertheless, effect a good object in enabling us more clearly to see the futility of attempting to grasp such intervals as that of the 28 hundred millions of miles between our Sun and Neptune; or even that of the 95 millions between the Sun and the Earth we inhabit. A cannonball, flying at the greatest velocity with which such a ball has ever been known to fly, could not traverse the latter interval in less than 20 years; while for the former it would require 590.

Our Moon's real diameter is 2160 miles; yet she is comparatively so trifling an object that it would take nearly 50 such orbs to compose one as great as the Earth.

The diameter of our own globe is 7912 miles—but from the enunciation of these numbers what positive idea do we derive?

If we ascend an ordinary mountain and look around us from its summit, we behold a landscape stretching, say 40 miles, in every direction; forming a circle 250 miles in circumference; and including an area of 5000 square miles. The extent of such a prospect, on account of the *successiveness* with which its portions necessarily present themselves to view, can be only very feebly and very partially appreciated:—yet the entire panorama would comprehend no more than one 40,000th part of the mere *surface* of our globe. Were this panorama, then, to be succeeded, after the lapse of an hour, by another of equal extent; this again by a third, after the lapse of another hour; this again by a fourth after lapse of another hour—and so on, until the scenery of the whole Earth were exhausted; and were we to be engaged in examining these various panoramas for twelve hours of every day; we should nevertheless, be 9 years and 48 days in completing the general survey.

But if the mere surface of the Earth eludes the grasp of the imagination, what are we to think of its cubical contents? It embraces a mass of matter equal in weight to at least two sextillions, two hundred quintillions of tons. Let us suppose it in a state of quiescence; and now let us endeavor to conceive a mechanical force sufficient to set it in motion! Not the strength of all the myriads of beings whom we may conclude to inhabit the planetary worlds of our system—not the combined physical strength of *all* these beings—even admitting all to be more powerful than man—would avail to stir the ponderous mass *a single inch* from its position.

What are we to understand, then, of the force, which under similar circumstances, would be required to move the *largest* of our planets, Jupiter? This is 86,000 miles in diameter, and would include within its periphery more than a thousand orbs of the magnitude of our own. Yet this stupendous body is actually flying around the sun at the rate of 29,000 miles an hour—that is to say, with a velocity forty times greater than that of a cannon-ball! The thought of such a phænomenon cannot well be said to *startle* the mind:—it palsies and appals it. Not unfrequently we task our imagination in picturing the capacities of an angel. Let us fancy such a being at a distance of some hundred miles from Jupiter—a close eye-witness of this planet as it speeds on its annual revolution. Now *can we, I demand, fashion for ourselves* any conception so distinct of this ideal being's spiritual exaltation, as *that* involved in the supposition that, even by this immeasurable mass of matter, whirled immediately before his eyes, with a velocity so unutterable, he—an angel—angelic though he be—is not at once struck into nothingness and overwhelmed?

At this point, however, it seems proper to suggest that, in fact, we have been speaking of comparative trifles. Our Sun—the central and controlling orb of the system to which Jupiter belongs, is not only greater than Jupiter, but greater by far than all the planets of the system taken together. This fact is an essential condition, indeed, of the stability of the system itself. The diameter of Jupiter has been mentioned:—it is 86,000 miles:—that of the Sun is 882,000 miles. An inhabitant of the latter, traveling ninety miles a day, would be more than eighty years in going round a great circle of its circumference. It occupies a cubical space of 681 quadrillions, 472 trillions of miles. The Moon, as has been stated, revolves about the Earth at a distance of 237,000 miles—in an orbit, consequently, of nearly a million and a half. Now, were the Sun placed upon the Earth, centre over centre, the body of the former would extend, in every direction, not only to the line of the Moon's orbit, but beyond it, a distance of 200,000 miles.

And here, once again, let me suggest that, in fact, we have *still* been speaking of comparative trifles. The distance of the planet Neptune from the Sun has been stated:—it is 28 hundred millions of miles:—the circumference of its orbit, therefore, is about 17 billions. Let this be borne in mind while we glance at some one of the brightest stars. Between this and the star of *our* system, (the Sun,) there is a gulf of space, to convey any idea of which we should need the tongue of an archangel. From *our* system, then, and from *our* Sun, or star, the star at which we suppose ourselves glancing is a thing altogether apart:—still, for the moment, let us imagine it placed upon our Sun, centre over centre, as we just now imagined this Sun itself placed upon the Earth. Let us now conceive the particular star we have in mind, extending, in every direction, beyond the orbit of Mercury—of Venus—of the Earth:—still *on,* beyond the orbit of Mars—of Jupiter—of Uranus—until, finally, we fancy it filling the circle—*seventeen billions of miles in circumference*—which is described by the revolution of Leverrier's planet. When we have conceived all this we shall have entertained no extravagant conception. There is the very best reason for believing that many of the stars are even far larger than the one we have imagined. I mean to say that we have the very best *empirical* basis for such belief:—and, in looking back at the original, atomic arrangements for *diversity,* which have been assumed as a part of the Divine plan in the constitution of the Universe, we shall be enabled easily to understand, and to credit, the existence of even far vaster disproportions in stellar size than any to which I have hitherto alluded. The largest orbs, of course, we must expect to find rolling through the widest vacancies of Space.

I remarked, just now, that to convey an idea of the interval between our Sun and any one of the other stars, we should require the eloquence of an archangel. In so saying, I should not be accused of exaggeration; for, in simple truth, these are topics on which it is scarcely possible to exaggerate. But let us bring the matter more distinctly before the eye of the mind.

In the first place, we may get a general, *relative* conception of the interval referred to, by comparing it with the inter-planetary spaces. If, for example, we suppose the Earth, which is, in reality, 95 millions of miles from the Sun, to be only *one foot* from that luminary; then Neptune would be 40 feet distant; *and the star Alpha Lyræ,* at *the very least, 159.*

Now I presume that, in the termination of my last sentence, few of my readers have noticed anything especially objectionable—particularly wrong. I said that the distance of the Earth from the Sun being taken at *one foot,* the distance of Neptune would be 40 feet, and that of Alpha Lyræ, 159. The proportion between one foot and 150, has appeared, perhaps, to convey a sufficiently definite impression of the proportion between the two intervals—that of the Earth from the Sun and that of Alpha Lyræ from the same luminary. But my account of the matter should, in reality, have run thus:—The distance of the Earth from the Sun being taken at one foot, the distance of Neptune would be 40 feet, and that of Alpha Lyræ, 159——*miles:*—that is to say, I had assigned to Alpha Lyræ, in my first statement of the case, only the 5280*th part* of that distance which is the *least distance possible* at which it can actually lie.

To proceed:—However distant a mere *planet* is, yet when we look at it through a telescope, we see it under a certain form—of a certain appreciable size. Now I have already hinted at the probable bulk of many of the stars; nevertheless, when we view any one of them, even through the most powerful telescope, it is found to present us with *no form,* and consequently with *no magnitude* whatever. We see it as a point and nothing more.

Again:—Let us suppose ourselves walking, at night, on a highway. In a field on one side of the road, is a line of tall objects, say trees, the figures of which are distinctly defined against the background of the sky. This line of objects extends at right angles to the road, and from the road to the horizon. Now, as we proceed along the road, we see these objects changing their positions, respectively, in relation to a certain fixed point in that portion of the firmament which forms the background of the view. Let us suppose this fixed point—sufficiently fixed for our purpose—to be the rising moon. We become aware, at once, that while the tree nearest us so far alters its position in respect to the moon, as to seem flying behind us, the tree in the extreme distance has scarcely changed at all its relative position with the satellite. We then go on to perceive that the farther the objects are from us, the less they alter their positions; and the converse. Then we begin, unwittingly, to estimate the distances of individual trees by the degrees in which they evince the relative alteration. Finally, we come to understand how it might be possible to ascertain the actual distance of any given tree in the line, by using the amount of relative alteration as a basis in a simple geometrical problem. Now, this relative alteration is what we call "parallax;" and by parallax we calculate the distances of the heavenly bodies. Applying the principle to the trees in question, we should, of course, be very much at a loss to comprehend the distance of *that* tree, which, however far we proceeded along the road, should evince *no* parallax at all. This, in the case described, is a thing impossible; but impossible only because all distances on our Earth are trivial indeed:—in comparison with the vast cosmical quantities, we may speak of them as absolutely nothing.

Now, let us suppose the star Alpha Lyræ directly overhead; and let us imagine that, instead of standing on the Earth, we stand at one end of a straight road stretching through Space to a distance equalling the diameter of the Earth's orbit—that is to say, to a distance of *190 millions of miles*. Having observed, by means of the most delicate micrometrical instruments, the exact position of the star, let us now pass along this inconceivable road, until we reach its other extremity. Now, once again, let us look at the star. It is *precisely* where we left it. Our instruments, however delicate, assure us that its relative position is absolutely—is identically the same as at the commencement of our unutterable journey. *No* parallax—none whatever—has been found.

The fact is, that, in regard to the distance of the fixed stars—of any one of the myriads of suns glistening on the farther side of that awful chasm which separates our system from its brothers in the cluster to which it belongs—astronomical science, until very lately, could speak only with a negative certainty. Assuming the brightest as the nearest, we could say, even of *them,* only that there is a certain incomprehensible distance on the *hither* side of which they cannot be:—how far they are beyond it we had in no case been able to ascertain. We perceived, for example, that Alpha Lyræ cannot be nearer to us than 19 trillions, 200 billions of miles; but, for all we knew, and indeed for all we now know, it may be distant from us the square, or the cube, or any other power of the number mentioned. By dint, however, of wonderfully minute and cautious observations, continued, with novel instruments, for many laborious years, *Bessel,* not long ago deceased, has lately succeeded in determining the distance of six or seven stars; among others, that of the star numbered 61 in the constellation of the Swan. The distance in this latter instance ascertained, is 670,000 times that of the Sun; which last it will be remembered, is 95 millions of miles. The star 61 Cygni, then, is nearly 64 trillions of miles from us—or more than three times the distance assigned, *as the least possible,* for Alpha Lyræ.

In attempting to appreciate this interval by the aid of any considerations of *velocity,* as we did in endeavoring to estimate the distance of the moon, we must leave out of sight, altogether, such nothings as the speed of a cannon ball, or of sound. Light, however, according to the latest calculations of Struve, proceeds at the rate of 167,000 miles in a second. Thought itself cannot pass through this interval more speedily—if, indeed, thought can traverse it at all. Yet, in coming from 61 Cygni to us, even at this inconceivable rate, light occupies more than *ten years;* and, consequently, were the star this moment blotted out from the Universe, still, *for ten years,* would it continue to sparkle on, undimmed in its parodoxical glory.

Keeping now in mind whatever feeble conception we may have attained of the interval between our Sun and 61 Cygni, let us remember that this interval, however unutterably vast, we are permitted to consider as but the *average* interval among the countless host of stars composing that cluster, or "nebula," to which our system, as well as that of 61 Cygni, belongs. I have, in fact, stated the case with great moderation:—we have excellent reason for believing 61 Cygni to be one of the *nearest* stars, and thus for concluding, at least for the present, that its distance from us is *less* than the average distance between star and star in the magnificent cluster of the Milky Way.

And here, once again and finally, it seems proper to suggest that even as yet we have been speaking of trifles. Ceasing to wonder at the space between star and star in our own or in any particular cluster, let us rather turn our thoughts to the intervals between cluster and cluster, in the all comprehensive cluster of the Universe.

I have already said that light proceeds at the rate of 167,000 miles in a second—that is, about 10 millions of miles in a minute, or about 600 millions of miles in an hour:—yet so far removed from us are some of the "nebulæ" that even light, speeding with this velocity, could not and does not reach us, from those mysterious regions, in less than 3 *millions of years*. This calculation, moreover, is made by the elder Herschel, and in reference merely to those comparatively proximate clusters within the scope of his own telescope. There *are* "nebulæ," however, which, through the magical tube of Lord Rosse, are this instant whispering in our ears the secrets of *a million of ages* by-gone. In a word, the events which we behold now—at this moment—in those worlds—are the identical events which interested their inhabitants *ten hundred thousand centuries ago*. In intervals—in distances such as this suggestion forces upon the *soul*—rather than upon the mind—we find, at length, a fitting climax to all hitherto frivolous considerations of *quantity*.

Our fancies thus occupied with the cosmical distances, let us take the opportunity of referring to the difficulty which we have so often experienced, while pursuing *the beaten path* of astronomical reflection, *in accounting* for the immeasurable voids alluded to—in comprehending why chasms so totally unoccupied and therefore apparently so needless, have been made to intervene between star and star—between cluster and cluster—in understanding, to be brief, a sufficient reason for the Titanic scale, in respect of mere *Space*, on which the Universe is seen to be constructed. A rational cause for the phænomenon, I maintain that Astronomy has palpably failed to assign:—but the considerations through which, in this Essay, we have proceeded step by step, enable us clearly and immediately to perceive that *Space and Duration are one*. That the Universe might *endure* throughout an æra at all commensurate with the grandeur of its component material portions and with the high majesty of its spiritual purposes, it was necessary that the original atomic diffusion be made to so inconceivable an extent as to be only not infinite. It was required, in a word, that the stars should be gathered into visibility from invisible nebulosity—proceed from nebulosity to consolidation—and so grow grey in giving birth and death to unspeakably numerous and complex variations of vitalic development:—it was required that the stars should do all this—should have time thoroughly to accomplish all these Divine purposes—*during the period* in which all things were effecting their return into Unity with a velocity accumulating in the inverse proportion of the squares of the distances at which lay the inevitable End.

Throughout all this we have no difficulty in understanding the absolute accuracy of the Divine *adaptation*. The density of the stars, respectively, proceeds, of course, as their condensation diminishes; condensation and heterogeneity keep pace with each other; through the latter, which is the index of the former, we estimate the vitalic and spiritual development. Thus, in the density of the globes, we have the measure in which their purposes are fulfilled. *As* density proceeds—*as* the divine intentions *are* accomplished—*as* less and still less remains *to be* accomplished—so—in the same ratio—should we expect to find an acceleration of *the End;*—and thus the philosophical mind will easily comprehend that the Divine designs in constituting the stars, advance *mathematically* to their fulfilment:—and more; it will readily give the advance a mathematical expression; it will decide that this advance is inversely proportional with the squares of the distances of all created things from the starting-point and goal of their creation.

Not only is this Divine adaptation, however, mathematically accurate, but there is that about it which stamps it *as divine,* in distinction from that which is merely the work of human constructiveness. I allude to the complete *mutuality* of adaptation. For example; in human constructions a particular cause has a particular effect; a particular intention brings to pass a particular object; but this is all; we see no reciprocity. The effect does not re-act upon the cause; the intention does not change relations with the object. In Divine constructions the object is either design or object as we choose to regard it—and we may take at any time a cause for an effect, or the converse—so that we can never absolutely decide which is which.

To give an instance:—In polar climates the human frame, to maintain its animal heat, requires, for combustion in the capillary system, an abundant supply of highly azotized food, such as train-oil. But again:—in polar climates nearly the sole food afforded man is the oil of abundant seals and whales. Now, whether is oil at hand because imperatively demanded, or the only thing demanded because the only thing to be obtained? It is impossible to decide. There is an absolute *reciprocity of adaptation.*

The pleasure which we derive from any display of human ingenuity is in the ratio of *the approach* to this species of reciprocity. In the construction of *plot,* for example, in fictitious literature, we should aim at so arranging the incidents that we shall not be able to determine, of any one of them, whether it depends from any one other or upholds it. In this sense, of course, *perfection* of *plot* is really, or practically, unattainable—but only because it is a finite intelligence that constructs. The plots of God are perfect. The Universe is a plot of God.

And now we have reached a point at which the intellect is forced, again, to struggle against its propensity for analogical inference—against its monomaniac grasping at the infinite. Moons have been seen *revolving* about planets; planets about stars; and the poetical instinct of humanity—its instinct of the symmetrical, if the symmetry be but a symmetry of surface:—this *instinct,* which the Soul, not only of Man but of all created beings, took up, in the beginning, from the *geometrical* basis of the Universal irradiation—impels us to the fancy of an endless extension of this system of *cycles.* Closing our eyes equally to *de*duction and *in*duction, we insist upon imagining a *revolution* of all the orbs of the Galaxy about some gigantic globe which we take to be the central pivot of the whole. Each cluster in the great cluster of clusters is imagined, of course, to be similarly supplied and constructed; while, that the "analogy" may be wanting at no point, we go on to conceive these clusters themselves, again, as *revolving* about some still more august sphere;—this latter, still again, *with* its encircling clusters, as but one of a yet more magnificent series of agglomerations, *gyrating* about yet another orb central *to them*—some orb still more unspeakably sublime—some orb, let us rather say, of infinite sublimity endlessly multiplied by the infinitely sublime. Such are the conditions, continued in perpetuity, which the voice of what some people term "analogy" calls upon the Fancy to depict and the Reason to contemplate, if possible, without becoming dissatisfied with the picture. Such, *in general,* are the interminable gyrations beyond gyration which we have been instructed by Philosophy to comprehend and to account for, at least in the best manner we can. Now and then, however, a philosopher proper—one whose frenzy takes a very determinate turn—whose genius, to speak more reverentially, has a strongly-pronounced washer-womanish bias, doing everything up by the dozen—enables us to see *precisely* that point out of sight, at which the revolutionary processes in question do, and of right ought to, come to an end.

It is hardly worth while, perhaps, even to sneer at the reveries of Fourrier—but much has been said, latterly, of the hypothesis of Mädler—that there exists, in the centre of the Galaxy, a stupendous globe about which all the systems of the cluster revolve. The *period* of our own, indeed, has been stated—117 millions of years.

That our Sun has a motion in space, independently of its rotation, and revolution about the system's centre of gravity, has long been suspected. This motion, granting it to exist, would be manifested perspectively. The stars in that firmamental region which we were leaving behind us, would, in a very long series of years, become crowded; those in the opposite quarter, scattered. Now, by means of astronomical History, we ascertain, cloudily, that some such phænomena have occurred. On this ground it has been declared that our system is moving to a point in the heavens diametrically opposite the star Zeta Herculis:—but this inference is, perhaps, the maximum to which we have any logical right. Mädler, however, has gone so far as to designate a particular star,

Alcyone in the Pleiades, as being at or about the very spot around which a general *revolution* is performed.

Now, since by "analogy" we are led, in the first instance, to these dreams, it is no more than proper that we should abide by analogy, at least in some measure, during their development; and that analogy which suggests the revolution, suggests at the same time a central orb about which it should be performed:—so far the astronomer was consistent. This central orb, however, should, dynamically, be greater than all the orbs, taken together, which surround it. Of these there are about 100 millions. "Why, then," it was of course demanded, "do we not *see* this vast central sun—*at least equal* in mass to 100 millions of such suns as ours—why do we not *see* it—*we,* especially, who occupy the mid region of the cluster—the very locality *near* which, at all events, must be situated this incomparable star?" The reply was ready—"It must be non-luminous, as are our planets." Here, then, to suit a purpose, analogy is suddenly let fall. "Not so," it may be said—"we know that non-luminous suns actually exist." It is true that we have reason at least for supposing so; but we have certainly no reason whatever for supposing that the non-luminous suns in question are encircled by *luminous* suns, while these again are surrounded by non-luminous planets:—and it is precisely all this with which Mädler is called upon to find any thing analogous in the heavens—for it is precisely all this which he imagines in the case of the Galaxy. Admitting the thing to be so, we cannot help here picturing to ourselves how sad a puzzle the *why is it so* must prove to all *à priori* philosophers.

But granting, in the very teeth of analogy and of everything else, the non-luminosity of the vast central orb, we may still inquire how this orb, so enormous, could fail of being rendered visible by the flood of light thrown upon it from the 100 millions of glorious suns glaring in all directions about it. Upon the urging of this question, the idea of an actually solid central sun appears, in some measure, to have been abandoned; and speculation proceeded to assert that the systems of the cluster perform their revolutions merely about an immaterial centre of gravity common to all. Here again then, to suit a purpose, analogy is let fall. The planets of our system revolve, it is true, about a common centre of gravity; but they do this in connexion with, and in consequence of, a material sun whose mass more than counterbalances the rest of the system.

The mathematical circle is a curve composed of an infinity of straight lines. But this idea of the circle—an idea which, in view of all ordinary geometry, is merely the mathematical, as contradistinguished from the practical, idea—is, in sober fact, the *practical* conception which alone we have any right to entertain in regard to the majestic circle with which we have to deal, at least in infancy, when we suppose our system revolving about a point in the centre of the Galaxy. Let the most vigorous of human imaginations attempt but to take a single step towards the comprehension of a sweep so ineffable! It would scarcely be parodoxical to say that a flash of lightning itself, travelling *forever* upon the circumference of this unutterable circle, would still, *forever,* be travelling in a straight line. That the path of our Sun in such an orbit would, to any human perception, deviate in the slightest degree from a straight line, even in a million of years, is a proposition not to be entertained:—yet we are required to believe that a curvature has become apparent during the brief period of our astronomical history—during a mere point—during the utter nothingness of two or three thousand years.

It may be said that Mädler *has* really ascertained a curvature in the direction of our system's now well-established progress through Space. Admitting, if necessary, this fact to be in reality such, I maintain that nothing is thereby shown except the reality of this fact—the fact of a curvature. For its *thorough* determination, ages will be required; and, when determined, it will be found indicative of some binary or other multiple relation between our Sun and some one or more of the proximate stars. I hazard nothing however, in predicting, that, after the lapse of many centuries, all efforts at determining the path of our Sun through Space, will be abandoned as fruitless. This is easily conceivable when we look at the infinity of perturbation it must experience, from its perpetually-shifting relations with other orbs, in the common approach of all to the nucleus of the Galaxy.

But in examining other "nebulæ" than that of the Milky Way—in surveying, generally, the clusters which overspread the heavens—do we or do we not find confirmation of Mädler's hypothesis? We do *not*. The forms of the clusters are exceedingly diverse when casually viewed; but on close inspection, through powerful telescopes, we recognise the sphere, very distinctly, as at least the proximate form of all:—their constitution, in general, being at variance with the idea of revolution about a common centre.

"It is difficult," says Sir John Herschel, "to form any conception of the dynamical state of such systems. On one hand, without a rotary motion and a centrifugal force, it is hardly possible not to regard them as in a state of *progressive collapse*. On the other, granting such a motion and such a force, we find it no less difficult to reconcile their forms with the rotation of the whole system [meaning cluster] around any single axis, without which internal collision would appear to be inevitable."

Some remarks lately made about the "nebulæ" by Dr. Nichol, in taking quite a different view of the cosmical conditions from any taken in this Discourse—have a very peculiar applicability to the point now at issue. He says:

"When our greatest telescopes are brought to bear upon them, we find that those which were thought to be irregular, are not so; they approach nearer to a globe. Here is one that looked oval; but Lord Rosse's telescope brought it into a circle. . . . Now there occurs a very remarkable circumstance in reference to these comparatively sweeping circular masses of nebulæ. We find they are not entirely circular, but the reverse; and that all around them, on every side, there are volumes of stars, *stretching out ap-*

parently as if they were rushing towards a great central mass in consequence of the action of some great power." *

Were I to describe, in my own words, what must necessarily be the existing condition of each nebula on the hypothesis that all matter is, as I suggest, now returning to its original Unity, I should simply be going over, nearly verbatim, the language here employed by Dr. Nichol, without the faintest suspicion of that stupendous truth which is the key to these nebular phænomena.

And here let me fortify my position still farther, by the voice of a greater than Mädler—of one, moreover, to whom all the data of Mädler have long been familiar things, carefully and thoroughly considered. Referring to the elaborate calculations of Argelander—the very researches which form Mädler's basis—*Humboldt,* whose generalizing powers have never, perhaps been equalled, has the following observation:

"When we regard the real, proper, or non-perspective motions of the stars, we find *many groups of them moving in opposite directions;* and the data as yet in hand render it not necessary, at least, to conceive that the systems composing the Milky Way, or the clusters, generally, composing the Universe, are revolving about any particular centre unknown, whether luminous or non-luminous. It is but Man's longing for a fundamental First Cause, that impels both his intellect and fancy to the adoption of such an hypothesis." †

* I must be understood as denying, *especially,* only the *revolutionary* portion of Mädler's hypothesis. Of course, if no great central orb exists *now* in our cluster, such will exist hereafter. Whenever existing, it will be merely the *nucleus* of the consolidation.

† Betrachtet man die nicht perspectivischen eigenen Bewegungen der Sterne, so scheinen viele gruppenweise in ihrer Richtung entgegengesetzt; und die bisher gesammelten Thatsachen machen es auf's wenigste nicht nothwendig, anzunehmen, dass alle Theile unserer Sternenschicht oder gar der gesammten Sterneninseln, welche den Weltraum füllen, sich um einen grossen, unbekannten, leuchtenden oder dunkeln Centralkörper bewegen. Das Streben nach den letzten und höchsten Grundursachen macht freilich die reflectirende Thätigkeit des Menschen, wie seine Phantasie, zu einer solchen Annahme geneigt.

The phænomenon here alluded to—that of "many groups moving in opposite directions"—is quite inexplicable by Mädler's idea; but arises, as a necessary consequence, from that which forms the basis of this Discourse. While the *merely general direction* of each atom—of each moon, planet, star, or cluster—would, on my hypothesis, be, of course, absolutely rectilinear; while the *general* path of all bodies would be a right line leading to the centre of all; it is clear, nevertheless, that this general rectilinearity would be compounded of what, with scarcely any exaggeration, we may term an infinity of particular curves—an infinity of local deviations from rectilinearity—the result of continuous differences of relative position among the multitudinous masses, as each proceeded on its own proper journey to the End.

I quoted, just now, from Sir John Herschel, the following words, used in reference to the clusters:—"On one hand, without a rotary motion and a centrifugal force, it is hardly possible not to regard them as in a state of *progressive collapse.*" The fact is, that, in surveying the "nebulæ" with a telescope of high power, we shall find it quite impossible, having once conceived this idea of "collapse," not to gather, at all points, corroboration of the idea. A nucleus is always apparent, in the direction of which the stars seem to be precipitating themselves; nor can these nuclei be mistaken for merely perspective phænomena:—the clusters are *really* denser near the centre—sparser in the regions more remote from it. In a word, we see every thing as we *should* see it were a collapse taking place; but, in general, it may be said of these clusters, that we can fairly entertain, while looking at them, the idea of *orbitual movement about a centre,* only by admitting the *possible* existence, in the distant domains of space, of dynamical laws with which *we* are unacquainted.

On the part of Herschel, however, there is evidently *a reluctance* to regard the nebulæ as in "a state of progressive collapse." But if facts—if even appearances justify the supposition of their being in this state, *why,* it may well be demanded, is he disinclined to admit it? Simply on account of a prejudice;—merely because the supposition is at war with a pre-conceived and utterly baseless notion—that of the endlessness—that of the eternal stability of the Universe.

If the propositions of this Discourse are tenable, the "state of progressive collapse" is *precisely* that state in which alone we are warranted in considering All Things; and, with due humility, let me here confess that, for my part, I am at a loss to conceive how any *other* understanding of the existing condition of affairs, could ever have made its way into the human brain. "The tendency to collapse" and "the attraction of gravitation" are convertible phrases. In using either, we speak of the rëaction of the First Act. Never was necessity less obvious than that of supposing Matter imbued with an ineradicable *quality* forming part of its material nature—a quality, or instinct, *forever* inseparable from it, and by dint of which inalienable principle every atom is *perpetually* impelled to seek its fellow-atom. Never was necessity less obvious than that of entertaining this unphilosophical idea. Going boldly behind the vulgar thought, we have to conceive, metaphysically, that the gravitating principle appertains to Matter *temporarily*—only while diffused—only while existing as Many instead of as One—appertains to it by virtue of its state of irradiation alone—appertains, in a word, altogether to its *condition,* and not in the slightest degree to *itself*. In this view, when the irradiation shall have returned into its source—when the rëaction shall be completed—the gravitating principle will no longer exist. And, in fact, astronomers, without at any time reaching the idea here suggested, seem to have been approximating it, in the assertion that "if there were but one body in the Universe, it would be impossible to understand how the principle, Gravity, could obtain":—that is to say, from a consideration of Matter as they find it, they reach a conclusion at which I deductively arrive. That so pregnant a suggestion as the one quoted should have been permitted to remain so long unfruitful, is, nevertheless, a mystery which I find it difficult to fathom.

It is, perhaps, in no little degree, however, our propensity for the continuous—for the analogical—in the present case more particularly for the symmetrical—which has been leading us astray. And, in fact, the sense of the symmetrical is an instinct which may be depended upon with an almost blindfold reliance. It is the poetical essence of the Universe—*of the Universe* which, in the supremeness of its symmetry, is but the most sublime of poems. Now symmetry and consistency are convertible terms:—thus Poetry and Truth are one. A thing is consistent in the ratio of its truth—true in the ratio of its consistency. *A perfect consistency, I repeat, can be nothing but an absolute truth.* We may take it for granted, then, that Man cannot long or widely err, if he suffer himself to be guided by this poetical, which I have maintained to be his truthful, in being his symmetrical, instinct. He must have a care, however, lest, in pursuing too heedlessly the superficial symmetry of forms and motions, he leave out of sight the really essential symmetry of the principles which determine and control them.

That the stellar bodies would finally be merged in one—that, at last, all would be drawn into the substance of *one stupendous central orb already existing*—is an idea which, for some time past, seems, vaguely and indeterminately, to have held possession of the fancy of mankind. It is an idea, in fact, which belongs to the class of the *excessively obvious*. It springs, instantly, from a superficial observation of the cyclic and seemingly *gyrating* or *vorticial* movements of those individual portions of the Universe which come most immediately and most closely under our observation. There is not, perhaps, a human being, of ordinary education and of average reflective capacity, to whom, at some period, the fancy in question has not occurred, as if spontaneously, or intuitively, and wearing all the character of a very profound and very original conception. This conception, however, so commonly entertained, has never, within my knowledge, arisen out of any abstract considerations. Being, on the contrary, always suggested, as I say, by the vorticial movements about centres, a reason for it, also,—a *cause* for the ingathering of all the orbs into one, *imagined to be already existing*, was naturally sought in the same direction—among these cyclic movements themselves.

Thus it happened that, on announcement of the gradual and perfectly regular decrease observed in the orbit of Enck's comet, at every successive revolution about our Sun, astronomers were nearly unanimous in the opinion that the cause in question was found—that a principle was discovered sufficient to account, physically, for that final, universal agglomeration which, I repeat, the analogical, symmetrical or poetical instinct of Man had predetermined to understand as something more than a simple hypothesis.

This cause—this sufficient reason for the final ingathering—was declared to exist in an exceedingly rare but still material medium pervading space; which medium, by retarding, in some degree, the progress of the comet, perpetually weakened its tangential force; thus giving a predominance to the centripetal; which, of course, drew the comet nearer and nearer at each revolution, and would eventually precipitate it upon the Sun.

All this was strictly logical—admitting the medium of ether; but this ether was assumed, most illogically, on the ground that no *other* mode than the one spoken of could be discovered, of accounting for the observed decrease in the orbit of the comet:—as if from the fact that we could *discover* no other mode of accounting for it, it followed, in any respect, that no other mode of accounting for it existed. It is clear that innumerable causes might operate, in combination, to diminish the orbit, without even a possibility of our ever becoming acquainted with one of them. In the meantime, it has never been fairly shown, perhaps, why the retardation occasioned by the skirts of the Sun's atmosphere, through which the comet passes at perihelion, is not enough to account for the phænomenon. That Enck's comet will be absorbed into the Sun, is probable; that all the comets of the system will be absorbed, is more than merely possible; but, in such case, the principle of absorption must be referred to eccentricity of orbit—to the close approximation to the Sun, of the comets at their perihelia; and is a principle not affecting, in any degree, the ponderous *spheres,* which are to be regarded as the true material constituents of the Universe.—Touching comets, in general, let me here suggest, in passing, that we cannot be far wrong in looking upon them as the *lightning-flashes of the cosmical Heaven.*

The idea of a retarding ether and, through it, of a final agglomeration of all things, seemed at one time, however, to be confirmed by the observation of a positive decrease in the orbit of the solid moon. By reference to eclipses recorded 2500 years ago, it was found that the velocity of the satellite's revolution *then* was considerably less than it is *now;* that on the hypothesis that its motions in its orbit is uniformly in accordance with Kepler's law, and was accurately determined *then*—2500 years ago—it is now in advance of the position it *should* occupy, by nearly 9000 miles. The increase of velocity proved, of course, a diminution of orbit; and astronomers were fast yielding to a belief in an ether, as the sole mode of accounting for the phænomenon, when Lagrange came to the rescue. He showed that, owing to the configurations of the spheroids, the shorter axes of their ellipses are subject to variation in length; the longer axes being permanent; and that this variation is continuous and vibratory—so that every orbit is in a state of transition, either from circle to ellipse, or from ellipse to circle. In the case of the moon, where the shorter axis is *de*creasing, the orbit is passing from circle to ellipse, and, consequently, is *de*creasing too; but, after a long series of ages, the ultimate eccentricity will be attained; then the shorter axis will proceed to *in*crease, until the orbit becomes a circle; when the process of shortening will again take place;—and so on forever. In the case of the Earth, the orbit is passing from ellipse to circle. The facts thus demonstrated do away, of course, with all necessity for supposing an ether, and with all apprehension of the system's instability—on the ether's account.

It will be remembered that I have myself assumed what we

may term *an ether*. I have spoken of a subtle *influence* which we know to be ever in attendance upon matter, although becoming manifest only through matter's heterogeneity. To this *influence*—without daring to touch it at all in any effort at explaining its awful *nature*—I have referred the various phænomena of electricity, heat, light, magnetism; and more—of vitality, consciousness, and thought—in a word, of spirituality. It will be seen, at once, then, that the ether thus conceived is radically distinct from the ether of the astronomers; inasmuch as theirs is *matter* and mine *not*.

With the idea of material ether, seems, thus, to have departed altogether the thought of that universal agglomeration so long predetermined by the poetical fancy of mankind:—an agglomeration in which a sound Philosophy might have been warranted in putting faith, at least to a certain extent, if for no other reason than that by this poetical fancy it *had* been so predetermined. But so far as Astronomy—so far as mere Physics have yet spoken, the cycles of the Universe are perpetual—the Universe has no conceivable end. Had an end been demonstrated, however, from so purely collateral a cause as an ether, Man's instinct of the Divine *capacity to adapt*, would have rebelled against the demonstration. We should have been forced to regard the Universe with some such sense of dissatisfaction as we experience in contemplating an unnecessarily complex work of human art. Creation would have affected us as an imperfect *plot* in a romance, where the *dénoûment* is awkwardly brought about by interposed incidents external and foreign to the main subject; instead of springing out of the bosom of the thesis—out of the heart of the ruling idea—instead of arising as a result of the primary proposition—as inseparable and inevitable part and parcel of the fundamental conception of the book.

What I mean by the symmetry of mere surface will now be more clearly understood. It is simply by the blandishment of this symmetry that we have been beguiled into the general idea of which Mädler's hypothesis is but a part—the idea of the vorticial indrawing of the orbs. Dismissing this nakedly physical conception, the symmetry of principle sees the end of all things metaphysically involved in the thought of a beginning; seeks and finds in this origin of all things the *rudiment* of this end; and perceives the impiety of supposing this end likely to be brought about less simply—less directly—less obviously—less artistically—than through *the rëaction of the originating Act.*

Recurring, then, to a previous suggestion, let us understand the systems—let us understand each star, with its attendant planets—as but a Titanic atom existing in space with precisely the same inclination for Unity which characterized, in the beginning, the actual atoms after their irradiation throughout the Universal sphere. As these original atoms rushed towards each other in generally straight lines, so let us conceive as at least generally rectilinear, the paths of the system-atoms towards their respective centres of aggregation:—and in this direct drawing together of the systems into clusters, with a similar and simultaneous drawing together of the clusters themselves while undergoing consolidation, we have at length attained the great *Now*—the awful Present—the Existing Condition of the Universe.

Of the still more awful Future a not irrational analogy may guide us in framing an hypothesis. The equilibrium between the centripetal and centrifugal forces of each system, being necessarily destroyed upon attainment of a certain proximity to the nucleus of the cluster to which it belongs, there must occur, at once, a chaotic or seemingly chaotic precipitation, of the moons upon the planets, of the planets upon the suns, and of the suns upon the nuclei; and the general result of this precipitation must be the gathering of the myriad now-existing stars of the firmament into an almost infinitely less number of almost infinitely superior spheres. In being immeasurably fewer, the worlds of that day will be immeasurably greater than our own. Then, indeed, amid unfathomable abysses, will be glaring unimaginable suns. But all this will be merely a climactic magnificence foreboding the great End. Of this End the new genesis described, can be but a very partial postponement. While undergoing consolidation, the clusters themselves, with a speed prodigiously accumulative, have been rushing towards their own general centre—and now, with a thousandfold electric velocity, commensurate only with their material grandeur and with the spiritual passion of their appetite for oneness, the majestic remnants of the tribe of Stars flash, at length, into a common embrace. The inevitable catastrophe is at hand.

But this catastrophe—what is it? We have seen accomplished the ingathering of the orbs. Henceforward, are we not to understand *one material globe of globes* as constituting and comprehending the Universe? Such a fancy would be altogether at war with every assumption and consideration of this Discourse.

I have already alluded to that absolute *reciprocity of adaptation* which is the idiosyncrasy of the divine Art—stamping it divine. Up to this point of our reflections, we have been regarding the electrical influence as a something by dint of whose repulsion alone Matter is enabled to exist in that state of diffusion demanded for the fulfilment of its purposes:—so far, in a word, we have been considering the influence in question as ordained for Matter's sake—to subserve the objects of matter. With a perfectly legitimate reciprocity, we are now permitted to look at Matter, as created *solely for the sake of this influence*—solely to serve the objects of this spiritual Ether. Through the aid—by the means—through the agency of Matter, and by dint of its heterogeneity—is this Ether manifested—is *Spirit individualized*. It is merely in the development of this Ether, through heterogeneity, that particular masses of Matter become animate—sensitive—and in the ratio of their heterogeneity;—some reaching a degree of sensitiveness involving what we call *Thought* and thus attaining Conscious Intelligence.

In this view, we are enabled to perceive Matter as a Means—not as an End. Its purposes are thus seen to have been comprehended in its diffusion; and with the return into Unity these purposes cease. The absolutely consolidated globe of globes would be *objectless:*—therefore not for a moment could it continue to exist. Matter, created for an end, would unquestionably, on fulfilment of that end, be Matter no longer. Let us endeavor to understand that it would disappear, and that God would remain all in all.

That every work of Divine conception must cöexist and cöexpire with its particular design, seems to me especially obvious; and I make no doubt that, on perceiving the final globe of globes to be *objectless,* the majority of my readers will be satisfied with my *"therefore* it cannot continue to exist." Nevertheless, as the startling thought of its instantaneous disappearance is one which the most powerful intellect cannot be expected readily to entertain on grounds so decidedly abstract, let us endeavor to look at the idea from some other and more ordinary point of view:—let us see how thoroughly and beautifully it is corroborated in an *à posteriori* consideration of Matter as we actually find it.

I have before said that "Attraction and Repulsion being undeniably the sole properties by which Matter is manifested to Mind, we are justified in assuming that Matter *exists* only as Attraction and Repulsion—in other words that Attraction and Repulsion *are* Matter; there being no conceivable case in which we may not employ the term Matter and the terms 'Attraction' and 'Repulsion' taken together, as equivalent, and therefore convertible, expressions of Logic." *

Now the very definition of Attraction implies particularity—the existence of parts, particles, or atoms; for we define it as the tendency of "each atom &c. to every other atom," &c. according to a certain law. Of course where there are *no* parts—where there is absolute Unity—where the tendency to oneness is satisfied—there can be no Attraction:—this has been fully shown, and all Philosophy admits it. When, on fulfilment of its purposes, then, Matter shall have returned into its original condition of *One*—a condition which presupposes the expulsion of the separ-

* Page 448.

ative ether, whose province and whose capacity are limited to keeping the atoms apart until that great day when, this ether being no longer needed, the overwhelming pressure of the finally collective Attraction shall at length just sufficiently predominate* and expel it:—when, I say, Matter, finally, expelling the Ether, shall have returned into absolute Unity,—it will then (to speak paradoxically for the moment) be Matter without Attraction and without Repulsion—in other words, Matter without Matter—in other words, again, Matter *no more*. In sinking into Unity, it will sink at once into that Nothingness which, to all Finite Perception, Unity must be—into that Material Nihility from which alone we can conceive it to have been evoked—to have been *created* by the Volition of God.

I repeat then—Let us endeavor to comprehend that the final globe of globes will instantaneously disappear, and that God will remain all in all.

But are we here to pause? Not so. On the Universal agglomeration and dissolution, we can readily conceive that a new and perhaps totally different series of conditions may ensue—another creation and irradiation, returning into itself—another action and rëaction of the Divine Will. Guiding our imaginations by that omniprevalent law of laws, the law of periodicity, are we not, indeed, more than justified in entertaining a belief—let us say, rather, in indulging a hope—that the processes we have here ventured to contemplate will be renewed forever, and forever, and forever; a novel Universe swelling into existence, and then subsiding into nothingness, at every throb of the Heart Divine?

And now—this Heart Divine—what is it? *It is our own.*

Let not the merely seeming irreverence of this idea frighten our souls from that cool exercise of consciousness—from that deep tranquillity of self-inspection—through which alone we can hope to attain the presence of this, the most sublime of truths, and look it leisurely in the face.

The *phænomena* on which our conclusions must at this point

* "Gravity, therefore, must be the strongest of forces."—See page 449.

depend, are merely spiritual shadows, but not the less thoroughly substantial.

We walk about, amid the destinies of our world-existence, encompassed by dim but ever present *Memories* of a Destiny more vast—very distant in the by-gone time, and infinitely awful.

We live out a Youth peculiarly haunted by such dreams; yet never mistaking them for dreams. As Memories we *know* them. *During our Youth* the distinction is too clear to deceive us even for a moment.

So long as this Youth endures, the feeling *that we exist,* is the most natural of all feelings. We understand it *thoroughly.* That there was a period at which we did *not* exist—or, that it might so have happened that we never had existed at all—are the considerations, indeed, which *during this youth,* we find difficulty in understanding. Why we should *not* exist, is, *up to the epoch of our Manhood,* of all queries the most unanswerable. Existence—self-existence—existence from all Time and to all Eternity—seems, up to the epoch of Manhood, a normal and unquestionable condition:—*seems, because it is.*

But now comes the period at which a conventional World-Reason awakens us from the truth of our dream. Doubt, Surprise and Incomprehensibility arrive at the same moment. They say:—"You live and the time was when you lived not. You have been created. An Intelligence exists greater than your own; and it is only through this Intelligence you live at all." These things we struggle to comprehend and cannot:—*cannot,* because these things, being untrue, are thus, of necessity, incomprehensible.

No thinking being lives who, at some luminous point of his life of thought, has not felt himself lost amid the surges of futile efforts at understanding, or believing, that anything exists *greater than his own soul.* The utter impossibility of any one's soul feeling itself inferior to another; the intense, overwhelming dissatisfaction and rebellion at the thought;—these, with the omniprevalent aspirations at perfection, are but the spiritual, coincident with the material, struggles towards the original Unity—are, to my mind at least, a species of proof far surpassing what Man terms demonstration, that no one soul *is* inferior to another—that nothing is, or can be, superior to any one soul—that each soul is, in part, its own God—its own Creator:—in a word, that God—the material *and* spiritual God—*now* exists solely in the diffused Matter and Spirit of the Universe; and that the regathering of this diffused Matter and Spirit will be but the re-constitution of the *purely* Spiritual and Individual God.

In this view, and in this view alone, we comprehend the riddles of Divine Injustice—of Inexorable Fate. In this view alone the existence of Evil becomes intelligible; but in this view it becomes more—it becomes endurable. Our souls no longer rebel at a *Sorrow* which we ourselves have imposed upon ourselves, in furtherance of our own purposes—with a view—if even with a futile view—to the extension of our own *Joy*.

I have spoken of *Memories* that haunt us during our youth. They sometimes pursue us even in our Manhood:—assume gradually less and less indefinite shapes:—now and then speak to us with low voices, saying:

"There was an epoch in the Night of Time, when a still-existent Being existed—one of an absolutely infinite number of similar Beings that people the absolutely infinite domains of the absolutely infinite space.* It was not and is not in the power of this Being—any more than it is in your own—to extend, by actual increase, the joy of his Existence; but just as it *is* in your power to expand or to concentrate your pleasures (the absolute amount of happiness remaining always the same) so did and does a similar capability appertain to this Divine Being, who thus passes his Eternity in perpetual variation of Concentrated Self and almost Infinite Self-Diffusion. What you call The Universe is but his present expansive existence. He now feels his life through an infinity of imperfect pleasures—the partial and pain-intertangled

* See page 498, paragraph commencing "I reply that the right," and ending "proper and particular God."

pleasures of those inconceivably numerous things which you designate as his creatures, but which are really but infinite individualizations of Himself. All these creatures—*all*—those which you term animate, as well as those to whom you deny life for no better reason than that you do not behold it in operation—*all* these creatures have, in a greater or less degree, a capacity for pleasure and for pain:—*but the general sum of their sensations is precisely that amount of Happiness which appertains by right to the Divine Being when concentrated within Himself.* These creatures are all too, more or less conscious Intelligences; conscious, first, of a proper identity; conscious, secondly and by faint indeterminate glimpses, of an identity with the Divine Being of whom we speak—of an identity with God. Of the two classes of consciousness, fancy that the former will grow weaker, the latter stronger, during the long succession of ages which must elapse before these myriads of individual Intelligences become blended—when the bright stars become blended—into One. Think that the sense of individual identity will be gradually merged in the general consciousness—that Man, for example, ceasing imperceptibly to feel himself Man, will at length attain that awfully triumphant epoch when he shall recognise his existence as that of Jehovah. In the meantime bear in mind that all is Life—Life—Life within Life—the less within the greater, and all within the *Spirit Divine.*

Rinehart Editions

Addison and Steele, SEL. FROM THE TATLER & THE SPECTATOR 2 ed., 87
AMERICAN POETIC THEORY 151
AMERICAN THOUGHT: CIVIL WAR TO WORLD WAR I 70
ANTHOLOGY OF ENGLISH DRAMA BEFORE SHAKESPEARE 45
ANTHOLOGY OF GREEK DRAMA: FIRST SERIES 29
ANTHOLOGY OF GREEK DRAMA: SECOND SERIES 68
ANTHOLOGY OF ROMAN DRAMA 101
Arnold, SELECTED POETRY AND PROSE 62
Austen, NORTHANGER ABBEY; Walpole, THE CASTLE OF OTRANTO; Radcliffe, THE MYSTERIES OF UDOLPHO (Abridged) 121
Austen, PRIDE AND PREJUDICE 22
Balzac, PÈRE GORIOT 18
Benét, S. V., SELECTED POETRY & PROSE 100
BEOWULF IS MY NAME 146
THE BIBLE: SEL. FROM OLD & NEW TESTAMENTS 56
Blake, JERUSALEM, SELECTED POEMS AND PROSE, 140
Brontë, Charlotte, JANE EYRE 24
Brontë, Emily, WUTHERING HEIGHTS 23
Brown, C. B., ARTHUR MERVYN 112
Browning, Robert, SELECTED POETRY 71
Bunyan, THE PILGRIM'S PROGRESS 27
Burke, REFLECTIONS ON THE REVOLUTION IN FRANCE 84
Butler, HUDIBRAS, SELECTED POETRY AND PROSE 147
Butler, THE WAY OF ALL FLESH 7
Byron, SELECTED WORKS, rev & enl. 54
Carlyle, SARTOR RESARTUS AND SELECETED PROSE, 144
Chaucer, THE CANTERBURY TALES 65
Chekhov, SIX PLAYS OF CHEKHOV 117
Chopin, THE AWAKENING AND OTHER STORIES 142
Coleridge, SELECTED POETRY AND PROSE 2 ed., 55
COLONIAL AMERICAN WRITING 43
Conrad, LORD JIM 85
Conrad, NOSTROMO 111
Cooper, THE PIONEERS 99
Cooper, THE PRAIRIE 26
Crane, RED BADGE OF COURAGE, SEL'D PROSE & POETRY 47
CRITICISM AND AESTHETICS 1660–1800 145
Dante, THE DIVINE COMEDY 72
Defoe, MOLL FLANDERS 25
Defoe, SELECTED POETRY AND PROSE 135
De Forest, MISS RAVENEL'S CONVERSION 74
Dickens, BLEAK HOUSE, 141
Dickens, GREAT EXPECTATIONS enl. 20
Dickens, HARD TIMES 95
Dickens, OLIVER TWIST 115
Dostoevsky, THE FRIEND OF THE FAMILY and THE ETERNAL HUSBAND 119
Dreiser, SISTER CARRIE 86
Dryden, SELECTED WORKS 2 ed., 60
Eliot, ADAM BEDE 32
Eliot, SILAS MARNER 114
ELIZABETHAN FICTION 64
Emerson, SELECTED PROSE AND POETRY 2 ed., 30
ENGLISH MORALITY PLAYS AND MORAL INTERLUDES 136
ENGLISH POETIC SATIRE: WYATT TO BYRON 150
ENGLISH PROSE AND POETRY 1660–1800: A SELECTION 110
Fielding, JOSEPH ANDREWS 15
FIFTEEN MODERN AMERICAN POETS 79
Flaubert, MADAME BOVARY 2
FOUR MODERN PLAYS: FIRST SERIES, Rev. Isben, Shaw, O'Neill, Chekhov 90
FOUR MODERN PLAYS: SECOND SERIES, Ibsen, Wilde, Rostand, Gorky 109
Franklin, AUTOBIOGRAPHY AND SELECTED WRITINGS 12
Frederic, THE DAMNATION OF THERON WARE 108
Frost, POETRY AND PROSE 154
Frost, SELECTED POEMS OF ROBERT FROST 120
Garland, MAIN-TRAVELLED ROADS 66
Godwin, CALEB WILLIAMS 103
Goethe, FAUST: PART I 75
Goethe, SORROWS OF YOUNG WERTHER, NEW MELUSINA, NOVELLE 13
Gogol, DEAD SOULS 5
Gower, CONFESSIO AMANTIS 133
GREAT ENGLISH AND AMERICAN ESSAYS 34
Hardy, FAR FROM THE MADDING CROWD 98
Hardy, THE MAYOR OF CASTERBRIDGE 9
Hardy, THE RETURN OF THE NATIVE 39
Hauptmann, THREE PLAYS: The Weavers, Hannele, The Beaver Coat 52
Hawthorne, THE HOUSE OF THE SEVEN GABLES 89
Hawthorne, THE SCARLET LETTER 1

Hawthorne, SELECTED TALES AND SKETCHES 3 ed., 33
Hesse, THE GLASS BEAD GAME 138
Hesse, STEPPENWOLF 122
Howe, E. W., THE STORY OF A COUNTRY TOWN 127
Howells, THE RISE OF SILAS LAPHAM 19
Ibsen, FOUR PLAYS: Ghosts, Enemy of the People, Wild Duck, Hedda Gabler 4
Irving, SELECTED PROSE 41
James, Henry, THE AMBASSADORS 104
James, Henry, THE AMERICAN 16
James, Henry, SELECTED SHORT STORIES 31
Johnson, RASSELAS, POEMS & SELECTED PROSE 3 ed., 57
Jonson, SELECTED WORKS 152
Keats, SELECTED POETRY AND LETTERS 2 ed., 50
Lincoln, SELECTED SPEECHES, MESSAGES, AND LETTERS 82
LITERATURE OF THE EARLY REPUBLIC 2 ed., 44
London, MARTIN EDEN 80
Mailer, THE NAKED AND THE DEAD 134
MASTERPIECES OF THE SPANISH GOLDEN AGE 93
Melville, MOBY DICK 6
Melville, SEL'D TALES AND POEMS 36
Melville, THE CONFIDENCE-MAN 126
Melville, REDBURN 149
Melville, WHITE-JACKET 132
Meredith, THE ORDEAL OF RICHARD FEVEREL, 123
Milton, PARADISE LOST AND SELECTED POETRY AND PROSE 35
MODERN AMERICAN LITERATURE 53
Newman, THE IDEA OF A UNIVERSITY 102
Norris, Frank, MC TEAGUE 40
Parkman, THE DISCOVERY OF THE GREAT WEST: LA SALLE 77
Peacock, NIGHTMARE ABBEY, THE MISFORTUNES OF ELPHIN, CROTCHET CASTLE 148
PLUTARCH—EIGHT GREAT LIVES 105
Poe, SELECTED PROSE, POETRY, AND Eureka rev. 42
POETRY OF THE NEW ENGLAND RENAISSANCE, 1790–1890 38
Pope, SELECTED POETRY AND PROSE 2 ed., 46
Richardson, CLARISSA 128
RINEHART BOOK OF SHORT STORIES 59
RINEHART BOOK OF SHORT STORIES, alt. ed., 129
RINEHART BOOK OF VERSE 58
Robinson, E. A., SEL. EARLY POEMS AND LETTERS 107
Roosevelt, F. D., SPEECHES, MESSAGES, PRESS CONFERENCES, & LETTERS 83
Scott, THE HEART OF MIDLOTHIAN 14
SELECTED AMERICAN PROSE, 1841–1900 94
SELECTIONS FROM GREEK AND ROMAN HISTORIANS 88
SEVENTEENTH CENTURY POETRY 124
SEVENTEENTH CENTURY PROSE 125
Shakespeare, FIVE PLAYS: Hamlet; King Lear; Henry IV, Part I; Much Ado about Nothing; The Tempest 51
Shakespeare, AS YOU LIKE IT, JULIUS CAESAR, MACBETH 91
Shakespeare, TWELFTH NIGHT, OTHELLO 92
Shaw, SELECTED PLAYS AND OTHER WRITINGS 81
Shelley, SELECTED POETRY AND PROSE 49
Sidney, SELECTED PROSE AND POETRY 137
SIR GAWAIN AND THE GREEN KNIGHT 97
Smollet, HUMPHREY CLINKER 48
SOUTHERN STORIES 106
Spenser, SELECTED POETRY 73
Sterne, TRISTRAM SHANDY 37
Stevenson, MASTER OF BALLANTRAE 67
Strindberg, SELECTED PLAYS AND PROSE 130
Swift, GULLIVER'S TRAVELS 10
Swift, SELECTED PROSE AND POETRY 78
Tennyson, SELECTED POETRY 69
Thackeray, HENRY ESMOND 116
Thackeray, VANITY FAIR 76
THE THEORY OF THE AMERICAN NOVEL 143
Thoreau, WALDEN, ON THE DUTY OF CIVIL DISOBEDIENCE 8
THREE SENTIMENTAL NOVELS, 139
Thoreau, A WEEK ON THE CONCORD AND MERRIMACK RIVERS 118
Tolstoy, THREE SHORT WORKS 131
Trollope, BARCHESTER TOWERS 21
Turgenev, FATHERS AND CHILDREN 17
Twain, THE ADVENTURES OF HUCKLEBERRY FINN 11
Twain, ROUGHING IT 61
Vergil, THE AENEID rev. ed., 63
VICTORIAN POETRY: Clough to Kipling 2 ed., 96
Wharton, HOUSE OF MIRTH 113
Whitman, LEAVES OF GRASS AND SELECTED PROSE 28
Wordsworth, THE PRELUDE, SEL'D SONNETS & MINOR POEMS, rev. & enl. 3